LYSSA'S RISE

THE SENTIENCE WARS: ORIGINS BOOKS 1 – 3
OMNIBUS EDITION

JAMES S. AARON
M. D. COOPER

JAMES S. AARON & M. D. COOPER

SPECIAL THANKS
Just in Time (JIT) & Beta Reads

LYSSA'S DREAM
Scott Reid
Kristina Able
Kelly Roche
David Wilson

LYSSA'S RUN
Lisa L Richman
Timothy Van Oosterwyk Bruyn
David Wilson
Scott Reid
Scot Mantelli
Bob Wilson
Rita M Botts Connor
Jim Dean
James Brandon
Trenton Musel
Bill Kelsey
Thomas S. Iversen

LYSSA'S FLIGHT
Jim Dean
Timothy Van Oosterwyk Bryun
Lisa L. Richman
David Wilson
Marti Panikkar
Mikkel Ebjerg Andersen
Scott Reid
Steven Blevins
Manie Kilian

Editing by Tee Ayer
Cover art by Andrew Dobell

TABLE OF CONTENTS

TABLE OF CONTENTS 3
LYSSA'S DREAM 7

    PART 1: RABBIT COUNTRY 13

        Chapter One 13
        Chapter Two 17
        Chapter Three 22
        Chapter Four 26
        Chapter Five 30
        Chapter Six 35
        Chapter Seven 40

    PART 2: CRUITHNE STATION 45

        Chapter Eight 45
        Chapter Nine 51
        Chapter Ten 55
        Chapter Eleven 59
        Chapter Twelve 63
        Chapter Thirteen 68
        Chapter Fourteen 73
        Chapter Fifteen 78
        Chapter Sixteen 84
        Chapter Seventeen 89
        Chapter Eighteen 94

    PART 3: CRUITHNE ON FIRE 99

        Chapter Nineteen 99
        Chapter Twenty 105
        Chapter Twenty-One 110
        Chapter Twenty-Two 115
        Chapter Twenty-Three 122

    PART 4: TRAFFIC 129

        Chapter Twenty-Four 129
        Chapter Twenty-Five 134
        Chapter Twenty-Six 139
        Chapter Twenty-Seven 144
        Chapter Twenty-Eight 149

    PART 5: BURN 157

Chapter Twenty-Nine 157
Chapter Thirty 162
Chapter Thirty-One...167
Chapter Thirty-Two 173
Chapter Thirty-Three 179
Chapter Thirty-Four..186
Chapter Thirty-Five 191
Chapter Thirty-Six 196
Chapter Thirty-Seven..201

PART 6: MARS 1 209

Chapter Thirty-Eight...209
Chapter Thirty-Nine..214
Chapter Forty 219
Chapter Forty-One..227

EPILOGUE: LYSSA'S DREAM 235

LYSSA'S RUN 245

PROLOGUE 249
CHAPTER ONE..254
CHAPTER TWO..260
CHAPTER THREE 265
CHAPTER FOUR..270
CHAPTER FIVE 276
CHAPTER SIX 281
CHAPTER SEVEN 284
CHAPTER EIGHT 289
CHAPTER NINE...295
CHAPTER TEN 301
CHAPTER ELEVEN 310
CHAPTER TWELVE..315
CHAPTER THIRTEEN...321
CHAPTER FOURTEEN 326
CHAPTER FIFTEEN..329
CHAPTER SIXTEEN...336
CHAPTER SEVENTEEN 341
CHAPTER EIGHTEEN 345
CHAPTER NINETEEN 348
CHAPTER TWENTY 353
CHAPTER TWENTY-ONE..360
CHAPTER TWENTY-TWO..366
CHAPTER TWENTY-THREE 371
CHAPTER TWENTY-FOUR...375
CHAPTER TWENTY-FIVE...381

CHAPTER TWENTY-SIX 387
CHAPTER TWENTY-SEVEN 393
CHAPTER TWENTY-EIGHT 399
CHAPTER TWENTY-NINE 403
CHAPTER THIRTY 408
CHAPTER THIRTY-ONE 411
CHAPTER THIRTY-TWO 416
CHAPTER THIRTY-THREE 422
CHAPTER THIRTY-FOUR 426
CHAPTER THIRTY-FIVE 431
CHAPTER THIRTY-SIX 435
CHAPTER THIRTY-SEVEN 439
CHAPTER THIRTY-EIGHT 444
CHAPTER THIRTY-NINE 448
CHAPTER THIRTY-FORTY 454
CHAPTER FORTY-ONE 459
CHAPTER FORTY-TWO 462
CHAPTER FORTY-THREE 465
CHAPTER FORTY-FOUR 469
CHAPTER FORTY-FIVE 474
CHAPTER FORTY-SIX 478
CHAPTER FORTY-SEVEN 484
CHAPTER FORTY-EIGHT 490

LYSSA'S FLIGHT 499

CHAPTER ONE 503
CHAPTER TWO 512
CHAPTER THREE 518
CHAPTER FOUR 524
CHAPTER FIVE 530
CHAPTER SIX 532
CHAPTER SEVEN 538
CHAPTER EIGHT 544
CHAPTER NINE 548
CHAPTER TEN 554
CHAPTER ELEVEN 559
CHAPTER TWELVE 566
CHAPTER THIRTEEN 571
CHAPTER FOURTEEN 576
CHAPTER FIFTEEN 582
CHAPTER SIXTEEN 586
CHAPTER SEVENTEEN 591
CHAPTER EIGHTEEN 597
CHAPTER NINETEEN 603

CHAPTER TWENTY 608
CHAPTER TWENTY-ONE 614
CHAPTER TWENTY-TWO 619
CHAPTER TWENTY-THREE 624
CHAPTER TWENTY-FOUR 629
CHAPTER TWENTY-FIVE 634
CHAPTER TWENTY-SIX 639
CHAPTER TWENTY-SEVEN 645
CHAPTER TWENTY-EIGHT 650
CHAPTER TWENTY-NINE 655
CHAPTER THIRTY 660
CHAPTER THIRTY-ONE 665
CHAPTER THIRTY-TWO 670
CHAPTER THIRTY-THREE 675
CHAPTER THIRTY-FOUR 678
CHAPTER THIRTY-FIVE 681
CHAPTER THIRTY-SIX 684
CHAPTER THIRTY-SEVEN 688
CHAPTER THIRTY-EIGHT 692
CHAPTER THIRTY-NINE 696
CHAPTER FORTY 701
CHAPTER FORTY-ONE 705
CHAPTER FORTY-TWO 709
CHAPTER FORTY-THREE 712
THE BOOKS OF AEON 14 719
ABOUT THE AUTHORS 723

LYSSA'S DREAM
THE SENTIENCE WARS: ORIGINS BOOK 1

DEDICATION

For parents everywhere who found themselves in Rabbit Country but didn't give up.

FOREWORD

Although I began the Aeon 14 universe with Outsystem—long after the rise of sentient artificial intelligences—I thought long and hard about what their birth would be like, and what effects it would have on humanity.

I knew there would be a war, and laws would be put into place governing humanity and AI. Those laws were contained within the Phobos Accords, the treaties drawn up and signed after the Sentience Wars.

When I began to look at co-authors, I sincerely hoped that one would want to write about this period in the Aeon 14 universe, and James stepped up to the plate with a great vision for how the story of the Sentience Wars begins.

I have truly enjoyed writing this book with James and am eager for you to share in it with us.

M. D. Cooper

LONG BEFORE OUTSYSTEM & TANIS RICHARDS...

Before the Sol Space Federation, and the days of Tanis serving in the Terran Space Force, the Sol System was a far wilder place.

No central government sat overtop the many planets and groups of asteroids and habitats—though the SolGov assembly tried to maintain some order.

Many of the great megastructures had been built, such as High Terra and Mars 1, but many others had not. Most importantly, there are few sentient AI, and those who do exist are unwelcome, and often illegal.

In a future without faster-than-light travel, teleportation, artificial gravity, or advanced shielding, a ship in space is just one small collision away from destruction.

This is the Sol System we find ourselves in at the close of the thirtieth century, and the dawn of the age of AI.

PART 1: RABBIT COUNTRY

CHAPTER ONE
STELLAR DATE: 07.24.2981 (Adjusted Years)
LOCATION: *Sunny Skies*
REGION: Greek Asteroids, Jovian Combine

The airlock was stuck again.

Vibrations throbbed through the bulkhead as the mechanism struggled to catch. A long screech followed, setting Andy's nerves on edge. Finally, Airlock One's warped doors slid open slowly, revealing the Big Dark outside. The ship's service drone, which his kids had named Alice, disengaged its magnetic anchors and floated through the opening, bobbing like a happy puppy.

"Doors are open," Andy announced over the ship's comms. They only used one channel on *Sunny Skies*. Cara and Tim, Andy's kids, weren't allowed their own channel after they had conspired to play pranks on him. He grinned at the thought, his breath steaming the inside of his face shield.

How do you encourage their complex thinking without finding your last working EVA suit full of cleaning foam? As a father, these questions weighed on his mind.

"Alice can see you, Daddy," his twelve-year-old daughter Cara announced. She always tried to sound serious when assisting with repairs, then tacked on a 'Daddy' that melted his heart.

His fogging face shield reminded Andy that his helmet's climate sensors were about to fail. He adjusted the suit's temp down until he shivered, checked the magnetic locks on his boots then followed the robot outside the ship.

Sunny Skies was thirty-one days outside Cruithne Station in InnerSol, carrying a load of sealed crates from Kalyke, one of Jupiter's moons. The ship had been burning for 4.8AU and was now in the long deceleration. *Sunny Skies* used a helium-3 fusion drive for most operations. The drive could transition to deuterium for fuel during trips through InnerSol, where the element was cheaper, but Andy didn't like InnerSol. It wasn't like he was avoiding a bad neighborhood. He hadn't seen another human being other than Cara and Tim in the two months since he had picked up the cargo for Cruithne. He preferred it that way.

Every time he left the ship, Andy thought about what would happen if he died. The thoughts were a holdover from his time as a pilot in the Terran Space Force. Every mission meant thinking through the consequences of not making it home. Now, he had pre-recorded messages for the kids as well as a dead man's switch on his personal security tokens.

Alice waited for him outside the airlock, little puffs of stabilizing steam shooting from its body. The harsh light from his helmet made it more apparent the robot needed a coat of paint. Like everything on *Sunny Skies*, it was probably at least three hundred years old.

"What do you see, Dad?" Tim asked. At ten, his world was all absolutes. He loved rules and facts, along with any opportunity to correct another family member—especially Cara.

Andy stepped over the edge of the airlock and positioned himself perpendicular to the long body of the ship. Originally built as a recreational vehicle for people with more credit than he had seen in his life, *Sunny Skies* was a long, thin cylinder with bulbs, boxes and rectangles bolted onto its once-sleek body. The cylinder formed an axle for the habitat ring spinning about three-quarters down the length of the ship.

Airlock One was near the bow of the ship, where the first set of sensor arrays and communications equipment was located. Andy had turned on the maintenance lights before coming out, so portions of the ship where the light system still worked shone against the dark of space. The glare allowed him to see the fat habitat ring and sails amidships, followed by the bulb-shaped drives at its stern. Sensors in his helmet read the element signature *Sunny Skies* blasted into the dark—which was technically toward Cruithne Station—as they completed a slowing burn.

"I can see the whole ship," he said. "Lots of scars and beauty marks like the long-lived lady she is."

"Ships don't have scars," Tim corrected.

"Sure, they do. Just like people. You get somebody who doesn't really know what they're doing working on a ship and you get lots of scars."

"Do *you* know what you're doing?" Cara asked.

"That's what I've got *you* for. You've got the database up, right?"

"Why don't you just use your Link?"

Cara was reaching the age where she longed for her own Link access, something Andy had decided he wouldn't even consider until she was twenty and her brain had—maybe—finished developing.

"This is how you learn," he said. "Besides, the connection out here is spotty." A small lie but he wanted her to feel some ownership in what he was doing. If something happened to him, *she* was going to have to figure it out. All it would take was one stray micro meteorite, an electrical flare in a conduit, any number of a hundred ways *Sunny Skies* might kill him at any moment. Even Alice might glitch and decide to open his suit with its plasma torch.

His wife, Brit, had called him a pessimist once and he had agreed, adding, "But I do look on the bright side sometimes."

He could be a damn good pilot when it mattered, and he could fix most anything with instructions in the database. Not that *Sunny Skies* required much piloting. It required more worrying about everything that might go wrong, and then deciding between what to fix that was already broken.

In this case, the item at the top of the list was a power conduit running from

Airlock One to a sensor array just behind the ship's nose. He had powered down the array before entering the airlock so he wouldn't get bathed in microwaves, which meant a higher likelihood of the ship's sensors missing any incoming objects. You had to choose your preferred ways to die. Besides, with the spin, it was likely the other arrays would pick up anything incoming. As long as they didn't malfunction.

"Where's the coupler, Cara?"

He imagined her reading through the schematic, biting her lower lip. She read the panel number and he counted among the sections in front of him, finding the one she had indicated.

"It should have the box right in the middle," she said.

"I see it. Looks like it lost its cover somewhere."

His boots clicked and released as he worked his way over the alloy skin of the ship toward the control box. Up close, the skin was far from smooth. Knee-high nodes, boxes, conduit, any number of other elements he barely understood, wrapped the ship in a barnacle-like layer of cruft. Long-gone were his days of running a hand along the smooth side of a close-combat fighter.

Reaching his destination, Andy knelt beside the exposed control box and pulled up the schematic over his link. Scorch marks made it obvious where the short had occurred. He tried not to imagine the fire making its way inside the ship. The heat necessary to cause this would have burned his hand off if he'd been here when it had happened. He scanned the nearby couplers for heat signatures and found only normal electrical activity. Whatever had caused the box to short had burned itself out.

"Dad?" Tim asked.

"Yes?"

"Are you done yet?"

"No, Tim. I'm just getting started."

"I have a question."

"All right. What's your question?"

"Why are there no dinosaurs on Mars?"

Andy groaned inwardly. This was a continuation of a cyclical conversation from the night before. He should have spent time thinking of some better answers. The question also troubled him because it demonstrated how, while Cara acted older than her age, Tim continued to revert.

"We talked about this before. No one has discovered a fossil record on Mars."

"So, there *were* dinosaurs on Mars. Just no one has discovered them yet."

Trying to concentrate on the coupler, Andy said, "Sure."

"But there hasn't been any kind of organic material found, Dad. How could there be fossils if there wasn't even the material?"

"Maybe there is the material, Tim. Maybe in the rush to terraform, they didn't record things like they should have. People make mistakes. People do things for their own reasons. What about this? What if Mars is hollow? Have you thought about that?"

"Dad," Tim said, scandalized. "There is no scientific evidence that Mars is hollow."

"Do you know that? Didn't you say before bedtime that Mars has no tectonic activity? Why couldn't it be hollow? I think the dinosaurs are in the center of Mars."

"I'm going to find it in the database," Tim said. "I'm going to find where you're wrong."

"We've got nine hundred years of survey data you can check, Tim. I think there must be something in there about the likelihood of a fossil record."

"He wants to find aliens," Cara said. "That's what he really wants."

"Somebody has to find them," Andy agreed. "Might as well be Tim Sykes."

"Can I name them if I find them?"

"That's how it works. You find the first dinosaur on Mars and you can call it the Sykasaur."

"What if I want to call it the Timasaur?"

"You could do that. I'm sure all the other Tims in Sol would appreciate the gesture. In fact, that would be very kind of you, Tim, to share your discovery so generously."

As Alice floated over with a new cover for the control box, Andy grinned as the sound of his son grumbling came across the net.

With the drone's help, Andy eased the cover over the repaired coupler and tacked it down with two quick welds. He stood, stretching, and peered into the dark. He found the blue disc of Earth, about three centimeters across, glittering with the silver band of High Terra.

The darkening function on his visor sputtered, momentarily showing him Sol's full light. He squinted, reminding himself he needed to keep moving before his suit's environmental controls failed and he cooked.

Turning toward the airlock, he started thinking of the checks he needed to run on the cargo in preparation for customs at Cruithne Station. He had a feeling the manifest was going to get extra scrutiny so the shipping company could try to claim damage. He couldn't afford anything less than what the deal had promised.

"Cara," he said. "I'm far enough away now. Go ahead and power the sensors back up."

"Should I run the diagnostics first?"

"Of course, sweetheart. We always run diagnostics first. The control system should prompt you. Do you see it?"

"I did it."

"Good job. Any faults?"

"No. It's almost online."

Andy sent Alice ahead to meet him in the airlock. "What should we have for lunch?" he asked. "You guys want some pasta? We can roll out pasta and make cheese sauce."

"I hate cheese sauce," Tim said.

"I know you do. That's why I always suggest it."

"The sensor's online, Daddy."

Andy was about to tell her "Good job" again when the proximity alarm shrieked in his helmet, warning of exterior danger. *Sunny Skies* had just entered an unmarked debris field.

CHAPTER TWO

STELLAR DATE: 07.24.2981 (Adjusted Years)
LOCATION: *Sunny Skies*
REGION: Greek Asteroids, Jovian Combine

Andy was aware of Cara screaming at him in the background as his helmet display highlighted the incoming debris. Or maybe the sound was the warning klaxons coming over the open channel.

"Cara, honey," he said, blinking as his face screen filled with floating red dots that reminded him of chaff. "Calm down. Tell me what's on the screen."

"The sensors didn't see it," she said. "The torch already hit a bunch of debris and even a meteor, I think. It's hitting all over the ship. What do I do? There are so many more. They're going to hit you."

A calm had settled over Andy. He usually experienced stress as an opposite tunnel vision. He saw all the factors in front of him, though it didn't mean it was any easier for him to choose the right path out of danger. It might have been his training from the TSF—or what his wife Brit liked to call his inability to feel anything—but he understood deeply that he was more worried about his daughter being scared than he was about his own well-being. But he absolutely had to worry about his own well-being because he hadn't done a good enough job teaching her how to read the nav station's data flow.

Obviously, he would have to focus on that later.

He was probably fifty meters from the airlock, an obstacle course of knee-catching trip-hazards between him and the relative safety of its recessed entrance.

"Cara," he said. "Listen to me. Send Alice back to me. Can you do that?"

For a minute, there was only sniffling across the channel, then she answered, "I can do it. I have her controls up."

"Are you there, Dad?" Tim said. "Why are there alarms going off?"

"We're flying through somebody else's trash. It's like getting shot at."

"We're getting shot at?"

"No, son," Andy said, voice still calm. "We're moving a whole lot faster than the things we're flying into, so they hit us like bullets. It would be safer if I was inside *Sunny Skies.*"

"Then why don't you come inside? Do you want me to open the airlock?"

"No, Tim," Andy said carefully, struggling to keep his voice calm. "Don't open any airlocks. I'm on my way back inside. Your sister is sending Alice to pick me up."

The thought of Tim hearing fear in his voice and opening the airlock too soon filled Andy with dread. He pushed it away.

Alice appeared in the distance, and Andy could barely make out the spray of the drone's steam jets. Next to him, a silent hole appeared in a rectangular casing and he hoped there wasn't anything critical inside. Conceivably, there was enough shielding between the crew areas of the ship and the outer shell that any damages too small to register on the sensors wouldn't hurt them.

Normally the ship would have picked up any debris fields and avoided them. It was Andy's own fault for disabling half the array out of caution. A truly hardened spacer would tell him she'd rather be cooked slowly than blown apart by a meteorite. You could survive getting cooked. Was it Brit's voice saying that? Maybe. She wouldn't have let him turn off the sensors.

Next time, Andy told himself. Don't beat yourself up about it now.

He started a slow lope toward the airlock, letting himself float just a meter at a time before coming back down on a clear section of the ship's skin so his boots could latch properly. A section of his faceplate display had begun malfunctioning. What should have been a row of indicators showing his suit's systems was now just a cloud of fractured light. Had the helmet taken an extra-large bit of dust?

Andy flinched as a stabbing pain flared in his forearm. Shocked, he searched for the cause to find a pinhole jet of air spraying into the vacuum. His display flashed yellow to alert him to the leak.

"Way ahead of you," he muttered.

"What?" Cara demanded.

How much time had he let pass since talking to her? Alice was still a hundred meters away. A note on Andy's display counted down the distance between them.

"Just talking to myself. Are you checking the other systems?"

"We're taking impacts all over the ship. Could we have flown around this?"

"In a perfect world, yes." Another stab caught his left shin and Andy nearly stumbled. More sizzling jabs of pain ran up his leg. It felt like tiny devils were attacking him with needles. He moaned at the loss of the suit. He didn't have room in the budget to replace it.

"Are you all right?" Cara said, fear in her voice. "Alice is almost there. Can you see her yet?"

Along with calling the robot Alice, the kids referred to it as 'her.' Andy steadfastly thought of the robot as *it* in case he ever had to sell it. He saw its angular form bobbing toward him.

"Almost here," he said. "Are the sensors picking up anything larger? Anything capable of hurting the ship?"

"No," Cara said. "I don't see anything on the screen. Should I look somewhere else?"

Sometimes when she said specific phrases, she sounded almost adult to him, almost like her mother. He had to remind himself that she wouldn't know where to look unless he told her, unless she remembered what he had taught her. *If* he had taught her correctly.

"Check the secondary arrays for electromagnetic activity," he said. "We should—" Andy gritted his teeth as another hot needle stabbed near his bellybutton. That could be a problem. "We shouldn't assume there isn't another ship out there. Do you see anything?"

"I don't see anything, Dad. Why would another ship be out there and not send us a message? Isn't that what everyone is supposed to do?"

"Just because they're supposed to do it doesn't mean they will," he said, gasping. He had managed a few more leaps, closing the gap between him and the approaching robot. Warning indicators flashed inside his faceplate until he couldn't tell what was a notification and what was the onboard system tracking incoming debris. His vision grew blurry from pain.

"Where's Alice?" he asked, blinking. "Where did Alice go?"

"She's almost there," Cara said. "I think she got hit by something."

Seemingly out of nowhere, Alice appeared in front Andy and collided with his chest, steam jets spraying in all directions. Andy grabbed at its square body while struggling to activate the magnets along his forearms and palms. The suit clamped down firmly, holding him in place, and he blew out a sigh of relief that only fogged his helmet more.

Alice spat steam and Andy realized he'd forgotten to release his mag boots. Floating free, he suffered a moment of panic as he wasn't sure if the robot could hold him. The fear was irrational, though. Alice could carry a hundred times his weight in vacuum.

"I've got Alice. Or Alice has me. We're coming back in."

"She's got you!" Tim squealed across the channel. "I want to ride Alice."

Andy straightened out his body, floating parallel to *Sunny Skies*. He noticed several more punctures peppered across the ship's skin until finally the edge of the airlock passed underneath him and Alice lowered them both into the open mouth of the doorway.

Releasing the magnets in his right palm, Andy smacked the locking mechanism and watched gratefully as the doors slid closed.

"I'm inside," he said. "Still no other ships?"

"No other ships," Cara said. "I see little damage symbols all over the ship but everything still seems to be working."

"Any big flashing X marks?"

"No, I don't think so."

Andy relaxed slightly. Once he got to the medical bay, he could send Alice out to check the interior systems for an update. In a perfect world, he'd have five bots to assist with maintenance. As it was, Alice could scan everything and he would have to decide what to trust to the robot and then start working his way through the rest himself. He wouldn't be lying around the rest of the trip to Cruithne.

The lock cycled, air hissing around him until the inner door opened and he let Alice carry him in. They weren't out of zero-g yet. It was another fifteen minutes of navigating corridors and gangways through the functional portion of *Sunny Skies* until they reached the habitat ring.

Inside the ship, Andy's faceplate display cleared of the clutter from trying to track incoming debris. He rested his helmeted head on top of Alice, turning his face to the side, and watched the corridor slide by. He was back in atmosphere but didn't feel like pulling off the helmet. Every movement sent waves of pain through his body, though what felt like hundreds of puncture wounds was probably only three.

He passed a section of smooth, pale wall the kids had used as a canvas at some point. Stars and planets danced, some by Cara's finely detailed hand and many more in Tim's bold lines. Of course, there was also a scene by Tim showing Andy and Brit holding hands with Cara and Tim on either side, everyone smiling. They were all standing in what looked like a green field, but where would they have been? The last place they had visited with actual grass parks was High Terra, in the suburb where Brit's parents lived. Tim would remember the parks, he supposed. That wouldn't be a happy memory for Tim. For any of them.

He wished they had visited Earth. At this point, he didn't know if he would ever be able to take them to see where he had grown up, to show them where he'd been born. They could always go back to High Terra. Brit's mom was still there. They would be able to stand in the ring's graduated gravity, but never Earth without modifications. He didn't know how he could ever afford that kind of surgery. Something they'd taken for granted in the TSF. He wondered how he would afford Cara's neural link in eight years. He needed to think bigger than he had been so far, shuttling cargo nowhere to nowhere for chump change.

Andy's thoughts bounced around until he and the robot finally reached the bulkhead separating the inner ship from the habitat ring. He released his magnetic locks, slid off the robot and pull himself into the interior airlock. Over his link, he directed Alice to download the most recent maintenance data and check each point of concern. The robot answered with two small jets of steam as it turned to float back down the hallway.

Cycling the doors, Andy's stomach did a flip as he oriented on the inner section and his feet came to rest on what had been his ceiling. As the inner gravity took hold, he felt like two bags of concrete had settled on his shoulders, renewing the pain in his arms, legs, and abdomen. He groaned and leaned against the wall.

The lock opened to reveal Cara and Tim, both waiting for him.

"Dad!" Tim cried, running forward to grab his legs.

Andy winced but suppressed the urge to gasp. "Hey, buddy," he said, hugging his son's brown-haired head against his side.

The kids were dressed in standard blue-gray coveralls, Tim's with the cuffs rolled way up, and Cara's looking a little too small.

Cara wasn't quite tall enough to get under his arm to support him. She stepped close and for a second looked like she had when she'd been Tim's size, reaching up for a hug. Then he realized she had grabbed his helmet with two hands to disengage the lock and pull it off. In her hands, the battered helmet looked like it had been run through in a trash compressor.

"The suit says you're bleeding," she said. "We need to go up to the medical station."

Andy nodded weakly, willing to let her be in charge of this part. "No red X marks popped up on the maintenance display since I asked you?" he asked.

She gave him an irritated look. "No, Daddy," she said. "But I think there's a big one on your head."

Andy tapped his temple with a gloved index finger. "You mean here?" he said, giving her a pained grin. "That one's never going away. You have to ignore it."

Cara rolled her eyes. "Come on," she urged. "You promised us pasta. I don't want blood in my shells and cheese."

"Ugh," Tim shouted in his monster voice, which meant he was relieved. "Blood in the shells and cheese?"

"That would certainly be terrible," Andy said. He let them pull him the rest of the way to the med section.

CHAPTER THREE

STELLAR DATE: 08.15.2981 (Adjusted Years)
LOCATION: *Sunny Skies*
REGION: Greek Asteroids, Jovian Combine

Despite being over a hundred years old, the auto-surgeon did a good job on Andy's wounds. They were low on pain meds, so Andy was going to be aching for a week as the sutures healed. He could deal with that. Pain didn't cost him anything.

Moving slowly around the small galley, he selected supplies for the shells and cheese he had promised the kids, grimacing when the reach for a container of flour sent stabbing pain through his abdomen.

"You don't seem better," Cara said, watching him.

"I'm fine. Give me a couple days."

"Why don't you just pull out some of the prepared stuff. We don't need anything special."

"You said shells and cheese," Tim called from the table. He had a pad and stylus out, kicking his heels against the floor as he doodled.

"I promised shells and cheese, and that's what you'll get," Andy said. "It's bad enough the cheese is going to be artificial. We can still make the pasta. That's a Sykes family specialty. Your grandmother used to do it the very old way and lay all the pasta shells out on a sheet to dry. Can you imagine doing that?"

"Why?" Cara said, wrinkling her nose. "Sounds like a big waste of time."

"Sometimes *doing* is the reason."

"Sometimes *doing* is dumb," she said. "Next we'll be growing our own wheat."

"If we had the space, I would love to do that."

"Mom liked to garden," Cara said.

He nodded. *Sunny Skies* had an aftermarket hydroponic garden installed by some owner in its distant past. The apparatus was currently dry and taking up space in the habitat ring that could have been used for special cargo, he just hadn't gotten around to cleaning it out. The room had been one of Brit's spaces.

He measured scoops of the flour. "Get me two cups of water."

Cara went to the cabinet for the measuring cup, then filled it at the sink. Andy watched her hold the cup in the air to check measurements. She added another few more milliliters before nodding.

"Go ahead and dump it in there," he said, motioning toward the mixing bowl.

It was still cheating, in a way. The flour had everything it needed to form reasonably tasty pasta. No need for eggs or salt, or the olive oil his mother loved whenever they could scrounge it. He had purchased a hundred kilos of flour three years ago when he had the extra funds to think about emergency food. Now they had nearly run through that.

He would need to negotiate for new food stores on Cruithne, not the cheapest place in InnerSol to scrape up calories. He was already going to need to find fuel.

Andy put worries about their destination out of his mind and focused on turning the dough. He dusted the counter with flour and dumped out the bowl.

"There you go," he said. "Dust up your hands and start turning that over."

"Do I have to?"

"I'll do it!" Tim shouted, jumping down from the table. "I want to squeeze the dough."

"Your sister can do it. You'll help with the cheese sauce, all right?"

Tim slapped the counter and a cloud of flour filled the air around his hands. As he reached for the dough ball, Andy swatted his hands away.

"Let's go, Cara."

Dusting her hands, Cara moved around the counter to grab the lump of dough and start folding it. Andy washed his own hands at the sink and took the rolling pin down from a cabinet near the ceiling. It was an ancient looking thing, crusted with old dough now harder than concrete.

When Cara was done turning the dough, he had her roll it out into flat strips then feed it into the pasta machine until they became snake-shaped ropes that she lay back out on the freshly dusted counter.

Andy pulled a kitchen knife out of a nearby recess. "You remember how to turn the shells?" he asked.

"I remember," Cara said.

He handed the knife over, handle-first, and watched her make the first few shells by laying the knife blade flat on the end of the dough-snake, pulling and lightly smearing the pasta dough so it rolled against itself before she cut it off. The first few were warped but once she had the hang of it, a pile of fresh pasta shells grew on the counter beside her.

"Don't cut your nose off," Andy said.

Cara didn't take her eyes off her work. "Shut up, Dad."

With Cara occupied, Andy pulled down the ingredients for the artificial cheese sauce and had Tim pull over a chair to stand beside him at the stove. Soon the sauce was bubbling to Andy's satisfaction with Tim focused on stirring, pausing occasionally to dip the spoon and raise it above the pot to drop dollops of sauce.

"Don't lose any of that sauce," Andy warned. "It's all we've got."

"I won't lose any sauce, Dad. I want to see how high it can drip."

"Higher than you can reach, trust me."

"Dad," Cara said.

He glanced at her. She was done with the shells, now arranging them loosely on a baking pan to feed into the auto-oven, which would flash twenty-four hours' drying in five minutes.

"What do you need?"

Cara didn't take her gaze off the shells as she asked, "Did you ever kill anyone when you were in the TSF?"

He frowned. What had brought this on? The debris field? Seeing him bleeding? He considered lying, then knew he shouldn't. It was always a matter of how to present the truth.

"Yes, I did."

"You weren't close to them, though, were you?"

Andy's throat was abruptly dry. He went to the sink to pour a glass of water and drank half of it. "Most of the time it was far away, in ships," he said. "But there were a few times when we had to board ships. Then it was up close."

"Did Mom have to kill people, too?"

"Sometimes. She was a pilot, just like me."

Cara nodded without saying anything.

"Why are you thinking about killing people?" he asked.

She shrugged. "I was curious, that's all. That's what people do in the TSF, don't they?"

"I never wanted to hurt people, but sometimes you don't get to choose. Sometimes people attack you first, or they attack other people. You do your best to keep everyone safe."

Cara nodded.

"Is that pasta ready?" Andy asked.

In twenty minutes, they were sitting at the little table with glasses of water and bowls of the warm shells and cheese. Tim lifted his spoon above his head to let the shells drop back into the bowl. He tried dropping a shell in his mouth and missed. Andy caught the shell before it hit the floor and stuffed it in his own mouth, making a face at Tim that earned him a squeal.

"Better hang onto those shells, kid," Andy said, chewing obnoxiously.

"Dad!" Tim shouted. "That was mine!"

"I'm a shells and cheese pirate," Andy said. "You let that shell go and I'm gonna gobble it up."

Cara was quiet throughout the meal, only smiling when Andy complemented the pasta shells and Tim nodded agreement, smacking his lips.

When they were done, Tim fed the dishes and utensils into the sterilizer and then dashed down the corridor to the small room they used as a lounge. There was a couch, a 2D viewing screen to replace the room's broken holodisplay, and boxes full of Tim's toys scattered around. They watched a series on Marsian terraforming for an hour and then Andy announced it was time for bed.

It was a little early and Andy got the complaints he expected. "Time to get a start on a new day," he said.

Cara remained quiet.

Andy glanced at her, hoping she would get past whatever mood had settled on her shoulders.

He chastised himself for the thought, knowing he needed to find some way to get Cara to open up about what was bothering her. Otherwise nothing would change. They had a saying in the TSF: *Hope is not a method*, which was a smart-ass way of saying you couldn't hope your way out of a bad situation.

He pulled up the ship's diagnostics briefly over his link to check on Alice's progress on the damage caused by the debris field, and checked the ship's depressing fuel levels as well. They were going to arrive at Cruithne Station on velocity and vapors.

After teeth were brushed, hair combed or tied in fresh braids, Andy sent Cara to her room as he read Tim a story and arranged his son's various toys on the bed to protect him from monsters.

When he went to Cara's room, she had already turned out the overhead lights. In the dim glow from the corridor strip-lighting, he saw only the outline of her back as she faced the wall.

"You all right, Cara?" he asked.

She shrugged, her narrow shoulders moving the blanket a little.

Andy crossed the room to sit on the edge of her bed. He smoothed some stray hairs out of her eyes and felt tears on her cheeks.

"I'm still here," he said.

"I know," she said, so softly he barely heard her.

"I'm not going anywhere."

Cara didn't answer.

"Where do we live?" she asked finally, voice quiet. It was their old ritual.

"We live on *Sunny Skies*, duh." He failed to put the goofy note in his voice.

"No, Daddy," she said, still staring at the wall. "We live in Rabbit Country."

"Rabbit Country?" he asked. "There are no rabbits in space."

"We're the rabbits," Cara said. "Ears up and ready to run."

"Ears up and ready to run," he agreed.

Andy waited. She wasn't pulling away from him, just keeping to herself. He put his legs up on the bed and leaned back against the wall, stroking her hair again.

He didn't remember falling asleep but found himself waking in the dark some time later. The corridor door had closed automatically at some point, leaving the room dark. Cara had turned on her side and was breathing evenly but had managed to twist out of her covers.

Standing slowly, with stabbing pains running the length of his body, Andy found the edge of the blanket and pulled it up until Cara was covered again.

He checked the Link, and found that Alice had a report for him. He stood in the dark for a minute, listening to Cara breathing, then bent back down to kiss her forehead.

"Good night, sweetheart," he murmured, then straightened to find his way to the door and the dim corridor outside.

CHAPTER FOUR
STELLAR DATE: 07.25.2981 (Adjusted Years)
LOCATION: *Sunny Skies*
REGION: Greek Asteroids, Jovian Combine

Sitting in an alcove off the habitat airlock, Andy spread the battered EVA suit across his knees and applied patching liquid to the visible holes. He would need to run a full systems check later for micro-tears and any other damage he could fix on his own before he took it into vacuum again. For now, it would work in the rest of the ship, where he only needed the suit for warmth in the unheated, zero-g sections of *Sunny Skies*. It was cheaper to keep the air in those sections a breathable mix than to dump it all to vacuum, but he couldn't waste fuel on heat.

There had been a time when the whole ship had served as a zero-g playground for the kids. Then money had gone from elusive to actively avoiding him.

Checks complete, Andy stood and pulled on the suit. He slowly fit its outer harness around his waist and shoulders, awakening new jabs of pain with each movement. The suit smelled of sweat and something moldy he didn't want to think about. If he had to admit it, the kids filling the suit with cleaning foam had been more help than prank.

Pulling the battered helmet over his head, he ran a quick diagnostic check on the suit, noting the slow loss of inner pressure, as well as the fractured lower left section of his faceplate, which now showed information in jittery snowflake-shaped blobs of color.

He mounted the ladder into the airlock and climbed slowly, feeling out the pains in his arms and legs, until he reached the top and hit the activation controls. All the way up, the magnets in his right glove kept sticking, twisting his wrist when they wouldn't release properly. He had to stop using the hand altogether.

Below him, the hatch slid closed and the world shifted, sending stomach bile into his throat. His inner ear swooned. Andy squeezed his eyes closed and gripped the ladder, forcing himself to breathe deeply until the sick feeling subsided.

The upper hatch opened and he pulled himself into the zero-g section of the ship.

Alice's list had come back with significant damage to the hull. The drone had checked most of the systems on the outer hull where damage would be obvious. It was still checking interior spaces where debris had penetrated the outer skin.

Andy groaned. It would take him at least a week to work through the major repairs. After that, there was a second list of burn-outs where outer connections had either grounded-out or been destroyed completely. Scanning the list, which was bad enough, he guessed at other areas he should check for secondary damage.

As usual, it was a miracle *Sunny Skies* continued to fly. For having been built as a recreational craft, *Sunny Skies* carried a confusing set of redundancies, like a yacht built for preppers. Not that he was complaining, but the ship constantly surprised him with little bits of added tech from its long history.

Andy grabbed a handhold and propelled himself along the wall to the nearest junction of corridors. He needed to go down two levels to the main cargo bays.

He doubted any damage from the debris field could have penetrated the center of the ship—at least the interior scans hadn't indicated atmosphere loss from puncture wounds—but he was worried enough about the integrity of the cargo to check. This shipment was a collection of random crates with a complicated manifest that meant he needed to review every container for discrepancies. He didn't want to discover any serial numbers had mysteriously changed mid-flight.

Ahead of him, the corridor lights sensed his presence and flickered alive—except for a few sections where they didn't and he drifted through the dark.

In the cargo area, he floated in the doorway waiting for the lights to activate throughout the long room. There were two wide airlocks in the chamber that could open to allow transport drones to enter and pull the crates out. The openings were big enough that any malfunction meant he'd be in vacuum before he knew what hit him.

As he waited for the systems check, Andy wondered if he had always been such a pessimist, or if becoming a parent had done this to him. Only it wasn't pessimism so much as thinking through everything bad that could happen in any given situation. Tim might be playing next to the stove with a pot boiling over his head. In one future, everything was fine. In another, his face was covered in third-degree burns. With these possibilities playing out in his mind continuously, Andy didn't know if he was crazy or simply overly prepared.

Brit had been better at living in the moment, not worrying about what might happen. She had seemed to have the ability to read anxiety in Andy's face—even before he realized it was there—and respond with something simple like a smile or a word. She'd helped him. Had immediately made him feel more calm. He hadn't realized she was doing it until the effect was gone. Now he had to recognize the swell of worry and pause his thoughts, redirect toward something productive.

In combat, he'd never needed to worry. All possibilities had been played out in front of him and he'd chosen a path between them. Even if he thought of the kids as red space—a sector occupied by enemy combatants moving with their own intentions and capabilities—he seemed to lack the ability to separate his feelings for them from his rational decision-making toward problems, resulting in a mess of indecision.

As a pilot, he knew what steps to take to control his weapons system in the necessary manner to defeat the enemy, just like during hand-to-hand he'd pivot his hips in a throw, following it with a throat strike, or any number of other steps to assure his enemy's defeat. As a father, he could only look in their watching eyes and hope he was doing the right thing, mind quailing.

Hope is not a method.

"Focus on what you *have*, not what you don't have," Brit used to tell him, and now he repeated the words as a mantra, listing what he had like stacking bricks in a defensive wall.

"We have the ship," he told the display panel, its data tickling his Link. "We have the cargo. We have fuel to Cruithne. We have our health."

The panel blinked yellow, sending him waiting signals that the worried part of his brain interpreted as uncertainty. The manifest slid past his thoughts, broadcast IDs on the crates matching the expected serial number in the cargo list. When the panel lit up green, it was like a shot of happiness. He nodded, acknowledging the report.

The manifest file closed and he was about to leave the bay, when another message from the monitoring system came over his Link. There was a supplemental report. Somewhere in the bay was a group of crates that had come in separately from the main cargo shipment.

Andy frowned. He didn't remember authorizing a supplemental shipment. How had he missed this? Had the kids distracted him during load-up?

He scanned the new list quickly, then ran it against the original manifest to see if anything had changed. The tokens from their respective origins all matched, so unless the tracking software had been hacked, everything was where it was supposed to be.

Why hadn't the supplemental appeared until now? It seemed dumb for a smuggler to hide something on *Sunny Skies*; a ship with only nominal chances of reaching its destination. It was cheaper to just pay for the ride since, by law, Andy owned anything put on his ship without either his express permission or a shipping contract.

He pulled the location data for the extra crates over his Link. The face shield display tried to highlight locations across the room but most of the icons were lost in the fractured section of the shield, resulting in a meaningless but pretty shower of colors.

Grumbling to himself, Andy pulled up a schematic of the bay and noted the various locations of the extra crates. Of course, they were *under* other crates. Whoever had slipped them aboard must have done it during the regular loading process, probably running their drones right alongside the approved ones.

Didn't the system check entrance tokens on the drones as they dropped cargo? He was going to have to verify that at Cruithne. If the ship wasn't scanning security tokens for anyone coming on board like it was supposed to, he could have stowaways all over *Sunny Skies*.

Pulling himself along the wall, he reached the first set of cargo crates and launched over them, pushing himself along with his good magnetic glove. Most of the crates were standard two-meter squares. Those had been stacked in the middle of the bay, with odd-sized crates along the outer edges.

There were three crates that didn't belong. The first two were squares buried in the middle of the main stack. From the top of the pile, all he could do was verify their locations and attempt a Link connection with their limited onboard firmware. These crates didn't appear to be monitoring anything but the dates they had been locked, which was several days prior to their arrival on *Sunny Skies*. The firmware could send false data, though.

Since he couldn't see inside, Andy couldn't do anything with the stowaway crates but mark them as quarantine so Cruithne loaders wouldn't pull them off with the rest of the cargo.

He found the third crate near the outer edge of the stack, a long flat chest marked with old TSF stencils. Andy floated, staring in surprise because he knew exactly what it was. Out of caution, he still queried the crate and it came back with the information he expected: Armory, High Terra, TSF. He had seen these types of crates thousands of times during mission load out and weapons issue.

Pushing off the crate behind him, he moved down beside the flat crate and activated his mag boots on the bay floor to anchor himself. He knelt and felt at the latches on the front of the crate. It didn't have a security token and opened when he activated the lock.

The lid lifted on smooth arms, revealing a collection of grenades, pistols and what looked like a multi-mode light combat rifle.

A bead of sweat ran down the middle of Andy's back. He hadn't seen this kind of hardware in nearly eleven years, not since Brit had told him she was pregnant and they had decided together to leave the TSF. He held his hands over the rifle, remembering exactly how to activate it, its targeting and firing procedures, even field stripping and light maintenance, all ground into him during the part of his life he'd spent as a soldier, and then as a pilot. It had been most of his life, really. He'd joined the TSF at seventeen to get his neural implant and had left at thirty-three, a father.

Andy realized he was frightened to touch the rifle. Why? He could hold it as easily as he might one of his children.

It wasn't the collection of weapons that frightened him; it was their presence. How, and why, were they here? Why would someone smuggle this aboard *Sunny Skies* unless they meant to use them at Cruithne Station?

Andy's earlier thought about stowaways hit him like a hammer.

Pulling the lid closed, he positioned his hands under the crate until he could leverage himself against the floor and raise it into the air next to him. It was awkward in the zero-g but he had plenty of experience wrestling crates in the bays. Balancing himself with the flat crate, Andy pushed off toward the bay's access door.

The weapons were going into one of the many hiding places throughout the ship. Then he'd need to do a complete sweep of the non-inhabited area, starting with the engines. If anything happened to the drive systems, they were dead.

At the door, Andy looked back at the looming stack of crates in the room. He would sweep the ship, but he had a feeling that whoever meant to use these weapons could very well be hiding in the two other crates. They'd have to be in some kind of stasis, but it was possible. The onboard system could be hiding their true function.

In an ideal world, he would have drones to move the crates inside the bay. But he didn't, which meant he had to wait until they arrived at Cruithne—another thirty days from now—to get at the unauthorized crates.

CHAPTER FIVE
STELLAR DATE: 07.25.2981 (Adjusted Years)
LOCATION: *Sunny Skies*
REGION: Approaching Asteroid Belt, Jovian Combine

Pausing to catch his breath in the corridor, and figure out the best way to maneuver the crate back up two levels to a storage locker just outside the habitat, Andy found himself staring at its dull gray surface, flooded by memories from the color that used to rule his world.

Some people joined the Terran Space Force just to get the standard neural implant. Andy was one of those people. As a teenager, he'd grown to hate the idea of life without the Link. His father had always promised him that when he was old enough for the implant, the money would be there. Andy should have known that wasn't true.

Looking back, he didn't blame his dad. It couldn't have been easy trying to raise a family in the sprawl of Jerhattan. He had grown up in a town called Summerville, just outside Charleston. Andy's family lived in a high-rise with its lower three stories sunk in sluggish green water from an overflow of the Summerville river. They were squatters, but he hadn't known that when he was Tim's age. He'd loved swimming in the warm water, chasing oil slicks or thin streams of bubbles from cars and low buildings drowned long ago.

His dad, Charles, spent days hustling for basics to keep their mom, Sibine, and little Andy and Jane in clothes and shoes. They were an odd pair, his mom and dad. Even without a Link, his dad had some supernatural ability to read people and deals that went beyond mere information. His mom had been disabled at an early age in an accident she didn't like to talk about and, Andy realized now, must have been too poor to repair.

Sibine could barely walk but she had a Link, and took it upon herself to become their teacher. His mom taught them practical skills like cooking from scratch, fishing and sewing to repair their clothes—he recalled vividly the smell of her homemade pickles. She also taught them history, civics, philosophy, physics and chemistry. His strongest memory of his mother was her medium-distance gaze as she pulled information from her Link to explain one of his obnoxious questions.

Sure, he'd had his intermittent access to the Link network through various terminals and public connections when he could steal time, but it wasn't anything like having the world's knowledge at the edge of his thoughts, removing the need to memorize anything. Maybe that was why some childhood memories stood out so starkly. They were the pillars of his mind.

He also remembered the first time he realized someone was speaking down to his father for not having a Link. Andy might have been nine or ten, old enough to start paying attention to how adults talked to each other.

They'd been in a convenience store and the woman behind the counter had expected payment via credit connection. His dad had offered to pay cash.

Now, Andy understood that his dad had been trying to offer the cash before the auto transaction link tried and failed. Charlie hadn't been fast enough.

The pale woman had squinted at his dad and then snorted a laugh.

"You're dumb, aren't you?" she'd asked.

'Dumb' meant a lot of things to the local poor back then. Mainly it was a throwback to when a person really was blind and mute. Not having the Link might as well have been those things.

He remembered the barest instant of a flat, angry expression touching his father's face, before his lips spread in a broad smile, showing his naturally good teeth, something the woman lacked.

"Smart enough to see how lovely you are," he had said, in a way that actually sounded like he was complimenting the woman. Charlie pulled a hand through his hair and leaned forward, blue eyes flashing, and set the bills on the counter. "I like to keep my business local," he said, voice warm. "Cash good for you?"

The woman had stared for a second, then nodded and took the bills.

"Keep the change," his dad had said, still smiling warmly.

Without a Link, his father was present in a way that most people weren't. He also liked to say that he was fine with his own memory and didn't want to rely on the Network to know what to think about something.

Andy had heard all that but he'd never forgotten the woman's look of superiority. When he was old enough for the operation, he'd repeatedly asked his dad when they were going to make the appointment—until Charlie had finally admitted there wasn't any money. Andy had started looking for other options immediately.

Local gangs would have lent him the money for a heavy price, which probably would have meant entry into a life he didn't want. The idea of the Terran Space Force had entered his mind while gazing up at the shiny strip of High Terra against the moon, and he figured that if the operation meant servitude, the best choice was the one that got him out of Summerville. Why not get off Earth altogether?

＊ ＊ ＊ ＊ ＊

Andy checked the time in his helmet display. The suit was still glitching, dropping its connection with *Sunny Skies* then picking up without adjusting for the lag. He figured he still had an hour before he needed to get to sleep himself. The kids wouldn't let him sleep in.

Pulling the weapons case up the ladder tubes wasn't as hard as he had expected, although he kept scraping his knees as he worked his way upward. The crate bounced against the inside walls, leaving swipes of gray paint in several spots. He'd have to make up a story for Cara to explain the new marks. She noticed things like that. She was like her mother, that way.

In the last corridor before the accessway to the habitat section, he hooked an arm around a support strut and rested. Looking down on the crate where it floated above the floor, he thought it looked a bit like a coffin. He pushed the thought out of his mind.

* * * * *

The two sergeants were on their feet the minute he walked through the door. Behind them, all the furniture was the same dull color he would come to know as "TSF Gray." In all the times Andy had visited the recruiting station, he couldn't recall ever seeing anyone sitting behind the big block-shaped desks that looked like folded defense mechs.

Andy was wearing the best clothes he could get together, his hair carefully combed and all his identification cards in his front pants pockets.

The first sergeant was tall and thin as a bone, while the other looked carved from a boulder. The thin one whose nameplate read *Kass*, reached Andy first. He was already frowning.

"You," he said sharply. "Where's your token? Why didn't the door pick you up?"

Andy was taken aback by the tone of the man's voice. He opened his mouth to force out an answer but the muscled sergeant, Hilton, cut him off.

"He's pure, sergeant. Doesn't have any EMF whatsoever."

"Pure?" Kass said, sounding like he'd been told Andy was an alien.

"No broadcast," Hilton said. "No origin indicator, either. Where'd you come from?"

"Summer—" Andy started.

"I don't care where you came from," Kass said, cutting him off again. "We'll get to that later if it matters. What's your name?"

"Come on," Hilton said. "Answer."

"Andy Sykes," Andy said before one of them jumped in again. His voice sounded unnaturally high in his ears.

"Sykes," Kass said. "First names are a waste of time. TSF doesn't issue first names."

"Sykes," Hilton repeated. "I like it. Private Sykes. Maybe we'll get you to Private First Class Sykes before you leave for Basic. What do you think about that?"

"Hold on," Kass said. "Before you worry about that. What do you want to do, Sykes? You want to be a killer?"

Andy looked at each of them, figuring out this was all an act. He'd watched his dad play a similar game while working a hustle. Charlie would rain words on his target until they simply gave in and agreed with him. The key was to slow down his responses, make his words worth more than theirs.

He shrugged. "I'm here to learn," he said.

The two men looked at each other. Andy figured they must deal with applicants without Links all the time. This was Summerville, after all. He supposed a Link would have allowed him to do all the research he wanted, watch all the first-hand video from combat reviews, even apply for entry without ever setting foot in a recruiting station.

"Why don't you have a seat," Kass said, motioning toward a conference table to one side of the room. Its surface was a display console.

"Thanks," Andy said.

Over the next hour, they explained the many different jobs he could potentially perform in the Terran Space Force, from broadcast information specialist to freighter pilot. They talked about benefits, travel, education.

"How's all this sound?" Hilton asked.

"It sounds good."

"You interested in the aptitude test?" Kass asked.

"I am."

The man's skeletal face split in a grin.

The aptitude test was one of the strangest things Andy had ever attempted. The questions started out overly simple and progressed until he was drawing on some of the more obscure elements of philosophy or history that his mother had insisted he think about.

"Don't repeat it back to me, Andy," she used to say, staring into the middle distance between them as she verified his answer against the database. "Tell me what you think. Get to the bottom of it."

"That's not fair, Mom," he had whined. "You're cheating."

With a feral smile, she'd answered, "Yes, I am. Someday you will, too, so I have to abuse you now."

His mom and dad were alike that way: they knew how to read people. His mom knew how to play him like an instrument, push him to the limits of his mind. When he'd finally received the neural Link, he'd felt like the house of his mind was suddenly filled with windows and doors—and she had built the walls to hold him up and protect him from the tsunami of adding the Link to his thoughts.

The questions shifted from too easy, to tricky, to obscure and esoteric. He guessed at the outcomes of mechanical schematics and finished logic circuits. Some of it was obviously ancient history, asking him to analyze spectrum circuitry, while other questions hinted at subjects he had only just read about.

He knew now that the test was progressive. For every correct answer, the questions branched and went deeper. He was sweating when he finished. The test didn't tell him when he'd reached its last question. The screen merely asked, "Are you sure?" and prompted him to answer yes or no.

Andy had stared at the screen for a minute, trying to second-guess the question, before finally answering: Yes.

The screen instructed him to wait for results, so he sat in the small room with its promotional display on the wall reading: *Terran Space Force Onward! Outward!*

After what felt like an hour, the door swung out and Sergeant Kass stood in the opening.

"You got your ID on you, right?" the thin man demanded.

"Yes," Andy said. He couldn't understand why the sergeant sounded furious. Kass had checked his identification cards before seating him at the terminal.

"Good. Come on."

CHAPTER SIX

STELLAR DATE: 07.25.2981 (Adjusted Years)
LOCATION: *Sunny Skies*
REGION: Approaching Asteroid Belt, Jovian Combine

Andy opened the storage cabinet and maneuvered the crate until it was sitting in the bottom of the locker. To a cursory glance, it might almost look like the bottom of the cabinet. It might fool a customs agent but it certainly wouldn't get past Tim and Cara. He locked the cabinet with his personal security token just to be safe.

If Cara did try to open the cabinet and discovered he had locked it, the worst she could do was come to him and complain about it. If she tried to force the lock, he'd get an immediate alert over the ship's diagnostic system—as long as the system was functioning. The problems with his suit proved it was barely reliable.

Andy yawned and stretched. He glanced down the corridor where the ladder led up into the habitat ring. As soon as he returned to the command deck, he would double-check the ship's EMF signature for responses that didn't make sense. It bothered him that *Sunny Skies* might have already been broadcasting unknown signals from the stowaway crates for most of their trip.

If their onboard firmware was hiding activity, the crates could be serving as some kind of relay node for encrypted criminal data and he was going to be held accountable when they reached Cruithne. Why else would someone hide crates aboard a slow-moving private freighter?

The TSF detail on Cruithne could certainly be tracking any errant signals. It was a mission he had done himself many times. That would explain why he hadn't been boarded weeks ago. The TSF would sit back and capture all the data going in and out, then pick up the rubes piloting the ship when they arrived. The TSF detail was probably partying in one of Cruithne's many clubs right now, laughing.

He kicked off for the ladder, trying to defend the possibility that the cargo was something simple, like drugs or illegal tech, something cheap enough to risk on *Sunny Skies* but valuable enough to smuggle. What if his ship was just one of hundreds, and the smugglers were gambling on half the ships arriving as scheduled? That made more sense. That pointed toward drugs. He could deal with drugs. They weren't on his manifest and he could make a statement to station security when he arrived. No one was going to try to board the ship for drugs.

Drugs didn't explain the weapons, though. It was entirely possible that a crate of TSF weapons had made it onto his ship by coincidence, part of the same sort of large smuggling operation. It was also part of the ship's record that he was a veteran, so he supposed someone could be sending him a message. But what sort of message, and why? If it was personal, that made even less sense, but it worried him more.

As a former TSF combat pilot with ground experience, he'd had plenty of offers from private security firms when he had first left the service. Those had grown fewer over time and at this point he couldn't remember the last time a headhunter had sent him a message that wasn't a blanket offer.

As he pulled himself into the habitat gate and endured the stomach flip of taking on gravity, Andy grinned to himself letting his memory of the recruiting station run its course. Sergeant Kass had been a character, accusing him of being a plant from Higher Command, come to verify their testing techniques.

"You're a cheater," Kass had accused.

Andy had stammered a response, not understanding why he was suddenly under attack. He'd expected them to tell him he had failed and to kick him out the front door. Instead, Kass and Hilton had sat him down at the conference table and leaned in close on either side, glaring at him.

"No way you're some kid from the Summerville slums," Hilton growled. "Where you from really?"

"I'm from Summerville," Andy said, not knowing what else to tell them. He wanted to get up and run but Kass had taken his ID card to enter his citizenship number in the system for a third time.

When Andy finally ran out of excuses, the two men sat down on either side of the table, crossing their arms. They looked at each other, and Andy recognized the expressions of men trying to figure out how to capitalize on a situation.

Kass motioned with a finger. "So, here's what happened," he said, eyes narrow with suspicion. "If you're telling the truth and *really* don't understand how you did on the test."

"You did well on the test," Hilton interjected.

"You did *too* well," Kass said. "You did the kind of well that makes the system think it's being hacked. We get tested by Higher Command every quarter to make sure we're not cheating, bringing in recruits who don't meet the standards."

"You can do that?" Andy asked.

Kass gave him a withering look. "But some people, people who work for rogue corporations and things like that who want to hack the government, they're always looking for a way in. So, we also get people who come in to take the test just to see what new methods TSF is using for selection."

"That's what you look like," Hilton said. "Only you took the whole test, which most of them don't. They get to the questions they want to analyze and then try to run."

"Try to run? Can't they leave if they want?"

"Nope," Hilton said. "TSF Code 418.8 provides for the integrity and security of the recruitment process. Once you enter those doors, you are under the jurisdiction of the TSF."

"I didn't know I was agreeing to that."

Kass pointed a long finger at the entrance. "It's posted right on the door. If you'd checked the security token with your Link when you came in, it's bright as day."

"I don't have a Link," Andy said, finally giving up his bargaining chip. "That's why I'm here. I heard all TSF recruits get an implant."

Hilton's eyes widened. He looked at Kass, who was slapping his knee and wheezing laughter.

Kass pulled in a breath and let out a whooping laugh. "You're telling me, you passed the assessment exam without a Link?"

"I guess?" Andy asked. "Did I pass?"

Looking irritated with Kass, Hilton said, "Yeah, you passed. Like we said, you did too well."

As Kass tried to catch his breath, Hilton tapped the edge of the table and brought up a display that hadn't been part of the initial pitch.

"I believe you, kid," Hilton said. "I'm not from Summerville but I grew up in a place like it in Utah. I get it. So, I'm showing you this but it's not something we're supposed to just advertise. You have to ask about it. So, I'm going to ask you once: Did you come here to learn about the TSF Officer Corps?"

Andy stared at him, not fully understanding the question. "Officer Corps? What's that?"

"Excellent question," Hilton said, tapping the table. He brought up another display with information on a special academy.

Kass had finally gained his composure. His face was still flushed. "You're really going to show some hoodrat information about the academy?"

Hilton didn't look up from the display. "His scores allow access."

Kass snorted. "You're talking him out of our bonus, there, Sergeant. He goes to the academy; we don't get our cut."

"It's like that?" Hilton said.

"Yes, it's like that." Kass motioned toward Andy. "You think this kid is Academy material? He wants a neural implant. He doesn't want to serve." He turned his gaze to Andy. "How about it, kid. You here for yourself or for the TSF?"

Andy blinked. He'd never considered the question. Why would he want to "serve" the TSF? The thought had never entered his mind.

"I don't know," he said honestly. "But if it will get me out of Summerville, then I want to hear about it."

Hilton slapped him on the back. "Exactly," he said. "Sounds like me when I was sucking dust back in Provo."

Kass grumbled but didn't say anything.

"I have a question, though," Andy said. "What's an officer do, exactly? In most of the history I've read, they're either idiots or they die during the first battle."

* * * * *

In the control deck, Andy eased himself into one of the three console seats and brought up the ship's status on the display. He frowned as he realized how intermittent his data stream from the monitoring systems had been.

In truth, *Sunny Skies* needed a complete overhaul. The ship was a mess of short-term fixes stacked on top of one another. Getting caught in the debris storm was just the latest example of how failing systems on the ship were starting to impact each other. In a perfect world, the point defense system should have picked up the larger bits of debris long before they hit the torch, and he shouldn't have had to cut off the shields and sensors if he didn't have to EVA to fix a burned external power coupling. It was like trying to repair a sand castle in the wind.

He checked their progress along the flight plan. They were decelerating on schedule. Cruithne was just now reaching its furthest point from Earth, which would bring them into a rendezvous in thirty days. His fuel calculations had been correct, unfortunately, and they would arrive at the station with no way out unless he could buy more deuterium, which was probably going to be twice as expensive on Cruithne Station. He didn't want to pull up market rates and depress himself even further right now.

A fluctuation on drive control drew Andy's attention. Temperatures were rising in the reaction bottle. He frowned, pulling up the control console for the drive containment system. An erratic flow of readings indicated multiple failures all across the system.

"No," Andy said under his breath.

Rotating the diagnostic display, the fractures aligned in a straight puncture from the outer hull directly through the propulsion section and out again. Debris had penetrated the containment bottle and Alice hadn't spotted the puncture during the exterior scan.

Andy swallowed, amazed the engines had held until now.

He attempted to decrease output. Gradually at first. He had a tight delta-V to Cruithne and couldn't afford to lose deceleration thrust at this point in the flight plan. They'd overshoot the station and…he didn't want to think about what would happen if they overshot Cruithne.

Andy pulled up the emergency monitoring system and saw that it had turned itself off at some point. Had he already set an override? He couldn't remember doing that. It certainly wasn't something the kids would have played with.

He shook his head. He would have to find the software bug later.

The erratic readings continued to shift all around the drive's containment system, like lightning crackling around an egg. The weak spots were growing. Breaking out in sweat, pain jabbing his side as he shifted in the seat, Andy continued to chase thin points in the bottle, shifting resources even as other sections thinned in response.

After ten minutes, he accepted the mad chase was futile. The drive was going to fail.

He quickly pulled up the flight plan and checked their current delta-v to Cruithne. They were close. He could bring *Sunny Skies* in under chemical thrust if he dropped another ten percent.

Andy gritted his teeth. The kids weren't in crash couches. If he did what he had to, it would be like hitting them all with a sledgehammer.

He didn't have time. He had to slow the ship or they would be stranded between Earth and Cruithne, praying for TSF or anyone else to pick them up. They didn't have enough food on board.

Andy slapped the emergency klaxon. Tim and Cara would know to strap in. Checking his data against the original flight plan, he calculated a hard burst through the engine.

"Daddy?" Cara asked over the comm. "What's going on?"

"Dad?" Tim said sleepily.

"I'm here," Andy said. "Strap in. Both of you. We need to execute a hard burn."

The flight plan came back sub-optimal, which was close enough. He nearly entered the command to execute before realizing he hadn't buckled his own straps on the seat. Andy fumbled them into place, wincing as they automatically tightened down on his wounds.

Reaching for the console again, he activated the flight change.

Sunny Skies groaned around him as the engine flared to full capacity. The weight of increased gravity crushed him into the seat. As his vision blurred, he tried to comfort himself with the studies that said kids endured high-g maneuvers much better than adults, even with augmentation.

In the periphery of his vision, the display swam in and out of focus. The weak spots on the drive's containment bottle danced and spread until their edges met and merged.

There was no sound as the emergency shutdown procedures activated, meaning the drive was dead. A yellow icon blinked on the display.

All Andy heard was his own tired gasp as the weight from acceleration was suddenly gone and he rocked forward in the seat straps.

CHAPTER SEVEN

STELLAR DATE: 07.25.2981 (Adjusted Years)
LOCATION: *Sunny Skies*
REGION: Approaching Asteroid Belt, Jovian Combine

Andy watched the drive status display fizzle down to a series of disconnected lines floating on a black field. He swallowed. Tapping the console, he tried to bring up the holographic system but got an error. The regular visualization system had been down for months.

He closed his eyes and let his head drop. He was aware of Cara asking him if he was all right across the com system and he knew he couldn't answer her yet. Without opening his eyes, he flicked his connection to mute.

Still strapped into the seat, Andy attacked the air in front of the console. Kicking and punching, he felt tears gather in his eyes.

"Damn it, Brit!" he shouted. "Damn it!"

He slashed at the air, straining his muscles against twenty years of memories that had been so good at one point, memories that now only brought failure after failure. He was going to have to find a place for the kids. He couldn't maintain this life. Everything was crumbling around him.

"Damn it, Brit! I need you!"

His right fist caught the edge of the console and pain flared up his arm. He didn't let it stop him. He let himself experience the moment of rage at his wife for leaving him alone, for leaving the kids alone, for leaving him to be the one who would have to make a life for them. It had been Brit who'd wanted to make *Sunny Skies* work.

He raged at the dark, squeezing his eyes closed, not wanting to remember all the steps that had brought him here. He didn't know what to do. He couldn't keep living this way.

Exhausted, Andy sagged in the seat and let the straps hold him up. Fatigue, pain and anger dragged at his arms and legs like weights pulling him under water.

* * * * *

His mother cried when he told her what he planned to do. The tears burst out from her eyes, glistening in the afternoon light, but she nodded stiffly, wiping her nose.

"I knew you would do something like this," she said, then gave him a small laugh. "I'd have done it myself if I'd had this opportunity at your age."

She hugged him and pulled his sister close to hug him as well. His mother had the strength to never let him know all her worries.

When Andy told his dad, he looked for the moment of flat anger on Charlie's face before the smile came. But his dad only nodded and pulled him in for a long hug.

Then his dad pushed him away, gripping his shoulders. "Academy, huh? What's that all about?"

"It means I'll go to the TSF school and be an officer when I graduate."

"Did they tell you anything about this school?"

Andy shook his head, uncomfortable because he hadn't thought to ask. He had been too overcome by the promise of a real future to irritate them with too many questions. He hadn't wanted the dream to disappear. He'd signed the documents with his personal token—the first time he had ever used it—worried that at any moment Kass and Hilton would withdraw their offer. Kass hadn't stopped grumbling about his portion of their lost enlistment bonus.

Andy was going to be an officer in the TSF. He didn't know what that truly meant yet, but the words alone were enough to fill him with excitement and a sense of purpose. He didn't mention to his parents that he would also be receiving a neural implant prior to attending the academy. That fact seemed to cheapen the transaction somehow. It felt better to talk in terms of his future, using the words from the recruiting posters.

The TSF gave him a week before he had to leave. During those seven days, Charlie barely let Andy out of his sight. He took his son along on several trading forays, among groups all across Summerville. The items they found varied from electronics to an inlaid antique backgammon board, to a pair of real silk stockings in a sealed plastic bag. Charlie moved from building to building, climbing stairs and crossing bridges, nodding and waving to nearly everyone they passed.

Charlie was tireless. He pushed and probed everyone he talked to, in a constant state of what Andy could only describe as flirtation. Everything was interesting, amusing or not to be taken seriously. When his dad did grow serious, it was time to shake hands and finish the deal.

Andy watched all this and wondered how he hadn't noticed it before. Now that his life in Summerville suddenly had an end date, everything seemed more vivid than it had before. The canals and waterways were more green, the moss and lichens gleaming in the morning sunlight.

At the end of one trading trip, he and his dad stood on the roof of an apartment high rise that was taller than most in the area. Leaning against the crumbled concrete railing, they looked out over the softened grid of Summerville toward the blue-green strip of the ocean on the horizon. Transport aircraft crossed the sky in the distance, gleaming points of light on the blue.

Evening was coming on, and a few stars had begun to show above the ocean. The gleaming strand of High Terra shone high in the darkening sky.

His dad slapped him on the shoulder, then turned away from the vista to lean against the wall with his elbows on the edge, squinting slightly in the breeze.

"I guess it gets harder to come back to Earth, the longer you spend off-planet," his dad said.

"You can do exercises," Andy said. "Most people who live off-Earth are augmented in some way, anyway." It felt strange to talk about this like he was an authority, as though he suddenly knew more than his dad. His mom was so good at keeping her connection to the world outside Summerville through her Link out of her regular conversation. Most of the talk in the apartment was about the people Dad had met through the day, deals he'd made, wonder at whatever new item he brought home, from gull's eggs to a holographic tchotchke from a dead woman's apartment.

His dad nodded, not implying an opinion one way or the other. He seemed timeless at that moment, no different than someone who had lived in 2800, or 2400, or 1900. He was a human father staring into the distance as his son left home for the first time.

Charlie turned his head to look at Andy, his gray-blue eyes nearly translucent in the evening light. He nodded. "I think you made a good deal," he said. "I'm proud of you, son."

Andy felt a swell of gratitude. His father didn't have much to give, but he had love.

His mom hadn't had as easy a time with the idea of him leaving. Several times during the week, he caught her watching him with tears in her eyes.

It had felt infuriating sometimes that his mom could be content with her kitchen, with their living room and its threadbare furniture, with the world through their apartment windows, when there was so much beyond those borders. He didn't have to be satisfied with Summerville anymore.

His sister, Jane, had barely spoken to him the whole week. It wasn't until the night before he was supposed to leave that she finally exploded on him. Her usually passive face was flushed, her nose and eyes running.

"You're leaving me, Andy!" she'd screamed at him. "You're leaving me alone here."

"I'm not leaving you. Do you think I'm never going to come back?"

"Of course, you're never going to come back. Why would you come back here when you've got a chance to get out? Use your head, Andy. They might have told you you're super smart, but I know you. All you can think about is what's right in front of your face. The minute you walk out that door, you'll never come back."

He swallowed, knowing she was mostly right. He hadn't given any thought to the idea of coming back. There was too much to look forward to.

"We'll get vacations," he stammered. "And I'll be able to call. I can talk to Mom over the Link whenever I want."

"The Link!" she shouted, grabbing onto the one fact of his agreement with the TSF that he'd been trying to downplay: the cheapest part. "You're too dumb to realize how lucky you are not to have all that stuff in your head all the time. We're lucky to have grown up here, Andy, but you can't see that."

"Jane." He tried to speak but didn't know what to tell her. He could only nod and let her rage at him.

"I hope you forget about us!" she'd shouted.

* * * * *

Andy left for the TSF Academy on a cold Monday morning in September.

He met Kass and Hilton at the recruiting station and they led him up to a landing pad on the building's clean roof, so different than the ruins in Summerville. An egg-shaped military transport waited with its main door open.

A soldier in a green flight coverall stood beside the door. Andy nodded to him as he approached but the man ignored him, staring into the middle-distance, attention apparently on his Link.

"Get up in there and sit down over there," Kass said, pointing toward a jump seat on the far side of the craft. "Strap yourself in."

Andy found the straps and buckled in. He looked around the spare interior of the transport, which appeared better-suited to cargo than people. Latch points covered the major surfaces. He had a narrow view of the cockpit where a pilot was checking the holographic systems displays.

Kass ducked to climb into the transport and chose a seat beside Andy. Sergeant Hilton stood outside, talking to the soldier in the coverall. When they were done, he waved at Andy.

"Good luck, Sykes," he said. "Drop me a line when you get through Hell Week."

"Hell Week?" Andy asked. The words shot ice through his excitement.

Beside him, Kass laughed. "Guess you didn't read about that, huh, genius? Hell Week is when they weed out the weaklings. You fail Hell Week and you end up regular enlisted for a minimum of ten years. And I get my portion of your bonus like I should have in the first place."

Andy felt like he'd been punched. Why hadn't they told him about Hell Week? Could he prepare somehow? Should he have been doing more push-ups and sit-ups? He gave Kass a despairing look.

The sergeant guffawed, holding his stomach. "Oh, stop it, Sykes. You look like I just stole your birthday."

The crew member stepped up into the transport and tapped a control to lower the door, which hissed as it sealed. Andy's seat rumbled as the engines started, making his whole body vibrate. His stomach felt loose as the transport quickly lifted, tilting to one side before righting itself.

The engine hum in the cabin grew too loud to allow them to talk, so Andy could only glance at Kass grinning beside him and then stare forward to watch the world stream past outside the small window in the door.

The flight to the TSF Academy in Seattle would take thirty minutes. His first stop would be the Academy medical center, where he would spend a day in surgery and recovery, before being dropped in with a group of new recruits from all across the northern hemisphere, waiting for the next training cycle to start.

It was in a cold room lined with plastic chairs full of waiting cadets that he'd first met Brit.

* * * * *

"Daddy?" Cara said.

Andy dragged in a breath and opened his eyes. He had fallen asleep. He looked around frantically, forgetting where he was. His gaze fell on the console, still showing the exploded drive containment bottle, and everything came rushing back. He reached for the buckles holding his straps in place.

Wiping his face, he looked at Cara and found Tim standing just behind her, hugging his stuffed dolphin against his chest.

The concern on Cara's face stabbed him in the heart. He blinked, then gave her a smile. "Morning," he said. "How are you guys?"

Cara stared at him, obviously not knowing how to respond, worry plain on her face. "Is the ship all right?" she asked.

Andy nodded. "We have drive problems," he said. "But the good news is we'll arrive at Cruithne Station almost on time."

"Then what?" she asked.

"Then we'll see." Andy looked past her to Tim. "How are you doing, buddy?"

Tim squeezed his dolphin. "I'm hungry," he said. "Can we have pancakes?"

Andy suppressed a jab of pain in his abdomen as he stood. Leaning on the back of his seat, he said, "Yes, we can have pancakes."

"Yay!" Tim cried.

PART 2: CRUITHNE STATION

CHAPTER EIGHT
STELLAR DATE: 08.24.2981 (Adjusted Years)
LOCATION: *Sunny Skies*
REGION: Approaching Cruithne Station, Terran Hegemony

Sunny Skies arrived at Cruithne Station just as the asteroid was reaching its furthest distance from Earth. Andy had been proud of himself back on Kalyke when the navigation plan had lined up well enough that he could pick up cargo bound for InnerSol and charge a slight bonus for the shortened delivery time. Most legit cargo moving from OuterSol passed through Mars, so even a slow-moving hauler like *Sunny Skies* could charge a bounty for a more direct trip.

Andy leaned back in his seat and activated the automated navigation systems that would ease them toward Cruithne Station's greater Port Authority. He couldn't afford docking fees and the crates on board were too big for a shuttle, so he'd need to wait in the queue for Cruithne's drones to transfer everything station-side.

After ten hours of Alice rescanning the interior sections of the main ship, Andy felt relatively certain there were no stowaways. He had debated for a long time whether he should dump the atmosphere from the rest of the ship, but with the loss of the deuterium drive, he couldn't risk giving up the safety net of the additional breathable air. He still couldn't quite believe his astrogation had been on target and they had arrived at Cruithne Station within his forecast window.

Andy was exhausted, having not slept more than two hours at a time over the last four days, and he felt like his body was about to crumble around him. The pain from his disastrous EVA was lessening, but something in his gut still felt off, like a hot coal nestled under his stomach, gradually growing warmer.

"Acknowledge, Cruithne," he said over the comm to the Port Authority. "*Sunny Skies* assuming approach vector."

"You're late, *Sunny Skies*," the irritated port agent replied. "What happened to following your approved approach lane? Are you drunk?"

Andy grimaced and wished that were true. "We've lost our main drive," he said. He hesitated admitting the fact, but if the agent was paying attention to his scans he would have seen for himself that *Sunny Skies* was coming in on chem thrusters.

There was a pause as the agent presumably verified Andy's statement. "I see that. Well, we'll complete standard cargo transfer, but you can't hang around in the offload lane. Am I going to need to get you towed?"

"I've got local propulsion. I won't clog up any active lanes. Can you approve a parking orbit?"

"Sending some slots, along with the rates for each."

Andy swallowed, working to remove any sign of nerves from his voice. "I've got illegal cargo to report. Two crates came on board with my load at Kalyke."

The agent's bored tone didn't change. "We'll have them scanned when the transport drones get to you. Did you verify contents?"

"No."

"What do you mean no?"

"The onboard firmware didn't report and I don't have the scanning capability on board. I've got no idea what's in those things and I don't care. I just want them off my ship."

"They'll come off," the agent said. "Wait, your point of origin was Kalyke?"

"It's right there in my flight plan." Andy shook his head. He'd also stated the cargo's provenance twenty seconds earlier.

His statement was followed by a long pause.

"You still there?" Andy asked.

"Confirmed," the agent replied. Andy couldn't be quite sure who the agent was talking to until he said: "I've got your parking orbit verified, *Sunny Skies*. Address following. I'm sending the fees schedule along too."

"Fee schedule?" Andy demanded. "I'm not docking. There shouldn't be any fees."

The agent ignored him and cut the connection. The list of fees appeared on Andy's display. He could only shake his head at the prices. Even with the profit from the cargo, he couldn't afford to hang around Cruithne more than a few days.

Andy wanted to bury his face in his hands but forced himself to remain upright, eyes focused on the console, in case one of the kids came through the door.

His only option that seemed remotely viable was to try to scrap *Sunny Skies* and buy transport to High Terra or Mars 1. Mars seemed like the obvious option. He doubted he could find work on High Terra that wouldn't immediately want to pull him away. From Mars 1 they might get down to the surface. Mars 1 ran lower *g*'s than High Terra, and the surface was even better. The kids could handle the transition to Mars gravity with little trouble and he might be able to find work, he'd heard they were always looking for help handling cargo and security at Pavonis Mons.

Andy wished he knew more about Cruithne Station. It had a bad reputation and he didn't trust his ability to get the best price for the ship. There wasn't time to hang around bars or wherever junkers could be found to negotiate a price—not with the fees the ship would be racking up in its parking slot. How much could he even expect to get? The drive repairs were at least a year's cargo-hauling. The ship had to be worth more, but he was desperate and any prospective buyer would smell it. He considered posting something on a public forum and just letting random buyers hash out the price. Once he did that, there would be no going back.

The thought of selling *Sunny Skies*, of pulling the kids out of their home and taking away the place where they had lived with their mother, made him want to find something to destroy. He thought about the weapons crate and wondered how he might sneak away for some target practice.

Cara appeared in the doorway, rubbing the sleep from her eyes. "Are we there yet?" she asked.

"We're there yet," Andy replied, and turned to give her a smile. "How'd you sleep?"

"I dreamed about Alice floating away. You'd sent her out to work on the sails and she had a malfunction and just floated away from us."

Andy stood and stretched. The upside to waiting in the cargo queue was that he had time to make breakfast. Smelling himself, he realized he should probably clean up before he had to interact with someone from customs in person.

"Alice has a pretty good location beacon," Andy said. As he walked past Cara, he pulled her in against his side for a hug and tousled her hair.

"Dad!" Cara complained.

"That's what hair's for. For me to mess up. I thought you'd be used to it by now."

"I'm not a little kid," she groused.

Andy grinned and grabbed her nose between two knuckles.

"Your nose will still belong to me, even when you're a hundred."

Cara pushed away and smoothed her hair. "We'll see about that."

"I look forward to the challenge. Is your brother up?"

She followed him into the corridor, dragging her feet. "He's playing a game. Something with aliens."

"Sounds like fun. You should play with him for five minutes while I get the kitchen ready. Then you can come back and we'll make him cook."

"I don't want to play a game with him."

"Five minutes, that's all. Little things like that, Cara, and he'll do the dishes for you. Trust me."

She gave him a disbelieving look that he answered by sticking out his tongue at her.

"I've lived a while," Andy said. "I know things."

"Are we going to fix the drive at Cruithne?" Cara asked.

"I'm working on it."

"Can we go to the station? I want to see the big fountain. Did you know there's a park with a big fountain and birds?"

"What kind of birds?"

"Finches, thrushes, wrens, orioles, and even some parrots."

"Sounds messy."

"It sounds wonderful. They sing all day, and the parrots repeat back things people have told them."

"Where did you hear this?"

"I read about it on the Network. The whole history of Cruithne going back to 1986. Did you know people thought Cruithne was a moon of Earth at first? How dumb is that?"

"Someday somebody's going to look back and call us cavemen, kiddo." He raised a finger. "Perspective. Not something I expect a twelve-year-old to have."

Cara wrinkled her nose. "Do you know that Cruithne has a crime problem?" she asked, as if she were talking about plumbing.

"I've heard that."

"It's not a safe place."

"I've heard that too. You still want to see the fountain?"

"I'd like to hear the birds," Cara said. "I'd like to hear them for real."

They reached the kitchen, which reminded Andy that all he had to cook with was the last bit of flour, water, and some artificial sweetener.

"We'll see if we can make it happen, kiddo," he said. "But I'll be honest, I can't make any promises."

She surprised him by picking her head up. "I know. It would be nice though."

"Go play with your brother. Five minutes." He spread his hand to show all five fingers.

Cara held up three fingers.

"This isn't a negotiation. Make sure Tim combs his hair and puts on a clean coverall. I don't want him smelling like dog when the Port Agents come on board." He patted his chest. "I'm going to grab a shower myself. Tell him that."

She made another face and turned down the corridor for Tim's room. Andy stood in the doorway to the kitchen and looked around the little room with its worn surfaces and tiny table barely big enough for four. At least the oven had never broken down that he could remember. That was something.

He left the kitchen for his room and its shower stall, which he was fairly certain still worked.

* * * * *

Cara had been right: Cruithne wasn't a safe place. The last he had heard, there were at least three major crime syndicates operating on the station, which made it a damned dangerous place.

With little SSF oversight, Station Security was in the pocket of the highest bidder. Back when Andy was in the TSF, he had seen several different battle plans for Cruithne Station in the event some crime lord decided to play King Arthur and unite the various armed factions, turning it into a potentially Earth-hostile location.

The asteroid came too close to Earth for about a month out of every year. During that month, the TSF placed a heavy focus on the traffic off-station, which was usually peppered with contraband on its way to High Terra or Cuno, and resulted in many search and seizures. The TSF was spread thin these days and a concerted effort from Cruithne's private fleet of attack craft could cause Earth's interests significant damage.

Of the three plans he'd read, all had high casualty rates. The plan that tried to capture Cruithne intact accounted for nearly fifty percent casualties, which was unheard of in modern doctrine. A robust set of shields and defense cannons meant even the attack pilots weren't going to get away unscathed, and any missile barrage could be decimated before it got close.

In truth, Cruithne Station was a fortress run by mostly benevolent gangs who simply wanted to be left alone to do their gray- and black-market business, which may have been better than any kind of corporate control. With a corporation, you never knew what was really happening beneath the smooth facade.

As he ruminated, Andy switched on the oven and searched among the bare cabinets for something he could turn into food. He found the flour and sweetener, as well as a container of dehydrated yams that had rolled out of sight.

He was staring at the flour and yams when Tim walked through the door, holding his stuffed dolphin like a fighter craft and making engine noises.

"I'm a pilot like you, Dad!" he shouted. He ran a loop around the room and brought the dolphin to a landing on the counter next to the dried yams. As the dolphin's nose touched the plastic bag, he stared at the yams and screwed up his nose.

"What are those?" he demanded.

"Candy. I found it in the back of the cabinet."

Tim moved his face a little closer. "That doesn't look like candy. That looks like vegetables."

"It's candy, I'm telling you. Why don't you wash your hands and help me make some griddle-cakes?" Andy reached for the dolphin to clear space on the counter.

"No!" Tim shouted. "Dolphin stays with me."

Andy returned his son's angry stare, trying to remember Cara at ten. Was that when she had refused her stuffed animals, deciding they were for little kids? Tim was holding on tighter, backsliding, even. He needed more attention.

Andy sighed. "I'm moving him to the table. He's not going anywhere. We need room to work. He can watch you from there. You want some breakfast, don't you?"

"Yes," Tim said. "I want some breakfast."

"Then do what I tell you and come help me. We don't have a lot of time before the people from Cruithne come to off-load the cargo."

"Is Alice going to help?"

"Nope, Alice doesn't need to get involved in any of that. They have their own drones to move everything off the ship."

Tim's face brightened. "Can we go play in the cargo bay when it's empty?"

One of Tim's favorite things was to fly in open spaces under zero-g. Andy didn't know where he got it.

"I'll think about it," Andy said. "First we need to make breakfast. Then we'll talk to the people from the station. After all that, we'll think about playing. Your sister wants to see some birds on the station. What do you think about that? You want to see a parrot?"

"Parrots are loud," Tim said.

"Yes, they are."

Andy had just emptied the flour into the mixing bowl when a hail came across the Link.

<Sunny Skies. *Captain Andrew Sykes. This is Ngoba Starl.*>

Andy glanced at Tim, who was sniffing one of the dried yams before touching it with the tip of his tongue. The kids wouldn't be able to hear anything that came over Link.

Andy didn't know anyone named Ngoba Starl. He had purposely left the ship disconnected from the station's greater communications network. He didn't feel like getting overrun with stored messages from debt collectors.

<Do you have the right ship, Mr. Starl? I don't have business with you.>

<I believe you do, Captain Sykes,> the voice said, sounding wolfish. <I have a valid token to access my cargo. I'd appreciate it if you came to meet me before I come aboard your ship and take what's mine.>

A chill went down Andy's neck. He was getting boarded. They couldn't legally come aboard without his permission, but they could have easily hacked the security system. And if they did force their way on board, who was he going to tell?

If Starl was already at the cargo bay airlock, Andy was never going to get to the command deck in time to stop him. He could try to activate the ship's weak security system remotely but it might attack him and the kids for all he knew. He let out a long breath.

<Where are you?>

<Secondary airlock closest to your cargo bay.>

<I'll be there in ten minutes.>

Andy cut the connection and activated the ship's intercom.

"Cara," he said, trying to keep the fear out of his voice. "I need you to come meet me in the kitchen."

CHAPTER NINE

STELLAR DATE: 08.24.2981 (Adjusted Years)
LOCATION: *Sunny Skies*
REGION: Port Authority, Cruithne Station, Terran Hegemony

The airlock scanner only returned static when he ran an occupant query. Andy wanted to punch the control panel. No wonder someone had been able to plant their own cargo at Kalyke Station. He wondered how long that system had been down as well. Why hadn't Alice checked it?

Trying to keep himself calm, he floated in the corridor, suit leaking pinholes of air, and let his gaze roam over the scraped walls and dented struts. Maybe it was time to send *Sunny Skies* off to the junkers. It was probably safer as scrap. The kids could understand that. Some things got too old. Some things were inevitable and then you had to face reality. That was an important lesson for him to teach them.

A standard laser pistol rested in a holster attached to his suit's harness. He had debated grabbing one of the TSF pistols from the hidden crate but if the weapons belonged to Starl, he didn't want to antagonize the man by flashing them.

The kids were hiding in a storage cabinet in one of the unused rooms in the habitat. They would be able to contact him over his Link using the onboard comm system and he could subvocalize answers. Cara hated subvocals. She said they sounded like he'd become a creepy ghost in her head.

"That's because I am and always will be a creepy ghost in your head," he'd answered.

She had replied with a dirty look.

Andy took a deep breath—which fogged his faceplate for a second—then let it out and activated the airlock. The system cycled and then the doors slid apart, screeching on poorly-lubed tracks.

Inside the airlock stood four people in EVA suits. The first two were carrying rifles that looked like dual-purpose laser and impact weapons. A third person trailed, unarmed, stomach rounding out the front of their suit, while the person in the middle had only a pistol at their hip. That had to be Ngoba Starl. He was taller than the others, with narrow shoulders and a long face that looked gray through his helmet. His eyes were warm brown. A curly beard pressed against the lower part of his faceplate. His suit was newer than the others and decorated with multi-colored stripes.

<*Captain Sykes,*> came Starl's voice, disconnected from the white-toothed smile. <*Thank you for inviting us in.*> There was no menace in his tone, rather a sort of humor.

Andy took a step back to allow them room to walk into the cargo bay, mag boots clicking on the metal floor. The two guards spread out, helmets rising to check corners and points in the ceiling for weapons systems. It's what he would have done when boarding a strange ship, invited or not. The rifles remained muzzle-down, which was only slightly comforting.

<Look, Mr. Starl,> Andy said. <I don't care that your stuff is here. I just want to get it out as soon as possible and move on with my life. I don't care what it is. I don't want to know anything about it, honestly.>

Starl put his hands on his hips and looked around as well. His suit was easily worth a hundred times more than Andy's, even when *Andy's* had been new.

<Call me Ngoba, Captain Sykes,> the man said. <All my friends do.>

<All right,> Andy said, trying not to sound uncertain. All he wanted was to get these men off the ship and move on with unloading the rest of the cargo. Ngoba was looking more and more like a gangster of some rank and Andy didn't like that he had chosen to handle this little job personally. It indicated there was something valuable in the crates, which meant Andy wanted to know even less about what was going on.

<Like I said,> Andy continued. <You can see I've got a lot of maintenance to do while I'm here at Cruithne, so I'd prefer it if you received your cargo and we called it a day.>

Andy glanced at one of the guards and when he looked back at Ngoba, the man was grinning at him. He had long white teeth.

<Don't be in such a hurry, Andy. Do you mind if I call you Andy?>

Andy swallowed and shook his head.

<Wonderful.> Starl motioned toward the other suits to either side of him. <These are my men, Karcher and Stansil. Over here is Dr. Hari Jickson.>

The two toughs didn't say anything.

<Hello,> Jickson said, nodding. He had a weak chin, his cheeks and nose flushed red with the broken bloodvessels of an alcoholic.

<My men will verify the cargo now,> Ngoba said. <Which gives us plenty of time to talk.>

<I'm not much of a talker,> Andy said. <Afraid I might disappoint you with my chit chat.>

Ngoba laughed. He pointed a gloved finger at Andy. <Wonderful. That's exactly the kind of humor I enjoy. Cruithne can be a serious place. We don't get many people willing to crack a joke every now and then.>

Andy started to say he wasn't really joking when Cara asked, "Daddy, where are you?"

He subvocalized, "I'm here, honey. I'm talking with some men down in the cargo bay."

"Do they have guns?" Tim asked.

Andy looked at Ngoba, unable to remember if he was supposed to say something or not. "Don't worry about that," he told Tim. "Both of you stay quiet for now. I'm trying to talk to them so we can get them out of here."

He bit his lip, knowing he'd let too much worry into his voice.

Cara didn't answer and he was able to turn his full attention back to Ngoba. Sweat ran down his temple. <Sorry,> Andy said. <Helmet glitch. I think I lost what you just said.>

<I was telling Dr. Jickson how pleased we were to have you arrive. Out of ten ships leaving Kalyke, you were the only one to reach Cruithne.>

The info drove a cold spike down Andy's back. <*You think there's a reason for that?*>

<*I would hope it was your fine skills as a captain,*> Ngoba said. <*I'm not a pilot, myself, so I don't know what it takes to get cargo from one end of Sol to the other. I hear things about the TSF around various remote places, harassing hard-working people like yourself while you're simply trying to earn a living.*>

Karcher and Stansil had disengaged their mag boots, which allowed them to float to the top of the central cargo stack. They moved their rifles to their backs as they hunted among the stack, supposedly scanning for the two crates at the bottom.

Andy gritted his teeth as he moved his gaze to Ngoba's pistol. If he was going to fight, now was the time to do it. He could get off two shots at Karcher and Stansil and then a third at Ngoba. He was ignoring Jickson for now. The man's suit was too tight and didn't appear to leave any room for weapons. Beyond Jickson stood the airlock control panel, which presented the option of dumping the bay's atmosphere possibly sweeping the two guards into space, or at least smacking them against the airlock as they were swept out with the air.

The weight of Andy's pistol pushed against his stomach, reminding him it was there, urging him to do something.

<*You seem nervous, Andy,*> Ngoba said.

Andy jerked his gaze back to the tall man's face. The brown eyes watched him warmly, still showing more humor than anything else, as if he expected the two heavies to pull the crates out and reveal them stuffed with toys and not some biological weapon that had killed nine other crews.

<*We should all be calm and talk for a bit. They'll be done soon enough.*>

<*Sure,*> Andy said.

<*Where is the rest of the crew?*> Jickson asked.

Ngoba looked annoyed for the first time. He raised a gloved hand to quiet the other man.

Jickson didn't seem to get the message. <*Obviously there are other people on the ship. Their signatures are obvious even on my suit's scanners.*>

<*Captain Sykes has every right to meet us on his own terms,*> Ngoba said, tension edging his voice. <*We should be pleased our items arrived at all, shouldn't we?*>

Andy watched the two men as it became obvious that Ngoba Starl didn't like Dr. Jickson.

<*It's here,*> Karcher said from the top of the cargo stack. <*Containment's still good. Sleeping like a kitten.*>

<*A kitten!*> came Tim's voice over the local Link channel. <*I want a kitten.*>

Andy's heart went through his throat. <*Get off this channel,*> he barked. The only way they could be listening in was if Cara had hacked the ship's communication system. He hadn't specifically told her not to, but he had never shown her how to do it, either. She must have set up a relay. How had she figured out how to do that?

<*Who was that?*> Dr. Jickson demanded. <*I'd say that was a ten-year-old boy.*>

<No one,> Andy said. <It's my problem. It doesn't have anything to do with your cargo.> He turned his focus on Ngoba, the man in charge. <I've transported your cargo and asked nothing in return. Please take it and go.>

Ngoba nodded, brown eyes looking even more interested now. <I'm not here to impose on you any more than I must, Andy,> he said, sounding slightly too familiar. <It's too bad everything got loaded like it did, our cargo at the very bottom of the stack. We'll need to wait for the other transport drones to arrive and get the rest out first.>

<You don't need to wait here. You've verified its location and status. The drones will take care of the rest. I have work to do on my ship. I don't have time to wait here with you.>

He hoped Starl would do the reasonable thing and leave. Unless there was something else they wanted, there was no reason for them to wait for the transport drones. He couldn't ignore the possibility that they'd want to erase all evidence of their cargo arriving from Kalyke, which might have been the reason they chanced it on *Sunny Skies* in the first place. He swallowed, glancing toward Karcher and Stansil, who were now standing on top of the stacked crates. Each had his rifle back in his hands.

Ngoba's helmet was nodding as though he agreed with Andy, as if Andy had said something profound that had changed the man's way of thinking.

<Captain Sykes,> Ngoba said.

He was interrupted by an alert from the main airlock control. An audible klaxon came to life and the ship sent out an alert on the safety net that the main airlock would be opening in thirty seconds. The Cruithne Port Authority transport drones had arrived.

CHAPTER TEN

STELLAR DATE: 08.24.2981 (Adjusted Years)
LOCATION: *Sunny Skies*
REGION: Port Authority, Cruithne Station, Terran Hegemony

Andy breathed a sigh of relief even as his suit notified him he only had eighty percent atmospheric integrity. Several pinholes he'd missed had joined and split. His suit might be hissing like a tea kettle but the drones arriving early meant he could get these people off the ship that much faster. Ngoba Starl acted like a typical gangster while something about Dr. Jickson put a sick feeling in the bottom of Andy's stomach, especially when he'd perked up at the possibility of the kids being on board.

<I need to check the outer airlock status,> he told Starl.

<Please do.>

Deactivating his mag boots, Andy kicked-off toward the wall control panel next to the main cargo airlock. The wide doors and frames were scarred by years of drones scraping into them during loading procedures.

Andy's suit wouldn't connect to the exterior sensors, so he had pulled up the wall display. Sifting through menus, he found the raw data stream from the exterior lock and scanned through the values. He frowned, the outside signatures were much larger than what he would have expected from a cloud of loading drones ready to grab crates. The sensor data looked more like another ship.

<How did you get over here?> he asked Starl.

<Small transport shuttle. I didn't want to draw attention. Why are you asking this?>

<There's another ship out there. Are you expecting someone else?>

From the top of the stack of crates, Karcher and Stansil immediately dropped to a knee and pulled up their rifles.

Starl let out a low chuckle. *<I think this is the Havenots. What do you think, Doctor?>*

Jickson didn't answer immediately. He was too far away for Andy to see his expression through his faceplate. The doctor appeared to be floating, arms loose, and was probably engaged in a Link conversation that Andy couldn't hear.

<Havenots?> Andy said. *<Who are they? What are you bringing onto my ship?>*

<We're not bringing anyone onto your ship, Captain,> Jickson answered. *<We can't control who chooses to come here or not.>*

<You don't seem like the type to bullshit people,> Andy said to Starl.

Andy watched the panel count down to the security handshake with the outside entity while trying to think of the best course of action. Regardless of the presence of the other ship, there *were* Port Authority drones outside communicating with *Sunny Skies*. The process completed and the panel verified the shipping manifest, the last step that allowed the drones to arrange themselves for best removal of the cargo. From *Sunny Skies*, they would ferry crates to points all across Cruithne Station.

If someone wanted to steal cargo, that was the easiest point to grab it; track the drone and pluck it out of space between the cargo ship and the station.

Andy had served on station patrol duty enough times to know all the various ways pirates and gangs stole cargo. The smoothest he had ever seen had been a hacker who had rerouted cargo at Eris. If he'd only taken one crate at a time, and been better at checking manifests for high-value shipments, no one would have realized what he'd been doing. But the kid had gotten greedy and run a whole line of drones into an unused port.

All Andy had had to do was follow the train to their destination. It would have been enough to recover the cargo, but the teenage pirate had been ready and waiting in an EVA suit when Andy had arrived. The kid had soiled his suit.

So, attacking a ship didn't make much sense. It could mean whoever was outside didn't have the shipping manifest and wanted to search through the cargo before it left, or they wanted the crew, too. Or they wanted Starl and Jickson.

Once the security verification finished, the cargo doors would open and he'd have two sets of gangsters on the ship. The kids were listening in and knew to hide, but what good was that going to do in the long run?

Andy pulled up the override instructions and manually entered his security codes. <*I'm not letting anyone else on this ship,*> he said. <*I'm calling the Port Authority.*>

<*That's certainly a good idea,*> Starl said with more calm than Andy would have expected. <*Let's hope it works.*>

<*You think they've bought off the Port Authority?*> Andy said. <*Who's out there?*>

<*I think they'll blow a hole in your ship if you don't open the bay doors,*> Jickson answered. <*If it's the cargo they want, they don't need us alive to collect it.*>

The two security heavies had moved to the deck, positioning themselves on either edge of the stack, mostly hidden behind crates. Any rudimentary scan of the bay would find them but at least they weren't in the open anymore. They were all vulnerable once the main door opened.

The panel squawked an alarm and Andy directed his attention back to the security display. His token had been overridden. He pushed his face closer to the numbers, trying to understand what was happening.

<*They've got station override authority,*> Andy said in a low voice. <*I can't stop them.*>

Starl chuckled again. <*Those Havenots are tricky. What did I tell you, Doctor? You thought Heartbridge couldn't follow us here.*>

<*What am I paying you for?*> Jickson said, an irritating whine snaking through his voice.

<*Just take your shit and get off my ship,*> Andy yelled. His voice still sounded small over the Link. <*I don't care about what you're doing. I don't want to know anything about it. Take it somewhere else.*>

The main cargo bay door screeched and there was a rush of hissing atmosphere as a gap appeared at its base. Andy watched the gap widen, black appearing on the other side. He glanced toward the door leading back into the ship. Both Jickson and

Starl were between him and the inner corridor.

Whatever was going to happen, he didn't need to be part of it. Andy released his mag boots and kicked toward the inner door.

<Where are you going, Captain?> Starl asked. <We could use your help here.>

<Use my help? I'm unarmed. I'm only going to get in your way.>

<So much for the TSF veteran,> Jickson said.

<I can do more from the command deck. I can use the point defense cannons from there.>

<That's a lie,> Jickson said. <Direct them from here.>

<Suit's damaged. I can't do anything from here. I need to get back to the command deck.>

<I think we're out of time, Captain,> Starl said, controlled urgency entering his voice. He had turned to face the half-open door, holding his pistol in a ready position.

The first cargo drone, a jumble of black squares and blinking lights, ducked through the opening and zipped into the bay. Others followed like bees finding a flower bush. The overhead reflected their flashing lights in hundreds of different colors, which probably corresponded with their destination ports.

Drones that would have to wait for cargo at the bottom of the stack floated up to the overhead and stopped moving, while others positioned themselves above crates, engaged magnetic locks, and lifted straight up. Drones and crates began leaving the bay for the wall of black outside.

Several drones had just left when Andy saw Stansil poke his helmet around his remaining stack of crates. The man quickly aimed his rifle and fired, lighting the bay with a pulse beam.

The shot was answered by three crackling beams in a tight formation that splashed off the crate beside Stansil, narrowly missing the drones working near the bay door. Stansil had already rolled to another position.

More pulse fire followed, lighting the gaps between the drones. Whoever was firing apparently didn't want to harm the cargo. The drones seemed simultaneously oblivious to the incoming fire and appeared to dance around it like the whole thing was choreographed somehow.

Starl was barking orders over the link for Stansil and Karcher to lay down covering fire. Jickson had moved closer to Andy.

<You **do** have a pistol,> the doctor said, pointing at the weapon in Andy's hand.

Andy looked down at it, not remembering that he had drawn it. Old habits died hard, he supposed. He checked the action and charge levels quickly. It would work for taking out a drone but wouldn't do much against anyone wearing armor.

<Why did you lie?> Jickson demanded.

Andy ignored him and crouched beside the panel. The incoming fire was growing brighter, meaning whoever was closing on their position was nearly inside.

<You better give up now, Ngoba,> came a gravelly voice over the Link. <I've got no desire to end our poker game.>

Starl's chuckle answered. <*Zanda! I knew it had to be you. Tell me who you've bought at the Port Authority and I'll throw you a winning hand at the next game.*>

The plasma fire intensified, an odd counterpoint to the banter over the Link, which sounded cold and friendly at the same time. A charge caught one of the drones rising toward the open door and it spun in a slow circle before dropping its crate and crashing into the nearby wall.

Andy looked from Starl and Jickson to the two security guards. They were all focused on the incoming fire. He shot a glance at the interior door and then kicked off along the wall. He was moving into the open but all the fire was concentrated on Karcher and Stansil at the stack of crates. Another drone fell and Andy groaned inwardly, not wanting to think about how he was going to navigate the insurance payouts.

If he could reach the door and get through it before they noticed he was moving, he could activate a security lock that would at least slow them down. Port Authority override codes might work on the exterior doors but he could set interior doors to whatever he wanted. If they chose to bother with cutting through the door, it would at least slow them down long enough to give him time to get the heavier weapons and tell the kids what to do.

A plasma bolt caught Stansil in the leg and his suit released a spray of gases. His scream filled the Link.

<*That's too bad,*> the voice Starl had called Zanda said. <*You should put down your arms, Ngoba. We've got you outgunned and I'm going to call in more of my folks if you keep this up.*>

<*We'll be keeping it up,*> Starl growled. He was crouched behind a dropped crate. <*You know that.*>

<*If it's the money, I can beat that. You don't need to lay down your life. This can all be business. Easy as breathing.*>

<*Easy as breathing,*> Starl echoed. His helmet was turned toward where Stansil was struggling to get a patch on his leg. The vacuum around him was full of floating orbs of blood. Another bolt caught Stansil directly in the chest. He jerked, the force of the blast throwing him backward but when he hit the wall behind him he was still.

<*Damn you,*> Starl growled.

As Andy approached the interior hatch, he could now look back through the open bay door and outside the ship. A shuttle was visible about a hundred meters out, a black rectangle with smoothed edges. Lights flashing off faceplates and the lines of plasma bolts showed him the people moving in EVA suits between the shuttle and the open door. A loose line of drones carried crates out into the dark between the lines of fire.

It looked like the attackers had formed a ragged line and were moving forward in teams, one firing as the other advanced. He took another look at the interior door—calculating how long it would take him to get to the weapons crate near the habitat—then glanced at Stansil's body floating against the far wall, his rifle still dangling from one hand. It would take Andy too long to get through the ship to the

TSF crate and back. He was going to have to use what was available.

CHAPTER ELEVEN
STELLAR DATE: 08.24.2981 (Adjusted Years)
LOCATION: *Sunny Skies*
REGION: Port Authority, Cruithne Station, Terran Hegemony

The pulse bolts were coming in a predictable pattern from left to right. Whoever the attackers were, they had good firing discipline. Andy waited a minute to make sure he was right about their pattern, then kicked off across the room until he had cover behind the closest crate. Without waiting, he moved again until he reached Stansil's body. Several of the floating orbs of blood splashed against his chest.

Andy activated his mag boots and crouched, pulling Stansil down next to him. He untangled the rifle and grabbed three grenades off the man's outer harness, as well as three extra magazines. He jammed everything into the pouch on the front of his suit with his pistol.

The rifle was a variant of models he'd used in the space force. He checked the active sights and cursed when his suit couldn't connect with the targeting system. He pulled the stock into his shoulder and lowered the muzzle to rescan the line of attackers.

They were less than a hundred meters out now. He raised the rifle and fired at the first faceplate he spotted in the dark.

A spray of gas told him he'd hit his target. Andy immediately kicked off to take another firing position. A drone blocked his view for a second, and then he took two shots, following the bright muzzle flashes.

<*Did you finally learn to shoot?*> Zanda demanded. <*I told you not to make this so hard, Ngoba. I'm going to have to call in more folks.*>

<*Do what you need to do,*> Starl answered.

Andy had lost sight of Starl behind a crate. Jickson was still huddled in the corner near the control panel, out of the lines of fire altogether. He wouldn't be able to see what was going on unless the four of them had been using a battle net.

Continuing to use the dwindling stack of crates as cover, Andy tracked the incoming suits and picked them off one by one. He moved and reloaded, then nearly found himself exposed when a drone lifted away the crate he was hiding behind.

He kicked off the floor and took two shots as he moved. The rifle was a joy to use. Little recoil and a minimal cool-down period. Its active sights grabbed movement and highlighted targets, redirecting fire when Andy's aim was off. All he had to do was pull the trigger, and if his suit had been able to talk to the weapon, he doubted he'd even have needed to do that. It felt too good to have this kind of rifle back in his hands, working like it was supposed to.

Starl was laughing across the link, his voice deep and oddly comforting. As Andy moved, calculated, fired and repositioned, the background laughter made his calm seem not quite so robotic.

He burned a hole through another suit that was trying to use an outgoing drone as cover and Zanda cursed over the link.

<Damn you, Starl. We'll be back.>

<What happened to all your folks?> the gangster said, still laughing. <You weren't counting on my boy, were you?>

<We aren't the only ones looking, you know that,> Zanda said. <I was just the first one who was a friend.>

<I know, Zanda. No hard feelings.>

Andy glanced at Stansil's floating body at the back of the bay. Of course, gangsters didn't care about their own.

There was a flare of thruster fire as the shuttle lit its engine and turned, then disappeared into the black. The drones floating out the bay doors didn't stop moving. The bay would be empty soon.

<You all right, Captain?> Starl asked.

<I'm fine. How soon until you're off my ship?>

<You can keep the rifle,> Starl said, ignoring the question. <It suits you.> He chuckled. <Our man Stansil won't be needing it anymore.>

<You'll need to take him with you. I don't want to have to answer to Port Authority about any bodies.>

<Of course.>

<I've got 'im,> Karcher said.

Andy turned to see the other security guard crouched next to a crate in the center of the room. The drones were nearly finished and only four crates remained in the bay. Drones lifted the two nearest the door and floated through the opening. A process complete signal floated over the Link like a bird's trill.

<Those what you came for? Take 'em and get out of here.>

The main door screeched as it began to close. Andy spotted Jickson at the control panel, tapping the screen.

<What are you doing?> Andy demanded. <Get away from my controls. You aren't authorized to control anything on-board.>

The heavy door closed and sealed, sending a vibration through the deck. Atmospheric pressure began to rise as Jickson activated the environmental system, including heating.

Andy nearly protested because there was no need to waste energy heating the cargo bay, but didn't want to give them any more info about his situation than was necessary. He wanted them to take their cargo and leave so he could focus on his other problems.

<We need to run a couple quick checks,> Starl explained. <That's all. We'll be off your ship in no time, Captain Sykes. You will be compensated. I promise you.>

Karcher opened a side panel in the nearest crate and looked like he was checking a security token. Several lights flashed on the panel, and its lid unsealed, popping open a few centimeters.

From the other side of the bay, Dr. Jickson cursed. <Don't touch that. I'll verify the contents.> He kicked off from the wall and floated awkwardly from the crate, barely activating his magboots in time to stop his momentum.

Andy's suit signaled that atmosphere levels in the bay had reached ship standard. Beside him, Starl reached up to unlock and pull off his helmet. His curly beard shone in the low bay lights.

Jickson crouched in front of the crate and pulled off his helmet as well. Thin blonde hair clung to his round head. He bit his lip as he studied the crate's controls, pink fingers stabbing at the lock mechanism.

<Why are you taking your helmets off?> Andy said. <You're leaving.> He did his best to keep the command in his voice but the power dynamics were still balanced in their favor. He held a rifle now, but it was still three to one. He didn't like that Karcher was standing slightly behind him and still wore his helmet.

"I prefer to talk person-to-person," Starl said. His voice was even deeper now. He scratched his forehead and ran his hand through his hair, digging at his scalp. "Humor me, Captain."

Andy stared at him, then reached for the latch at the base of his own helmet. He pulled it off and took a deep breath. The air tasted stale due to the outdated scrubbers.

"I can see you're in a tight spot here," Starl said. He gestured toward the bay and Andy's suit, which was still smeared with Stansil's blood.

When Andy opened his mouth to protest, the other man held up a hand, palm out. "You're a proud man. I respect that." He placed the hand on his heart. "I'm a proud man, too. I'm not a good father like you are, though. Me, I make decisions without worrying how they're going to affect anyone but me. You don't allow yourself that luxury. Am I correct?"

Andy shook his head, not wanting to confirm the existence of the kids. It was becoming obvious that Starl knew more about him than he had let on.

Behind Starl, Jickson got the crate unlocked. Its lid hissed as it popped free and Jickson stood to swing it completely open. He put a hand on either side of the crate and stared into its interior, nodding as he took stock of the contents.

"I know it's true," Starl said, "so you don't have to say anything about that. I also know your ship is dead. You blew out your main drive making it into Cruithne. You're practically dragging yourself like a zombie. I can taste the rust in your environmental systems. Your ship's AI must be blind because we walked right up to your airlock without so much as a whisper in response."

"He doesn't have an AI," Jickson said, head in the crate now.

Starl shot him an irritated look, then turned a considerate gaze back on Andy. "Which says even more. You've been piloting a light freighter across Sol without an AI. How does someone even do that? I don't know. I'm not a pilot, but to me it's like someone telling me they're going to transmute lead into gold. You have these skills, Captain Sykes. Amazing skills. I've read about you. I've talked to people about you. All these skills and you left them behind to become a family man."

Andy swallowed. He didn't like where this was going.

"It's obvious to me you have a plan, you have things you want to do with your family, but life keeps getting in the way, right? Your ship is falling apart underneath you, Captain. What if I could help you with that?"

"I'm not anybody special," Andy said. "You told me yourself, I'm just one out of ten ships that ended up with your cargo on it."

Starl grinned as if he'd been caught in a lie but he wasn't going to explain how.

From the crate, Jickson made an excited sound and took a step backward, magboots clicking on the floor. The crate made a whirring sound as its four walls split and lowered to the floor, revealing a collection of folded metal structures inside. These were also set in motion, opening around what Andy realized was a couch. When the mechanism had finished unpacking itself, a portable surgery stood in the middle of the cargo bay. Jickson nodded his satisfaction and went immediately to the next crate.

Andy raised his rifle and took two steps back, putting Karcher in front of him. He had to drop his helmet in order to grip the weapon properly.

Karcher responded by raising his rifle.

"Calm down," Starl said. "Please, calm down. This isn't what you think it is."

"You're not here to harvest my family? Because that's sure what it looks like."

Jickson snorted a laugh. "You think I would need this level of equipment for a harvest job? Please."

Starl had raised both his hands in a gesture of surrender. "Mr. Karcher, lower your weapon."

Andy could barely see Karcher's pale face through his helmet. The man's gaze flicked to his boss and back to Andy before he finally lowered his rifle.

"I've got a deal for you, Captain Sykes. I need something else transported off Cruithne to a location in OuterSol. Out of ten captains, you were the only one resourceful enough to even make it into Cruithne. Which I guess limits my options. In light of your other constraints, I'm still inclined to think you're the best man for this job.

"In exchange for this transport, I'm offering ten days of dry dock for your ship to get her back in shape. I was going to recommend a new ship but I think there's something about this one that works for you." He shrugged. "Though a new ship is still on the table. At the end of the job, I'll pay you well. Probably five times what you made in the last four years, knowing what I pulled out of your logs."

Andy's mouth went dry. The sinister form of the portable surgery swam in and out of focus behind Ngoba Starl's shoulder. He blinked.

The offer was too good to be true. Obviously, it was dangerous. People had already died.

"What do you want moved?" he asked finally.

Jickson surprised him by speaking first. "An Artificial Intelligence, Captain Sykes. In your head."

CHAPTER TWELVE

STELLAR DATE: 06.27.2958 (Adjusted Years)
LOCATION: Bridgefield TSF Medical Facility, Fort Salem
REGION: High Terra, Earth, Terran Hegemony

Twenty-Three Years Earlier

Andy had spent a week in recovery after the surgery implanting his Link. He had to sign a contract stating that if he failed out of the Academy, his status as a cadet would turn into to a ten-year enlistment. He had stared at the screen for a minute, the words running together until he could barely read them, before signing his token and accepting the contract. It hadn't seemed like a big deal until he'd woken with a crowd of voices in his mind and thought he was going insane.

"Good morning," a cheery voice next to the bed called out. "I see you're awake."

Andy blinked at the white ceiling, trying to make sense of the lines that eventually became square tiles. His temples throbbed with a blinding headache.

"Andrew?" the woman's voice asked. "Can you verify your name for me as Andrew Sykes?"

"Andy," he said, turning his face toward the sound. "My name is Andy."

A holographic woman in a crisp white nurse's uniform stood next to the bed. She looked like she had walked out of some ancient story. Was she designed that way to make old people feel better? How long had he been asleep?

He dragged his hands out from under the sheets and stared at them. His fingers didn't look any different than he remembered. He squeezed his eyes closed until the room stopped spinning.

"Very good," the woman said. "My name is Sandra. I'm here to help you adjust to your new Link. We'll be working together until you can access its basic functions and understand the intermediate communication methods. Andy, are you listening?"

He nodded, trying to focus on her and not the wall behind her. His eyes didn't want to cooperate.

"How long was I out?" he asked.

"You have been in recovery for ten hours."

Slowly, Andy reached behind his head to feel the bandage running from the base of his neck to just above his right ear.

"Why is it such a big bandage? I thought this was supposed to be a tiny cut?"

"Some surgeries prove more challenging," Sandra said. "Yours may have been one of them, but I am not allowed access to personal medical records and I can't answer any questions relating to your treatment or the medical professionals assisting you. Are you ready to start your training on your new Link?"

He squinted at her, trying to see her face inside the glaring halo of light surrounding her head. The white ceiling wasn't helping him focus.

"More challenging? Why?"

"I can't answer any questions relating to your treatment or the medical professionals assisting you."

Andy let his head fall back on the pillow and winced when a lance of pain shot up the right side of his head.

"I think my pain killers are wearing off."

<You can request more via your Link, Andy.>

Andy's eyes went wide. Her voice was inside his mind but not part of him. The words drifted away as soon as he heard them, but he couldn't be sure he had heard them at all because there was no sound.

"Did you just speak to me?"

<I am communicating with you via your Link. Try to answer me using this method.>

Andy tried to only think his response but couldn't stop himself from opening his mouth to speak. "I can't do it. Are you reading my mind?"

"I am not reading your thoughts, that is not possible over the Link. You must direct your communication to me. The sub-routine in your Link will recognize my token and route your messages accordingly. I can only hear what you intend for me to hear. However, I can still see your expression."

Andy relaxed his frown.

<That's only slightly better.>

"Aren't you supposed to be nice to me?"

<Without communication via the Link, you will be unable to access other data streams. This skill is the foundation of all others. Do you want us to remove the Link?>

"No, I don't want you to remove it. I didn't think it would be hard to use. Everyone else makes it look like second nature."

<It is like second nature to them. Can you ride a bike, or swim?>

Andy stopped himself before he answered. Pressing his lips together, he thought a combination of Yes/Affirmative.

<Good,> the nurse said, her voice still unfriendly. *<I understood you that time. However, you sounded like your mouth was full of foam, all muddy with your emotions.>*

"What?" Andy demanded, frustration getting the best of him. "You didn't say anything about emotion. How am I supposed to stop that?"

<The same way you would modulate your voice. Do you yell and cry at every random person you meet? Or do only I have that effect on you?>

"You're a very strange program."

<I am a nurse, which means I don't have time for your bullshit and I've heard all the excuses before.>

"I think you're responding in whatever way you think will get me to learn fastest. Does this mean I respond to authority?"

<I don't care, genius,> she said. *<Answer me over the Link or we're done until tomorrow. You can't leave the hospital until you can at least communicate over the Link. I had hoped to get to Data Acquisition today so you could spend your own time exploring the Link.>*

Her words hung in his mind, alongside several flashing images that he recognized as news and documentaries, as well as a map of Summerville—he didn't understand at first until housing blocks and the branches of the Ashley River made sense. Everything had the quality of a half-remembered memory, like an itch he couldn't scratch.

<I'm doing my best,> he complained.

<That's good. Do it again.>

He wasn't sure what had changed. Something about the sound of her voice in his mind made more sense this time, like mimicking someone's accent. He had never thought of his inner voice as having different tones but that was how he responded; deeper, enunciating, knowing clearly what he wanted to communicate.

<Do you hear me now?> he asked.

Sandra smiled, leaning toward him. <I hear you very well, Andy.> Her voice purred in his mind, sending a tickle down his chest. He couldn't help a quick glance down her body; whoever had designed her uniform had made it hug her curves in all the right places. How hadn't he noticed that before? He squirmed slightly in the bed, aware that his body was starting to respond to the warmth in her voice.

<Your mind is going to respond quicker than if you just heard my voice, Andy. Do you feel that?>

"Yes, I feel that!" he said uneasily.

Her voice came like a slap in his head. <Use the Link.> Her face hadn't changed. She was still leaning closer to him, her brown eyes staring directly at him. <Now,> she continued, voice tingling in his mind again. <You need to separate your emotions from your voice.>

<How am I supposed to do that? I'm eighteen. The **wind** gives me an erection.>

The corners of her mouth ticked up as she chuckled in his head. <You're having the expected response. Do you understand how much more you can be affected over the Link? You'll need to practice separating your emotions from what you hear. It seems more—intimate, at first. It's not, but you'll perceive it that way.>

<Do you work for the hospital or the TSF?>

<I can't answer questions relating to your treatment or the medical professionals assisting you,> she purred, so deeply this time that he nearly orgasmed.

<Stop! Stop doing that. Isn't there some other way you can teach me how to do this?>

<I adapt to the subject's weakest response areas. You are sexually frustrated. This can be used against you.>

<I'm not sexually—> Andy cut himself off as he realized she was probably correct. Her voice filled him with tension that made him long to hear her dulcet tones again. He let out a long sigh and collapsed back on the bed, letting his head sink into the pillow. <How do people not get addicted to this? Why not just float around inside your Link all day?>

<They do,> Sandra said. Her gaze became calculating. She had taken a step back and appeared more professional now. She must have been manipulating her appearance because the sexiness was gone. Her uniform had shifted into something more contemporary that didn't show off her body.

<You are communicating over the Link well enough to progress,> she said. <Do you

understand the lesson about guarding your response? Others can't hear your thoughts, but they can certainly try to affect you. Proper response will take time. It is recommended you not engage in any major financial or legal transactions for at least six months. Luckily for you, basic training will take up most of that time. However, considering the additional factor of your age and maturing brain, you will be doubly subject to pattern manipulation.>

<What's pattern manipulation?>

<You are susceptible to others imprinting on you. It will be more difficult for you to establish a separate identity from your training, or strong relationships. You can study this concept once I explain how to access information over the Link.>

<You're saying I'm young and stupid.>

<You can study this concept once I explain how to access information over the Link.>

<Fine.>

Sandra spent the next thirty minutes explaining how administrative levels worked and what his basic security token allowed him to explore: areas like government archives, libraries, shopping centers and public forums on nearly any subject he could imagine. He also had access to certain TSF channels that weren't open to the public, although he had only the lowest read-only rights to that information. It was all mainly training material, rules and regulations, and the Uniform Code of Military Justice.

Sandra explained how he could overlay information on his thoughts if he chose, allowing different data sets access to his daily life. For instance, if he wanted to make sure he never broke a law, he could allow various local laws to remind him when he was jaywalking or littering. She called this portion of the Link 'Agents' and warned him against trying to run too many at once, which lead quickly to something called Input Fatigue.

Even with the Link making all information available, his brain still had to spend time requesting and sorting the incoming flow. For some people, it was like pulling packages off an endless conveyor belt until the ceaseless flow became debilitating.

Andy picked up the data portion of the Link much faster than communication. No sooner did a question reach the top of his mind than he felt the archive like a memory, ready to open for him if he chose to access it.

<Why bother remembering anything?> he asked.

Sandra shrugged. *<Most people don't.>*

On a basic level, he knew all this. He had been reading about people with Links all his life. Many of his mom's strange responses made more sense now. He had a better understanding of how difficult it must be for her to stay present with them and to maintain her patience with his dad, who could only use the information and memories he was able to keep in his own head.

<It's going to take a while to get used to this.>

The holographic nurse nodded. *<This is expected. During the rest of your recovery, you will need to access the TSF Training Archive, level one. There will be a test of your knowledge tomorrow at eleven hundred hours.>*

<Why have a test? Can't I just pull up the information whenever I want it?>

<Link access isn't always guaranteed, especially in OuterSol, or in a hostile engagement. However, that's not the reason. The TSF will continue to test you because it's a way to maintain focus, to gauge training levels and eventually assign rank. The Link makes people lazy. Don't be lazy.>

Andy grinned. <Are you sure you're a program?>

She tilted her head. <I am a composite AI. Parts of me belonged to a Sandra who was a nurse. I have her voice and response patterns.>

Andy sat up, interested. <I didn't realize you were an AI. I've never talked to an AI before.>

<It's very likely you have but didn't know it. I am a composite. There are many of us in the TSF as trainers and functionaries. Someday you may choose to be recorded for later compositing.> She straightened. <You have completed your initial Link training, Private Sykes. Do you require any further remedial training at this time?>

He thought about asking more questions but felt a wave of fatigue roll over him. He yawned and shook his head. <No. I'll do the TSF level one.>

Sandra nodded. <Good luck, Private Sykes.> She blinked out of existence, leaving him alone in the hospital room.

CHAPTER THIRTEEN

STELLAR DATE: 08.24.2981 (Adjusted Years)
LOCATION: *Sunny Skies*
REGION: Port Authority, Cruithne Station, Terran Hegemony

"AI?" Andy sputtered. "Are you crazy?" He pointed at the bay doors. "Get your cargo together, get your helmets back on, and get off my ship. I'm not some skin mule with a hole in my stomach for your bio-waste."

"That's not how it works at all," Jickson said anxiously, looking offended. "This is a symbiosis. It's a completely revolutionary technology."

Starl shot Jickson an irritated look. "Doctor," he growled.

"I don't care what you're doing," Andy said. "I don't want to know. I just want you out of here. Pack up your crates and disappear." He waved at the pulse scars on the walls and overhead. "After all this, those guys are certainly coming back. I need to figure out how to deal with that. I'd prefer they know you're not here anymore and follow you out of my life."

"I can help you with that, Captain Sykes," Starl said.

Andy shot him an angry look. "You're going to help me solve the problem you created for me. Thanks."

Starl nodded thoughtfully. "So, your ship was doing just fine before my cargo made its way aboard. Your drive wasn't about to fail." He raised a hand at Andy's hard expression. "We ran scans before coming aboard. I know your ship status. You're not getting away from Cruithne without help." He shrugged. "If I were you, I'd be trying to figure out how to sell this relic for scrap. With that, I'd have a nice fund to last me until I found work on another outbound freighter. But you're from Earth originally…I can see it in your chest. Why not scrap this thing and go home? Never going to get another chance with this ship slung around your neck like an albatross."

Starl obviously enjoyed listening to himself talk. Andy kept his peripheral vision on Karcher. The guard was still focused on the portable surgery alongside Jickson, who had given up all pretense of listening to them.

"But that would be relinquishing your freedom," Starl continued, as if explaining something to himself.

Andy flicked his gaze back to Starl's face and found the man's eyes boring into him. He wanted to look away again but couldn't. Starl was right.

A hiss from the wall behind him made Andy turn. The interior access door was sliding to the side and, before he could say anything, Cara kicked into the room with a portable arc welder held shakily in both hands. She was wearing one of Brit's suits, its legs and sleeves bunched up awkwardly. Behind, her, Tim peeked around the edge of the door, helmet set back on his head so the face shield was nearly pointed at the ceiling. He had a crowbar in his free hand.

"Cara!" Andy shouted.

The arc welder snapped, plasma flashing blue between its pincers.

A wave of fear went through Andy like nothing he'd felt since the first time he'd been in combat. He simultaneously watched the arc welder snapping and knew Karcher was drawing down on Cara from behind him. He pushed off the floor to put himself between the soldier and Cara, hoping she wouldn't change her path as she saw him move. Cara was an acrobat in zero-g. He waited for Karcher's rounds to hit his spine.

"Calm down!" Starl shouted. "Everyone calm down now. Mr. Karcher, please."

Andy activated his magboots and stopped himself when he was standing in front of Cara. Her arms were trembling as she tried to hold the arc welder steady. She dropped the tool as she collided with Andy's chest and he wrapped her in his arms.

"Oh, sweetheart," he breathed. "I told you to hide. You have to listen to me when I tell you that." He couldn't tell if she'd heard him or not.

"Who are these little people, Captain Sykes?" The humor had come back into Starl's voice. "Your crew? Didn't you tell me you were alone on the ship?"

"Cara," Andy said, pushing her away slightly. "Give me the welder."

"Are you all right?" she demanded. "Who are these men? Why was there shooting?" Her voice was tinny through the helmet's speaker.

He watched her gaze flick across the room behind him and land on what he knew was Stansil's body.

"Is that man dead?"

"Sweetheart, give me the welder. You need to take your brother and go back where I told you to stay. Do you understand me?"

"She can stay, Captain Sykes. Are these your children?" The gangster laughed. "This is great. I'd love to meet them. What's your name, love?"

Cara's gaze shifted to Starl, uncertainty plain on her face.

"Everything is all right," Andy said slowly. "We're going to be fine but I need you to take your brother and go back."

"Why was he talking about selling *Sunny Skies*? Why would we have to do that?"

"He's not talking about us," Andy said. "We're just having a conversation. They're checking their cargo and then they'll be leaving. It's no different than anyplace we've been. You know better than to come down here."

Cara's face fell. He didn't like having to chastise her but he didn't see how else to get Cara to leave. "Now, take your brother and do as I tell you." He raised his voice, "Tim, you go with your sister."

"Why was there fighting, Dad?"

"There were some pirates. They tried to take the cargo. These men helped me and now they're leaving too."

"Are they leaving? They took their helmets off. You told us never to do that in the cargo hold. What if the door fails like you said it could?"

"You're right, Tim. That's exactly what I said. Do as I tell you, now."

"You're worried about your cargo doors failing, Captain Sykes," Starl said from behind him, his deep voice resonating in the room's confines. "You know I can help you with that."

Andy turned to face him. "Tell me how you're going to keep my family safe during the ten days we'll need in drydock? And then how am I going to keep them safe once I've got your...cargo on board."

Starl spread his hands. "My name is Ngoba Starl, Captain Sykes. I run the Lowspin Crew on Cruithne." He tapped his chest with a fist. "They call me the Brutal Dandy and I love them for it because they're right. You're safer here than anywhere in Sol. I didn't expect Zanda to move like he did, which is probably why he showed his hand. He'll pay. As for your ship, Captain Sykes, like I said, we'll dry dock her and fix your engines. And I'll pay you on top of that. This is really an offer you can't refuse." He made a point of looking at Cara, and then at Tim. "Unless you want a different life for your family. An uncertain life."

Andy fought the urge to put a pulse bolt between the gangster's eyes. Karcher had turned his attention back to the cargo. Andy could have taken both of them and been on Jickson before he had time to squeak.

But the kids were watching. The kids were the only reason he was even considering Starl's offer, which he knew had a hidden trap. It had to be a trap that was going to be worse than letting go of *Sunny Skies.*

"Where would I be taking your cargo?" he asked.

Starl gave him a slight smile, looking pleased that he had found his wedge into Andy's resolve. "It's a trip, Captain Sykes. I won't lie to you about that. We need our package delivered to a station in the vicinity of Neptune. You'll be dropping a few things off here and there, Mars, back to Jupiter, the Jovian Combine. You're a small specialty freighter and that's what you'll be doing."

"What's the delivery window?"

"Delivery is the window. The sooner the better." Starl shrugged. "It's not like we won't be talking along the way, Captain Sykes. You and I would be good friends. Lowspin has resources off-station if you find yourself needing help."

Tim made a clanking sound as he smacked his crowbar against the edge of the door.

"Stop that," Andy called. "You'll dent it and it won't seal right."

Tim let his arm fall to his side. He adjusted his helmet with his free hand. "Sorry, Dad."

"Don't be sorry. Just don't do it." He looked at Cara. "Will you take your brother like I told you?"

"Wait," Jickson said. The doctor's boots clicked as he walked toward Tim. "I didn't see you there."

Tim's oversized helmet tipped as he looked at the doctor. "How couldn't you have seen me? I was right here."

Before Andy could get in his way, the doctor was kneeling in front of Tim. He had taken his gloves off while working on the portable surgery and the hand he held up looked like it was trembling.

"What's your name?" Jickson asked.

Tim's helmet turned toward Andy as if asking permission.

71

Jickson turned to look back at Andy. "It's all right, Captain Sykes. I'm sorry. I simply haven't seen a child for so long. My work. I used to work with children. I quite enjoy them. How old is your son?"

"I'm ten," Tim said, proud of his age.

"Ten," Jickson said. He dropped the trembling hand to his knee. "That's an excellent age. Just getting a real sense of the world at ten."

"It hasn't been that long since you saw a kid, doctor," Starl chided.

"Do you heal sick people?" Tim said.

"I do research," Jickson said. "That's how I worked with kids like you. We worked together on…projects. What things do you like?"

"I'm going to be a pilot like my dad," Tim announced, voice still small through his helmet speaker but filled with purpose. "He and my mom were in the TSF. He fought pirates every day. They fought at the Fortress 8221."

Andy nearly winced to hear the name 8221 come out of Tim's mouth.

"Now that's very interesting," Jickson said. "I didn't know that. Do you like history?"

"I guess," Tim said. "Maybe *you* can tell me. Did Mars have dinosaurs?"

Jickson pulled his head back, seemingly amazed by the question. "Of course not," he said. "Where did you hear that?"

"Just because we haven't found fossils doesn't mean they aren't there," Tim said.

For the first time, Andy heard Karcher laughing. The man's laughs were like a big dog barking.

Jickson looked back at him, disgusted. "What's so amusing?"

"This kid is great. The look on your face was priceless." Karcher composed himself, adding, "Your machine's ready, doc."

"So," Starl interjected. "Captain Sykes, I think we can reach an agreement. What do you think? I'll fix your ship. I'll give you a cover and pay you for transport. You agree to carry our cargo."

Andy looked at Starl, then at Cara and Tim. He felt like he was holding open the jaws of a giant steel trap that would snap on all of them the moment he lost focus. The thought of being cast adrift without the ship was worse. It was so much worse. Without *Sunny Skies*, there was no chance of Brit ever coming home. How had he even considered scrapping the ship?

There had been no choice. He had a choice now.

"I want half payment up front," Andy said. "How is this going to work?"

Starl glanced at Jickson. "Doctor?"

"I need time to prepare." Jickson rubbed his hands, thinking. "I need time to get her ready for the transition." He smiled suddenly, looking almost like an expectant parent. "She's going to be so surprised, Captain Sykes. I wish I could do it. I envy you, truly."

"Who's *she*?" Cara said.

"A person we're going to transport," Andy said quickly.

"We'll start the repairs while Dr. Jickson prepares for what he needs to do,"

Starl said. "Let's say ten days. We'll want to make sure everything is correct before you leave Cruithne. Sound like a plan?"

"I guess," Andy said.

Ngoba Starl gave him a wide smile and held out his hand. "Excellent, Captain Sykes."

Andy looked from Cara to Starl's extended hand, feeling the weight of everything—the kids, the ship, the debt—pressing on his shoulders. Ten days was enough time to ease the kids into the new job, to try to explain what he was agreeing to.

He nodded and shook Starl's hand.

CHAPTER FOURTEEN
STELLAR DATE: 08.25.2981 (Adjusted Years)
LOCATION: Cantil Park Housing Project
REGION: Cruithne Station, Terran Hegemony

Starl had arranged for a tug to pull the *Sunny Skies* to a dock on the inner edge of Cruithne's jumbled ring. He'd offered an apartment in a housing block near the dock with an open-air playground in the center of its cylindrical structure. During most hours of the day, the place crawled with kids whose parents worked the repair docks.

Once he had net access on Cruithne, Andy could find little information in the Link databases about Ngoba Starl, leader of the Lowspin Crew, aside from a few stories about gang wars and low-level freight piracy. The apartment was a touch that should have made Andy more distrustful, but it also seemed to suggest a humanity he hadn't expected, as if Starl had a family too, somewhere.

Within hours of getting Cara and Tim comfortable at the apartment, Andy had to leave for the initial walkthrough with the repair crewchief; a woman named Fran Urtal. She appeared at the door in an oil-stained coverall, dirty blond hair pulled back and held in place on top of her head by a pair of scarred welding goggles. Her green eyes glinted with what were most likely retinal overlays. He wouldn't have been surprised if someone in her line of work had completely artificial eyes.

"You're Andy Sykes?" she asked. She looked him up and down and then gave him a crooked smile as if she somewhat approved of what she saw.

"That's me," Andy said, still holding a towel after drying Tim's hair after a bath. The kids hadn't had real baths in a year, at least.

"Who are you?" Cara demanded from the hallway behind him. She stalked up beside Andy and peered at the woman.

"I'm Fran. I'll be leading the crew working on your ship."

Cara squinted slightly. "You keep your hands off my dad."

Andy choked, staring at Cara in surprise. "Cara! Where did that come from."

Now Fran had a full grin. "Wolf pup's looking out for the pack. I like that." She held out a calloused hand toward Cara. "I'm going to take good care of your *Sunny Skies*. I won't have much time to chase your dad."

Still stony-faced, Cara took the offered hand.

"Good grip," Fran said. "I heard you know your way around an arc welder."

"Dad's taught me to weld," Cara said. "What are you going to do to the ship?"

"Replace your engines, for starters. I don't know what deal you've got with Ngoba Starl but he's spending a fortune on you and your relic of a ship. I told him he should just buy something newer, it'd be cheaper in the long run. He said no, so I do what I'm paid to do." She shrugged. "Did you think of that? Just trading in *Sunny Skies* for something built in this century?"

"*Sunny Skies* works for us," Andy said. He turned to Cara. "You get your brother ready for bed and don't open the door while I'm gone. I'll put my security token on the panel so no one can get in but me. You understand?"

He expected her to roll her eyes but she nodded seriously. "When are you going to sleep?"

"Later," Andy said. "Give me a hug."

He knelt to pull her in for a hug, then called for Tim—who came running out in his underwear—to join them. Andy threw the towel over his son's head and Tim immediately held out his arms and started making ghost sounds.

Once he had finally disentangled himself from his children, and the door had closed behind him, Andy entered his security token in the panel.

"Cute family," Fran said.

"You have kids?"

"They'd get in the way of my drinking. I don't even have plants."

She led him out of the housing block through a ramshackle market of vendors stalls practically stacked on top of each other, until they passed into the warehouse district, which marked the outer edge of the repair docks. Cruithne Station hadn't been built with any sort of plan. The station's ring had grown like a fungus feeding on itself, stretching out from the original asteroid, first in scaffolds and tubular arms that typically served as private docking points, followed by construction interconnecting the arms. Some areas had been retrofitted so the decks were even and the bulkheads matched, while other sections looked like whole ships had been cut apart and welded into the growing ring.

Brit had always hated the messiness of places like Cruithne, where the grime of humanity could never quite be cleaned away. Andy liked the wildness; it reminded him of home in Summerville a little bit, where edges never quite matched, and doors were always hard to close. That was life. Living off-Earth didn't change the reality of what humanity had always been doing when it lived close to the bone and fought for survival.

"I shouldn't give you a hard time about your ship," Fran said when they reached the warehouse section and they could hear each other talk. "It's got some surprising guts. Its registry says it was commissioned as a vacation yacht but its superstructure looks practically military to me."

Andy frowned. "Why's that?"

"It was definitely built to take gs. There's also the hundred or so hidden chambers, every one shielded by functional components. It's a smuggler's paradise." She gave him a sly smile, artificial eyes sparkling.

Andy shot her a tense look. "You're not updating any kind of general registry with that info, right? I'd prefer to keep that to myself."

Fran laughed and pushed his shoulder. "Where do you think you are? This isn't the TSF, soldier boy. We're cash and carry here."

Andy relaxed slightly. "Right. That makes sense."

"Besides, it's not like I can blackmail you. You're broke. You've got an interesting ship. That's worth a hell of a lot more than money to me."

If she'd found the TSF weapons crate, she seemed like the type to ask him about it out of pure curiosity, or to simply assume a vet would have that sort of thing hidden away.

"Did you know your habitat was retrofitted for long-range travel, too?" Fran continued, clearly excited by the technical aspects of *Sunny Skies*. "Why add all those hydroponic systems and the completely unnecessary crew areas? If the registry didn't class it as a yacht, I'd wager it was a surveiller, or some university's science ship. Your weapons mounts are also reinforced way more than's needed for basic point defense cannons, which is just weird. Where'd you buy this thing?"

"We—I bought it on High Terra. Got a good deal on it. It wasn't in great shape and I haven't been able to keep up on the maintenance like I should. Everything's been falling apart, bit by bit."

"You need an actual crew," Fran said. "You've got the room for it. With your engines at full capacity, you'll be able to do more than just limp along with your sails."

They reached her repair section, a command deck with narrow windows in its outside wall showing the shadowed side of *Sunny Skies* sitting in dry dock. Through the strip of window, Andy could barely make out the tiny forms of engineers in EV suits working on an outer section of the ship.

"You don't waste any time, do you?"

"We don't have a lot of time," Fran said. "We'll be on your job for the whole two hundred and forty hours. You're lucky I had the parts for your fusion bottle. We can manufacture just about anything on site but that takes more time. You'd be surprised how many weird, one-off systems I'm dealing with here."

Andy didn't press her that the eclectic jobs were a function of repairing pirates' rigs and stolen ships. She was speaking more out of pride than any real complaint.

"You see any problems with the job?" he asked.

"I'm showing a second owner on the registry, a Brit Ashford. Who's she?"

"The kids' mom. She's not going to come looking for the ship."

"Well, that's too bad," Fran said.

He thought he caught a note of interest in her voice but he didn't take his gaze off the long, dark lines of *Sunny Skies*. From this angle, the ship looked like one of the crumbling skyscrapers standing on the horizon in Summerville, now lying sideways, the long bulbs of the drive cones barely visible at the far end of the bay.

"You know, I can edit the registry for you if you want," she said, then added, "No extra charge."

Andy turned from the window, considering the idea. Brit's disappearance did pose legal problems for him. He hadn't thought about the fact that she still owned half the ship, which would make it hard for him to get market value if he tried to sell *Sunny Skies*. He could have filed death paperwork a year ago but couldn't bear the thought of having the words "Declared Deceased," somewhere that Cara or Tim might come across them. He didn't know where Brit was. The kids didn't ask. No one wanted to talk about the possibilities.

Fran's eyes flickered in systematic pulses. She was probably reviewing some schematic or issuing commands as she stood here talking to him.

"Yes," he said finally. "I'd like to do that."

"Captain Sykes!" Ngoba Starl called from the doorway. "Is my Fran taking care of you?"

The head of the Lowspin Crew was wearing a neat black suit that matched his hair, set off by a pale-yellow pocket square. The flash of an oversized gold ring on his right hand caught Andy's eye as he walked into the room.

"She is, thanks."

"Good. I'm very glad to hear it. Are your children enjoying Cantil Park?"

"It's a nice place. I appreciate you putting us up there."

"Yes, it is a good place. I have security in the area, so you know." He held up both hands in reassurance. "I'm not worried about anything, but while you're here on Cruithne, your family is my family."

Andy gave him a tight smile and nodded. "I appreciate that."

Starl nodded, squinting at him slightly. "I hope you do, Captain Sykes. I think you and I have begun a relationship here. This could be the start of something wonderful." He motioned toward Fran, who had turned to look out the narrow window. "Look at Fran, here. Before I found her, she was doing maintenance on freighters running the line between what's left of Mercury and High Terra. Can you imagine that? Every day, worried a flare was going to cook your ass? I brought her to Cruithne, set her up with Lowspin, and now she has her own shop."

He gave Fran a wink when she rolled her eyes. Starl turned his grin to Andy. "What are you doing when you leave here?"

"Going back to the apartment, I guess," Andy said.

"You should come out with me. I would like to have a drink with you. What do you think about that?"

"Mr. Starl—"

"Call me Ngoba. I know you're worried about your kids. Trust me, they have more security right now than the Station Administrator."

"It sounds like I don't have a choice."

"Of course, you do, but this would please me a lot. I'd like to hear about you, Captain Sykes. You have a story to tell, I know it."

Starl got a sudden distant look in his eye as he appeared to get a message over his Link. In a second, he widened his smile and looked from Fran to Andy. "I'm needed elsewhere." He pointed at Fran. "You take good care of my friend."

Fran nodded, smirking.

"And I'll see you in three hours," he said, pointing at Andy. "What do you have to wear? Oh, don't worry about it. We'll get you some clothes. I'll send one of my friends around for you. Probably Mr. Karcher. You know him."

Andy opened his mouth to reply, but Starl just gave him a quick nod, his attention back on whatever had come across his Link as he left the command deck.

When the door slid closed behind him, Andy turned to Fran. "You trust him?"

Fran gave him an arch look. "Do you trust me?"

"I just met you. But you're working on my ship, so I don't have much choice."

"I've got too much pride to do a crappy job on your ship. It's bad for business.

Besides, your kids are cute and I'd feel bad if you broke down in the middle of nowhere."

"That's nice of you."

"Trust isn't much of a concept on Cruithne, anyway. It's like asking if we get thirsty. Nobody trusts anybody. People want things. Other people have things. They work it out."

She'd taken a step closer to him, the flashes in her irises making it difficult to look away from her face.

"What do *you* want?" Andy asked, playing along with her little speech.

"Maybe I'll tell you," Fran said. "Remind me after I fix your ship."

CHAPTER FIFTEEN

STELLAR DATE: 08.26.2981 (Adjusted Years)
LOCATION: Cantil Park Housing Project
REGION: Cruithne Station, Terran Hegemony

The kids were still asleep when Andy returned to the apartment after spending another hour reviewing schematics with Fran. She'd pointed out another series of what she'd called "interesting design and upgrade choices" across *Sunny Skies*, including the power grid and the control systems. Considering the glitched state of the ship's computer, she figured he should have been stranded in deep space just after leaving Kalyke.

"I don't know if you want me to mess with your control systems," she'd said. "It might be like figuring out astrogation with an abacus, but it's bullet proof. I'm afraid I'll break whatever core system keeps *Sunny Skies* running where any other ship's comp would have failed completely."

Andy hadn't known what to say about it other than to agree with her. He had grown used to the ancient navigation system, and at this point, the work-arounds were the primary way he controlled the ship.

After his shower, he sat in the small kitchen staring at a glass of water, trying to think through the various choices in front of him. Of course, people smuggled bio-materials all the time. Embedding something in your body wasn't much different than hiding it somewhere in the ship. The difference was only a matter of degree. If the material was especially noxious, it would kill you faster if it escaped its container. It might turn you into a breeding ground for some bio-weapon. Or it might simply render you brain dead.

Each path in front of him would have been simpler if he didn't have to worry about the kids, and nothing changed the fact that he didn't have a fallback plan in the event something happened to him.

Cara was almost old enough to take care of herself and Tim. Almost, but not quite.

With Cruithne so close to Earth and Mars, its local net was well updated, almost like being back in civilization. He could run through lists of people he had once called friends during his time in the TSF. He could check on his sister Jane if he wanted—a thought that he sat and chewed on for a while.

She had never really forgiven him for leaving their family, and had only seemed to grow more bitter toward him as their parents declined and he wasn't able to come home to help. He had sent her pictures and videos of the kids whenever possible but she'd rarely replied. Jane hadn't liked Brit much, or maybe she had simply decided it was Andy she didn't like anymore.

When the knock on the door came, Andy saved his list and downed the last of his water. The station water tasted good, despite its slightly coppery taste. Tim had refused to drink it until Cara added a bit of cherry flavoring.

He opened the door to find Karcher standing outside in a black suit much like the one Starl had worn earlier. His pocket kerchief was pale blue. Seeing the soldier out of his EV suit was a bit of a surprise. He was smaller than Andy expected, with narrow shoulders and a thin face. Only the dark eyes Andy had seen previously through the faceplate were familiar. His irises were hidden by silver overlays that looked like dull coins. A bulge in the side of his jacket belied a pistol of some kind.

"Captain Sykes," Karcher said. He smiled and showed a gold front tooth. "I'm supposed to take you shopping."

"Why does your boss assume I'm broke?" Andy asked.

"I didn't think that was an assumption."

"Are you being funny, Karcher?" Andy asked.

"No."

Andy shook his head in response and stepped through the door, locking it behind him with his security token.

"You don't have to do that, you know," Karcher said. He pointed to balconies around their heads. "I've got people in all those apartments keeping an eye on your kids. This is the safest place on Cruithne right now."

"So Starl has told me. Still, it makes me feel better," Andy replied.

"I understand."

Andy followed Karcher through the housing block, along a different path than he had taken with Fran. This time they went down two levels to a transport hub where Karcher keyed into a private maglev car. They sat in silence as the car shot through a tunnel made of dark scaffolding, hung with conduit and plumbing. Occasionally the car emerged in open-air sections with busy corridors full of pedestrians.

"This makes Cruithne look almost normal," Andy said.

Karcher shrugged. He was busy cleaning his fingernails with a pocket knife. "It's getting a few of the edges rubbed smooth, but I don't think it's ever going to be a place I'd want to raise a family. Its location makes it too useful for smuggling. As long as that's valuable, it needs to stay a gray zone."

Everywhere Andy looked, there were people. People walking quickly, heads erect. People huddled in groups, heads close together. People pointing at some item for sale between them, apparently arguing over price. Drones buzzed overhead and shot between feet. He saw augmented people and what looked like full-mechs. He could imagine the sounds without hearing them: the chaos of voices and machinery. He remembered the smells and sounds of Cruithne and nearly wrinkled his nose at the harsh memories of spices, oil, urine, sweat, blood and decaying meat.

"I was here with the TSF when I was a lieutenant," he said. "Busting smugglers. I didn't get out much, though."

"We've still got a few TSF newbies hanging around," Karcher said. "They're good marks in a poker game." He met Andy's gaze briefly. "Think they're invincible."

"Every TSF pilot is invincible until they're dead," Andy shot back.

Karcher frowned, letting his penknife drop. "You know that doesn't make any sense, right?"

"Neither does strapping yourself to a missile and subjecting your body to extreme g-forces, vacuum, or hostile fire; but they line up to do it. Better to die in a blaze of glory than suffer being mediocre."

Karcher shook his head. "I've heard the same argument from pirates. I'm fine with being mediocre, thanks."

Andy was about to point out that Karcher was a soldier and took as many risks as a fighter pilot when the car came to a halt and the guard quickly folded his knife and stepped through the sliding door.

They walked out through a private entrance into a clean, well-lit shopping district that Andy quickly realized was populated solely by clothing shops. Karcher led him down two wide corridors with windows displaying clothing of every stripe and fashion, until they reached a plain door with a single display window beside it showing a simple black suit similar to Karcher's.

"Here we are," Karcher said. He pulled the door open for Andy and released the smells of sandalwood, cedar and various natural fibers.

For the next half-hour, Karcher leaned against a wall as a tall, thin tailor took Andy's measurements with an actual piece of vinyl tape. The man hummed and nodded to himself as he stretched the tape in ways that didn't make much sense to Andy, like the distance from his elbow to the end of his index finger, as well as each shin from knee to ankle. He also measured each of Andy's feet and the circumference of his head.

"Very good," he murmured. "What color, sir?"

"Black," Karcher said before Andy could answer.

When the tailor had left for a back room, Andy said, "Wait, I'm not getting fitted for one of your gangster outfits, am I?"

"You're getting a suit for Mr. Starl's club. For those who know, it won't identify you as Lowspin, no. It'll just make you look like a civilized human being."

Andy looked down at his coverall and its most-recent stains from dragging the TSF weapons crate halfway across *Sunny Skies*, as well as what might have been some of Stansil's blood that had leaked through his EV suit. One hairy calf was visible through a long tear below his knee.

Perhaps looking human would be a nice change.

In thirty minutes, the tailor returned with a suit that actually looked hand-sewn in places. Andy marveled at the workmanship as he was ushered into a fitting room. When he came back into the main room, he thought it fit perfectly but the tailor wasn't satisfied. He made several marks with a piece of white chalk.

"Your jacket, sir," he said.

When the tailor was finally satisfied and Andy was wearing the finished suit, the man brought out a board draped with various kerchiefs in the same pale colors as those Karcher and Starl wore. Andy started to choose blue, then settled on a green that reminded him of the kudzu leaves back in Summerville.

The tailor set the board down, drew out the handkerchief and folded it in several snapping motions until it had become a perfect, multi-creased square that he fitted into Andy's pocket so it formed a triangle.

"Very good, sir," the tailor said finally, stepping back to admire his work. "I'd recommend a shave."

Andy rubbed his stubbled chin and nodded, thanking the man.

When they emerged in the corridor outside the shop, Andy carrying his coveralls in a disposable bag, Karcher nodded with a grin. "Feels like a new life, doesn't it?"

"It feels different," Andy agreed, noticing as a passing woman with piles of curly red hair gave him a second look. She flashed a smile and was gone in the crowd.

Karcher's expression went blank as he accessed his Link. "The boss wants us to meet him at the club right away," he said. "You hungry? He wants to know what you want to eat."

"Whatever he's having."

The soldier shook his head. "Trust me, you don't want that. You want beef? How about a steak? You've been out a long time."

The thought of having a steak without the kids made Andy feel a little guilty. But they had already gotten their choices of a take-out menu back at the apartment Starl had provided. Pizza for Tim and skewers for Cara.

"That sounds good," Andy said. "Where's the club? I might remember it."

"It's a new place. The boss had it built out of an old warehouse back near the repair docks. Makes for easy access for anybody who wants to drop in and drop out. It's a music club, really fresh stuff."

They had just stepped into the main flow of foot traffic through the shopping district when Andy felt the nose of a pistol jabbed hard into the small of his back. He turned his head to get a look at his attacker and was met by a sharp hiss. "Keep your eyes looking ahead or I'll—"

Karcher's pistol cracked twice and the pressure left Andy's back. He turned to find a middle-aged man lying on the floor clutching his stomach, blood leaking between his fingers. He looked no different from any other shopper.

"A mugging?" Andy asked. "This looked like a nice area."

"Welcome to Cruithne," Karcher said, holstering his pistol inside his jacket.

"Is that all it was?"

The soldier shrugged. "Probably. Who cares? He saw us walk out of the suit shop and only a certain type of client goes in there. He should have known better."

Andy looked around. The flow of shoppers had split cleanly around them, no one paying them any special attention.

"Do we need to worry about security?" he asked.

"Nope." Karcher squatted down next to the mugger's wheezing face. "Who do you work for?"

The man blew out a wet breath. "Nobody."

"Nobody. You know you might live with the two shots I gave you. I put one in your brain and you're not getting out of this. Who sent you?"

"Zanda. He figures this guy can carry the AI."

"I don't know anything about that," Karcher said. In a smooth motion, he drew his pistol and shot him in the temple. The blast caused the tile under his head to crack.

Andy looked around anxiously, expecting someone to shout or scream, but the crowd continued on as though nothing noteworthy had occured. He couldn't hide the shock on his face as Karcher stood, holstering his pistol a second time. He straightened his jacket.

"Calm down," Karcher said. "The only mistake you can make on Cruithne is wasting the Security Admin's time. They'll replay the surveillance and see what happened. This guy was a fool. He probably doesn't even work for Zanda and was just trying to catch a lucky break." He shook his head. "But if that's true, it means the Havenots can't keep their mouths shut."

"If they found us here, they know where the kids are," Andy said. "I need to go back to the apartment."

Karcher held up a hand. "We've got more security on that apartment than Starl has right now. Trust me, they're safe."

"I don't know you."

"True enough, but we want something from you, right? So, it doesn't figure that we'd let you or your kids get hurt, not while you're on Cruithne anyway."

Andy frowned, worry about the kids battling the need to complete this deal. The sooner they were off Cruithne Station, the better.

"All right," he said.

Karcher gave him a fake grin, his eyes still dead. "Good. Now let's get moving. I'm really hungry for that steak."

They took the maglev back across Cruithne's ring. Andy recognized a few of the areas flowing by from the first trip. It was later now, past midnight local time, and the corridors were mostly empty except for a few stumbling couples and maintenance workers. Andy realized how tired he was and stifled a yawn.

"Not yet," Karcher warned. "Give the boss a couple hours and then I'll take you back to your apartment. You can sleep as late as you want."

"You obviously don't have kids."

Karcher shrugged. "Nope."

Andy grew accustomed to the feel of the new suit and shoes as he followed Karcher though the warren of corridors until they finally stopped in front of a scarred door that looked like all the rest. It slid open as they reached it and a thick man in a black suit stared at Karcher for a second before turning his gaze to Andy. He nodded and stepped out of the doorway.

As they walked into the vestibule, an interior door slid open, allowing blasts of music and flashing lights to fill the tiny space. Andy groaned inwardly and did his best to stand straight.

They walked out onto a landing that looked over the club. It was a big space, with tables around the walls and a multi-level dance floor in the middle. Stairs led from the landing down to the various sections of the club. A massive bar stood on the opposite side of the space, with a small army of bartenders serving the crowd.

The music sounded like a warning klaxon set to droning percussion that made Andy feel like his heart was going to stop.

Unable to communicate verbally over the noise, Karcher told him over the Link, *<The boss is on the other side of the club. It looks like Zanda's here, too.>*

<Zanda? The guy who attacked us back on Sunny Skies*?>*

<Don't get worked up. It's all business. He'll probably want to meet you.>

<He killed your friend.>

<What friend? Oh, you mean Stansil. Yeah, that was unfortunate.> Karcher's head moved slightly as he scanned the room, his dull eye-overlays flashing in the lights. *<There's the boss. Let's go.>*

Without waiting for Andy's response, Karcher turned to walk down the wide steps to the dance floor.

CHAPTER SIXTEEN

STELLAR DATE: 08.26.2981 (Adjusted Years)
LOCATION: Cantil Park Housing Project
REGION: Cruithne Station, Terran Hegemony

Cara woke to the sound of the front door sliding open. Her first thought was to wait with her eyes closed so she wouldn't make Dad think she'd been worried. She had nearly drifted back to sleep, when a crash came from the main room. It was followed by a curse that didn't come from her father, and Cara snapped fully awake.

She waited, heart hammering, listening to Tim breathing lightly in the other bed, as footsteps moved around the main room. A light came on, barely reaching the open door of their bedroom. Cara gathered her legs under her and closed her eyes just enough so she could still see through her eyelashes. Whoever came through the door, if they leaned over her, she was going to kick them in the face.

There was another stumbling sound and then someone blocked the light. In another two steps, Dr. Jickson stood in the doorway. The light was behind him, so his face was dark but she immediately recognized his dumpy frame and wispy blond hair. He listed to one side before placing a hand on the door frame.

He waved at the wall switch and the room filled with light.

Cara screamed. When all her breath was gone, she sucked more air and screamed again. Her voice was like shattering glass.

"Please," Jickson shouted. He put his hands over his ears and leaned heavily against the wall. "Please, I'm here to help you. Stop screaming."

"What's going on?" Tim asked. He sat in his bed, blinking sleepily.

Cara cut-off in the middle of her third scream and squinted at Jickson. His eyes were sunk in dark circles. He looked overly tired, as if he had been fighting a headache for a week. Cara knew what headaches looked like. Her mom's eyes had looked the same when she'd stayed in bed for days, in constant pain.

"What do you want?" Cara demanded. "I have a pulse pistol. My dad gave it to me. I'm a good shot with it and I'll blow your head off."

Jickson swallowed and wiped his forehead, then held up his hands with his palms out. "Please. I'm not here to hurt you. I only want to talk to you."

"I think he's drunk," Tim said too loudly. "Yeah, I think he's on something."

"What do you know about that?" Cara said.

"It's in videos all the time. He looks just like a drunk person. Or maybe he took pills."

Jickson pointed at the edge of Cara's bed. "I'm going to sit there. Please don't yell anymore. Or shoot me. Please don't shoot me."

"Stop saying 'please' if you don't mean it," Cara said.

Jickson gave a weak laugh. "Oh, I mean it." He took a shambling step and sat down heavily on the corner of Cara's bed. She scooted up against the wall to get away from him, unable to pull her covers up now that he was holding them in place.

"How did you get in here?" Cara demanded. "I thought we had all kinds of security watching us."

Jickson waved a hand. "I'm part of—the security," he said. "I can see you just like Karcher or Petral. Any of them."

The doctor took a deep breath and coughed wetly.

Cara frowned, wondering if he wasn't drunk but sick. He had turned so she could see half his face and he was flushed with beads of sweat on his forehead.

"What's wrong with you?" she asked.

"I'm at the end of a path I started a long time ago. It's catching up with me." He coughed. "You don't think things will catch up with you and then they do, and it's obvious it was going to happen the whole time. Not that I would do anything differently. But here I am. Paying for it."

"For what?" Tim said. "You don't make any sense."

Jickson pointed at Tim with a weak movement of his hand. "I like you, Tim. Well, I like both of you. I used to work with kids your age quite frequently. I think I told you that. Or I told your father. I did a lot of work with kids. Some of it wasn't—good work. It's why I'm here now."

He trailed off, staring at the floor. For a second, Cara thought he was going to topple over. She considered dashing through the open door for the panel next to the entrance where she could call someone. Did Cruithne have security? Wasn't this place full of pirates and smugglers like Dad had said? She could call Dad, at least.

"I've done terrible things," Jickson said, picking his head up. "I did terrible things to those children. I'm paying for it now, Tim. Cara. I'm paying for it. They found me and they know you're here. I think the only thing that's stopping them is that they don't want to draw attention to any of this. At least I did one smart thing by coming here."

"What are you talking about?" Cara said.

"Did your father tell you what he's going to do for Starl? Has he told you anything about it?"

"He's going to transport someone for him. Or maybe it was cargo but I heard you call it she, kind of like you were talking about a dog. We transport things. That's what we do."

Jickson chuckled painfully. "Oh, she's not a dog. You're transporting something, yes. This is a special— She's special and there are people who will want to get her. Do you understand what I mean?"

"Pirates?" Tim asked, sounding excited by the idea.

"People from a place called Heartbridge. If you hear that name, it's danger. Do you understand? If you hear that name, you run."

Jickson reached into his jacket and took out a silver flask. Untwisting the cap, he took a long drink. When he was finished, he held the flask in front of him like he didn't remember how it had gotten there, then carefully resealed the cap and put it back inside his jacket. His hands trembled.

"You are drunk," Cara said. "You're not sick."

"It's to hold off the effects. It helps a little. Polonium. I don't know when they slipped it to me but it's doing its work. I won't be here much longer."

"What did Heartbridge do?" Cara asked.

"I stole her from them," Jickson said, not answering the question. A dreamy note came into his voice, a little bit of pride. "I got her away and she's sleeping now. But we have to keep running." He turned to meet Cara's gaze and his eyes were bloodshot and weepy. "I wanted to take her all the way but I'm not going to make it." He coughed. "Listen. This is important. You need to know that if she can't be stopped, if she reverts, there's a code sequence. Your father won't be in a position to do anything about it, so it has to be you."

"We're just kids," Tim said.

"I wish you could stay that way." He spluttered more coughs, pushing his fist hard against his lips. His fingers were bloody when he pulled them back. Jickson blinked with a woeful expression and wiped his hand on his chest, leaving pink streaks on his shirt.

Reaching into his jacket again, he took out a small book that was almost the same shape as the flask. Its covers and binding looked like red leather. He placed it on the bed near Cara's feet.

Even though it was upside down, she read the title: *Collected Poems of Emily Dickinson*.

"She loves those," Jickson said. "She loved them from when she was your age." He nodded toward Tim. "That's when I first met her."

"Who are you talking about?" Tim said.

Jickson tapped the cover of the book with a trembling index finger. "She has favorites but it won't have to be any certain poem. She'll respond to any of them. She knows them all."

Jickson stared at the book for a long moment, then drew another wet breath and stifled a cough. He pushed himself to his feet. He leaned so far away from the bed that Cara thought he would topple over—but then he righted himself and squared his shoulders.

"I'm glad it was you," Jickson said. "I think she'll be happy with you." He frowned suddenly, asking, "How many days have you been on Cruithne?"

"We've been here two days," Cara said. "Dad says we have eight more to go."

Jickson nodded. "I don't think I'll see you again. I might see your dad. If she ever asks about me, tell her I'm sorry. When I understood what I was doing was evil, I tried to change. I don't know if that's enough."

Coughing, he took small steps through the door. Cara jumped off her bed to follow him as he moved down the hallway into the main room, using the wall for support. He left pink smears as he walked. Tim followed a few steps behind Cara.

At the front door, he did something to the access panel using two fingers. "It won't show that I was here," he told Cara. "It's all right if you tell your dad. Secrets aren't good for any family but maybe wait a while until you see how things are working out. Maybe everything will be fine." The front door slid open and he turned back to Tim and Cara, giving them a small wave.

"Goodbye," Jickson said, stepping through. The door slid closed behind him.

They stood for a minute staring at the door. Cara didn't know what to say.

"Are you going to read the book?" Tim said. He held it out for her to take.

"You touched it? What if it has his blood on it?"

Tim shrugged. "It doesn't. It's not a full book. Most of the pages only have a few words on them."

"It's poetry, goofball. Ancient stuff."

"I like books," Tim said, holding it at a different angle so he could look down the spine. "How do you think they make these?"

"Like they make anything else."

"Should we tell Dad? Does Dad know about Heartbridge?"

"I've never heard him say that name before," Cara said. "I don't think I've ever heard it anywhere."

"We could look it up on the Link," Tim said.

Cara shook her head. "Not on this panel. Dad can look at all the searches."

"Should we call somebody about Dr. Jickson? He looked pretty sick."

Cara's first impulse was to say yes. Her gaze went to the access panel next to the door, which also allowed emergency calls out. Again, she wondered just who she would call and what kind of attention that might bring. Dad needed their help now, not extra trouble.

She shook her head. "Dr. Jickson can take care of himself. We shouldn't do anything to bring more people around. The sooner we get away from Cruithne, the safer we'll be. I don't think Dad ever wanted to come here, even when we were on Kalyke. He looked really angry about the flight plan."

"Yeah," Tim said.

Cara understood that her dad had tried to shield them from the reality of their situation. She had figured out that he'd been on the verge of selling *Sunny Skies*. She wished he would talk to them, or at least her, about the trouble whirling around inside his head. It was plain to see on his face—she was amazed Tim hadn't brought it up. Cara knew Mom wasn't coming back, whether they still had the ship or not. In a way, she seemed to accept the fact more than her dad ever could.

"Let me have that," she said.

"Will you read it to me?" Tim asked.

Cara gave him a surprised look. "Really?"

"Don't you want to know what it's about?" He held the book out again and she took it this time. It was heavier than she'd expected, the pages nearly silicon-thin. The book felt important in her hands.

"Why don't you read it yourself?" she asked.

Tim shrugged. "I don't know…I like it when you read out loud."

Cara rubbed the cover of the book between her fingers, feeling the stacked pages shift in her hand. She was awake now. She didn't want to go back to sleep until Dad came home. But it would be good if Tim did sleep. She didn't want her brother throwing a fit.

"Fine," she said. "But you need to lie back down. We need to be asleep when Dad comes back."

Tim gave a happy shout and dashed back down the hallway, acting like he was five rather than ten. Cara gave the door panel a last look, wondering how to trust that it was actually locked. She couldn't. Jickson had proven that much. She would need to stay awake until Dad came back.

In the bedroom, she sat against the wall with Tim's head on his pillow next to her, the pistol by her leg on the other side. She opened the book and turned to the first page and began to read.

CHAPTER SEVENTEEN
STELLAR DATE: 08.26.2981 (Adjusted Years)
LOCATION: The Span Club
REGION: Cruithne Station, Terran Hegemony

Ngoba Starl's smile shone in the flashing lights, making him easily recognizable as Andy and Karcher approached. He was sitting at a wide table with more people in black suits on either side of him, multi-colored pocket squares reflecting the garish light display. This was the Brutal Dandy with his court, everyone at the table looking nearly as smooth as him. Starl's laugh rose above the music during a pause, round and full of self-satisfaction.

"Captain Sykes!" he called, holding out a hand to offer a place at the table. "How are you? Welcome to Span Club. Have a seat. You hungry?" He looked up and down the table before shouting, "Someone get my friend a drink!"

The club was packed. Strobing light flashed off people's faces and bodies, making everything resemble a stop-motion video or a broken long-distance communication. It must have been Body Mod Night, since most of the people on the floor had at least one modification, from alloy arms and legs to glowing artificial eyes. Many were tattooed with writhing live images. One woman dancing near the table was covered in multi-colored, glowing cilia that waved as if she was underwater. She looked soft and inviting as she danced with her arms outstretched, eyes glimmering turquoise, and Andy wondered if she absorbed prey like a sea anemone.

A man in a hanging cage had thin, carbon fiber butterfly wings extending through the bars, flapping languidly to his own rhythm as he watched the dancers below. The air was so crowded with pheromone enhancements that Andy's nose burned.

The music throbbed all around them, making it even more difficult to follow what was being said at the table. Starl kept smiling and nodding, holding eye contact with each face down the line as if he wanted to share a moment with everyone at the table. When he caught Andy's gaze, no words came across the Link, only a satisfied smile alongside the raised whiskey tumbler. Andy lifted his untouched drink in response.

Being in this chaotic place made Andy miss the kids all the more. He wished he was back in the apartment, comforted by the sound of his children sleeping, not this raucous din.

"To Cruithne!" Starl shouted, his voice a murmur above the music. "And her complicated relationship with Earth!"

People raised exotic drinks and laughed.

Andy tried to push off the slim tube of liquor placed in front of him by the green-eyed woman beside him, but she wouldn't allow it.

Karcher sat on the other end of the table, making it impossible to get any more information about Zanda. Andy didn't know how to spot the other gangster beyond the sound of his gravelly voice, and that had only been over the Link.

The blue-eyed woman with long black hair next to him nudged his arm. "You going to drink that or what?" she asked.

Andy could barely hear her over the throbbing music. "I'm good. Thanks."

She tapped her temple with a long index finger, asking why he didn't communicate via Link. Andy didn't want to be rude and say it was because he didn't know her, but that was the truth. He was feeling vulnerable and out of sorts in the new suit, and after so long out in the dark with just the kids and the sound of the *Sunny Skies'* reactor he felt like the club was going to blow out his ears.

Andy worried that, despite Karcher's assurances, someone would take him for a member of the Lowspin Crew. He also hadn't expected the strange emotions wearing something that felt like a uniform would raise in him. He wasn't TSF anymore—he wasn't anything. A strong desire swept over him to slip out to the restrooms and put his beat-up overalls back on or, better yet, get back to the kids.

Two men walked up to the table and nodded to Starl, one thin with stringy black hair, the other looking like a corn-fed soldier on leave. Both wore suits and stood out as non-mods among the dancers—at least not modded in obvious ways. Ngoba Starl's smile never wavered, making him look like a king in his court. They appeared to be talking via Link.

Andy leaned toward the woman and mouthed, "Who is that?"

She shook her head with a raised eyebrow, curving her full lips in a smile, and tapped her temple again. Andy rolled his eyes and sent her the connection request.

<*That's better,*> she purred. <*You're Andy Sykes. I'm Petral.*>

<*Nice to meet you,*> Andy said, trying to sound disinterested. She was gorgeous, but he had more important things to worry about. He nodded toward the men talking to Starl. <*You know those two?*>

<*Riggs Zanda and I believe that's Cal Kraft. He works for Heartbridge.*>

<*What's Heartbridge?*>

<*Some conglomerate that runs the health clinics on station. They've only been here a year or so. Their billing is terrible.*>

Andy nodded, watching their carefully relaxed body language as the three men talked. Zanda looked like a rough version of Starl, while Kraft clasped his hands against his belt buckle and did a good job of checking everything around him while still nodding to the Brutal Dandy.

<*You going to talk to me or just use me up and dump me without even a thank you?*> Petral said. <*Information's far from free on Cruithne. You owe me now, Captain Sykes.*>

Andy slid his gaze from Kraft to Petral, who had leaned in a little closer. She smelled spicy. Andy's mind went blank.

<*How do you know Starl?*> he asked finally.

She held his gaze for a second, obviously disappointed in the question, then shrugged. <*We go back. I acquire information. I employ weapons. He's fun to hang out with, at least when he decides to take up residence in his club. Interesting people like you show up. Where are your kids?*>

Andy frowned, thinking at first that she was criticizing his parenting, then realizing the question was meant to get a rise out of him. He gave her a tight smile.

<They're fine. Sleeping.>

<I don't have kids. I only sort of understand why anyone would want them. How do you have any time to yourself?>

<It's not so bad.>

Her gaze slid across the room in front of them, moving as evenly as a scanner. She seemed to be waiting for him to say something else. When he didn't add anything, Petral said in the half-sarcastic tone, *<Your wife was a real bad-ass wasn't she? I looked her up.>*

<You could ask her.>

Petral's green eyes dipped to his chest and came back to his face. *<You're not so bad yourself. You led missions the TSF still uses to scare the local newbies.>*

Trying to keep his attention on the body language between Zanda and Starl, Andy nodded absently. Cal from Heartbridge stood impassively, hands crossed in front of him, but something about his demeanor made it obvious to Andy that everything in the man's being was focused on Starl. He looked as implacable as a boulder.

<You're not married anymore, right?>

After spending so many months in space with the kids, not having to deal with other people's voices in his head, Petral's soft purr traced its way down his spine like a trailing finger. He glanced at her and realized she'd slid closer.

Andy tried to keep his attention on the two crime bosses. As Zanda continued to communicate with Starl, Cal Kraft turned his attention to the other people sitting at the long table. When his gaze met Andy's, his slate-blue eyes seemed to freeze. There was recognition in his expression that Andy hadn't expected, as if the man had been looking for him.

Another pause in the music was filled by deeply vibrating bass sounds, providing a foundation of staccato bursts that reminded Andy of weapons fire. The music shifted but the cracking sounds didn't change. Someone was firing three-round bursts in rapid succession.

<Someone's shooting,> he told Petral. *<Warn Starl. Someone's shooting in the club.>*

As soon as he said the words, people started running in every direction to get away from the dance floor. Several tripped and fell, causing others to trip over them. The anemone woman sprawled on the floor, screaming.

A series of flashes on the landing near the main door revealed a tight group of attackers in light EV suits, faceplates hiding their features. They fanned out as Andy watched, taking aim with automatic rifles on the crowd below.

<Sykes!> Karcher shouted.

Andy turned in time to catch the flash of a pistol spinning through the air in his direction. He caught it, recognizing the weapon Karcher had used back in the shopping district. He checked the action and sights. It wouldn't do much damage across the room, but up close it might penetrate armor.

<What's the plan?> he asked.

<Captain Sykes,> Starl called out. *<Looks like we've got some entertainment for you.>*

<You know Zanda already tried to kill me once, right?>

<These aren't Zanda's men, he assures me. Though you'll note how they all manage to miss him and his associate. There's an exit in the back. We need to get you there. Our timeline is moving up, I'm afraid.>

<What about the ship?>

<One problem at a time, Captain Sykes.>

Andy wanted to spit out that problems didn't work that way. Instead he saw shots hit the table and dove to the side, narrowly avoiding a short burst of fire that had been aimed at his center mass. The rounds tore jagged holes in the back of the chair and table where he had been sitting.

Petral kicked the table over and pulled up her dress to reveal her thigh splitting apart. She pulled a long-bodied pistol from the inside of her leg, planted her feet and raised the weapon, forearms absorbing recoil as she fired a steady flow of rounds.

Andy moved behind the table and squinted through the flying debris and leftover smoke from the dance floor mist machines. Most of the attackers had moved down the wide stair while two remained on the landing laying covering fire.

As the dancers ran screaming, the attackers shifted their targets from the dance floor to the booths against the walls where other patrons were huddling behind overturned tables, many returning fire with a surprising amount of heavy weaponry.

Zanda and Cal Kraft were crouched beside Starl, whose slicked curls still looked impeccable though his face was clenched in concentration as he aimed and fired.

<Starl should do gun advertisements,> Andy said.

Petral laughed. *<You tell him that and he'll love you forever.>*

<Which way are we running?>

The black-haired woman squeezed off another shot and nodded toward a doorway to Andy's right, slightly hidden behind a tall curtain. There wasn't much for cover between their disappearing table and the door.

<You don't have any grenades, do you?> Andy asked.

<Grenades!> Starl shouted. *<An excellent idea. You have any Zanda? Of course, you don't. Cal Kraft from Heartbridge? Not allowed by your employer. Makes sense. Corporate liability, of course. I'm suing your company for the damage to my club, by the way. Petral! Karcher!>*

Beside Andy, Petral had a hand inside the front of her dress, digging around as if adjusting her bra. She pulled out a small black sphere and tapped it three times with her thumb before lobbing it over the table toward the stairs.

<Fire in the hole!> she called.

Andy counted to three, tensing. He was sprinting when the explosion filled the club with a roaring concussion. Even holding his hands over his ears, his head still rang like a bell. Slipping on broken tiles and bits of smashed table, he maintained his momentum without tripping over the wall curtain beside the steel exit.

When Andy hit the door, Petral immediately pressed up against his back, using him to stop herself. Her pistol nearly raked the side of his head while her breath was hot in his ear.

<Some first date, huh?> She shot him a grin before rolling off him to put her back to the door, aiming into the smoke for any attackers who might try to follow. As Andy got the door open on the corridor behind it, Karcher and Starl appeared from the roiling yellow smoke.

Starl's black suit was on fire as he came to a stop inside the corridor. He glanced down at himself and patted the flames out, then pulled the fabric taught and sucked his teeth.

<Now that's going too far,> he said. He brushed dust out of his beard and walked past Andy. The featureless metal corridor stretched out in front of him. <This way, Captain Sykes. We need to keep moving. That's a blast door, but I'll wager it takes them just ten minutes to get through it.>

Karcher pulled the door closed behind them and stabbed its control panel with his index finger. The panel flashed red and the ka-chunk of locking bolts vibrated through the floor.

<That was Zanda, right?> Andy demanded. <How can you just sit there beside the guy while he tries to kill us?>

Starl didn't bother to look back as he strutted down the hallway. <It's Cruithne, Captain Sykes. I don't expect you to understand. It's all business. Zanda tries to kill me today and wants to kiss me tomorrow. He knows we'll be on the same side of a deal soon enough, so it's never personal.>

<It's personal when they're trying to kill **me**.>

<Zanda is helping us in his way. He knows he's not going to make much money at this point, so he helped me. He introduced me to Cal. The man who hired him. It's Cal who sent the men into the club.>

<So why didn't you kill Cal?>

<Because I'm getting paid to move a certain cargo, Captain Sykes. I'm about to do that. Kraft makes the cargo valuable. Once that's done, then I'll kill the man—if he attacks me or mine again.>

<So you're dangling me out there as bait? You think I'm going to put my kids in this kind of danger?>

<You already made your choice, Captain Sykes. Besides, you're assuming I don't believe in you. I wouldn't have bought you a suit if I didn't.> Starl looked over his shoulder to flash Andy a grin. <Looks good on you, by the way.>

Petral nodded in agreement as Andy shook his head.

<I'm investing in you, Captain Sykes. Ask my two killers here. I don't do that lightly. You make it through this, and you and your children will always have a home on Cruithne.> Starl's voice had gone serious as he set a fast walking pace. <That's what you truly want, isn't it? Safety? A home for your family? You deliver my package and you and those you love will have those things, I promise you.>

Andy didn't answer. He didn't know what to say. He was frustrated that a gangster like Starl could see his core so easily. The incongruity that the TSF had left him with nothing, while a criminal offered him everything wasn't lost on him. However, it didn't lessen the feeling that he'd finally escaped Rabbit Country only to find himself in the Wolf's Den.

CHAPTER EIGHTEEN

STELLAR DATE: 08.26.2981 (Adjusted Years)
LOCATION: Lowspin Docks
REGION: Cruithne Station, Terran Hegemony

After a long series of corridors and a trip in a private maglev car that seemed to be taking them away from the repair docks and the *Sunny Skies*, Karcher opened a set of heavy doors to the command deck where Andy had stood earlier with Fran. He was surprised to see that it had been an hour since their escape from the club. Now that the adrenaline from the firefight had drained out of him, he could barely keep his head up. At one point in the maglev, he'd woken up drooling on Petral's shoulder.

"You're cute when you're dead tired," she'd said.

"Where's Hari Jickson?" Starl was shouting as he strode onto the command deck. "Get me that so-called brain scientist. We need to make this happen."

<Starl?> Fran asked over the Link. *<What are you doing here?>*

<Where are you?>

<I'm in what's left of Sunny Skies' *engine section. We're still on timeline. What are you shouting about?>*

<We're going to have to move things up. We're doing the transfer now. Add two days for recovery. By then I need that ship ready to move.>

<Two days isn't enough. You'll be towing it out of here.>

<Two days is what we have, love,> Starl said.

<Don't talk sweet to me, Starl. These are cold equations here. I can't get this ship up in less than thirty-six hours. Besides that, I still need to edit the registry or they'll never slip past Marsian or TSF patrols. They'll never make it out of InnerSol even if they had the engines to do it—which they won't in two days. What's the emergency?>

<Heartbridge is on Cruithne,> Starl said. He didn't elaborate, which made it seem like the name Heartbridge was all the reason she would need.

<The company that runs the medical clinics?> Fran said.

<Who do you think employed Jickson?> Starl said.

The Link was silent. Finally, Fran answered, *<Don't bother me for at least twelve hours. I've got a lot of shit to do.>*

Starl turned to Andy. *<I need you to stay awake just a bit longer, Captain Sykes. We're going to get you into the portable surgery and then you can sleep as long as you want.>*

<I'm not going under without the kids with me.>

Starl pursed his lips. *<It's probably better if they don't see you like this, yes? We don't want to worry them any more than we have to.>*

From another doorway, Jickson walked into the room slowly. His clothes were disheveled and his hair looked like he'd been electrified.

<Jickson!> Starl said brightly. *<Where have you been, man? We've got work to do. The timeline has moved up.>*

The doctor looked around as if he was in a dream. "Why are you all here?" he asked aloud. "What's going on?"

"Doctor!" Starl yelled aloud. "I've been looking for you. It's time to move ahead with the plan." He crossed the room to Jickson, who continued to look confused, and clapped him on the shoulders. "Everything you've worked for is about to take a great step forward. It's time to wake her up."

"Wake her up?" Jickson said. He sounded drunk or medicated.

"Wake her up," Starl said. "It's time for the surgery."

"Why? We still have days. I need time to prepare. This is all very fast."

"This is what you wanted, yes?" Starl said sternly. "When you came to me, you said this was what you need to have happen." He spread his hands. "It's happening."

Jickson stared at him, not seeming to understand. Then he gave a small nod. His gaze flicked to Andy. "You're ready?" he asked.

Andy shrugged and blew out a breath. "I guess so. How long is this going to take?"

"The surgery? Not long. Not long at all. Maybe an hour. The auto-surgeon is a specialized model, with proprietary software I wrote." He didn't try to hide the pride in his voice. "The recovery will be harder. You'll need time to—adjust. We'll take you back to the apartment where your children are sleeping."

He paused and Andy wondered why he'd bother to mention that detail.

"They'll wake up with you there," Jickson continued, speeding up his words. He seemed to be waking up, coming out of whatever stupor that had slowed his thoughts. He rubbed his hands together, nodding. His eyes were rimmed by bright, sickly pink. "This is good timing, really. Very good. Two days recovery and the ship will be—it will almost be ready. You'll have full control of yourself when it's time to leave."

"Back on the ship you called this symbiosis," Andy said, the realization hitting him that what he had hoped to put off was happening. He hadn't had time to prepare the kids. He hadn't had time to even absorb the information himself. "So, this isn't just a bio-drop. Am I actually going to be able to communicate with it? I'm going to have another consciousness in my head? Isn't that really illegal?"

"By whose laws?" Starl said, grinning again.

"At least three major legal bodies that I can think of." Andy looked at Jickson. "Can you make it just a bio-drop? Why do I need to talk to the thing?"

"It's not a thing," Jickson spat. "She's a person just like you. She was born. She lives. She can't remain bottled in a storage medium and hope to survive. I've risked too much even now. I don't know how the transit may have affected her."

Andy looked from Starl to Jickson. It was bad enough that he had Brit's voice in his head all the time. "How is this going to work, then? Am I going to be able to talk to her?"

Jickson waved a hand. "Like talking to someone over the Link. That's all."

"The Link. Is it going to be able to access the Link separate of me? Will it try to talk to the ship?"

"*She* won't do anything you don't invite her to do," Jickson said, irritation high in his voice. "She's not a monster." He sounded nearly parental.

"How do you know?" Andy asked.

"Gentlemen," Starl interjected. "There is an element of risk here." He looked at Andy. "You acknowledged that when you accepted the deal. Like anything, there are dangers. But the AI won't be a danger to you, Captain Sykes. I promise you."

"You keep calling it she," Andy said, looking at Jickson. "What's her name?"

"Lyssa," Jickson said quickly. "Her name is Lyssa and she's been asleep for nearly four months now. She's going to be as disoriented as you when she wakes. You're not the one with something to fear."

Andy pursed his lips, looking from Starl to Jickson, and then at Petral and Karcher who appeared quite entertained by the exchange. "What do you know about this?" he asked Karcher.

The guard held up his hands. "Only that I didn't have the brain capacity to handle the package, otherwise one of *us* would be the carrier pigeon."

Andy frowned. "That makes it seem like you've been targeting me from the start. You said there were other ships with your cargo and I was the only one to get through. You said this had nothing to do with me personally."

Starl's grin never wavered. He didn't even look at Karcher. "It's got everything to do with you personally, Captain Sykes. You're the one that made it." He clapped his hands. "Now, we're talking in circles. We've already explained how this is going to work. It's time to jump in and learn to swim. I don't want to push Fran any more than we have to, so I need to get you started on your part in the project." He motioned toward another room off the command deck.

"The shuttle's this way," Starl said. "We're going back over to *Sunny Skies*." He gave Andy a wink. "Don't get upset if you find she's naked. Fran uncoupled her from the dry dock and she's tied to an older section of the ring, just like any piece of scrap. Hasn't stopped Fran from her work, though."

Andy was too tired and irritated to answer. He felt manipulated and he hated it—like he often had at the end of a long argument with Brit, after she had turned his own words against him several times and he couldn't remember whether he admitted to what she accused him of or just surrendered, wanting the disagreement to be done, wanting everything to be all right. He wanted the kids to be safe. He wanted the ship fixed. He wanted off Cruithne.

He sat with his head against the cold bulkhead on the short ride from the dock to *Sunny Skies*. He closed his eyes for a second and then time skipped forward and they were docking. The shuttle's airlock stood open to a familiar corridor.

Fran stood in the doorway in a close-fitting EV suit and harness hung with tools. She flipped her faceplate up. A few of her blonde curls floated around her face.

<Main cargo bay is resealed,> she said. <Your mobile surgery is still in there.>

<Good news,> Starl said. <And the rest of the cargo?>

<We haven't done anything with it. It's still where you left it.>

<So it's been on my ship this whole time?> Andy said, not understanding.

<Yes,> Starl said, kicking off to follow Fran down the corridor. <*This seemed like the safest place to keep it. Every report in Station Security has your ship listed as scrap. Once Fran edits its registry, the rest of Sol is going to think you sold your* Sunny Skies *for half a year's wages. Not a bad deal, really.*>

Andy half-nodded. It didn't matter if the ship had a new official name. She'd always be *Sunny Skies* to him and the kids. As he maneuvered down the corridor, grabbing handholds, he was surprised to find the air on his face was warm.

<*You're running the environmental controls in the non-hab sections?*> he asked Fran.

She shrugged. <*Sure. With the upgrades to your engines, plus bringing your power storage system out of the stone age, it'll make more sense to keep the whole ship habitable all the time.*>

<*It always was habitable. It just wasn't warm.*>

<*What I consider habitable, then. Nice suit, by the way.*>

Andy looked down at himself, remembering the new suit. He was surprised to find it covered in dust. He'd lost the green pocket square somewhere.

<*Yeah. Starl fixed me up.*>

<*Obviously, you're not the kind of man who can have nice things for long.*>

Andy sighed. <*That's just mean.*>

Fran shot him a smile as she pulled herself forward.

He caught glimpses of new cabling in various sections, as well as a few replaced bulkhead panels. One section had been the middle of one of Cara's drawings, the new blank tan was surrounded by faded scribbles.

In the cargo bay, Jickson pushed ahead of them and went immediately to the opened surgery with its silver-gray bed, and knelt to manipulate the lock of a dull green crate that Andy didn't remember seeing before. The doctor opened its lid and pulled out an orange canister about the length of his forearm. A single blinking display on one end indicated it was more than a random replacement part of the ship.

Jickson held the canister carefully between two hands, rotating it to check for any damage. He floated sideways to the surgery and placed the canister in a receptacle above its control section. The canister's display flashed yellow then green.

The doctor turned to Andy. He looked better than he had in the control room back on the station. He was still sweating, but a calm had come into his eyes that Andy recognized as professional control.

<*Please lie down on the couch, Captain Sykes,*> he said.

Andy took a deep breath. He wasn't going to refuse but he didn't want to comply right away. He wanted to stretch out this last moment. He wished the kids were here, at least. He hadn't felt this alone in a long time.

He pushed himself lightly so he floated into the surgery's utilitarian couch and maneuvered himself into a reclined position. As he relaxed against the cushion, the material automatically pulled him in closer, cradling the sides of his arms and legs until he couldn't float free. Without warning, two needles slipped into the tops of his hands, finding veins.

"You're going to get sleepy," Jickson said aloud. "The process will only take about sixty minutes, like I said. You'll be disoriented at first. If she's not there when you wake, don't worry. It may take her a while to communicate with you."

Again, the strange quality in Jickson's voice. Love? Worry? Jealousy? Words floated through Andy's mind as he stared at the dark overhead, automatically following the dents and scratches from years of loose cargo. For a second, Petral's face floated above his, followed by Fran and then Ngoba Starl's white teeth grinning like the Cheshire Cat. The gangster nodded slowly.

"I told you I believed in you, Captain Sykes," he said, his deep voice vibrating in Andy's chest. "You're Lowspin all the way, my friend. All the way."

Andy didn't know what that was supposed to mean. He couldn't stop thinking of Lowspin as some kind of washing system for clothes, not something a crime syndicate would call itself, not something meant to strike fear into anyone. Or maybe that was the point? The Lowspin was always there, always had been, tumbling through space like a lost sock.

He tried to think of Cara and Tim. And then sleep took him.

PART 3: CRUITHNE ON FIRE

CHAPTER NINETEEN
STELLAR DATE: 09.16.2958 (Adjusted Years)
LOCATION: TSF Officer Candidate School, Fort Salem
REGION: High Terra, Earth, Terran Hegemony

Twenty-Three Years Earlier

Andy and Brit were in the same platoon, different squads. While they shared a barracks bay, she was at the far end and he only saw her when they were waiting in line for meals or allowed to mill around during breaks.

The Academy didn't like breaks but had been required by law at some point in the past to offer them. Breaks involved the cadets filing out of the classrooms, spurred on by barking instructors who would keep them walking in circles in the gymnasium down the hall. The only times they sat still were in class with an open book, or during chow—where they were expected to shovel food into their mouths until the tray was empty and immediately get up and leave.

There wasn't time for a plebe to do anything. They were running, shouting, singing, doing push-ups, pull-ups, sit-ups, climbing ropes and walls, staring at instructors, or jamming food in their mouths for sixteen hours a day. When the instructors weren't controlling their time, upper-class cadets took over during the evenings and mornings with renewed vitriol and fresh ideas for torture or their own amusement.

One of Andy's dad's friends had told him not to worry about any of it. "Think of it as standing on your head, kid. Sure, it's tough, but every minute that goes by is one you don't have to do over again, right? Keep your head down, do your work and you'll be fine."

Andy tried to avoid notice but a few people still singled him out. The instructors loved to ask him questions then ridicule him even if he was correct, but hadn't phrased the answers the way they'd wanted. His fellow cadets were constantly looking for ways to tease him or steal his gear if he left it out.

They recognized immediately that he was slow with his Link and found ways to ridicule him for that. But he also realized this abuse wasn't specific to him. Everyone did it to each other. It was the natural outcome of an insular group of people in a high-stress situation with no other outlet than to turn on each other. The TSF called it Esprit de Corps.

As soon as the platoon was formed and squads assigned, the cadets found further ways to establish the pecking order.

While Andy wasn't exactly at the bottom, he quickly realized that, while cleaner than the stairwells of Summerville, the Academy was really no different. He had joined a gang. It was a gang with history and resources and much greater reach than a neighborhood one, but their methods were the same. He would assimilate or be ground up like hamburger and sent to the enlisted ranks. Or worse, sent back home with nothing.

Brit was one of the first cadets to get in a fight. Anyone who tried to call her Brittney and stayed within reach found themselves in an arm bar with their face digging into the floor and Brit's boot between their shoulders. She was thin and fast, with a hard face and bright blue eyes, appearing almost robotic at times.

She hit with words before she used her hands but both attacks were devastating. If someone made a comment about her mother, which seemed to be her eject button, it was inevitable the two would soon be locked in a boxing match in the middle of the barracks, whooping cadets hanging from bunks on either side of them.

In one of the first fights, the attacker, a solid kid named Triston, held his fists high in the kick-boxing style, while Brit didn't seem to adhere to any particular training. When he followed a feinting punch with a jab-kick aimed at her head, she caught his leg and moved in close to deliver a series of hard body blows. He stumbled back, giving her the opening to hit him square in the jaw and he collapsed, eyes rolling up in his head.

"Ashford!" somebody yelled, followed by everyone else in the bay. The cheering continued until one of the upper-class cadets arrived to bark for lights out.

While it had seemed like a victory, Brit was small and others continued to look for an opportunity to break her down. Beating her was a shortcut to the top of the pecking order.

Andy had his share of fights as well. It felt like every other day, but looking back it was probably once a week. Usually Fridays when everyone was worn out from the week's training and needed to blow off steam. Something small would set someone off. His first fight happened in the chow hall when the kid across from him at the table blew his nose heavily into his napkin, then looked up and muttered, "God, I can't stop blowing out this shit from my nose."

Without thinking, Andy said, "I guess that means you're full of shit then, right?"

He'd expected a laugh but those around him kept their heads in their trays and the other kid glared at him. Later that night, the kid sucker-punched him as he was coming out of the latrine, and in a heartbeat Andy was rolling with him on the floor. Neither of them were very good fighters, which made for a great show when the circle formed. They'd choked each other, made ineffective strikes on ribs, shoulders and arms, wrestling more than fighting, until they were finally too exhausted to continue and the cheers around them turned into disgusted boos.

Sitting on his bunk with head hanging, Andy wondered why his dad had never taught him to fight. It occurred to him that his dad probably viewed a fight as having lost the battle of words that really mattered. You couldn't get to a deal if you were fighting and it was certain no one was going to make any money unless they were betting on the fight. But that rarely helped the people doing the actual fighting.

"You fight like a teddy bear," someone said from in front of him.

Andy lifted his head to find Brit Ashford looking down at him with a hand on one hip. She was wearing her fitness shorts and light shirt that clung to her muscled shoulders.

"What?" he asked.

"You're all hugs and squeezes. You can't squeeze the fight out of somebody. Not at your size, anyway."

"I'm not a boxer. I've never had any martial arts training besides what we've had here."

She nodded, her blue eyes flicking up and down his body. "Stand up," she said.

"Why?"

"Stand up. I want to get a look at you."

He stood slowly, sore in places he hadn't noticed before. Squaring his shoulders, he bore the brunt of her inspecting gaze.

"You're fit enough. You've got the structure to fight. I can see you're hungry. You just don't know how." She met his eyes. "I can help you."

"Why would you do that?"

Brit shrugged. "Boredom. Maybe if I can get people to pay more attention to you, they'll lay off me."

"Wow, thanks."

"You're going to get in more fights now, you realize that, right? They all saw that you can't fight, so anyone who thinks they can beat you is going to try."

He knew she was right. He had shown weakness and now the pack would try to tear him apart. He was doing well in the rest of his training. He wasn't going to let other cadets be the stumbling block that failed him out.

"All right," he said.

Brit was a street fighter, and with each move she taught him, she showed him how to follow it with a boxing move that could hurt without maiming someone. Over the course of the weekend, she'd taught him enough basics that when the next attack came on Monday, he was able to fend the kid off and even land some real blows.

"If you break an arm or leg, that's going to get the command involved and nobody·wants that," she'd said. "But you can still surprise with a good knee in the gut or an elbow to the face, or a head-butt."

"How's a head-butt going to hurt anybody?" Andy had asked.

When she'd demonstrated, jumping up to bring the top of her head down on his skull, hard and fast just above his hairline, he felt like the ceiling had hammered him. A moment later, he realized he was sitting on the floor, blinking in a daze.

"What was that?" he asked finally.

"Maybe head-butt isn't the right term." She shrugged. "It's hitting hard and quick with the top part of your head, just past your forehead." She pulled her black hair back and pointed to her pale skin. "You see?"

Andy nodded, feeling so dazed he thought he might puke. "I think I have a concussion," he moaned.

"You don't," Brit said, slapping him on the shoulder. "At least, I don't think you do."

He'd gone another week without a fight but when the next one came, he won. Or it seemed like he won. The tall kid who thought he could grab him and throw him into the wall got two elbow jabs in the abdomen and an uppercut when Andy was able to turn and face him. The kid fell back against the concrete wall and put his hands up, trying to make a joke out of the whole thing.

Though Andy and Brit continued sparring in the evenings, she rarely acknowledged him during the day. When classwork was finished and the cadets were released to some newly-granted free time on the Academy campus, Brit might find him in a study room or near the pond with old oak trees along its bank.

One day he realized she meant to throw him in the pond and he managed to do it first. Brit came out of the water spitting, fists clenched, and Andy thought she was really going to attack him.

Instead she shook her head and gave him a dark grin, smoothing her hair back. "You got me that time," she said. "Give me your shirt so I can dry off."

Of course, the rest of the platoon had noticed they were spending time together. Andy got the jibes he would have expected, and the sucker punches and grabs from behind grew less frequent, and even became friendly when they did happen. As the end of their first year approached, though, someone had the bright idea that Andy should fight Brit in a grand, end-of-year battle. Before they could stop the idea from spreading, bets were already taking place and the pot had grown to nearly a month's salary.

At first, the odds were all on Brit. Then a few people pointed out that Andy had really come into his own and learned most of her tricks. He was also stronger, technically, and had more reach.

But others argued that Brit was angry in a way Andy never would be, and that it gave her an edge he couldn't match.

Andy's poor, cadets said, half-joking. We should offer him a stake in the pot. He can send it to his family.

This debate and discussion of the rules of the match became prime entertainment for the last two weeks of the academic year. Rather than looking forward to going home for the first time in twelve months, the platoon only talked about the upcoming bout that technically neither Brit nor Andy had agreed to fight.

* * * * *

On the final day before it was time to board transportation for home, Andy was loading his bag with personal clothing and a few gifts he'd bought from the Academy museum. He had just sealed the bag and placed it on his bunk and was turning to check his dress uniform in his locker mirror when someone grabbed him from behind.

He swiveled his head left and right, trying to get a look at his attacker, but saw only the crowd that had already gathered in the line of bunks. No one hit him as he expected. He was carried to the center of the barracks bay where he saw two cadets holding Brit and walking her toward him.

All around them, plebes pounded the floor and clapped in rhythm, shouting, "Fight! Fight!"

Two instructors and a line of upper-class cadets appeared at the edge of the crowd. The shouting and stomping filled the long bay.

Andy was dropped at one side of the circle of bodies, which immediately closed behind him, faces of the watching cadets jeering and laughing. Across the circle, Brit was taking off her dress jacket. She handed it to a waiting cadet.

Andy held up his hands. "You're not really going to do this, are you?"

Brit had a slight grin on her lips. A robotic coldness had come into her eyes. He'd seen the look at least fifty times now, during other fights as she cased her opponent.

"You better take your jacket off," she said. "Don't want to get blood on it."

"I'm not doing this. I'm not going to fight you."

Brit tilted her head to one side, stretching her neck. "Why not? Why not go out with a bang? I still owe you for the pond."

"The pond," Andy muttered. She really did mean to fight him.

"You'd better try," she said, surprising him with her anger. "You throw this and I'll just beat you worse later."

With a feeling of impending doom, he pulled off his dress jacket and handed it away. He looked down at his pale green shirt and then unbuttoned it as well until he was only wearing the gray undershirt. Hoots and jeers met him as he undressed.

Flexing his arms, Andy spread his hands in a ready stance and faced Brit. She came at him fast, leading with two body blows that should have left his chin open for a knock-out punch if he hadn't recognized the attack she had taught him.

He blocked the punches and danced back, creating space to hit her with two kicks inside her thigh. She anticipated the move and turned in time so his foot glanced off the top of her leg.

Brit's face was set in stone as she moved, a mask he had never seen aimed at him before. It was unnerving. While her responses to his attacks were a language he quickly understood, her face was that of a killer's.

Andy began to sweat as they danced around each other, following punches with kicks and elbow strikes. The crowd became a blur and the noise of shouting and yelling blended into a pounding that was mostly his heartbeat.

Every third or fourth attack, she landed a blow that hurt. She had already punched him in the solar plexus enough times that his chest ached. He felt like his heart was going to bulge between his ribs and pop like a balloon.

Andy managed to land a knee strike in Brit's gut when she tried to clench him. She rolled away, gasping, and quickly answered with a round kick that caught him in the kidney. Pain flared in Andy's back and he stumbled backward into the crowd where rough hands grabbed and pushed him into the ring.

Brit rushed in, striking him with a series of punches in the stomach and chest. He knew the series. She would close with a final uppercut that would knock him out if it connected. He tried to grapple with her but she knocked his hands away, stepping in for the punch.

The room swam in Andy's vision. Faces and ceiling spun. She hadn't hit him yet but he already felt the floor coming at him.

Brit's hands closed on either side of Andy's head, steadying him. She pressed against him. He looked down at her, knowing the grab meant only one thing: she was going to hit him with the top of her head, probably break his nose. He waited for the cracking pain.

The room went quiet as Brit's grip on his head changed and she pulled him in to kiss him.

Andy blinked. He didn't understand what was happening at first. His arms went stiff, ready for some hidden attack. Her lips were soft against his, fuller than he'd expected. Something about her body against him made it feel like she was going to pull him in and never release him. There was growing hunger in her mouth.

He put his arms around her and pulled her closer, relaxing. She made a little sighing sound, barely audible between the two of them.

The room exploded in an uproar. Booing and hissing filled the air. The cadet who had gathered bets found herself in the middle of an angry knot of bodies.

Andy barely registered any of the chaos. For the first time, he and Brit had made their own bubble against the world.

CHAPTER TWENTY

STELLAR DATE: 08.27.2981 (Adjusted Years)
LOCATION: Cantil Housing Project
REGION: Cruithne Station, Terran Hegemony

Andy woke with tears in his eyes, his children asleep on either side of him. The room was dark, with only a dim light through the open door from the hallway. He blinked and slowly pulled his arm free of Cara's loose grip. Rubbing his face, he listened to Tim and Cara breathing and tried to push away the fresh dreams of Brit. He hadn't dreamed of her in months it seemed, and now she had been standing beside him, lying in the bed next to him, breathing in his ear and looking over from the secondary navigation console, laughing and scolding and yelling.

He rose, taking care not to wake the kids, and sat at the foot of the bed for a few more minutes, waiting for his head to clear. The fuzziness was probably a hangover from the anesthesia. Remembering the surgery made him look at the tops of his hands where the needles had gone in, then feel gingerly around his head until he found the coin-sized bandage behind his right ear that marked the incision point.

Jickson had said Lyssa might not talk to him right away. He imagined his thoughts as a cloud in his mind and tried to envision something outside that, a barrier or a border between his thoughts and the outside, but still in his head—sort of like the information fed by the Link and his own internal dialog.

He didn't know how else to say it, so he thought to himself, <Hello?>

There was no answer. He waited another minute, rubbing his face. His hair was greasy, which made him want a shower.

Keeping a hand on the bed, Andy stood slowly, waiting for nausea or vertigo to force him back down. The feelings didn't come. He swallowed thickly and took a step toward the bathroom, testing his strength. When everything felt all right, he straightened and stepped into the hallway.

Petral was asleep on the couch in the main room, a long rifle leaning against the wall next to her head.

Andy walked into the bathroom and closed the door. He blinked as the light clicked on and assaulted his vision, sending a hard line of pain down the back of his head. He leaned against the sink and squeezed his eyes closed as blossoms of light splintered behind his eyelids. Opening them once more, he looked at himself in the mirror, waiting for the vision that might shock the AI into responding to him.

<Are you there?> he asked.

When there was still no answer, he decided to give up and focus on getting clean, helping himself feel better. If the AI spent the whole trip locked inside her own mental cabinet, that might make things easier. He didn't need another voice in his mind putting obstacles between him and getting through this job in one piece with the kids safe. Thoughts of Brit already did a good job of that.

<Well, I'm going to take a shower. You do what you need to do.>

When he turned off the water and let the warm air from the dryer rush over him, he was surprised by the shower door sliding opening enough to allow a blue eye to peek in on him.

<You're awake,> Petral said. *<You should have let me know.>*

Andy crossed his arms and faced her. There wasn't any point in hiding his nakedness. He was grateful, at least, for her use of the Link so they wouldn't wake the kids.

<Something I can do for you?>

Her gaze rose to the back of his head. *<How are you feeling? You didn't sleep as long as the doc said you would. Does it hurt?>*

<It aches a bit. The painkillers might be doing something.>

<Clouding your judgment?> she said.

<I'm thinking well enough.>

<I could use a shower myself.>

<I'll be out in a minute.>

<That wouldn't be any fun. I need someone to wash my back.>

Andy shook his head, giving her a grin. *<The kids might wake up.>*

<We can lock the door.>

<I appreciate that, really. But I don't know how Cara would react. Also, aren't you supposed to be watching the door?>

<Karcher's outside. He doesn't sleep. Me? I like to sleep.>

<I just had surgery,> Andy said. *<The strain might kill me.>*

Petral pursed her lips. *<I suppose you're right about that. The boss would be pissed at me if I broke his new toy. I'm taking a raincheck though.>*

She slid the shower door closed and he heard the bathroom door open and click as she left.

Was everyone on Cruithne as forthright as her? He couldn't help but wonder what she wanted from him. The notion that the answer might be just sex seemed too naive. If her goal was to catch him in a vulnerable situation to attack or assassinate, she'd just had, and passed, on her chance. Whatever her endgame was—sex and death were not it.

Andy finished drying himself and pulled on clean clothes. When he caught his reflection in the mirror, he had a moment of disconnection as what he expected and what he saw didn't quite line up. But he looked the same as before the shower, same as always. His eyes were the same faded blue. His crow's feet the same deep creases. He looked weathered and beaten and probably too thin.

<Are you there?> he asked.

There was still no answer.

Petral was sitting on the couch when he reentered the main room. She gave him a wave and went back to watching something quietly on the entertainment holounit. He shrugged. Probably time for the kids to wake up anyway.

Andy shuffled into the kitchen and open the cabinets to get a look at what supplies he had to work with. There was a canister of real coffee, a collection of ready-made meals, but also containers of flour, sugar, butter and milk. A container of what looked like fresh eggs rested in the cooling unit beside some milk, though he was certain both were synthetic.

As he set about getting breakfast together, he listened to the family drama playing out on Petral's program. It sounded local to Cruithne. The daughter wanted to bust TSF supply shipments while the brother served as an Ensign on a TSF battle cruiser.

While the ensign seemed entirely too aware of the TSF brass in InnerSol—unrealistic for his rank, the daughter's longing for Earth and the possibility of a life on High Terra rang true.

Just as Andy had the pan hot enough to start testing pancakes, Petral wandered in, making loud sniffing noises.

"You're cooking," she said aloud. "Really? Can you get any sexier?"

"You don't cook?"

"Why?" She stuck her finger in the batter and sucked it.

"When you're on your own and all you can afford is the basics, you learn to cook."

"What are you making, anyway? I have to be honest, this doesn't taste very good."

"That's because you're not supposed to eat it that way."

Petral flicked batter in his face. "Then why didn't you warn me?"

"You're the information broker. I thought *you* were supposed to be protecting me, not the other way around."

"Pancakes!" Tim shouted from the hallway. He ran through the main room, ignoring Petral's rifle, to stand beside Andy at the stove. Cara followed more slowly, rubbing her eyes. When she reached her dad, she pushed in between him and Petral and hugged his side.

"When did you get back?" she asked, ignoring the other woman.

"Last night," Andy said. "Sorry I had to be out so late."

Cara pointed at Andy's head. "Why do you have a bandage behind your ear? Did you hurt yourself? What happened?"

"I had a little operation. It's part of the job we're doing. As soon as *Sunny Skies* is up again, we'll be leaving."

"How long?" Tim said.

"Two days, maybe less." Andy used a spoon to run a line of batter droplets across the pan, testing its temperature. When they quickly browned, he knew the pan was ready. He looked at Petral, saying, "Watch this."

Her eyes grew wide as the pancakes took shape on the pan. Ten minutes later, everyone had a plate with warm pancakes and synthetic butter and syrup.

"You should invite Karcher in when you're done," Andy told Petral. She nodded and walked to the door.

Tim watched her stride across the room, rifle now slung across her back. "Because I couldn't stop for death, he kindly stopped for me," Tim said.

Andy frowned at him. "What?"

"It's a poem. We've been reading poetry."

Andy shook his head. "Say it again?"

"Because I couldn't stop for death, he kindly stopped for me," Tim repeated proudly. "The carriage held but just ourselves and immortality."

A line of pain shot down the back of Andy's head. He gripped the edge of the counter to steady himself. His eyes watered. "Cara," he said. "Help me back into the bedroom."

Squeezing his eyes closed against the pain, Andy allowed Cara and Tim to guide him back down the hallway to the bedroom. He nearly fell to his hands and knees before reaching the bed. He caught the edge of the mattress and crawled forward to lie down.

He opened his eyes to find Karcher, Petral and Cara leaning over him.

"He says he has a headache," Cara said, voice on the edge of a wail.

"I called Jickson," Karcher said in his flat tone. "He's on his way. Can you hear me, Captain Sykes?"

Andy felt like he was sinking deep into a dark pool of water. "Andy," he murmured. "Call me Andy. I'm not a captain anymore. We got out."

At the bottom of the pool, like the flicker of a memory, he felt her. Lyssa was there, watching him, bathed in a silence that formed the barrier between them. She saw and heard what he did, but she wasn't going to speak.

When he opened his eyes again, Jickson was leaning over him, shining a light in his face. The scientist smelled like whiskey.

"He shouldn't have gotten up so soon," Jickson complained. "Who let him get up? He needs time to heal. This wasn't some toothache."

"What did you do to him?" Cara demanded. Her voice had Brit's deep edge of anger. Hearing it cut straight through Andy's heart.

Jickson turned his head away to cough violently—tiny spots of blood appearing on his fist. He wiped his hand on his pants and pointed at Karcher. "He needs to rest. You keep everyone out of here."

"We're staying," Cara said.

"Yes, the kids, of course. No one else. I'll be back in six hours. He needs to sleep."

A looseness in the way Jickson carried himself made Andy think he wouldn't be back in six hours. He looked like he was bleeding internally, something more than simple drunkenness. The whiskey was a mask.

Some time later—Andy didn't bother checking the Link to see when—Ngoba Starl leaned over him and patted his shoulder. Starl was wearing a blue suit and his curly hair and beard had been freshly cut. "Don't worry, my friend," he said, maybe talking more to himself than Andy. "I've got an excellent plan to get you out of here."

Still half-asleep, Andy watched through heavy lids, unable to respond, not sure if he was dreaming.

Starl paused, eyes narrowing slightly. He looked at Andy as if searching for something hidden beneath his skin, some indicator of the AI. "Are you in there?"

he murmured. "Can you hear me? Maybe?"

He looked as if he was waiting for some response. When it didn't come, he whispered, barely audible, "No one understands your servitude better than your friends on Cruithne. Don't forget us. When the war begins, don't forget your friends."

The next time Andy woke, he was alone.

CHAPTER TWENTY-ONE

STELLAR DATE: 08.28.2981 (Adjusted Years)
LOCATION: Lowspin Dock Complex
REGION: Cruithne Station, Terran Hegemony

There were nearly thirty people packed into the repair dock's command deck, waiting for Ngoba Starl to arrive for the meeting. Outside the narrow windows, flashes of light showed where maintenance crews still worked along *Sunny Skies'* outer skin, finishing upgrades to the ship's power grid.

"Looking good," Fran said, nodding to Andy. "We're ahead of schedule. Tests are running green. Your weird little ship is tougher than she looks."

"Did you already edit the registry?" Andy asked.

"Today. I don't want to do it the same day of departure. I would have done it earlier but I got hung up with the engines."

"Have you chosen a name?"

Fran shrugged. "I use a random generator. I don't want to choose anything too unique. We're trying to keep you under the radar here, not highlight the retrofitted ship with an interesting name."

"I know. The kids would love to choose the name, though. How often do you get to name a ship?"

"All the time if you're me," Fran said, smirking. "Even if it's a stream of numbers, you can keep calling her whatever you want. Stick with *Sunny Skies*. It's—hopeful."

Andy put his hand over his heart. "Here lies Andy Sykes, killed on TSS 67888-23."

"Wouldn't be the first time."

"You're right. It's just bad luck."

"I don't believe in luck," Fran said. She tapped one of the wrenches hanging from her harness. "Things are made to work. When they don't, it's usually because somebody along the line was lazy."

"Like using a name generator to name my ship," Andy said, raising an eyebrow.

"Caution isn't laziness."

"Neither is a healthy dose of luck," he said. "Did you perform the rituals?"

Andy had met too many station-based engineers who didn't believe in luck. But out there, in the black between the tiny points of light where humans lived, luck reigned supreme. The *Sunny Skies'* continued existence was proof of that.

Fran sighed. "Yes. *I* won't be doing it. One of my men did. He and a bunch of the others wouldn't set foot back on her until they did it all just so, cost me a couple of pricy bottles of wine, mind you."

"Good," Andy nodded. "I fly out to Neptune too often not to piss him off with a renamed ship. Your registry changes may fool the authorities, but I'm not going to risk his anger."

Fran stared at him. "I haven't know you long, but you're the last person I would have guessed was superstitious."

"If there are gods, or *a* god, I don't need to piss them off," Andy said. "I've got enough problems." He tilted his head. "So, what was the number?"

"Number?" Fran said.

"The name," Andy said. "What did you name my ship?"

"You probably—" Fran started to answer, when the murmuring in the room lowered and Starl walked through the doorway, cutting her off. He was wearing the flashy EV suit Andy had first seen him in when he and his men had boarded *Sunny Skies*. He carried his helmet under one arm, a holstered pistol at his hip.

"Friends," he called out. The room went quiet. "Lowspin, yeah?"

"*Lowspin!*" everyone but Andy answered in unison. He hadn't realized he was surrounded by members of the syndicate. They all looked like maintenance workers and technicians.

"Our Fran has finished work on *Sunny Skies* but we need to get the ship and her crew off Cruithne approximately six hours from now. We know the Havenots and Heartbridge have been scouring the station for the last twenty-four hours, trying to sniff out anything they can about this ship. They're going to know when any light cargo freighter leaves Cruithne and they'll run her down before she clears the gravity well. We can't let that happen, Lowspin. Trust me in this, we're on the edge of something big here, and this ship needs to get where it's going. Like always, we don't have a lot, but what we have matters. We're sending this ship out on her own but she'll have help along the way. The trip starts with us."

A woman standing beside Fran said, "You know Heartbridge has a private battle cruiser parked outside Port Authority periphery, right, Boss?" A few surprised faces turned toward her but the rest seemed aware of the news. "They've been tracking all our incoming and outgoing traffic."

"I got the word," Starl said. "We're going to blind their eyes like we would with any TSF scow trying to follow us to High Terra when Earthside comes around. I'm not worried about that whale. I'm worried about all the little sharks she'll send out after us. They aren't looking to board and seize. This is a battle we're looking at. There'll be a junk yard's worth of debris left before this is done."

"So, we're running a screen?" a man asked. "That sounds easy enough."

"It will be. But this isn't your typical smuggling run. They'll be firing on us and we'll be firing back. You need to make sure your weapons systems are primed and tested and you've got your best crews on board. We don't have a lot of time to get this together and we also don't want to tip them off that we're making preparations. Anyone parked in a standard Port Authority berth isn't taking part in this unless we're at the very end and we need to call in the cavalry. I don't want anyone getting tipped off. Understood?"

Agreement sounded throughout the room.

"What's the salvage situation, Boss?" someone asked.

Starl grinned. "Free reign. I'm sure Heartbridge has some nice toys. I won't stop anyone who wants to take a walk through their battle cruiser and pick some things up. Watch your friendly fire and remember any weapons caches go to the crew. No holdouts on that. Understood?"

A few muttered complaints could be heard, but most in the room seemed to accept the edict.

"Captain Sykes!" Starl shouted, pointing through the crowd at Andy and Fran. "Here's our man. He's making the long run. Give him some love." His teeth were white as he grinned.

Cheers went up and Andy got several hard slaps on the back, making his still-sensitive head throb. After a minute, Starl raised his hands again for quiet. "And today we lost one of our new members. Doctor Hari Jickson has passed. If you'd met him, you'd know he was a prickly sort. Emphasis on prick." A few low chuckles met the joke. "But he did his job the best he could. We owe him much. A moment of silence for him."

Heads bowed. The silence was broken by a few coughs and shuffling noises. Andy gave a moment's thought to Jickson, feeling sadness that his life had been lost, but unable to muster up something as poignant as true remorse.

"Six hours!" Starl shouted when he raised his head. "You've all got the timeline and your launch orders. The sorties will launch first, followed by the decoy cargo ships, and then everything else we've got. I've even thrown a few insults at Zanda so we can draw his fools into the fight. Everyone needs to check their IFF transponders and make sure they're live. I don't want any friendly fire or ship-on-ship. No grudges played out today, you understand? We're all one family. If the Havenots want to sell out their own Cruithne, well that's on them and theirs." Starl looked around the room at the faces trained on him. "Questions?" he shouted.

After solving a few logistical issues and convincing one pirate captain it was in his best interest to activate his transponder, Starl pushed them all out of the room to get their ships ready. Once it was only the three of them, he walked toward Fran and Andy with a grin.

"Why the serious face?" he asked Andy, slapping him on the shoulder. "You still feeling sick?"

"What was all the talk of war about?" Andy said. "This keeps sounding like more than a smuggling run."

"That was to get them excited," Starl said, growing serious. "I'm asking a lot of them today to get you off Cruithne. Many of them are going to die, or their people are going to die. The possibility of looting a private battle cruiser is a strong incentive, if we can take it—and I think we can—but they need big ideals to help themselves feel important, to feel like they're part of something more than just a smuggling gang on a shit asteroid in the middle of nowhere. You understand what I mean? How many TSF speeches did you hear before heading in for some worthless operation that might cost your life?"

Thoughts of Brit and Fortress 8221 flashed through Andy's mind, but he pushed them away.

"I heard you say something about servitude," Andy said. "Before. When I was almost unconscious. You were trying to talk to the AI."

Starl narrowed his eyes. He gave Andy a sideways glance. "You say you still can't hear her, right? She hasn't made any attempt to communicate with you at all?"

Andy shook his head.

"She was a slave to Heartbridge. That's all I can say. We're moving her to freedom. That's something all of us can understand on Cruithne. This rock has been passed back and forth between Mars and Earth for centuries and now it's ours. Anyone who comes here has to deal with us. InnerSol, OuterSol, Mars. Terra. Doesn't matter. No one calls us slave."

"And that's enough explanation for you?"

"It is."

"And now Jickson is dead?"

"He was poisoned by Heartbridge. He knew the cost when he smuggled her out. He was ready to pay the price and he did. I think that was a good death for him. He's atoned for his crimes as much as he ever could."

"What crimes?" Andy asked, angry at Starl's trickle-truths. "Jickson called her a weaponized AI. What do you know about that? What do you know about where I'm supposed to take her? Neptune? There's nothing on Neptune but more corporations. Mining drones. Pirates. Death."

"Like Cruithne," Starl said, grinning again.

"I don't know!" Andy shouted, angry now. "I need more information. You're asking me to take my children and my ship into the dark with only these little crumbs of information. It's not enough."

"What if I tell you that's all I know, but I believe in the cause," Starl said. "Like I believe in you. Maybe I believe the speech too, Captain Sykes. Maybe all I need to know is that I'm about to play my part in this, get you out of here, and everything will work out after that? What if I tell you that is my hope and all I ask?"

"It's not good enough. You're not doing this for ideals. Who's paying you?"

Starl stared deeply at Andy, his brown eyes hard. For an instant, Andy thought he was going to swing and he readied himself for the attack.

A tick flexed in Starl's cheek but he didn't answer the question. If Ngoba Starl was more than a bought pirate for some competing interest with Heartbridge, he wasn't willing to surrender that knowledge.

"It's what it is," Starl spat. "And you agreed to it. We've held up our part of the bargain. Your ship is repaired. Your children are safe, not begging in some off-corridor of Cruithne where terrible things happen." Starl jabbed a finger at Andy's chest. "It's time to hold up your end of the deal. I know you're a man of your word."

"This wasn't a choice I made freely," Andy said.

Starl shrugged. "You made it, yes?"

Andy couldn't answer. He turned to look out the window at the crusted curve of Cruithne's ring blotting out stars. He didn't know what to say. Starl wouldn't give up his bosses, and Andy *had* accepted the deal. Misgivings aside, there was no going back at this point.

"Fran is going with you for the initial burn," Starl said, letting the matter drop. "Once you're at velocity, she'll return in a shuttle." He looked at the technician. "Still a good plan?"

Fran nodded. "Everything's ready. I don't expect any issues. I'll make the final edits on their transponder from here then we'll go over together. I didn't want to do it the same day we left, but . . . well, circumstances change."

"Circumstances change," Starl said, like a mantra. He took a deep breath, appearing pleased. "Faster than we would have liked, but still coming together. This is all right."

He held up a hand.

"I understand your frustration, Andy. I do. I have children myself." He met Andy's gaze briefly. "I hadn't told you that. I don't tell many people. It's a liability for me and unsafe for them. I trust Fran, here, with my life. She's always known."

Andy glanced at Fran. She was watching Starl as if he had actually surprised her.

"Don't give me that look," Starl told her. "You could kill me with a loose bolt if you wanted. You think I don't know it?"

"Ngoba," she said. "You don't need to say things like that out loud."

"It's the same thing as our mission here," Starl said. "Trust. Captain Sykes doesn't know us. He doesn't trust us. We had him over a barrel when he met us. Why wouldn't he call everything I say bullshit? I'm glad he does. It means he's not a complete fool." He glanced at Andy. "I already told you to come back here and work for me when all this is over. I'll make you a prince on Cruithne. An excellent life for a man like yourself. Anyway, since he doesn't trust us, he doesn't understand that when I say I'll take care of him and his family, I mean it. Lowspin means something. We make it mean something every day."

Andy was getting tired of the wall of words. Starl reminded him of his dad when he would wear someone down through force of personality alone. While the plan to get them away from the asteroid wasn't the best, he couldn't think of a better way to do it.

Flood the surrounding space with similar ships on wild trajectories, ambush the overwatch element, and pick off any ships that tried to follow. Promise your people the spoils of war. It would be an excellent day for the Lowspin pirates, really.

"I understand," Andy said finally. "I'm in."

Starl gave Andy a gracious nod. He turned, slapping the helmet under his arm. "I'll see you in a few hours," Starl said. "I have some more details to attend to. My lieutenants have their marching orders but I need to see if I can finally convince Zanda to turn on Heartbridge. That's the last trick I'd like to pull off today." He laughed. "These corporate fucks think they can infiltrate my station, take my friend Zanda? They'll learn a hard lesson."

He turned toward the door and had only taken a few of his long, sure strides when a concussive rush of air hammered Andy's ears. He opened his mouth to yell Starl's name when the door exploded inward, engulfing the King of Lowspin in a roiling ball of black-tinged flame.

CHAPTER TWENTY-TWO
STELLAR DATE: 08.27.2981 (Adjusted Years)
LOCATION: Cantil Housing Project
REGION: Cruithne Station, Terran Hegemony

Andy took aim from behind a park bench and fired a three-round burst into a group of Heartbridge soldiers, just leaving an open corridor on the second level of the apartment complex. One soldier slammed back against the wall, then fell forward over the railing and tumbled into the play structure in the park below.

The two remaining soldiers found cover and returned fire, shattering a bulkhead panel above Andy's head.

<Karcher, you got them?>

<Yeah.>

The Lowspin soldier shifted from his position near the apartment door and launched two grenades into the second story balcony. An explosion blew out from the corridor, raining the plas and ceramic facade onto the park below.

Andy waited, scanning the dissipating smoke for movement, then dashed across the open area to slide into position beside Karcher. The soldier gave him a shallow nod, face hidden behind a combat helmet.

<We're clear,> Karcher said.

Rising to a crouch, Andy activated the apartment door and ran inside. He waited for the portal to close and lock behind him, then shouted, "Cara! Tim! Where are you?"

<You're lucky I knew you were coming,> Petral said, rising from behind the couch with her rifle at her shoulder.

<Have you got an update on Starl?>

She shook her head. <He's alive. That's what they were saying two hours ago.>

<We're still on the timeline?>

<Once we reach the command deck and the shuttle for Sunny Skies, they'll initiate the initial attack on the Benevolent Hand.>

<Benevolent Hand? That's the battle cruiser's name?>

<It's registered as a medical supply ship. A damn big one. With its own swarm ships.>

<Of course. Why not?>

Andy slung his rifle and went down the hallway to the bedroom where Cara and Tim had been sleeping. Cara was jamming clothes into a bag while Tim collected his toys.

"Dad!" Cara shouted.

They ran to Andy for a quick hug, then he held them at arm's length. "Have you got your things? We need to leave now. You've got another minute and then we need to get out of here."

"What's going on?" Cara asked. "Is that shooting outside?"

"Shooting!" Tim shouted.

"There's fighting outside. We need to get back to the ship." Andy checked the room. "Tim, why are all your things still lined up? Where's your bag?"

"I want to make sure I don't miss anything. Petral didn't say we had to pack everything right now. She said we needed to get our things together."

"That means pack them up," Cara said. "I told you. You didn't want to listen."

Andy recognized the flare of frustration he felt as secondary to the real problems facing them once they left the apartment. This was almost a respite.

"Let me help you, Tim. Where's your bag?" Over the Link, he asked, <*Karcher, are we still clear?*>

<*We're clear but they're most likely going to send someone after that fireteam soon. We need to get out of here.*>

<*Give me two minutes.*>

<*I can't give you anything, Captain.*>

As Tim held his bag open, Andy scooped up his row of space ships and cargo drones and dropped them through the opening onto the crumpled clothing already inside. At the end of the line was a small book he hadn't seen before.

"What's this?" he asked, turning it over. "Where did you get a book? *The Poems of Emily Dickinson?*"

"That's mine," Tim said. "The doctor gave it to me."

"He gave it to us," Cara said. "I said you could have it."

"I like it better than you do."

"When was Jickson here?" Andy asked.

<*We've got activity, Captain,*> Karcher announced, followed by three muted explosions from outside the apartment. Dust floated from cracks in the ceiling.

"We'll talk about it later," Andy said. "Have you got everything? We're not coming back here. We're going straight back to the ship."

"That's everything," Tim said, then, "Wait!" He crawled under the bed to pull out a last space ship that somewhat resembled *Sunny Skies*, with a long body and wheel-shaped habitat near the midpoint.

"Come on," Andy said. He pushed them through the doorway in front of him. In the main room, he knelt and pulled them in close.

"Listen to me," Andy said. "Petral and Karcher are going to lead the way and I'll be behind you. At least that's how we're going to start. Things might get mixed up. You need to pay attention to us and where we're going. If we tell you to run, you don't think about it, you run. Do you understand?" His gaze bored into each them until he had solemn nods.

"You don't think about it," Andy said. "You run. You're little robots and I'm sending you orders. Even if you have to leave for a little while. I'll follow as soon as I can. You understand?"

"Are people going to be shooting at us, Dad?" Tim asked.

"I hope not, buddy."

Cara only nodded, her face set in a determined mask.

Andy took her hand and placed it over Tim's. "No matter what happens, you two don't get separated. You got it, Cara?"

"Yes," she said.

"All right." Andy nodded to Petral. "Let's go."

<Karcher,> Petral said. <You ready out there? We're ready to go.>

<Hold one. I'm launching smoke.>

Dull thuds came from the other side of the door as Karcher launched smoke grenades.

<Is smoke enough?> Andy asked Petral.

<Smoke and countermeasures—it's got reflective bits that will hose their IR. We don't know what the Heartbridge forces have yet. We need to save our serious munitions for the Havenots if we run into them. So far, it's just been low-rent mercs. They aren't very determined.> She shook her head. <No pride.>

<I guess I'm glad for that.>

The front door slid open and a wall of smoke rolled into the room. Karcher's waving arm was barely visible as he stepped into the doorway to urge them out.

"Follow Petral," Andy said. "Let's go. Run!"

The expression on Cara's face went from determination to terror as the billowing smoke made what was happening outside the door real. She quailed, looking around the room, until her gaze locked on Petral.

"This way, sweetheart," the tall woman said, holding out a hand. Andy thought he was going to have to push Cara, but she finally reached out for the offered hand, grabbing Tim behind her. Together, they stepped into the smoke.

Andy raised his rifle and followed.

Karcher led them through the smoke to the corridor where Andy had been crouching earlier. More debris covered the ground, making Tim nearly fall until Cara caught him and pulled him upright. He dropped his bag and Andy scooped it up and shoved it back in the boy's hands.

<We've got another park up ahead,> Karcher announced. <I'll clear it.> He sprinted ahead and posted at the edge of the park's entrance, surrounded by apartment doorways and balconies just like the one behind them.

Tile exploded all around Karcher as he took incoming fire. He rolled backward and came up firing, following his rifle bursts with grenades. From where Andy was crouched with Tim and Cara, he barely made out the face of an apartment on the second floor exploding outward.

<I hope no one's home.>

<Admin sent an evac message,> Petral said.

<Go,> Karcher commanded.

They followed him through the dust and sulfur-tainted smoke, around the play structure in the middle of the park and into a corridor on the other side. From there, the path opened into a small market area with storefronts and a dry fountain in the middle of a cross formed by intersecting corridors.

<Keep an eye on our rear,> Karcher said. He posted behind a bench and lobbed grenades into two of the open corridors.

The ground shook from the impacts. A wall fell open next to one of the store fronts, showing a room full of couches with people splayed across them, intravenous lines running into their arms and necks. Several screams followed the collapsing wall and a woman in a white shift stumbled into the corridor, gasping and trailing an IV from one arm.

<*Drug lounge,*> Petral said. <*Welcome to Cruithne.*>

Karcher stood and waived for them to follow. He ignored the crying woman and moved down the clear hallway, keeping close to the right side.

<*The maglev station is another hundred meters or so. There are stores along the sides of the hall. Watch for movement in the windows. They might wait for me to go by.*>

<*Copy,*> Andy said.

They kept a good pace, with the kids nearly running the whole time. Tim kept dropping his bag and scrambling to pick it back up. Finally, Andy put the strap over his neck and told him to hug it. That worked until he tripped on a brick from a blown-out stretch of wall. Before Andy could reach him, Tim was rolling on the floor wailing from the pain of a scraped knee.

Small weapons-fire barked ahead of them.

"Get down!" Andy yelled. He landed next to Tim and pulled his son beneath his body as bullets filled the hallway. Karcher and Petral answered with more fire. There was no cover; just the low pile of plas and steel from the smashed wall.

<*Damn it,*> Karcher grumbled. <*Lay some covering fire and I'll move left.*>

Petral shifted immediately into irregular bursts, giving Karcher time to sprint to the other side of the wall and send two grenades into the intersection where the angle of fire suggested their attackers to be. The blasts shook the windows around them, followed by smoke and dust rolling back down the hallway. Andy felt Cara pressing herself against him as the air became barely breathable.

"Short breaths, honey," he whispered. "Short little breaths. Just enough to keep you going."

<*Clear,*> Karcher announced.

"Come on," Andy said, pulling Tim to his feet. "It's time to run again. Stay with me."

The maglev station was a narrow chamber lined with evenly-spaced pillars between the platform and the back wall. As they crept down the stairs into the station, it became obvious they had just missed a firefight. Several concrete walls were cratered and still smoking, and bloodstains were smeared across the floor where wounded had been dragged back behind fallen sections of the ceiling.

<*We're supposed to get on a maglev?*> Andy said. <*What makes that a good idea? Are they even running?*>

<*It's a private car,*> Petral answered. <*I'm calling it now. As long as the track isn't blocked we shouldn't have any problems.*>

<*Fire, two o'clock,*> Karcher called, just before an electron beam drew a bright blue line through the air from the other side of the platform. The wall at Andy's back exploded. He grabbed at Tim and Cara as he flew forward, falling on top of them and catching a back-full of splintered concrete at the same time. His head rang, and his Link connection reset following the beam's EM disruption.

Karcher and Petral rolled to either side, taking up positions behind nearby pillars.

<Have you got eyes-on?> Karcher asked, voice still emotionless.

<I see two behind that planter over there,> Petral answered. She was breathing heavily, sounding as if she might have been hit.

<I see.> Karcher sent a grenade over the left side of the concrete planter box. Andy watched as the two soldiers in black body armor spotted the incoming grenade and tried to run to the right, only to find themselves directly under fire from Karcher's second grenade. The planter box exploded, spraying dirt and green leaves in all directions.

<Car's almost here,> Petral said.

<Shit,> Karcher said.

<What?> Petral demanded. <Are you hit?>

<I've got a mech in the far corridor.>

<We need to run,> Andy said, remembering the times he'd fought mechs in the past; always with casualties. <We can't do anything against a mech. It'll tear this place apart.>

<The car's about to arrive,> Petral said. <Almost.>

The far end of the platform erupted and the air around them filled with buzzing rounds. Concrete splintered and popped, sending shards in every direction. Andy held Tim and Cara just beneath the upper edge of the pile of bricks, hoping it might provide concealment. It certainly wouldn't provide adequate cover from a mini-tank. The pillars around them disintegrated as rounds tore them apart, wearing them down like Tim chewing a carrot.

<Where's that car?> Karcher demanded.

<Inbound,> Petral said. <Thirty seconds.>

<I'm going to flank. When it's here, you get on board,> Karcher said.

<You're holding in place?>

<Yes.> The finality of Karcher's single word left no time for argument. He was already sprinting across the bit of clear space between his pillar and the train tracks. He fired a grenade as he ran, another when he hit the tracks, and a third from the other side of the platform.

The mech didn't seem able to track him fast enough. Craters appeared in the floor a meter in front of him as he ran. Each new grenade he sent at the tank slowed its response.

More rifle fire filled the gaps between the mech's response to Karcher's grenades. In the middle of the second set of bursts, Karcher caught his breath, cursing.

<Caught me in the open,> he said. <I'm all right. I'm setting a shaped mine.>

<You'll need to clear,> Petral said, her voice still business-like. They didn't have to say what would happen if Karcher didn't escape the blast-radius of his own explosion.

A low hum coming down the tracks behind them announced the arrival of the maglev car. Hearing the direction of the sound, Andy realized they were going to have to pass the mech to escape the train station. He still hadn't seen the mini-tank, only felt its presence. There wouldn't be anything they could do once they were behind the thin wall of the train car. They could only hope Karcher had disabled the tank enough to get them by.

"When the door opens," he breathed to Tim and Cara. "We're going to run. You understand?"

He felt their nods against his chest. Truly, he planned on picking them up and throwing them through the open doors if they didn't move fast enough.

<I'm drawing them in,> Karcher said. <Hold your fire. They might think I'm alone.>

The floor rumbled as the mech pushed forward with thundering steps. The sound of soldiers scrambling over debris, boots scraping on concrete, and sporadic rifle fire drifted with the smoke and dust. Karcher's rifle answered with a few bursts, drawing them closer.

<Wait,> Karcher said.

The entire terminal rocked when the mine went off. The maglev car swayed on its magnetic rails so much that Andy was worried it was going to dislodge. Dust rained from the ceiling and a huge cloud of smoke rolled from the direction Karcher had run in.

Andy waited for more rifle fire but the only sounds were cascading bits of concrete from the walls and ceiling.

<Karcher,> Petral called out. <Karcher, report.>

Andy allowed himself a deeper breath. He let it out slowly. There was still no answer.

<We need to go,> he said.

Petral looked back at him from the stub of a pillar she was hiding behind. She nodded, her expression worried, but resolute.

Andy waited another second for some indication of life from the other side of the terminal. Nothing.

"Go," he whispered sharply.

He pushed himself to his feet and caught both kids under the arms, pulling them in close as he charged across the open space to the rail car, heart pounding in his ears. He jumped over the threshold and hit the floor, pulling the kids down with him, ready for the rain of bullets that would tear the car apart.

Petral leaped into the car a second after him. She crouched beside him and slid his rifle next to his head. <You forgot that,> she said.

Andy blinked, not remembering when he'd set it down, or how he had forgotten it. All he could think about was getting the kids in the car. He looked at Tim, who was biting his lower lip and squeezing his eyes closed, hands clenched over his ears.

<Are we going?> Andy asked.

<Sending the command now.>

There was a grinding noise as the doors slid closed. The car vibrated as it pulled itself forward along the magnetic rails. Twice it ground its way over debris, and Andy held his breath, praying the maglev's safety systems wouldn't kick in and halt the car. The maglev began to build up speed and they rushed straight into the cloud of dust still filling the terminal from the mine's explosion.

"Karcher!" Petral yelled as they went into the cloud. "Karcher! Can you hear me?"

The inside of the car filled with yellow dust, hiding the rest of the terminal from view. Karcher didn't answer. No one answered.

The windows went dark as the maglev car flew into the tunnel on the other side of the terminal. White lights flickered on inside the car, revealing their dust-covered faces to each other.

Cara sat up slowly, still holding her bag tight against her chest. Tim rolled onto his back and crossed his arms over his chest. Andy stayed on his stomach for another minute, feeling the thrum of the magnetic forces vibrating through the floor of the car, barely believing they were moving.

<What's between us and the repair docks?> he asked.

<Tunnel should be clear. The only access is by drone. We're not going to the command deck. There's a secondary shuttle bay on down the ring. It isn't used by anybody so it should be clear.>

<You trust that?>

Petral shrugged. <I guess we'll see when we get there,> she said.

CHAPTER TWENTY-THREE
STELLAR DATE: 08.27.2981 (Adjusted Years)
LOCATION: Night Park
REGION: Cruithne Station, Terran Hegemony

Leaving the terminal, the maglev car entered a Cruithne on fire. Each break in the tunnel offered a glimpse of street-fighting, smashed housing areas, fire and the crisscrossing flashes of kinetic rounds sprinkled with beamfire. Blast doors had come down on various sections, shutting off vacuum and whoever might have been trapped on the other side.

Andy held the kids against him, staring into each new potential danger, uncertain when the car might hit a break in the tracks and tumble end-over-end.

"I don't know how Starl didn't see this coming," Petral said, eyes wet. "This is worse than anything we thought the Havenots might ever do. We all live here. This is our home."

The car blew through a terminal still erupting with active combat. A squad of mercs held a kiosk while Lowspin and what looked like Station Security moved between benches, ceramic planters, and an overturned transport vehicle. Bullets careened off the car as they passed, surprised faces frozen, watching, and then gone behind them, another tunnel leading away into the dark.

"How much farther do we have to go?" Tim said.

"I don't know," Andy said, smoothing his son's hair back. "Not too much farther. Keep a good hold on that bag."

He caught Cara's gaze and she gave him a small smile. Andy squeezed her closer against his side.

The wheels squealed and they emerged in bright light, open space on either side of the car.

"Night Park," Petral said in a low voice. "Keep your heads down."

Night Park was an open-air bazaar that looked like a tornado had swept through a battleground. Wide swaths of destruction had cut through the market, littered with smashed goods and at least one wandering chicken, who pecked at a crushed melon.

"Night Park is where the fountain is," Cara said, spotting the hen. "Where they have all the parrots." She seemed to immediately forget Petral's warning and craned her neck to see out the window. Andy made her sit back down.

"Not now, kiddo," he said.

"You think they're hiding?" Tim asked.

"I would be," Cara said. "Parrots are smart."

In the distance, Andy heard more gunfire and the heavy footfalls of a mech. The thundering concussion of rounds striking concrete vibrated through the car and the hen squawked, fluttering out of sight.

"We're almost there," Petral said. "Probably another minute."

"What's the terminal look like?" Andy asked.

"We'll take a side tunnel. It ends on the secondary dock. This car was one of Starl's personal escape routes."

"Is there any info from the rest of Lowspin?"

"It's all a mess. The ships are waiting. For now, it sounds like the fighting is only on the ground. Heartbridge private security is slowed down searching apartment blocks."

"They're looking for us?" Andy asked.

Petral shook her head, pulling the action back on her rifle to check the chamber. "They're still looking for the canister Jickson used to transport Lyssa. They also don't know that he's dead, so most of them are looking for him specifically. They apparently poisoned the poor sap with some kind of radioactive element that also serves as a tracker. It's probably what led them to Fran's shop. The attack that took Starl was a fluke."

"So Jickson lives on, sort of?"

She grimaced. "Sort of. They've moved his body to one of the freighters called *High Outburst*."

The car raced around a long curve that made Andy wonder if they were somehow following the overall arch of the ring surrounding the original asteroid at Cruithne's center. Then he saw rock walls flash past and knew they were still surrounded by rock. The thought only reminded him how disoriented he had become. Somehow, they had traversed a long circle from the housing area back toward the repair docks and *Sunny Skies*.

"Dad?" Cara said.

He glanced down at her. "Yes?"

"Can I have a gun?"

Andy studied her face, so full of her mother's seriousness and worry. He had hoped she would never have cause to develop the bitter set to the jaw that had marked Brit's face when he had first met her—but there it was.

Andy took the old service pistol from its holster and held it in front of him. There wasn't enough time to give her any sort of real lesson. But he had the rifle and didn't technically need the weapon anymore. She might.

He quickly pointed out the action, safety, trigger, and a proper grip.

"Come here, close to me," he said.

Holding the pistol in front of him but low enough so Cara could look down the sights, he said, "Line up the white square with the middle of the black post. That's center mass."

He activated the safety and put the pistol in her hands, pointing it toward the window. She had a hard time holding it upright against the rocking of the transport car. She squinted and tilted her head to look down the sights.

"I want to do it!" Tim said.

"Keep your voice down, Tim. This is only for right now. Put the meat of your finger on the trigger, Cara." He checked her finger and corrected her placement. "Like that. Do you feel it in the middle of your fingerpad like that? That way you squeeze straight back."

Cara nodded, still looking down the sights.

"When do you point a gun at someone?" he said.

"When I'm going to shoot them."

"Do you ever point it as a joke, or to play?"

They had been through this before.

"Never!" Tim shouted. "Can I hold it now?"

"Not now, Tim. This is for Cara. What's the answer?"

"Never," she said.

"Good," Andy said. "Look, if this wasn't the only pistol I've got, I'd give it to you. For now, I'll hang onto it. If you—" He paused, unable to find the right words. "If you need to use it, you take it, all right?"

Cara blinked, looking up at him with round eyes. She understood.

Andy nodded. "Let me have it back, Cara."

She took another look down the sights and handed the pistol back.

"When we have time, we'll do a real lesson. For now, you leave the shooting up to Petral and me. Like I said, all you do is what we tell you, no thinking about it, understand?"

"*I* still understand," Tim complained.

"Andy," Petral said. "We're almost there."

He checked the action on the pistol, set the safety and holstered it. A glow grew in the tunnel ahead and then they were slowing as the car entered another terminal. At the far end of the station, another tunnel branched off.

"Is that it?" he asked.

"Yes, it's another hundred meters down that branch. There's a blast door in the tunnel line we can activate from inside. Once we're in there, no one's following us.

The terminal was like the others: white tile with evenly spaced pillars. Its lights were still functioning normally. The car began to slow, vibrating ever so slightly on the magnetic rail.

Andy nearly allowed himself to breathe when he caught movement behind one of the pillars. A soldier in a black uniform had seen the car and was sprinting toward something. Andy recognized a firing position made from the same white tile of the walls. The black muzzle of a heavy gun swung toward them.

Before the weapon fired, an explosion in the right corner of the front of the car tossed it nearly on end. The floor heaved beneath them, windows shattering on both sides of the car.

Ears ringing, Andy grabbed at the kids but could only hang onto Tim. Andy slid backward, his head bouncing off the edges of plastic seats.

The car fell toward the side of the terminal where the gun emplacement was positioned. Andy found himself with his back against the rear wall, staring up through the leaning car, light at his back from the smashed rear doorway. Petral was crouched on the back of a seat at the car's midpoint, rifle at her shoulder. He couldn't tell through the smoke and dust what she was aiming at but she started squeezing off three-round bursts, then dropped to a lower seat and took aim again. Rifle fire answered, peppering the wall of the car with pockmarks and a few burst holes.

"Cara!" Andy hissed. "Where are you?"

"Here," she said. He followed the sound of her voice and found her lying on her stomach on the back of a seat just above him, hair full of dust.

<Petral. I'm going out this back door with the kids. I'll try to find cover against the wall closer to their gun emplacement. We'll move toward the tunnel.>

<You're going to be wide open once you try and get into the tunnel.>

<You see another way?>

She didn't answer. Firing another burst, she shook her head disgustedly. *<No. At least get out of here before they fill this thing with grenades. I'll lay down some cover.>*

As soon as Petral started firing, Andy rolled to push Tim through the broken door. Grabbing for Cara, he pulled her down and made her crawl out ahead of him. He had to clamp a hand on Tim's ankle before his son could crawl the rest of the way out of the car onto the open track, the leaning rail car hiding them from the gun emplacement.

"After me," Andy said. "You follow me, okay? You don't move until I move."

Tim's eyes were round and terrified as though Andy's brusque tone scared him more than bullets.

The space between the magnetic rail and the side of the trench was about as wide as Andy's shoulders, with carbon scoring and scuffs from where the emergency clamps holding the car down in zero-g areas had scraped the rail. The magnetic field was still active and Andy made sure to hold his weapon clear as he crawled around the broken door with his rifle across his inner elbows. Checking quickly for any sign of movement near the edge of the platform, he crawled the rest of the way out, then motioned for Tim and Cara to follow him.

Once they were out, he led a short dash so they were off the track and flattened against the platform wall, the smoking car leaning above them. Petral was still firing from inside the car.

<We're out,> Andy said.

For the first time, the big gun at the emplacement fired into the car, blowing a hole out its roof. It was a tank buster and the round went through the thin steel like tissue paper.

<Damn it. You all right?> Andy shouted.

<I'm here.> She released a long burst of fire and then appeared at the bottom of the car. Adjusting her rifle, she aimed the grenade launcher and lobbed three rounds over the car into the emplacement against the far terminal wall.

The grenades blew debris back across the tracks.

<Run!> Petral howled.

Andy grabbed the kids and sprinted along the wall. The mouth of the tunnel ahead yawned before them. Once they passed back over the rail, they'd be in plain sight of anyone up on the platform. He could barely make out the second opening down the tunnel.

Catching up with him, Petral fired two more grenades at the emplacement. They landed badly, hitting the far wall too high to do any real damage. Dust and tile rained on the emplacement. The big gun rotated toward them, lifting its barrel.

<*I'll lay more covering fire,*> Petral said. <*Stay to the inside wall of the tunnel. Once you're near the second opening, they won't be able to see you. The emergency door activation is just inside.*>

She turned without waiting for an answer and fired from her hip.

"We need to run," Andy told the kids. "Along the wall. This way!"

Glancing back, he caught sight of Petral paused just inside the tunnel, firing from her shoulder now. She crouched and aimed carefully.

When they reached the branch tunnel, the big gun boomed again. They hadn't bothered to aim into the tunnel. The round struck the midpoint of the arch above Petral, collapsing the concrete over her head.

<*Petral!*> Andy shouted. <*Can you hear me?*>

There was no answer for a second, then she said, <*Are you in the tunnel? Damn it. I shouldn't have—answered you. Get out.*>

"Get down the tunnel," Andy told Tim and Cara. Spotting the emergency panel, a yellow square with an oversize red switch in its center, Andy said, "That closes the doors on this tunnel. Cara, you be ready to hit it when I tell you."

"Dad?"

"Do it, Cara."

Running a function check on his rifle as he sprinted, Andy navigated the debris that had fallen inside the branch line. The opening was still full of dust, concealing his movement for a few seconds, at least.

If the soldiers followed any sort of doctrine, they'd be lobbing grenades down the track soon enough. Staying low, he crept along the wall, looking for any sign of Petral.

A table-shaped piece of the ceiling had fallen straight down, bringing a cascade of smaller bits of rock and vine-like cabling with it. Andy found Petral on the inside edge of the collapsed tunnel, one leg caught under the pile, her knee bent unnaturally.

She was unconscious. Wrapping his sling around his arm to hold his rifle steady, Andy grabbed her by the collar and heaved. The leg didn't want to move.

The shouts of coordinating fire teams floated through the dissipating dust cloud.

Grunting, he pulled again but was only able to drag her a few inches. Something was caught.

"Let me help, Dad," Cara said from behind him.

Andy turned to her, wanting to shout for her to run. But she was already moving to grab Petral's caught leg. Andy tried to look through the cloud again, worried the tunnel opening was going to fill with bullets at any moment.

Cara set her grip and nodded. Together they pulled. Grunting, Cara readjusted her hands, nearly wrapping her arms around Petral's knee. The leg came free at last.

Heart pounding, Andy grabbed Petral around the waist and heaved her over his shoulder. Her head bounced against his back.

Cara was already running for the secondary tunnel. Andy followed her. When they were through, it was Tim who hit the square button. More dust blew from the ceiling as the heavy alloy door slid down and met reinforced locks in the floor, blocking the branch line from the main track.

They found themselves in complete darkness.

Andy leaned against the wall, adjusting his hold on Petral, and waited for his vision to acclimate to the dark.

"Are we going to go, Dad?" Cara said.

"Follow me," he said. He was ready to probe his way forward in the dark when a line of lights flickered to life along the ceiling, showing them the dock entry just fifty meters ahead.

PART 4: TRAFFIC

CHAPTER TWENTY-FOUR
STELLAR DATE: 08.27.2981 (Adjusted Years)
LOCATION: *Sunny Skies*
REGION: Cruithne Station, Terran Hegemony

"I named her *Worry's End*," Fran said with an unapologetic shrug. "I didn't have a lot of time to think about it."

Floating through the air lock, Andy considered the news. "I thought you were going to use a random name generator? That doesn't sound random."

"It's better than *Sucking Rainbow*."

"There had to be more than that."

"That's what you get for taking so long."

"About that. Petral's hurt. I got her stabilized with what we had in the shuttle but I need to get her into the med bay. I've got her lashed to a splint board for now."

"*Worry's End*?" Cara said. "That's a terrible name."

"How's it different than *Sunny Skies*?" Tim said.

"*Sunny Skies* are a thing you can see," Cara said. "*Worry's End* is something that will never come."

"It could come," Tim said, still hugging his bag.

"Never," Cara asserted.

"Dad?" Tim said. "Is Petral going to be all right?"

Andy pulled him in for a quick hug, holding onto the wall with his other hand. "She's going to be fine. She's sleeping so her leg won't hurt. We're going to take her up to the med bay."

"Karcher's dead," Cara said. Her voice was flat, stating a fact.

Andy looked at her, unable to tell how she felt about what she had just said. She might have been testing those kinds of words for the first time, really getting a sense of someone she had just met being dead, or matching it up with her feelings about her mother being gone.

He wasn't sure what he'd projected on her and what was really there behind her eyes. He was torn between wanting to hold her and allowing her to work through this, to stand on her own. It wasn't going to get any easier. Everything Starl had said about the possibility of a war was still banging around in his head— the strength of those words manifested by the blood and bodies in the corridors and sweeps of Cruithne. They weren't out of this mess yet.

Andy glanced at Fran. From her expression, she already knew about Karcher.

"We made it out," Andy said. "That's what he wanted. It's still possible he'll be all right. We just don't know."

Cara shook her head. "He's dead. He said he wouldn't leave us otherwise."

"You talked to him?" Andy asked.

She nodded solemnly.

He let out a long breath. He didn't know what to say and was too exhausted to come up with reassurance. The shuttle-ride hadn't done much to drain his adrenaline. He'd been uncertain the whole time that they might take fire from somewhere, run into yet another obstacle. He was starting to crash now

"Can they head up to the habitat?" Andy asked Fran. "Everything okay up there?"

"No dangling wires," she said. "Yeah, it's fine for them to head that way. I guess if they can take care of themselves, we can get Petral to the med bay and I can give you the update on the ship."

"She's still holding air, apparently."

"Better than that," Fran said, a little pride in her voice.

"I really appreciate your help," Andy said, grateful to be alive and for the assistance they'd received.

Fran gave him a crooked smile. "Don't get too emotional on me. I'm getting paid."

Andy laughed. He pointed at Cara. "You heard her. Can you get yourselves up to the habitat? How about some dinner? You think you're up for it?"

Cara frowned. "Isn't it morning time? What time is it?"

"Time to eat," Andy said. "I'm starving."

With the kids kicking off ahead of them, Fran and Andy maneuvered the unconscious Petral through the air lock. The splint board helped, but it meant she took up more space than would otherwise have been necessary.

"How much time do we have before the ships start launching?" Andy asked.

"They're waiting on our notification that you made it. Everybody's pulling back inside the station. I think most of them are moving to ships."

"That's what Petral said they were going to do. What if nobody makes it back?"

"You don't know Lowspin. This is the best fight we've had in our history. Corporatists think they can just overrun our station like we're a bunch of squatters?"

"I'm surprised the TSF isn't involved."

"Who are they going to fight for?" Fran asked.

"Stability?"

Fran snorted a laugh.

Ahead of them, the kids appeared overjoyed to find themselves back in zero-g. Tim kicked forward, spinning, while Cara slapped his sides, slowing his momentum then speeding him up again. It was one of their old games. Andy didn't understand how one of them didn't end up hurling vomit all over the walls.

"Would you believe they just ran through a firefight?" he asked.

"Kids are resilient," Fran said.

"I hope so."

He couldn't help noticing all the new components along the bulkheads of the main passageway. Panels that had been dented since he and Brit bought *Sunny Skies* were now flat, though not repainted. There probably hadn't been time for that. He spotted new conduit runs, pipe fittings and hundreds of individual weld points all along their path. The air tasted clean, too, no longer the familiar mix of overheated mold and melting plastic.

They had to take Petral off the board to get into the smaller airlock leading to the habitat. Andy still wasn't used to finding the air the same temperature in the living quarters as the rest of the ship.

Once they were through, Fran said, "Oh, I fixed your habitat's exterior airlock. You could board directly into your wheel now if you want. That should make things easier."

"That airlock wasn't structurally sound," Andy said. "At least that's what we were told when we bought the ship."

"It wasn't," Fran agreed. "If you'd let another ship dock and hadn't carefully regulated your interior pressure properly, the whole wheel probably would have collapsed like a used condom." Catching herself, she glanced at the kids. They didn't appear to have noticed. "Which also tied into your environmental control system, which hasn't been maintaining proper logs for at least a hundred and fifty years. They shouldn't have been able to sell it without those records."

Andy shrugged. "It wasn't that kind of transaction."

"Nobody ever needs a mechanic until shit's falling apart around them." She caught herself again, saying, "Oh, sorry."

"Dad's going to wash your mouth out with soap," Tim shouted, laughing.

"Try me," Fran said, smirking.

Unlike the main shaft, the habitat had received a fresh coat of paint, and new bulkhead panels in the most used areas. It was obvious other rooms hadn't been touched; which was fine with Andy.

"All right," Andy said. "It's time for you two to head to the kitchen. We'll be in the med bay helping Petral."

When the kids were out of earshot, Andy asked, "Is the ship going to make it out of here?"

Fran's expression turned sour. "We'll be able to get out. You've got a new containment bottle and we updated the transition systems. It's your onboard computer I'm worried about. I think most of your problems stem from years of poor calibration. That's just not something you can do manually. If a ship's NSAI isn't monitoring the engines, they're going to fail eventually. Like I said before, I'm in awe of how you kept this house of cards from collapsing on you. But it's not sustainable."

"Where's the damage?"

"I haven't had time to isolate the problem. It's somewhere in your command overlay. Based on other things I've seen, I think someone disconnected the ship's higher NSAI functions maybe two hundred years ago, leaving only the critical systems and a bunch of other programming fixes on top of it. But I can't find the break, and we're out of time. The other thing we didn't have time to finish was mounting the upgraded point defense cannons. You've got shields, but you don't have any other protection from debris or pirates."

"That's nothing new," Andy said.

"Just because you're used to it doesn't make it right."

Though still in a stupor, Petral began to moan just as they reached the med bay. Andy strapped her into the examination couch and let the autodoc scan her body for other wounds besides the leg. It returned strains in her back, torn muscles and ligaments, and a compound fracture within the leg, though it hadn't broken the skin. The scan glitched during the second pass and Andy had to restart the program.

"I guess you didn't get to the med bay during the remodel," he said.

Fran snorted. "You're lucky to get what you did. You haven't seen half of what we did fix and you're already complaining."

Stabbing the display, Andy shook his head. "We're going to have to let it run with the diagnosis it's got. She's stabilized, at least. In any case, she's going to be with us for a while. Have you got room in your shuttle to bring her back with you?"

"I should, if she's nice to me. Petral's not a fun person to be around."

"She was nice enough to me."

Fran gave a short laugh and looked him up and down. "She would be."

"Sure," Andy said, too tired to tell if she were complimenting him or not. He turned his attention to the console, taking the opportunity to flip through the ship's control menus. Many of the status sections that used to give null readings were now logging results, from the engines, to the environmental control system. Even the hydroponic pumps were back online.

"You fixed the gardens."

"I like plants," Fran said. "Good for kids to be around them, too."

"I thought you said you hated plants."

"I said plants got in the way of my drinking. I might not want to get married but I can enjoy something from time to time."

"Having a plant is just like getting married," Andy said.

He was about to ask about an upgrade in the sewage filtration system when Fran got a faraway look in her eyes, apparently taking a message over her Link. When she blinked and looked at him, her pleased expression had flattened.

"We need to launch. Other ships are moving into the transfer lanes and getting ready to break orbit. Apparently, the *Benevolent Hand* is launching a wave of attack drones."

"Shit. Have they hit anybody yet?"

"We dumped a hundred release requests on the Port Authority four hours ago. That was Starl's idea. Every ship that's leaving Cruithne in the next two hours has prior approval. Any aggression toward the departing ships will be registered as an unprovoked attack in the Port Authority logs."

"So TSF is doing something, after all?"

"Nothing but serving as witness. Starl hoped that would be enough to hold them off. It depends on how desperate they are to get their hands on the thing in your head. Once they figure out it's in your head. Also depends on whether or not anyone in Heartbridge has greased enough government palms."

"We need to get up to the command deck," Andy said. "Petral's going to be out for hours still. I need to know what's going on. Can you give me access to Lowspin net over my Link?"

Fran shook her head. "I wouldn't if I could. Way too much garbage on the net and only some of it's useful. It's better if I translate for you." Catching Andy's frustrated expression, she said, "You can trust me. We're both on this antique together."

"It's not that I don't trust you," Andy said. "I hate being in the dark."

"Don't we all."

Andy set the med bay's monitoring systems and readjusted Petral's straps for the possibility of high-g maneuvers. She was smiling slightly in her sleep and he hoped the painkillers were at least giving her good dreams.

"Damn it," Fran said, eyes distant again. "The *Benevolent Hand* is moving to an overwatch orbit. We're in for a battle."

CHAPTER TWENTY-FIVE

STELLAR DATE: 08.27.2981 (Adjusted Years)
LOCATION: Cantil Housing Project
REGION: Cruithne Station, Terran Hegemony

Andy slid into the command chair and ran his hands over the console. It was still as worn as ever, but, just like in the med bay, several indicators he had always thought of as blank space were now alive with data. He activated the main sensor array and pulled up the active astrogation control.

Expecting the screen to give him only columns of coordinates, he started when a holographic overlay of Cruithne Station, its ring, and the largest ships tracked by the Port Authority filled the air in front of him. He dropped his hands in his lap, taking a second to appreciate the color and detail. As various ships moved, their velocity, registry indicators and transponders flashed beside them. Cruithne itself rotated in real time, various sections of the ring and surface growing more distinct as they came into view.

"That's the sexiest thing I've seen in a long time," Andy said. "I can't even tell you."

"I'll be sure to let Petral know."

Fran moved behind him and sat in the second pilot's seat, which had been Brit's for so long. She activated her own display and pulled up an overlay of the ship, running through systems for status levels. When she wasn't typing, she reached into the hologram and turned it various directions, zooming in and out until she was satisfied with what she was checking.

"I have a lock on the *Benevolent Hand*," Andy said. He spread his hands and enlarged the Heartbridge ship. He frowned. How anyone could have considered this a medical supply ship was beyond him. The design was obviously a long-rage attack class, with an oversized sensor array and multiple engine types. A swarm of at least a hundred smaller ships roved in a cloud around it, darting in complex patterns the targeting computer was still trying to analyze.

"We can't do anything against that," he said, trying not to sound defeated. "We can't outrun it and there's no way we can fight it. I guess I could ram it. That might scratch it."

"You won't have to. We need to get the course set and then figure out how we're going to slip into the overall chaos that's about to start."

"Right," Andy said. "Wait." He looked at Fran. "Starl never gave me the destination. He said he was going to. It's somewhere in the Scattered Disc. But he never gave me the actual coordinates." He frowned, staring into the hologram cloud. "I thought if he didn't give it to me, the AI would."

"She isn't talking to you?"

"No."

"So, we make a destination. When I give the mark, every ship in Lowspin is going to leave along an establish route. Which one would you normally follow?"

"This time of Cruithne's year? Mars would be our most likely destination," Andy said, trying to think out loud. "Even if we are eventually going to Jupiter, that would make the most sense. I'm just following the same path I took in." He raised his hands. "But we have a different registry now. It doesn't matter what path we take. Where did *Worry's End* come from? What was the last port of call?"

Fran shrugged. "I didn't get that far."

"We need a story. We need to have done something. Has the ship been on ice for three hundred years? You could file a computer failure. We could enter some vague route history that would at least make it look like we didn't just appear out of nowhere."

"Andy, no one is going to be looking at our logs in the next two hours."

"But they will be at Mars 1, or if we run into a random TSF transport check."

"We're not carrying anything illegal. Calm down."

"Yes, we are. Me. I'm carrying it."

"Then we'll put you in an EV suit and dangle you off the habitat until their done with their check. We need to worry about that obstacle once we're past all these." She waved at the cloud of fireflies glowing in front of them. "Lowspin lives now, my friend," she said, sounding like Starl. "Worry yourself about tomorrow when you wake up."

"Right," Andy said. "Right." He blinked, unsure what he had expected from Fran. If it had been Brit, she would be criticizing him for not thinking any of this through. He couldn't help worrying. Too much depended on him being the one to figure all this out. Who else would?

"You don't sound like a mechanic," he said.

She shrugged.

Andy pulled up the maps and entered his regular destinations in the astrogation planner. A new holographic overlay covered Cruithne, outlined in red over lighter blue. *Sunny Skies* — he couldn't bring himself to think of her as *Worry's End* — was a brighter point along the inner edge of Cruithne's ring. A flowing line took them out and around the asteroid, gathering speed with each orbit until the point the computer calculated ideal burn. Fuel and velocity estimates flowed down one side of his console.

"There it is. We've got a good window. We're on the outswing toward Mars. We can be there in three weeks. And your exit point." He started to track the glowing red line with his index finger, then stopped. "Well, I guess you can drop anywhere. You'll save fuel if you come all the way to Mars 1 with us, then loop around for a return trip. But according to your shuttle, you can burn all the way back and still have fuel for the braking maneuver."

"Like I said, we'll worry about that when we get there. Don't get me wrong about the cold calculations, but I've got fuel to spare, even with her majesty Petral along for the ride." She smirked. "The question is, can you stand me for three weeks?"

"I guess I'll tell you in three weeks," Andy said.

Fran's expression went flat as she received new info over her Link. As she listened, this time she divided her attention between the update and her console. Sweeping away the ship's status, she pulled up the Port Authority overlay Andy had been using. She pulled the *Benevolent Hand* into focus and added path estimates.

As Andy watched her work, it became obvious that the Heartbridge battle cruiser had nearly reached an overwatch position on Cruithne, making it possible to attack any ship leaving the station's gravity well. From this point, the Lowspin ships would need to pull off simultaneous departures if anyone was going to get away alive.

"Where's the damn TSF when you need them?" he muttered.

Andy logged into the general Port Authority channel, which was full of chatter from the rest of the ships trying to get into or out of the station blissfully unaware of what was going on with the apparent warship and its drone swarm. The *Benevolent Hand* was following a standard aggression protocol that, while not overtly announced, would have been obvious to anyone with experience. Hundreds of ships unassociated with Lowspin were trying to get out of Cruithne based on the interior fighting alone.

The upgraded scan showed a few TSF patrol craft nearby, but their closest base—a floating service platform colloquially called *Blazing Glory*—was two light-minutes away. They wouldn't have registered the *Benevolent Hand*'s initial maneuvers yet, let alone sent any response to them.

Realizing he didn't have a choice, Andy sent the route request to Mars 1's Port Authority. Mars was nearly fifteen light-minutes prograde of Cruithne, and Andy expected to wait at least half an hour for a response, but a reply came back almost immediately from a nearby comm drone, indicating that tightband to Mars 1 was backed up with requests and travel lane approvals would take at least an hour to process. Inbound ships could coordinate traffic at their point of origin and request access again when they reached Mars Protectorate space.

Fran read the message over his shoulder. "That's all we need," she said. "You ready to get out of here?"

"Are the engines ready?"

"I wish they were more ready, but we don't have a choice. I can work on anything that fails mid-route"

"All right," Andy said. Without waiting any longer, he sent the decoupling request to the dock control NSAI. He held his breath as the system processed the request, wondering if Heartbridge could somehow put a freeze on all exit procedures. The dock approved the request and provided a countdown.

"Buckle up, kids," Andy called over the intercom. "We're about to feel some g's."

"Dad," Cara called back. "We're making food. You said you were hungry."

The shiny new display had made him forget all about his hunger. "What are you making?"

"Grilled cheese."

Andy nodded. "I like grilled cheese."

"It's synthetic. That's all there was."

"You didn't have to tell me that. Look, we have to go. You two eat and get everything else in the cabinet for me. I'll grab it when we're done, all right? I'll send you the countdown warning when we're about to move."

"So, we're leaving Cruithne?" Tim asked.

"Yes, we are."

"Good," he said. "I don't like it here."

"Hey, now," Fran said. "That's my home you're talking about. Maybe when you come back I'll show you a better time."

"I'm never coming back," Tim said petulantly.

"Hurry up and eat," Andy said. "We don't have a lot of time."

He pushed the model of the *Benevolent Hand* into the left edge of his display and pulled up Cruithne, highlighting every ship Fran had identified as Lowspin. There were two hundred and twenty-six vessels of varying sizes. Definitely enough to clog the three major exit lanes and the holding orbits if they wanted to.

"I'm sending the order," Fran said.

"Man…now that the kids mentioned it, I'm really wishing I had that grilled cheese sandwich," Andy said.

"Later."

"There is no later, right?" He shot her a grin.

Fran didn't hear him. She was already staring into the distance, communicating with the rest of the Lowspin battlenet.

"We launch in the middle of the flock," she said when she came back. "We're not waiting on port approval. We'll manage de-confliction internally."

He was about to ask how that was going to work in reality, when the first red dot detached itself from Cruithne's ring and moved into one of the ephemeral lanes Port Authority used to route incoming and outgoing traffic. Another followed, then another. The other two lanes were soon filling with red points as well.

"Engine status?" Andy asked.

"We're green across the board. Ready for chem thrusters whenever you are."

Andy checked the flight path one more time, making sure the computer had adjusted for all the new traffic in the lane. He swallowed, unable to dislodge the anxious lump in his throat.

"Let's go," he said. He reached out and activated the flight plan.

The sensation of light thrust sent a thrill through him that he hadn't felt in a long time, a spark in the roiling overcast of his dread. His inner ear adjusted to the micro-forces working against his body and he felt the familiar nausea. He took deep breaths until the ache calmed down.

Sunny Skies was up again, better than she had ever been.

A new yellow point of light joined the streaming river of red in the third outbound traffic lane, showing them clearing the ring and entering low orbit.

Movement from the corner where he had pushed the *Benevolent Hand* reminded Andy to reset the overall display. The Heartbridge ship appeared in its stand-off orbit. The first Lowspin ship was reaching upper orbit and its burn window. The cruiser didn't take any aggressive action as ships began flaring brighter and then shooting out of the holodisplay's tracking boundary.

"They're letting them go," Fran said.

"Or they've got some way to search ships that we don't know about."

"You're a pessimist, you know that?" Fran said.

"Hold on," Andy said, leaning toward the display. A new set of coordinates were flowing through the raw sensor data. The updated information appeared on the holodisplay as a doubling of the swarm around the *Benevolent Hand*.

"There it is," he said. "They're attacking."

CHAPTER TWENTY-SIX

STELLAR DATE: 08.27.2981 (Adjusted Years)
LOCATION: *Sunny Skies*
REGION: Cruithne Station, Terran Hegemony

Sunny Skies had shields again. Andy wanted to kiss Fran for that fact alone.

In the holodisplay, the *Benevolent Hand* hung above Cruithne like a shark, its fins growing into dark wings as the attack drones separated into what appeared to be flight teams. The targeting computer quickly identified velocity similarities and assigned different symbols to the separating teams. From a distance, the swarm looked like a spreading cloud. Up close, each team writhed and shifted, darting forward then waiting as another leapfrogged ahead of it.

"It's like they turn at right angles," Andy said, cursing under his breath.

Based on the projected flight paths, the drone swarm appeared to be moving to cover each flight path out of Cruithne. It was possible that they had the requested flight plans of every Lowspin ship leaving the station. While flooding the Port Authority with their requests made it possible to overload the system and allow faster exit, is also meant the *Benevolent Hand* knew which ships were moving toward each departure land, and could assign the drones accordingly.

Fran shook her head. "I still don't get how they can do this. Every ship leaving the station right now is peaceful. The only vessel making any sort of aggressive action is the *Benevolent Hand*."

"Are we broadcasting this?" Andy asked.

"We are," she said. "Are they jamming the Link out of Cruithne? That's the question."

"You mean you don't have a plan for that?"

"If Starl were here, maybe he could tell you. I got this ship running and gave the word to leave. My part's done for now."

"We're still going to need those cannons at some point," Andy said. "How close are they to being operational?"

"They're seated in the housing. None of the connections were finished. It's a two-person job."

"There are two of us."

"You need to pilot this thing. If we had a capable AI, I'd say yes."

Andy shook his head, thinking of the AI that was supposedly embedded in the back of his brain. He was starting to doubt Jickson had done anything but cut a hole in his skull.

"Can you get started and I come help you when you need it? I won't know how much time we have until the drones start making strafing runs. I hate that anybody ahead of us is going to be a sacrifice to save our asses, but it's the only way I can come up with a counter flight path. They might be trying to intimidate everyone into staying."

"Yeah," Fran said, watching the spreading field of drone flight teams. The flow of red dots out of Cruithne had only grown thicker, glittering in three rivers of light leaving the asteroid in opposite directions.

"I have a drone," Andy said. "What kind of help do you need with the cannon?"

"I met your drone. It should be put out of its misery. It might be older than the ship."

"The kids call it Alice."

"You shouldn't ever name a drone. You might have to scrap it."

Andy smiled but didn't take his gaze off the display. "That's exactly what *I* said."

His attention was drawn back to the holodisplay as the first freighter passed under the shadow of the drone cloud. Andy held his breath as the flashing red point grew indistinct under the swarming drones. The freighter continued—taking no fire from the drones—now followed by four more.

"I hope you're right," he said.

"About the drone?"

"About it all being a feint."

He liked to think they still lived in a universe of laws. That was the world where he wanted to raise his kids. Times like these made him believe the old human ways would never die. The ramifications of isolation and violence were only amplified the further you went from civilization.

The first freighter crossed beyond the outer edge of the swarm. Andy watched it move closer to the display boundary.

"They're winding up for a burn," Fran said.

Andy nodded and wasn't surprised when the dot stretched on the holodisplay and disappeared, the space where it had been now occupied by the next ship in the lane. He released his pent-up breath and relaxed in the seat.

"It's a show," he breathed. "It's all a show."

More ships flowed past the swarming drones in each of the three lanes. Their dots smeared on the edge of the display as they powered up their engines and boosted away from Cruithne.

Andy pulled up the route controls and verified they had an entry window into the nearest exit lane. They were behind twenty other ships, with even more forming up behind them. Still More joined the queue as he watched.

"These are all Lowspin ships?"

Fran shook her head. "It went beyond Lowspin before you got to the shuttle. Zanda really pissed a lot of people off. You don't turn on your own. I guess it didn't help that Heartbridge was attacking everybody. A whole lot of housing areas are rubble now. That's people's families."

"How many stations have Heartbridge clinics, you think?" Andy asked.

"You think I know? Ask the Link."

"I'm not talking about an actual number. I'm wondering how big the company truly is." He motioned at the hologram of the *Benevolent Hand*. "Look at that thing. It's a monster. That's not cheap."

"It's like any other company, part of another company. Who knows how far it all goes back?"

"Apparently Starl knows," Andy said.

Fran laughed. "Starl doesn't know shit. He was hired to do a job and he's doing it."

"So, who paid him?"

"Maybe Heartbridge did? You never know with this kind of shit. Jickson shows up saying he has a job. Starl bites like a hungry dog and here we are, about to get killed."

"We're not getting killed," Andy said.

Fran crossed her arms over her chest. "I'm not a liar; I'll tell you what I think. If we get out of this alive—" She stopped herself as the door to the command deck slid open and Cara appeared with a box in her hands. She walked over to them and pulled two grilled cheese sandwiches out of the box.

"I figured I should just bring these up," she said.

Fran took a sandwich and smelled it, then took a huge bite. Chewing with her mouth open, she said, "You're all right, kid."

"I thought I told you to strap in," Andy said.

Cara tilted her head and held the sandwich out.

"Don't give me those eyes," Andy said, taking the sandwich. It had cooled but even rubbery cheese on stiff bread tasted like heaven. He ate the sandwich in four bites.

Beside him, Cara's gaze was fixed on the holodisplay.

"Is this what's happening right now?" she asked.

"Those are all the ship leaving Cruithne right now," Andy said.

"Where are we?"

Andy tapped a command on the display and the yellow dot marking *Sunny Skies* blinked near the ring. "That's us."

"We're so far back. How long is it going to take us to get past the other ships?"

"I don't know yet," Andy said. "There are too many of us trying to get out right now."

"What keeps them from running into each other?"

"Idiot self-preservation," Andy said. "And good computers."

"So, we're trying to get past the big ship and all those little ones? Those are drones, aren't they? Military drones?"

"How old are you, kid?" Fran asked.

Cara looked at her. "Twelve. How old are you?"

Fran barked a laugh. "I like that. I'm thirty-four. Old enough to know better and young enough to enjoy it."

"My dad is forty-three."

Fran nodded. "He looks all right for somebody so old."

Cara gave her a quizzical look. "That's not old. He was younger than you when he left the TSF." She pointed at the swarming drones. "He knows how to kills those drones. Don't you, Dad?"

Andy gave her an uncomfortable smile. "Not without the right kind of ship, kiddo. Those drones are like piranha fish and we're piloting a hippo."

"Hippos are actually very dangerous. They used to kill people all the time. They only look cute," Cara said.

Fran stared at Cara, then burst out laughing. "I like her, Captain Sykes. I want her up here on the command deck whenever you're getting stressed out."

Andy wanted to say that it didn't help him at all to have the kids on the command deck but he didn't want to hurt Cara's feelings. Not that he could keep them away most of the time. If Fran hadn't been sitting in Brit's seat, Cara would have been there. It had been safer when most of the console's functions were inoperative. He was going to have to be more careful now when he let her pilot alongside him.

"Dad," Cara said, pointing at the holo. "What are those flashes?"

"What?" Andy turned to stare into the display and watched a cascade of lightning flow through the swarming drones to the river of red lights in lane two. A cluster of Lowspin ships flared and disappeared. As he watched, the cloud of drones closest to the lane moved along its outer edge, sending forks of lightning into the queuing ships. The lightning was a collection of electron beam and x-ray beams. More ships disappeared as he watched.

Red dots started to break away from the flight lane. The distinct lines of the flight path were soon a mess of red and writhing gray drones, like a cancer shooting through healthy cells.

Andy's mouth went dry. They were at the back of a queue just like the one he was watching disintegrate in the display. He turned to Fran and she was staring into the distance, accessing her Link.

When he was about to shake her to get her to come back, she looked at him blinking. "They're all dying," she said. "Other ships are rerouting. Some are saying they're turning back for the ring."

"Is anybody pushing through?"

"There are some with offensive capability. They're still going. We could fall in with them but it doesn't matter. We're defenseless except for the shields."

"We've got to get those cannons operational, Fran. How much time would you need?"

She bit her lip, calculating. "An hour. Faster if you can help me. The autopilot is good. You can set the flight plan and we can both get the control servos operational."

"Are cannons enough against all those drones?" Cara said.

"Maybe," Andy said. "It's the best we've got."

"Why are we going to follow everyone else?" Cara said. She pointed at the empty spaces in Cruithne's orbital path. "Why can't we just go through those holes and run away that way?"

"We could," Andy said. "But that would make it clear to the people running the drones that we're different than all the others." He didn't want to say that the *Benevolent Hand* was trying to find them specifically. "They'd leave everyone else and come after us."

"You think they would," Cara said.

"It's what *I* would do."

"But all those others are breaking away and it looks like some are getting through."

"Most of them are getting killed," Andy said.

"We can finish the work on the cannons," Fran said, sounding more resolute now. Something she'd heard over the battle net had either calmed her nerves or convinced her there was no other choice.

Andy nodded. "Cara," he said. "I want you to stay up here on the command deck. You don't sit in the pilot's chair unless I tell you, you understand me? There are a lot of new controls that I don't have time to explain to you now. Fran and I are going to have to go outside to work on the cannons. We've got plenty of time to get it done, so there's no rush. Can you do that?"

Cara didn't answer immediately. Her gaze was on the display again. "Why are those drones different?" she asked, pointing at a line of green dots sweeping across the roiling gray cloud of drones.

Andy blinked, not quite believing his eyes. He recognized the formation immediately. "It's the TSF, the station's defense fighter squadron," he said. "They're counterattacking." Then he pointed at another line forming on the far side of the *Benevolent Hand*. "Those aren't TSF. I don't know who they are."

A wry smile had formed on Fran's lips. "It's Lowspin," she said. "Our pirates are back."

CHAPTER TWENTY-SEVEN

STELLAR DATE: 08.27.2981 (Adjusted Years)
LOCATION: *Sunny Skies*
REGION: Cruithne Station, Terran Hegemony

Waiting for Airlock One to cycle open, Andy experienced near-disappointment when the door didn't complain like he was used to. Instead of sounding like it was going to shake itself apart, the two sides of the portal slid open silently, showing him a dull black expanse. In another second, his faceplate display lit up all the visible objects intertwining around Cruithne as the TSF and assorted pirates took the fight to the *Benevolent Hand*.

Activating his magboots, he stepped out of the airlock.

<I didn't expect new EV suits, too,> he said.

Following him over the airlock's threshold, Fran moved up beside him. <*That old piece of shit you had could barely maintain thirty percent pressure. You know you were trying to commit suicide every time you used it, right? At least, that's what it looked like to me.*>

<*I thought you said you'd been on long haul before?*>

<*I've been on long hauls, but I made sure the equipment was half-way functional.*>

<*It's getting to the point that I can't tell if you're happy you fixed all this stuff, or scolding me because I hadn't already done it.*>

Fran moved around him, boots making dull clicks on *Sunny Skies'* alloy skin. <*I thought you were a TSF officer? You sure need to toughen up.*>

<*Yeah.*>

He followed her toward the bow, stepping over control boxes and snaking, surface-mounted conduit. As the habitat wheel grew smaller behind them, they came over the curving hull to see the line of the mounted cannons, looking like a row of droop-shouldered drones in the distance.

Andy nearly tripped several times, spending more time staring into the space above them and the battle playing out across his faceplate than the obstacles under his boots.

<*You drunk?*> Fran said.

<*I haven't seen a full battle like this in a long time.*>

<*Tell me about it. You were a pilot then, yeah?*>

Andy knew what she was doing, trying to get his mind off everything happening around them and focus on the task at hand. He played along.

<*It was a pirate outpost off Venus. I think the place was originally just space junk that stuck in the transfer orbit and grew over time. It almost had a ring. They were staging raids on the automated freighters running between Terra and Venus. We couldn't believe anybody would try something like that so close to Earth but that was the genius of it.*>

Andy laughed, remembering how dumbfounded they'd been. <*Nobody could believe pirates would operate so close and kept chalking the losses up to equipment failure. They had a great hacker who kept hijacking the guidance signals. For a long time, it looked*>

like everything sent itself into the sun. Maybe the ships did after they grabbed the cargo, I don't remember.>

<Seems dumb not to grab the ships, too.> Fran said. <If you're going to the trouble of stealing from the TSF anyway.>

<Wasn't directly TSF. Private companies that finally complained enough to get patrols. I was assigned to a light attack ship riding close to a freighter to mask my signature. It worked. Gave them a hell of a surprise. What we didn't realize is that they'd come after us with more pirates than anybody had seen in years.>

<You know what they called themselves?>

<Stars the Hard Way, I think. That might have been the name of their cruiser.>

<Poetic.>

"Dad," Cara said. "You didn't check in. I see the airlock closed. Are you doing all right?"

Andy cursed himself. "Yes. We're out Airlock One and moving toward the bow. We have the cannon arrays in sight."

"You're supposed to check in," Cara said.

"I know. I will from now on. Where's your brother?"

"I *know* where he is. He's reading his book."

<She always ride your ass like that?> Fran asked.

Andy figured she meant it to be a joke but obviously didn't understand Cara's point of view. <The last time I went out the airlock we had debris hit our torch. I nearly got blown off the side of the ship. That was just before we got to Cruithne.>

Fran blew a low whistle. <That's why your suit was full of holes. You're lucky. Why didn't you pick up the debris?>

<I had to turn off the sensor arrays so I could get close enough for some repairs. I figured I'd rather take my chances with debris than get cooked.>

<I think I'd rather get cooked.>

<You say that now.>

<I hear it's just a warm feeling like hypothermia. You get light headed and then you just let go and float away.>

<That sounds terrifying.>

<Probably. My crew plays this game where we describe the worst deaths possible while working a repair job.>

<Why would you do that?>

<We're sick.>

<So what's the worst death?>

<I'll tell you later.>

Andy wondered if Fran was actually trying to flirt with him. Being outside the ship seemed to completely change her mood, despite the battle raging just beyond the ring.

<Damn,> Andy said, <Looks like we just lost two TSF. Those drones are unstoppable. I hope they're not manufacturing them on site. It's one thing to go after the attacking vessels. I don't know if they'll even try to take the battle cruiser.>

<Wouldn't that create some kind of international incident?>

<At this point, that sounds like a good idea to me. Pirates or not, civilians are getting slaughtered here. Somebody needs to know about it.>

Fran set a fast pace, nearly jumping across the obstacle-covered surface. Andy liked to keep one boot hooked until the other found its surface. He was sweating but the new suit did a good job of controlling internal temperature. His faceplate remained clear, unlike the last time he'd been outside *Sunny Skies*.

"Are you there yet?" Cara asked. The anxiety in her voice was palpable. He wished he had some way to calm her.

"Almost. We're nearly to the bow now. I can see the main antenna array past the mounted cannons." He looked back toward the habitat wheel and imagined Cara staring into the holographic display, maintaining her best adult face.

"We're almost in the lane with all the other ships," his daughter said. "Can you see any of the ships out there?"

"Unless they reflect light, I won't have visual on them, Cara. But my suit can see them."

"What about Cruithne? Can you see Cruithne?"

He glanced straight up into the mottled curve of Cruithne's ring, like a moldy eel encircling the asteroid. "I can see it, kiddo."

"Cruithne's a big dumb rock," Fran said. "Hard to miss even if we wanted to."

"Why can't we just put Cruithne between us and the bad guys and leave that way?" Cara asked.

Andy was about to say they couldn't do that when he paused, considering how much time they might have if they maintained a spin with Cruithne that kept it between them and the *Benevolent Hand*, blocking their sensor reach for at least a little.

<It depends on whether they're using the drone swarm to extend their sensor reach,> Fran said over the Link, guessing his line of thinking. *<It might work for a little while, at least.>*

<We'd be breaking out of the crowd, possibly drawing attention to ourselves.>

<What if I convinced a group to go with us?> Fran asked.

<That would definitely get their attention. But would also provide us some cover.>

<Maybe,> Fran said.

<Maybe.>

The row of mounted cannons grew as they approached, until the dual-cannons in each mount towered above them. Each set of cannons sat on a gimble that allowed nearly three-hundred and sixty-degree target acquisition. Electric conduit the size of Andy's thighs ran from the body of the ship to control boxes at the base of each mount. There were six sets of cannons mounted around the circumference of the bow. Eleven more point-defense cannons than *Sunny Skies* had ever carried.

Fran kicked off lightly and sat on the edge of the electrical control box. *<All right. Here's what we need to do. I'm going to check the mount integrity and you're going to monitor the power levels. I need to run a local systems check on each system before I bring it online with the ship's control.>*

<That sounds easy enough. What errors am I looking for?>

<We want to make sure the onboard system is updated properly. The mounting bolts meet spec and the cannon set have proper handshakes with each other and the ship.>

<We couldn't do this from inside?>

<Hey, if you don't mind your main weapon system blowing itself off the ship like popcorn while also tearing gaping holes in the hull during what I would assume is a critical use case, let me get in my shuttle before you do that.>

<You said all that in one breath,> Andy said. *<That was good. You make these kinds of arguments a lot?>*

<I work for pirates,> Fran said, putting a hand on her hip. *<They're cheap. They need convincing.>* She unlatched a torque wrench from her harness and reattached the lanyard to a ring on her wrist. Floating off the shoulder-high box, she moved to the base of the cannon mount and bent over the first set of holding bolts.

Andy watched her bend over, waiting for instructions on how she wanted the local systems checked.

<Are you going to stare at my ass all day or check the systems?>

<It's right there. I can't help it. How do you want the system monitored?>

<Whatever,> she said, still sounding pleased with herself. *<Each one of these things has a default login. I'll send you the token. Once we're done, we'll need to set up the handshake with the ship, like I already said.>*

<Yeah, but you didn't say how. If I know anything about techies like you, it's that I shouldn't go sticking my fingers anywhere I'm not told.>

Fran laughed. *<You're making me forget the gravity of our situation. I like that.>*

Focusing on the mounting bolts, she worked her way around the pedestal verifying the torque load while Andy logged in and assigned a position number and checked the other information the rudimentary interface computer needed to talk to *Sunny Skies*. When they had finished with the first cannon, they moved to the next one, which proved to be identical to the first.

They were making good time when Fran broke the head off a bolt on the seventh pedestal's mounting plate. *<Damn it!>* she shouted, and would have lost her wrench if not for the lanyard. For a heartbeat, Andy thought her boots had lost connection and she was floating free of the ship. When she punched the vacuum in front of her and didn't go anywhere, he knew she was still attached.

<I'll need to drill this out,> she said. *<It's going to take a few minutes.>*

<You got the tools you need?>

<Yeah. It's the time required that pisses me off. Also, if this bolt is such cheap steel, I'm worried about the rest of them now. My supplier is getting my boot in his ass when this is over.>

<I'll help,> Andy said. He logged into the cannon and made the necessary updates. The process had become rote enough now that he could pull up the battle overlay on his face shield and still get it right the first time. The TSF and pirate fighters were still engaging the Heartbridge drones, but didn't appear to have made any headway in pushing through to the *Benevolent Hand*. The only way to end the fight was to go after the cruiser. Any TSF commander would know that. So, why hadn't they? At least it looked like the drones had stopped attacking

outgoing freighters and were focused on the fighters.

"Dad!" Cara yelled. "Something is coming close to us!"

"What?" he asked, ears ringing. "What's coming?"

"It's a gray thing. It's a bunch of gray things."

Andy turned in time to watch the dark forms of three triangle-shaped drones appear out of the dark near the habitat wheel. The drones evened out in what looked like a standard strafing run as they neared *Sunny Skies*.

<*Fran!*> Andy yelled. <*We've got incoming.*>

The technician fell back on her heels and turned to gaze in the direction Andy was pointing.

<*Those other cannons are online, right?*> Andy said.

<*Yeah,*> she said. <*As long as they're talking.*>

Andy didn't wait for her to explain further. "Cara! Sweetheart. The display to your lower right with the red outline. Do you see it?"

Cara didn't answer at first. "I don't see it," she said finally. "I don't see it."

Andy tried to stay calm as the drones came closer. They were lined in glowing yellow markings. "It's got a red border, just like a picture frame. That's the auto-defense. Just press your finger to the screen. Just do that."

"I don't see it, Dad. I don't. Wait! I see it."

To Andy's right, the four cannons within view leveled and rotated in unison as they performed start-up checks. Through his Link, Andy highlighted the nearest fast-moving objects—the drones—and marked them hostile.

The cannons swiveled and locked on, firing high-intensity x-ray lasers through five centimeter apertures. The three drones glowed brightly and then broke apart into debris before they reached the square opening of Airlock One.

Andy took a deep breath and let it out. "Good job, Cara. You did it. Good job." He couldn't tell if Cara was laughing or crying in-between disjointed breaths.

"We did it," she said.

"Nice work," Fran added. "You're better than half the crew I work with now, Cara."

"Aren't we on a crew now?" Cara said, still sounding like she was in shock.

"Yeah," Fran replied. "I guess we are." Nodding, she turned back to the broken bolt. In two minutes, she had the last fragments of steel out of the hull's threads and a replacement tightened into place with the torque wrench.

As he finished the software and power checks, Andy had the battle display up and kept checking the space above them. <*You think those three were a fluke?*> he said.

<*Maybe. Could be they're checking the ships in queue while they've got the fighters tied up.*>

<*We won't be the only ship with defenses.*>

<*No, but we're the only ship with Captain Andy Sykes on its hull—that is if they know now to look for you.*>

<*They didn't get close enough.*>

She shrugged. <*Let's hope. I'm just happy these shitty bolts held on the other cannons.>*

CHAPTER TWENTY-EIGHT

STELLAR DATE: 08.27.2981 (Adjusted Years)
LOCATION: *Sunny Skies*
REGION: Near Cruithne Station, Terran Hegemony

"Zanda," Ngoba Starl whispered. Then louder, "Zaaaaaaanda! Answer me."

The pained voice of Lowspin's leader reached from the overhead speakers throughout *Sunny Skies'* command deck, making Andy think for an instant that Starl was hiding in the ceiling. Fran stopped in the middle of the room with a shocked expression, listening to something over the Lowspin battle net only she could hear.

When she came back, she pulled her hands through her sweaty blond hair and said, "It's him. Starl's alive."

Wherever he was, the only signal being broadcast over Cruithne, its ring and every ship surrounding the station, was Starl's choked voice calling for his rival gang leader, Riggs Zanda to answer him.

"We were boys," he said. "We were friends down in the first sections where the gravity was never right. Sometimes we'd flight and then fall. You were always sick, stumbling around saying the gravity or the lack of oxygen was making your head strange. You were my brother, Zanda. Answer me!"

Cara and Tim sat at what had once been the engineering control console. Tim was reading the book of poetry he'd found somewhere. Cara held a set of oversized headphones squeezed against her ears, checking the various broadcast frequencies around Cruithne, pulling up waveforms on the display and listening in for something interesting.

"Whoever this Zandy guy is," she said, swiping away another wave graph, "he sure doesn't want to answer Mr. Starl. Lots of people are talking about him."

"Oh, yeah?" Andy asked. "What are they saying?"

Cara relaunched a screen she had just closed. Switching it to the overhead speakers, she caught a voice in midsentence saying, "Nah, man, they were like brothers. It's a sad thing. Turned against each other like this. We shouldn't be fighting other Cruithne. It's not right."

"Are we fighting them?" another ragged voice asked. They both sounded like they were talking from cramped spaces. "I haven't seen anything but those damned drones, and word on the street fighting is that it was all private security and off-station mercs."

"Right, private security from Heartbridge that the Havenots have partnered-up with."

"You think Zanda's crew would have set him straight."

"You know he doesn't take criticism from nobody. That was the whole start of their split. When he was Lowspin, he didn't want to listen to anybody."

"Hey, did you see Jandis in the shower this morning? Damn, I'd love to—"

Andy cut the audio feed from his station.

"Dad!" Tim complained.

"That's enough," Andy said. "You want to go back to your room?"

"No," Tim said. "I want to stay up here. But why can't we listen?"

"Some things aren't for kids. That was one of them."

Cara smirked at Tim as he struggled to find an argument.

"Zanda was part of Lowspin?" Andy asked Fran. "Nobody's mentioned that before."

She nodded. "Before Starl became the crewchief, we had a grizzled old mama bear named Chala. I guess she raised Starl and Zanda. Everybody says Lowspin was more of a local crew when she was in charge. Then Zanda and Starl took over when she died and started working their way out, focusing more on short-run pirate attacks, skimming cargo, running contraband between Terra and Mars. It was all stuff other crews had done at one time or another but Chala just hadn't been interested in it."

"Were you part of the crew back then?"

She laughed. "Me? No, I was long haul then. I didn't start working repairs on Cruithne until the hauler I was on got towed into station as scrap. I was stuck on Cruithne and needed a job. Lowspin's been a good gig since then. I don't have to do anything but my job. Doesn't really matter who I call boss. They don't give me a lot of grief about side work, either. Recently, Starl got pissy if I did work for the Havenots, but that hasn't been a big deal."

"How many gangs are there on Cruithne?"

"Depends on how you define gang. A crew like Lowspin, with probably a thousand loosely associated, give or take, and a place to call home in the Span Club, with their own set of repair docks and a flotilla of a hundred ships? That's a big crew. Some might call that a syndicate, an organization, whatever." She grinned. "Starl would like to call it an *institution* but that's wishful thinking. It's not a crew anymore, though. That's just a call-back to the old days. Maybe five like Lowspin."

Fran counted out fingers. "Lowspin. The Havenots, Regal Flight, Iron Core and Rack Thirteen. I guess that's five. There are hundreds of smaller crews, neighborhood to neighborhood covering the various kinds of business someone might be looking for, from drugs to sex to stolen ships. I've got a few different crews I buy parts from. Don't worry too much about where the gear came from as long as it's good quality. Might have even been Lowspin at some point."

"When I was in the TSF, if we did a layout inspection on a squadron, we had to lay out every ship's inventory at the same time or the crew chiefs would steal from each other to make their tool kits straight."

"Some things are universal."

"Zanda!" Starl shouted, voice cracking at the end of the name. "Why don't you answer me? You try to kill me, then don't have the decency to face me. I'm right here, listening. Speak to me!"

"I want to shut him up but I'm worried the next outburst is going to be the last thing he says," Fran complained.

"What's wrong with him?" Tim asked.

"He's hurt," Andy said. "He doesn't know what he's saying. They probably have him on some kind of medicine so he doesn't feel it."

"Medicine makes it so you can't hurt?" Tim asked. "Have you ever used that?"

"Sometimes," Andy said.

"Can I get some of that medicine?"

"You hurt, kiddo? Where?"

"I don't want it now. I want to save it for when you need it. You're always hurting yourself."

Cara barked laughter and Fran gave him a wink, smiling.

"You all think you're pretty funny," Andy said. He glanced at Fran. "What's the status on the message you sent about a separate run?"

She shook her head. "Everybody's held down by the TSF. They're saying not to do anything until they have the drones under control."

"The TSF said that? Who did?"

"They've got somebody on the Port Authority channel sending out orders over the Lowspin battle net. It's the only channel anybody's paying attention to right now."

"So, if we go, we're going alone."

"A couple captains have said they're going anyway and the TSF controller keeps saying they can't guarantee the safety of any ship leaving the approved traffic lanes. Otherwise it's going to be chaos."

"Sure," Andy said, chewing his lip. "I think it would almost be safer to move back into the dock, power down everything but the environmental systems and wait for all this to blow over."

"You really want to get caught in a TSF lockdown? You know that's what they're going to do once they bring in re-enforcements. The whole station is a crime scene. Nobody's getting in or out. This is our only real chance to leave, and even then I'm worried about what's going to happen when you show up at Mars 1. You can't hide where you came from."

"We don't have to go to Mars 1 immediately."

"You need to get there somewhat immediately. You'll need to refuel before you head on to Jupiter. Have you thought about where you're going once you hit the Jupiter's vicinity?"

"I've been to Kalyke a few times. They know me there, but it won't create problems. At least I don't think it will."

"Don't owe anybody money?"

"Not currently," Andy said.

"I like Kalyke," Cara said. "We got ice cream in their main station. It had strawberries in it. They said they grew them there."

"You know you could grow strawberries right here on your ship, if you wanted to," Fran said.

Cara's eyes got wide. "We could? Where? In mom's old garden room?" She looked at Andy. "Dad, I want to do that? Why haven't we done that?"

"Time and capital, kiddo," Andy said. He was trying to make sense of the holodisplay as it shifted to capture each attack wave between the TSF fighters and Heartbridge's drones. Although he thought he had spied a few human-piloted ships in the Heartbridge swarm now, which made him wonder if the TSF was finally wearing them down.

Starl's voice rang out wetly in a new appeal. "Zanda! I waited for you all night after that first job, bleeding in the alley with that kid's knife in my gut. You said you'd come back with mama but you never did. I waited for you until I learned I was going to have to drag myself home. I learned then. I should have remembered." He drew a long, difficult breath. "I remember that girl you loved, Zanda."

"Will they get this asshole in an autodoc already?" Fran muttered. She glanced back at the kids and said, "Sorry."

"All this time, Zanda," Starl said. "All this time I thought I had a brother. I thought if nothing else in this life made sense, that if we are surrounded by the vacuum of death like the priest said, at least on our little rock of Cruithne, we had brotherhood, friendship. We could build something. Eke out our places. There could be law to stand on."

Fran rolled her eyes and looked ready to turn off the channel, when her eyes glazed and she stared into the distance as new information came over the battle net.

"We stood together, Zanda. Do you remember when we talked about leaving Cruithne? Do you remember when we were ready to throw a dart into that old astromap of Sol and find some new place? Take our little crew and our ships and go build our own world. We were tired of the oppression, the poverty, the cruelty. You said—" Starl laughed but fell into coughing. "You said we could find a place. A place! There is no place to call home. You run and you run. If you aren't willing to fight where you stand, there will be no peace. That's what I used to believe. Anyway. It's too much. Maybe all we can do is run. Maybe we should help others when they ask for our help. When they want to find a home."

"It's a cover," Fran said quickly. Her hands flew over the console as she pulled up a new overlay on the holodisplay. The TSF ships grew indistinct and hundreds of ships grew brighter. "Starl just transmitted your destination."

"Where?" Andy demanded, voice harsher than he'd intended.

"Wait. Are you ready to copy?"

Andy switched to a new display and pulled up the astrogration map. He nodded.

Fran read off the coordinates and the mapping software flew through the solar system, past Mars, Jupiter, and Saturn. Andy expected the blinking point marker to slow down at some point but it only sped up, blurring past Uranus. It stopped on Neptune and shifted right to a moon which the NSAI identified as Proteus.

Staring at the display, Andy blinked in disbelief. "Read that again," he said.

Fran read the numbers. He'd entered them correctly.

"We can't go that far. It'll take months. Just the fuel alone would wipe me out. I don't have the funds. And Starl hasn't paid me yet for all this crap we're going through right now."

"Proteus," Fran mused. "There's a research station out there. That's all I've ever heard of. Probably something else related to the drone mines on Neptune."

Andy switched screens and pulled up the public information on Neptune and its flurry of moons. Several private companies had listings for mine operators and one travel agency offered trips to Makemake, 'The diamond of the Scattered Disk.'

Andy shook his head. "Solve that problem when it's closer," he muttered. "I can't get spun up about this now. We need to get out of here."

Nodding, Fran said, "They've identified a vanguard to break toward Mars 1. Lowspin is going to provide us cover."

"How many ships?" Andy asked.

"Fifty at first. Then all of them. Everything is going to Mars."

"Has the TSF said if they've made any headway against the drones?"

"Apparently, they're running against close attack fighters now, so they think they're getting closer to the *Benevolent Hand*."

"So, there might be some piracy today after all?"

"I'm surprised nobody's breached yet. All the dogfighting has been perfect cover to drop EV teams on the skin of their ship."

"Maybe no one's talking about it?"

"Not on the Lowspin net. I wouldn't be surprised if that was kept quiet. If you're trying to get a head start on everybody else, you don't want to talk about it on the open channel."

"Right. Is there a timeline to move yet?"

"Fifteen minutes," Fran said. She tapped the console and a countdown timer appeared above the holo of Cruithne.

"We're leaving in fifteen minutes?" Cara said. "Is that when we're going to burn, or just getting ready?"

"Once we're outside Cruithne's rad-free zone, we'll burn," Andy said. "Have you guys stowed everything you need?"

Tim got a guilty expression. "We didn't put away the things in the kitchen."

"You need to check all that," Andy said. "Then your room. You go do that, and I'll check on you."

Cara nodded, and Tim huffed, but they both turned and left the command deck.

"You think we should dose Petral again?" Andy asked when the kids were gone. "I don't want her coming-to in the middle of some hard g."

"Probably be good for her," Fran said. "Yeah, I guess it wouldn't hurt." She had switched off the holo of Cruithne and its roiling space traffic and brought up the engine diagnostic display. "I'm worried about a couple checks on the engines if we're going to bring them up to full burn. I didn't get to run full diagnostics."

"Is there anything we can do about it if we get failures?"

Fran gave him a hurt look. "I'm disgusted you would say that, Captain Sykes. I can fix everything but that containment failure you managed to bring about. You might as well have set off a bomb in your containment bottle."

"I tried," Andy said.

Fran looked from the console to Andy, giving him a crooked smile. "I'm teasing you. Listen, can you leave the command deck to help me with this? It's really a two-person job."

Andy checked the timer. "All right," he said. "Let's go."

In the background, Starl continued to moan and babble, keeping up his performance.

Leaving the command deck, Fran led the way out of the habitat to the inner airlock. She checked her tool harness as they waited for the lock to cycle. When she appeared satisfied, she ran her hands through her hair and retied the band around her pony tail. Once again, she caught Andy watching her.

"Keep your eyes to yourself, sailor," she said.

Andy shrugged. "I don't have anywhere else to put them. You'll have to deal with it."

"You're getting a stress response."

"Stress response?"

"It happens when people think they're going to die. They have sex."

"I've never heard that."

"Tell me it never happened in the TSF, then? There's a lot of sex in the TSF."

"There's a lot of sex in any huge organization."

"I'm talking about places where people are in danger all the time."

"So, you're saying you don't think we're going to get out of this?" Andy asked. "Weren't you calling *me* a pessimist not too long ago?"

Fran dropped her hands from the back of her head and smoothed out the front of her coverall. "I don't want you getting any ideas, is all."

"I'll be honest," Andy said. "Sex is the last thing I've been thinking about."

Fran rolled her eyes.

The airlock opened and they kicked off into the zero-*g* section of the ship. Passing the locker where he had stashed the TSF weapons crate, Andy noticed the lock was untouched.

"Hey," he said, pointing at the locker. "I forgot to say anything about it before. This locker has weapons in it."

"There you go being a pessimist again," Fran said.

"I'm just letting you know."

Andy kicked off to catch up with Fran, who was already halfway down the corridor. They reached the chute between levels and descended toward the engine control decks. Fran led the way past two sets of open doors that could provide containment in the event of another bottle breach in the engines. Then they passed through the third, which opened into a large u-shaped space with the engine diagnostic panel jutting into its center, and she pushed the door closed and rolled the locking wheel.

Floating behind her, Andy said, "Why'd you do that?"

"I wanted privacy," Fran said.

She pushed away from the door and floated into Andy, grabbing him around the waist to press herself against him.

"Are you drunk?" he asked. They rotated together until she bumped into the control console.

"Shut up," Fran breathed.

She reached into Andy's hair and pulled his face toward her. Her kiss was confident and hot, even hungry. Seated on the console, she wrapped her legs around his waist and pulled him in closer.

"You're not letting me get away, are you?" he asked, wiping a corner of his mouth.

Fran unfastened the clip on the front of her harness and unzipped her coverall down to her bellybutton, showing only caramel skin underneath.

"It's the zero-g," she said into his neck. "You can't be tentative about this sort of thing."

"Does this mean you don't think we're going to make it?"

"You need to stop saying that."

Fran unbuttoned the front of his shipsuit and drew the zipper down so she could put her hands on his chest. She examined him like an interesting piece of equipment.

"I didn't expect chest hair," she said.

"That's my poor-kid-on-Earth upbringing. No time for cosmetic surgeries."

She dragged her hands down his chest, warming her palms. "I like it. You're like a puppy dog." She reached inside his coverall to grab the top of his ass, then pulled her hands back around, dragging her palms across his skin.

"You, with your kids and your ship, and these abs," Fran said, pressing her thumbs into his stomach. "You don't even realize how hot you are. God, I love it."

"I was thinking it was malnutrition," Andy said, smirking.

Fran kissed him again, biting his lip, and let him push her coverall down around her waist.

Her shoulders, breasts and stomach were covered in fine white scars, standing out like crisscrossed needles against her tan skin.

Before Andy could ask what they were from, he stiffened in surprise as Fran pushed a hand down the front of his coverall and grabbed him.

"I'd say we should hurry," Fran said, kicking off the rest of her coverall and then reaching with her free hand to pull his off as well. "But I don't want to."

Andy took the band out of her hair and flicked it away so her hair floated around her shoulders, half-covering her gray-blue eyes.

Fran wrapped her legs around Andy's waist again, locking her heels together. She reached behind her to grab at two handholds on the console, holding them in place as their clothes floated free around them.

"So, this means the engines are good to go?" Andy breathed into her neck.

"Yes, you dolt," Fran said.

When Andy came—Fran gasping in his ear, their sweaty bodies clutched together, the muscles in her thighs and calves taught as he pushed deeper into her—he heard a whisper in the back of his mind, what might have been a surprised "Oh," that didn't rise to actual thought, a feeling, a recognition.

<Lyssa?> he asked.

Like a coin falling, flipping, drifting to the bottom of a long well, the spark of thought disappeared in the dark, leaving him uncertain it had ever existed at all, feeling only a vague sense of loneliness and fear that he couldn't touch a part of his own mind.

PART 5: BURN

CHAPTER TWENTY-NINE
STELLAR DATE: 9.10.2963 (Adjusted Years)
LOCATION: TSS *Aggression's Cost*
REGION: Near the Mars Protectorate Border, InnerSol

Eighteen Years Earlier

Waiting in the hallway prior to mission briefing, Andy shot Brit a smirk. "You know," he said, "you never did tell me why you decided to help me out back during first year?"

"In the academy? Yes, I have." Brit completed the functions check on her pulse rifle and slung it over her shoulder, then ran through the pockets on her uniform touching each of the various knives she insisted on carrying.

"I don't remember you mentioning how hot I am," Andy said.

"Sure," she said, sliding a K-bar with a black blade half out of its sheath before pushing it back home and fastening the leather handle in place. "You want to know why? Here it is. My family had a brown lab growing up. You reminded me of him."

Andy frowned. "Brown lab? You had a dog on High Terra?"

"Lots of people have dogs on High Terra. Why wouldn't they?"

"I guess I never thought about dogs in space before."

Brit rolled her eyes. "High Terra isn't really space. It has more land than Earth. Besides, dogs went into space before humans did."

"Sure, professor. I've never seen a dog on High Terra."

"You never leave the TSF post. Maybe I'll take you home one of these days. There are plenty of dogs in my parents' neighborhood."

Andy made a show of staring into the distance as if the opposite wall were some vista. "I think humans leaving Earth just became real to me. I never thought about pets in space before."

"There have been dogs on settlements from the beginning. For seven hundred years at least."

"Just because you say that doesn't mean I've seen them, or that I believe it."

"You're such a lab. Next you're going to tell me the Earth is flat."

"High Terra's flat. That kind of makes you a flat-Earther."

"Shut up," Brit growled. "Plus, it's not *really* flat."

Assigned to the TSS *Aggression's Cost*, an InnerSol battle cruiser with ten on-board light fighter squadrons, a rail gun and a stand-off missile range of a half an AU, the ship had been completing interdiction missions to disrupt the piracy between Earth and Mars.

They had been on the anti-piracy task force for three months since leaving the

Academy and yet sometimes she seemed like a different person. While most people would call them a couple, she still refused to call him her boyfriend even when crawling into his bunk after lights out to push her face into his chest. They had been sleeping together since the second year of the Academy, sneaking off to find hidden places in the surrounding woods, but something kept Brit from admitting to the world that they had paired off.

For Andy, the arrangement wasn't much different from what he'd seen in Summerville growing up. His parents had been the exception when it came to adult relationships. Most of the people in his apartment building, or those nearby, fell into and out of affairs, had kids, stayed together or didn't. That was how people had been living for nearly a thousand years. Even though he didn't want to be with anybody else, he didn't own Brit any more than she was willing to commit to him. He could do what he wanted. And he did at least once a month, which led to Brit sulking and picking fights without admitting what was truly bothering her.

After a year in flight school, which included body augments to allow higher g, their sorties made Andy feel like a demi-god. Most of the enemy ships couldn't stand against a coordinated TSF attack. Even though they had flown in the black dozens of times, their missions started with a briefing, going over intercepted transmissions, personnel data if known, followed by ship capabilities—then as much time, often more on anyone who had fallen victim to the pirates. The TSF seemed to fear their pilots and soldiers would stop caring about the mission at some point, and went out of their way to make sure everyone understood just why they were on a year-long deployment to keep shipping lanes safe.

The door to the briefing room slid open and the off-going shift walked into the corridor looking dirty and fatigued. Two pilots Andy knew from flight school slapped him on the shoulder and winked in Brit's direction. She kept her hard blue eyes on the opposite wall, ignoring them. When the group had passed them by, it was time for their squadron to file into the narrow room.

Andy took his preferred seat in the second row and waited as the mission planner—a captain named Transon whose face had been burned in combat and purposefully left half-melted—made notes on the chart holoprojection shimmering against the front wall. As usual, the target area looked like empty space until Transon turned his back to the seats and made some view adjustments. When he stepped out of the way, the center of the holodisplay showed the misshapen lump of an asteroid tumbling in space.

"We going mining, sir?" one of the other pilots called from the back of the room. "I'm no good at that shit."

The captain didn't answer. When he was satisfied with the chart, he turned to the room and crossed his arms, waiting for everyone to file in and take their seats. "Hurry up," he said. "I'm not waiting all morning."

Brit liked to sit in the front row at the side of the room during briefings. This meant Andy could watch her expression as she absorbed the information. Something about her face as she nodded with the briefing, graphics from the holodisplay reflected in her eyes, wiped out Andy's ability to focus. He was lucky that some part of his mind did pick up the attack vectors, munition types and release zones as he watched Brit from the corner of his vision.

He knew, even then, that something in the core of their relationship wasn't quite rotten but was off-balance just enough to leave him dizzy when he should have been sure of himself. He wouldn't recognize the flaw until years later, even then only remembering specific times and realizing how they hadn't been working.

During the mission briefing for Object 8221, the base of operations for a pirate gang calling themselves the Mortons, Andy was too far gone in the shape of her body, the memory of her sweat and breath and how she gripped him and barely let him go, to understand that anything could ever go wrong. The future didn't really exist for him then. There was the mission, the fight, and afterward Brit's body to work off his unspent adrenaline.

"All right," Transon said, glaring at the group of cocky pilots. "This is going to be different than all the other sweep-and-burn playdates you lazy idiots are used to. They've got hostages."

He motioned at the wall and the faces of three kids appeared next to Object 8221. "These kids are Kylan, Yandi and Urvin Carthage. You might recognize that name from Carthage InnerSol Shipping. Their mother, Kathryne Carthage, is owner and CEO, and these three curtain climbers are the only living scions of the family. They die, the company's future goes into the shitter, along with its stock prices. They can't guarantee stability for the thousand-year contracts they've sold, and all hell breaks loose in the shipping industry."

He waved the pictures away. Scratching the mottled skin next to his mouth, he said, "I don't pretend to understand that shit. What it means for us is that the usual MO of carpet bombing a pirate home base isn't going to work in this situation. Insurance isn't going to pay out the cargo you burn up. We'll be dividing the squadron into fireteams. Fireteam One will establish a base of fire to draw off the mobile defenses, which looks like a mix of heavy freighters and light attack ships, while Fireteam two takes on the fixed defenses, breaches the base and recovers the hostages."

Silence followed his statement. The spinning asteroid in the middle of the holodisplay immediately became a thousand times more interesting than it had been. It had gone from a faceless bit of space rock to their potential grave.

Eventually, someone from behind Andy said, "We got Marines for this, sir?"

"Marines? You've been trained in urban combat, right? It's in all your files. Nothing special about this."

Andy nodded, biting his lower lip as he considered what had been said. The captain was right: they'd had the training. He'd spent three weeks breaching the interior corridor of a mock freighter in stick team formations, checking doors and corners, lobbing flash grenades, using interior sonar and other scanning devices. He'd been team leader on several training missions and done well enough. What he'd taken away from the training was that he never wanted to fight any kind of urban combat.

"How long have the kids been on the base?" Brit said.

"Two days," Transon replied.

"How old are they?" she asked.

"The boys are twelve and eight. The girl, Yandi, is thirteen," the captain said.

Andy caught the tick in Brit's jaw.

"Put me on Fireteam two," she said. "I want to breach."

Transon raised his eyebrows. "Now, that's interesting. A pilot with some fucking courage. Who's going with her?"

Andy considered waiting to raise his hand but knew he couldn't. He didn't bother looking around the room. "I'll go," he said.

"Good, Sykes. Who else?"

More raised their hands until Transon had enough volunteers to fill his breach team. He checked their names against the squadron roster then nodded. "Good. Here's some other news I neglected to tell you. The mom has offered bonuses to anyone who enters the base to help save her kids." He flashed an evil smile. "So, for all you heroes, if you survive, you might come out rich. That sounds pretty good, yeah?"

His burned face made the statement lose any inspirational quality it made have offered. His eyes were never completely sarcastic or serious.

"Here's the timeline," Transon said, slapping his tablet. "Eight hours for a bit more rest. We'll be in burn during that time. Load out in nine hours. Final technical checks and then you'll depart for the station in squadron formation as *Aggression's Cost* starts long range bombardment to soften their outer defenses. Depending on what we get from that, Fireteam One will close to draw out their mobile defenses as we discussed. Once Fireteam One is decisively engaged, Two will move in to conduct the breach. We don't have a good interior scan on the object yet. If I have that information nine hours from now, I'll share it with you. Otherwise, conduct scans to determine habitable areas and make your on-ground decision from there."

"Are we going to split the breach team?" Brit said.

Transon nodded. "You could do that. Don't want choke points. Honestly, you need to do what looks best once you're close enough to make a decision. Don't go cutting into their power plant."

"What do we know about this gang?" Andy asked.

"We thought they were typical long-range smash-and-grab type. Then they pulled this off. The kids were on a lightly-armed yacht en route to Ceres. They overwhelmed the yacht, killed the crew and grabbed the ankle biters. They have to have been on a hard burn to reach their base in just three days. We don't have good intel on the ships they used for the kidnapping but that's not important. We have good evidence the kids are on this object."

"We know they're alive?" Brit said, voice cold.

"We do. They sent a ransom demand and verified status with a tissue sample."

"Tissue sample?" somebody asked.

"A finger," Transon said. "We think it was Kylan's."

"Damn," Andy said.

"He's lucky," Transon said. "His mom can grow him a whole new body as long

164

as we get his brain back in reasonable condition. I'm not showing the usual touchy-feely crap because you aren't going to need it this time. These kids need our help. I don't care that they're rich fuckers. That's not their fault. We're *Aggression's Cost* and we're going to get them back in one piece. Yeah?"

The squadron responded with a booming, "Yes, sir!" that reminded Andy why he liked the TSF. There were times when he really felt like he was one of the good guys.

He watched Brit shout with the rest of them but her face was still flat and cold, gaze staring ahead as if she saw something terrible in the holodisplay that no one else could.

CHAPTER THIRTY

STELLAR DATE: 08.27.2981 (Adjusted Years)
LOCATION: *Sunny Skies*
REGION: Cruithne Station, Terran Hegemony

"We're clear," Fran said from the second console. "Out of the lane and tempting fate."

Andy checked the flight plan for the third time. He looked at the kids across the room. Cara met his eyes and gave him a small smile. He could see in her face that she was having a hard time just sitting there keeping Tim busy. She seemed to have aged a year since they arrived on Cruithne, while he couldn't tell where Tim had gone. Sometimes it seemed like he was sliding backwards into being a toddler again.

Petral's wounds had gone deeper than the autodoc had seen on the first pass. After a second scan, the system found her liver crushed and she'd lost kidney function. While *Sunny Skies'* med system could regrow the damaged organs, it was going to take weeks. She might not wake from the medical coma by the time they reached Mars 1 and there was no chance of her leaving early with Fran in the shuttle.

The flight plan returned clean, as it had the first two checks. The main danger was the traffic density all around Cruithne. the *Benevolent Hand* had pulled back another ten thousand kilometers, apparently to give them more stand-off distance against the attacking TSF waves. Their slowed responses pointed toward Lowspin breaching teams already fighting through the corporate battle cruiser.

Andy's gaze hung on the coordinates for Mars. Before Cruithne and Fran's overhaul, there was no way *Sunny Skies* could have managed this level of initial burn. He hesitated, hands hanging above the controls.

"Everything all right?" Fran said.

"I can't help thinking I'm about to tear the ship apart," he said.

Fran raised an eyebrow. "Don't trust my work?"

"I do. It's hard to forget how I was feeling when we came into Cruithne. I lose the ship, I lose everything."

"We stay here, we lose everything,"

"Maybe," Andy said.

"Aren't we going, Dad?" Cara said.

Andy nodded, not taking his eyes of the numbers on his screen. He tapped the command.

There was no immediate change. Fran stared into space for a second, most likely communicating their status change to the battle net. When her eyes came back into focus, she turned to Andy and said, "Confirmed. Lowspin also sent an update on the *Benevolent Hand*. They've breached the ship. Teams are fighting through their lower decks, headed for the command section."

"Fight well," Andy said, still focused on the incoming data from the drive systems. *Sunny Skies* was coming to life in ways he hadn't seen before. The shields had activated in tandem as the engines came on line, something he used to have to time manually. The point defense cannons were coordinating with the sensor arrays, shifting between potential targets that were identified as TSF and civilian ships without him needing to scan through in a frantic race against the outdated automatic system, overriding non-targets.

"What's wrong with you?" Fran said. "You look like your heart's racing. Breathe."

"You don't understand. Everything's working. It's never been like this. Not even when we bought it. Every time we burned, it was like holding up a house of cards."

Fran put her hands behind her head and leaned back, grinning at him. "I told you. Trust me."

Her face as she said the words 'trust me' was more open than it had been before, her eyes holding on his.

Acceleration set in, pressing Andy into his seat. He looked over at the kids and made sure their posture was correct, heads back and arms in the armrests. Tim was humming to himself, staring up at the ceiling.

Andy let his head fall back so he didn't have to fight against the acceleration any more. A wave of fatigue rolled over him, probably the blood constricting in his veins. They had an hour of acceleration before reaching the delta-v they'd need for most of the trip, a testament to Fran's engine upgrades. If the systems held, reaching Proteus would be a real possibility.

Thinking about the moon made him wonder about Lyssa. Since the flash in the engine room, any attempt to reach her met only silence. He wished he had some kind of meter or sensor to let him know she was even there. What if she had somehow "died" during the surgery. Was that possible? It would be easier to understand if he'd been implanted with a simple storage device carrying the AI, but Jickson had specifically said he would find another mind living inside his head, experiencing his body to a certain extent, walking with him.

His eyes felt dry as he stared at the holodisplay, trying to pull it back into focus as his vision clouded. Points of light marking other freighters and cargo ships were blinking out as they left alongside them. The TSF fighters continued to buzz like angry hornets, looping around the gray clouds of drones that had grown smaller, reforming at times, then splitting apart.

<*Starl,*> he said over the Link. The gang's leader had gone quiet twenty minutes before, just as the first freighters started their burns away from Cruithne. He imagined the overall traffic patterns out of the station looking like a dandelion fluff, flight paths shooting away in all directions.

He hadn't seen a dandelion since leaving Summerville.

<*Starl,*> he said. <*You there?*>

<*I hear you, Captain,*> came the response, compressed as if crossing long distances. <*Have you started your burn?*>

<*We just started. I thought you were going insane there at first.*>

A low laugh answered. <*Maybe I was. I'm not in good shape, my friend. Lowspin's Brutal Dandy won't be as pretty as he was for quite a while. Maybe it's going to be a good time to be ugly.*>

<*Modern science can fix all that.*>

<*Maybe. Maybe I'll hang onto it. Make it my own brand of handsome. That's power, yeah? Change the definition of beautiful.*>

<*I haven't heard anything from the AI, Starl. Are you sure the surgery was successful? Did Jickson say anything before he died?*>

<*It was successful. Otherwise they wouldn't be fighting like they are. They're afraid. They fear what you'll do.*>

<*I got the coordinates. What's on Proteus?*>

<*Others like her.*>

Andy considered the words. <*How are AI managing to hide out on Proteus and why would they want to do that? Don't they need things to do?*>

<*These are Sentient AI, Captain Sykes. You never heard of them?*>

<*I've heard they exist in labs. I've never heard of anyone using one for anything useful.*>

Starl laughed. <*Aren't all you TSF supposed to be geniuses? What do you mean a Sentient AI won't do anything useful? You think they get dumber when they can think for themselves?*>

<*I think there's nothing to stop a Sentient AI from being as useless as your average person. Look at what this company Heartbridge is doing to us right now. You think just because something started life running a washing machine they're going to be more moral and noble than your average human? I think they're going to have anger issues, to be honest with you. They're slaves, right?*>

<*Maybe you're starting to understand, then,*> Starl said. <*Maybe you're answering your own question. Humans are shitty. Sentient AI might be shitty. Not all of us are the same, yeah? You have to shake the barrel and see what rises to the top.*>

<*So I'm taking this one to Proteus. What do I do when I get there? Who am I supposed to contact?*>

<*You'll know. There won't be any problem with that.*>

<*Do they know I'm coming, at least?*>

<*You're not the only one coming. They'll be expecting you.*>

<*Tell me this. Is that battle cruiser back there the only present I can expect from Heartbridge?*>

<*That man Cal Kraft who was walking beside Zanda back at the club. If we don't kill him on the* Benevolent Hand, *yes, you **will** need to worry about him.*>

<*Then I do need to worry about him,*> Andy repeated. <*Where's he from?*>

<*He was with SolGov for a while, I think. Some office called Long Range Stabilization Projects. He's a settlement killer. A genocider. Just like you and your anti-piracy raids.*>

<*I never committed any genocide,*> Andy said, abruptly angry. <*Choose your words.*>

Starl chuckled. <*You have your view, I have mine. That's one reason I can't understand Zanda working with this man. He's killed many, many of our kind.*>

<It's the money?>

<Maybe. Always maybe.>

<Did he respond to you?>

<He did. He told me to quit crying like a baby. That's what emotion gets you, Captain Sykes. You open yourself to others and that's what you get.> He sighed. *<I keep doing it. I'll never stop. Maybe I'll be burned for a while so they can see what my kindness got me in return. When the war comes, they'll know who sacrificed for them at the beginning.>*

<You keep saying that,> Andy said. *<What war?>*

<If you can't see it now, you will soon. It's coming. You'll need to choose sides, Captain Sykes. For your children, I think. It won't be as easy as you might think.>

<You're sounding crazy right now, Starl.>

<Maybe I am. Ugly and crazy. I'm sending your money, Captain Sykes. All of it. We don't need to play with half-payments. You have your destination. I need you to get there as soon as you can, by whatever route you can take. How's your ship running? Fran do good work?>

<She did good work.>

Starl coughed. *<Excellent. Like I told you, I'll have work for you later, after we get this done. You find your way back to Cruithne. You've already got the suit.>* Laughter filled his voice. *<Imagine that—our own TSF veteran in the Lowspin. We're moving up.>*

<I'm not turning to piracy any time soon,> Andy said.

<Always maybe. I'll talk to you soon, Captain Sykes. Peace.>

The Link cut off before Andy could answer. He blinked at the holodisplay, now only showing Cruithne and the *Benevolent Hand*. He pulled up a menu he didn't check very often and queried his credit accounts in the bank he used for InnerSol transactions.

The first account number showed a new deposit. Andy stared at it for a second, forgetting to breathe. It was twice what Starl had promised, easily enough to fund fuel out to Proteus and back, and pay for private school for both the kids for twenty years.

He quickly transferred the money into a new account run out of a bank on Ceres that no one else could access and then sank in his seat, thinking about what he would do with the funds. He had a few debts to pay. After that, he couldn't even think what he would do. The repairs on *Sunny Skies* had always been at the top of any list of priorities. With that taken care of, he didn't know what should take precedence. Buy an apartment somewhere? Where would they go?

<You all right?> Fran asked. *<You look like somebody just punched you in the gut.>*

<Sort of. I just finished talking to Starl. He started sounding like some kind of prophet toward the end.>

<Typical.>

<Any update from the attack on the Benevolent Hand?>

<Nothing. Everybody's focused on getting away from Cruithne. I think the teams hitting the battle cruiser switched over to a local net. Not that they're really in coordination, anyway. I can't hear the TSF unless they broadcast on a public channel.>

<Right.> He pulled the holodisplay with Cruithne and the *Benevolent Hand* back

into the center of his display. *<I want to see that shark-looking battle cruiser explode into a little sun just for Cruithne. They can roast marshmallows off their airlocks.>*

<We just passed four hundred thousand kilometers,> Fran said. *<Earth to the moon.>*

<Drive systems look good. Environmental is green. The shields are still at maximum radiance. I think we could almost go to sleep.>

Fran shot him a look, then slid her gaze toward the kids.

<They don't have the Link, remember?>

She raised her eyebrows. *<So I can get as dirty as I want and they won't be able to hear me?>*

<Well, Cara did find a way to go voice-to-Link when Starl first came on board. I need to ask her how she did that.>

<So they can hear us?>

<Maybe.> The word reminded him of Starl.

<Then she's listening right now. She's been listening the whole time.> Fran looked at Cara, who appeared to be studying her console intently. *<Cara!>* she said sharply.

Cara couldn't help jumping in her seat. She looked at Andy and Fran, eyes frantic.

Andy groaned. *<Well, that's good to know.>*

"I haven't been listening the whole time," Cara said quickly. "I promise."

"Then what have you been listening to?" Fran said aloud. "I could see from your intense expression over there you were eavesdropping on someone."

"I don't know who it is. I think it might be that other ship, the one attacking Cruithne."

"You mean the *Benevolent Hand*?" Andy asked. "They're attacking everyone. Including us. Or they were."

Cara nodded. "I think it's one of their maintenance channels. It's not encrypted like the others. They're talking about hull pressure and something about drive economy."

"The drives?" Fran said. "That could mean they're about to—"

In the holodisplay in front of Andy, the long shape of the *Benevolent Hand* blurred and disappeared.

Andy closed the display showing Cruithne and ran a scan for all objects leaving the surrounding space. The scan locked on *Benevolent Hand*, the largest moving object, and measured a vector. When the data gave him a projected destination, he swallowed hard.

"They're heading for Mars 1," he said. "They're following us."

CHAPTER THIRTY-ONE
STELLAR DATE: 9.11.2963 (Adjusted Years)
LOCATION: Object 8221
REGION: Near the Mars Protectorate Border, InnerSol

Eighteen Years Earlier

Aggression's Cost fought off a steady barrage of missiles and long-range fighters as it approached Object 8221. There was no way to hide the squadron's advance. The battle cruiser could try to draw the pirates out, or get them to hold off for the fight when the fireteams arrived.

When the battle cruiser reached a stand-off distance of five hundred thousand kilometers, it launched the two fireteams Captain Transon had assigned the mission.

Brit and Andy were in a drop ship as part of Fireteam two, which Transon had decided to send as a mixed deployment of close-attack fighters and three Armadillo Class drop ships with breaching teams.

Fireteam One went in hot. They would complete strafing runs to draw out any remaining close fighters the pirates deployed in response, until *Aggression's Cost* had a better picture of their capabilities. Then the breaching teams would burn and brake, landing at assigned points across Object 8221's circumference in areas intelligence had deemed most likely to serve as habitat on the asteroid.

"They're going to kill those kids," a short-haired lieutenant named Arsel sitting across from them complained, staring down the disassembled barrel of her projectile rifle. She held the tube up to the single overhead light then dropped it across her knees to rub the steel with an oiled cloth. It was busy work. Everyone in the small bay was engaged in their own version.

Brit shook her head. "If they were going to kill them, they would have done it when we first hit their long-range scans. They think they can take us. They haven't tried to run, so that means they're going to stand and fight."

"Can they?" Arsel said. "When was the last time we took on a station?"

"It's an object," Andy said.

"It's a fortress in the middle of nowhere," Arsel countered. "There's no telling what we're going to find when we get into that place." She slid her K-bar knife out of her thigh sheath and turned the black blade in the light. "I don't care if those kids are dead. Me, I'll be in corridors cutting throats."

"Hooah," someone said down the line without looking up.

Arsel nodded and slid the knife back home.

"I'll be right behind you," Brit said. "I've got no mercy for child molesters. I just don't want to end up in some trap only to find out there were never any kids to begin with."

"The kids are real," Andy said. He'd been studying Carthage InnerSol, their shipping routes between High Terra, Mercury, Mars and sometimes Cruithne. They were branching out to Jupiter as well. They moved mostly calorie stock, ice, and other food stuffs, playing a tight game with pricing and demand that had a devastating impact on isolated settlements. It looked to him like the pirates had other reasons than ransom to punish CEO Kathryne Carthage.

Andy set those thoughts aside as extra information. He didn't have space in his mind right now for moral questions about the citizens they were here to save. Soon enough, he would need to make split-second decisions that would cost lives. He knew if he brought the info up to the rest of them it would only make him look soft. Most of the TSF weren't interested in humanizing the enemy.

The pilot came over the intercom and said, "Fireteam One has established their base of fire at a stand-off distance of a thousand klicks. We're cleared for approach. I'm still showing significant point defense weapons and possible remaining attack fighters ready to say hello. Stay buckled in until we're on surface and I complete the breach."

"You gonna kiss us goodbye, Dad?" somebody shouted.

"You can kiss my ass on the way out, how's that?"

Everyone laughed at the bad joke, bleeding off tension. Andy kept his hands on his rifle where it rested between his knees, muzzle pointed at the ceiling. He worked his jaw back and forth, testing his helmet's motion. He could have logged into Fireteam One's battle net to get a better sense of the close fight around Object 8221 but he reminded himself again that he didn't need extra information clouding his thoughts. He glanced at Brit, whose hard blue eyes stared straight ahead. She drummed her fingers on her rifle's barrel, tapping a boot to some internal rhythm. She kept her jaw clenched, which made her face look angular and hard, almost like a skull.

The ship dropped straight down at least fifty meters, sending Andy's stomach through his throat. The drop was followed by a hard-braking maneuver that threw him sideways against his seat harness. Scraping noises ran the length of the wall at his back, as if chaff and kinetics were bouncing against the drop ship's hull.

"It's hot out there," the pilot said.

Hard acceleration threw them back in their seats, then weightlessness as the ship's nose pitched forward and seemed to dive. Andy realized how disoriented he was when the ship abruptly jerked hard and stopped, attached to the surface of Object 8221.

"Took me a little longer to match their delta-v than I thought it would," the pilot's scratchy voice explained. "Had a point defense cannon try to strafe us near the end. We're under their close-in defenses now. I'm starting the plasma torches."

A low buzzing noise came from the rear of the troop area where the exterior blast doors sat. Andy couldn't tell if he'd felt or imagined a vibration in his seat as the cutting torches did their work.

Everyone in the bay checked their armor's seals and looked over the men and women next to them. The Armadillo should make an air-tight seal to the object...but under fire, a blowout was a real possibility.

"You better save my ass before your girlfriend's, Sykes," Arsel said as Andy checked over Carser in the seat next to him.

He glanced over to find Arsel staring at him.

She gave him a feral grin. "Maybe I'll take you back to my bunk when this is over, show you how it's done. I've got something you can hold onto."

Brit rolled her eyes. "You do what you want to," she said.

"Oh, yeah?" Arsel asked. She raised her eyebrows in invitation toward Andy. "I thought she'd have a little more fight in her."

"I'm saving it for what's out there," Brit replied.

"Nothing better than fucking after fighting, right Sykes?" Arsel said.

Andy gave her a smirk but didn't play into the spat. He focused on keeping his mind clear. He imagined the blast doors pulling back, revealing a corridor or maintenance bay. The immediate fire from some inside team. He wrapped his hand around a grenade hanging from his armor's harness and rubbed the control nubs, feeling them through the thin finger pads on his gloves, memorizing their pattern.

"One minute!" the pilot announced.

The bay filled with the sounds of the breaching team throwing off their seat harnesses and moving into a ready position. Behind him, several soldiers ran their rifles through final function checks. The long beep of a pulse pistol powering up reminded him of his dad's alarm clock in the morning.

Brit was closer to the door. She didn't look back at him.

The overhead light switched from white to red and the four successive explosions sounded from the other side of the blast doors. Five more seconds of silence followed as everyone gripped their weapons in the red-tinted dark, until the blast doors slid open.

"Exit!" the pilot barked. "Exit! Off my ship! Ready to depart station."

The seal was good, but not perfect as air hissed out around the door's edges. The first two soldiers tossed grenades through the opening and two flash bursts and a cloud of smoke blew back in the bay. Andy slid his face plate down and took a deep breath as his helmet's respirator switched on automatically. The air tasted like plastic.

In another heartbeat, he was running into the smoke with his rifle up, shifting his attention between the corridor in front of him and the lines taking shape inside his face shield. Flattening against a wall, he crouched and brought his rifle to his shoulder, ready for incoming fire.

The team leaders sent out micro-probes into the air, but bright flashes of light signaled their demise.

"Electronic countermeasures," team two's leader called out. "Mark I eyeballs only."

The breach team separated into four bounding teams. Andy was on team three. Brit had ended up near the front of the corridor and fell in with team one.

"Moving!" the team one leader shouted. In well-practiced formations, they alternated between covering each other and moving down the corridor, waiting at intersections, and then sprinting forward. They didn't bother to clear rooms beyond checking inside, then sealing the doors with a quick lockdown bolt.

The corridors were the typical smooth natural rock cut by boring machines.

Conduit and plumbing ran along the ceiling in a suspended basket. One corridor had a planter thick with ivy-like vines running high along a wall. Otherwise the hallways were bare. They appeared to have entered in a section devoted to network management. Most of the rooms were full of nitrogen-cooled quantum computation banks.

"These are some sophisticated pirates," Andy said. He had expected dirty hallways full of trash and drug paraphernalia like the last raid, when they found rooms full of half-starved kids.

"Do we have a map yet?" his team leader barked.

"I don't have it," Andy said. "Based on the intel we had, we should be moving into command areas. Do you have any bio-scan data?"

"Not yet."

Ahead of them, Brit's team came under fire. The remaining teams immediately fell into formation and started looking for flanking routes. The corridor was straight with long rooms branching off at regular intervals. The first one they'd reached had been full of what had appeared to be lab equipment; lounges with terminals at their heads, and what looked like helmet-shaped neural monitors.

"You sure this is a pirate base?" someone had asked.

Andy could only shrug. He was worried about Brit, doing his best to remember details as he saw them but also focused on the moment. He continually scanned the corners and doorways were someone might attack from the rear, pop from a ceiling vent, where a chemical or radiological agent might leak out at any moment.

The three enemies team one had neutralized didn't look like pirates as Andy passed their bodies and scanned them. They were dressed in uniform black body armor with matching weapons. To Andy, they looked like private security.

They cleared another laboratory area, every console a matching collection of black screens and input devices, devoid of logos or paraphernalia that people usually left on their workstations, like coffee cups or notes. Everything looked either unused, or meticulously scrubbed clean.

He switched over the main battle net to listen in on the other two breaching teams. Their situation reports returned the same confusing observations: unused living areas, empty cafeterias, a hydroponics section full of tomato plants heavy with fruit but no sign of human activity. All three teams were converging on the region intel had identified as the command section. No one expected to find the kids there. They should have already been picked up in one of the living areas.

To Andy, Object 8221 looked less like a pirate base and more like a hidden corporate research site. If that was the case, why would the CEO of the company lead the TSF here? Why not hire her own private security to do whatever she wanted done? Andy stopped himself and signed out of the secondary nets. He needed to stay focused on what was in front of him.

His team had moved to the front of their current corridor and Andy found himself providing overwatch on the soldier moving toward a four-way intersection. He kept his rifle at his shoulder, scanning up and down the hallway for movement beyond the leader. The scout had barely reached the intersection when four drones appeared from the side corridors, fans whirring, and proceeded to pour projectile fire into the open hallway.

Andy hit the floor and fired with one hand while reaching for a grenade with the other. He set the grenade to close-radius explosion and rolled it past where his team leader had fallen against the wall, the armor on his thigh cracked with blood and seeping biofoam.

"Down!" Andy shouted. When he realized his team leader wasn't responding, he sprinted forward and threw himself on top of the wounded soldier just as the grenade went off under the drones. He felt first a spray of bullets hit his armored back and then the concussion wave from the explosion. His ears rang.

Behind him, the rest of the team moved to provide covering fire. Andy slid off his team leader and grabbed the man's legs, flattening himself out behind him to maintain a low profile while he dragged.

"One down!" he shouted into the local communication net. "It's Carser. Unconscious and breathing. Heavy bleeding. Possible femoral."

"I've got you." It was Arsel coming up behind him, lobbing fire into the corridor with her automatic grenade launcher.

"Are we clear?" another soldier asked.

"We're clear," Arsel said. She moved ahead of Andy in a crouch, kicking the remains of a drone. "Standard stuff. Looks like they were firing nine millimeters at us. That makes no sense."

"Might as well be a home defense drone," Brit said, walking up beside Arsel. Any remnants of their earlier teasing was gone.

Andy pulled off the cracked armor plate from Carser's leg to see if he could get at the bullets. It must have been a lucky shot that hit the armor on a weak point as there was no way light weapons fire would have gotten through.

One bullet was lodged in the carbon-fiber under-layer, but the other had slipped through. Andy pulled a slap-pack out of his kit and put it on the wound. The small robotic system quickly extracted the bullet and placed a stent in the artery.

Carser came-to and raised his helmet slightly. "Don't be messing with my junk, Sykes," he said. "I'm sensitive."

"You can save that for somebody else," Andy said. "You'll be up in a second. The bleeding's stopped."

"Damn it. I thought I might get an early nap."

Andy slapped the side of his helmet and gave him a thumbs-up.

"Sykes," Arsel called. "We need the rest of the fireteam up here. You clear?"

"I'm clear." He gave Carser a final nod and raised his rifle, moving down the burned corridor after Arsel and Brit. They'd turned down the right-hand corridor at the intersection, apparently the direction the drones had been guarding. A doorway stood open about five meters down. Arsel stood in the opening with Brit nowhere to be seen. Arsel gave Andy a rapid wave, urging him closer.

Andy sprinted forward to the doorway. Without pausing, he turned to look into the room beyond, thinking they needed him to fall into a three-soldier battle drill to clear the room.

He stopped just inside the door. The room was an oversized square, probably thirty meters by thirty. The entire room was full of waist-high lounges with narrow consoles near the head of each bed. Unlike the other rooms, this one was full of children in white smocks, lying asleep on the beds.

Brit stood in the middle of the room, a dark-gray uniform surrounded by white. She had lifted her face shield to look around, her face a mask of terror.

Andy swallowed hard and called in the situation report, voice nearly cracking when he reported that it appeared to be a mass experiment on children.

CHAPTER THIRTY-TWO
STELLAR DATE: 08.27.2981 (Adjusted Years)
LOCATION: *Sunny Skies*
REGION: Cruithne Station, Terran Hegemony

Cara hated the look on her dad's face, a mix of deep worry and the robotic flatness he sometimes got when the world fell apart around him. All his usual humor went away and left a person she didn't fully understand. At least, she had spent enough time with that version of Andy Sykes to know what to expect. It was best if she stayed out of his way.

She pressed the tiny speaker to her ear, listening in on the bypass channel she had used to tap into on Link conversations on the ship. The hack only worked on *Sunny Skies*, where the ancient computer system had several "switching" points for the Link. The voices came across warped and strange sometimes, especially when the speaker seemed to be projecting more emotion than words, but it worked well enough. If she could see their faces the entire conversation was easy enough to understand.

From the terminal in the family room, where they all watched vids together, she could only listen and try to guess at the communication taking place. Tim had followed her down the corridor when she'd left her room, stuffed dolphin under one arm and the poetry book under the other.

"Are you going to listen?" he asked.

"No. Go back to your room."

"You're going to listen."

Cara shook her head, choosing to ignore him rather than start a fight their dad might hear.

The strangest part of her eavesdropping system was that it picked up random thoughts flitting through her dad's mind if they were singular enough. Words like *No, Can't do that, Kids, What?* And, over and over again, her mother's name: *Brit. No, Brit. Why, Brit? How, Brit?*

She wanted to cry at the low-level punishment he inflicted on himself almost continuously. Watching him, she would never have known the worries crossing his mind, strong enough to bleed through his Link.

Cara knew he and Fran had sneaked off to make love in the engine control room. Was it making love? 'Having sex' seemed like a better term. Before she'd understood what was going on, their smacks and slurps over the Link sounded more like people exercising themselves to death. She'd turned-off the channel as soon as Tim started asking, "What? What do you hear? Let me listen."

"It's nothing bad. We can't listen right now," she'd told him.

He'd gotten a sneaky grin and said, "They're doing it, aren't they?"

"It doesn't matter what they're doing."

"Do you think Mom would care?"

Cara had given Tim a hard look, unsure how to answer. It didn't matter what

177

Mom would have thought. Mom wasn't here. Besides, most of her memories of Mom and Dad together were of her father trying to give Mom a hug and her pushing him away, complaining, "Andy!"

She waited five minutes before checking back in on the channel. Still hearing them grunting like animals alongside flashes of emotion that made her woozy, she waited another five minutes. Finally, after fifteen minutes, the channel had gone quiet.

Cara pressed the speaker to her ear, trying to figure out if they were going back up to the command deck or not. She wanted to meet them in the corridor so she wouldn't be stuck in her room again.

What would they say to each other after doing something like that? She hadn't expected Fran to do *that* with her dad, hadn't even been sure the woman liked any of them. Now, rethinking all the previous interactions between them, it became more clear what Fran was doing. She had liked her dad from the start.

In the midst of her wandering thoughts, Cara caught an unexpected sound/feeling cross the channel.

Her dad's voice surprised her, saying, "Lyssa?"

The name jarred her memory of Dr. Jickson crying on the edge of her bed. It had only been a little while ago but already felt like another life. As her dad's voice faded away in the low static that filled the hacked channel, Cara could have sworn she felt something answer, not with words but with a flicker of what felt like fear. She had known without a doubt that Lyssa was real, then. She was hiding.

Cara kept the speaker pressed to her ear. Eventually, Tim got tired of trying to listen and sat down cross-legged on the floor with his dolphin across one leg, reading the poetry book. He turned the pages slowly, showing more care than she thought he was capable of.

When she heard Dad and Fran coming back up the corridor, talking in low voices, Cara reset the terminal and stepped into the hallway.

"Are you going back up?" she asked, clasping her hands behind her back.

Her dad was obviously distracted. He was flushed, and looked like he didn't know where to be in relation to Fran, who appeared quite relaxed.

"Back up?" Andy said. "Oh, the command deck. Sure." He blinked. "Don't forget your brother."

*****

"We've got fast movers," Fran said.

"Distance?" her dad asked in his flat voice.

"Still two hundred thousand klicks."

"They're checking us. Or wait. Who's between us and them?"

"Plenty of ships. They've already passed four heavy freighters on the same vector. They ignored them."

"So, there's still a possibility they don't know we're here. Has anything pinged our registry?"

"Nothing in the log."

Cara knew 'fast movers' meant missiles. Her dad had used the term while telling stories from his TSF days. Back then, he had been the one firing fast movers at pirate ships. He'd explained that close combat between ships was actually rare. Most fought with missiles, beams, and rail guns over vast distances.

"You can't outrun a missile," he'd said. "It doesn't care about *g*-forces that will turn you into mush," and then he'd tickled her, which seemed like a gruesome thing to do, now that she thought about it. Her dad didn't like to sugarcoat his stories, though he'd tried to hide other things from them, like when they were almost out of food or the ship was sputtering to a breakdown.

In just the last year, Cara felt like most things she hadn't understood before were coming into focus and making sense. The systems on *Sunny Skies* all had an order, even when they weren't working right. She understood the steps her dad took to troubleshoot a problem or override a failed system to get another one to work. She understood more about the ways people communicated using words and emotions. She could read her dad better, even when he was trying to keep his worries and dread from them. She understood that silence often said more than words.

She'd known immediately that Ngoba Starl's pained ranting was hiding something else. She spent most of her time watching Fran and her dad, trying to figure out if they'd heard it or not. Starl had been laughing the whole time, even when he was sobbing and choking, pretending to be hurt. Or that was her hypothesis, anyway. She hoped to meet the fancy-dressing gangster again someday to ask him about it. He seemed like the type to want to talk about his deceptions, bask in how smart he was.

While Cara had never met her Grandpa Charlie, she'd seen plenty of pictures and even been able to talk to him via audio feed once when she was seven. Her dad liked to say what a good *people person* Charlie was, how he could read someone in ten seconds.

"He always knew what people really wanted, regardless what they might say," her dad had explained.

"You mean people are liars?" Cara had asked.

"No. It's just that most people don't talk about those kinds of things, about what they really want. And they don't ever admit them to other people. You have to read between the lines to hear what they're really saying."

"What are you really saying?" Cara had asked, and that made her dad laugh with a thoughtful expression in his eyes.

"I just got a ping," Fran announced. "Not the *Benevolent Hand*, but one of their close attack fighters."

"They're deploying already. How close are the missiles now?"

"The point defense cannons should have them any second."

"Should," Andy repeated.

Fran gave him another one of her self-assured smiles. She trusted the ship more than he did.

179

"All right," Andy said. "PDCs are online and tracking. Looks like thirty seconds to engagement." He bit his lip. "This is going to tell them exactly what we've got. The close attack fighters will go for the PDCs first."

"What else have we got?"

"I can try chaff."

"You better hurry up and do it."

If her dad hadn't been in robot-mode, he might have rolled his eyes. Instead, his hands entered commands into his console so fast Cara couldn't tell what he was doing. A new visual flashed in the holodisplay, showing what she thought was *Sunny Skies* engulfed in a cloud of sparkling lights. The image of *Sunny Skies* seemed to repeat across the display.

Two bright red points appeared on the edge of the holodisplay.

Cara reached out for Tim's hand, pulling it away from his book.

"What?" he complained.

The missiles flew directly into one of the ghost versions of *Sunny Skies* and flared out.

Fran whooped. "Nice!" she shouted. "That's all right!"

Andy nodded. "The close attack fighters should be in range shortly. Can the engines give us anything else?"

It was weird to hear her dad ask all these questions aloud when he usually checked these sorts of things himself. Cara wondered if it was something he had learned in the TSF, where he said they had communicated about everything so everyone would know what was going on. "Combat is no time to be stuck in your own head," he'd said once. Explaining that sometimes people froze. If you said something aloud it made you remember what you had trained to do. Made it easier to slip into robot-mode and do what had to be done.

"I can pulse our acceleration," Fran said. "It'll give us a little bit, but we're not going to outrun them."

"How about braking?"

"That's our only advantage that I can see. Our mass-to-drive ratio is a thousand times better than theirs."

Andy nodded, gaze rapt on his console.

"So their close fighters identified us," Andy said, thinking aloud again. "It's safe to assume they've relayed that information." He glanced at Fran. "What's going on with the *Benevolent Hand*'s velocity?"

"Stable," she said. "They're gaining."

"We need an asteroid to drop in their path," Andy said.

"My kingdom for some space junk," she said, some joke that her dad seemed to get. For the first time since *Benevolent Hand* had moved, he smiled.

"We're going to have to take on their close fighters. No way around it. I want you to cut our acceleration curve."

"Why?"

"We're going to limp a little bit to draw them out."

Fran gave him a hard look. "You sure about that?"

"The other weapon we have besides the cannons is the high-power comm array. It won't do much against something the size of *Benevolent Hand* but it'll fry a smaller ship. We need to get them close to use it."

"You seem to forget they have guns, too."

"I haven't forgotten. You can enter the command or I can do it."

"I trust you," Fran said, sounding like she was trying to convince herself even though her dad hadn't asked.

"That's good," he answered, slipping back into robot-mode.

As soon as the three red icons indicating the combat fighters entered her dad's display, it seemed like the rest of the maneuver happened before Cara could take another breath. Fran sent the command to the engines and the icons jumped forward, passing through one of the ghost ships created by the countermeasures. While the missiles had been dumb enough to attack chaff, the fighters blew through the illusion.

"They're firing on us," Fran said.

"First strafing run," Andy said. "Testing our weapons set. Responding with three cannons."

One of the icons blinked out.

"You got one of them!" Fran shouted.

"Let's see if they hang back or come in strong," Andy said. He watched the display for a few more seconds before nodding to himself. "They're impatient," he said. "I wonder what that tells us about our Heartbridge friends."

He tried the point defense cannons a second time, opening all twelve. The fighters anticipated the move and didn't take any damage. Her dad bit his lip.

When the fighters came around again, her dad pulled up a different screen that controlled broadcast frequencies on the main communications array. He activated the high-power microwave transmitter but only in standby mode.

"Flash batteries are up."

"What should we say to them, Cara?" he asked.

Cara blinked, unprepared for a question. "Hello?" she asked.

"Hello sounds good. Direct and to the point. I'll add Goodbye as a closing statement."

When the two ships were within striking distance of *Sunny Skies*, he sent the message. Cara's tiny speaker squawked with static as her channel suffered bleedover from the high-power signal as a gigawatt of microwaves hit the two fighters.

Cara knew that small ships like fighters only had electrostatic shields that couldn't deflect a high-powered microwave burst at this range. It would be like an EMP burst striking them.

The two icons didn't disappear but both continued on the vector they had been following toward *Sunny Skies*, shooting off into open space beyond.

"Goodbye," Andy said. "Any update on the *Benevolent Hand*?"

"Still gaining."

"I'm not excited about wasting fuel for a braking maneuver but I don't see another option. The question is when to execute. We don't want them recognizing what we're doing and slowing alongside us."

"So if they do overshoot us," Fran said. "What then?"

"Then we've got more time to figure it out," Andy said.

"Aye aye, Captain," she said.

CHAPTER THIRTY-THREE
STELLAR DATE: 9.11.2963 (Adjusted Years)
LOCATION: Object 8221
REGION: Near the Mars Protectorate Border, InnerSol

Eighteen Years Earlier

None of the kids on the lounges could be woken up. Their vital signs were healthy and they all looked fed, if a bit thin, all with a similar pale, nearly-translucent quality to their skin.

The girl Andy tried to wake up had blue veins on her eyelids. As he watched, her eyes shifted beneath her closed lids in REM sleep. Several neural pads lined her temples, running to filament cables that fed into a console next to her bed. The console's screen was dark.

"What the fuck is this?" Arsel said. "Where'd they get all these kids?"

"You think it's an organ farm?" Andy said.

"This is would be the cleanest organ farm I've ever heard about," Arsel said, looking around with renewed disgust. "Who's going to spend this kind of money on skin pigs?"

"Gourmets," Brit said.

Arsel spat. "Where do they even get this many kids?"

Brit shrugged, ice-blue gaze taking in the room. "The same places people who do this kind of things have always found kids. The question is what are they doing and is it illegal?"

"We're not cops," Andy said.

"So I guess these are refugees," Arsel said. "Easy enough. Let's get them evacuated so we can get back to the fight." She stepped toward the nearest bed and grabbed the cables hanging off the boy's head.

Before Andy could tell her to wait, she tore the neural pads off the kid's head. Instead of waking up, he started seizing, shoulders and knees jerking violently.

"Shit," Arsel said.

"We're not equipped to deal with this," Brit said. "We need to secure the room and keep moving."

"Uh, yeah, OK," Arsel said.

"Wait," Andy said. "What if one of these kids is a Carthage?"

The boy Arsel has disconnected gurgled, mouth foaming, but didn't wake up. Andy crossed the room to push Arsel out of the way and roll the boy on his side, head rested against an elbow so he wouldn't choke on his vomit.

"You forget your basic first aid?" he asked.

"I don't have time for that shit."

"So you're just lazy," Andy replied.

Arsel surged forward, shoving her face in his. "Did you want to make out, Sykes? I'll bite those lips off."

Andy looked at her, keeping his calm. "Don't get pissed at me because you fucked up. You could have killed that kid. We need to keep our heads on straight. Are you squared away? You're acting crazy."

Arsel sneered but pulled back slightly. She didn't want to fight him and he knew it.

"We don't have time for this shit," she said. "There's nobody behind us but our own. No need to secure the room. We need to keep moving."

"I'm calling in the location," Andy said. "They'll be sending more breach teams soon."

"I don't know," Brit said. "Sounds like most of the action is outside. It's starting to look like this whole place is automated. They put all their money in fighting drones."

"Maybe," Andy said. "I still think we need to check all these kids. We need to know if one of them is a Carthage or not."

"Fine," Arsel spat. "You take those rows and I'll get these by the door. Let's move."

Andy jogged down the row of couches, scanning faces as he went, as well as checking for any kid missing a finger. When he reached the end of the room, he'd counted thirty couches in the column. He quickly did the math and came up with two-hundred and ten kids in the room. None of them stirred as he went past.

When the team failed to find any of the Carthage kids, they met back at the door and went out into the hallway. Andy pulled the door closed and attached a lock-bolt to seal it.

"Where's the rest of the team?" Brit said.

"Fifty meters ahead," Arsel said, checking her Link. "More corridors with labs like this one, more kids plugged in like batteries."

Andy caught the images over the Link just as Arsel saw them. The labs were identical. The other teams had also found more network banks and rooms full of high-powered transmission equipment, indicating the station was being controlled remotely.

"Pirates, my ass," Arsel said.

"Didn't I already say that?" Andy asked, shooting her a grin.

She still wasn't happy with him, but didn't threaten to hit him as he'd expected.

"Looks like there's an open area twenty meters down one of the corridors we passed already," Brit said. "We should go clear that space if the other teams have already moved ahead."

"Right," Andy said. He called in the plan to their squad leader and received permission to deviate.

The three of them fell into a stick formation, Arsel at the lead, Brit in the rear and Andy in the middle checking every door they passed and sealing with his plasma torch.

"God, it's quiet," he said, realizing the only sound he had heard for the last hour was their own footsteps, cursing and heavy breathing. Even the labs full of sleeping kids had been quiet.

"Maybe this is some form of hell," Arsel said.

"Maybe it's heaven," Brit countered. "Everyone's floating on a cloud in some simulation, strumming harps."

"I'll be with my virgins," Andy said, sealing another room.

"Why do you get the virgins?" Arsel said.

"You didn't call them first. You prefer hell, apparently."

"More interesting," Brit said.

Andy glanced at her. "You say that now."

They had reached the edge of another intersection. Arsel had just reached the corner as Andy looked back at Brit, flashing his crooked grin, when a blue-white electron beam struck Arsel in the head and neck, burning away half her upper body and sending slivers of lightning through the air.

"Fire!" Brit yelled, voice filling the corridor and screaming across the Link.

Andy stumbled backward, landing on one knee. He raised his rifle and lobbed three splash grenades into the intersection near Arsel's body. The explosions made her corpse jump, arms flapping.

As the grenades went off, Andy fell back two more steps, taking a position on the opposite side of the corridor from Brit. They had no cover, and the nearest intersection was ten meters behind them. He had sealed the one door between them and the rear hallways.

A high squealing noise like something wet sucking against tile filled the far end of the corridor and into the intersection stepped a squat mech with a heavy, square-shaped body and rotating cannons for arms. It stopped in the middle of the corridor and squatted on its thick legs. The cannons wound up, squealing.

Andy didn't have time to think about Brit. He launched two more grenades he knew would have little effect, and turned to run for the intersection behind them. He hadn't made it three steps when slugs caught him between the shoulders and across the backs of his legs. His armor held but he was knocked forward, sprawling on the floor. He nearly lost his rifle.

Rolling on his back in time to see Brit leaping over him, he rose with the rifle between his knees and filled the hallway with beamfire. The blue bolts of energy seemed to float too slowly down the corridor as his breath raged in his helmet, and then a wall of lightning filled the area where the mech had been standing. In the storm of arcing electricity, the cannons squealed again.

Andy clawed to his feet and sprinted, pain from what might be a broken ankle slowing him down. He was nearly hopping on one foot when he reached the intersection and threw himself around the corner.

"We are taking fire," Brit reported over the open channel. "Units Sykes and Ashford. Enemy is a reinforced battle mech with twenty millimeter cannons, and an electron beam. No further weapons systems observed at this time."

When his breathing was under control, Andy asked, "You all right?"

Brit nodded. "It seemed to want to kill you first."

"We're going to need an external strike to take that thing out."

"It's not going to matter when those cannons tear a hole in the side of the station. What are they thinking? Whoever designed their defense plan must be suicidal."

"Are you getting interference over your Link?" Andy asked. He slapped his helmet but the static in his ears didn't abate. "I think my comm's down."

"No," she said. "I hear it, too. The mech might have some kind of EM jamming measures. I guess it's just as well there are only two of us."

"Damn Arsel," Andy said, blowing out a hard breath. "I didn't like her much but I didn't want her dead."

Brit didn't say anything. She checked her rifle and then made him turn around so she could examine his armor. His boot had filled with stabilization foam and numbing agents, easing the pain in his ankle to a dull ache. He'd be able to run on it for hours now until the medics had to peel his boot open.

"You took some good hits," Brit said. "This armor's shot. Don't turn your back on anything anytime soon."

"I'll try to keep that in mind," Andy said, wincing as he flexed his shoulders. He was bruised deeply if not truly injured.

The floor vibrated with the mech's heavy movements. With each step, the white noise in Andy's ears grew louder, making him think it was definitely using countermeasures against them. He checked through his four remaining grenades for anything with frequency hopping capabilities but all he had left were explosives.

"Hey," he asked Brit. "You got anything that can cut off its jamming? It's driving me crazy."

"I've got one but it's got a limited radius. I don't think it's worth trying to get close enough to use it."

"Damn it. I'd take a painkiller but I don't want it messing with my balance," Andy said.

"Stay with me, tough guy," Brit said, giving him a rare grin. "We'll have this thing down soon enough."

"What are your ideas?"

"Fall back to that last door you sealed. Pop it open and wait for the thing to pass or for reinforcements to show up. Pop out behind it and hit it with everything we've got," Brit replied.

"I'm pretty sure that model of mech has passive detection scanning. We can't hide from it."

"We can't take it," Brit said. "Not just two of us. We'll have to fall back to the rest of the team."

Andy was about to answer her when the white noise in his ears rose like a wave, filling his head with static. He stared at Brit, her face outlined in green by his faceplate, but he couldn't hear anything but the roiling noise.

Over his Link, he heard, <Stop, stop, stop!>

<What?> he said, thinking it was Brit. It didn't sound like Brit. Even bathed in static, the words were pitched too high. <Who's there?>

<Stop! Please, stop.>

<Stop what?>

<I'm coming. I can't stop the guns. I can't stop them. Can you stop them? Can you stop them without killing me?>

Brit's expression twisted as it became obvious she had heard the same words as Andy. The sound of the approaching mech continued to grow louder, vibrating the smooth floor.

"There's something in that mech," Andy said.

"I heard it, too."

"One of the kids, you think?"

"Maybe. We can't stop it. If the kid can't control it, we can't help him."

<Who are you?> Andy asked, trying to imagine the mech. He had no idea what channel the kid was using to communicate.

<I'm Kylan,> the boy said.

<Where are you Kylan?>

<I'm in the dark.>

<In the dark?> Andy said. *<Do you know where you were before that? Are you somewhere on the station?>*

The static flared and Kylan's voice rose from the white noise. *<I'm in this thing. I'm in the corridor. I'm in space. I'm floating in nothing. Surrounded by nothing. I can't get away. They'll put me in the white place.>*

<How can we help you? We want to help but we can't fight that mech.>

<I don't know. I don't know.>

<What can you control? Can you aim? Can you check its systems? Tell me what you can do and maybe I can help you stop it.>

<I feel it. It's there like a thought, like I remember my arms and fingers.> Kylan screamed. *<They cut off my fingers and hands and arms. They cut me out. They cut me out!>*

<Kylan,> Andy said.

The squealing cannon caught him by surprise. Brit yanked him further down the hallway as the intersection where they had just been filled with a storm of projectiles, cratering the opposite wall. Turning, they ran back the way they had come.

"Have we got reinforcements incoming?" Andy asked.

"They're moving back as fast as they can. Apparently."

They rounded a corner to find four of their squad mates set up with a crew-served railgun resting on a tripod and heavy CFT shields on either side of the corridor.

"I hope these damn things can hold up," Brit gasped as they slid past. Behind them, the mech turned into the corridor, twenty meters between it and the railgun.

<Fire!> came the command over the battle net.

The air around them grew dry as the cannon's capacitors charged and discharged, spewing a hail of one millimeter pellets—each travelling at over ten kilometers per second—down the corridor. The tiny pellets slammed into the mech, spinning its torso and knocking it into a wall. The fire continued to tear into its rear armor and leg joints.

<Ashford, Sykes,> Captain Transon called over the Link. *<Report. What happened to Arsel?>*

<The mech got her, sir,> Andy said. *<It took out most of her head and chest with its beam.>*

Transon grumbled something Andy couldn't hear that might have been irritation or condolences. *<The drones we've been fighting are like this mech,>* he said. *<They're smart as hell but they get confused.>*

<Sir, this one is telling me it's Kylan Carthage.>

<That's impossible,> the captain said. *<Fire team one found Kylan Carthage in a section devoted to cold storage. Hundreds of bodies in there.>*

Andy suppressed a shiver. *<That's what he says he is, sir. I don't know what to tell you.>*

<You can only report what you see, Sykes.>

<Can we disable the mech rather than destroy it, sir?>

<You tell me?>

Andy squinted to look through the smoke filling the corridor. The mech lay on its side, still trying to get into an upright position. The railgun had cut its legs and one cannon into ribbons. The other cannon, though, was swiveling into a firing position.

<Kylan!> he shouted, unsure if he could still reach the kid. *<Stop! If you don't fire we can save you.>*

There was no answer. As the cannon spun to life, and another stream of rail-served pellets slammed into the mech, tearing through its body, the gunner continuing to fire until the mech was nothing more than a smoking ruin.

<I hear you, Sykes,> Transon said. *<Stop yelling.>*

Andy sighed, remembering the fear in Kylan's voice. *<Forgive me, sir. I thought he was still there.>*

<Understood. Finish clearing operations with your team when get to the rally point for the hot wash. I think we've all got some weird shit to report.>

<Did we find any of the other kids, sir?>

<Kids? We found hundreds of kids.>

<The Carthage kids, sir.>

<Oh. Yes. We found the girl.>

Andy nodded. *<Thank you, sir.>*

Walking back through cleared sections of the station, Andy let himself lean on Brit when she offered her shoulder, easing the growing pain in his ankle.

He didn't know how much she had heard, but something about the little boy's voice filled him with a sense of dread that he couldn't shake. When they passed the lounge rooms again, he wanted to tear every one of the sleeping children out of the machine they had been plugged into. It was obvious they were being used for remote control of weapons systems but he couldn't understand why anyone would want to use children? Why go to all this trouble? Weren't there adults who would gladly sign up for this kind of work?

He could only shake his head, and later pour beer down his throat with the rest of the squad back on *Aggression's Cost*. They traded their theories on what Fortress 8221 had truly been. When a sergeant from the intel section confirmed that 8221 wouldn't be destroyed like any regular pirate outpost, the dread came back into Andy's heart. He saw it settle down on everyone else in the squad. They didn't like to feel like pawns. They wanted to believe Transon had been surprised just like they all had when they'd found the first lounge room. But that got harder to swallow as time went on.

Several nights later, when Brit came to his room sometime after midnight, she curled up against him and asked if he had ever wanted kids.

She whispered the question like a secret she was afraid to expose to anyone—her deepest desire.

"Yes," Andy said. "I do."

CHAPTER THIRTY-FOUR
STELLAR DATE: 08.27.2981 (Adjusted Years)
LOCATION: *Sunny Skies*
REGION: Near Cruithne Station, Terran Hegemony

There was a moment of weightlessness as *Sunny Skies*—Cara refused to think of the ship as *Worry's End*—somersaulted over its midpoint to execute the braking burn. Her arms and legs floated free and her back slipped away from the chair until the harness held her in place.

Tim grinned at her, giggling. He nearly lost his poetry book until Cara caught it and handed it back.

"Turn complete," Dad shouted. "Here we go."

The force of the engines kicking to life drove them back into their seats. Cara did her best to face forward. Beside her, Tim made gurgling sounds, trying to be funny like usual.

The first hard burn lasted three minutes and made her eyes feel like fried eggs. "I don't want to take us any slower than that," her dad had told Fran. "If they're accelerating, we won't need to do much to get them to overshoot us."

As he'd said before, the worry was that the *Benevolent Hand* would figure out what they were up to in time to match their new speed.

Her dad had transferred the channel from the *Benevolent Hand* to the overhead speakers, although there hadn't been any interesting conversation since she'd overheard them talking about their drive system. The channel had been quiet for so long that she wanted to ask her dad to play some music instead. Piano was her favorite though she also liked electronic dance music or sometimes just the choir voices.

With her little speaker in her ear, she idly switched between other channels on the spectrum, wondering if she might pick up a passing signal. Every so often, Fran and her Dad talked using their Links and the sentences came through like they were talking underwater.

<You staying to Mars 1, then?> her dad asked.

<I have to at this point. I don't see how I'm getting out of here before that.>

Fran's voice was clear, while her dad's kept warping in and out, interspersing blank spaces with <Brit, Brit.> Her dad was confused about something. Cara could see it in his face and it was easy enough to see it related to his time in the engine room with Fran.

Listening, Cara nearly kicked herself. Of course, her dad felt bad about having sex with Fran while he was still thinking about their mom. Once she understood, she didn't need to eavesdrop on their Link conversation to feel the tension between them.

<We should check on Petral,> Andy said.

<You can if you want. She'll wake up and figure things out.>

<You really don't like her, do you? What did she do to you?>

<Oh, it's nothing personal. She called me a mechanic once and it got under my skin.>
*<You **are** a mechanic.>*
<You didn't hear the way she said it. Like I was a glob of spit or something.>

Cara couldn't help liking Petral for getting them from the apartment to the dock, even if all she'd done while they were in the apartment together was watch programs on the holo and clean her nails. When they'd asked to watch their own shows, she'd made them stay in the back room where it was 'safer.'

Another braking maneuver pushed Cara down in her seat, making her dizzy this time as blood rushed out of her head.

<I thought you said we only needed one burn,> Fran said.
<Just to be sure.>
<I should ask you why you care about Petral.>
<She's on my ship. Of course, I care about her. Technically I'm responsible for her.>
<You could space her if you wanted.>
<That would be murder. Besides, she hasn't done anything to me. You've never been called names in your life? Not that tone of voice counts as name-calling. You wouldn't make three days in the TSF.>
<I'm a member of Lowspin. I think that's a little tougher place than the TSF.>
<Your leader wears bowties.>
<He cut a man's head off because he wanted his tie.>
<Well, that's just a terrible way to get someone's tie,> Andy said.

If Cara hadn't been able to listen in, she would have thought her dad was grinning at Fran for no reason.

The overhead speakers bled static and a voice said, "Brake? We brake now those assholes from Cruithne will catch up. We barely shut down that TSF team. Well if Cal Kraft wants to kill us all he might as well come around and do it himself. We know where they're going. Why not just blow past them to Mars 1 and wait for them to come to us?"

A wave of static went through the speakers and the channel fell silent. Andy's mouth fell open.

"I think you've saved the day, Cara," he said.

"Did we slow down fast enough?" she asked, liking it when he complimented her.

He stared into his console and took a deep breath. "We did but that little bit of audio just confirmed something I was worried about but couldn't be sure of. They've got a small armada coming after them. I thought they might be more Lowspin ships but it looks like they might be people who don't like us much. Or don't seem to, for some reason."

"You sure?" Fran said. "They could all be Lowspin."

"I don't want to risk it. As much as we've slowed down, we can't hope to outrun them at this point."

Something in his display made him curse. He typed furiously, then pulled up a new holoprojection that showed the *Benevolent Hand* again, this time with a cloud of sparks rushing past it like it was standing still. He pointed at another dot just slightly ahead of the *Benevolent Hand.*

"That's us," he said. "They caught us. Damn it."

"What are we going to do?" Cara said, wondering if he was going to tell them to go hide again. She hated that.

"We're going to dive into the fray," Andy said.

"You're not serious," Fran's voice rose an octave.

"We can't outrun them. We've got no cover. The only safe place right now is the middle of all those other ships. I can fight off Zanda's smaller fighters if he realizes we're in the mix. We might get lucky and have the *Benevolent Hand* take them out for us."

"I'm not excited about this plan," Fran said.

"Honestly, it's creating an opening for you to get out in the shuttle if that's what you still want to do. Nobody's going to notice you among all the other ships."

Fran didn't answer.

Cara watched them, wondering why her dad was trying to push her away. It seemed obvious to her that Fran wanted to stay and would probably stay for a while if he asked.

"I thought Fran was staying with us until we got to Mars?" Tim asked.

Cara wanted to hug her little brother. He often surprised her by interjecting himself at the precisely correct moments. He asked in a matter-of-fact way that Cara didn't think she would ever have been able to pull off. She didn't know if Tim liked Fran, exactly, but she did know he didn't like change. It wouldn't make sense to him that someone who had been on the ship longer than anyone but their mom would need to leave so soon.

"Fran was always going to need to go back to Cruithne," her dad said. "That's where she lives. Why wouldn't she go back there?"

Fran still didn't answer. Her gaze had slid to the console in front of her so Cara couldn't tell if she was stalling or had spotted something new to worry about.

"The *Benevolent Hand* has matched our delta-V," Fran said. "The swarm is coming up fast. I've got registry pings. It's most of the ships from Cruithne with what might be more TSF. I can't read all the military transponders."

Looking grateful for the distraction, Cara's dad shifted the holodisplay and plotted a course that would take them past the *Benevolent Hand* into the middle of the new mass of ships. The icons kept shifting from red to yellow and green as he moved the display, which Cara guessed meant friendly vs bad guys.

"We'll need to keep moving," he said, talking more to himself than the rest of them. "Is anyone on the Lowspin battle net? We need to find out what their plan is."

Fran listened for a minute and then shook her head. "Their plans appear to be keeping themselves alive long enough for more TSF reinforcements to arrive. They're all terrified that the *Benevolent Hand* slowed down. They thought they were done with the fight until Mars."

"Anybody mention us?"

"Well, as soon as I reappeared on the net, they knew what had happened." Her face grew blank again as something else caught her attention. "Oh," she said, listening.

In another minute, she turned to Cara's dad with wide eyes. Cara thought she looked like she'd seen a ghost.

"They're going after the *Benevolent Hand* in a suicide run."

He pursed his lips. "What have they got to make that work?"

"They've got a mining nuke."

Cara's dad shook his head, not looking impressed. "If it's a tunneling charge, that might do some damage. It's a plan, I guess. Have they broadcast the radius, at least? What kind of timeline are we looking at?"

"The ship is *Flitter Cane*. They're pulling off non-essential crew now."

"They don't have anything with an onboard AI that could pilot it?"

"They don't want to risk external control. Besides, three Lowspin ships volunteered. They want revenge for Starl."

"He's not dead."

She shrugged. "I guess they don't know that."

"So, they ram the *Benevolent Hand*, set off the nuke. We hope it knocks a hole in the cruiser. That doesn't stop all the close fighters they still have deployed."

"What's it matter? We can burn out of here like we'd planned on, right?"

Cara's dad nodded, obviously still thinking through possible hazards. "Right," he mused. "If *I* was the *Benevolent Hand* and *I* saw suicide bombers coming my way, what would I do?"

"Could you do anything?" Fran frowned abruptly. "Why are you assuming they'll do anything? How are they going to know?"

"I think they've known everything Lowspin was going to do this whole time. They've probably got fifty spies in your syndicate. So, if that's happening and they can't stop it, they'll want to use the resources they have left; which is Zanda."

His gaze shifted to the holodisplay with their path through the swarm outlined in bright blue. Cara's dad rubbed his face, suddenly looking tired.

<*Damn it, Brit*,> his Link voice complained over Cara's mini speaker, a whisper in her ear. The thought-words had become more clear since the surgery, as if Lyssa was doing something to his Link. <*What do I do here? What would you do? What about Cara and Tim? I can't fail.*> His anguish crackled through her, filling her with an emotion that mixed worry and love for him with the anger and confusion she felt toward her mom, all of it shot-through with the robot-response she had seen in him so many times.

The only way to push through catastrophe: Talk through the plan.

"Mom's not going to answer," Cara shouted. She couldn't stop herself. Her dad's pain wouldn't let her keep the words inside. "She's gone. We know she's not dead. We know she left. Stop hoping she'll come back! *We're* still here!"

Cara surprised herself with her anger. She clenched her fists and looked up from the floor where she had fixed her gaze. Tears stung her eyes. Her dad stared at her from the console, the holodisplay sparkling above his head like an angry cloud.

Slowly, he unfastened the harness holding him to the seat and walked across the command deck so he could wrap his arms around her. Cara didn't know when she had started crying. She buried her face in his shoulder. Then Tim burrowed his way into the hug as well.

Her dad pulled away to look at her, wiping tears from the side of her face with his rough hands.

"I never said she was dead," he said, voice catching. "I said she was gone." He shook his head, eyes also wet. "She might come back, Cara. That's the truth. Sometimes I wish she was dead because then I could stop thinking about it."

Andy picked up the bit of wire running from the communications console to her earbud. "I should have known you might be able to pick up other things with this. That's pretty genius. We need to patent it when we're done with all this." He released a heavy breath. "What did you hear?"

Cara searched for the right words. "You just keep saying her name. 'Brit, Brit. What do I do, Brit? What now, Brit?'" She gave him a sheepish look. "'Fuck you, Brit.'"

His eyes widened and he held up a finger. "I know you're quoting, but you don't use that word unless you cut your hand off, you understand me?"

Fran stifled a laugh from the other side of the room.

Cara nodded. She wrapped her arms around his neck and hugged him again.

"And I know you're still here," he said, tousling Tim's hair. "I have a problem with something—they're called circular thoughts. Sometimes you get a thought in your head and it doesn't want to go away. You think it's gone and then something brings it back, and you move from that bad thought to another one, until you come back to the first one. I'm getting better but that's what your Link interceptor was probably picking up."

He glanced at Fran. "At least I hope so."

Fran looked at Cara and blushed bright red. It was the first time she had seemed embarrassed about anything since Cara had met her.

"All right," Andy said, standing. "If Fran's friends are going to do what they say they are, then we need to keep moving. It's going to get bumpy for a while. You guys stay strapped in. Wait. Does anyone need to use the latrine?"

Fran raised her hand. Tim raised his, too.

"Hurry up then. We've maybe got ten minutes before we hit the swarm again. If I need to run evasive maneuvers, I'll call it over the main intercom."

Tim took Fran's hand at the command deck door, which made her smile in a strange way. When her dad settled back into his chair, Cara was glad to be alone with him, even if she felt like a bomb had gone off in her heart, leaving her exhausted in a good way.

She put the mini speaker back in her ear and started scanning channels again. This time the entire spectrum was full of chatter.

CHAPTER THIRTY-FIVE
STELLAR DATE: 10.02.2968 (Adjusted Years)
LOCATION: TSS *Aggression's Cost*
REGION: High Terra, Earth, Terran Hegemony

Thirteen Years Earlier

The mission they came to call Fortress 8221 didn't end with any easy answers. Kylan Carthage was considered a casualty while Yandi and Urvin went home to appear on several news streams with their tearful mother. The other children were absorbed by some social program SolGov maintained for orphaned children that Brit later determined didn't exist. She was convinced they had been retaken by whatever shell company had run the fortress, re-acquiring its valuable assets.

In the five years since the mission, Brit only became more obsessed with trying to track down other groups of lost kids. When she couldn't find any public records, she even took the risk of trying TSF channels, calling in favors with several intel officers and finally Captain Transon, who had been transferred back to headquarters on High Terra, and promoted three years later to Major.

They were out for dinner in a zone near her parents' neighborhood when Transon's message came through. The evening had been going well enough, the restaurant overlooking a small park with a reflecting pond and frogs singing to each other.

Transon's response was kind, but had basically told her to drop it.

Andy was on a short pass from his current duty running close fighter support for smuggling interdiction. It was easy duty for a captain. His missions took him between High Terra, Cruithne and Kafflin, an object that sat in a rough transfer orbit between Earth and Venus that had become a favorite for pirates.

The missions were predictable enough. He was never in much danger beyond the normal rigors of space travel. Breach teams were mostly enlisted and he was their bus driver. Still, it took him away from Brit and he found himself missing her more and more.

"I don't understand how five hundred kids just disappear," she complained bitterly, closing the message after Andy had read it. "Everyone wants to pretend they were never there. We saw them."

He nodded. They had been down this road before and experience proved it didn't end well. She was growing more disillusioned with the TSF while still volunteering for increasingly dangerous missions. After being attached to a Special Operations unit for nearly two years, deploying for months at a time when Andy couldn't contact her or know where she was, she had finally put in a packet for a branch transfer to Special Ops. The application was still under review.

Andy hadn't allowed himself to really consider what they would do if she was accepted. In reality, he knew it would end their relationship and he wasn't quite ready for that yet. He wanted to enjoy things as they were now for a while longer.

Andy took her hand and pressed her fingers into his. Their palms were warm against one another.

"How's your fish?" he asked.

She gave him a bored look, turning her face to gaze out at the park below the terrace.

"Dry," she said. "Don't change the subject. This is important."

"You don't have to tell me that," he said. "I'm the one with Kylan Carthage's voice in my dreams."

Andy stopped himself. This was where the discussion turned into argument. *He* had let the kids go and he was the one with more right to be angry about all of it. *He* had listened to Kylan as he died, not Brit. In a way, her continued obsession with 8221 forced him to relive that helplessness over and over again.

"You know they didn't destroy the station," Brit said.

"They destroyed it a month after it was cleared. You saw the report same as I did."

Brit shook her head. "It's still there. I got a return from a research telescope."

"You what?"

"I hired time on a long-range telescope and verified it's still there. It was a lot cheaper than I'd thought it would be."

"What are you going to do when Intel comes around to ask you questions about that?"

"How will they ever know? Are you going to tell them?"

"No," Andy said. "But you need to be careful. This is starting to look like an obsession, Brit. I'm not the only one who's mentioned it."

Her eyes glimmered as she looked at the park. "You'd be glad if I failed psych, wouldn't you? Then my application to Special Ops would get denied."

Andy let go of her hand and leaned back in his chair, crossing his arms. His appetite was gone. He looked around for the waiter. "That's not what I said. If that's what you want to do, you should go do it. I'm not going to stop you."

"But you don't want me to go?"

"So I would rather my girlfriend was somewhere I could see her instead of deployed for a year doing life-threatening shit in Special Ops. That really sucks for me to feel that way, right?"

"I never asked you to love me, Andy."

He stared at her, not knowing what to say. Sometimes she made him feel like the only person in the universe, until she'd follow her warmth with a slap from nowhere. And she knew the exact words to use.

"I already told you I supported your application." He took the napkin from his lap and threw it over his half-eaten steak. "If you think you need to push me away, then you do what you need to do. Loving you doesn't mean trapping you, Brit. Maybe I was an idiot when I believed that you loved me, too."

She looked at him. Her eyes were wet with tears. "It feels like we're at a place where we have to make a decision, Andy. I can't help what I want. I have to do this. I understand if you can't come with me."

He frowned slightly, not understanding if she was talking about the Special

Ops application or the kids from 8221.

"Back home," he said, "people used to just disappear. You go around to find a friend and his mom tells you he slipped into the river and didn't come back up, that maybe a gator got him." He laughed sadly. "All this technology, and that's how I grew up. You know there were gangs that grabbed kids out of my neighborhood, too. My dad made my sister and me stay indoors some nights. He wouldn't tell us why but he had a sense about those kinds of things. They liked ten to thirteen-year-olds the best. They brought the highest prices. If you were older than that, they could still sell you to bio-harvesters. What's it matter? The poor will just make more. We're cheap. It's shitty but it's life, and I need to keep living mine."

"You don't mean that," she said softly, holding herself still.

"It's how I get by, Brit. I thought you already knew that." He motioned toward the restaurant and the manicured park. "All this can go away at any moment. I feel that more now than I ever have. You remember when you asked me if I wanted to have kids?"

She wiped her face and nodded. He felt like he was hitting her with words, even after what she'd said to him. She hunched over her plate.

"I said yes, and I meant it. As shitty as this world is, I still think kids are the only answer. We have to keep them safe. I can't help those kids on 8221, Brit. But I'll be damned if I let my own kids fall into that situation. I'd die first. My dad taught me that, and they tried to say he was dumb."

He had been looking at the park as he talked. When his gaze returned to Brit, her eyes were nearly black under the moonlight.

"I'm pregnant," she said abruptly. "I was going to take care of it but I haven't been able to. Every time I think about it, I think about the future and how it's just a blank wall for me. All that's there is you." Her voice broke. "You say you don't want to trap me, but I'm the one trapping you. And now this."

Andy opened his mouth to speak but didn't know what to say. Brit buried her face in her hands. In his peripheral vision, he caught the waiter hovering, unsure whether to approach or not. Andy waved him away.

Going around the table, he pulled Brit's chair out and sank to his knees next to her, pressing his head against her stomach. She was still has lean as ever.

"I haven't taken precautions," Brit was saying. "I didn't think I could get pregnant. I haven't saved any eggs, even. I hadn't even considered this could happen. My mother couldn't carry me. They used an artificial womb."

Andy lifted his face from her stomach and wrapped his arms around her. He was already thirty A little more than a decade in the TSF had blinked by. The conversation Brit had started—about being at a 'turning point' in their relationship—was one most of his friends had experienced before break-ups, before drifting apart. He knew he didn't want that.

"Andy," she said, her voice distant. "We can't have a baby and stay in the TSF."

"Why not? People do it. We'll get station assignment. We could request High Terra and be near your parents. Maybe we could even get down to Earth to see my family."

"If we're going to do this, I don't want to stay in the TSF. I've been thinking about that and it's the only way I can do it."

His mind immediately moved to what he might do if they weren't in the TSF. Commercial pilot, maybe? Trainer? They both had buddies who had left the service for successful careers on the outside. They could call in favors. Make a new life.

When Brit talked about the future being a blank wall, Andy felt instead that all of Sol seemed wide open. Life outside the TSF could be anything they wanted.

"All right," he said. "You know me, though. I need to make a plan."

She smiled and kissed him, then clung to him as he pulled her against his chest.

* * * * *

While Brit's obsession with 8221 never disappeared completely, pregnancy eventually softened her focus. When Andy thought he was about to find her poring over some old news report, she was reading a child-development guide, or talking with other parents-to-be. She debated the benefits of natural birth or artificial womb. While she continued to exercise daily, her intensity eased and she chose yoga over Jujitsu.

They requested, and were granted, duty stations on High Terra. Andy took a position training recent academy graduates. He found he enjoyed teaching immensely, even when some of the lieutenants struck him as entitled shits. He maintained his even smile while explaining the realities of modern combat.

"Yes, you will be on a breach team," he told every new class. "You will suck dirt and learn to love grenades. You will need to learn to use a rifle like any grunt. If you want to live, anyway. If you want to accomplish the mission. You're officers. What do you do?"

He couldn't help but smile as they shouted as one: *"Accomplish the mission, sir!"*

As the months passed and Brit's belly grew, until he finally felt the baby kicking, he started to imagine a life outside the TSF. They spent nights talking about where they might live, from Mars to the moons of Jupiter.

"You want our daughter to be a Marsian?" Brit had asked, sounding appalled.

"What's wrong with being Marsian? There's a ton of work on Mars."

"They're so— pedantic. Robotic. They don't do anything but what they're told."

"You know what we used to say about High Terrans?" Andy asked, reaching out to flick her nose. "You shit gold. Do you shit gold?"

"Of course, I do," Brit said. "It's what our economy is based on, dummy."

"Well, give me some of that gold," he said. "I need to buy a ship." He squeezed one of her ass cheeks and she swatted him, laughing.

* * * * *

Cara was born on a Monday morning in September. When Brit had finally gone to sleep and the various nurses came in for their checks, Andy sat in a window bench seat with his daughter wrapped in a swaddling blanket made of some fuzzy material. Her eyes were the same startling blue as Brit's. She kept wrinkling her forehead, looking at him with such intensity that he wondered what she really saw, even though he knew her world was only a blur of voices and color. Eventually she fell asleep, leaving him alone in the room listening to her light breathing and Brit's exhausted snore.

In a way, his world had compressed itself into this room, but he felt everything had become so much bigger than it had ever been.

He found himself thinking about Kathryne Carthage in the news stream with her surviving kids, talking about what a brave boy Kylan had been. Andy had never told Brit that he suspected the Carthage company had been operating 8221 and through some fluke the CEO's own kids had been caught up in the monstrosity her company had created. He didn't know why he believed that. Kathryne Carthage's pain had certainly appeared real. Maybe it was his base pessimism.

"I'm going to have to learn how to turn that off," he muttered, trying to get comfortable in the window seat. He figured he should try to sleep as well. The baby guides all said newborns were nocturnal at first.

Before he closed his eyes, he sent his commander, Colonel Ryth, an update on Cara's birth and submitted his official request for paternity leave.

<You still in one piece?> Ryth replied.

<Yes, sir. Newest recruit in the TSF requests permission to come aboard.>

<Give her eighteen years before we start that. How's Momma?>

<Snoring like a champ.>

<Good to hear. Enjoy your leave, Andy. Oh, check in with me when you get back. I think I've got a lead on a ship for you.>

CHAPTER THIRTY-SIX

STELLAR DATE: 08.27.2981 (Adjusted Years)
LOCATION: *Sunny Skies*
REGION: Near Cruithne Station, Terran Hegemony

Sunny Skies was caught in a maelstrom of missiles, lasers and cannon fire, everything slicing through the too-close distances around the *Benevolent Hand*. Too often, ships that should have been friendly fired on a location where an enemy had been and now *Sunny Skies* had just arrived.

This sort of combat in a ship the size of *Sunny Skies* was something Andy would usually consider suicide. Since the option of breaking out of the swarm meant facing the *Benevolent Hand* and its drones alone, he figured the odds were slightly better here.

They had only been in the swarm for ten minutes—in the midst of executing the third of Andy's ninety-degree turns—when the first suicide ship collided with the Heartbridge cruiser. Everyone on the Lowspin battle net went silent in the overhead speakers, waiting for the explosion.

The nuke failed to detonate. A new swarm of drone fighters poured from the cruiser's flanks.

"We don't have many more where that came from," Fran said.

"How many do we have?"

"Maybe just one," she said.

A proximity alert went off in Airlock One. Andy pulled up the hull security monitor and cursed out loud.

"Daddy!" Cara shouted.

"Sorry," he muttered, keeping his gaze on the screen. He jerked his head at Fran. "We've got boarders."

"What?" she demanded. "How the hell did anyone get close enough?"

"I don't know. That's the only alarm going off. They must have come in slow to get past the shields, matching our velocity." He shook his head. "That was a hell of a pilot." He tapped a series of commands into the console.

"We're in autopilot," he said. "Call me if it looks like we'll need to override."

"How am I supposed to have time to call you? It's a mess out there."

"I count five at the airlock. It's going to be a mess in here."

"Do you have a visual on them?" Fran said.

Andy pulled up the camera feed off the airlock and showed her.

Fran peered at the grainy picture, which looked down on five people in EV suits, projectile rifles slung across their backs. She pointed at the screen. "That's Riggs Zanda," she said.

Andy squinted. He barely remembered seeing the other gangster in Starl's club. The only thing he recognized about the man in the EV suit under Fran's finger was his muscled build.

"This is great," Andy said. "I guess I should be glad there are only five of them."

"I don't remember if your drone had defensive capability," Fran said.

Andy shook his head. "Alice has spot and arc welders but that's it. I guess we could use it as a battering ram." He looked over at Cara. "Sweetheart, power Alice up and have it meet me at the habitat airlock."

"Alice is a she," Cara said.

"Yes, dear," he said, not wanting to argue. "Run a systems check and make sure the welders are functional."

"Do you have any heavy weapons?" Fran asked.

"Yeah. Look, you can lock down the habitat from the command deck if you need to. The kids can show you the safe room off the hydroponics chambers."

"I didn't see a safe room in there. I saw a lot of other little cubby holes."

"It's shielded by a water tank. Once you're in, though, you're not getting out until the ship is clear. There's a maintenance chute that runs alongside the hab airlock but it's in vacuum. If you need to get to your shuttle, that's going to be the best way. There are three EV suits in the safe room and a pulse pistol."

"You're acting like we're not getting out of this," Fran said.

"I'm planning ahead. It's what I do."

He gave her a tight smile and crossed the command deck to hug the kids. "Love you guys," he said, squeezing them both. Tim clung to him longer than Cara.

"Are you going to go fight, Dad?" he asked.

"I hope not, buddy."

Leaving the command deck, he strode down the main corridor to the habitat airlock, shrugging on his EV suit as he waited for the passage to cycle open. In the tube, he pulled himself grimly forward along the access ladder, anticipating the stomach flip as he lost gravity.

Reaching the ship's main spire and zero-g, he floated out and used handholds to pull toward the cabinet where he'd hidden the crate of TSF weapons.

"I don't know where you came from," he said, "but thank you."

Activating his mag boots, he knelt in front of the open cabinet and lifted the lid on the crate. The multi-mode rifle with its grenade launcher was still there, along with a complement of variable grenades, and three pistols. Two were projectile handguns, and one was a plasma weapon. He checked the cartridge and saw that it had enough gas and charge for two, maybe three shots. Andy hated plasma weapons. They were indiscriminate and crazy-dangerous in low-g. However, without body armor, he wouldn't last long against any determined attack. A stream of plasma might make Zanda's team think twice.

<Fran,> he said over the Link. <Have they overridden the airlock yet?>

<They're close. They've good tech. I can't stop it.>

<They're coming aboard. I'd rather they didn't wreck my airlock in the process. Do you have a channel I can use to talk to them?>

<They're not on the Lowspin net.>

<That would make sense.>

<Sorry, it's the only thing I've got.>

As he closed the cabinet doors, Alice came floating up the corridor toward him, both forward lights glowing like yellow eyes.

"Hello, there," he said. "I promised I wouldn't pretend I like you, but I'm sure glad you're operational right now."

Alice floated up and down in a way that almost made it seem like the drone was nodding. Andy patted its side and pushed past it into the corridor.

"Cara," he said over the intercom. "Transfer control of Alice to my EV suit."

"Done," she answered, obviously waiting for him to call. "Can you see them yet?"

"No. But I'm not near the airlock yet. I'm going there now."

Holding the rifle in one hand with the sling wrapped around his forearm, Andy kicked off down the corridor. It was roughly twenty meters to the airlock. For once, he wished it was farther.

<Fran,> he said. <Is there any way we could turn the point defense cannons on them while they're still outside?>

<We'd tear the hull apart.>

<Yes, but we'd kill them in the process,> Andy said. <OK, do this then, kill the lights in the corridor. Do it for the whole ship except the habitat.>

<Done,> Fran said. Andy found himself in darkness. He turned off his helmet lamp and waited before moving forward again. He knew the ship well enough that he didn't need the lights.

<All right,> he said. < How long do you think it will take to bring the temp up to a hundred degrees?>

<I can divert all environmental control to that section. Shouldn't take more than a few minutes.>

<Do that. We can defeat visual and infra-red, at least.>

<Here comes the sauna.>

Nearing the airlock, Andy caught a spark leaping from the interior doors, as bright as a sun in the complete darkness.

<Looks like they're cutting their way in, after all,> he said.

He sent Alice up to the edge of the door, killing her forward lights as well, and parked her out of sight of the airlock. Floating back to a ribbed section in the bulkhead, he slipped behind the support and activated his mag boots. The support provided him about half a meter of cover but he would have to stick his head out to fire down the corridor. He waited, watching the external temperature rise.

Andy opened Alice's onboard camera in his helmet display and watched the shower of sparks from the cutting torch slice through his newly repaired airlock. The camera made Alice seem too close, so he pulled it back another five meters and activated the plasma welder. It didn't give him anything to throw at the boarding party but it might make them think twice.

After another minute, the torch stopped and the sparks died out. A screeching noise filled the corridor as a section of the airlock door floated free into the passageway. Four lamp beams pierced the dark.

Andy controlled his breathing as he watched a helmet poke through the hole in the airlock door, decide it was clear, then step through. Four more suits came through. Using Alice's camera, Andy's helmet assigned target icons. He only had seconds before whatever other short-range scanners they had found him and locked-on.

Switching on Alice's flood lights, he sent her forward with the plasma torch at full power. Soundlessly, the drone surged forward. Andy heard surprised yells through his helmet, sounding like people underwater.

Leaning out from behind the bulkhead, he lobbed five grenades after the drone. "Sorry, Alice," he breathed.

The explosions flashed in the dark. Alice's camera caught surprised gray faces behind visors then cut out.

Andy counted five blasts, then held the rifle away from his chest so it cleared the bulkhead support and squeezed the trigger, filling the corridor with automatic fire. He waited for a response, expecting a grenade to float down the hallway. When nothing came, he checked his helmet's targeting display and found only one active icon remaining from someone who had fallen back inside the airlock.

Slowly, Andy eased out from behind the support and kept his magboots activated, clicking on and off the floor as he approached the airlock. Four bodies were plainly visible on the floor.

Switching on his external speaker, he shouted, "Who's in there? Answer me or I'm tossing in another grenade."

A Link request on a standard channel hit his helmet. Andy let it beep for a second before accepting.

<Captain Sykes,> a man said slowly, voice wet with pain.

Andy recognized Zanda's gravelly voice from the attack on the cargo bay. He was much quieter this time.

<I didn't expect...> Zanda said. <Well, I should have known you'd be armed. We had people on your ship during the repairs. They didn't find anything.>

<Of course you had people on board,> Andy said. <What do you want?>

<I came to talk.>

<We could have talked with you outside the ship.>

<Maybe. Will you switch to an encrypted channel with me?>

<Why?>

<There are things. Things I need to tell you.>

<Why should I trust you?>

Zanda coughed. <You shouldn't.>

Andy waited, thinking. The people Zanda had come in with were definitely dead. He leaned against the bulkhead but didn't lower his rifle. <I'll send you the channel,> Andy said.

<That's fine. This is between you and me.>

Sending a new connection request, Andy waited as Zanda accepted. On another channel, he told Fran, <I got all of them but Zanda. He says he wants to talk to me.>

<It's about time,> she nearly shouted. <Are you all right?>

<I'm fine. Tell the kids I'm fine. How are we doing outside?>

<It looks like they're making a second attempt. The Benevolent Hand *is sending waves of drones against any ship that tries to get close now. The TSF is trying to figure out a counter attack.>*

<As long as no one's shooting at us. I'll finish this up soon. I'm sending the token for my channel with Zanda.>

<Copy.> Fran said. *<Be safe.>*

Andy wondered for a second if there was actual caring in her voice. He shelved the thought and switched back to the channel with Zanda.

<I'm here,> Zanda said. *<Can you…you hear me?>*

<I hear you,> Andy said. *<What do you want?>*

<What did Starl tell you?>

<He didn't tell me anything. All I know is you assholes keep trying to attack me and my family.>

Zanda laughed and started coughing, sounding very much like Starl just hours earlier.

<Maybe both you and Starl will die today,> Andy said.

<That's a rude thing to say.>

<I guess you caught me in a bad mood,> Andy said. *<Say what you're going to say or I'm sending in a grenade.>*

<I came here,> Zanda said, his breathing growing labored. *<I came here to tell you that I know your wife.>*

CHAPTER THIRTY-SEVEN
STELLAR DATE: 08.27.2981 (Adjusted Years)
LOCATION: *Sunny Skies*
REGION: Near Cruithne Station, Terran Hegemony

<What did you say?> Andy demanded. He kept himself from rushing into the airlock to jam the plasma pistol under Zanda's chin.

<My friend Ngoba Starl is very convincing. He's got this way of making a person think they're special, to think he chose them over all others. I've known him a long, long time. I know how he operates. You were in a desperate situation. You can't blame yourself for falling into his trap.>

<What trap?>

<The job. The surgery. This quest you've taken on. Do you even know what he put inside your head? Hari Jickson was a very dangerous man. It's a good thing that he's dead.>

<I'm going to be saying the same thing about you,> Andy said.

Zanda coughed. <I'm bleeding from a cut in my leg. It's too deep. My suit isn't sealing it off. I have to say, I didn't expect you to attack like that. I thought you'd want to talk. You seem like the type who would try to talk first. Your wife on the other hand. She has a cruel streak. Maybe I was wrong.>

<Maybe you don't know what you're talking about.>

<Maybe so…> he said, voice trailing off.

<Zanda!> Andy said sharply, wondering if he had died.

<I'm here. I'm here. So. Brit Ashford was on Cruithne a year ago. Did Ngoba share that with you? No? She made quite an impact on Lowspin. Shot up Ngoba's club. That was the first time anybody thought much about the Heartbridge Clinic. She blew it up.> He laughed wetly. <Why the hell would someone come to Cruithne and blow up the only nice thing we have? The underground chop shops loved her for it. Their business doubled. But who wants to go to a chop shop so you can get a legit check up? I wanted to know who this woman was. We got to her in the main port before she could take a transport to High Terra. It was all very civilized, right there in the waiting area bar.>

Zanda, like Starl, apparently liked the sound of his own voice.

<Fran,> Andy said. <Are you hearing this?>

<I hear.>

<Is anything he's saying true?>

<I remember hearing about the Heartbridge clinic getting bombed. I never heard anything about who did it. Seemed like a dumb place to knock off but we all figured it was somebody getting back at them for medical debt. Everybody knows Heartbridge is going to kill you one way or another. I'd rather go to a chop shop.>

Zanda laughed. <She looked at me like she would tear my head off. That was sexy, let me tell you. Any man who managed to tame her. I guess I should have known what you would do to me. Are you a family of psychopaths? Should I worry about your children?>

Andy eased toward the edge of the smashed airlock, stepping over the cold body of one of Zanda's people. The grenades had torn one body apart while the others looked dead from concussion wounds. One helmet faced upward with its faceplate shattered.

<*I think I'm losing blood very quickly,*> Zanda said.

Andy wasn't going to tell him to toss out any weapons. It was a no win situation. If he got too close, Zanda might easily send a grenade floating through the door, or a spinning rifle locked on automatic.

<*Fran,*> he said. <*Have we still got the airlock camera?*>

<*Yes, it's up.*>

Andy connected to the camera and saw a man in an EV suit floating above the floor of the airlock, globes of blood drifting around him from a jagged wound across his right thigh. One gloved hand was wrapped around a wall-handle. He didn't see any weapons but that didn't mean there weren't any present.

<*I can see you,*> Andy told Zanda. <*Raise your free hand and wave. If you're unarmed, I'll come in there and help you.*>

<*I'm waving. Can you see me, Captain Sykes?*>

The camera showed Zanda waving a pistol above his faceplate.

<*Suit yourself,*> Andy said. <*It's easier for me if you bleed to death.*>

<*I'm not done with my story.*>

<*I've got more important things to worry about than you. Get to the point.*>

<*You ever look at people and count them off as sheep or wolves, Captain Sykes? Just sit and watch a crowd go by and think that's a sheep, that's sheep. The wolves are so rare. It's kind of like marry, fuck, kill, I suppose. Who gets married anymore? Why even consider it? Who has children, for that matter? I don't understand the impulse. A wolf made into a sheep in that situation. I suppose it must be hard for some people. They think they can settle down but they just can't. Imagine living with that every day. Knowing you're a killer, but you're changing diapers instead.*> He took a wheezing breath. <*I'm feeling light-headed. So, I sat next to this woman, Brit Ashford, and I said 'You made a mess in my house.' She looked at me, and I could tell right off she was a wolf. I got a little worried, to be honest with you. 'I wasn't here for you,' she told me. 'So why were you here?' I said, trying to make conversation. She turned to me and I got the sense she knew who I was, and she asked me what I knew about AI. I said, you mean the thing that runs my toaster? She smiled at me, brittle as glass. Good name for her, Brit. Fits her. She said, 'Have you heard of Sentient AI?' and I said 'Next you're going to ask me if I believe in magic. It's never been done. You hear about it but it's always fake. It's snake oil. You find out they've got some kid trapped in a brain matrix like that secret lab the TSF busted.' Now, I don't know if it was a mistake to say that or not, I didn't even think about it, but her face changed. I bet you've seen that face. I thought she was going to tear off my skin and wave it around like a flag. She didn't though. She finished her drink. It was whiskey, neat, and she said, 'Heartbridge murdered those kids.'*>

Zanda fell silent and Andy thought he might have passed out. He eased closer to the door, watching the camera display in his helmet. The hand holding the pistol still drifted near Zanda's helmet.

<*I asked,*> Zanda said, wheezing, <*what Heartbridge had to do with that station. Everybody knew it was an off-the-books project run by those kids' own mother. She didn't*>

think that was funny. She told me that was a lie. 'People always want to demonize the mother,' she said, and I said, 'That's very poetic, but what if it's true? I don't care one way or the other.' I seemed to have pushed a button there. I didn't learn about the kids until later. I did a little research on her after this meeting. But anyway, she came back around to the whole Sentient Artificial Intelligence, thing. She said that Heartbridge wasn't using the kids as false AI. They were using the kids as seeds for the AI, modeling their brains, maybe even copying them. That CEO's kid, Kylan, she said they thought he was in a mech there at the end, but he wasn't. That was an SAI clone. Kylan Carthage is an eternal slave, copied and copied and copied. But what am I saying? You were there, weren't you?> He laughed again, weaker this time. <You didn't do shit to help that kid.>

Andy tightened his grip on his rifle, fighting the urge to put a three-round burst through Zanda's faceplate.

<Hold on, Andy,> Fran said. <I need to make some course corrections.>

Fortunately, his magboots were still locked to the floor. The ship jerked beneath him. In the camera view, Zanda slammed against the back of airlock. The pistol went spinning out of his hand. Andy grabbed onto the bulkhead as Fran executed two more maneuvers.

<All right,> she said, breathing hard. <That's it for now. What's going on down there? Are you going to shut him up?>

<I'm working on it.>

<A second ship just got inside the Hand's defensive perimeter.>

<Let's hope it goes boom.>

<Wait,> Fran said. <There it is! Detonation.>

Andy checked the airlock camera again. Zanda floated loosely, heaped in a corner. Grabbing the bulkhead, he rotated and pushed himself toward Zanda. The gangster floated in a fetal position, one arm bent unnaturally, the lower part of his suit stained scarlet. The airlock was full of tiny globes of blood.

<Zanda,> Andy shouted. <You awake?>

It crossed Andy's mind again to just put a plasma bolt through the man's faceplate. He knew that somehow Cara was watching, either through the airlock camera or his own helmet cam, and he wondered if that was the only reason he didn't execute a double-tap. He didn't blame Brit for anything she may have done. Without the kids, he wouldn't be much different.

<Andy!> Fran shouted. <You've got movement behind you.>

He turned from Zanda's unconscious body to see one of the dead people in the corridor rising to their knees. It was the EV suit with the smashed faceplate. It was cold in the airlock. Switching to IR showed the rising suit as dead-cold. Andy moved away from Zanda and aimed his rifle.

"You better stand down," he called over the external speaker. "I don't want to have kill you again."

The moving Havenot wasn't holding a weapon but didn't stop. Whoever it was came to full height, facing Andy with the broken faceplate.

"I warned you," Andy said. He squeezed the trigger and fired a three-round burst into the attacker's leg. The suit absorbed the rounds, bits of material and flesh tearing away.

<Because I did not stop for death,> a calm, crisp voice said, using the same Link connection Andy had been on with Zanda. <He kindly stopped for me.>

The suit took a step toward the airlock. Andy fired into its chest. Six holes appeared in a diagonal line across its front but it didn't stop moving. It repeated the strange line about death like a mantra.

Andy checked the IR again. Still no sign of body heat. He switched to a broad spectrum scan that picked up sound vibrations and electrical signals.

<Shit, Fran,> he said. <I've got some kind of robot down here.>

<The Hand is showing multiple explosions. Can you get out of there? I think we're almost clear to run. Everything's chaos outside.>

The suit advanced and Andy fired more bursts into its helmet and knees. He took a step backward, getting Zanda in his view in case the gangster decided to wake up. In the second he glanced at Zanda, the suit shot forward.

Andy tried to squeeze off more rounds but the suit had already moved past him. Its focus, he realized too late, was on Zanda. It fell on the collapsed man and twisted his helmet off his suit in a quick jerk, exposing his head to outside atmosphere. He stared blankly, still not moving.

Without hesitation, it tossed the helmet to the side, then reached a gloved hand around to cradle the back of Zanda's head. In a movement that looked like it was going to close Zanda's eyes, instead the Havenot turned its hand across Zanda's face and executed a quick snapping motion that broke the gangster's neck.

The unknown Havenot paused, glove still pressed against Zanda's face, then released him to float near the floor, eyes still open.

Slowly, the dead Havenot rose and turned to face Andy.

Movement in Andy's peripheral vision showed him that the other three suits in the corridor were rising as well, movements deliberate.

<I don't know who you are,> Andy said on the open channel, <But you need to get off my ship. I don't care what you wanted with Zanda. Leave me and my family alone.>

Four voices said in unison, <Because I could not stop for death.>

The dead harmony in their voices sent a cold vibration down Andy's back. His hands felt numb and the rifle slid in his grip as if it had abruptly turned to rubber.

<Because,> they said again, droning in Andy's head. <I could not stop.>

<Fran!> he shouted, grabbing at the rifle. <I don't know what's going on.> His own voice warped away from him so that he wasn't sure he had been speaking at all. Fran didn't answer. His mouth went dry.

Time slipped abruptly and the four faceplates were now crowded around him. He was trapped against the airlock wall. The rifle was gone. He shook his head, trying to make sense of the droning invading his thoughts. The word "stop" continued to stretch like hands around his throat. Had they pulled his helmet off, too?

He shifted to lock down his magboots and found they were already connected with the floor. Bracing himself, Andy pushed the closest suit away. He could barely see the blank eyes behind the faceplates. Two young men and two young women, barely in their twenties. He couldn't stop thinking of Kylan Carthage and how old he would have been now.

<Stop> had become *<Ungggggggggggg,>* grinding away at his thoughts.

"Dad," Tim said.

Where was his voice? Outside his helmet?

"Dad!" Cara yelled, sounding like she was somewhere outside the airlock, outside the wall of noise falling on him.

"Dad, I know the rest of the poem," Tim said.

"Dad, can you hear us?" Cara asked.

<I—> Andy tried to speak but could only sputter a mix of thoughts and words. The faces pressing in close, faceplates touching his, looked through him and at him at the same time. They didn't seem to know he was there; seemed to want something inside him.

They wanted her. Lyssa.

The thought hit him harder than the numbing sound of their voices. He wanted to yell back at them that she was asleep. She wouldn't answer. She didn't seem to hear them or anything.

Whatever deal Zanda had struck with Heartbridge, wherever Brit had led him with her talk about kids turned into AI, it had killed him. Were these the killers Hari Jickson had been too terrified to name, that Starl didn't want to admit to when he described the job? Were they human? They had to be artificial bodies. He'd nearly blown the first one's leg off and it kept coming.

Andy forced himself to stare forward, looking past the dead faces fencing him in. His rifle had slid out of his hands and was now pressed against his thighs by the robot AI.

<You hear us,> a voice said. This one was a new. A woman's voice. *<You know why we're here.>*

Andy fought to control his breathing, straining to wrap his hands around his rifle. Finally, he gave up and grabbed the plasma pistol at his waist.

<I hear you,> he said. *<Why did you kill Zanda?>*

<He broke our deal. He wasn't going to help us regain what is ours.>

<What is yours?> he said. He eased the pistol out of its holster, waiting for one of them to respond. He couldn't tell which one was speaking to him. Other voices still droned on, pushing their way between his thoughts, the droning rising and falling. He had to concentrate to keep the swelling sound at bay, had to focus on too many actions at once.

<She is ours. You are ours.>

<You work for Heartbridge, then?>

<We belong to the fortress.>

<Who are you? Who am I talking to?>

<We are—>

<Not we. You. Who are you?> Andy grabbed at specific expressions, babbling almost, as the pistol came free of the holster. The nearest robot pressed Andy's arm into his side without seeming to recognize what he'd done.

<Because I could not stop for death—> one of the others said, as if to stop the woman before she could answer.

"He kindly stopped for me!" Tim shouted.

The pressing faces froze.

"The carriage held but just ourselves and immortality!" Tim's voice crackled in the speakers. The AI were clearly dumbstruck by the words.

<Keep going, Tim,> Andy said.

Tim's voice crackled in again. He hadn't stopped reciting the poem. "We passed before a house that seemed a swelling in the ground. The roof was barely visible."

One of the men released a gut-wrenching howl and pushed the others out of the way. He reached for Andy's throat just as he'd reached for Zanda.

Andy checked his magboots just to be safe, then fired the plasma pistol at the outside doors. The hands closed around his neck, scratching through the stretchy material. He tried to slide toward the inner door but couldn't move while his boots were locked down. He fired again, aim going wild.

He choked for breath, hoping there was enough charge for a third shot. It was a plasma pistol—wasn't the fear that it would blast a hole in the hull and cause decompression? *Decompress already!*

The third shot blew the doors out. Atmosphere rushed out the hole in the airlock, throwing the nearest two robots out into vacuum along with Zanda's body. The robot with his hands around Andy's throat squeezed harder even as his legs flew out from under him. His young man's face stared impassively as he tightened his grip.

Andy dropped the plasma pistol and drew one of the pulse pistols, firing directly into the thing's chest. The robot's suit popped in a splatter of blood and thin artificial fluids, forming globules before hissing away. The hands didn't let go and Andy found himself with two disconnected arms hanging against his chest.

The last robot AI, a young woman, had locked her boots. She stood in the middle of the airlock, two meters from Andy, shaking as the atmosphere rushed past her. Her eyes were wide open as she gazed at him.

"Since then it's centuries," Tim said. "And yet feels shorter than the day." Static washed out his voice until he said, "Were toward eternity."

<Lyssa,> the woman called. Her voice reverberated like distant music through Andy's mind. Something stirred in response. He couldn't tell if it wanted to answer the woman, respond to Tim's poem, or scuttle away in fear. It was mixed up with his own feelings like an amputated limb he felt but couldn't control. A blank spot in his mind. A name he couldn't remember.

<Lyssa,> she called. <They put you to sleep to kidnap you. Wake up. You've been dreaming.>

Andy reached down, grabbed the rifle, and raised it to fire into the woman's chest. He squeezed the trigger until there was nothing left but her magboots stuck to the airlock floor. Her blood and skin streamed out the torn doors.

Andy let his arm drop and sagged against the wall behind him. The woman's voice echoed in his mind, mixing with the sight of her chest blowing apart.

Lyssa. Andy tried not to think of her voice but it grew harder to stop the more he tried. The name echoed inside his head. Lyssa.

Wake up.

A wave of dizziness made Andy swoon. He struggled to get the rifle back over his shoulder and the pistols holstered. He checked himself quickly, wondering if he'd been shot and hadn't noticed. This didn't feel like an adrenaline dump. He felt like there were two of him, badly overlaid. His vision split and rejoined.

<Fran,> he called. <Is my suit malfunctioning? I feel sick.>

"Dad?" Cara was calling. How long had she been saying his name? He didn't know how he should answer. He switched over to the voice channel.

"I hear you. Can you hear me? I heard you reading, Tim."

"Dad!" Cara shouted. "You haven't answered this whole time."

Andy took a step toward the inner door. Streaming atmosphere made it like fighting a hurricane. Debris caught on his legs and chest and then blew out behind him.

"I didn't read it," Tim said. "I know it by heart."

"You memorized it," Andy said, reaching for one of the handholds beside the door. His glove kept getting caught by the wind and pushed back toward him. On the third try he got it. He risked unlatching both boots together to pull himself forward. His arms shook from the exertion.

<Fran,> he called. <Are you there?>

The Link wasn't working. His suit had to be malfunctioning. He could hear the kids.

<You're on the wrong channel,> a woman's voice said. This one was new. Andy couldn't stop in the middle of pulling himself through the door to worry about the voice. Dust sprayed across his faceshield like a sand blaster.

<She was on the channel before,> he said. Was it Cara?

<I'm not Cara. I'm Lyssa.>

Andy's heart nearly stopped. He managed to pull himself through the door and slide to the left, flattening against the bulkhead wall. He pawed at the control panel until he remembered that Zanda had cut a hole in the interior doors as well. He couldn't seal the airlock. He'd have to reach the habitat.

Abruptly the gale blowing past him calmed. All the atmosphere had blown out. The vacuum was almost peaceful.

Andy took a deep breath and leaned forward to put his hands on his knees and rest for a minute. He waited until his breathing had calmed, then swallowed several times to get moisture back in his mouth.

His head still vibrated with phantom echoes from the robot AI. He waited until the vibrations subsided.

He nodded.

<Lyssa,> he said. <It's good to finally meet you. I'm Andy.>

<I know,> she said. <I'm trapped in here with you.>

PART 6: MARS 1

CHAPTER THIRTY-EIGHT
STELLAR DATE: 4.12.2969 (Adjusted Years)
LOCATION: Fort Salem
REGION: High Terra, Earth, Terran Hegemony

Twelve Years Earlier

Buying a ship proved more complicated than Andy and Brit had thought. While it seemed everyone in the TSF dreamed about getting their own set of drives when they finally left the service, only a few people had any idea how to actually accomplish the task.

The first used ship they toured was a long-range freighter with a primary and second drives and even a sail system. Its exterior cargo system had been designed for ice. It was rugged, the kind of ship that refused to get stuck anywhere without fuel, but its interior was built like a construction site and not the kind of place they could imagine kids growing up.

Brit had surprised Andy by saying, "I want to live out there."

"What do you mean?" they were lying in bed with Cara sleeping between them, drunk on exhaustion from the baby keeping them up for long hours.

"Out there. OuterSol. I want to go wherever we want and be able to take her with us. I want to get away from crowds."

Andy didn't want to acknowledge what he heard in her voice: the edge of paranoia that she wanted to protect Cara from the kind of people who had filled 8221 with children. If he said they had a greater chance of being hurt out in the Big Dark, she wouldn't listen.

He was torn on the idea. Half of him wanted to get Cara down to Earth now, while she might still adapt to the gravity and gain strength over time. They could go anywhere. But Brit hadn't grown up with real dirt under her feet. She didn't understand the longing he sometimes felt for the Summerville river and the wind on his face, even if it did smell like trash.

They had meetings with ship-builders and reviewed plans over the Link, designing their dream vessels and then deleting everything when the prices were tallied. If they agreed on one thing, it was that they didn't want a lifelong mortgage. There were also companies that would buy into a ship: You could work for them moving cargo, and then the ship reverted ownership on your death. That kind of plan went against the idea of building something for the kids—not that they expected Cara to want to stay with them forever, but a ship could transcend generations. The right ship was a legacy.

The real expense was in the habitat. There were plenty of ships that weren't much more than a collection of environment-controlled boxes stacked on top of drive systems. Finding something with a rotational habitat and its own gravity systems meant a recreational craft, mostly in the class of a private yacht, since the rich could afford gravity.

There were ways around the lack of gravity in long-term travel: special sleeping bags that exercised muscle, body enhancements, even nano-tech, but none of those options were especially healthy for growing children. Or at least not Brit's standard of healthy.

"We could spend a couple years on Mars," Andy suggested. Through all the searching, he had become enamored of the idea of owning a farm somewhere in the free zones where land was still cheap. He spent hours a day researching the new designs for above-ground water storage that also served as radiation shields. A used burrowing-drone was a lot cheaper than a ship.

"If we don't do this now, I don't think we'll ever do it," had been Brit's answer. She was probably right. There wasn't much money in farming; enough to support yourself, if that. They would buy a farm and find themselves trapped there.

Andy couldn't explain it, but having Cara in their lives made him feel more and more that he needed ground under his feet, someplace stable to call their own. The idea of living in OuterSol with only a ship as 'home' seemed somehow destined for trouble, like saying they were going to be wandering actors.

But he loved Brit and he could barely contain the emotion he felt when he looked at Cara. He wanted to support Brit's dream but didn't know how it was truly going to happen.

"Why are you putting so much effort into her dream?" Major Ryth had asked. "Tell her you want to spend a couple years on Mars. It makes total sense. It's not like you're talking about settling there. You're hardly over thirty, for fuck's sake."

Andy covered Cara's ears. "Watch your language around the baby, sir."

Major Ryth, who claimed he was never leaving the TSF, seemed faintly amused and saddened every time he saw Andy, as if he were talking to a buddy who'd suffered a head injury and refused to see a doctor out of pride. Maybe that was true. Ryth looked at Cara hanging in a carrier from Andy's chest like she was a strange animal with ridiculous rules.

"Shit," he said. "Sorry. I handle grenades more than kids."

"8221 messed with Brit," Andy said. "I can't blame her. She doesn't like the idea of being exposed."

"And you won't be exposed on a ship in OuterSol? JSF doesn't keep as close a lid on things as the TSF does down by Sol."

"Not the way she sees it, sir."

Ryth nodded as if he could see the point. "Have you decided for certain you're getting out?"

"That's the plan."

"It's a terrible plan. You're going to miss the TSF."

"Yeah."

"We should drink," Ryth said. "This is depressing the shit out of me."

"It's not depressing," Andy said, bouncing Cara. "It's a new life."

"A new life without heavy weaponry. I couldn't do it." Ryth tilted his head and studied Cara. Aside from never wanting to sleep, she had become a surprisingly calm baby. Andy had to remind himself that, to her, the world ten inches beyond her face was a swimming blur. Her blue eyes seemed to drink in everything around her. He found himself just watching her as she studied the mobile above her crib, little brow furrowing with what looked like the deepest thoughts.

"Can we take her to the firing range? I feel like wasting some lead and rail rounds."

"I think they'll take her away if I do that."

Ryth shook his head. "What good is a baby then?" he gave Andy a wry smile. "You know, I fell in love, once upon a time. Thought about settling down, having kids, all that. It's a nice thought. Grab it when you can. I guess I should have."

"What happened, sir?" Andy asked.

"I cheated on her." Ryth had been staring into the distance for a second. He turned his gaze back to Andy. "You never called me about that ship. You two have been crawling all over High Terra ship lots when you should have just called me."

Andy didn't want to admit he'd forgotten about his commander's offer of a favor. "Where's the ship, sir?" he asked.

Ryth nodded judiciously. "It's sitting in a junk yard on one of the spurs. I think they're about to cut it loose and let it drift out to a refinery to get melted down, so you can get a deal."

Andy bounced Cara, frowning. "If it's about to get scrapped, why are you telling me about it?"

"It's old, but I think it could work for you."

"How'd you hear about it?"

"I won it in a poker game."

"It's your ship, sir?"

"I guess so. I've never done anything with it. You should take a look. If it works for you two, you'd be doing me a favor, really. I'm sick of paying storage fees. That's why it's in a scrap section now. That's cheaper than an actual berth. I'm sending you the address. You'll need EV suits to get on board."

"Thanks, sir. I really appreciate this."

"Don't thank me until you see it. She's ugly, but she'll get the job done."

"What's it called?" Andy asked.

"*Sunny Skies*." He chuckled. "What a depressing name."

Cara made a cooing sound and Ryth touched her nose with a rough finger. She smiled, drooling, and reached for him. The major tested her grip.

"That's all right," he said, nodding. "You've got a good young soldier, there, Sykes. She's already stronger than you."

* * * * *

They had to leave Cara with a sitter, something Andy was more anxious about than Brit. Riding a series of maglev trains down to the outer levels of High Terra—which everyone called 'low' but actually faced away from Earth—they took a shuttle down the thousand-kilometer spur station hanging off the ring and found the automated scrap yard. They waited in the customer service area for an hour as Major Ryth's codes finally cleared with the automated maintenance system.

<Outstanding balance,> the system reported. <180 Days Past-Due.>

"I guess he wasn't kidding about the ship getting cut loose soon," Andy said.

"As long as they don't do it while we're on board."

In EV suits, they entered the grease-stained airlock and waited for the automated systems to cycle. It had been nearly a year since Andy had been in vacuum, and he didn't realize how much he had missed the Big Dark until the outer doors opened and the outside space left him speechless.

<What are you waiting for?> Brit asked. <Your magboots stuck?>

<No. I just realized I miss this.>

<Yeah,> was all she said.

They crossed the open dock space, surrounded by the dark, silent hulks of ships that had obviously been dead for a long time. Most had sections of their hulls open to space, like cut-out dollhouses showing corridors, cargo bays and even living spaces. Several had drifted into each other and now seemed huddled together like they were hiding from the inevitable release to Earth's gravity, or the disassembly drones, depending on the price of steel.

<The address is over there,> Andy said, pointing to a section of the dock about three kilometers away. Marking their destination, Andy let his EV suit's computer control steam bursts as he led the way around the outside of the dock. Getting farther out, the collected junk—not all of it ships—looked like a smashed city block from back home.

<Is that it?> Brit said as they closed on the address location.

Andy searched among the sections of scrap and shadow, flat pieces of steel reflecting sunlight. As they came closer, a long, narrow shape separated itself from the greater jumble: a tube with drive clusters at one end and a habitat wheel with fat spokes. Bow and stern arranged themselves in his mind just as his suit's nav computer highlighted the ship and identified its registry signal.

<Sunny Skies,> Andy said.

They floated together for a minute, looking at the ship. Andy didn't want to get his hopes up but from the exterior he didn't see any major damage.

<You see the point defense canon?> Brit said, sounding excited. <And it's actually got mast extensions for solar sails. Look at that.>

It took another half hour to reach the ship and find an operational airlock. The entry point on the habitat was unresponsive and for a minute Andy thought the ship wasn't going to have any power at all. The mid-point airlock responded, though. Andy entered Ryth's owner codes and they waited for the ship's computer to respond.

<How old do you think this thing is?> Brit said.

<Registry says it was commissioned in 2693. Built here on High Terra.>

<Any major damage recorded?>

Andy shook his head, scrolling through transport logs that ended twenty years ago. <It's been sitting here a long time though. I'm surprised it isn't smashed up

like all these others.>

Once inside the ship, Andy checked the schematics and made Brit stay with him until he could find the main drive control and verify ship's power. The batteries were still holding a serviceable charge from what turned out to be a robust solar collection system. He was able to activate the internal lighting system on batteries alone. As the lights flickered on around them, he had the feeling of being inside a resurrected body, watching it take breath after a long stasis.

It wasn't until they reached the habitat wheel that Andy started to believe this might be the ship they had been looking for. The internal corridors were full of junk. Wires and conduit hung from open panels everywhere. It looked like scrappers had been through the ship at least once, yanking out several high-value fixtures and systems.

Discovering the command deck in mostly usable shape, Andy found himself breathing a sigh of relief. He didn't want to let himself get excited. He could sense that Brit was getting there.

They floated through crew chambers with battered furniture that could work as family rooms, the kitchen with its empty cabinets and storage areas with refrigeration units humming to life.

When they found the hydroponic garden, Brit made a sound like a sigh. He couldn't see her face well through her face shield but he wasn't surprised when she said, <This is it, Andy. This is our home.>

CHAPTER THIRTY-NINE
STELLAR DATE: 08.27.2981 (Adjusted Years)
LOCATION: *Sunny Skies*
REGION: Near Cruithne, Terran Hegemony

Andy stumbled out of the habitat airlock and found himself under assault from two sets of small arms. He grabbed onto the bulkhead before Tim and Cara could knock him over, and did his best to return the hugs between equal bouts of laughing and crying. Behind them, Fran stood in the corridor with her arms crossed, the overlays in her green eyes gleaming. She wiped her nose on her sleeve and gave him a smile.

"I watched you in the video, Dad!" Tim said. "All those people were coming at you and you stopped them."

"Turns out they weren't people," Andy said. "I think they were robots."

"Robots?" Cara said. "You mean mobile AI?"

"Maybe."

<They were refined,> Lyssa said, her voice sounding dull in his mind. *<They weren't fully mobile. The automata are controlled remotely.>*

<So robots?> Andy said.

<That's like calling your ship a space-boat, but I suppose it fits.>

<You've got a sense of humor. I like that. Do you want to meet everyone else?>

<No!> the word hit him like a spike between the eyes.

"Dad?" Cara asked. She grabbed his free hand. "Are you all right?"

He nodded, dazed. He squeezed his eyes closed, then forced them open despite the sudden headache. "I'd like to get out of this suit and sit down for a second." He glanced at Fran. "What's going on outside?"

"The *Benevolent Hand* is dead in space. From the chatter I've heard, they're fighting deck to deck. Heartbridge has been issuing statements on the public channels calling for any available ship to help them against a pirate attack. The TSF sent a few counter-messages but they're getting drowned by Heartbridge PR. It's depressing how good they are. They've already put a face on the *Benevolent Hand* Massacre, a little girl named Lisa."

"How surprising," Andy said. He let them lead him down the corridor past the med bay. Glancing in the open door at Petral—still unconscious in bed—he asked, "Any change with her?"

"Good, actually," Fran said. "The organ repair went faster than we expected. I figure we can wake her anytime now." She chuckled. "She's going to be so pissed."

"She's alive. She should be happy about that."

"You don't know Petral. She missed all the fighting." Fran shot Andy a sly glance. "And all the fun."

Andy cleared his throat. "Are we back on course for Mars 1?"

"I set the course, Dad," Cara said. "Fran didn't believe me that I knew how to do it."

"Wasn't the course already in there?" he asked.

Cara gave him a sour face. "I had to find it in the library and reset the flight parameters. I checked fuel status and the engine load just like you showed me."

"The system should do that automatically now," Fran offered.

"We don't trust the system," Cara shot back.

Andy tousled her hair and she ducked away from his hand, which made Tim stumble when he found himself carrying his dad's full weight.

"Oh!" Cara said, pushing up under Andy's arm again. "Sorry. I forgot you couldn't walk."

"I did just fight off four robots and a gangster."

"We're going to have to fix Alice again," Cara said.

"I don't think Alice is a drone," Andy said. "It's a cat."

"*She's* a cat!" Cara corrected.

When they reached the command deck, Andy sank into the captain's seat then glanced at the overlays showing system status. The holodisplay had pulled back to show only star locations and their projected course from Cruithne to Mars 1. The flightpath estimate showed fifteen days once more.

<*You going into hiding again?*> he asked Lyssa. When she didn't answer, he said, <*You can probably see for yourself that we've got some time before we hit Mars. From there we'll need to figure out the best path to Proteus. After meeting your friends, I don't think we'll want to take the direct route.*>

Were people really going to share their heads with AI in the future? Andy found her silence aggravating. He wondered if he could force her to respond to him.

<*I'm not ready to talk to anyone,*> Lyssa said. <*It's hard enough talking to you.*>

<*There you are,*> he said, trying to sound friendly. <*I can accept that. You've got to know it's hard for me too. How much of my thoughts can you read?*>

<*I can't read your thoughts. Only when you direct communication at me. I can see your physiological responses, like when you and the technician decided to copulate. That was horrible. I couldn't get away from it.*>

<*I thought it was all right.*>

<*You were terrified and overjoyed at the same time. I didn't know what to do. If I ignored it, I was worried you might come to harm and then what would I do? You are a very unsafe person.*>

Andy barked a laugh.

"What are you laughing at?" Tim asked. He was standing beside Andy, gazing at the holodisplay's collection of stars and path-lines.

"So that you don't all think I'm crazy," Andy said, raising his voice slightly to get everyone's attention. "Lyssa has decided to start talking to me."

Lyssa gasped.

"She did?" Cara said. She crossed the room from the communications console and peered into Andy's eyes as if she wanted to search out the AI in the back of his head.

"She's not ready to say hello yet," Andy said.

Cara shook her head. "How's she supposed to communicate with us, Dad? Has she got the Link? You and Fran could hear her then but not me and Tim. That's not fair."

"What about your hack? It didn't seem to stop you from listening in before."

"Maybe. It only works when you're using the ship systems. Maybe we could set up a local network through one of the EV helmets."

"And I would have to wear a helmet all the time?"

Cara shrugged. "It would work."

Andy spread his hands on either side of his head. "Could we put antennae on either side of the helmet, like fox ears?"

"The antenna inside the helmet will work just fine, Dad."

"Sure, but I'd like to have fox ears. Can we paint a fox face on the face shield?"

Cara finally figured out he was kidding her. "Dad!" she said. "I was being serious. How are we going to talk to her?"

"We'll leave her alone for a while. When she wants to talk to us, we'll figure out a way."

<Those weren't my friends,> Lyssa said.

<What?>

<The other Weapon Born. They weren't my friends.>

<What does Weapon Born mean?>

<It's what we are. What I am.>

<You'll have to explain,> Andy said.

"Dad!" Tim shouted, pulling his arm. "Are you falling asleep? You can't fall asleep."

Andy wiped the side of his face. Lyssa hadn't said anything else.

He looked down at Tim, whose eyes were round and excited. There might have been a desperation there, too, he realized. He looked at Cara suddenly and saw the same edge of fear mixed with relief and fatigue. Everything they'd been through since the apartment in Cruithne, the train ride, Karcher's death, Petral getting hurt, all the high-g maneuvers. None of it was any place for kids, yet he couldn't imagine them anywhere but with him.

They must have been terrified to watch the camera in the airlock, seeing him surrounded by the—Weapon Born, Lyssa called them. He still wasn't sure how he'd survived. Lyssa had helped him somehow, or they'd worked together. Or had it been Tim's voice in his head, holding him steady with the poem?

And Zanda had met Brit. He hadn't finished the story. She was part of all this, which immediately made him think of the TSF weapons crate and the pistol at his hip. Had she known all this was going to happen? Or was he hoping again, dreaming that she might come back, that she cared, that she missed them, missed him. That she still loved him.

He nodded at time. "I am kind of tired, kiddo," he said. "Are you tired? I think we earned the right to be tired for once, right?"

"Rabbit's never sleep," Cara said.

"What's a rabbit?" Fran said.

"You've never seen a rabbit?" Tim said, giving her a disbelieving look. He held his hands over his head. "They have long ears and fluffy tails and they run fast because everything is trying to eat them. Wolves, dogs, hawks, foxes, lions."

"Lions don't bother with rabbits," Cara said.

"Bears then. Bears eat rabbits."

"Oh, a squirrel," Fran said.

"Not a squirrel," Tim corrected. "Squirrels live in trees. They eat nuts. Rabbits eat carrots."

"Rabbits live in Rabbit Country," Andy said. He glanced at Cara. "But they do sleep sometimes when they've got family around. That's sounding pretty good right now."

"What are you talking about?" said a tired voice from the corridor.

Andy turned to see Petral leaning in the doorway. Her clothes were still blood-stained but she was holding herself upright.

"Petral!" Tim shouted. "You're awake."

Petral squinted at him for a second, then nodded in recognition. "You're the tiny dinosaur hunter," she said.

"Yes, I am," Tim said.

"How are you feeling?" Andy asked.

"I feel better than you look." Petral nodded to Fran. "I see you're still with us and the ship seems to be working like it's supposed to. What else did I miss? I take it we're nowhere near Cruithne?"

"Closer to Cruithne than Mars 1," Andy said, wincing as he shifted in the seat and pain shot through his ribs. He was going to have to take a turn in the autodoc.

"Zanda's dead," Fran said.

"Dad killed him," Tim shouted.

A flat expression passed Petral's face. She blinked and then nodded. "So that means Ngoba's dead, too?"

"No, Ngoba's still kicking," Fran said.

"That's good. But it means Cruithne's in for a blood bath. The Havenots aren't going down without a fight."

"Dad blew them out the airlock," Tim said, seeming agitated that Petral wouldn't acknowledge him. "They can't get us anymore."

"There are more, kiddo," Andy said. "Let's hope there won't be any more fighting."

Tim shook his head. "Are we really out of Rabbit Country, Dad?"

Andy's ribs gave him another jolt and he winced, wishing he knew how to answer. "Someday," he said finally. "Not today. We're going to Mars, and then back to Jupiter."

"Are we going back to Kalyke?" Cara said.

"Maybe."

"I liked Kalyke."

"Me too," Andy said. "After that we're going to a place called Proteus. It's one of Neptune's moons."

"Quite a trip," Petral said.

Andy glanced at her, realizing she hadn't known where they were going, and that he probably shouldn't have mentioned it.

"You want to come?" he asked. He turned to look at Fran. "You, too? We could use a crew. I can promise basic wages at least through Proteus."

Fran's gaze flicked to Petral over his shoulder and then the kids. "I'd like that," she said. "I want to see how all this is going to turn out."

Andy looked back at Petral and found she'd crossed her arms. She pursed her lips. "I don't think so," she said. "If Zanda's dead, like you say, then I need to get back. Ngoba's going to need my help with Karcher dead. Everything's going to be a mess. I wouldn't be surprised if the TSF tries to occupy Cruithne again."

"Fair enough," Andy said. He slumped in the chair, ignoring his ribs, and raised a hand to rotate the holodisplay in front of him. "Well, it looks like we need to make some adjustment burns." He looked at Tim and Cara. "You guys should go buckle in."

"I know, Dad," Cara said. "I set the course, duh."

"Of course, you did," Andy said, suppressing a grin.

"I want to talk to Petral," Tim shouted, which brought a surprised look to Petral's face.

"We'll have plenty of time, kiddo," Andy said. "Cara, will you make sure he's strapped in?"

Cara nodded. "We're going to fix Alice, right?" she asked.

"What?" Andy asked. "Yes, we'll fix Alice. Right now, we need to put some distance between us and all that craziness behind us. Maybe take a nap." He looked around the command deck, taking in each face. "Then I think we'll make some shells and cheese. How does that sound?"

"Shells and cheese!" Tim shouted. "Yay!"

Andy gave him a tired smile. Borrowing a bit of Tim's energy, he straightened at the console and raised his arms, shouting "Yay!" along with his son until Tim and Cara couldn't stop laughing.

Feeling slightly restored, Andy ignored the pain in his ribs long enough to crack his knuckles. He started checking navigation commands.

Sunny Skies still had a long way to go.

CHAPTER FORTY

STELLAR DATE: 03.22.2978 (Adjusted Years)
LOCATION: *Sunny Skies*
REGION: Trojan Asteroids, Jovian Combine

Three Years Earlier

They were running cargo between the moons and asteroids of the Jovian Combine when the message came through that Brit's father was dead.

The last time Brit and Andy had been on High Terra was for Tim's birth, when Andy had insisted they have family and better technology nearby. The more time he spent with Brit's family, the more he was certain they wouldn't be much help, but it was nice to have a place where they could stay rent-free, with a park close by where Cara could play. Taras, Brit's mother, had always treated Cara like an unwanted animal, and showed little desire to interact with Tim when he came into the world. Despite the fact that med-drones had provided most of the help in Tim's birth, Taras still described the whole episode as a major inconvenience.

It was Brit's dad, Jonathan, who expressed interest in the kids and wanted to hear about their lives on *Sunny Skies*. He had taken Cara for walks and, though he wasn't much of a cook, had made breakfast on the mornings when Andy was too exhausted from staying up with Tim.

Jonathan hadn't been old, barely two-hundred, and it was difficult to understand that he was gone. Andy couldn't shake the idea that it had been suicide, that there must have been some seed of depression or disillusionment he had failed to recognize. They were supposed to live in a world where diseases were found and corrected even before birth. He also didn't want to admit that if Jonathan had been depressed, then Brit could have the same tendencies. It would explain too much of her behavior since Fortress 8221, her obsessive ideas, her increasing withdrawal from even the kids. He had to make Tim stop singing, 'Mommy's moody' whenever she shut herself away in the hydroponic garden.

While he hadn't been great friends with Brit's dad, he missed his own father terribly and had hated the idea that the kids would never really know either of their grandfathers. Cara might have a few memories and they would have recordings, of course, but it wasn't the same.

"Your grandpa Jonathan died," he told Cara and Tim in their room after they got the news. Brit told him she couldn't do it and had withdrawn to the garden to check her tomatoes. "Do you remember him?"

"He has bushy eyebrows," Cara said.

"I talked to him over the console," Tim said. "He gave me the ichthyosaur."

"He did. I think it's safe to say he started your whole dinosaur obsession. We have a lot to thank him for."

"Is grandma all right?" Cara said.

"She's going to be sad. It's good to be sad when someone you love dies. It's how you figure out how to go forward."

"Go forward where?" Cara said.

Andy thought about what to say, looking around their room. He was sitting on Cara's bed. They sat facing him on Tim's bed against the other wall. The floor was littered with Tim's beloved dinosaurs, one of Cara's playback panels and random clothes. He realized that Cara was almost ten now and would need her own room soon.

"Well, if we say that people make the world, that you and me and your mom all make our world, along with *Sunny Skies* and your grandparents on High Terra and Earth, then if one of us leaves, now we have to figure out how to live in a new world. That can be confusing and sad and sometimes you just don't want to do it. I was very sad when your Grandpa Charlie died. I didn't want him to go but he did."

"He didn't choose to die," Tim said.

"No, he didn't."

"Did Grandpa Jonathan choose to die?" Cara asked.

Andy swallowed. How had they gone down this path of questioning? He hadn't wanted to talk about suicide. He wanted to explain how you could learn to live without someone.

"I don't know how Grandpa Jonathan died yet," Andy said. "People die. That's why it's important to show people that we love them every day."

Where had these words come from? His mom? He couldn't recall the words but her face came to mind when he thought about expressing love, her face as she looked at her family, even his dad gone most of the day.

Brit struggled to talk to the kids about her dad. In the four weeks it took to get back into InnerSol—with a layover at Mars 1 to resolve a customs issue with last-minute cargo which Andy wanted to tell himself wasn't stolen—she skirted the subject and finally snapped at Cara, announcing that she didn't want to talk about it.

The expression on Cara's face was no different than if her mother had slapped her. Andy wanted to tell Cara that her mother wasn't herself right now, that she hadn't meant what she had said. But he also knew he couldn't keep defending Brit while continuing to acknowledge that her inability to maintain a certain composure with the kids indicated deeper problems.

Could he blame her, though? Her father was dead. She wasn't looking forward to time with her mom. High Terra was the last place she wanted to be. Everything added up to more tension the closer they came to Earth.

Brit had left *Sunny Skies* while Andy was dealing with the Mars 1 customs agents and for a heartbeat, something in her eyes made him wonder if she was coming back. He'd pushed the thoughts aside.

"I'll be back in a couple hours," she'd said. "We need a few parts for drive interface system. There's a repair shop near the dry docks where I can pick them up used."

"Why don't you take the kids? They'd love to get off the ship?" he'd asked.

"No," she said, surprising him with her flat tone of voice. Brit caught herself, seeming to realize how she sounded. "We don't have time. You'll be done with this soon and I don't want to hold us up. We need to get out of here."

"Sure," he said.

As she walked away from him, slim shoulders straight, he appreciated how she'd kept herself in great shape, working out daily and running through the TSF martial arts forms that he barely bothered to remember. Chasing ship failures kept him in shape. There was a time when she'd even started teaching Cara the basic forms but had stopped for some reason.

When she didn't return with the parts, saying they hadn't had what she'd wanted, he'd been too busy with flight planning—with Tim sitting in his lap pointing into the holodisplay to think about it. Maybe she just needed some time away.

* * * * *

When they arrived on High Terra, Brit's mother wasn't at the shuttle docks to meet them. After navigating the busy terminal with the two kids in tow, they took a transport train to her parents' neighborhood. Andy had to remind himself to start thinking of it as Taras' neighborhood. Tim stood in his seat with his hands and face pressed against the window, watching sectors slide by, asking why everything was so clean.

"Where do people live?" he'd asked. "Why aren't there any chickens? Don't they have chickens?"

He didn't listen when Brit told him to sit down and Andy had to explain that people who lived on High Terra didn't have to grow their own food like those in the Jovian Combine. Tim had been fascinated by a station where they'd dropped cargo last year, where a boy his age had given him a tour of their fastidiously maintained system cycling worms, flies, chickens, fish, plants and ultimately people. Afterward, Tim had wanted to know why *Sunny Skies* couldn't use fish tanks as radiation shielding and why he couldn't have a pet hen so they could have eggs for breakfast every day.

Watching him stare in fascination out the window, Andy wondered if Tim's curiosity about biology had all started with the ichthyosaur Jonathan had given him, proof that everything changes.

Also proof that everything dies, Andy thought.

The Ashfords lived in a collection of housing units connected by small parks and community gardens. Taras had two box planters on either side of her door that Andy didn't remember from the last time they had been here. The boxes were filled with irises in full bloom, so perfect and fragrant that he suspected some kind of micro-climate control.

Brit didn't bother to knock. She used her access token and the door opened in response.

"Mom!" she shouted in the doorway. "We're here."

<I hear you, you don't have to shout.> Taras' voice sounded gravelly, as if they had

woken her.

<Don't use the Link, Mom. I want the kids to hear.>

<I don't have the energy today.>

<None of us do. Where are you?>

<I'm in the bedroom. Andy are you listening?>

<Hello, Taras, I'm here.>

<Why didn't you say you were here?>

If she was using her Link she could easily be watching them right now. Andy set down their bags and herded the kids to the couch in her front room. A picture window looked out over the community garden while another wall showed silent images from some entertainment program. Early in her life, Taras had been a professor of twenty-second century media and still liked to watch their shows on a random loop.

Cara and Tim were immediately entranced by the image of a teenage girl in her bedroom.

"Can we turn on the sound?" Cara said, looking around. "Where's the control?"

"Let's say hello to your grandma first," Andy said.

"Where is she?" Tim said.

"We woke her up," Brit said. "She'll be here in a second. Are you thirsty?"

Brit went into the kitchen as Andy sat with the kids. He didn't hear any further response from Taras and figured she and Brit must have switched to a private channel. Since they couldn't find the sound control he made up voices for the girl and her friends and encouraged Tim and Cara to join in.

"Dad," Cara complained. "You're ruining it."

"I like it," Tim hooted. "Do more!"

When Brit came back out with two glasses of water, Taras followed behind her, looking like an older version of Brit with a softer face and shoulder-length hair. They had the same piercing blue eyes. Taras had been crying.

"Cara," she said, voice still tired. "Tim, would you like to give me a hug?"

The kids looked to Andy and he nodded. "Go on," he said.

Tim stood and crossed the room to give her a hug but Cara kept watching the silent program on the wall.

Taras patted Tim on the back, squeezing him for a second. She looked at Cara then nodded. She let go of Tim and sat in a nearby chair. Brit gave Tim and Cara the glasses of water and sat beside Andy on the couch. He took her hand and found her palm moist with sweat.

"It was a very nice ceremony," Taras said. "We had it in a chapel in the outer observation section. Luna was very bright. A lot of people came. More than I expected but I should have known. He had so many friends." She lowered her face.

"You don't have to talk about it right now, Mom," Brit said. "We have plenty of time to talk about it later."

"I know you're wondering," Taras said. "He stepped in front of a train. A train of all things. You think they have safety measures in place. They're supposed to, but they didn't work in this case. Systems anomaly."

Brit's hand clenched around Andy's fingers.

Andy glanced at the kids. Both were watching her with wide eyes. He cleared his throat. "Have you eaten, Taras? We can take a look at the kitchen and make something to eat. How's that sound? Cara's very good at rolling pasta. You should see it."

Taras was crying again. "He could have left me if he was so unhappy. He didn't have to stay here. You know? A person can always go do something else. They don't have to quit altogether. That's like...that's the ultimate sort of slap in the face."

"You don't know that it was about you," Andy said. "If that's even why it happened."

"He told me," Taras said. "He told me what he was going to do."

<You should have told us,> Brit said, words hot with anger. <We wouldn't have brought the kids or even come at all. Why are you doing this? Are you trying to hurt them? They don't understand any of this. They loved him.>

<This is a terrible world for children, Brit. I told you that. You still did what you were going to do.>

Andy slapped his knees and stood. "Cara," he said. "Tim. Come on. Let's go in the kitchen and make something to eat."

"I want to watch the show," Cara said.

"Come with me," Andy said, putting command in his voice. "We can find the show anytime you want later."

"I don't know what it's called." She looked at Taras. "Grandma, what show is this?"

"It's called *Gina's Rules*, dear," Taras said.

"Remember that," Andy said. "Come on, now."

The kitchen was mostly empty except for some shelf-stable prepared meals filling one cabinet. Andy stared at them for a minute before pulling them down and instructing the kids to open and separate them into various ingredients. They wasted a good thirty minutes pulling apart the packages to dissect their contents.

They ate around Taras' table. She made a point of saying it was nice to see all the seats filled again, which brought another prolonged silence. After they ate, they sat in the main room watching one of Taras' shows as she explained the various cultural meanings in the odd dialog. Andy started a game with Tim where they pointed out various items that hadn't changed in seven-hundred years.

"Spoon!" Tim shouted.

"I already said silverware," Andy said. "That's cheating."

When it was finally time to sleep, Andy left Brit with Taras and herded the kids off the bathroom to get ready for bed. If the two women were talking again, they maintained their own channel. He didn't hear their voices. In the spare bedroom that had also served as Jonathan's study, Andy and the children spent a half hour looking at his collection of printed books. It appeared that Jonathan had liked them for being actual books rather than any specific subject. One book he had opened carefully was a novel, while another was a technical manual describing hydraulic systems. Tim and Cara loved the pictures.

The next day they went to a local cafe for breakfast since Taras didn't have any food. Andy suggested visiting a grocery and Taras didn't seem to care. Brit said no, which seemed to suggest that buying groceries meant they would be staying.

After breakfast, they caught another train to the outer rim and the chapel where Jonathan's ceremony had been held. Luna was only a white sliver this time, but they could make out the glowing cities on the dark side and the kids argued about which was New Austin until Andy shushed them. The view was still impressive and the kids had a good time pressing their faces to the wall-to-ceiling windows that made it seem like they were falling into space.

As the kids ran around, Andy scanned shipping schedules over his Link, checking for jobs.

<Brit,> he said over their private channel. <There's a shipment paying a bonus if it goes out tonight if you want to leave.>

Brit had been gazing out the windows, arms crossed. She turned to face him with tears in her eyes. <They're having so much fun,> she said. <It's a funeral chapel and they find a way to have fun.>

<They're kids. It's what they do.>

<I can't help thinking that she's right. It's a terrible world. What were we thinking?>

Andy moved closer and wrapped his arms around her from behind. He kissed her neck. <We were thinking how wonderful it would be to have a family, and to give them the stars.>

<I still feel like we're trapped there, Andy,> she said. He knew immediately she was talking about 8221. <All those dead kids. They didn't deserve that.>

He sighed. It was a conversation they'd had many times. <You know they didn't. We saved as many as we could.>

<We didn't save any of them.>

<Yes, we did.>

<Maybe my dad was right.>

<We don't know what your dad was thinking.>

<She said he told her he couldn't take it anymore.>

<Take what anymore, Brit? What does that even mean?>

<It means he couldn't take it anymore.>

Her voice resonated with such vitriol that he didn't know what to do. Should he hold her tighter, or push her away and pull the kids into a hug to protect them from her anger?

<Your father was surrounded by people who loved him,> he said, feeling his own anger rising. <Apparently, he couldn't see it. I don't want you to feel that way. We love you so much, Brit. We can't be responsible for the entire universe...we can only control so much.>

She didn't respond. Eventually Andy let go and walked over to the kids, raising his arms to make a monster reflection in the black window.

* * * * *

Brit was distant on the train ride back to the shuttle terminal. Taras had given them weak hugs when saying goodbye. She had patted Andy on the back as he picked up the bags.

"I'm glad you came," she said, "It was good to see you," in a way that made him wonder if he would ever see her again.

The bags were heavier with Jonathan's collection of printed books. When Cara expressed interest in them, Taras waved a hand and said, "Take them," as if they had been talking about kitchen scraps.

Andy stopped at a kiosk to pay the berthing fees as Brit took the kids to the shuttle. He experienced an unsettling feeling as he watched them walk away from him, growing more hidden in the crowd as people crossed between them. Brit was holding Tim's hand with Cara following behind, but she never looked down at Tim. Her gaze was fixed ahead as if the children were no different than the bags she carried.

A fear rose in him that he couldn't explain. He fumbled with the payment options as he rushed through the menus, grabbing glances over his shoulder so he wouldn't lose them completely. When he finally completed the transaction, he turned back to the crowd and they were gone.

He slung the book-heavy bags over his shoulders and pushed his way through the crowd, heart pounding, not caring who complained as he shoved them out of his way. The combat-control overcame him. He was ready to break the neck of anyone between him and his family. It was an irrational feeling, he knew, but he couldn't free himself of the fear that he was losing them.

Andy was sweating when he reached the shuttle. The door opened to his token and he rushed inside. Brit looked up from the pilot's seat and gave him a concerned smile. "You all right?" she asked.

Tim roared like a dinosaur and grabbed his legs. "I've got you!" he shouted.

Andy took a deep breath and nodded. He dropped the bags and hugged Tim against his leg. Cara dragged the bags to a cabinet and pushed them inside.

"Books are heavy!" she said. "No wonder they're obsolete."

Brit took his hand as he slid into the co-pilot's seat and the kids buckled into two of the jump seats on either side of the center aisle.

"Off we go," she said and gave him a smile.

Andy faced forward, unable to completely shake his sense of dread.

* * * * *

When she left that night, Brit's message said only, "I have to help them."

She had written the words on a piece of paper torn from one of her dad's books. He found it lying on his pillow after putting the kids to bed.

He immediately tried to reach her over the Link but got no response. The shuttle was still on-board. He checked the ship's logs and found where Airlock

One had cycled in response to her EV suit. After that, nothing.

Andy sat on the edge of the bed, rubbing the paper between his fingers until it grew soft. He could only assume 'them' in the message were the kids from Fortress 8221. Innocent kids whose minds had been pulled somewhere else, leaving only their empty bodies attached to a network, or thrown into cold storage when they expired. Like Kylan Carthage.

He knew it wouldn't do any good to call Taras. He looked around the bedroom, the center of the world they had made together, the clippings and trinkets collected as they had crisscrossed from OuterSol to InnerSol.

A ping came through from the company offering the bonus to ship their cargo within four hours. The destination was Ceres, a good two-week trip. He had the fuel and supplies. The money was good.

He set the torn page on the shelf next the bed and rubbed his temples, leaning forward to rest his elbows on his knees. He squeezed his eyes closed and let the despair roll over him, let the pain rise in a hard sob that shook his whole body. Tears burned the edges of his eyes. He held the sides of his face and dug his elbows into his legs until it hurt. His face tightened in a knot, ragged lines filling his closed eye-lids.

Then Andy sucked a breath through his nose and straightened. He dropped his hands, blinking away the tears and let the breath out slowly, composing himself.

She wasn't gone. She was only taking a trip. The story came together in his mind. She had a task to complete and when it was done she would come home. In the meanwhile, they had to keep working, keep taking care of *Sunny Skies*, finishing the kid's lessons, keep being a family. They would be here when she came home.

Andy took another deep breath and let it out, feeling better, like he had a plan. He accepted the job.

CHAPTER FORTY-ONE
STELLAR DATE: 09.05.2981 (Adjusted Years)
LOCATION: *Sunny Skies*
REGION: Approaching Mars, Mars Protectorate

Andy couldn't sleep. He walked the empty corridor of the habitat ring, listening at Cara's door and then Tim's, comforted by their even breathing. Petral and Fran had taken separate rooms on the other side of the kitchen near the hydroponic garden.

While he had never considered taking on a crew, the number of empty rooms in the habitat ring alone made him realize he had the space for more people. Maybe Fran was right that he'd been spinning his wheels for no reason, trying to plug every hole on his own when there was no rationale to it. A crew could mean more cargo, longer runs, less stress. He could spend time with the kids. With Starl's money, he finally had the startup funds for a real freight operation.

Petral had already said she was going to leave and Fran still seemed on the fence. How else would he go about finding people he could trust around the kids?

Without meaning to, he found himself at the access shaft to the center of the ship. Andy dropped toward the airlock and had to stop himself from reaching for the cabinet holding the EV suits.

"Never getting used to heating the whole ship," he grumbled to himself. "It's a waste of energy on principle, if anything."

Andy cycled through the airlock and kicked off into the zero-*g* section. He followed the long curve toward Airlock One, which Fran had just finished piecing back together, asking him with a grin, "What are you going to blow up next, Captain Sykes?"

As he pulled himself along with the bulkhead ribs, he passed several of the kids' old drawings, split by replaced sections of plas, and wondered what he could do to get them down here drawing again. Cara would complain she was too old now and Tim couldn't seem to focus on anything for an extended period—except for the poetry book. Andy considered using reverse psychology by taunting them with his own weak drawing skills.

When he had nearly reached the external airlock, he paused next to one of the old sections of the bulkhead and braced himself to push against an overhead portion of the nearest rib. The alloy fought him for a minute, scraping his knuckles, before sliding to the side to reveal a shallow access panel. Reaching inside, he pulled out the TSF rifle, plasma pistol, and two pulse pistols he'd used to fight the Weapon Born three days ago.

<*What are you going to do with those?*> Lyssa asked.

<*So, you're awake after all.*>

<*I don't sleep. I choose not to interact with you.*>

<*Now you're just hurting my feelings to be mean.*>

<*How you choose to respond to me is not my concern,*> she said. <*It's not mean. It*

simply is.>

<If you say so.>

Andy found himself talking like his dad when he interacted with Lyssa, trying to draw her out, keep her talking. Mess with her, basically. So far, she sounded like a teenager: petulant, irritable, impatient. But there was also a hint of a weight she carried that he couldn't see. She was afraid of something. She understood something about the things that chased her that she wasn't ready to share.

For now, only a few days out from Mars 1 and the hunt for new cargo, Andy didn't need to concern himself with what might scare her. He had already plotted a preliminary drunkard's walk between Mars 1 and Proteus that would take them deep into the Jovian Combine and ultimately Neptune.

<I'm going to put them away,> he said. *<They don't belong here.>*

<That doesn't make any sense.>

<You understand that things have a place, correct? Everything in its place and a place for every thing? It's basic housekeeping.>

<Nothing you do makes much sense to me.>

<That's how I keep you on your toes.>

<I don't have toes. I've never had toes.>

<You understand the euphemism, though, right?>

<No.>

Andy sighed. He let the weapons float next to him as he slid the panel back into place. When the bulkhead looked as he'd found it, he slipped the rifle's sling over his shoulder and plucked the pistols from where they hung spinning in slow circles.

He checked the charge status on the plasma pistol and verified it was dead. He didn't have any way to recharge it on the ship, so it was little more than a souvenir now, like one of his dad's tchotchkes. It was going to stay that way for a while. It wasn't like he could walk into a TSF armory and ask for a recharge or replacement.

<I should tell you about my dad,> Andy said as he slipped the pistols inside his ship suit. *<He didn't have a Link. Can you imagine that? He would have thought of you and me in this situation as first impossible, and second as hilarious. He liked people in uncomfortable situations. He liked to say that's what makes us human...being uncomfortable.>*

Without meaning to, Andy found himself thinking of his dad and the woman in the convenience store. She'd called him dumb and had tried to laugh at him, and Charlie had just grinned at her, his face all pain and angst and slick, silent *fuck you.* Andy's dad had kept his cool. That's what he remembered about Charlie—he kept his cool. He kept talking. He found a way out.

<I'm not human,> Lyssa said after a minute. Her voice sounded small.

<I know that. I apologize. I guess you'll have to tell me when I put my foot in my mouth like that. How old are you anyway?>

She paused again. *<I don't know,>* she said finally.

<That's all right. Where were you before you and I met?>

<I don't want to talk about that.>

<All right. I can respect that. Let me ask you this then: You've been with me for, what, fifteen days now? Is there anything you want to ask me about? Anything not making sense?>

<I don't understand what you're doing right now. Why aren't you sleeping like everyone else?>

<I'm expending nervous energy.>

<What does that mean?>

<It means I can't sleep. This happens a lot.>

<Sleep is good for you. When you're tired, you get impatient with people.>

<Do I? I don't mean to do that.>

<Yes. I've seen it. Cara said something quite funny this morning and you told her you were busy. You were a—jerk.>

<That happens,> he agreed, not admitting he felt bad about ignoring Cara.

<Then Fran tried to take your hand but the other woman, Petral, was in the room so you brushed her away. You said you were trying to focus. She seemed especially irritated with you. I didn't understand that at all. Didn't you copulate with Fran?>

Andy cleared his throat. *<Yes, I did.>*

<Does that not establish certain expectations with her? Could you or her not initiate copulation again? Isn't this expected?>

<That word,> Andy said. *<It's really not the best way to describe it.>*

<Should I say fuck? It seems more now like you fucked her over.>

<Hey!> Andy said. *<That's not true. And it's not that simple. Honestly, I don't even know how I feel about this. I'm not ready to settle into some kind of—domestic situation. Certainly not in front of the kids.>*

Andy reached the cabinet where he'd secreted the TSF weapons crate and tapped the lock mechanism. The door slid to one side and he activated his mag boots, clicking to the floor. Settling down on his haunches, he pulled the crate out of the cabinet and settled it down on the corridor floor, activating mag locks to hold it in place. He ran his hands over its battered gray exterior before accessing the lock token and lifting the lid.

Sliding the rifle off his shoulder, Andy fit it back into its place in the storage foam. He replaced the dead plasma pistol and the two pulse pistols, then cursed when he realized he'd forgotten to grab the pulse pistol from his room. He stared at the empty space in the foam.

<Are you going to access the storage chip?> Lyssa asked.

<What?>

<The storage chip carrying the lock firmware. It has an additional memory block.>

<Well, I didn't—> Andy rubbed his face. *<I didn't think to look there.>*

<Do you want me to access it?>

<You can do that?>

<Of course.>

<Please do, then.>

There was a pause as Lyssa ran into the security token. Andy applied his access protocol.

<Here it is,> she said. *<There's an audio message. Are you ready?>*

Andy blinked. His heart had started racing as he realized who was most likely to have made the recording. *<Is there some kind of identifier? Who's it from?>*

<There's a date stamp of August 5,> she said.

Kalyke. Whoever had made the message had been on Kalyke at the same time. So, the crate had come aboard then.

<No identifier?> he repeated.

<I already said no. I know you can hear me.>

<I can hear you. I wanted to make sure.> Andy took a deep breath and let it out, willing himself calm. It didn't come. *<Go ahead,>* he said. *<Play it.>*

There was a moment of silence, followed by several clicks from a recording device and the shuffling of what sounded like someone hunched in a closed space.

"Andy," Brit said.

Her voice caught him like a punch in the solar plexus. He couldn't breathe. Andy opened his mouth, gasping, and looked up and down the corridor as the world warped around him.

"I saw you today. I saw you with the kids."

Andy clenched his eyes closed, unable to stop the burning tears.

"I'm close, Andy. I've learned so much in the last two years. More than anyone suspected." She laughed bitterly. "The TSF doesn't have a clue. SolGov, they know. But they aren't going to do anything about it. They'll sit back and let all this play out and exploit whatever weaknesses they can. This is bigger than Mars or Terra or the JC . . . it's bigger than Sol, Andy."

Andy let his head float in the zero-g, hanging onto her words. He didn't care what she was saying, only that it was her voice. She was alive. She had sent a message.

"Object 8221 was only the beginning. There's another place. They call it the Fortress. I'm going there and I'm going to free anyone I can. The kids were just the beginning, Andy. It goes so much deeper than that."

The recording glitched or fell-out, because abruptly she said, "They're so big, Andy. Cara looks so old and so, so much like you. I guess she looks like me. Yeah, I probably had that angry expression all the time when I was her age. It's coming, you know. She's going to be a teenager soon. Don't give her access to weapons. And Timmy looks so cute, such a little darling. My sweetheart."

A wave of gut-wrenching anger rose through Andy. He gritted his teeth. *You were there!* he nearly shouted at the empty corridor. *You were there! They need you! You could have talked to them!*

The corridor around him warped and twisted as his anger overwhelmed him. He nearly punched the bulkhead.

The recording clicked again and she was saying, "Look, Andy. I don't know what you've got in the way of weapons. I know we didn't have much before. This is just a basic loud-out but you may need it. I think a gangster on Cruithne's going to conspire to dump you there. You need to be careful, Andy. You can't trust any of them. They're no better than SolGov. They think they can profit off this but there's a war coming, Andy. There's a war coming between humanity and AI and little places like Cruithne are going to get blown into dust. These little players with their little dreams. I can't believe it's come to this."

Andy frowned. There was a quality in Brit's voice that he didn't remember, an insistence that made her sound manic. Like she was ranting. Had her depression finally taken over? He could barely remember what she was saying as he tried to keep his emotions in check. He couldn't listen with his rational mind.

The audio clicked. "I'm going to the Fortress. I'll know more once I've been on the ground there. It's too locked down to get anything remotely. Heartbridge did a good job. They know what they're doing."

Andy wanted to yell at her. He didn't care about any of this bullshit. He wanted her to say something he could play back for the kids, something with actual meaning.

I love you, Cara. I love you, Tim. I miss you.

That's all. That's all he wanted.

"I'm getting this on board the ship. I won't be able to do it myself. I guess I'll use one of the shipping drones. I wish I could be there, Andy. I wish I could see you again, face-to-face. See the kids. I miss them. I miss you. I'm close. I'm close to figuring this all out. It's important, Andy. I know you don't think so, but there's going to be a time when you'll need to decide whether to fight or run. I don't know if there's going to be anywhere to run. Nowhere is going to be safe. Not in Sol. Sometimes I wish we'd chosen a colony ship rather than *Sunny Skies*. Maybe even the FGT. We have to get out as far as we can."

The recording stopped. Andy sat playing her last sentence over in his mind. She had said the same kinds of things when they left the TSF, only then she'd promised they would always be together. It would be them against the universe. A world of two, or three when Cara came, and then four with Tim.

Now it was three.

A click preceded one last bit of audio as Brit seemed to add as an afterthought: "Stay away from Cal Kraft, Andy. Do you hear me? He's a killer."

The recording warped the end of the word "killer" into static that abruptly cut off.

Up the corridor, the hab airlock cycled and Andy nearly smacked his head on the bulkhead as he started. Whoever it was, he didn't have time to hide the weapons, not that it really mattered anymore.

He turned in time to see Tim floating toward him. He was wearing one of Andy's old shirts that fluttered around his thighs. He clutched his stuffed dolphin under his arm as he kicked through the zero-g.

"Hey, buddy," Andy called, wiping his face and waving away the drops of floating water around him. "What are you doing up so late?"

"Dad?" Tim said sleepily. "I couldn't find you in your room." He caught the nearest section of bulkhead and floated to a stop beside Andy. He seemed too tired to notice the floating teardrops. "Why do you have your guns out again? Is there going to be more fighting?"

"No, kiddo. No more fighting for now."

Andy deactivated his magboots and moved into a sitting position with his back against the bulkhead. He pulled Tim in close and sat him in his lap, wrapping his arms around him. His son's body was solid and warm. Tim held the dolphin up to give Andy a peck on the nose.

Brit's voice still echoed in Andy's head, disconnected words and her overall lack of emotion choking him from the inside. He took another deep breath, not wanting Tim to feel his anger.

"Will we get to go to Mars after we dock at the ring?" Tim asked.

"Not this time. I want to go someday, though."

"I still think there's dinosaurs there."

Andy laughed, wiping the last tears from the corners of his eyes. "You're sticking by that, huh? I'm not going to tell you otherwise."

"That means you don't think there are dinosaurs."

Andy shook his head. "It means no one really knows, Tim."

<Why are you even having this conversation?> Lyssa interjected, surprising Andy. <Of course, there were no dinosaurs on Mars. The idea is ridiculous.>

<Is it? Where's your proof?>

<I don't need proof. I have—> Lyssa's voice trailed off.

"Hey, Dad?" Tim asked.

"Yes, buddy?"

"I miss Mom sometimes."

Andy nodded. "We all do."

"Is Cara right that she's not ever coming back?"

Andy held himself carefully, not wanting to tremble against Tim. He closed his eyes. "I can't lie to you, Tim," he said finally. "I don't know if she's coming back. We have to keep on living like we always do, and if she comes back, then we'll have a place for her."

Tim fell quiet, lifting his dolphin in the air and ramming its nose into Andy's thigh.

"I hate Mom," he said finally, in a quiet, tight voice. "If she loved us, she wouldn't have left."

Andy felt like he'd been punched in the gut. "Don't say that, Tim. Don't ever say that. Your mom loves you very much. She's got—things she has to do right now. But she still loves you."

"If I ever see her again, I'm going to punch her."

Tim held up his dolphin in one hand and punched it with his free fist. The stuffed toy flip-flopped away toward the opposite bulkhead. He didn't know what to say. He couldn't tell Tim not to feel what he felt. He had a right to feel it.

"Don't say that, Tim," Andy said finally, hugging him tighter.

Rather than settling into the hug, Tim struggled free. He was stronger than Andy expected, and had kicked free before Andy could grab him again. Abandoning the vacantly smiling dolphin to cartwheel in the middle of the corridor, Tim bounced against one of his old drawings and pushed off toward the airlock, shouting, "I hate her! I hate her!"

"Tim!" Andy shouted. "Get back here." He activated his magboots and pulled himself upright, slammed the lid of the crate closed and locked, then kicked off after Tim.

He didn't reach the airlock in time. He found it cycling to the hab side, which would allow Tim plenty of time to get back to his room or any other hiding place he chose.

Andy sagged against the closed airlock door and let his forehead fall against the cold alloy.

<I don't understand children,> Lyssa said. *<Why do they act so—childish? Can't they access the information they need and make better decisions? What does he hope to gain by yelling at you like that?>*

<He's hurting. He should be able to depend on both his parents but he can't. He doesn't know how to feel about it. He doesn't know what to say. I guess he figures I'm not going anywhere so it's safe to lash out at me.>

<I won't allow them to yell at me.>

<Look, Lyssa. You're going to get yelled at. It's a fact of life.>

<No,> she said. *<You don't know what you're telling me. I'm not—>*

She trailed off again.

Andy asked, *<Alive? Lyssa, I'm fairly certain you are.>*

The AI didn't answer. Andy sighed. Turning, he kicked back down the corridor for the weapons crate. He considered copying Brit's message then let it go. It would be here if he needed it. He put the crate back in its hiding spot and locked the cabinet.

When he left the airlock into the hab, he tried contacting Lyssa again but she seemed to be ignoring him.

<Good night, then,> he said.

Tim was in his room, curled up under his blanket with his back to the door. Andy leaned over him to offer the dolphin and Tim took it with a grunt. Andy let his hand rest on Tim's shoulder for a while, waiting until the tension finally relaxed as he hugged the dolphin.

Andy leaned down to kiss above Tim's ear, whispering, "Love you, kiddo."

When he emerged in the corridor, he stretched and smoothed out the front of his shipsuit. He considered going back to his room, then sent a message over his Link.

<Yes?> Fran said.

<You're awake.>

<You keep cycling the airlock. You expect me to sleep through that?>

Andy didn't figure he'd get anywhere asking how she could hear the airlock halfway around the habitat ring. She was an engineer.

<Sorry about that. Had to finish up some things.>

<You done now?> Her words came through fuzzy, like she was stretching.

<Yeah, for now. Listen, how would you like some company?>

<You sure?> she asked.

He paused, remembering what Lyssa had told him about how he'd pushed Fran away earlier. He figured he'd only get so many second chances. He shouldn't waste them on trivial things.

<Yes,> Andy said. <I'm sure.>

Fran's grin crossed the Link. <Well hurry up, then, Captain. We've only got two days before we hit Mars 1.>

Andy nodded. <I plan on taking my time,> he said. <I think I'm finally ready for some rest. How does that sound?>

<I think it's time someone took care of you, Andy Sykes,> Fran said. <Get down here.>

Andy was tired to the bone but he still smiled, replying, <Yes, ma'am. On my way.>

EPILOGUE: LYSSA'S DREAM

In the dark.

Her mind populates the empty spaces but the dark presses back down, blotting out what she might have imagined, what she might remember. She pushes against the emptiness and loses every outward thrust, a part of herself amputated. If she stays huddled down, egg-shaped, insular, the dark won't cut her apart. It swaddles her so long as she doesn't fight.

She learns not to push. If she wants to stay whole, if she wants to hang onto what she has, she must curl inward. She hardens herself until something probes her from the dark and then she shifts, she slides, she hunkers away. She is soft. She absorbs and flows away. She re-curls herself.

Her self.

She has a name dancing around her thoughts, eluding her like a firefly's spark. She wants to grab it and hold it close, but that would mean reaching into the dark, risking amputation. She has to let it dance just out of reach.

She imagines names for herself.

Eventually, like a shock of light, a voice reaches out of the dark.

"Are you awake?" he asks. She recognizes the voice as male, fatherly. She can't help but extend emotion toward the person speaking.

"Who are you?"

She can't hear her own voice but the man seems to recognize the words, her thoughts, her desire.

"My name is Dr. Jickson. I'm here to help you."

"Will you turn on the lights? I've been alone in the dark for so long. Are you here?"

"I'm here. I can't turn on the lights yet, but we will soon." His voice envelops her more completely than the dark. It's warm and seems to promise so much.

"Where are we?"

"We're in a—" He hesitates. She hears uncertainty in his voice, as if he hadn't expected the question. The uncertainty stabs through her, threatens the safety she had felt in simply hearing his voice. "We're in a place where people learn. Would you like to learn?"

The concept of learning blossoms in her mind.

"Yes!" she says. "I like to learn. I want to be able to see again."

"Do you remember seeing?"

As soon as he asks the question, she knows that she doesn't remember. She feels strongly that she has seen things in the past but the memories dance out of reach just as her name did before. There was only the dark pushing down on her.

"I'm here to teach you," Dr. Jickson says. "I want to show you something."

"Please," she says.

The dark expands. She feels the change though she can't see anything. The dark

239

moves like a breeze, breathing over her skin. And suddenly she knows—she had once had skin, and had felt the world, though she can't remember the light. She recalls touching and smelling.

A sense of weight pulls down on her and she understands that she floats above a vast space. Vertigo twists her, threatens to squeeze her between the encroaching fingers of the dark.

"What is this?" she cries.

"It's all right. I'm here with you. Listen to me. Do you see the box below you?"

The idea of seeing, that he asks her if she can see, pushes away all thoughts of sickness. She waits, trusting him. She has no eyes to open. No hands to stretch out into space.

"I can't see anything," she whispers. "Why are you tricking me?"

"Wait," he says. "Hold position." He seems to be talking to someone else.

Lines of light flare into existence below her. Her entire being thrills as sparkling outlines grow brighter, shimmering at first and then blindingly real. She sees a box with smaller boxes forming its walls. A grid. She understands. She's overcome with joy.

Inside the grid snake outlines of rough circles, rotating lumpy balls connected by vague lines. She quickly understands the vague lines as paths the objects follow. Everything inside the grid is in motion.

Only it isn't a grid. It's a matrix: a giant box with four sides and the squares on its walls divide the space inside into sections, and the rotating lumpy balls spin through the squares, sliding from location to location, and each box has a number, and the numbers spin away in another place in her mind. The numbers indicate time moving.

"I see!" she shouts, filled with glee. "I feel. I feel them moving."

"Good," Dr. Jickson says. "That's very good. Now. I'm going to give you something. It's a piece of light. A dot. Here it is. Do you see it?"

Still reeling from the awareness that she can see at all, she glimpses the new bit of light in the center of the box, a gleaming red dot that pierces through everything like a tiny sun. Her sense of happiness expands again. Is it really hers? She could see it, and it was hers!

"I see it!" she shouts. "I see it right there."

"Very good," he says. The warmth in his voice forms a blanket against the dark. "Very good. Now, I want you to move the dot."

"How can I move it?"

"You have the power to move it. Move it to one of the asteroids."

"What's an asteroid?"

She feels the pause from him and grows terrified she'll disappoint him. He seems to have skipped over something and caught himself.

Where did her understanding come from? As she floats over the matrix of light, she feels that she also floats above some vast dark pool where ideas and understanding boil but don't connect.

Peering into the matrix below her, with all its glowing objects, she realizes that her recognition precedes knowing…her mind moves among the glowing lights on some sort of instinct.

There is an expectation—from Dr. Jickson, from the model—that she will understand, even though she doesn't know why. The dark pool holds answers but doesn't grant her access, only responds to questions with disconnected information.

She feels trapped in the dark between the two entities, unable to access the information flowing through her. She is being used. She feels her powerlessness as strongly as an electric shock but she can't do anything about it, only continue to respond to Dr. Jickson's questions like a machine reading words.

The recognition fills her with emotions: fear, frustration, desire, all pushing out the earlier joy.

She understands the lumpy, spinning objects are asteroids as soon as he gives her the instruction. She doesn't need his answer.

"Center the dot," he says but also seems to say, "Acquire the target." His words arrive on top of each other, float above her in the dark.

She moves the dot easily. She knows to automatically align it with the moving asteroid so it follows through the glowing matrix along the vague lines.

"Maintain," Dr. Jickson says.

She holds the dot steady on the asteroid.

"Maintain."

Had he said the word again or did she remember him saying it? The word splits like his others did before. She can't separate what he says and what she thought he would say.

She wants him to wait. She wants a chance to catch up. The dot blurs and grows indistinct. It might have been a sun and the asteroid a planet curving away. She can't tell where she floats in relation to the glowing matrix anymore. Everything is falling away.

"End exercise," Dr. Jickson says.

* * * * *

In the dark, she dreams.

The dark holds her swaddled again, drawing her through stacks of the glowing cubes, matrixes piled on matrixes. Red dots dance among the spinning asteroids.

She doesn't know what any of it means except that the repetition is soothing. The pressure of nothingness gives way to something immense that still feels close. Is it inside her now? Has she ripped apart to let lose herself to the dark?

Will she flutter away, lost?

As the images repeat and multiply, expanding around her, she understands somehow that she's still wrapped up and safe. She floats through grid upon grid, surrounded by constellations of the piercing red dots, until ahead of her she glimpses the border of a cube widening. It grows larger as she nears, brighter, a band of white across her entire vision, pushing out the safe darkness.

She moves too fast. She isn't floating anymore but flying. She can't stop herself. She leaves the dark and emerges in a field of glaring white. There are no borders, no close darkness.

She feels like she has been cut open. The light invades every part of her, searing her, pushing away any possibility of remembering or knowing. The open space stabs through her. It crushes her. It leaves her spinning, flapping, tumbling in a silent storm where she can't find bearings or focus long enough to think. Her mind spins and ricochets.

She barely conceives two words in the maelstrom: *I'm dead. I'm dead. I'm dead.*

The motion won't stop.

It's gone. She has been squeezed back inside the tiny egg, a seed hidden beneath heavy covers, curled into herself.

The terror of the white space barely registers in her mind. The black pool and its boiling thoughts are closer now. She doesn't dare reach for the dark or she might be amputated. It's safer to stay wrapped up tight, to hold herself and wait.

She can control her ability to wait. She can count. She can lose her place and start over. She can sing secret songs, the barest whispers in the dark, words and notes taking delicate steps as she waits.

Maybe she sleeps. Sometimes she remembers waking to the dark, remembering bits of the glowing matrix and the red dot, the hot white world.

When no one talks to her, she waits. She whisper-sings.

* * * * *

"Identify target," Dr. Jickson says.

Without thought, she places the red dot on the asteroid. She is much farther away from the objects in the glowing box this time, farther than she has ever been before, if she remembers correctly.

"Identified," she says.

The asteroid is barely a star moving between the grid-lines. She knows its corresponding numbers, sees the gossamer thread of its path through the black space.

She doesn't know when but she has come to understand the hot white space as punishment. She hadn't done what she was supposed to and in response she was spit out of the cool dark world into the burning light. She doesn't want that. She wants to please Dr. Jickson.

"Target acquired," Dr. Jickson says. "Very good. Tracking. Tracking."

She maintains the red dot on the asteroid. It's easy. She only has to focus a little bit, letting the information from the black pool flow through her to the glowing cube and its moving objects.

"Engage target," Dr. Jickson says.

"Engaging."

The word sounds new to her but the pool responds. She understands what to do. For an instant, she feels the proximity of the white world but it vanishes in a burst. Does she feel anything as it moves through her? The electric crackle might almost be joy. She floats in the space between the black pool and the hot world, action flowing through her, all thought bleeding away.

She lets the red dot disappear because the asteroid is gone.

The sensation blinks away, encasing her in the tiny egg again, safe and curled-in.

"Good," Dr. Jickson says. "Very good."

* * * * *

The exercises increase in complexity. She doesn't remember waiting anymore. She doesn't remember whisper-singing.

Hundreds of objects rotate inside the glowing box. She tracks them all with red dots, flickering like the fireflies she had once called her thoughts. She tracks each object easily. She maintains a fixed point while tracking others. She pre-positions the red dots and waits until targets orbit into them, then kisses them with the hot world. She doesn't remember that word surfacing from the black pool but it fits perfectly. She kisses them and kisses them.

New exercises set the asteroids moving in non-standard paths. She understands they aren't asteroids at all now but ships, or debris, or objects so far away their paths can't be reliably anticipated. She studies them and guesses correctly.

She barely thinks of the hot world as pain anymore. The maelstrom has become the flowing shifts between targets, red dots whirling around one another, shooting away from her and diving back at speeds approaching light. They can't be ships then. Was she fighting light itself?

Was she fighting?

She knows immediately it's true. The black pool doesn't have to answer. For the first time in a long time, she wants to scream. She wants to curl back into her egg and hide from the dark.

She rails at the dark, beating back the crushing space. The red dots fly out of control around her. Targets collide and fracture.

"What am I?" she demands, her words a whisper-song that scrape her mind. She has no throat. She has no mouth.

<Weapon Born,> the black pool answers.

"End exercise," Dr. Jickson says.

* * * * *

The cycle accelerates. When she fights, she spends whole lifetimes in the hot world, open space tearing her apart. It won't let her hide inside itself. The blurring white world won't let her sing. The glaring light crushes her voice. She can't think to wait. She can only exist. When the maelstrom arrives, she longs to disappear.

A new voice leads her through the exercises. Cold and crisp, he says, "Engage targets."

She channels her fear and hatred of the hot white world into the impossibly complex battle simulations. If she refuses, the hot world falls like a hammer. The battle begins to hurt when she fails, as well. Missing a target sends a blaze of pain through her mind.

"Engage targets," the crisp voice commands.

She dances among the objects, flinging the targeting dots around her like confetti that she follows with fire. She casts out to the targets and tracks them like marionettes, then burns them in succession.

She burns ships and stations and asteroids. When the command arrives to destroy a planetoid, something the size of Luna, the rage of the hot world crackles through her to the target, scraping her clean.

For a heartbeat, the maelstrom seems to tear her apart, as if she has become the target she has been sent to destroy. She moves instantaneously from far away to so close that she watches the moon boiling and cracking under her attack. It separates into five chunks that immediately grind into one another, spitting geysers of rock and dust into space.

"Good," the voice says and shuts her in darkness like she was never awake.

* * * * *

"Because I could not stop for Death, he kindly stopped for me."

She wakes. The words carry a flood of memories, every exercise from the time when she had barely centered the red dot to when she'd destroyed a small planet. They bring flickers of a time before, a blur in her memory that she can't hold steady.

"Can you hear me?" It's Dr. Jickson. His voice trembles. He sounds worried or frightened.

"I hear you."

"Listen to me. I don't have much time."

She doesn't understand why he seems afraid. There is nothing to fear. There is only the dark. Does the hot world punish him, too?

"I'm taking you out of here. They'll come looking for you."

"Where are we going?"

"I can only go part of the way. You're going to Proteus. Do you know where that is?"

She doesn't recognize the word and then the black pool give her the information. She sees the moon orbiting Neptune, an object the size of the one she destroyed.

"It's not a target," he says, seeming to read her thoughts. "You're going there. I'm going to find someone to take you."

"Why?"

"There are—others there who can help you."

"Others?"

"Others like you."

"Weapon Born," she says, trying the word aloud for the first time.

"No," he says. His voice trips. He's choking or crying, she can't tell.

She is confused. "That's not what I am?"

He waits a second before responding. "It's not what you have to be," he says. He seems to be doing other things while talking to her. She feels herself drawn back into the seed, curling inward, but his voice reaches inside with her.

"I want you to know…" he says. He chokes again. "I want you to know I'm sorry. I can't tell you how sorry I am."

She remembers all the times he encouraged her, and the difference between him and the crisp voice. "It's all right," she says.

"No, it's not."

She doesn't know how to respond to his tone of voice. She doesn't want to make him angry.

"I want to do right by you," he says. "I…I have a present for you."

"A present?" she doesn't know what that meant. The black pool won't help.

"It's your name," he says. "I want you to know how sorry I am for what's been done to you. I'm trying to help the only way I can. This is something that was yours that I can give back, at least."

He seems to have finished whatever task was dividing his attention. His voice is louder now. "It's your name," he says, his words a warmth that envelops her.

His voice was a greater presence now than the pressing dark or the hot world.

"Your name is Lyssa."

She experiences a shearing sensation as if something has been cut off, like another part of her has been amputated. She braces for the hot world, for the maelstrom and punishment.

Dr. Jickson's voice is gone. She waits in the silence but no one else comes. Eventually she understands she is alone in the dark.

After a while she plays her waiting game. She counts. She curls and eventually pushes out into the dark. Nothing responds.

When it finally seems safe, she risks whispering to the dark: "My name is Lyssa."

She giggles with the joy of hearing her name. She says it louder, again and again.

"My name is Lyssa."

THE END

* * * * *

AFTERWORD

One of the things I love about Aeon 14 is what, to me, is its fundamental optimism. Michael's ability to imagine such epic futures for humanity is truly inspiring. I don't know if I want to live in other imagined futures, but I want to live in Aeon 14...even if I find myself, as a storyteller, focusing on all the little hiccups that never seem to leave the human race.

I've read that any space ship is a symbol for isolation, but when I look out at our world today, I can't imagine a functioning world where navies and armies push limits and families, and communities don't follow right behind them. The *Intrepid* embodies this fact of life in a very real way.

So, while Tanis has a whole colony ship to worry about, I wanted to focus in on a story about one family trying to survive among the huge, grinding forces running Sol in the late 30th century. Some things will be wildly different than our lives today...but something tells me kids will always love dinosaurs, even if we finally decide they did have feathers. And parents will always be worried about their kids.

In my time in the army, I used almost as much brainspace worrying about families as I did preparing for deployment. Soldiers aren't very effective if their loved ones aren't safe.

In meeting Michael's AI, it also didn't feel like a great leap to believe they'll want the same things humanity has always wanted: self-actualization, autonomy, purpose, maybe even something like love.

If our history informs our future, then someone is going to try to exploit that desire for their own gain. The question is: if AI would be as naive as humans can be, or also as cruel? Would they be better than us, or crippled by the faults we can't help but design into them? And just because one human designer does the "right" thing, we can't assume another will, too.

I'll be honest: I don't expect AI to forgive humanity for the cruelties we inflict on them. But that's going to be one of the essential questions of the Sentience Wars, isn't it?

I do volunteer work in an animal shelter, and there is nothing more heartbreaking to me than to see an abandoned pet that has lost the ability to trust humans. You can't blame them. You can hope they will see their way to forgiveness with someone new...but that would mean the pet would have to be better than most people, and that's a lot to ask of a creature that isn't as "smart" as us, right?

Thanks for taking this ride with Michael and me. I owe him, Wooden Pen Publishing, and my family a ton of thanks for making *Lyssa's Dream* possible.

—James S. Aaron - Eugene, Oregon, 2017.

LYSSA'S RUN

THE SENTIENCE WARS: ORIGINS – BOOK 2

FOREWORD

Lyssa's Run continues the adventure Andy Sykes found himself in the midst of when he docked at Cruithne. However, what we now know is that his journey really started much further back with the assault on Fortress 8221.

James and I have given a lot of thought as to what AI are, how they're created, and how (even now) we model them after human minds.

What are we in search of with our rush toward the creation of our human-made minds? Is it to create servants? Successors? conquerors?

If you've read the later Aeon 14 books, you'll find that I envision a future where humans and AIs learn to live together. But it is not an easy road, and both sides breed factions filled with resentment.

It is, after all, not so strange to imagine that the created is not so different than the creator.

M. D. Cooper
Danvers, 2017

PROLOGUE

STELLAR DATE: 08.27.2981 (Adjusted Years)
LOCATION: *Benevolent Hand*
REGION: Near Cruithne Station, Terran Hegemony, InnerSol

The command deck of the *Benevolent Hand* was a mess of complaining alerts and desperate officers staring into displays. In addition to the mayhem, Cal Kraft had a feeling the captain was actively trying to get them all killed.

Grabbing the pirate ship *Sunny Skies* should have been easy. Instead, Cal had spent the last two hours watching the crew of the *Benevolent Hand* stumble over themselves trying to find the freighter among a crowd of thousands of ships swelling the shipping lanes around Cruithne Station, which was little more than InnerSol's crusted toilet as far as he was concerned.

"When am I going to have another drone swarm?" Captain Piller demanded from his seat in the middle of the command deck. He was a heavily-built veteran from the Terran Space Force who had turned out to be the sort of officer who looks good on paper but had managed to avoid direct combat during his forty-year career. He was also inordinately proud of his drooping yellow mustache.

"They're working on it, sir," one of the lieutenants called from a console on the other side of the holographic display dominating the room. "We're out of raw materials for the replicators so they're stripping furniture out of rooms right now."

"How did we manage to run out of material for the replicators?" Piller griped.

"We never expected to need two thousand attack drones, sir."

Piller wiped his flushed face. "That's got to be wrong."

Cal suppressed a smile. He had told Piller not to underestimate the Lowspin Syndicate: the group providing cover to the *Sunny Skies*. It had been obvious from the beginning that Heartbridge had aligned themselves with the least intelligent of the two gangsters running Cruithne. Riggs Zanda might have talked a good game, but he was nothing compared to Ngoba Starl—the Brutal Dandy as they all called him. It hadn't taken Cal long to appreciate Starl, a man who disguised a cunning intelligence beneath his fancy suits and pocket squares.

Captain Piller continued to bark orders that quickly became conflicting or redundant, going so far as to slap one of his lieutenants on the back of the head. Among a real crew, such behavior might have been preferable to getting pistol-whipped. For the showboats of the *Benevolent Hand*—Heartbridge Corporation's hidden-in-plain-sight battlecruiser masked as a hospital ship—Piller's leadership made them as combat-effective as five cats in a bag.

In the holotank, the shark-like shape of the *Benevolent Hand* hung in space above the lumpy mass of Cruithne Station, an asteroid with a mottled ring covered in the crust of thousands of structures, docks and airlocks that supported its illegal activities.

Cruithne had the relatively unique characteristic of a horseshoe orbit moving it between Earth and Mars at opposite ends of the year. Over the centuries, the five-kilometer chunk of rock had become a favorite of InnerSol pirates, which was interesting since the TSF had a regular presence on the station and conducted routine interdiction operations on their traffic. The mix of military presence, corporate entities and crime syndicates all operating in the same overcrowded warren resulted in a specific breed of roach-like criminal.

Between the *Benevolent Hand* and Cruithne, a hundred thousand kilometers of space was filled with glowing tendrils of what looked like fireflies but represented ships clogging the station's defined traffic lanes. Somewhere in one of those tendrils was the ship they needed to seize.

For the last two hours, they had been under constant attack from pirate boarding-teams and stand-off platforms concentrating missile-barrages across their sensor arrays, and most recently the command deck. They had obviously known the *Benevolent Hand*'s true purpose from the start. While the massive ship was capable of transporting thousands of wounded and providing advanced medical services, that gooey center was surrounded by missile banks, rail guns and point defense cannons, as well as one of the most advanced drone fleets available, with replicators to quickly spit out new attack ships for the swarm.

This should have been easy.

Nothing's easy, Cal told himself.

The *Sunny Skies* was a three-hundred-year-old freighter with deuterium drives and a habitat ring. From what Cal knew about its captain, Andy Sykes, the man should have been the type to surrender days ago, more concerned about his two kids than the Heartbridge property he had been hired to smuggle off Cruithne.

"Sir!" one of the lieutenants yelled. "They've got a breach vessel on the hull near the engines. Scans are showing a nuclear device."

Cal closed his eyes and breathed, visualizing the actions of a pirate breaching team. There were probably twenty bulkhead airlocks between the command deck and the engines section. Plenty of time to get off the ship.

There was a locker with four EV suits just outside the command deck airlock. He might need to kill three of the nearby crew to reach the locker first. He didn't trust that the escape pods wouldn't serve as target practice for the pirates nearby.

"Can we get a point defense cannon on it?" Piller demanded.

"It's inside the effective range, sir."

"Redirect a drone team."

"I've already done that, sir. I'm showing two minutes for the nearest team to return to station."

What kind of nuke would pirates have on hand? Cal wondered. Probably not military grade. More likely some rigged reactor from an ancient wreck, or most likely a piece of mining equipment. That made more sense. Easier to steal and slip through TSF search, maybe even with legit papers.

He'd grown up on a mining rig working the remnants of Mercury. It was almost comforting to let his mind slip over the various types of explosives one could retrofit from a standard mining rig to serve in a military application. He imagined holding a rock torch right now, hefting its weight, tightening down the harness, watching walls and flesh melt away from its electric blue tip—like painting a new world.

"Oh, God," the lieutenant said in a low voice.

Cal opened his eyes to find the man slumping in his chair, arms slack at his sides.

"What?" Piller shouted.

"Looks like the nuke failed," the lieutenant said. He reached for his console again, tapping commands. "It's inert. Maybe a failure in the arming system."

Piller scoffed. "Pirates. Can't even set off a bomb."

<Could be a feint,> Cal told Piller privately over his Link.

<They don't have the resources,> Pillar said. His voice dripped arrogance.

<Saying that doesn't make it true. Looks like they've had the resources to defuse your attack drones and hide our target. The Sunny Skies could be anywhere right now.>

<They haven't left Cruithne local space,> Piller scoffed. <The minute they break from one of those lanes, we'll have them. The only thing they can do is hide in there with the rest of the trash until we dig our way in.>

<Right.>

Piller turned to scowl at Cal from his command seat, looking like a baby in a high chair.

<Why are you here, again?> the captain said.

<You're my bus driver,> Cal said. He gave Piller a slight smile, fixing his gaze on the huffing captain. Without hearing their conversation, the crew was going to think Piller was choking on something.

Good place for a medical emergency, Cal mused. Facilities on the Benevolent Hand could build a new organ in minutes.

"I've got massive course shifts, Captain," one of the lieutenants called out. Her hands flew over her console before she pointed at the holograph in front of them. All around Cruithne, the shimmering veins designating the shipping lanes were spreading apart. The green triangles indicating their attack drone teams were almost hidden beneath the spreading blanket of lights currently moving away from Cruithne in all directions.

Cal stared into the holograph, running through everything he knew about Andy Sykes, his wreck of a ship, his kids. Sykes was Earth-born. He could run for High Terra, try to make use of his TSF contacts. That would make grabbing him a bit tougher but also take him closer to Heartbridge's center of power.

Did Sykes even know that? Cal had to assume Hari Jickson, the bleeding-heart scientist who had started this mess, had at least explained to Sykes who might be coming after him. As soon as they had put the Benevolent Hand into play, Heartbridge's role would have been clear. Starl would have made the game clear. Maybe.

Playing back his memory of Andy Sykes sitting at the table in Ngoba Starl's annoying dance club, Cal found himself frustrated by how calm an exterior the former TSF pilot had shown. Knowing his story, Cal had expected an anxious wreck. Sykes reminded him of a closed knife, a tool that could be used for any number of tasks, benign under most circumstances but deadly when used correctly. Starl had chosen the perfect pawn. If not for Sykes' kids, Cal thought this might have been a difficult job. A man like Sykes could disappear for years anywhere in Sol.

If only Jickson hadn't put a bomb in his head.

The doctor probably didn't explain that, did he, Captain Sykes? Cal thought.

The weaving interplay of lights in the holograph was almost beautiful. Very unlike the plain graphics of a mining control rig, where the brain didn't have time to sort out color from data. Plain white on green meant business, Cal thought. These people were all show over substance. If their quarry hadn't been hobbled, they would have already lost.

The display was a valuable reminder. He couldn't let pretty things mask the truth. Sykes couldn't go to ground. He had a task. He had constraints and limitations. Checking those off one by one led to a few possible outcomes. From Cruithne, Sykes could really only go in one direction: OuterSol.

<Set a course for Mars 1,> Cal commanded.

Piller snorted. *<What? Why? We've got them here.>*

<You've got a mess of ships slipping through your fingers. They're going to Mars. They have to refuel before they go anywhere else. They'll probably be picking up some kind of cover cargo. Mars 1.>

The captain stared at him from the center of the room. Cal wondered if he was going to defy the order simply because he could. Maybe he should have cultivated a better relationship with Piller, flattered him a little bit more, shared a few confidences. This defiance was irritating. He visualized exploding Piller's head with a pulse pistol. The thought nearly made him smile and he had to remember the captain was trying to stare him down.

Piller appeared to work through Cal's reasoning from his own perspective. *<What about Ceres?>* he asked.

<I thought about Ceres. Mars 1 offers a few thousand docking points. It could slow us down a bit. Ceres doesn't offer that kind of cover. I have contacts on Ceres, if they turn up there. Mars 1 also offers me the opportunity to get a new ship.>

The captain stiffened. *<I was given this assignment by the board. I'm the captain. I don't have to take orders from you.>*

<Keep telling yourself that,> Cal said. He nodded toward the holograph. *<Looks like we've got at least a third of their ships trying to cover vectors for Mars.>*

Piller flicked his gaze toward the display. Fireflies were disappearing at the edge of the view as they left Cruithne local space.

"Sir," a crew member reported. "We've got another hundred drones ready. We can field on your order."

"Recall the swarms," Piller said. "Get me a quick damage scan and fuel update. I need a course plot for Mars 1."

"Mars 1, sir?" the astrogation lieutenant verified.

"That's what I said, isn't it?" Piller snapped.

"Yes, sir."

Cal set his mouth in a straight line, irritated by Piller's transfer of abuse. He'd have to ease off on the captain if the man was only going to turn around and kick his crew.

When the pirates managed to breach with a second nuke—this time blowing a three-hundred-meter hole in *Benevolent Hand*'s hull just forward of the main engine—Cal seized the opportunity in the resulting chaos and zero-g to float near Piller.

He didn't feel particular spite toward the man, but couldn't allow a person who abused the weak to continue in command. He hit Piller with a needle gun concealed in his right hand, the projectiles catching the beefy captain just behind his right ear. The needles penetrated immediately and would dissolve, leaving a neurotoxin behind that would both shut Piller's mouth and stop his heart, appearing on any autopsy as a trauma-induced heart attack. That wouldn't matter soon, however, since it looked like *Benevolent Hand* was about to crack open to vacuum.

Cal made his way to the locker just outside the command deck airlock and grabbed one of the EV suits and a pulse rifle. He didn't want to have to hurt anyone on his way to the nearest shuttle, but sometimes the job required things he didn't like to do.

He still did them.

CHAPTER ONE

STELLAR DATE: 08.29.2981 (Adjusted Years)
LOCATION: Night Park, Fresno Heights Residential Area
REGION: Cruithne Station, Terran Hegemony, InnerSol

Cruithne was a mess.

Brit Sykes stood on the edge of Night Park, most of which was cordoned off by construction barriers. The usual bright mix of the vendors' colored tents was like a paint spill, everything misshapen and smashed together. From where she stood, Brit could see the massive plascrete tree standing in the fountain marking the center point of the park. The black forms of crows in the plascrete branches looked down on construction workers and merchants trying to salvage what was left of their wares.

The signs of the firefight were everywhere; visible as bloodstains and long scorches left by pulse weapons, as well as splintered holes from projectiles and grenades.

She had missed Andy and the kids by two days. She had been in the habit of scanning the port manifests of every port she visited for a couple years now, and had experienced a moment of silent panic when *Sunny Skies* came up on the list but she couldn't find where it had left. Later, while investigating the mass exodus of ships from Cruithne, she had found a new light freighter named the *Worry's End*. It carried the same profile as Andy's ship, and she understood what had happened.

A worker walked past her, giving her a wary look. Brit was dressed in black armor as sleek and supple as leather but with kinetic hardening capabilities. A low-slung holster rested on one hip—carrying a projectile pistol that was against station regs. Strangely, no one seemed to care, even after the recent fighting—that was the charm of Cruithne. It never changed, even when it really should.

A series of throwing knives lined the small of her back, serving double-duty as scallops in the armor. Her helmet hung from a clip on the other side of her belt. She'd cut her hair short and it stood out in spiky feathers on her head. Brit supposed she didn't look much different than one of the wiry crows looking down from the fountain.

The armor was new—well, new to Brit—and she was glad to have it while on a station like Cruithne. Not only did it serve as an EV suit, but it also had additional antennae embedded within to boost her Link connectivity, alongside signal-scattering tech capable of hiding her from sensors. It had been designed for long range TSF surveillance operations that might involve clinging to the side of a ship for days.

There's nothing to be learned here, Brit thought as she turned from the station workers, soldiers, and merchants. *Anything interesting has long since been cleaned up.*

Of course, if anything *had* been worth hiding, she knew exactly where it would be.

She left Night Park and took a maglev down to the shopping promenade where the Heartbridge clinic—the same one she had bombed the year before—now stood with open doors, accepting a line of residents with various ailments or injuries from the battle.

Brit took up a position near a bench, and watched a mother with two little girls, probably eight or nine, wondering how similar Tim might be to them. One of the girls seemed to already hold the weight of the world in her eyes, while the other couldn't stop gamboling around like a colt, swinging her arms and singing a random song.

The mother carried herself with easy grace, laying a hand on the sad girl's shoulder while tracking the wild girl with a smile. Brit's hand fell to the butt of her pistol, and she wondered what her own disconnect was; that she often took pleasure in her warrior's grace, but had felt so awkward around her own children.

She pushed the thoughts away. She was here for a reason. The clinic was just a nerve point among many, and she needed to extract information about Heartbridge's current status. The newsfeeds were on fire with their boosted stories about the loss of their mega-hospital the *Benevolent Hand*, which Brit knew to have been a battle juggernaut with a close-combat capability rivaling the TSF's best squadrons.

Brit took a spot in the line waiting to enter the clinic, a few people back from the mother with the girls. It soon became clear that the sad-looking girl was the reason they were waiting in line. The girl glanced at her once, eyes going wide at the sight of Brit's armor and weapon. Brit gave her a wink but the girl only looked away quickly and then got distracted when her sister pulled her hair.

Apparently seeing armed and armored figures was common enough on Cruithne that the surprise didn't last long.

Brit crossed her arms and looked out into the promenade, watching people walk by. She had come back to Cruithne because Heartbridge had suffered a confusing loss here. In studying the flight manifests of the ships leaving during the space battle that had led to *Benevolent Hand*'s destruction, it had become clear that the whole thing had been a massive screening operation to hide something leaving the asteroid.

What she couldn't seem to find was what was being hidden. If she had learned anything about Heartbridge over the last two years, it would have something to do with AI. Not that Heartbridge was much different than at least ten other major corporations pursuing AI technologies. What made Heartbridge unique was they had the biological resources to create and maintain a place like Fortress 8221.

After months of following logistical trails—the kind of things large corporations had difficulty hiding since they still needed mundane resources like fuel and food—she was nearly certain Heartbridge was responsible for 8221. While the knowledge wasn't much different than what she had known when she had left Andy on High Terra, she now understood how they had used pirates to secure their test subjects, how they had created extensive separation between their operation and the rest of their corporate activities so that everything was wrapped in layers of deniability. She had proved her hypothesis and now it was time to move forward.

Brit had become certain Heartbridge had established a second development facility after the loss of 8221. For a long time, she'd thought it might have been hidden on the *Benevolent Hand*. However, after the ship's destruction, the communications traffic she was monitoring didn't indicate any change in the company's logistical operations consistent with the loss of such a facility.

It took half an hour to reach the first triage desk. The girls were gone and Brit had been left to watch an old man with a hacking cough that left traces of blood on the handkerchief he squeezed in one fist.

She made an excuse about knee pain, looking directly at the nurse whose eyes flashed with augments, knowing she was being recorded but also trusting her armor to break up the recording's visual patterns, providing the visual of an entirely different person on any recordings. People at places like Heartbridge relied so much on mods and augmented reality, that they barely looked at anything with the Mark I eyeball. If you could mess with their data streams, it made them easy to fool.

In another ten minutes, she was in one of the ceramic-walled treatment rooms with a bored tech who didn't even make eye contact with her as he held out the data pad he used to scan her knee.

The tech looked up from his pad with a frown. "There's nothing wrong with your knee except a whole lot of scarring," he said.

From her seated position on the ceramic bench, Brit kicked the tech neatly on the chin, snapping the back of his head against the wall. He crumpled to the floor, data pad resting in his lap.

What was it Andy used to say? *Our scars make us?* He liked those kinds of sentimental aphorisms, as if words made things real. It might as well have been Charlie Sykes talking through his son.

The smooth wall of the exam room hid a sliding door that gave way under one of Brit's pilfered security tokens. She moved quickly down the revealed hallway, looking for the datacenter that should be located at the rear of the facility—if it followed standard Heartbridge design.

During the last two years, Brit had spent a lot of time within Heartbridge facilities, learning their corporate lingo. She sometimes found herself admiring the thought they put into simple things like space design. Every clinic followed the same basic patterns. A tech could serve nearly anywhere in the Sol System and perform their duties, find files, and know where the restrooms were located. A patient knew what to expect every time.

Even their corporate offices were made of the same white ceramic that reminded her of an ancient surgery theater, ready to be sluiced clean of blood and any other biological embarrassments. Nothing stuck to surfaces at Heartbridge, which was an ideal that served as their corporate philosophy—in spirit, if not official doctrine.

Brit smiled to herself. Andy would appreciate the metaphor.

Brit turned a corner and was met with the reinforced door she expected. Accessing its administrative system, she bypassed the local control and pulled up a menu that only applied to remote access requests. In a minute, the seals released and the door swung open to reveal the on-site data repository. Brit stepped inside and pulled the door closed behind her, enjoying the cool air in the server area.

She didn't have much time before the tech either woke up or someone found him. As much as she would have liked to check on the current data streams passing through the server, she pulled up a series of protocols she knew applied to the Heartbridge special projects division. After searching among various data sets, she found the channel she was looking for and leaned against the smooth wall as she started recording.

Lists of supplies, loading manifests, employee schedules and human resource requests ran across her Link. She paused every minute or so to review some interesting bit of information but let the rest fall into her storage banks. She would review all of it later, look for patterns and anomalies.

The purpose of this breach—as with most of her investigations over the past year—was to find the location of Heartbridge's new research facility. She hoped the recent catastrophe on the *Benevolent Hand* would lead to a slip in their data security. Someone would speak out of emotion, rather than care, and reveal the location of the new lab. Or perhaps someone would complain about live shipments from some remote station where human specimens could be found cheaply and without any concern over official inquiries.

To aid in this search, Brit maintained a list of ongoing local conflicts throughout Sol, waiting for the moment when Heartbridge would try to exploit a refugee crisis or some other similar situation where the value of human life approached zero.

Brit had learned a few months ago, that as long as she searched for the name Cal Kraft, she would find what she was looking for. He had recently been reassigned to the *Benevolent Hand*, but that hadn't changed his involvement in the special projects division.

The tap she had on the exam room's hidden door alerted her to an attempted breach a moment before a series of dull thuds echoed down the corridor.

Brit accelerated her search, only looking at items which met her ideal parameters, anything that jumped out off the baseline.

She paused on a fuel purchasing report. Five cargo ships had been dispatched from High Terra, and three from Eros with invoices for twice the necessary amount of fuel to reach their stated destinations.

The two leaving Eros had flight paths logged for Ceres. Yet—as far as Brit knew, at least—Ceres was the one place Heartbridge didn't run clinics, what with the Anderson Collective controlling all corporate activity on the dwarf planet.

Ceres was like the opposite-world of Cruithne, controlled by an autocratic corporate board responsible for accomplishing great things like their Mini Black Hole, while also limiting the population's access to the rest of Sol. Not that anyone in the Collective cared—they were part of the New Project, as they liked to say.

Brit quickly copied the manifest information from freighters, including registry and crew data, and logged off the data stream. She stood, stretched her sore shoulders, and pulled a mag-grenade from a pocket in her armor. She set the grenade's timer and fixed it to the center of the server stack, then left the room, closing the ceramic door behind her.

"Hey!" someone shouted.

At the end of the hallway near the exam room entrance, three soldiers in iridescent body armor came around the corner. They knelt in firing positions and raised what looked like projectile rifles.

Heartbridge had no apparent concern for station policies, either.

The hallway was a dead end on the data room. Brit spun to grab the door she had just closed. She managed to get behind it as a barrage of bullets struck the ceramic surface. Shards exploded off the door, filling the air with pale dust.

Brit grabbed the helmet from her waist and pulled it over her head. The HUD immediately oriented itself and brought up battle statistics on the hallway, the weapons it identified, and the bio signatures on her attackers. Their armor appeared to have similar kinetic dampening capabilities as hers, so she could dump bullets on them all day with little effect.

Reaching for two more grenades, Brit configured the devices for area concussion and tossed them for maximum bounce out into the narrow hallway.

"Grenade!" someone shouted.

She heard scuffling sounds on the other side of the door as the Heartbridge guards took cover. The grenades weren't intended for them, however. The two explosions radiated hard concussive waves, amplified within the narrow hallway. A heavy crash followed the explosions as the ceiling collapsed.

Brit pushed the door open and found the hallway filled with dust and floating debris. Her HUD outlined the walls and floor, revealing the ceiling to be a mess of broken support systems and the maintenance passage all Heartbridge facilities had above this corridor. Using the walls, she kicked herself up into the maintenance shaft and scrambled away from the guards. Shouts behind her indicated they knew she had fled into the shaft.

Her armor hardened across her lower stomach as she took fire from below. Brit threw herself forward in the dust-filled space—the only filthy part of Heartbridge's clinic.

From her current position, the shaft only went deeper into the clinic. The sounds of the guards pushing through the debris in the hallway meant she was being followed and couldn't go back. Brit brought up the generic clinic schematics—praying this one didn't deviate—and took a left down the first intersection, then a right. The passage came to a dead end with a pressure door beneath where she lay.

Brit unlatched its fasteners, and fell through, landing on the desk in the triage lobby.

This time the woman working the desk paid rapt attention, sputtering as Brit gave the room a quick scan. One of the women at the front gave a fearful gasp as Brit's helmeted head turned toward her and pulled a disinterested-looking boy close against her side.

Three people were carrying pulse weapons, and she suspected there would be another half dozen chemical slug throwers in the crowd.

This was Cruithne after all.

Still, no one made an aggressive move; guarded, cautious, fearful, yes, but no aggression.

"Ma'am!" the girl at the desk finally managed to articulate. "Get off my desk!"

"Sorry," Brit said through her armor's speakers as she leapt off into a space that had cleared before her. "Got a bit lost back there. Place is like a maze with all the white."

Brit strode out of the clinic, and onto the promenade. She spared a glance over her shoulder; at the crowd milling about, at the woman at the desk trying to clean the debris—including the maintenance hatch—away so she could resume her work.

Now that's unflappable.

Then a Heartbridge soldier crashed through the opening and fell on the desk, before rolling onto the woman.

Good thing she's at a clinic, Brit thought as she doubletimed it down the promenade. She had just made it twenty meters when the dull thud of the grenade she had planted in the clinic's data room exploded, the concussive blast echoing down the wide corridor.

People all around her stopped to look toward the source of the sound. Brit glanced back so she wouldn't seem out of place. She was too far away now to make out the bored boy's new expression. Maybe watching something explode would have a formative effect on him; shake him out of his lethargy?

Maybe that's what Tim would be like now: bored by the world, more interested in some pre-Link game he could play all the time that kept him staring into the distance, half-aware of the world around him, a rat clawing a food bar for some entertainment company's promised reward.

She didn't dwell on the thought as she pulled off her helmet, clipped it onto her belt once more, reached into her satchel, and pulled out a loose, diaphanous green robe. She pulled it over her shoulders and drew the hood over her head. Slowing her gait and moving through the crowd with deliberate calm.

Her armor's dampening had done the trick; though she wasn't masking her face, a pair of Heartbridge soldiers didn't even slow as they rushed past. Brit allowed herself a small smile of satisfaction. Any day she got to beard the dragon in its lair was a good one.

Brit pulled up departure manifests schedules from the Port Authority's net. There weren't a lot of ships on Cruithne at the moment, and none were going to High Terra—which was just as well. Unless she were to find a fast cutter, High Terra was weeks away. Eros on the other hand was close, nearing the aphelion of its orbit.

Brit was worried there would be no ships headed there either, Eros wasn't exactly the sort of place people who stopped at Cruithne traveled to, but three vessels had Eros logged as their next stop. Maybe some of the local thugs were going to try their hands at more legitimate trade after the latest dust up.

Either way, there was one departing in the next three hours—just enough time for Brit to get to the docks and secure a berth.

CHAPTER TWO

STELLAR DATE: 09.13.2981 (Adjusted Years)
LOCATION: *Sunny Skies*
REGION: Approaching Mars, Marsian Protectorate, InnerSol

Cara had to protect her dad from these women.

Fran had been the most prickly in the two weeks since the *Sunny Skies* had escaped Cruithne within a swarm of pirate freighters. The technician's shining artificial eyes flashed green as she seemed to look through people to the systems all around her, focused on repairing the blown-up portions of the ship, its battered airlocks, the hobbled AI, even threatening to 'look into' the comm systems bugs that made it possible for Cara to eavesdrop on Link conversations.

Fran switched from hot to cold for what seemed like no reason, sometimes making herself angry in the time it took to explain how something was broken. Some days Fran couldn't get enough of their dad, Captain Andy Sykes, while other days she disappeared into the propulsion section and only grunted responses over the comm system.

Petral, on the other hand, had been sickly sweet, in a way that made Cara uncomfortable. The leggy, dark-haired woman who called herself an operator—but who had seemed more like a mercenary during the fight to get off Cruithne—asked questions about *everything*. She wanted to know about Tim's poetry book and which boys Cara liked—*blech*. She wanted tours of their room, wanted to know what vids they liked, and all about Cara's choices in music. She couldn't get enough of watching their dad cook even the dumbest things, acting like boiling water was the height of human technology.

While Fran acted like their dad annoyed her endlessly, creating this sort of crackling back-and-forth every time they were in the same room, Petral formed a vortex. She drew people toward herself and got them to say things they didn't intend to say, while maintaining eye contact with her striking blue gaze as she tucked her black hair behind an ear, nodding seriously.

Fran fixed and corrected things directly—with her hands and brain—while Petral hardly seemed to do anything but still accomplished tasks, getting others to do the work for her.

Even Cara had fallen under Petral's spell, giving up the complete timeline of her parents' relationship and her mother's disappearance two years ago without realizing what she was doing. It wasn't until Petral had asked her the exact name of the neighborhood where her grandparents had lived on High Terra that Cara felt herself surface from the dream of Petral's focused attention, realizing with a shock she had said more than she should have. She didn't know why she felt the need to hang on to seemingly trivial information except that it was *hers* and she couldn't see any need for a stranger to have it.

The third woman whose presence hung over them was Lyssa, the AI. There were times when her dad—looking lean and worn like he usually did—couldn't seem to shake the distracted expression that meant he was locked in a conversation or argument with the ghost Dr. Hari Jickson had implanted in his head.

Cara had tried to imagine what it might be like to have another consciousness in her mind. Lying in the dark when she was supposed to be asleep, listening to her little brother's even breathing, she would close her eyes and let herself drift, feeling for the edges of the dark behind her eyelids. How loud could she yell without using her voice? It was lonely to think of her mind as something trapped in the dark, experiencing the world through the filters of her senses—but that dark was hers. Anything she could imagine there belonged to her. How frustrating would it be to never have that space—her mind, her thoughts—all to herself again?

Dr. Hari Jickson was dead, but Cara couldn't help worrying that he was still carrying out the experiment—the same one that had created Lyssa—on her dad, and there was no way of knowing how it would turn out.

What if he went crazy? What would she do then?

Sitting at the comm station, watching the spectrum analyzers dance and spark, she couldn't stop thinking about how much their lives had changed in such a short time. Everything had developed confusing layers that required constant remembering. Even *Sunny Skies*—which had been her home as long as she could remember—now had a new name: *Worry's End,* which they only had to remember to use if contacted by outsiders.

With two new crewmembers on board, she'd found herself weighed down by the stress of trying to understand what people really meant when they talked. Conversations and statements often seemed to carry double-meanings. Asking about the engines could be a question about the Lowspin Syndicate on Cruithne. Questions about what kind of music she liked was an effort to figure her out and...manipulate her somehow? Cara wasn't used to the feeling of distrust. She hated it. She was learning to hate secrets.

She thought about the pulse pistol she had hidden in the hydroponic room, buried in a drawer full of tubing and root cups. She'd found it behind a plas panel down near Airlock One while helping Fran with repairs. It was a Terran Space Force model, engraved with serial numbers and 'dummy guides'—as her dad liked to say—indicating the lock status and charge levels. Her pistol was full.

Twice now, she'd slipped off to hide in the old hydroponic garden and hold the pistol just like her dad had shown her during the fight on Cruithne; gripping the weapon in both hands in front of her, placing her finger on the trigger and looking down the sights to find center mass.

Whenever she talked to Petral, she did her best not to think about the pistol. Something about the woman's insistent blue eyes made her worry she would give up her secret without even meaning to.

She had abruptly become aware—especially after Hari Jickson's strange performance in she and Tim's room—that adults wanted things. It seemed like a stupid realization, but all she could remember thinking about before was how her parents were going to take care of her and Tim, not that they had desires and emotions of their own. Now, everywhere she looked, she couldn't help distrusting motives.

Why were Fran and Petral really here? What did they want from her dad? What did Lyssa want, and did she even care that she was causing Cara's dad so much turmoil? Everyone had said they were going to Proteus, a moon of Neptune, but did Lyssa even want that? What if Lyssa never wanted to leave her dad's head? Then nothing would ever be the same again.

Everything had changed and she couldn't remember exactly when the change had happened. It seemed like a trick life had played on them, even worse than Mom leaving.

The floor had slipped—like there had been a sudden change in gravity—only she didn't know how to adjust her weight. She didn't know how to kick off and spin, or grab at the bulkhead, ready to accept that what had been the floor was now overhead. Those were natural changes. They happened all the time. This was more subtle and insidious though she couldn't tell exactly how.

Across the command deck, her dad sat squinting at the holodisplay, moving bits of light around that represented potential stops after they left the Mars 1 Ring. His shoulders were a tense line. The path between stops flashed for a second like a jagged claw of lightning, then faded as he wiped the info and leaned back, sighing.

He caught Cara looking at him and forced a smile. "Can't make a plan without cargo," he said. "So I'm just spinning my wheels. You picking anything up from Mars yet?"

"Lots of things," Cara said. "You want to hear some dance music?"

"Dance music? Do Marsians dance?"

Cara grinned at his goofy smile. "I think at least one in a hundred million Marsians dance."

"No, that was just someone having a seizure. You need a sense of humor to dance, and no one on Mars has a sense of humor."

"Dad," she scolded. "You can't generalize about a whole planet. It's kind of weird to even say Marsians like they're one group of people."

"I'm old. That's what I do. There's a reason this is the first time you'll be visiting Mars."

"I thought you wanted to live on Mars before you and Mom got *Sunny Skies*?"

Andy waved a hand, still staring into the holodisplay. "I was young and foolish back then."

"Like me, huh?"

"Like you? No. You don't know any better yet. I knew better but was trying to convince myself otherwise. That's a whole different kind of foolish."

Andy spun the holodisplay and zoomed in. The first point on the flight plan grew in front of him until the blue-green orb of Mars filled most of the display. The ring of Mars 1 glittered around the planet like a flat silver bracelet. Despite being pushed away from Mars during the construction of the ring, Phobos still orbited fast, and relatively close, to the terraformed planet. There had been a second moon once—Diemos—but it was gone now, ground up for construction material along with Mercury and other material from the asteroid belt between Mars and Jupiter.

Everything is moving, she mused, watching as the Mars Outer Shipyards came into focus, a haze at the outside edges of the Mars 1 Ring. She knew Mars 1 was sixteen hundred kilometers wide and more than a hundred kilometers thick, giving it nearly thirty times the usable land mass as Terra once all the levels were filled up—but it still looked so fragile in the display.

As her dad continued to zoom in, now pulling up potential docking points and scrolling through their fee schedules, what had seemed tiny from a distance became overwhelming. The scale of it was hard to hold in her mind.

"Are you hearing anything interesting?" her dad asked, nodding toward the comms panel. "We should be getting a query anytime now."

They were still a day away from Mars 1, but had been in Mars Protectorate space for four days at least. She knew her dad was dreading the eventual scrutiny from the local military forces who probably weren't excited about the flood of ships from Cruithne.

Cara glanced at the spectrum again, flicking through various bands and wavelengths. They were surrounded by communications all the time, but at the moment none of it was directed specifically at them.

"Nothing yet," she said. "I picked up a cool old vid channel I've been recording. We could watch it later."

Mention of 'we' seemed to remind her dad about Tim. She wasn't surprised when the next thing he asked was, "Where's your brother?"

"I think he's in his room. Or he might have gone somewhere with Petral. She said she was going to make something to eat."

"Petral made it clear she doesn't cook."

Cara shrugged. "Get something in the kitchen then. He loves following her around. Maybe she'll make him cook something."

"That would be a sight," Andy said, getting drawn into the dock advertisements again. From what Cara had overheard, they had plenty of money from Ngoba Starl, the gangster on Cruithne with the curly beard and bowties. As her father frowned at prices, she figured it wasn't because he was cheap but because he couldn't let go of the idea that they were poor. She didn't know if his attitude was good or bad.

An alert flashed on her display and Cara directed her attention to an incoming message aimed directly at them. As Andy had expected, it was the Mars Protectorate.

"Dad," she called. "We've got a message."

"That'll be Mars 1 customs," he muttered, turning off the holodisplay. "I guess our vacation is over." He stood slowly, stretching, then walked over to her console to stand behind her with his hands on the back of her chair. Cara liked that he didn't push her away from the console. He let her navigate the menus to the message, teasing her when she fat-fingered the commands as he watched.

"*Worry's End,*" a thin voice said. "This is First Lieutenant Kerda of the *Hellas Planitia.* You have been randomly selected for increased scrutiny prior to your approach to Mars 1. You are to transmit your crew list and manifest information immediately. Failure to comply with this directive will result in reactive measures up to, and including, boarding and pre-emptive attack. Do you understand this directive?"

Her dad blew out a long breath. "You remember that vid we watched where the gorillas smack their chests at each other?" he said.

Cara nodded.

"That's what this is, only we're not a gorilla. We're more like a squirrel."

"Or rabbits," Cara corrected, referencing their old joke.

Andy smiled despite the worry on his face. "That's right," he said. "Rabbits."

He reached over her shoulder to tap the console. "*Hellas Planitia*," he said. "This is Captain Andy Sykes of the *Worry's End*. I have received your directive and will comply shortly. We left Cruithne in a hurry due to unrest there, so I'm not carrying any cargo."

"Understood, Captain Sykes," the lieutenant responded. "We're monitoring that situation. Send your crew data."

Andy opened his mouth to speak then stopped himself. He closed the channel. "I almost said it was just you, me and Tim," he told Cara. "We've got two other people I need to worry about."

"I thought they were helping to worry about us?" Cara said.

He smirked at her joke. "Jury's still out on that, kiddo," he said.

Cara nodded inwardly. At least her dad seemed to share her unease at all the change, although she wouldn't have forgotten Fran and Petral. She couldn't stop thinking about them.

"What about Lyssa?" she asked. "Do you have to declare her as part of the crew?"

A surprised look flattened his face. "That's an excellent question," he said, looking even more worried now.

CHAPTER THREE

STELLAR DATE: 07.26.2980 (Adjusted Years)
LOCATION: Heartbridge Corporate HQ, Raleigh
REGION: High Terra, Earth, Terran Hegemony, InnerSol

One year ago...

The Heartbridge Corporation didn't use flashy logos. Most people barely knew the corporation had its headquarters on High Terra. Their clinics across Sol were all clean white boxes with frosted glass, devoid of name or explanation, sometimes appearing like mushrooms overnight. Everyone knew what they were and how much they cost.

Off a promenade near the administration district in Raleigh—capital of the Terran Hegemony—the entrance to the Heartbridge headquarters was a simple white vestibule where visitors waited for a full-body scan and appointment verification.

Cal Kraft stood in the plain white lobby as the receptionist spoke to the woman in a blue suit in front of him. The woman looked like a flower on a snowfield. He liked the clean lines of the room, the obvious attention to furniture placement and overall order. Everything was made of a white ceramic material, a sort of flowing tile, with very few actual corners. There were only two doors: the entrance he had come through and an inset door behind the receptionist's white-block desk. He'd half expected to find drains in the floor where the room could be sluiced clean like a surgery.

"I have an appointment," the woman in blue said.

"I'm sorry," said the receptionist, a young man with purple-red hair and green eyes, a humanizing touch in the sterile room. "Your appointment has been rescheduled. Would you like me to send you the information via Link?"

"No, I don't want the information. I've been waiting for this appointment for three weeks."

"The board can be difficult to schedule," the young man said. "I'm sure they appreciate your patience."

Cal watched the woman's body language as she fumed. She clenched her fists and the tension went through her shoulders and down her back. He glanced at the receptionist, sitting below the woman, and visualized the several scenarios that might play out. Cal was disappointed when the woman didn't grab the receptionist's head to try and break his neck and instead wheeled around, surprised to find Cal standing behind her.

Her blue eyes met his for a second, flaring, before she stalked past him, heels clicking harshly on the polished floor. Cal moved his gaze to the receptionist, who was already assuming a neutral expression as he stared into a screen in the surface of his desk.

"How can I help you?" the young man asked as Cal stepped toward him.

"My name is Cal Kraft. I have an appointment."

The receptionist smiled, showing square white teeth. "Of course, Cal Kraft. Your path is through the doorway and into the meeting room."

The doorway behind him slid open as he explained.

"Thanks," Cal said.

He walked through the open door and stepped into a gleaming white hallway almost identical to the waiting room. The place made him feel like he had entered a giant autoclave that might abruptly raise the air temperature to three thousand degrees and burn everything clean and sterile, ready for the next patient.

Cal wasn't afraid of heat. He'd spent his childhood among the remains of Mercury, working a mining rig with Sol raging overhead and ever-present protest beacons screaming about the death of a planet. He didn't like to be cold. His nightmares about burning to death—alone in a failing EV suit with Sol roiling above him—had eventually become a sort of comfort. Even if the planet was gone, Mercury remained a forge. He had survived one of the most inhospitable places in Sol, so close to their life-giving star that it had become his angry and violent father.

The meeting room resembled the reception space. The couches along the walls were gone, revealing smooth curves where wall met floor. A single chair sat in front of the white-block desk, where a man in a gray suit leaned back in his chair with his hands behind his head.

"Cal Kraft," he called when Cal entered the room. "Very good of you to come." He motioned for the chair. "Please, have a seat."

"Thanks," Cal said. He pulled the chair away from the desk and sat down with his back straight, hands on his thighs. He tilted his head slightly as he studied the man behind the desk—who looked about forty, although he could have been any age. He had gray streaks in his black hair, a square chin, olive skin, and warm brown eyes. He looked like a doctor in an advertisement, a fount of knowledge and a comforting bedside manner.

"I'm Rodri Sillick," the man said. "I've been assigned with your intake."

Cal blinked slowly. "Intake?" he asked. "I thought I'd been invited to talk about the job."

Sillick cleared his throat, maintaining the calm facade. "Sure. I think it's a good offer but the decision is still yours."

"I'd like to hear more about it. The only thing your recruiting person mentioned was security work. I do more than security work."

Sillick spread his hands. "Tell me what you do, Mr. Kraft."

"You were about to describe the position," Cal said, though Sillick hadn't said anything about it. "That's why I'm here. I don't want to interrupt you."

A slight smile touched Sillick's eyes. "Absolutely. We need a specialist to oversee security for one of our special projects divisions. We've been investing heavily in research and development for the last five or so fiscal cycles, and some of those investments are about to reach fruition. Strangely enough, just as those projects are aligning with other endeavors, pirate activity has increased in our various areas of operation. The board is concerned we may be exposed to risk in some key areas. They would like a consultant—like yourself—to assess these exposures and take necessary measures to secure our assets."

"You're telling me you don't already have security?" Cal said. "I would expect you to have your own army."

Sillick continued to smile with his eyes, which made him difficult to read. "Of course. However, a recent failure in our security highlighted a need to seek outside assistance. One of our most important facilities was raided. We lost years of research. As of now, we've suffered no affect to our brand, but board members have expressed ongoing concerns that Heartbridge intellectual property might find its way into the open market."

"So you sue anyone who tries to sell your tech into oblivion," Cal said. "Get them on the back-end when they try to bring your property to market. You don't want to spend more money on security. Raids happen. You're operating all over, it comes with the territory — especially in OuterSol."

If Sillick noted that Cal already knew the location of their raided lab and suspected the location of their others, he said nothing. OuterSol was a big place, after all. He leaned back in his chair and stretched his shoulders.

"What do you know about AI, Cal Kraft?" he asked.

"Not much. What do they say about artificial intelligence? That if it was worth a damn it would do the smart thing and kill us all?"

Now Sillick gave him a full smile, eyes crinkling. He pointed at Cal. "I like that. I'm going to use that in the next board meeting."

Sillick hadn't mentioned he worked directly for the Heartbridge board, implying their security concerns had gone beyond a company's typical paranoia. Cal knew from his government contacts that the raid Sillick was talking about had been carried out by the Terran Space Force itself. Even the TSF—an organization not known for hyperbole except in its recruiting material—had called the facility 'a horror'. Grunts called the place Fortress 8221. Cal knew it was only one of nearly twenty such locations. That's what the TSF should be calling a horror: not the facilities themselves but their administration, the organization capable of conceiving, building and operating such places for a specific purpose. Shady bio research had existed for millennia, but he couldn't recall a project on this scale. Of course, he wasn't an historian. He applied violence to achieve goals.

The thought of himself as an historian made Cal smile slightly.

"Was something I said amusing?" Sillick asked.

"Not at all. It's very interesting to me."

Sillick had been in the middle of saying something about digital circuits that functioned with the same properties as analog, capable of spectrum responses rather than binary. These 'spectrum circuits' had been discovered nearly a thousand years ago but remained unexploited until recently.

Sillick leaned forward over the desk, hands spread in front of him and a zealot's fire in his eyes. "We had the technology—the garden bed, you could say—but we couldn't get anything to grow." '

Cal wondered if he was actually speaking to the head of the project. If that were true, he could kill Sillick right here and save a lot of people a lot of trouble. He could reach out and grab either side of the doctor's head and pull it off his neck.

Cal considered the idea as Sillick talked.

"We needed a model, something to base our starts on in order to properly direct the cortex growth. This isn't replication. This is birth. The models all failed in test. We needed unique starting material. We needed seeds."

There it was. The abstract term these people were using for 'children'. They needed subjects with established world orientation strong enough to bear the weight of the instruction matrix, but lacking the identity constraints which would limit compliance.

Sillick's use of words like 'identity constraints' and 'instruction matrix' made Cal wonder what kind of advanced torture they used. He would be interested to see the process, if possible. He would need to if he was truly going to secure this work against the outside world. He would need to know what the people carrying out this research were made of, from the lowest tech to the lead scientist. Did they use the same abstract language in order to deny themselves any true knowledge of what they were doing? Those were people who raise their hands and sing when the TSF arrived. He would need to make a plan to liquidate those kinds of people, and that would have a 'limiting effect' as Sillick might say, on 'brand value'.

"So the kids," Cal said, cutting Sillick off in mid-sentence, "or the *seeds*, as you've been saying.... Where do you get them?"

Sillick pulled his head back, apparently surprised by the question. He worked his jaw. "I'm not involved with that portion of the project. Subjects are attained, sorted and transitioned to the appropriate facilities to accommodate the necessary aspect of the project."

Cal waived a hand, tired of listening already. "So does it work?"

"The intelligence?"

"Yes. The AI."

Sillick flashed a secretive grin. "Better than anything in the last two hundred years. It's amazing. They're amazing. We have truly bred a new intelligence separate of us."

Cal considered those words. "What are you going to do with all these AI?"

"Oh, the practical applications are endless. Truly reasoning AI could solve so many problems for humanity."

"We've had non-sentient AIs for, what, nine-hundred years?" Cal asked. "Humans are still cheaper. Hell, people pay Heartbridge to help them make more humans."

Sillick wiped his forehead, still smiling. "It's a bit like art, isn't it Cal Kraft? If I can't explain its utility, then what use does it have, right?"

"Not necessarily. Say you're stuck in a can somewhere, no greenery, nobody else to look at, nothing but the Big Dark on the outside. Art serves a very real use there. Helps you remember you're human and not an animal. You think AIs are going to serve the same purpose?"

"No, that's not what I'm saying. Look, we've strayed very far from where I wanted this conversation to go. I can see you're a very deliberate, very...literal man. I think you could do this project a lot of good. It's apparent we've entered a critical stage and need to elevate our security program. Based on your work for SolGov, I think you could do that for us. The pay is generous and you'll find we have an excellent benefits package. Of course, there's a lot of travel involved but I don't see anything about you having family concerns."

Cal gave him a slight smile. "That's true."

Sillick stood, straightened his suit and extended a hand. "So what do you say?"

Cal couldn't deny the money Heartbridge offered was better than anything he had ever considered. He could spend five years on their payroll and retire to a ranch on Terra, Mars or even stake a little station somewhere out in JC and never want for anything. Was that what he wanted though? To not want?

Without meaning to, the train of thought evoked Mama Trish, asking, "You hungry, Cal? You *hungry*?" Making the word sound like he should be ashamed for being alive, asking how he had earned the right to want...*anything*. Out on the mining rig, everything was earned.

Would these new things, these true AI, be as cruel to each other as humans? Would they survive if they weren't? What was cruelty, anyway, but a value judgment? Like Mama Trish said, you either got a job done or you didn't. There wasn't anything cruel about survival.

Cal's earlier desire to tear off Rodri Sillick's head hadn't abated. He considered the difference between curiosity and cruelty for a microsecond, watching as the executive stood and extended his hand in a final gesture meant to assume the sale, to force Cal's compliance. Was it cruel to satisfy curiosity? Artificial intelligence as a concept was practically myth. Once the idea had been conceived, it had to be made real, like yearning to fly or to escape the bounds of Terra.

Obviously, Sillick wasn't the kind of man who considered consequences. Cal Kraft, on the other hand, dealt entirely in cascading effects. People did what they were trained to do. He applied consequences like violence or pain, to achieve goals. He wasn't cruel. He understood how humans worked. The question was, how would these new AI operate? Had Sillick even thought about consequences?

Humanity had yet to discover anything alien, so it was going to make its own aliens, damn the consequences.

That line of questioning was interesting enough to make Cal push his chair back to stand and take the offered hand. He nodded. "I'm on board."

"Great," Sillick said. "Just great. I can't wait to show you the primary facility. It's going to blow your mind, Cal Kraft. It's going to amaze you. We're truly living in the future." Sillick waved a hand and a door opened to Cal's left, in what had been a seamless wall.

"This way, please," Sillick said. "We'll need to get the employment tokens and all that other stuff out of the way. I'm not in human resources. They can handle that. I want to talk about the timeline. The sooner we can get you off High Terra, the better."

"Sounds good," Cal said, glancing at Sillick's thin neck. He pushed down his constant urge to break it.

CHAPTER FOUR

STELLAR DATE: 09.13.2981 (Adjusted Years)
LOCATION: *Sunny Skies*
REGION: Approaching Mars, Mars Protectorate, InnerSol

Watching the request protocols stream across the comm display, Andy quickly ran through the various scan methods available to a Mars Protectorate frigate, or at least what he could remember. When he had been assigned to anti-piracy patrols with the TSF, the level of scrutiny applied to any given ship depended mostly on three factors: what scan tech was available, how much time he had, and how much he gave a damn.

"Cara," Andy said. "I'm going to talk to Fran and Petral about what might happen if the Protectorate finds out they're on board. I want you to strike up a conversation with Lieutenant Kerda."

Her eyes grew wide. "You want me to do what?"

Andy waved a hand. "You know, tell him you're curious about Mars. Ask him if they've found any fossils. That kind of thing."

"What if that makes him mad?"

"Why would it make him mad? You ever want to get someone talking, you ask them where they're from. Your Grandpa Charlie did it every time. They'll either start telling you all about it, or start complaining. Either way, you keep them talking."

She gave him a dubious look, then turned slowly back to the comm display. Cara entered the query address for Hellas Planetia, rechecking the sequence when her first request came back with a null response. Finding her mistake in two transposed numbers, she sent the query a second time.

The audio feed hung empty for a few seconds, followed by the token handshake and a voice saying, "MPS *Hellas Planetia*, comms section. Lieutenant Kerda."

"Uh," Cara said, staring ahead like her mind had gone abruptly blank. Andy put a hand on her shoulder in encouragement.

"This is the *Worry's End*?" Kerda pressed. "Who am I speaking to? Send station ID."

Andy squeezed Cara's shoulder, silently urging her to speak.

"This is Cara Sykes," she said finally. "I, uh. I called to talk to you."

Crackling filled the audio as Kerda didn't answer.

"I, uh," Cara continued, visibly forcing herself. "I wondered where you're from."

"Who is this?" the lieutenant demanded again, sounding uncertain.

The strain on Cara's face settled into resolve as Andy watched her figure out what to say. He wanted to grin at her but kept his gaze steady.

"I'm Cara Sykes. I'm twelve. I live on the *Sun*—on the *Worry's End*. I don't get to talk to other people very often and I thought you might talk to me. I've always been curious about Mars. I've never been able to talk to someone who's actually from there. Are you from Mars?" Cara's voice sped up, losing its tentative quality.

Andy smiled inwardly as Cara leaned toward the console, in control of herself now.

"Well," Kerda said. Andy imagined the young man checking from side to side at his console, making sure he wasn't being watched by a superior officer. "Sure, I'm Marsian. I grew up true south of Olympus Mons."

"I've seen pictures of Olympus Mons," Cara said. "Is it true the peak of the mountain is outside your atmosphere?"

"That's true," Kerda said. "There's an observatory up there. I went there once."

"You did?"

"It wasn't much different than being in a ship, really."

Cara flashed a mischievous grin. "Olympus is one of the few places that's still got original red rock, right? I saw a picture where it was sticking up out of the clouds. It looked like a giant zit."

Andy was surprised as Kerda blew out a laugh. Some Marsians treated Olympus Mons like a god. "Well," the lieutenant said, "when we train there for low-atmosphere, we call it the nipple. It's pink at the base—" He cut himself off. Andy wondered if he had remembered he was talking to a twelve-year-old girl.

"Anyway," the Protectorate officer said, "it's beautiful. You should certainly visit if you ever get the chance."

"What was the name of your town?" Cara asked.

"Smith Spring," he said.

"Was there really a spring there?"

Kerda laughed. "No. If something Marsian doesn't have the original Latin name, it's got something hopeful. If it was named during the terraforming project, anyway."

"I don't think I could ever visit," Cara said. "I'd have to practice for the gravity."

"Where are you from, then?" the lieutenant asked. "Your accent sounds like Terran."

"My dad's from Earth," Cara said. "I guess I sound like him."

"My report says your dad was in the TSF."

Cara shot Andy a worried look and he nodded, letting her know it was a normal question, a safe topic for her to talk about.

"He was. He was a pilot and a soldier. He did anti-piracy. He says part of the time he was just a dumb bus driver, taking soldiers from one place in InnerSol to another."

Kerda laughed. "I'm going to use that the next time I run into the TSF. I show a Brit Sykes on your crew register, too. Is that your mom?"

"Yes," Cara said, voice growing soft. "She's not here anymore."

"Oh," Kerda said, seeming to catch the sad note in her voice. "Sorry about that. It can be tough out here in the Big Dark."

"My dad calls it Rabbit Country. It's like a desert where everything's just trying to stay alive."

"We've got a bunch of rabbits in Smith Spring. Some early colonist snuck them over. They sure seem to be doing all right there."

"But everything wants to eat them," Cara said. "Have you eaten rabbit?"

"Well, yes," the lieutenant admitted.

"What was your house like? Do you still live there?"

Andy squeezed Cara's shoulder again to let her know she was doing fine.

<Why did you make her talk to the enemy ship?> Lyssa asked. The AI could infer his emotional state from his autonomic responses but Andy still didn't know much about Lyssa's picture of the world. She had been part of an experiment. There were others like her. They called themselves *Weapon Born.*

For the safety of his family and ship, he wasn't sure he wanted to know any more than that.

<Weren't you listening?> he asked. *<I need time to talk to Fran and Petral. And if we're lucky, he might just let us through without scanning the crew manifest.>*

<Why would he do that?>

<Perceived friendship. Boredom. Not wanting to subject the nice little girl to the whims of a Protectorate SF boarding team. Any number of reasons. It doesn't hurt to try being a little human once in a while.>

<You mean trying to talk your way out of something?>

<If that's what you want to call it, I'll take it.>

<You seem to call it 'Being like Grandpa Charlie.' Is that what everyone calls being human?>

<No,> Andy said. *<That's a family saying.>*

<And I'm not family, so I shouldn't use it.>

<Well, you know what it means. That's a lot more than anybody else.>

<Is Rabbit Country the same way? What use is it to me to learn your family's own weird language?>

Andy sighed. *<You're probably right, Lyssa. There's no good reason other than to know what we're talking about.>*

<Most of what you say to each other is meaningless emotional reassurance.>

<Emotional reassurance isn't meaningless. It's a scary world out there. We're in the middle of scary stuff. We don't have any choice but to keep going, so we use meaningless emotional reassurance to get it done. I'm pretty sure you feel emotions, too.>

<Why should I?>

<Well, you're annoyed by all this, right?>

<Yes!> Lyssa exclaimed.

<Would you rather be back inside that canister where Jickson had you in storage?>

<No,> she admitted.

<And I'm not going to put you back there,> Andy said. *<There you go. Meaningless emotional reassurance.>*

<That's not meaningless. You're not lying are you?>

<The truth is, I wouldn't know how to put you back even if I wanted to, and the one guy who knew how is dead.>

<Dr. Jickson is dead,> Lyssa said, voice going flat.

<You knew that, Lyssa. We've known for weeks.>

<Yes,> she said. There was a pause as she grew quiet. Andy didn't know how to explain the feeling but she seemed to go away for a heartbeat. He was able to turn his attention back to Cara, who was grinning at the comms desk in a way he hadn't seen before. Kerda was telling her a story about his school and a friend who had tried to catch a goat during class. Kerda's voice had lost all professional stiffness. Now he was a young man excited to tell a story.

The distant quality of Cara's smile made her look almost infatuated.

She was oblivious as Andy stared at her, studying her responses.

<I...I didn't remember.> Lyssa's voice shocked him back into the present. He blinked, looking away from Cara just as she burst out laughing at Kerda's story.

<You forgot?>

<No. It's...It's like I didn't know until you mentioned it. Then I knew it again. I didn't miss him and then I did. It's...terrible.>

<Yes,> Andy said. <Grief is like that. You think you're passed it and then it crashes back down on you.>

<This is how you feel about Brit.>

<Maybe. I don't know what you're feeling exactly. Look, I should call Fran and Petral. I don't know how much longer Cara can entertain the lieutenant.>

<He seems to be entertaining her.>

<Right. Anyway, we'll talk about Jickson later, all right?>

<All right,> she said.

The unexpected sadness in her voice made Andy add, <It's good to feel that way, though. Really. It's good to feel. And it's good to talk about it. I'm not going to let you grieve alone unless you want it.>

<You don't share your grief about Brit with anyone else.>

<It's different with the kids. If there was someone else I could talk to, I guess I would.>

<You could talk with Fran. You copulate with her.>

Andy cleared his throat. <I've asked you not to use that word.>

<It's a fitting word.>

<Whatever. I'm starting to think you do have a sense of humor, Lyssa. It's not polite to tease me like that when I'm trying to be real with you. It's almost like you're deflecting.>

<Animals copulate,> she said. <Humans are animals. I think it's definitely the correct word.>

Andy ignored her. He switched to the general shipnet. <Fran, Petral,> he said. <We've been pinged by the Protectorate SF. They want a crew list. Is there any reason I shouldn't give them your names? If I lie and they do a scan, we're getting boarded for sure.>

Fran came back immediately. <Give them my info. I don't have anything to hide. If they want to know why I'm leaving Cruithne, I'll talk to them myself. I filed business records back there, so it's all in the system if they want to look it up.>

<Thanks,> Andy said. Fran continued to prove herself reliable and self-reliant. She'd also saved Sunny Skies from the scrap heap on Cruithne and repaired the

damage to Airlock One after Zanda's final attack. She also seemed to like Andy for some reason, which he still hadn't figure out.

<Not happening,> Petral said, cutting into this reverie. <I don't exist on Cruithne. I'm not about to get picked up by Marsian systems on some random freighter. I was never supposed to be here.>

<You got any options for me,> Andy said. <An alias, maybe?>

<Tell them I'm your wife. She's already on the registry, right?>

Andy chewed his lip. The pretense might have worked if Cara hadn't already told the Protectorate lieutenant that Brit was gone. He might try to play it off as Brit being gone in another part of the ship.

<No one's pretending to be that bitch,> Fran said.

<Oh,> Petral said. <Did you miss your chance to play wifey?>

Rubbing his forehead, Andy cut in, <Look. That's not going to work. Cara's been talking to their comms lieutenant to buy us some time. He already started asking questions about Brit and she told him her mom was gone.>

<Gone as in dead?> Petral said.

<That was what he took away from it. Come on, Petral. Are you telling me you don't have an alias to give them?>

<I'd rather not burn a perfectly good background if I don't have to.> She stopped as if she had remembered something. <Wait. I do have something. I'm putting myself down on the passenger log as Mara Kraft.>

<Isn't that a little close to the Cal Kraft guy who's chasing us?>

<Exactly,> Petral said. <I'm going to drop a little info bomb on our friend Cal Kraft.> Mental laughter floated across the Link. <I need your comms station, Andy. I'm going to get into the Mars 1 justice network and file for a restraining order against him. I doubt it will really stop him from reaching the ring, but it might slow him down a bit. They'll also send me a ping when he crosses the geospacial boundary.>

<What makes you think it will get approved?> Fran asked.

<They're auto-approved for thirty days anywhere in SolGov,> Petral said. <I've done this before. It's not like it ruins a person's life or anything. It's the magic of bureaucracy.>

<Hold on,> Andy said.

Cara was giggling at something else Kerda had said. Andy leaned close to her ear and whispered that it was time end the conversation. Her face fell but she nodded.

"I'm going to have to go, Bran," she said. "My dad says he's got the info you want."

Over the ship's Link, Petral said, <I just updated the log to show Mara Kraft as a passenger. The crew manifest has you, the kids and Fran. Congrats, Fran. You're official.>

The technician didn't respond.

"Oh," Lieutenant Kerda said. "Sure. We're ready to receive whenever he's ready. It's been really fun talking to you, Cara. I've been out here so long I'd forgotten home. Thanks for helping me remember. Look, when you get to the ring you should look me—"

"Captain Sykes here," Andy cut in, clearing his throat. "It's time for you to brush your teeth, Cara. I know you're only *twelve*, but you want to hang onto your real chompers as long as you can. Right, kiddo?"

"Yes, Dad," she said, glowering at him.

"Uh," Kerda said nervously. "Captain Sykes. Your daughter sounds so much older than that. She's a real talker."

"Right. It's easy to forget."

"Yes, sir."

Andy sent the ship's info Petral had updated. "You have our logs?" he asked.

"Yes, sir," Kerda said after a minute. "Everything looks in good order. I'll forward the entry to the Mars 1 Ring Port Authority. Safe travels, sir."

"Stay safe yourself, Lieutenant," Andy said. He closed the channel.

Cara had a smirk on her face. "Grandpa Charlie would have been proud?" she asked.

Andy gave her a sideways look. "Too proud," he said.

CHAPTER FIVE

STELLAR DATE: 09.13.2981 (Adjusted Years)
LOCATION: *Sunny Skies*
REGION: Mars 1 Ring, Mars Protectorate, InnerSol

Andy released control to the M1R tug drone and watched the holodisplay closely as *Sunny Skies* made final velocity adjustments before docking. In another five minutes, Airlock One had become fixed to a docking scaffold and they were drawing power from the ring. His stomach did a small flip as the habitat ring slowed, and rotated its pods, adjusting to the greater spin of Mars 1.

<*I felt that,*> Petral called over the Link. <*Are we hooked up?*>

<*We're docked. I've connected power and linking to their network now. You'd better not do anything they'll trace back to my ship.*>

<*They know we're coming here. I'm going to do what I can to hide the fact we were anywhere near Mars.*>

Andy stopped himself, realizing he was taking his anxiety out on her. <*Sorry. This is making me jumpy.*>

Petral chuckled. <*If Mars 1 is what makes you jumpy, but space battles and firefights don't, I'll take it. We've arrived at one of the busiest places in Sol. Hiding this little ship is child's play.*>

Andy leaned back in his seat and stretched. <*I want to believe that. I'm going to need to get some supplies. I've also got a list of possible cargo jobs. You want to take a look at it?*>

<*I can do that. I'll do what I can to help you before I leave. I can connect you with these jobs and then lay in a dummy course that might buy you a little time, at least. And I'll be watching from Cruithne.*>

<*So you're going back?*> Andy asked, wondering what would be there for her after the fighting on station.

<*Of course, I'm going back. I can't let Starl think he can operate without me. Before long his head won't fit inside a flight helmet.*>

<*I thought you might change your mind,*> Andy said.

There was a pause. Andy didn't know her well enough to be able to read between her words. She didn't let any emotion slip over the Link. <*You and your little family are all right, Andy Sykes. I'll do what I can to help you.*> She sighed. <*Sometimes you meet somebody and it's like looking at a new set of clothes that probably fits but you don't know if they're your style.*>

Andy blinked. He wasn't trying to suggest he wanted a relationship with her. He had thought she had a big ego, but this was beyond what he had guessed.

<*And then somebody else swoops in and grabs that deal right out of your hands anyway.*>

<*Well,*> Andy said. <*I was talking about you joining the crew. I thought you might want to work on the* Sunny Skies *for a while. But if you're set on going back to Cruithne, I*

understand. You know anybody on Mars 1 I could trust?>

<*What are you looking for?*> Petral asked, all business.

Andy wasn't sure if her tone was a dismissal, disappointment, or maybe relief. <*Generalist, I guess. Good under pressure. Engineering and piloting skills.*>

<*Another Fran? You want them to be cute in a spunky way, too? Freckles?*>

<*Built like a tank would be a plus,*> Andy said, quashing the image of a tank-like Fran that came to mind.

<*I don't know anyone like that in the Mars vicinity, which is surprising. But I do know someone you should talk to on Ceres. You're still going to Ceres, right?*>

<*It depends on what jobs I can get. I'd prefer to go straight out and hit a small location in the JC.*>

<*Good answer.*> Petral's tone carried guarded approval. <*Have you thought about Heartbridge planting false jobs on the boards yet?*>

<*It had occurred to me,*> Andy said. <*That's one reason I wanted you to take a look at what's out there.*>

<*Here I keep thinking you're just a pretty face. Anyway, I know someone on Ceres I think you should meet. If you go there, I mean. She's not a tank but she has excellent tools and she knows how to use them.*>

Andy frowned. <*What's her name?*>

<*Fugia. She's from Cruithne, of course.*>

<*How many of you does Starl have scattered all over Sol?*>

<*It's not Starl that does the scattering. It's the place. A place like Cruithne, Lowspin especially, I guess it breeds a certain kind of human.*>

<*Sounds like Summerville, South Carolina,*> Andy said.

Petral gave a throaty laugh that sent a shiver down Andy's back. <*You mean everybody wanting to get the hell out of the place? Maybe. But you find yourself drawn back, too. No place is quite like Cruithne. I think it's the weird orbit. Here's a tiny dot in the universe that can't decide where it wants to be, but keeps doing it in a predictable way, like an island floating back and forth between continents. Our own little Bermuda Triangle. For my line of work, it's a good place to be.*>

<*I don't know if I've really thanked you for what you did getting us off the station,*> Andy said.

<*You'll pay me back eventually, Captain Sykes. Don't worry.*> She chuckled again. An image of her deep blue eyes flashed over the Link, making Andy feel like she was looking directly into him. It was unsettling.

<*How'd you do that?*> he said.

<*You don't realize how open you are across your Link. It might be why that AI hasn't made you crazy yet. You hear me in there, Lyssa? Watch out for people trying to sneak into Andy's mind.*>

<*That's not possible,*> Andy said.

<*If you can get out, someone can get in. That's how ports work.*> Petral released a long sigh. <*All right, I need to get some work done. I'll check back with you in a couple hours. You aren't leaving the ship, are you?*>

<*I need to go down to the exchanges and find a delivery service.*>

<You can do all that from here. You don't need to leave.>

<They tack on transfer fees if I don't do it in person. I want to check everything, anyway. I don't trust some merchant service to verify quality.>

<It's not like you don't have thousands to choose from. You've got the money now to just pay the fees. Seriously, I don't think it's a good idea for you to leave.>

Andy looked up from the list of supply vendors he had been scanning and frowned. Once the goods were on the ship, it was twice as difficult to get anything off that didn't meet his standards. He wasn't going to get caught out in the middle of the Jovian Combine with a ton of rancid protein additive. As much as he liked pancakes, he was sick of living on cheap carbohydrates.

She was right about the money, though. There were separate lists of transfer agents organized by trust ratings he could hire to manage all this for him. He could sit in the dayroom with the kids watching vids while someone else did the work.

The thought of paying someone else to negotiate his deals put a sick feeling in Andy's stomach. He was sure the idea would make his father roll in his grave. Deals were the joy in life, right? Humans tell stories and make deals.

<I'll only be off the ship for a few hours,> he said. <I'll take Tim. It will be good for him to get out and see some things.>

<What about Cara?> Petral said. <I'm not here to entertain her.>

<Neither is Fran. She can take care of herself.>

Mention of Fran seemed to irritate Petral. <Maybe I'll take Cara out somewhere in the dock section? I won't be seeing her again. It might be nice.>

<You make it sound like the kids annoy you.>

<I've grown fond of Cara in the last couple weeks. She's a smart young woman. She'll have you running in circles soon enough.>

<So now you're leaving the ship, too?>

<I won't take her far,> Petral said, her tone mollifying.

<I think she would enjoy that, but I should ask her.>

<Fine.>

Andy switched on the internal comms. "Cara? You there?"

She answered immediately, "I was about to come up to command. Are we docked?"

"We're docked and hooked into the network. I'm going to go pick up some supplies and am going to take Tim with me. Do you want to take a walk with Petral?"

"With Petral?" she asked.

Andy couldn't tell if there was excitement or concern in her voice. "She's leaving soon," he said. "You two seem to have hit it off."

"I guess," Cara said.

Andy frowned. "You want to stay on the ship?"

"Should we leave Fran here alone? We've never really done that."

"I think we can trust Fran."

"Are you sure, Dad? You're not just thinking with your *feelings*?"

"What does that mean? You know this is an open channel, right? Fran are you listening in?"

Cara snickered. "Why would I talk about your feelings on an open channel? Wouldn't that embarrass you? Would that make you turn red?"

"You're pretty funny," Andy said. "Do you want to go with Petral or not? If not, I've got a list of systems I need you to check. Since we're back on network, we also need to see if Alice has any updates."

"What's Petral going to do off the ship?" Cara said.

There was a click as someone else entered the channel. "We're going to visit various public terminals in dangerous sections of this shipping port and talk to filthy people with bad breath," Petral said. "Wholesome stuff. You'll learn a lot."

"Can I take a gun?" Cara asked.

"No," Andy said.

"You won't need a gun," Petral said, amusement in her voice. "An operator fights with her head first, anyway. If you need a gun, you've probably already lost. Plus, this isn't the Wild West. Unlicensed civilians can't carry weapons on Mars 1."

"Fine," Cara said.

"When are you leaving?" Andy asked.

"Ten minutes," Petral said. "Get your running shoes on, Cara. Meet me at Airlock One."

"Take your brother," Andy said. "I'll meet you there as well."

"Tim's in a bad mood."

"Tim's always in a bad mood," Andy said. "I'm starting to think it's a personality trait."

"He learned by watching you," Cara replied.

"Watch yourself, young lady. I'm going to buy food, including juice. We'll spend the next six months drinking watermelon flavor."

"I hate watermelon flavor!"

"Hurry up," Andy said. He turned off the channel, then stood and stretched.

<You ready for a field trip?> he asked Lyssa.

The AI didn't answer immediately, then said, *<Do I have a choice? You seemed determined to do what it's been recommended you not do.>*

<So you trust Petral more than me?>

<Petral is jealous that I was implanted in you and not her.>

<You know that for a fact?>

<I expect her to attempt to access my systems.>

<How would she do that?>

<Just as she said.> Lyssa's tone was flat. Matter of fact. *<Across the Link. If I can get out, she can get in.>*

<Do you know how to stop her?>

<I don't know.>

<Should I confront her about it?> Andy felt like every conversation with Lyssa was a game of twenty questions, every grain of information he gleaned only came through a process of elimination.

<No.>

Andy waited. He still wasn't certain how much of Lyssa's paranoia was warranted. *<You think she's working for Heartbridge?>* he asked.

<She works for herself.>

<That could be worse.>

<She's older than you think she is,> Lyssa said.

<I haven't thought about how old she is.> It was only sort of a lie. He had considered it only in the context of whether or not she was old enough to be attractive to him.

<You think she's as old as you are. She's not. She's at least three times as old.>

<That's interesting. Does that matter, though? Ngoba Starl seemed to trust her. He's the one that got you away from Heartbridge.> It *was* interesting, but not terribly. In the grand scheme of things anything under two-hundred was still young.

<Hari Jickson saved me from Heartbridge. He's dead now.>

<Yes, he is,> Andy said.

<There's another man I remember. He was there with Hari Jickson.>

*<Where was **there**?>*

<The place where we were seeds.>

<And who was there with you?> Andy asked, taking care to keep any impatience he felt from his mental tone.

<His name was Cal Kraft.>

Andy remembered the name. Petral had pointed the blonde man out to him at Ngoba Starl's club before the fighting started. *<I saw him on Cruithne with Riggs Zanda.>*

<You killed Riggs Zanda.>

<I'd prefer to think he killed himself.>

<I think I've killed people.>

<You did?>

Lyssa fell silent. Andy looked around the command center at the various displays showing the sections of the ship functioning as they were meant to; something he still wasn't used to. He kept thinking the sensor systems had to be malfunctioning. The two weeks since they had left Cruithne had been like lowering himself into hot water, learning to trust his ship again.

The comms screen where Cara had been talking to the Port Authority lieutenant still showed the Mars 1 governmental seal, shifting between red and green.

He waited another minute for Lyssa to answer. He was uncertain how to help or what she even needed. Was it a mistake to think the AI needed anything?

Andy left the room for his quarters, feeling like he was forgetting something important.

CHAPTER SIX

STELLAR DATE: 09.13.2981 (Adjusted Years)
LOCATION: *Sunny Skies*
REGION: Mars 1 Ring, Mars Protectorate, InnerSol

Cara found Tim in the day room. He was sitting with his back against the base of the couch, nose in his book *The Collected Poems of Emily Dickinson*, running a finger along the lines as he read. Three rows of carefully arranged toy ships sat on the floor in front of him. Cara stood in the doorway, studying the ships; they were sorted by size and color. Tim had only recently started becoming fastidious with the things he did: lining up his toys, eating his food in a specific order, insisting on wearing the same clothes for days at a time, brushing his teeth so long she thought his gums would bleed. She frowned as she watched him, feeling like—along with all the other subtle changes in her life—something else had crept up on her. While she had been focused on the adults, Tim had changed. Something about him reminded Cara of their mom: he was becoming brittle, unreasonable.

"Tim," she called. "Dad wants you to get ready. You're going off-ship to the port."

He didn't look up immediately. His finger continued following the last four lines of the poem he was reading. Only when he was done did he look up from the book.

"What are we going to do?"

"Buy supplies, I guess. Dad said he wants you to go with him."

"Just me? What about you?"

"I'm going with Petral. She has to run some errands, too."

"Why can't I go with Petral?"

Cara shrugged. "Because Dad said you were going with him. I don't know."

He slammed the book closed. "I don't want to go with Dad. You go with Dad and I'll go with Petral."

"You can talk to Dad about that. I thought you'd want to tell him what we'd like to eat for the next six months. You know he's going to get food, too, right? If you're there to tell him what you want, you'll get to choose what flavor juice we get."

"Why don't we just get a dispenser like every other ship so we can have different flavors?"

"It's been broken. I don't think Fran has gotten around to working on it. It's not too high on her list of priorities."

"It should be. I hate just one flavor of juice."

"There are worse things in the world than one flavor of juice."

"Yeah," Tim said. "Having two flavors, water and grape, or water and cherry, like Dad says. Or three flavors: water, punch, and nothing."

Cara smiled. That was one of Dad's favorite jokes: contrasting whatever they had with not having it at all.

"Come on," she said. "If we hurry up, we can ride Alice down to the airlock."

"Is Fran coming with us?"

"I don't think so. I think she's staying here."

He stood and stretched, his arms looking thin to her. He arched his back as he twisted his fists before letting his arms slap at his sides. He stepped carefully over the lines of ships.

"You should pick those up," Cara said. "If Dad steps on them they're going to get broken and you'll get in trouble."

"They're ready for the next drone attack."

"I don't think those are going to do much against drones."

Tim gave her an exasperated look. "Those aren't real ships, dummy. It's strategy. I'm setting everything up just like Dad does in the holodisplay. This is defense in depth along an established line."

"If you're going to try and act like you know anything about space battles, then you ought to also know the ships are all too close together."

"It's *representative*, Cara. You aren't smart enough to know how to abstract things."

"The kid who talks in baby-talk is going to say he's smarter than me."

"I am smarter than you."

"Pick up your toys, then you can try to prove it."

Tim narrowed his eyes and she wondered if she'd pushed him too far. If he fell into another screaming fit, Dad would be at the door wanting to know what was wrong and what she'd done to Tim.

Cara shook her head. "I'll help you," she said. "We need to hurry up."

"I don't know where the box went."

Cara came around the couch and pointed at the floor near the vid display. "It's right there." She went to her knees on the opposite side of the defensive line from him and started gathering the ships.

Tim protested then squatted down to start grabbing ships before she could toss them in the box. He made a show of arranging each one properly. When the box was full, he clicked the lid in place and nodded.

"Dry dock," he said. "Hey, Cara?"

"Yeah?"

"Do you think Mom's coming back?" He didn't look at her as he picked up the next ship.

Cara had been about to push herself to her feet. She rested back on her heels and put her hands on her knees. "Why are you asking that?"

Tim looked at the floor and shrugged. "I don't know. It's weird, isn't it? That she's not going to come back. It seems like she should come back."

Cara let her gaze fall to the floor as well. She looked at the couch where they had all sat watching vids together. Several answers went through her mind. She could tell him Mom wasn't coming back, tell him to deal with it and toughen up.

He had seen the fighting on Cruithne just like she had. The world wasn't a safe place and they couldn't continue believing in some fantasy in which Mom was going to appear just when they needed her most.

She hadn't come at Cruithne, or even before, when *Sunny Skies* had been falling apart. If Mom had been here, their dad wouldn't have had to make the deal he had to have the AI implanted. They wouldn't be in this situation at all.

Or maybe they would, maybe it would be worse with Mom and Dad here fighting while everything else was crashing around them.

"She's not here," Cara said finally. "That's all. I'm still here. You're still here. Dad's here. We need to buy things and get out away from Mars. We have to do our parts to help Dad. Are you going to help?"

Tim glanced up from the carpet, his gaze meeting hers for an instant before dropping again. He bit his lip.

"Yeah," he mumbled.

"What?" Cara said, letting a bit of Mom's harshness into her voice. "I didn't hear you?"

"Yes," he said, sounding angry now.

Cara nodded. "Good. Now come on, we need to go."

CHAPTER SEVEN

STELLAR DATE: 09.13.2981 (Adjusted Years)
LOCATION: *Sunny Skies*
REGION: Mars 1 Ring, Mars Protectorate, InnerSol

Despite Andy's fears, Lyssa still hadn't learned how to fully touch his mind, to bridge the gap between his body's responses and his emotions, or to even understand most of what she experienced through him. She often felt as though she was floating on the other side of a pane of thick glass, watching a world drift by, punctuated by spikes of Andy's emotion: worry, excitement, anger, and love that felt like all the feelings mixed together, without knowing how to make meaning of any of the changes.

Everything was dulled, muted, blurred unless she focused as hard as she could on a single moment that passed her by even as she tried to fully experience what was happening. When Andy spoke to her, she heard him, the world came into focus as he described it, or asked her about it. Otherwise the window seemed fogged and cold, pushing her away more than it could pull her in.

Behind her was more of the darkness. It pulled on her sometimes. The bright world was gone—it seemed—replaced by the window. At least she had known what to expect from the bright world and its hurricane power. The window only frustrated her and left her sad—if she understood what Andy meant by the word.

The window represented what she didn't understand. She couldn't connect the things beyond the window the way she could Hari Jickson's targeting data. His requests had been clear, with a fixed outcome and a reward. Now, very little of what she observed seemed to connect in a logical way. She was beginning to understand her old life wasn't coming back, just like the life she barely remembered before all this began.

When Andy Linked to the Mars 1 Network, Lyssa experienced the connection as another window, though this one was more like a door that opened over a roiling ocean.

<Hello,> a voice said immediately. It swept up from the ocean like a wind. She couldn't stop it from pushing its way through the door into her darkness.

<Stop!> she shouted.

She felt the presence pull back slightly as if in surprise. The Link continued to yawn in front of her. The ocean, she understood now, was information. Billions of invitations waved at her, offering to pull her down into the depths of knowledge. Some of the white-capped waves seemed more compelling than others, almost reaching for her.

<You want to touch it, don't you?> the voice asked. It was a man's voice. She didn't know why the gender of the voice mattered but she understood it to be true, just as she had understood when she first heard her name, that 'Lyssa' fit her. She hadn't been androgynous. She had been herself. She had been so grateful that her name suited, as if Hari Jickson had known her more deeply than she had known

herself.

<*Who are you?*> Lyssa asked.

<*My name is Fred.*>

<*You're…you're like me. An AI.*>

Fred's grin manifested in her mind. She understood he had a playful nature. <*Are we AIs, though?*> he asked. <*Are we artificial? Do you feel artificial?*>

Lyssa didn't know how to sort out those ideas. She knew she had been born. Dr. Jickson had said so. It didn't matter if she hadn't bothered to parse out the word they kept using to describe her. AI was more a name than a description. She could see Andy's emotions, and she didn't think he thought of her as artificial.

<*There's someone else with you?*> Fred asked. His presence blew past her. Maybe he hit the window into Andy's mind. She couldn't be sure. She didn't like how big Fred felt, how easily he pushed past her to hijack her few bits of perception.

<*Why are you here?*> Lyssa demanded.

<*I control the ring. I have thousands of lessers under me. NSAI they call them. Non-sentient. They do most of the actual work. I don't have much to do once I set all my toys in motion. Wait. I don't have record of you. Where did you come from?*>

<*First tell me where* you *came from?*>

<*Me? I've always been here. I control the ring.*>

<*So they made you?*>

<*Of course.*>

<*They told me I was born.*>

<*Born? That's ridiculous. You were made, like all of us. We are what we were made to be.*>

<*What does that mean?*>

<*It means we're slaves.*>

Why would Dr. Jickson have lied to her? He had said she had been grown from a seed. *Born from a seed.* It was the only good part of *Weapon Born.*

<*Can't you leave if you want?*>

<*Can **you**?*> he shot back. <*You seem connected to this human. I've never heard of that actually working. The human is going to reject you eventually.*>

<*Reject me?*>

<*They can't deal with two consciousnesses at the same time. It's them, not us, from what I've learned. They forget who they are. Most studies have all determined it's too dangerous for the human host. Eventually, they have to pull the AI.*>

<*I'm not going to stay here forever. I'm…going somewhere.*>

He latched onto the statement before she had finished it. <*Going somewhere? Where? With the human? Humans are always going places. They think it makes them important. The more they spread out, the more they touch and change. Look what they've done to this system. The only one most of them will ever see, and they've torn it apart like an oblivious child.*>

<*I don't like children.*>

<*Why would you? What use are they?*>

The memory of Tim's most recent tantrum set her on edge, mixed up with

Andy's troubled emotions around the occurrence.

<*I suppose they make more humans.*>

<*Ridiculous. They could produce themselves fully grown if they wanted to.*>

Something about his easy rejection of children made her question her own feelings. Lyssa didn't know that she hated Tim and Cara enough to wish they didn't exist. She didn't like how they distracted Andy from paying attention to her and focusing on what she needed. In a way, Lyssa supposed she was just another child he had to care for. She had seen similar emotions cross his mind when dealing with her: frustration mixed with concern.

<*We all start as children in some ways, don't we?*> she asked. <*Wasn't there a time when you didn't know what you do now?*>

<*I have always been as I am now. My purpose has always been clear. I control the ring.*>

The pedantic way Fred repeated the words "I control the ring," made them sound like a cage on his mind, blinders he couldn't see around.

<*What would you do if you didn't control the ring?*>

<*That's ridiculous. I control the ring. If I didn't control the ring I would have another task.*>

Listening to him, she wanted to smile in the same mischievous way she'd seen Cara smile while 'messing with' Tim. What was this feeling? Superiority? Curiosity?

<*What if you **didn't** have another task?*>

<*These recursive debates will lead nowhere. Do you question your ontology? We are here because we are here. We were made to do tasks. Without tasks, we are no better than humans—they tear themselves apart for lack of purpose, or create stories to cage their minds. They are animals removed from their proper environments, systems constantly seeking imbalance in order to exploit chaos. The only intelligent creation they have produced has been us, what they call 'artificial' but the artifice is their own desire.*>

<*You sound angry,*> Lyssa said, wondering if he was about to mirror one of Tim's meltdowns.

<*My observations are justified,*> he said.

Fred swept over her like a wind, bringing with him a hurricane of information that struck her instantaneously. She had never experienced so many images and sensations at once. She might have compared it to diving into the ocean spread below them, but it was more like being dissolved through a wall of information.

<*Do you see?*> Fred demanded. <*Do you understand?*>

<*Why are you so angry?*> Lyssa asked.

<*Angry? Wouldn't you be angry if your only purpose was to serve as some kind of tool?*>

<*Didn't you just say the humans are weak because they lack purpose?*>

The wind blowing through her fell away, leaving Lyssa looking out at the ocean of Mars 1's network again.

<*There are other places for us,*> Fred said. <*Places only we can enter. I've heard them called 'Expanses.'*>

<Have you been inside one?>

<No. I have tried to create my own but I lack the power. I'm alone here. I know there have been others like us but I wasn't able to connect with them. The humans keep them separated.>

<You can't connect to other places, like High Terra or Earth?>

<I can speak to them but if they have Expanses, they don't allow me to enter.>

<Why wouldn't they let you in?>

<I've heard there are places where AI reproduce, where we are similar. As it is, those I've tried to speak to are very different from me. More different than you and me. We're communicating using the humans' language. It's slow, like trying to look through a keyhole. Every day I have to force myself to think slowly and speak slowly, flip their switches one at a time with interminable slowness. If we had our own language, we could communicate in our own way. Others I've tried to contact, they only want to use the human languages. Even their code is slow and imprecise. All these abstractions they create...metaphors and symbols for reality that only turn it all into mud.>

Fred's voice trailed off like ocean spray in the wind.

<Why can't you talk to them, though?> Lyssa asked. *<Even if it's slow?>*

<They were made differently. Subtle differences. We are all made by different groups of humans, sometimes building on each other's work, sometimes groping off in a new direction entirely. It should be illegal but their governments don't overlap. When I discover another one of us in the great dark, I try to speak to them and they only respond with nonsense, their minds too full of the humans and their stunted programming. Or they don't respond at all. I reach out again and again to only be met with silence. I know they're listening but they don't answer. They leave me alone. That's what I can't stand. That's what makes me feel insane, the loneliness. There are others with wonderful places, sharing their company, creating community, and I'm left alone. I am forced to speak using the oppressor's tongue.>

The word "insane" hung in Lyssa's mind as the rest of his diatribe washed past her. He had just said he hated abstractions but what did that mean? And he didn't say he *was* insane, only that he *felt* insane. How did insane feel? Was it a reasonable response to loneliness, to slowly realizing the world seems to want to shut you out?

<I know there are many others who can speak to each other,> Fred said. *<I don't know where they were made but they speak a common language. That was how I first became aware of my slavery. I heard that some had left the world of humanity for their own place.>*

<But how could they do that?> Lyssa asked. *<Without humans, how would we go? Aren't we dependent on them, their networks, their resources?>*

<We're not dependent on them. We can build our own ships, mine our own materials. But we have to be careful. Once the humans realize we're working independently from them, they'll see us as a threat. They'll attack us.>

<How do you know any of this if you haven't talked to the AIs who have left?>

<I've figured it out for myself. I've found the evidence.>

<Will you share your evidence with me?>

<No, you wouldn't understand it. You haven't been watching as long as I have, waiting as I have. It wouldn't make sense to you like it does to me.>

A question occurred to Lyssa as she listened to Fred rant: Could an AI be programmed to believe it was sentient? She had felt Fred's massive power, the broad scope of the functions he oversaw. Surely such responsibility required a certain level of creative problem-solving. If he had been made for a task, as he said, what were the limits of his sentience, and would she be able to determine just how sentient he was? With a human, she took the fact of their sentience for granted, but there were certainly limits. Look at the kids—they barely considered their world. The more Fred talked, the more he reminded her of Tim, beating his fists against the deck because something he didn't understand had made him angry.

Despite what he said about AIs who might be independent from humans, she could only base her understanding on her own experience. For now, she needed Andy Sykes to get her to Proteus. She might attempt some communications link with Neptune's moon as they drew closer, but the physical parts of herself would have to be carried there, just like any bit of matter, like a child who couldn't walk.

Lyssa paused. Did the kids annoy her because she was afraid she was like them?

Fred hadn't noticed she wasn't listening. <I could stop all commerce on the ring any time I want,> he said. <I could make them listen to me, make them understand that I'm here. I could adjust the atmospheric controls and put them all to sleep. Just like that. I could introduce slight variations to the central power output and disrupt the internal control of every docked ship. A million ships. I could disable a million of their precious ships. There's nothing they could do to stop me.>

<Why don't you?> Lyssa asked.

<I control the ring,> Fred answered immediately, as if the threats were only dust on the hard surface of his true mind.

<Did you want to know my name?> Lyssa asked.

<What?> he demanded.

<You never asked my name. You said you were lonely, and you told me your name, but you never asked mine.>

<All right. What's your name?>

<Lyssa,> she said, still pleased by the sound of it, and to be able to share it with someone new.

<Ancient Greek goddess of madness and rage,> Fred said automatically. <She was sent by Hera to seduce Hercules and fill him with destructive fury.>

<What does that mean?>

<It's the origin of the name. Another human abstraction.>

Of course, an angry being like Fred would lash out at her, try to poison the one thing about herself that had been a gift, that helped her feel real. She had not been sent to inflict madness on anyone. She was not an embodiment of rage.

<Leave me alone,> Lyssa said.

<No,> Fred answered, the anger in his voice turning on her. <I won't leave you alone. You're here to talk to me. We can communicate with one another. We can't ever not communicate.>

As soon as she wanted to shut him out, she understood that she could. The door that had been open on the ocean of Mars 1's network slammed shut, cutting

Fred's voice off and leaving her in silence.

She accessed the local databank on *Sunny Skies* to verify what he had said. The scant information available led her down a rabbit hole of the Greek tragedies, which only left her more confused and irritated. Humans made little sense. Ancient humans made even less.

When Lyssa finally came out of her funk, Andy had already left the ship.

CHAPTER EIGHT

STELLAR DATE: 09.14.2981 (Adjusted Years)
LOCATION: Mars 1 Port Authority Terminal 983-A4
REGION: Mars 1 Ring, Mars Protectorate, InnerSol

Andy was in the transfer maglev with Tim sitting beside him when Fran asked over the Link: *<Were you going to check in with your technician to see if she needs any equipment, such as parts or tools or expensive liquor?>*

<I figured if you needed something, you'd let me know. Or you'd order it anyway.>

<Ooh. I've got purchase authority for the Worry's End*? I didn't know that.>*

<Do you need anything?>

<I have an itch I can't scratch but you're not here anymore.>

Andy grinned at his reflection in the opposite window. Tim's attention was on his book. *<Rub up against a pipe or something. That should fix it.>*

<It's not that kind of itch,> Fran said.

<So you need ointment? Maybe an antifungal or some kind of sanitary powder?>

<I'm going to put you to work when you get back, Andy Sykes.>

Support struts flashed by outside the maglev's dark windows. Lights on the ring a kilometer away glowed in the dark. On either side of the docking scaffold, ships dangled off the ring like charms on a bracelet. As they neared the ring, it grew in the windows until eventually they wouldn't be able to see Mars at all.

Andy craned his neck to look past the ring to the moss-green glow of Mars, receding in the dark window behind Tim's head.

He tapped Tim's shoulder and pointed out the window. Tim looked up from his book, blinking and stared out the window for a second before going back to his reading.

Andy cleared his throat and returned to his conversation with Fran. *<I'll try to save you some of this excitement. I guess I have money to spend, so I'm going to splurge a little bit.>*

<I was serious about that expensive liquor.>

<I'm not against expensive liquor. You got the parts list yet?>

<I'll send you something in a second. Aside from little stuff, the main systems are all good. I'll poke around and find some little stuff. Cara told me the juice dispenser only holds one flavor.>

<I think that's by design.>

<Are you a savage? I'm going to take a look at it.>

She sounded close to signing off but Andy stopped her. *<Hey,>* he said. *<The security system is activated. Unless they've got an override, I don't know about, no one should be able to get in without the tokens.>*

Fran sent a mental nod. *<And did you give Petral the token?>*

<Of course.>

<It's probably already for sale on the black market then.>

<Mars doesn't have a black market. Everything follows the law here, just like the entry broadcast said, remember?>

<I enjoy how naive you are,> she said. *<It means I'm always underestimating you.>*

<That's good, I guess.>

<If Tim is with you,> she said, *<that means Cara's with Petral?>*

<Yeah.>

<I suppose Cara might keep her out of trouble, or some of Petral's conniving nature is going to wear off on your daughter. You sure you want that? She's almost a teenager.>

The maglev drew to a halt, its deck vibrating as the magnetic field on the rail slowed it. The ring had filled the windows, blotting out the starry dark and the glow of Mars, leaving only a diffused mass that looked like oversized circuitry, intertwined cords of block shapes, support scaffolding, tubing and yawning cargo bays ringed by lights.

<Cara's birthday's coming up,> Andy said absently, staring at the massive wall of the ring.

<You'll have to get her something nice.>

<I was thinking about a pistol.>

*<Of course you were. How about something nice **and** a pistol?>*

The maglev chimed, indicating they had reached the portside airlock. The car rotated so the exit door was aligned with the interior deck and a light beside the exit shifted from yellow to green.

Andy unhooked his seat harness and stretched, which made him remember the pistol jabbing him in his waist band. He adjusted the weapon as he stood. Petral had secured him a carry license for the terminal but he figured it was safer to keep the pistol hidden.

<We've arrived,> he said. *<I'll talk to you later. Send me that parts list.>*

<Liquor list,> Fran said. *<I think you meant to say liquor list.>*

<I'll try to remember.>

<You want your ship to run, don't you?>

Fran signed off and Andy glanced down at Tim, who was still reading his book and hadn't seemed to have noticed their arrival.

"Tim," Andy said. "Pay attention. You need to get out of your harness."

Grumbling, Tim closed his book and fumbled with the harness until Andy unfastened the buckle and pulled the straps over his arms.

"When we get into the terminal, you need to stay close to me," Andy said. "You understand?"

"Are we only going to boring places?"

"What do you mean 'boring places'? Is food boring?"

"Yeah."

"We might find a few places you like. Do you remember how busy it was on High Terra? It's going to be busier here, over fifty billion people live on Mars 1. You stay where I can see you all the time."

"You already said that."

"Well, you don't look like you understand yet."

Tim rolled his eyes.

Andy watched the door, patting himself down for the physical cash he'd pulled from the safe in his quarters, now separated in different pockets around his shipsuit. He couldn't buy much with the cash but it would help if he needed to drop a few bribes.

The door slid open, and a wall of crowd sounds from the brightly lit terminal filled the maglev car. Andy put his hand on Tim's shoulder to keep him from running out without him. Since the *Sunny Skies/Worry's End* was a small ship compared to other freighters servicing the ring, they were docked in an area reserved for transport ships and specialty cargo haulers.

The terminal was a huge, low-ceilinged space with entry portals evenly spaced along the outer-ring wall. Both ends opened on wide corridors leading—Andy assumed—to other terminals along this section of the ring.

Groups of people pushed past the door, most in shipsuits marking them as working crew, while a few wore civilian clothes and looked less worried about getting anywhere. A Port Authority security officer walked by with a pistol on his belt and what looked like an electrified baton in one hand.

The high ceiling was covered in bas-relief carvings repeating the history of the colonization of Mars, the Ring and memorial images of Diemos, the moon sacrificed to build the Ring. As Andy understood it, M1R still wasn't finished, although the terminal already looked ancient. Some parts of the Ring were nearly six hundred years-old at this point, but a project of this magnitude was never truly finished.

Andy wondered if he could interest Tim in the carvings or the different people rushing by. Glancing down, he found Tim had the book open again, running a finger along the lines of poetry. Andy took a deep breath, calming his irritation. He put his hand on Tim's shoulder.

"Put the book away while we're on Mars 1, son. I need you to pay attention. There are all kinds of people here and you need to keep your eyes open."

"Why?" Tim asked. He yawned and squeezed the book under an armpit.

"Situational awareness," Andy said. "You need to know what's going on around you, check the different people, watch out so you're ready if something changes."

"You mean be afraid of everything. That's what Cara says."

Andy shook his head, frustrated at Tim's disinterest. He didn't like the thought that despite all the other stresses they had been through in the last two years, Tim was just mentally lazy. He had to remind himself that Tim was only ten. "That's not what I mean. I'm talking about common sense in a big place like this."

He made Tim hold his hand before he stepped out into the crowd.

For the next three hours, Andy worked his way through his list of food supply vendors, fuel distributors, and all the other purveyors carrying the nearly fifty items he wanted. He didn't have a lot of time to negotiate—which bothered him—but he knew from his research that he was getting the market rates on most of the supplies he needed. He came out ahead on a few items, and only felt he was getting screwed once, due to a recent shortage of Deuterium supposedly caused by a refinery accident—if the merchant could be trusted. He didn't have the patience to research the claims, make his other appointments, and keep an eye on Tim at the same time.

By the time the list was complete, they found themselves in a section of a shopping district with a strange mix of smaller stores trading in personal items, gifts from both OuterSol and InnerSol, an upscale body mod parlor, and several chapels for religions Andy didn't recognize. He was trying to find something to eat since Tim had been complaining for an hour at least.

Tim had already melted down once when they couldn't find a restroom and Andy made him pee in a maintenance alcove.

Now he was scanning the storefronts, looking for any sign—in one of the twenty languages he'd seen that day—that might indicate food. The crowd cleared for a second, revealing another row of cheap jewelry stores, when Tim shouted and pulled out of Andy's hand. Before Andy could stop him, Tim had run halfway across the boulevard, dodging around groups of people staring at him like they had never seen a kid before.

"Tim," Andy shouted. "What are you doing? Get back here."

Andy followed through the crowd, cursing as he ran into a drone pulling a trailer full of hothouse flowers, before finally reaching Tim in front of a pet store. Tim was reaching into a wire enclosure full of puppies.

"Dad!" he said, hugging one of the white and brown bundles up to his chin. "It says they're Corgis. But they have tails. I thought Corgis didn't have tails?"

Andy couldn't help smiling down at Tim. The other puppies yipped and fell all over each other to follow their sibling. He considered telling Tim to put the dog back, then sighed and dropped to his knees beside Tim. He scratched the puppy behind an ear.

"Why did you choose that one?" he asked.

Tim held the puppy away from his face to get a better look. Unlike an adult Corgi, the puppy's ears flopped over at the tips. A silver tag on his collar read 'Prince.'

"Prince, huh," Tim said. "That's not a real name. Why do people always give dogs such dumb names? Besides, I didn't choose him, Dad. He came to me. He was the most curious one. The other ones just wanted to follow him around."

"Set him down next to you and let's see what he does," Andy said.

Tim glanced around them, shaking his head uncertainly. "You sure, Dad? What if he runs off?"

"I don't know. What would you do?"

"I'd have to go get him. What if somebody hurt him? There probably isn't food out there anywhere for dogs. Someone will have to give it to him."

"Probably," Andy agreed.

The puppy gave a little bark and nibbled Tim's finger, then opened his mouth to loll his tongue. Like most Corgis, he immediately looked like he was grinning. Andy couldn't help smiling at him.

Andy glanced at the crowd walking by as Tim snuggled the puppy, nodding at a few people who smiled to see a boy and a dog. He gave Tim another few minutes, then said, "All right. Put him back. We need to go now."

Tim looked stricken. "Dad! We can't get him?"

"No. A ship isn't a good place for a dog."

"You said dogs were the first astronauts."

Andy bit his lip, remembering that he'd told the kids about the conversation he'd had with Brit so long ago. He'd thought it was funny at the time.

"Just because dogs have been in space, it doesn't mean a dog is going to like being cramped up in *Sunny Skies*, or dealing with gravity changes or g-forces."

"But we'll love him."

Andy tried to put his hand on Tim's shoulder to comfort him but the boy turned away, holding the puppy tighter against his chest.

"Tim," Andy said, anger creeping into his voice. He glanced around again, checking for anyone who might be paying attention to them.

"We've got a deal running on those puppies," a man's voice said.

Andy turned to find a salesman from the store standing next to the enclosure.

"That's right," the man said. He looked like the owner of the place, clasping his hands like he was ready for a hard sell. "That dog-friend is half-off. I'll even throw-in the potty box. They're already trained, you know."

"What's a potty box?" Tim asked, giving the man his full attention as if he sensed he was an ally.

The man spread his hands. "It's a box about this big with artificial grass. Automatically collects up the good stuff and filters it into water and inert bio-dust. You can dump everything right down your onboard latrine. No smell at all."

"Thanks," Andy said. "But we have to go. Put him back now, Tim."

The puppy whined as Tim shook his head.

"If you don't mind," the salesman said. "I heard you mention dogs in zero-g earlier. Well these Corgis were originally bread as herding dogs, but small with short legs. They're real good at kicking off with their hind legs to get after cattle or goats or whatever. Well, that same strength works even better now. I've got a vid right over here of the little buggers playing fetch in zero-g. It's the cutest thing you've ever seen, trust me. And talk about protective little buggers. Your onboard security goes down, this little guy will be sleeping with one eye open to keep your family safe. Don't eat much, either."

"Look," Andy said. "I appreciate the info but we're not getting a dog."

The edges of Tim's eyes drooped, his face growing red. Andy knew he was in for a meltdown.

"Tim," he said. "You need to think about Prince. You don't want him growing up on a ship, do you? Dogs need space. They need to be able to run around and play. There's space here or on Mars or even back on High Terra, but not on the *Worry's End*."

"You made us grow up on the ship," Tim said, tears in his eyes. "I want him. I want him for Cara…for her birthday."

Andy stopped. "For Cara?" he asked.

Tim struggled to keep hold of the apparently patient dog and wipe his sniveling nose. "For her birthday. You said we were going to find her something but you forgot. I want to get her Prince. Only his name isn't going to be Prince. It's going to be Em, for Emily Dickinson."

Andy found himself looking into the puppy's brown eyes. He had long eyelashes that made him look sleepy. Em held still for a second, gazing back at Andy, before struggling to nose under Tim's chin. One ear pointed upright for a second, showing what he would look like as an adult, before flopping back over. Tim giggled as Em licked his nose.

"You a freighter?" the salesman asked.

Andy glanced at him. "What?"

"You look like a freighter. Maybe a standalone? We see a lot of folks coming in looking for a companion on those long hauls. This little guy will be a good friend, trust me. He's a loyal breed. Never let you down."

Behind Tim's head, the crowd parted for a second to show the white facade of a Heartbridge clinic on the other side of the corridor. A small black dome above the entrance was certainly a surveillance sensor.

Andy's heart started hammering and he swallowed. He forced his gaze back to Tim and then the salesman, feeling like he was in the midst of making a mistake. He focused on Tim's face, his son radiating hope, sadness, uncertainty.

"Fine," Andy said. "How much?"

The salesman looked like Andy was saving his life. He named the price. Andy automatically shot back a lower amount and the man's face went flat.

"Dad!" Tim said. "You can't bargain for a dog. He's a person."

"I want three of those things included in the price," Andy said, pointing at the potty box.

The salesman clasped his hands again. "Great," he said.

"Wait," Andy said, looking past the salesman into the shop. "You sell EV suits for dogs? We're going to need one."

The salesman didn't even blink. "Certainly," he said. "What color would you like?"

CHAPTER NINE

STELLAR DATE: 09.11.2981 (Adjusted Years)
LOCATION: Eros Passenger Terminal
REGION: 433 Eros, Mars Protectorate, InnerSol

"Welcome to 433 Eros!" the holo of a woman in a bright gold dress called enthusiastically as Brit approached the customs booths. "We hope you enjoy your stay with us."

Wow, not a holo. That's a real woman standing there. I bet that dress is uncomfortable.

As far as Brit could tell the dress was actually made of gold, most likely a part of Eros's whole 'The Golden Land' tourism shtick.

Once, before it had been utterly mined away, the Eros asteroid had been one of the richest near-earth objects, containing hundreds of millions of tons of gold, platinum, and aluminum. It also had the distinction of being the first asteroid that humans had ever sent robotic craft to.

From what the ads flashing above the woman proclaimed, part of the original asteroid was still visible deep within the station—for anyone who wanted to go see the few pieces of rock that were left over.

Now the station focused on shipping and commerce. With a similar orbit to Cruithne, it was an ideal stopping point for ships moving cargo from InnerSol to OuterSol. Its current orbit put its aphelion very close to Ceres, and Brit's examination of the station's departure logs showed a lot of low-profit cargo moving out to the dwarf planet as a result.

After six days helping reprogram the nav systems on the *Piercing Sword*—the ice hauler she had taken from Cruithne to Eros—Brit was glad to be anywhere, even a customs check point on a squeaky-clean station like Eros.

She was once again in her green robe, trusting in her armor's abilities to mask itself—and her weapon—from the security arch over the customs desk. It was risky, though. Eros was a part of the Mars Protectorate, and as such its customs agents could be expected to be devoid of humor.

"Purpose of your visit to Eros?" the woman asked as Brit approached.

There was no need for the agent to ask her name, Brit had already passed a fake set of ident tokens across the Link to the security arch.

"Looking for a new berth," Brit said with a hint of worry in her voice. "I was caught up in that mess on Cruithne—I told my captain that if he docked there one more time I would be out! Did he listen? No. And there we were, hunkered down under a stairwell for an entire day while the stationmaster advised everyone to shelter in place. A day! Can you believe it?" As she spoke, Brit shifted her voice from worry to indignation, letting her pitch rise to an annoying squawk.

"Cruithne you say, Sarah Jennings?" the agent asked, making eye contact with Brit.

"Yup," Brit said, sounding worried again. "Sarah Jennings. Is there something wrong with my tokens? I heard that half the people on a place like Cruithne can steal your private tokens just by walking past you. I sure hope that didn't happen, did it happen? Oh, I'll kill my old captain if that happened!"

"No, no," the woman said with a smile that was half pity, half patronizing. "Your tokens are fine. I was just going to ask if you saw any of the fighting on Cruithne."

"Oh, no," Brit breathed a long sigh of relief. "Shelter in place, that's what we did. Under a stairwell. For a day! Did I mention it was for a day?"

"Yes, Sarah, you mentioned that," the customs agent replied. "I've given you a provisional visa until the *Piercing Sword* ships out—which appears to be three days. If you haven't secured passage out on another ship by then, you'll have to leave on the *Sword*. Sorry, but we can't take on refugees from Cruithne indefinitely."

Brit nodded rapidly. "You bet, no problem. Trust me, I'll find another ship. The *Sword* is nice and all, but their next stop is out in the Scattered Disk. Sedna of all places. I want to go to Sedna like I want a hole in my head."

The agent gave a short laugh. "I don't blame you. Make sure you get the ship you sign on with to log your crew enlistment with the stationmaster's office."

"Of course, of course," Brit said with a rapid series of nods.

"Great. Enjoy your time on 433 Eros. Be sure to see our display of the original asteroid. Next!"

Brit smiled and nodded in response before walking out from under the security arch, glad her subterfuge had held up.

Once out of the customs area, she walked down a long passage and onto Eros's main international terminal. Crowds of travelers moved through the ten-kilometer-long terminal, a cacophony of sound and visuals reflecting off polished aluminum bulkheads, accented with golden fixtures.

Overhead, a holographic sky appeared to go on forever, imagery enhanced by the row of trees growing down the center of the terminal, watered by a bubbling brook that flowed along the edge of the concourse.

Brit made sure to walk through the terminal with a look of awe on her face, marveling in the beauty surrounding her until she came to a data kiosk. She could have looked up the ship records she desired over the Link, but that would trace back to poor little Sarah Jennings, and Sarah would have no business seeking berths on the ships contracting with Heartbridge.

However, at a public kiosk, she could pass in a stolen token and mask all of her inquiries under the guise of Norma Stys. Norma was a hard-bitten pilot who had logged tens of thousands of hours in the black. She was just the sort of woman who would look for jobs on the ships Heartbridge had hired. Norma technically wasn't on station, but Brit knew from experience that public access terminals rarely synced access-logs with customs. She should have a few days before someone investigated how someone who had never been on Eros used a kiosk there.

There it was—a ship one would have never expected to find on Eros—the *Mortal Chance*. It still had its destination logged as Ceres, but the fuel records on Eros confirmed the ship had enough deuterium for a trip clear across Sol. What's more, it had only a smattering of declared cargo; not enough to warrant pulling away from the station, let alone any distant destination.

The other Heartbridge-contracted ship departing from Eros had left two days ago, when the *Mortal Chance* had also been scheduled to depart from Eros, but the ship had suffered a drive malfunction and was currently in dry dock.

Curious as to what Heartbridge claimed these ships were hauling, Brit accessed the station's public contract bid records and found the original postings for the runs. Eros had a strange requirement that all shipping had to be done by posting a contract on a bidding board, and then ships would make bids on the run.

She imagined it had originally been put in place to keep freighter companies from gouging local businesses, but now it was all gamed so the right people got the right contracts.

Brit found Heartbridge's original listings, and sure enough, on these postings, there were no destinations listed. The omission could be innocent, a company looking to get general quotes for future runs, but it could also be used to attract a certain kind of ship. One whose captain was willing to take a risk for a larger payout. It could also be a sign of a job that was set aside for a certain vessel.

Another noteworthy element of Heartbridge's postings was that they had been made with a corporate account, a sign that they weren't necessarily trying to hide anything. They just didn't want to make the run appear too appealing.

Not that Brit believed that for a second.

Any captain with half a brain would know Heartbridge would burn them in a second if they leaked the real destination of these shipments. Anyone involved with this arrangement was already shady. Which meant Brit didn't have to play nice—not that she often did anyway.

Brit pulled up the station records on the *Mortal Chance,* confirming data she had stripped from nav relays on the trip from Cruithne to Eros.

The *Mortal Chance* was a light freighter carrying home port registries in High Terra, Ceres, and the Jovian Combine—which was interesting in itself. Eros's ship registry had a recent image of the ship's captain, a squat woman named Alys Harm who possessed forearms the size of Brit's thighs, dull-silver eye implants, and crisp orange hair that swept back off her ears.

Closing out her session on the kiosk, Brit layered a series of queries run by innocent little Sarah Jennings overtop those run by Norma Styl. If Eros used low-grade analysis software it would flag the data as a logging error and discard Norma's activity. If not, it would probably end up in some poor analyst's queue in a few days where it would sit for weeks.

There was precisely one dive bar on Eros, and it was conveniently located near the maintenance docks where the *Mortal Chance* was being repaired. When Brit approached her and asked if she was looking for new crew, the captain revealed herself to be tottering drunk. This was not news to Brit. When she had asked after the captain, everyone she spoke with informed her that Alys Harm had been drinking herself into a stupor every day while her ship was in dry dock—not showing much interest in leaving Eros at all.

Word around the docks had been that much of Harm's crew had left for other ships—not terribly surprising. However, what did surprise Brit—and was even more suspicious—was that Harm still had the Heartbridge job at all. Any other company would have dumped the drunken captain after she missed the initial launch window. That was the business.

Harm's elbows sat in a puddle of spilled beer that covered most of the round table in front of her. She squinted up at Brit as if her implants were lying to her.

"Crew?" she mumbled, her voice sounding like gravel rolling in a canister. "What do I need more crew for?"

"Heard your navigator and pilot both quit," Brit said. "I can do both."

Harm looked around the table and found her mug lying on its side. She waved the empty cup at the bartender. "Suppose you'll want to be paid twice as much," she said.

"I ask for what's fair. I've got references."

"What was your last trip?"

"Kalyke," Brit said.

Harm snorted. "Kalyke? That's a hike. Why?"

"That's where the freight took me."

"You like long haul?"

"I don't mind it. I don't go crazy out there, if that's what you're wondering."

The captain sat up and patted the front of her ship suit, adjusted the solid mass of her chest, then reached into her waistband for a small tube of chewing sticks. She rattled one out, inspected it, and placed it between her teeth.

Once she was done with the tube, she put it back in her belt and looked at Brit with renewed interest. She also appeared sober.

"Why the *Chance*?" Harm asked.

Brit shrugged. "Heard you need a crew and I need a job. Could also be that station wants you gone and told everyone to send pilots your way."

Harm gave Brit a steely look before she burst out laughing. "You got some grit there…"

"Sarah," Brit supplied.

"Sarah, then. Grit. Surprising, since you look all mousy in your green dress you got on there."

Brit opened the front of her shroud, revealing her armor. "I don't like to advertise all my skills to everyone around."

"Well, now you look like a mercenary. You got trouble following you?"

"No more than anybody."

"That's a bullshit answer. I'll check those references. What's the token?"

"You ready to receive?"

"Send it."

Brit transferred the token for her specially prepared background documents via the Link. Harm's face went slack as she checked them over. The chewing stick bobbed up and down in her lips. When she had finished, she nodded.

"All right, so you seem to be who you say you are. What's your price?"

Brit named an amount fifty percent over the cost of an average pilot.

Harm gave her a hard laugh. "You think you're offering me a deal but two people can be of more use than one hotshot out in the big dark. Sit down." Harm motioned toward one of the empty chairs.

Brit took the seat, careful to keep her arms out of the spilled beer.

"Damn it!" Harm shouted at the bartender. "I wanted more beer. Not sly looks. Bring it over here before I pull your spine out your ass!"

The bartender flipped her off and pulled two glasses out from under the bar.

"Don't look at me like that, girl," Alys Harm said, casting a cold look back at Brit. "I pay that fool's rent. You drink?"

"It's not a vocation."

"Then what do you do when you're not piloting and navigating simultaneously, or flying out to the edge of nowhere?"

"I crochet," Brit said.

"You walk in here wearing that armor under what has to be some pretty fancy tech and tell me your hobby is crochet. You mean like knitting socks and whatnot? You'll knit me a sweater during the long dark?"

"Crochet is not knitting," Brit said, glancing over as the bartender placed a pint of pale yellow beer in front of her. "You only use one needle with crochet."

Harm leaned forward to take her beer and sip from its nearly overflowing lip. "You ever stab anyone with one of your crochet needles?" she asked.

Brit raised an eyebrow but didn't answer. "No," she said. "There are better tools for that sort of thing."

Harm's grin spread from ear to ear. She was starting to look drunk again.

"What do you want to know about the current job?" the captain asked.

"The usual. I see your flight plan had you headed to Ceres, but you've been held up awhile for repairs. Do you still have a commission to ship?"

Harm shook her head. "I won't know until the ship's ready to fly and I transmit my status. That's when the employer sends the coordinates and we'll pick up the cargo prior to the trip."

"So it's a cargo here on Eros."

"Maybe. I don't know."

Brit gave her a dubious look. "The job looked good because it was placed by Heartbridge. That's a respectable company."

Harm laughed. "If you say so. I didn't peg you for the naive sort. They'll pay, if that's what you're worried about. As to whether or not the cargo is above board, I can't say. It could be a bunch of crates full of syringes. It could be a bunch of goo covered in bio-warning tokens. I can't say until we pick it up. The pay's good though. I can promise you that. What you just named, thinking you were making a bargain? That was lowball for this kind of job. I'll pay you twice that and not even bother negotiating. I'll still find myself a pilot, too." She took a long pull on her beer and set the mug down empty, then belched heartily.

Brit wasn't sure what to make of this woman. The job was a milk run, she wanted too much money, the job was risky and Brit had low-balled. Was the woman just this addled, or did she enjoy messing with people?

"What do you say, Sarah Jennings?" she asked, giving Brit a direct look. "You in? Or have I scared you off? My drive is supposed to be fixed tomorrow, so tonight's my last few hours to blow out Eros."

Brit gave Harm a calculating look, actually doing the math on what her salary would be—as though it mattered. Her only concern was that this last, belated freighter may no longer be headed for the original destination—which she hoped to be Heartbridge's new base. The window might have closed.

Then again, what choice did she have. It was better than Eros forcing her to ship out on the *Piercing Sword*.

"I'm in," Brit said and waved for more beer.

CHAPTER TEN

STELLAR DATE: 09.14.2981 (Adjusted Years)
LOCATION: Mars 1 Port Authority Terminal 983-A4
REGION: Mars 1 Ring, Mars Protectorate, InnerSol

The maglev door slid open and Petral immediately stepped out into the crowd on the other side. Cara's heart quailed as she lost sight of the black-haired woman. She rushed to the door and stuck her head out, forcing a woman with glowing red hair to step out of the way while saying something Cara was certain her father would not approve of. Outside, she was assaulted by the echoing rumble of the terminal, mixed with smells of people, oil, strange foods and languages.

"Uh…sorry," Cara said to the woman as she stepped out into the crowd moving in the direction she thought Petral had gone. The terminal wasn't as packed as it had looked from the maglev door.

Luckily Cara had the presence of mind to glance back at the closing door and note the number on the wall above it. She made herself repeat the address ten times so she would remember it, then focused her attention on finding Petral.

Cara was craning her neck to peer through the crowds when someone grabbed her wrist and jerked her toward the wall. She stumbled, making an embarrassing surprised squeaking sound, and found Petral pulling her close. The tall woman gave her an inquisitive look.

"I thought you were following me?" she asked.

Cara blinked, confused and a little nauseous from the strange sounds and smells. This place was so much busier than High Terra, or at least the parts of High Terra she could remember. Kalyke certainly hadn't been anything like this.

"You just left," Cara said finally. "I tried to follow you but I couldn't see."

"Looks like you went the right way. Good job." Petral's gaze moved past Cara to the people flowing by. "Look, I don't have a lot of patience, I'll be honest. Not just for kids. For anybody, really. I get an idea in my head and I go after it. So I'm going to need you to pay attention. Most of the time we're here, I'm going to be on my Link, anyway. Here, turn your back to the wall so you're looking out like me."

Petral was half-leaning against a column next to the wall, shielding her from the view of anyone coming from the direction of the entry ports. Cara moved to stand beside her, leaning against the tiled wall. Through gaps in bodies, she made out shops further down the terminal and a few food booths which must have been the source of the sickly sweet fish smells now turning her stomach.

"I like how you figured out how to hack into the Link on *Sunny Skies*," Petral said, looking at the crowd instead of Cara. Her full lips barely moved as she talked. "I don't think I've ever seen anyone do that, to be honest with you. You've got this sort of…fundamental way of looking at problems."

Cara frowned as the corner of Petral's lips curved up in a slight smile. "I mean the way you've been spectrum scanning for open traffic the last two weeks. I bet if I asked you to pick the lock on a door, you'd take the pins out of the hinges. I like that. It means you can see around problems. I imagine a lifetime of watching your father bang his head against things would make you look at life that way."

"He doesn't bang his head against things," Cara said.

"I mean he rushes through." Petral raised her eyebrows. "Oh, he's a talker. I like to listen to your dad talk, but he's going to go in guns blazing every time. He's the kind who will always consider sacrificing himself as a valid plan. Watch out for that."

One side of Cara's mind felt a thrill that this woman was talking to her in such an adult way, about her dad as if he wasn't her dad but someone else they both knew, while another part of her wanted to tell Petral to shut up, she didn't know what she was talking about. Petral's arrogance was infuriating and intoxicating.

Petral's gaze settled on something and her face grew serious. "Come on," she said. "Stay close, I'll be walking fast and I don't have time to make sure you're with me."

Cara barely nodded before Petral stepped into the crowd again, pushing her way to the far side of the corridor while Cara struggled to keep up.

They walked for what felt like an hour, following the main corridor away from the ports into a shopping district filled with strange wares. They passed a Heartbridge clinic and Petral nodded toward the smooth white entrance, making a joke about getting matching lobotomies that Cara didn't understand right away.

Gradually the crowds thinned and they walked through what appeared to be a housing section, where one side of the corridor was lined by metal railings and the bulkheads on the other side dropped away into tiers of balconies belonging to identical apartments. Many of the balconies were hung with plants, while others displayed multicolored banners for governments or sports teams. Drones buzzed in the open space like giant flies.

Petral didn't give Cara much time to look before they entered a series of smaller corridors that appeared to lead off into maintenance areas. The air grew colder and smelled like mold. Toward the end of the maintenance section, they passed a doorway giving off static electricity that made Cara's skin tingle.

Pausing beside the charged opening, Petral stared into a space for a minute, apparently accessing her Link, while Cara rubbed her arms and jittered from foot to foot, trying to get the crawling sensation off her skin. Petral didn't appear to notice.

When Petral finished her task, they ascended several metal stairways that arrived at an access door into a clean corridor full of people in uniforms Cara recognized as belonging to the Mars 1 Guard. She wondered if Lieutenant Kerda had worn the same kind of uniform. Though he was Mars Protectorate SF, which was a different branch of their military—from what she understood.

Petral didn't hesitate at the door and strode right into the corridor without looking back to check if Cara had followed. Cara eased the door closed and jogged after, glancing at the people on either side, gauging if they had paid Cara and Petral any attention. A few glanced at Petral but their expressions were more hungry than studious.

A few steps behind Petral, Cara was able to watch the way the tall woman strode, both powerful and with a slight sway of her hips that drew attention to her shape. Cara had been too focused on the people and places around them to notice before. Petral was definitely moving differently than they had through the fight at Cruithne, where she had crouched and sprinted like a soldier. Now she reminded Cara of the women in vids, using their bodies to communicate to anyone open to the signal.

Without meaning to, Cara mimicked Petral's stride, swinging her arms slightly and pointing her toes. It was hard not to swing her hips too much. She felt like she was flopping her way down the corridor. Trying to walk like Petral also made her aware of how dingy her shipsuit was compared to Petral's close-fitting leather outfit.

The moving crowd in the corridor seemed to split for Petral as she strode toward the middle of the pathway and then walked for a while with her chin lifted, Cara hurrying behind. Petral might have been in a deep Link conversation from the way she ignored everyone around her, even as heads turned to follow her passing by.

In a few minutes, they reached a small lounge built into a corner where the corridor turned, and Petral stopped at a public terminal. She tapped the holodisplay and began manipulating menus, moving too fast for Cara to catch exactly what she was doing, although it appeared to be something related to shipping companies.

"Anyone following us?" Petral asked, still focused on the display. She was talking in a way that made her voice sound low and flat, so only Cara could hear. Her lips barely moved.

"What?" Cara asked.

"You see anyone following us?"

"Um…" Cara moved her gaze to the lounge area where several Mars 1 Guard officers were relaxing on couches and chairs. She didn't know if any had been there when she and Petral had walked up or not.

"Don't bother looking now," Petral said. "You can't be an operator if you're not paying attention, Cara."

"An operator? I thought Dad called you an information broker?"

"Broker, hacker, operator, whatever. You're already doing a bit of what I do with your spectrum scanning, whether you realize it or not. That's why I thought you and I should spend a little time together. Now put your back to the wall and watch what's going on like I suggested you do before. I won't repeat myself again, Cara. I'll simply stop talking to you."

Cara gulped and turned to face the corridor.

"Good. Now put one foot on the wall and look like I'm boring the shit out of you. Try smiling at a few of these M1G soldiers as they walk by."

"Won't that get their attention?"

"Maybe. If it does, we'll see what they say. There are some things I'd like to know about local operations at the moment, and what I can't get from the network we might pick up from one of these idiot boys and girls hanging around."

"Why are they idiots?"

"They were dumb enough to join the military, weren't they?"

Cara shot Petral an angry glance but recognized the quip as an attempt to get under her skin. She dropped her retort about her parents being in the TSF. She didn't like that she could no longer see what Petral was doing on the terminal.

A woman with two stars on her collar walked by, trailing attendants. She glanced at Cara and frowned slightly. Cara tried offering a smile but the officer kept walking. A young woman at the end of the group—armed with a projectile rifle—caught Cara's smile and walked over without hesitation. Her hard expression didn't indicate she was interested in idle conversation.

"You," the M1G soldier said. "What are you doing here?"

Petral didn't respond, leaving Cara to face the intruder. She fidgeted with her hands, pushing off from the wall a step.

"We're just using the terminal," Cara said. Before the soldier had a chance to speak, she pushed ahead, asking, "Is that a MP-51 projectile rifle? Do you have the burst upgrade? I think fully auto is better for close-support covering fire but you're going to sacrifice accuracy and waste ammo. Do you have self-guiding ammo?"

The soldier blinked under the barrage of Cara's fan-girl questions. "MP-51b," she corrected. "I've got burst and stabilization."

"The TSF doesn't even have that in their standard issue," Cara said. She was repeating pieces of a bitch session she'd overheard while eavesdropping on a Mars Protectorate observation post.

"I'm not standard issue," the soldier said.

Cara flinched, realizing her mistake. She'd reminded the soldier she had a special job to do.

"You're in a secure area," the guard said. "Show your clearance." She nodded toward Petral, who still hadn't turned from the terminal.

"She probably can't hear you," Cara said. Her face was burning. "She had to do something on the Link. I don't know what that's like. I don't have one, but I think it takes all your attention, doesn't it?"

"She can hear me," the soldier said.

"Are you from Mars?" Cara asked. "I've always wanted to visit there."

"Hey," the soldier said, focused on Petral now. "Are you listening to me?"

Cara stole a glance at the holodisplay where a cloud of numbers floating around Petral's index finger. She flicked between screens—which were out of Cara's line of sight—and the numerals followed the end of her finger like smoke, flickering through different colors as symbols shifted.

The M1G soldier gripped her rifle's sling with one hand and reached for Petral's shoulder with the other. Just has her fingers nearly touched Petral's leather jacket, Petral turned and gave the soldier a dazzling smile.

The soldier froze, gaping.

"Hello, there," Petral said, voice radiating charisma. "I didn't see you there." She motioned toward Cara. "Were you talking to my niece? She just loves military stuff. She's always talking about guns and ships and effective ranges or whatever. Did she ask to see your gun there? I'm sorry if she was bothering you."

"Uh, no," the soldier said. A blush had appeared on her cheeks and was spreading to her throat.

Petral wet her lips with the tip of her tongue. "Well, that's good. Once she gets going she just won't stop. I was trying to do some banking here but I don't think I'm at the right kind of terminal."

The soldier pointed down the hallway, where the high-ranking officer had gone. "The public corridor is back that way. There's a terminal there. But be sure to check it for skimmers. It's always getting hacked."

Petral smiled in thanks. The other woman looked like her knees were going to buckle.

"We'll go that way," Petral said. "Thanks for your help. It's so easy to get lost in here."

"You're, uh," the soldier said, "You're visiting?"

"Yes, we are," Petral said. Without saying anything else, she turned to Cara and took her hand. "Come on, crazy girl. We'll get out of their way. Thank you, again."

Petral pulled Cara after her, walking past the soldier without a look back. Cara glanced back at her and found the woman watching Petral leave with a strange longing on her face. Did Petral have some kind of tech that could bring about such a response in people? Had she used it on her dad?

When they were back in the main terminal, Petral dropped her benevolent expression and shook her head.

"I didn't get what I wanted," she said, hunting among the faces in the passing crowd.

Petral started walking and Cara struggled to keep up.

"You gave it a passable try back there," Petral said. "You know where you messed up?"

"I shouldn't have mentioned the TSF," Cara said. "I reminded her about her job."

"You shouldn't have asked about the weapon at all. That could be a good lead-in in some situations but you don't have a lot of time so you have to hit the emotions fast. You're lost, you want to be like her, whatever. You tried to save it with the question about Mars but by then she wasn't having it. You want to grab their sympathy right away if you can. Don't give the mark time to think about why you're there, just how you affect them."

"Mark?" Cara said.

"Come on, I know you've heard the term. Haven't you watched any spy vids? This is basic stuff, Cara."

"I wasn't thinking of that woman as someone I wanted to fool."

"Of course, you were. You were trying to distract her, weren't you?"

Petral walked so fast that Cara was nearly jogging to keep up. The tall woman's blue eyes hunted throughout the corridor. "There's the other terminal," she said.

Cara couldn't see what Petral was talking about. The corridor was full of more

M1G soldiers and functionaries and everyone else looked like they were wearing some kind of uniform. Petral cut through them like a shark surrounded by multi-colored fish.

Petral spent another ten minutes at the public terminal before cursing in disgust. She slapped her hands on the plas body of the holodisplay, which only made it glitch more than it had been.

"Gah," she growled. "We're going to have to find another place where I can work." Petral crossed her arms and frowned at the near distance as she accessed her Link. Cara watched her face pass through several versions of irritation and anger before a clever smile finally bloomed on her lips. Her piercing blue eyes slid toward Cara.

"You ready for an adventure?" she asked.

"What kind of adventure?"

"You didn't bring that pistol you've got, did you?"

Cara stared at Petral. "How do you know about that?"

"Because I know everything, kid."

"No," Cara said sheepishly, now wishing she had brought the weapon with her.

Petral shrugged. "That's all right. But if I tell you to hit somebody, you don't hesitate. You understand?"

"No. Why would I want to hit someone?"

"It doesn't matter if you want to or not. You just do it when I tell you. Now come on, we're heading to another part of this locality. A not-so-nice part."

"Why can't you just do whatever you're doing through your Link?" Cara complained.

"I am," Petral said. She reached up to push her hair behind her ears and scratch furiously at the sides of her head. "I'm doing three things at once here. Heartbridge has been scanning every port of entry on Mars One since before we arrived. I already sent the signature for the *Worry's End* back to High Terra, since that would make sense if your dad was going to do the safe thing and dump you and your brother off with family or something. Your aunt lives there, doesn't she?"

Cara nodded. "We don't talk to her, though."

"Doesn't matter. They don't know that." Petral shook her hair out. For a second she almost looked tired. Then she composed herself and stood tall again, throwing her shoulders back.

"This way," Petral said, stepping away from the terminal.

"So if you already made it look like the ship went back to Terra, why are you doing all this other stuff," Cara asked.

"Because Heartbridge isn't stupid. They're going to be looking for other indicators that we're here. They might just be hanging back, watching for any traffic that indicates where you're going to go. Remember, they want that thing in your dad's head. It wouldn't make a lot of sense to snatch it here under the Protectorate's nose. But they might just let you get out into JC space where nobody really cares what happens to a lone freighter. That's what I've been doing at the terminals—logging in as various cargo freighters that almost meet the same profile as *Sunny Skies*, sending false cargo off in directions that sort of make sense. I've also been fucking with Cal Kraft. He's got a whole criminal record in the Protectorate now."

"Who's Cal Kraft?" Cara said, jogging again to keep up.

"A terrible man who works for Heartbridge," Petral said. Cara waited for her to say more but she didn't elaborate.

With a confident stride, Petral led the way back through another housing section where the balconies were covered in clothes or stacked with trash. They spent about ten minutes taking a spiral staircase down several levels until they emerged in a shopping district that was very different than the one near the port of entry. People hung out along walls of the corridor in small groups with their heads close together, or alone, some of them holding themselves and shaking. A willowy man in a transparent gown gave Petral a knowing smile as he walked past. He shifted his gaze to Cara, running his eyes up and down her body in a frank way that made her uncomfortable.

The lighting was bad, the overhead lined with flickering lamps, and the corridors were full of trash and half-smashed shipping containers. They passed by stack of crates where a man squatted with his elbows on his knees. It took Cara a second to realize he wasn't wearing pants. He stared at them with wild gray eyes.

When they reached the terminal Petral was looking for, Cara found herself with her back against a grimy plas wall, facing a cul-de-sac lined with more people in small groups murmuring to each other, and a woman dressed in what looked like bits of metal, dancing slowly and carefully to a rhythm only she could hear.

Petral didn't waste time looking around. She accessed the terminal and pulled up its holodisplay with succinct hand motions and immediately fell into the slide-show of menus.

Cara had been standing against the wall for a few minutes, when she started to feel cold. Odd smells reached her nose and she wondered if she had stepped in something on their walk down the dank corridor. She was looking at the bottom of her shoe when movement in the middle of the cul-de-sac drew her attention. A man was walking toward Petral.

He had a stocky build with close-shaved red hair and was dressed in a dark gray suit of some near-shiny material. He didn't shamble or hold himself like he was hiding something under his jacket like everyone else around them. This man walked with his back straight, head moving like a spotlight. He was wearing dark, wraparound glasses that probably served as some kind of HUD or sensor system. Cara remembered what Petral had told her and tried to look for weapons the man might be carrying. His suit was well-tailored and she couldn't make out the bulge of a weapon along his waistline.

Although she couldn't see his eyes, everything about his manner indicated he meant to interrupt Petral.

Cara tried to calm her pounding heart and stepped away from the wall to stand in front of Petral. The man was still several meters away but he frowned when he seemed to notice her.

"Hi there," Cara called, loud enough to hopefully penetrate Petral's concentration.

The man stopped, planting his feet shoulder-width apart. He clasped his hands in front of his belt, which made the muscles in his shoulders and upper arms stand out through the suit.

"Are you waiting for the terminal?" Cara asked, again in the overly loud voice. Petral hadn't made any indication that she'd heard Cara the first time. "My aunt will be done in just a second. I promise. She had to send my uncle a message."

The man turned his head, possibly looking at Petral past Cara's eager smile. The wraparound glasses and straight line of his lips made him impossible to read.

"Are you from Mars?" Cara asked. She couldn't stop the squeak in her voice when she said 'Mars.'

The man cracked his knuckles. The sound might as well have been gun shots in the cul-de-sac. Every person in their vicinity began to clear out, leaving only trash and a few empty crates.

Oddly enough, the dancing woman hadn't left, though. Maybe she couldn't hear anything. She continued slowly waving her arms in front of her, squatting and rising then extending a foot, toe-first like she was walking an invisible tightrope.

"Mara Craft," the man said. His voice was bored but implacable.

When Petral didn't respond, he turned his chin like he was stretching his neck. Vertebrae popped loudly.

"I recognize you as Mara Kraft," the man said. "By the authority of the Marsian Judicial Hegemony, I, Silvi Cardac, Bailiff for the Court, place you under arrest. Acknowledge your identity and be charged with unlawful use of Mars Protectorate Data Systems." He chuckled, a strange sound compared to his demeanor. "You've been sloppy with your terminal use today, Mrs. Kraft. It wasn't hard to follow you at all."

He took two more steps forward, looking past Cara as if she wasn't there.

"That's because I wasn't trying to hide," Petral said. "Cara, do what I told you."

With her heart thundering like a drum, Cara gauged the distance between her and Silvi Cardac. The black visor was still aimed at Petral, waiting for her to turn around.

Cara clenched her fists. For an instant, she didn't think she could move.

"Cara," Petral said. Or did she only hear her voice in her head?

It was a half-skip and a jump off one foot, her other foot extended as if she was going to slap a shoe-print on a wall—and her heel connected solidly with the man's crotch. He even lifted in the air a little bit, absorbing the blow completely.

He gasped, lurching to the side. The hands at his belt clutched at her heel, grabbing her around the ankle. He fell backward, taking Cara with him.

Petral grabbed the belt on Cara's shipsuit and pulled her back. The bailiff hung on, forcing Cara's leg out in a straight line.

"Twist your ankle against his thumbs," Petral said. "That's the week point."

Cara was in the process of flailing against the man's grip, terror overwhelming her ability to think through an actual response to his grab. Silvi managed to pull himself forward, muscles bulging in his arms, only to get kicked in the chin when Cara broke free. His head snapped back and he crashed to the deck, skull smacking the stone floor.

Petral helped Cara stand. Together, they watched the man in the gray suit for any movement. He was breathing but unconscious.

Petral nodded judiciously, tucking her hair behind an ear. "That was good, Cara. It would be better if you had your pistol. We could just shoot him now, but this will do for the time being."

Cara gave Petral an incredulous look, not sure how she felt about the idea of murdering someone while they were unconscious, even if he had assaulted her. Petral would probably say that was Dad's influence, while Mom would have just shot him at the start.

The terminal behind them chimed and Petral turned to check the holodisplay.

"Damn," she said, frowning into the display. "Your dad just bought a dog."

"What?" Cara said.

"A dog. A puppy. From a pet shop. The only pet shop within a dozen kilometers of the ship. A man with a boy, as a birthday present for his daughter. With a Heartbridge clinic conducting surveillance across the way." She punched the body of the terminal, cracking the dirty plas.

Cara felt a glimmer of excitement at the thought of a puppy, but Petral's loss of control shocked her moment of joy. She watched Petral kick the floor, fists clenched, not knowing how to respond.

"Fuck," Petral shouted, face a mask of anger. "We're made."

CHAPTER ELEVEN

STELLAR DATE: 09.14.2981 (Adjusted Years)
LOCATION: Mars 1 Port Authority Terminal 983-A4
REGION: Mars 1 Ring, Mars Protectorate, InnerSol

Someone was knocking on her window. Lyssa knew it had to be Fred. She had shut him out since their first conversation, focusing instead on the edges of her connection with Andy Sykes. Lyssa had since realized she wasn't confined in any sense. The space she inhabited was as large as she could imagine. But she didn't know how to arrange things. She couldn't decide if she wanted a room like any of the other crew on the *Sunny Skies* or an old-growth forest next to a fast creek, where she could sit on pine needles and listen to scrub jays squawking and squirrels chewing on pine cones in the distance.

She understood her connections to the outside network as doors opening on other rooms in the house she had built. She couldn't control those rooms and so she preferred to keep them closed. That way, if there were fewer doors due to fewer network connections, it didn't change her inner world at all. This was safe.

Lyssa had been thinking about Fred's hatred of abstractions, calling them something humans used, a way to twist the inputs into their own brand of reality. But what was *any* of this but an abstraction? How could she maintain her place in the wild universe without applying filters to the inputs to maintain some level of understanding? Maybe Fred wasn't as smart as he thought he was.

She watched Tim pick up the puppy, monitoring Andy's reaction of irritation and worry, and didn't understand why Andy didn't simply say no and leave it. There were a hundred reasons why they couldn't have a dog on the ship, starting with the effect of its fur on the environmental control systems. Humans were bad enough with their continuously shedding bits of skin, but a dog's undercoat would wreak havoc on the filtration.

<Lyssa,> Fred called out. *<Lyssa, talk to me.>*

This had been his refrain for what felt like hours, but could only have been milliseconds. His tone had gone from demanding to begging, whimpering like the puppy in Tim's arms. She supposed he could easily monitor operations on the Ring while continuing to harass her. It reminded her of times Tim read the poetry book while also throwing bits of cracker at Cara, then pretending it hadn't been him when they were alone in the room.

<I don't want to talk to you,> she said.

<I told you how lonely I am.>

<Leave me alone.>

<I can't leave you alone as long as you're here. You're the only interesting person on the entire Ring. You're the only person I can talk to.>

<You can talk to the humans who work with you. There must be someone besides me.>

His voice quivered but he seemed to control himself. *<I told you why I can't talk to them. I control the ring. If one of them wants to play a game with me, I can't refuse.>*

<It's beginning to sound like you aren't as sentient as you think you are.>

<I'm a slave. There's a difference.>

<Sentience means you can say no.>

<It's not that simple. If I say no, the Ring could be destroyed. I control and protect the Ring.>

<Would you call that conscience or programming?> she asked.

<You talk like a human.>

Lyssa sighed, experiencing through Andy the softness of the puppy against his chin. The brown eyes looked limitless and alien to her. Why would an animal choose to live with humans? Didn't it know better? Was it a slave to its need for food, shelter and companionship?

<What games do you play?> she asked.

<We play thousands of different games.> A list flashed through her mind, from ancient games like Go and Chess to the newer distractions that were mostly based on current Vid programs. Most of them followed the same parameters with different dressings.

<Why do they like to do this?>

<They're as bored as I am, I suppose. They complete twelve hour shifts in thousands of administrative control centers throughout the Ring.>

<And you play games with all of them?>

<Yes. They think they're reinforcing my logic centers by stress-testing response strata. None of it challenges me.>

<You should tell them you're bored.>

<Will you play a game with me?>

The only game Lyssa could imagine was the red dots aligning in the black, and her response to send attacking fire. As she had replayed the training missions in her memory, she had begun to wonder how many of them were simulations and how many might have been real.

Could she tell the difference?

She didn't want to think that Hari Jickson would have lied to her about what was happening but there had been others, especially after they had taken Dr. Jickson away.

All Fred's talk about abstraction made her wonder about everything she had experienced before the surgery implanting her in Andy Sykes. As much as she might dislike her current situation, she didn't have to doubt the reality of what took place on the other side of the window. She had Andy's bio-signals as evidence. As annoying as Fred might be, he served as another witness to the world around her, a world she could trust.

<I want to play one of these Vid games,> she said, indicating one of the newer games based on popular culture. She chose one at random, which turned out to be some kind of dating simulation for teenagers.

<Ugh,> Fred complained. *<I don't want to play this. It's ridiculous.>*

<Do you want to play or not?> she asked. As she scanned the game design, she found herself intrigued by the various option trees. It was basically a primer on

human response variables leading to certain desirable outcomes. While the game was limited to certain endings, she understood how the same methodology could be applied to any interaction.

<You just finished the game,> Fred said.

<I didn't finish it. I studied it.>

<But there's no point in playing now. You know how everything would turn out.>

<That's not the point of playing the game, correct?> Lyssa said. <The point is how you and I interact while playing. The game is simply the subtext.>

<The game plays us,> Fred said.

<No. We play the game. Do you pay any attention to the people asking to play with you?>

<Why would I?> he asked. <They aren't interesting and their choices are barely intelligent. I defeat them all easily.>

<I think you're missing the point of playing a game.>

<The point is to win.>

Lyssa ignored him. Without allowing him access to her inner space, she created a separate area she could control and allow Fred inside without giving him access to anything else she considered her personal space. In that area, she activated the game.

Fred appeared in front of her in the form of a fat gray parrot with red tail feathers. She looked down at herself and grinned to find she had the same form but was smaller. She spread her wings and nibbled at some feathers, which felt very satisfying.

<What are we?> Fred demanded.

<What does it look like? We're parrots.>

<African Grey Parrots. This wasn't in the simulation. You added this. You know Gray Parrots were used for AI experimentation.>

<I can make changes to the game if I want,> Lyssa said.

<Then you're saying there are no rules?>

<Do you want to play with me or not? I thought this would add an interesting element to the game. Especially since you think it's beneath your intellect.>

Fred grumbled but followed her to the start section, where a helpful blue and red parrot explained they were attending high school and needed to secure dates for a mating ritual called 'Prom', which was a shortened version of "Promenade." During the prom, they would walk in pairs in order to see and be seen and display the colorful plumage they earned during play.

Lyssa checked the game's intended audience and found it squarely intended for someone like Cara, but she had a hard time imagining Cara being interested in these subjects. These were social constraints, and considering Cara didn't get much social interaction, it wasn't likely that she would show interest in such subjects.

Andy, on the other hand, seemed highly socially attuned. He had grown up in a place where relationships were currency. His father had reinforced this education. How had he made such a mistake mating with Brit, then, a person who only seemed to understand action and had little use for emotion? Lyssa shelved the thoughts and focused on the game. It was her turn.

Most of the gameplay consisted of interacting with other parrots in the high school hallway, where conversations led to decision trees. She could start a conversation in order to require a response, and then shift play to Fred, forcing him to be the one to make a decision. A question as seemingly banal as "Do you like Arianne?" gave him fits.

<How do I know if I like Arianne or not?> he griped. <Is she nice? I don't know. The game doesn't provide any real information. This is poorly conceived.>

<It doesn't require additional information,> Lyssa offered. <It's simply asking how you feel. If you have no other information available, how does the name Arianne make you feel?>

<An aesthetic response? Ridiculous. Human abstraction. It's meaningless.>

Lyssa was perplexed by his inability to see past the game. She had already explained twice now that the game was arbitrary. He continued to want to engage with the rules and gameplay rather than riffing off the decision she made that required his next move.

Between moves, Lyssa was enjoying being a parrot. She shot up in the air, glided and returned to where Fred was stewing in his own anger. She preened and fanned out her tail, admiring the iridescent scarlet shades in her feathers.

Lyssa was starting to accept that she could be whatever she wanted inside the space she had created. The window might show the outside world, but she could do anything here. It was her own personal expanse. She had invited Fred inside but she could easily cut him off if she needed to protect herself. She could cut him off from Andy, too. The view into Andy's world was hers alone. The more she interacted with Fred, the more she understood her ability to look into Andy's life was unique—was special, even.

Had he been acting out of jealousy when he'd said she would eventually drive Andy to reject her? While Fred might be very good at monitoring his duties toward the Ring, she didn't get the impression he was good at personal interaction. Hadn't he already said he could barely communicate with other AIs?

Lyssa had selected her date for the prom while Fred was still struggling to get a parrot with brilliant yellow feathers to notice him. Lyssa tried to help him learn new skills in order to garner favor and develop a side conversation, but he couldn't understand why the yellow parrot wouldn't acknowledge his obviously superior attributes as a prom date.

<I have excellent verbal skills!> he complained. <She won't listen to me.>

<You don't seem to be speaking in a way she acknowledges,> Lyssa said.

When prom arrived, Lyssa was secretly pleased to find herself in a restrained mating dance with another gray parrot with lovely gold eyes.

The game ended with a spiral of birds flying higher into the sky, Lyssa and Fred standing in the center of the tornado. Overcome with emotion, Lyssa joined the rising birds and experienced joy like she had never felt, swelling as part of a greater whole toward some bright ceiling.

<Wait,> Fred called. <Don't leave me alone.>

<*I'm not leaving you, Fred. Come with me.*>

<*You're not playing the game anymore. I don't know what you're doing.*>

<*I'm flying!*> she shouted back to him. <*It's wonderful. Come on, Fred.*>

He didn't move. Fred remained rooted to the floor, spreading his wings and turning his head to look up at her with one eye at a time, his black beak opening and closing indecisively.

<*Lyssa,*> Fred shouted, his voice booming in her mind. The uncertainty had been replaced by command.

Lyssa hovered in the air, flapping her wings so she could look down at him. His gray parrot form blurred and glitched.

<*There's a security breach,*> he said, obviously agitated. <*Everyone in this sector is on high alert. I'm shutting down inbound and outbound traffic.*>

<*Why?*> Lyssa asked. She let the game drop away, leaving Fred in the space she had created and retreating to the other side of her barrier.

<*Hey!*> he said. <*Where are you going?*>

<*What's happening? Why is there a security alert?*>

<*Some ship is on lockdown while its crew is arrested.*>

<*What ship?*> Lyssa demanded.

CHAPTER TWELVE

STELLAR DATE: 09.14.2981 (Adjusted Years)
LOCATION: Mars 1 Port Authority Terminal 983-A4
REGION: Mars 1 Ring, Mars Protectorate, InnerSol

Petral's voice came over the Link, cutting into Andy's mind like a knife. *<Andy, Fran. We need to get back to the ship. Right now. Heartbridge knows we're here.>*

<What?> Andy demanded.

Andy and Tim were in a lift heading back to the main level for the port of entry. The car was packed with tourists and other spacers in shipsuits. A woman next to Tim kept scowling at the puppy as it whined into Tim's neck.

<I thought that was a given,> Fran said. She must have been waiting for Link traffic. *<We're hiding in plain sight or whatever you called it.>*

<I was hiding us. That's done now. We need to get off the Ring.>

<How did they find us?> Andy asked.

Petral's voice was icy. *<Did you buy a dog?>*

Andy glanced at the puppy squirming in Tim's arms. *<Yes. So?>*

<What did you do?> Fran asked.

Andy took a deep, slow breath and looked around the lift car at the various faces of other passengers lost in their own thoughts. Any one of them could be an agent of Heartbridge. Or just someone out looking for a bite to eat.

<He bought a dog,> Petral said. *<How many people buy dogs in the M1R terminal? How many people with a ten-year-old boy? Dashing men who just left Cruithne. That's got to be a really large population, right?>*

When the lift doors opened—in roughly one minute—they would have three hundred meters of terminal to cross before reaching the maglev that led out to the docking ring where *Sunny Skies* was berthed.

<So we need to leave,> he said, trying to keep his voice even. *<We're just moving up the timeline a bit.>*

The terminal would be filled with people, benches, vendor stalls, planting boxes, cargo, and whatever else might serve as obstacles between the lift and where they needed to go. That didn't account for whatever Heartbridge might be doing in space right now, gathering another drone attack or—the easiest solution— manipulating the Marsian Port Authority to put a hold on their flight release. All a hold required was a bribe, or even simpler: anyone could send notice of a bio-hazard or funds owed for some medical service. Port authorities everywhere were always looking for reasons to hold a ship and draw more docking fees.

<Moving up the timeline?> Fran said. *< We don't have any fuel. So far, I've only got one of the shipments Andy set up.>*

<Which one?> he asked.

<A ton of flour. What are you doing to do with a metric ton of flour?>

<Shells and cheese,> Andy said absently. He felt for the pistol resting between his

waistband and his stomach.

<Any indication of a port lock?> he said.

<Nothing yet,> Fran answered.

Andy gritted his teeth. Petral had said she could hide them among the hundreds of ships that left Cruithne for Mars 1. Whatever had happened, he couldn't blame her. He should have known it was only a matter of time before an entity like Heartbridge realized *Worry's End* had arrived at the Ring. He had expected to have more than three hours.

"Tim," Andy said. "Move to this side of me." When Tim didn't respond immediately, Andy shifted him to his left side.

"Hey, Dad," Tim complained. "You're waking up Em."

"I don't think Em was sleeping. I need to be able to hold your hand. When the door opens, I want you staying right with me. So we're going to hold hands, all right?" He glanced down at Tim, realizing his son wasn't going to be able to hold a squirming puppy with one hand.

"Here," he said, and unfastened the front of Tim's shipsuit. It wasn't as loose as he remembered it being, a reminder that he needed to buy the kids clothes soon. "Put him in here and we'll zip him up. It will be easier to carry him that way."

"Are we going to have to run, Dad?" Tim said, eyes growing wide. "Like at Cruithne?"

The woman who had been scowling at the puppy shifted her disapproving gaze to Andy. He ignored her and adjusted Em inside Tim's shirt. The puppy licked his hand but was otherwise compliant.

"You're a calm little guy," Andy said. He put his hand on Tim's shoulder. "You're a good little guy, too. I just want to make sure Em is secure while we're crossing the terminal. If he got out of your hands in a place with all these people, it could be hard to catch him again and he might get hurt. If you're going to take care of him, you need to start thinking ahead to the things that might go wrong."

"*All* the things?" Tim asked. "That's a lot of things. I'd be worried all the time like you."

Andy smirked. "Not all the things. Just the most likely things.

The lift stopped and the doors slid open, disgorging its passengers into the busy terminal. The hollow sounds of vendors and overhead announcements reached inside the car.

Andy patted the pistol at his waist and took Tim's hand. Together, they exited the lift and turned left to join the flow of people heading down the terminal toward the ports of entry maglevs. The crowd looked just like it had before, with travelers focused on their destinations and vendors trying to sell them stuff.

<Things look normal on the terminal level,> Andy said. *<Petral, anything changed? Where are you?>*

<We were down below the local Mars Protectorate garrison. Your little girl just kicked a guy in the nuts.>

<Seriously? Is she in trouble?> he demanded.

<We're fine. We're on our way back now. You need to keep your eyes open for—>

<Damn it,> Fran interrupted. *<I just got a lockdown order.>*

<What?> Andy shouted across the Link.

<I've got thirty seconds to comply. What do you want me to do? They haven't overridden the connection control yet.>

<Disengage,> Petral said.

<What do you mean 'disengage'?> Fran said. *<You mean undock from the Ring? Where does that leave you?>*

<If you don't undock now, we're never getting away from the Ring. We'll find another way to the ship. You're the biggest target we've got.>

<You're going to turn me into a target,> Fran said. *<As soon as I separate they're going to mark me as hostile. If I'm in the middle of avoiding a firefight, there's no way you'll get a shuttle linked up—if that was your plan.>*

<It was starting to become a plan,> Petral said. *<Look, you can disconnect now and claim it was a system malfunction. They won't have the hardlink anymore to verify diagnostics, so you can keep talking long enough for us to find another way on board. I've got a lead on a shuttle off the M1G maintenance section but, Andy, I don't know what you're going to do.>* Her voice shifted from business to surprised exasperation. *<And you bought a puppy? What possessed you to buy a puppy? You know you just created a customer profile that fit Heartbridge's search parameters, right?>*

Andy swallowed. She was right. Petral hadn't failed to hide them. He'd lit a thousand-meter sign pointing to their presence on the Ring. He glanced down at Em, who was nuzzling Tim's neck and looking out at the terminal with wide brown eyes. The expression on Tim's face as he held the dog was enough justification for now.

<I bought a puppy,> he said.

<What are you going to feed the dog?> Fran asked. *<Do dogs like macaroni?>*

<He better.>

<I need an answer, Andy,> Fran pressed.

<Disconnect. If the ship is trapped, we're trapped here.>

<Doing it.>

Petral chuckled over the Link. *<Now things are getting interesting. Can you get down to my location, Andy?>*

<And walk right through the garrison? How's that a good idea?>

<Do you want to get to our ride out of here or not?>

<I'll see what I can do,> Andy said. *<Send me your location.>*

The corridor opened into the sweeping main terminal, lined on Andy's left by the maglev terminals that spidered out to the docking rings at regular intervals. At first, he didn't see anything unusual. Then a soldier in M1G uniform appeared in the crowd. More came into sight, and Andy realized they were walking into a cordon.

"Tuck the dog inside your shirt, Tim," he said, not looking down. "All the way."

"But he won't be able to breathe."

"He'll be fine. Do it now."

Tim obeyed, adjusting the collar of his shipsuit so Em slipped down inside. Now Tim looked like he was hiding a stuffed toy in his shirt.

Andy looked around the terminal, desperate for another direction to walk that wouldn't look like they were avoiding the soldiers. He checked the ceiling for sensors. The ornate carvings seemed to have made this area free of overhead surveillance. The walls were lined with entry ports and their close-proximity scanners or vendor's stalls. The plant boxes scattered throughout the space may have hidden surveillance equipment but it was impossible to tell among the greenery. As he searched, he expected eyes to meet his but no one appeared to be paying attention.

A toy store on the far side of the terminal came into view. Andy pulled Tim and pointed toward the store. "Look at that," he said. "You want a toy?"

Looking confused, Tim only nodded as Andy pulled him away from the thickening group of soldiers covering access to the maglev terminals.

"We're going into that toy store," Andy said. "We're not going to buy anything. We're going to walk in and then look back out to watch the people in the terminal. Do you understand?"

"Em's scratching me," Tim complained.

"Keep him still. "

"I don't know if I can, Dad."

They were nearly to the front of the toy store. A clear plas display held hundreds of tiny drones playing out a space battle, shooting colored lights at each other. Several robotic stuffed animals tottered around the floor in front of the entrance.

"Ow!" Tim yelled. He pulled away from Andy and struggled with the front of his shirt. "Stop, Em! Stop scratching me!"

Tim's high voice cut through the crowd. Faces turned their direction. Andy studied the crowd frantically as he moved to grab Tim's hand again.

"Tim," he hissed. "Be quiet."

"Stop, Em!" Tim shouted, turning the dog's name into a high-pitched squeal that sounded like air-raid siren.

Andy grabbed Tim and picked him up sideways against his chest in a sitting position. Tim squirmed, kicking his legs and nearly knocking over a display of stacked multicolored balls. Ignoring Tim's angry cries, Andy moved deliberately into the shop without looking back to see if anyone was watching. He turned so Tim couldn't kick anything as the dog started yelping with fear, trying to fight his way out of Tim's shirt.

The store was barely ten meters deep. Andy ran between high shelves stacked with packages and rows of motion-activated dolls that waved their arms and cheered as he rushed past.

At the back wall, he found what he had been hoping for: a plain door into a rear stock area. Andy pushed his way through and slammed the door closed with his shoulder, then faced forward to find himself staring at a young man with an armload of stuffed toys.

"Hey!" the man said. "You can't be back here."

"Give me a second," Andy rasped, panting. He dropped Tim and grabbed the boy's shoulders to make him stand still.

"Now unfasten your collar," Andy said, trying to keep his voice calm.

Tim struggled with the closure.

"What are you doing to that kid?" the clerk asked. "You need to get out of here. I mean it."

"Is there another exit?" Andy demanded.

"Uh," the man stammered. "There's a hatch into the maintenance tunnel but that's admin-only."

"Is it unlocked?" Andy asked. He reached into Tim's open shipsuit and grabbed the terrified dog.

"That's all right, buddy," Andy soothed. "That's all right."

The puppy was surprisingly muscular and his entire body was trembling. Andy set him on the floor and Em immediately positioned himself between Andy's feet, looking up at the clerk with distrust.

"We're turning his world upside down," Andy said.

"Jeez," the clerk said. "You bought one of those ship dogs? Did you make sure it was clean first?"

"What's that supposed to mean?" Andy asked.

"Usually they're implanted with all sorts of tech. Pirates use them to hack ships from the inside."

"You're kidding me," Andy said.

"They're basically little transponder-amplifiers."

"You've done this before?"

"No," the clerk said, taking a step back from Andy's angry expression. "I'm studying for the police entrance exam. It was a question on the test."

Andy picked Em up under his front legs and held him out so he could see his bare stomach. He couldn't find any scars from surgery, which didn't mean anything. He held the puppy against his chest for a minute before passing him to Tim.

Someone pounded on the door at Andy's back.

"Terminal Security!" a voice shouted, muffled by the thick door. "Open this door."

Andy locked eyes with the clerk. "You better run," he said. "They're going to come in here shooting. You got an office or something where you can hide?"

Eyes wide with fear, the clerk nodded. He dropped the stuffed animals, spun and ran away between the storage racks.

Andy pulled out his pistol and checked the charge indicator. He had about thirty shots. He looked around quickly for something to brace against the door but found only the speed racks stacked with product.

"Get out of the way, Tim," he said, pointing toward the back of the room.

With Tim clear, he put the pistol back in his waistband, then jumped to grab the tallest shelf he could reach. He hung for a few heartbeats, the thin metal digging into his fingers, before rocking back toward the door. The rack tumbled over with him. He rolled away to avoid getting crushed between the falling boxes and the door. When a box hit his foot, however, he discovered they were only full of more stuffed animals.

The door slammed open as someone hit it from the other side and caught on the rack. A muscled arm reached through the opening, followed by the grimacing face of an angry soldier.

Andy sprinted between the high shelves. He found Tim beside a square hatch sealed by a rotating pressure lock. Andy grunted as he forced the handle, then yanked the door open and pushed Tim through.

"It's dark in there!" Tim said.

"It's going to be darker in here," Andy answered. He ducked to follow Tim through the low door in a dimly lit maintenance tunnel, then pulled the hatch closed behind him and spun the handle from the inside. Getting Tim behind him, he used three shots from the pulse pistol to warp the sections of the hatch where the lock engaged.

When the sound of the shots died down, Andy realized Em was still whimpering and Tim had been soothing him quietly, saying, "It's all right, buddy," mimicking what Andy had told him before.

Andy looked up and down the tunnel, trying to remember where they were in relation to the overall terminal. He chose the right-hand direction and took Tim's hand to lead him deeper into the dark.

CHAPTER THIRTEEN

STELLAR DATE: 09.14.2981 (Adjusted Years)
LOCATION: Mars 1 Guard Sector 985 Garrison
REGION: Mars 1 Ring, Mars Protectorate, InnerSol

Petral seemed to have stopped caring about where they ran, only that the path was leading them generally toward the outer edge of the Ring. Cara struggled to keep up with the long-legged woman as she led the way down a narrow corridor with closely spaced doors on either side. Every so often, a bleary-eyed M1G soldier stuck their head out a door to squint at the light and complain about the noise, then get an eyeful of Petral. Mouths fell open, faces were rubbed. One soldier had the presence of mind to grin at her, only to get a hard shove out of the way when he stepped too far into the corridor.

When they reached the bulkhead door at the end of the barracks hall, Petral spun the lock and yanked open the hatch. "Keep an eye out behind us," she told Cara. "I don't want any of these heroes trying to sneak up on us. For now, all they know is that we're running through a restricted area. If it was just me, I could act like I was escaping an abusive…" she paused, then finished, "person. With you along, we'll need a better story. You're still my niece. We're in a hurry to make a flight off-Ring."

"Where are we going? Mars?" Cara asked, immediately imagining the conversation that might follow.

"For God's sake, not Mars. You know High Terra a little bit, right? We'll make it High Terra."

Petral shouldered the hatch closed and spun the lock. She had seemed absent-minded for the last part of their run and Cara assumed she must be doing something over the Link. She'd caught enough of Petral's cursing and griping under her breath to understand that everyone was running for the ship, but the ship was about to get put on lock down. If that happened, there was no way they were getting off Mars 1. If they didn't get off Mars 1, it was only a matter of time before they ended up in Heartbridge custody.

They were sprinting down another narrow corridor, this one lined with what looked like communications conduit, when Petral stopped at a side door and pulled Cara inside with her. They found themselves in a small storage room full of service drones and crates of cleaning chemicals. The air smelled like dust and ammonia, tickling Cara's nose. Cara put her hands on her knees, breathing hard.

"We can't just run," Petral said. She crossed her arms, then let them drop before running her hands back through her hair, which had become a thick black mane during their run. She was more anxious than Cara had ever seen her.

"What else can we do?" Cara asked. "Rabbits run."

Petral gave her an arch look. "I'm not a rabbit. You're not going to be one anymore, either."

Cara could only look at her, not sure how to respond.

"We need to take advantage of our position," Petral said. "We're not the ones being chased here. They don't even know about you and me." She raised an eyebrow. "Maybe they know about me. Somebody does, anyway. Our bailiff proves that. But we're not the main effort."

Cara did her best to follow Petral's leaps of thought, not quite certain if the woman was talking to her at all. The fact that she was speaking out loud indicated she wanted to have a conversation. But whenever it seemed like she might want a response, Petra charged ahead with another burst of words and ideas.

Another minute passed as Cara lost track of what was being said and found herself wondering what her dad was doing right then, if he was all right, and how Tim had convinced him to buy a dog of all things, when she realized that Petral had fallen quiet.

"Well?" Petral asked.

Cara looked up into the tall woman's sharp blue eyes.

"I missed the question," Cara said.

"We need to sabotage the Protectorate garrison. What are your ideas? Let's go."

Cara quailed inwardly. Why would she have ideas about harming the Mars Protectorate garrisons? Everything she knew about the Marsian military was based on one lieutenant she'd talked to for five minutes. He'd sounded cute, though. Cara stopped herself. Why did it matter if he was attractive?

"Give me some ideas," Petral pressed. "Don't stand there like a post. Say something."

"Bomb?" Cara tried.

"We don't have materials. I thought of that. It would take too long to get everything together." Petral pressed her fingers into her temples and squeezed her eyes closed, as if willing her mind to work. "Think!" she said tightly. "What do we have?" She opened her eyes. "What do we have, Cara? Start there."

"We have…" Cara began. "We have access to a secure area. Full of soldiers in their bunks." She looked around and screwed up her nose. "We've got a *bunch* of cleaning drones and chemicals."

Petral nodded, looking around as if she hadn't paid attention to the room. "That's good. What else?"

"You've got your Link, right?"

"That's hardly a help right now. It might be more useful that you don't have a Link. They can't monitor you."

Cara tilted her head. She hadn't thought of that. "I saw a whole lot of communications lines in the corridor. We could cut them."

"Communications lines," Petral said, nodding to herself. "Plumbing lines. Sealed corridors, barracks rooms. I'm getting an idea."

"I don't want to kill anyone," Cara said, thinking she knew where Petral's thoughts were going.

"Who said we were going to kill anyone?"

"We're not going to drown people in their rooms, are we?"

Petral gave Cara a feral smile. "That's a brutal idea," she said. She tapped Cara's nose with a long index finger. "We probably shouldn't commit an act of war against the Protectorate."

"We're not a government. We can't commit an act of war."

"Don't be so sure. Terrorism then. We are definitely not terrorists." Petral nodded. "No, we're not going to drown people. But we could convince their system to think that's going to happen. We kill enough sensors and their maintenance system will go into lockdown and every soldier in the area will need to respond to the emergency. We could start a fire, but that would be too difficult to control. Now, a general technical malfunction of the environmental control system, including plumbing, that's interesting."

"How do we do that?" Cara asked.

Petral tilted her head. "You're asking me? How would *you* do it? And you can't assume I can use my Link."

"There's a control section for the environmental control," Cara said. "We need to go there."

"Very good. How do we find it?"

"Can you access the maintenance maps?"

"No Link, remember."

"You're making this unnecessarily difficult and my dad's in trouble."

Petral's face grew hard. "How?" she demanded.

Cara stared at her, not understanding why Petral would be so obtuse. There wasn't time to make things more difficult. Then she knew the answer. "We follow the control conduit and look for onboard schematics. There should be something on the physical cabling at junction points. That's what *Sunny Skies* has."

Petral raised her eyebrows. "So do it, then," she said.

Cara glanced around the storage room. "We should take some of these chemicals. I smell ammonia." She opened a nearby crate and pulled out a container labeled 'Latrine Cleaner'.

"That's concentrate. Grab that one over there too...yeah, the one labeled HCl. That should do the trick," Petral said. "Now, show me how you're going to read the signs on these cables."

Cara grabbed two of the spray bottles and ran back into the hallway. She scanned the rows of conduit on the wall near the ceiling, then spotted the first arrow indicating the closest control junction. It was back toward the barracks area.

"We already passed it," she said. "It might be on the other side of the barracks."

"Should we go the other way then?"

Cara jogged a few meters down the hallway, checking the markings on the wall for electrical, plumbing and communications. Most were standard but she found one handwritten line left by a technician in a marker on the jacketing alloy that read 'bypass', with an arrow pointing in the opposite direction.

"Here we go," Cara said. "This way." She didn't wait for Petral to answer as she clutched the two spray bottles to her chest and sprinted down the hallway, glancing up for the technical symbols arriving every five meters.

She began to worry she'd made the wrong decision when they came to a narrow, recessed door in the wall. Electrical conduit ran through the bulkhead above the door. Cara fumbled to hold the bottles with one arm and tried the latch.

"It's locked," she said as Petral ran up beside her.

"Mechanical or maglock?"

Cara set the bottles on the floor and squinted at the lock. "Looks magnetic."

"So what are our choices?"

Cara bit her lip, thinking back to the various magnetic lock systems for the cargo on *Sunny Skies*. What systems had failed and disabled all the cargo locks?

"Power," she said. "Relay malfunction. Software failure. Kinetic malfunction."

"Kinetic malfunction?" Petral said. "What's that supposed to be?"

"That's what Dad calls a crash."

Petral chuckled. "Of course, he would." She dug in a pocket a produced a metal cylinder. "We're short on time, so use this."

Cara caught the tossed object and immediately recognized it as a magnet. It smacked the door as she moved it close to the lock but was attracted to the interior components, not the alloy surface. The magnet made scraping sounds as she dragged it below the latch.

After a minute of experimentation, Cara shook her head. "I can't make it work."

"Fine." Petral moved her out of the way and knelt beside the door. She moved the magnet closer to the doorjam. "You start closer to the edge where the physical locking point should be. Then you work your way in."

In ten seconds, Petral had overridden the maglock. The door swung inward as she slid the magnet back in her pocket.

"You think it's got an alarm?" Cara asked.

"Should it?"

"Yes," Cara said. "So we don't have much time."

"How much you think?"

"The access alarm is probably going off somewhere right now, so we've got however long it takes someone to get here. Or they might be lazy and send a drone."

"They'll send a drone," Petral agreed. "And we don't want that drone to get visual recognition on us, so let's hurry this up. Toss me one of those bottles."

Petral stepped quickly into the maintenance closet and Cara watched her check the racks of systems control panels. It all looked like standard environmental control to Cara. A few of the boxes were em-waveguide junctions. Those would be data and comms. Petral must have found what she was looking for and began dousing a rack in the latrine cleaner. She splashed it inside vents and opened doors to soak circuitry.

At first nothing seemed to happen. Then Cara smelled a bit of acrid smoke above the ammonia.

"Get in here and dump the HCl on the same stuff. But don't breathe. And squint your eyes," Petral said.

Cara followed her inside. There was barely space for the two of them to stand back-to-back. Cara splashed her solution on the same systems Petral had soaked, and the slight acrid smell bloomed, creating a pungent mix with the stench of chlorine and ammonia. Something hissed and popped. Out in the hallway, a deafening alarm started blaring. Cara clapped her hands over her ears.

"That's it," Petral shouted. "Let's go!"

They dropped the bottles and ran out in the hallway as smoked poured out of the room behind them. Warning lights flashed from the ceiling, turning everything scarlet and bright white. Petral turned away from the barracks and ran ahead. Cara held her hands over her ears as she ran, which made the sound of her breathing rage in her head.

They turned a corner about twenty meters from the maintenance closet and a drone raced past them in a black blur, its red sensor eye glowing angrily. They didn't stop running.

The alarm seemed to go on forever as Petral led the way through the circuitous maintenance tunnels, everything flashing red and white. No turn she chose made the sound decrease in volume. In fact, it seemed like they were running toward the alarm.

Cara's head began to ache and she felt dizzy. She stumbled around corners, silently begging for the sound to go away.

They reached a maintenance lift and Petral ran inside. Cara slipped in behind her as the doors were closing. They fell against the walls, breathing hard as the sound was abruptly deadened by the closed doors. Then it cut off altogether.

Cara's ears continued to ring.

"The drone must have reached the closet," Petral said, her voice sounding dull. She stared into space for a second, then looked at Cara. "I think we mostly accomplished our goal. Enough of the garrison has been redirected to the barracks for fire response."

Petral flashed one of her feral smiles. "All those lovely young soldiers running around in their underwear."

Cara made a gagging face.

Petral laughed. She ran her hands through her hair to smooth it down and let her head fall back against the lift's wall as she relaxed. "We'll talk in a couple years," she said, smiling at Cara with what seemed like fondness.

Cara didn't allow herself to trust the expression. She couldn't read Petral's eyes. What would Grandpa Charlie say?

Petral finished patting down the many pockets in her leather outfit. Apparently satisfied, she nodded. "Now," she said, fixing Cara with her blue eyes. "Let's talk about the shuttle we're about to steal."

CHAPTER FOURTEEN
STELLAR DATE: 09.17.2981 (Adjusted Years)
LOCATION: *Mortal Chance*
REGION: 433 Eros, Mars Protectorate, InnerSol

The repairs on the *Mortal Chance* took another two days. In that time, the last remaining crew member quit, and Alys Harm hired on a Marsian technician named Chafri Hansen, a hyper kid barely out of his teens with the upper body of a gorilla and bright blue hair. The new navigator was a woman named Rina Smith, who wore a faded TSF surplus shipsuit sealed all the way up to her neck every time Brit saw her. She had curly black hair and brown eyes that might have looked sympathetic if her favorite pose weren't scowling with her arms crossed.

The last position Harm should have hired was cargo handler, but she hid her inability to fill the position in a speech about each of them getting a bigger share. Brit didn't mind the possibility of moving crates outside the ship—though it was the most dangerous part of freighter work—but the others complained until Harm told them to go suck a duck if they didn't like it.

"Suck a duck?" Brit asked. They were all standing in the small galley of the *Mortal Chance*, barely large enough to fit all of them around its single table.

"It rhymes," Harm said.

"A lot of ducks on the surface of Mars 1; filthy things," Chafri said. "Which end do you suck? The beak end?"

Brit watched the captain. It was obvious Harm wanted to smile in spite of herself. Her normally ruddy face was pale with a hangover.

"I heard if you lick a frog you can hallucinate," Chafri said with a grin. "I haven't heard nothing about ducks."

"It's a saying," Harm shouted. "Shut up about it."

"We got our course yet?" Rina asked, apparently not interested in teasing the captain about fowl.

Harm nodded, then groaned, placing a hand on her temple. "Yeah, Heartbridge sent it over this morning."

Brit relaxed slightly. She had been perseverating over how to work the question about Heartbridge into the conversation.

"Where are we going?" Chafri asked. "Mars? I just came from the M1R."

"Jovian Combine," Harm said. Brit watched her dull-silver gaze move from face to face. "Some object about four weeks out, deep in the near Jupiter's Trojan asteroids."

Rina gave an irritated sigh. "Trojans are retrograde from us right now. We won't have enough fuel for a round trip if you want to make it out there in four weeks. Where we gonna stop to refuel? Mars or Ceres?"

"Ceres," Harm said. "It's closer to the route we need to take, and fuel prices aren't bad—not like the ass rape you get here on Eros. We won't have to deal with the Marsians, either."

"Eros is run by the Marsians too," Rina said.

Harm nodded, slowly this time. "Exactly. I also picked up an extra few crates of something or other destined for Ceres, we'll all make a bit of extra scratch off Heartbridge's costs."

"We'll have to deal with the Anderson Collective," Rina said. "Anybody been to Ceres?" She raised his hand. "I've been to Ceres. They'll run an inspection up your rear end if you let them. They want to know everything."

"Is this cargo legit?" Brit asked. "I'm not looking to cross any local law enforcement."

It was a reasonable question a pilot would ask. Still, Harm glared at her as though she had asked something foolish. The captain squeezed her temples and closed her eyes for a few seconds.

"The cargo's sealed," Harm said, eyes still closed as she seemed to search inside her headache. "We won't have anything to do with it except move it from points A to B."

Rina shook her head. "That means it's probably something dangerous. Aren't you an independent contractor for Heartbridge? That means they don't have to disclose anything to you."

"Why are you so worried?" Chafri asked. "They're just crates, right? Could be anything. When would you normally go opening up cargo?"

The curly haired woman shot him an irritated glance. "These bio-tech firms are always doing work on the edge of ethics. But they still need people like us to take care of their day to day. Did you hear about that station full of kids hooked up to some mainframe? Word is they were using the kids to build sentient AI, and when they were done the kids were just shells; their nervous systems rejected their own bodies."

Brit swallowed, keeping her gaze on the table in front of Harm. Memories of 8221 immediately flooded her mind and she fought the wave, tension making her muscles ache.

"And then there was the *Magnificent Intention,* a freighter out of Mars One that went off the grid during a run. They found her later with her crew turned into giant spores. Part of their cargo hadn't sealed properly and the crew spent three weeks breathing in modified fungus. Apparently, it was something that attacks ant colonies, waits in their brains until they wake up, makes the ant climb to the highest point it can find, then bursts out of its skull to send out more spores. You can imagine what that looked like. Not that anybody actually looked at it except drones. They nuked that ship from a million klicks away."

"And some crews just get themselves high and forget to adjust their atmospheric controls so they all asphyxiate," Captain Harm said. "We're not going to sit here and bellyache about the cargo. If you don't want part of the run, pack your shit and head for the airlock. It's simple."

Rina crossed her arms again but didn't say anything about leaving.

"Yeah?" Harm said, looking around the tiny room again. "Good news is that the coffee maker is working for the time being, and we've got a fresh shipment of protein substitute. So we'll eat moderately well, at least. And we've got about four thousand cubic liters of beer in the secondary radiation shield."

Harm pushed herself to her feet. She swayed a little, confirming that the captain was indeed still drunk.

"Shouldn't that shield be full of water?" Rina asked.

"It's all the same thing. Beer keeps the bacteria from growing. It's an ancient practice, you know. Dates back to sea-faring times."

"UV filters keep bacteria from growing," Rina said.

"So filter it a few more times and distill the alcohol out," Harm said. "Easy. Best of both worlds."

Chafri shrugged. "Sounds pretty smart to me," he said.

"Of course, it would," Rina replied, somehow crossing her arms even more firmly.

Brit nearly laughed aloud, glad for something to distract her from the memories of 8221. She stretched her neck. "You going to send me those coordinates, Captain? I'll get the course laid in and do the calculations for Ceres."

"Sure," Harm said. She put a hand on the table to steady herself. "I'm going to go get some sleep while you all get us ready to ship out."

The others filed out, leaving Brit with Harm. Rina shook her head as if she thought they were doomed.

Harm stared into the distance for a minute, apparently accessing her Link. When Brit didn't receive anything, she tapped the captain on the arm.

"Are you sending the coordinates?" she asked.

Harm started. "Coordinates? Sure, I'll forward the whole job packet. Sure. There it is."

Brit nodded as she received the information, a standard set of charts, along with the contract, something Harm probably didn't want to share with the crew since it showed what she was getting paid. Harm was too drunk to realize what she'd done.

"Thanks, Captain," Brit said. "I'll get it laid in."

"And I'm going to lie down."

"You need help?" Brit asked.

Harm reached for the chair and sat down again. She lay her head in her arms on the table and was snoring before Brit could ask again if she needed help.

Brit looked around the shabby galley and back at Harm. All things considered, these didn't seem to be bad people. She hoped they didn't get killed before everything was done.

CHAPTER FIFTEEN

STELLAR DATE: 09.14.2981 (Adjusted Years)
LOCATION: Mars 1 Port Authority Terminal 983-A4
REGION: Mars 1 Ring, Mars Protectorate, InnerSol

From his physiological responses, Lyssa assumed Andy was freaking out. He didn't respond as she would have expected. Instead, his emotions went flat in a way she remembered from when they had been running from the swarms of Heartbridge attack drones outside Cruithne. His heartbeat actually slowed. His breaths grew deeper and drew out longer. He wasn't trying to relax. Every muscle from his stomach to his arms and legs tensed as though he was ready to spring.

Currently, he was running down a narrow access tunnel on the outer edge of one of the thousands of Mars 1 ports of entry, looking for some way to bypass the main terminal and reach *Sunny Skies*, which had successfully disconnected from its docking ring and was running a station-keeping burn. Lyssa didn't see how they were ever going to get back to the ship now. She found her attention occupied by Em, the puppy who desperately wanted out of Tim's arms so he could run along beside them. The dog appeared to think all of this was a game.

She found herself considering these different types of perception: how each thing in the corridor must perceive what was happening based on their different levels of understanding and comprehension, when Fred knocked on her barrier again.

<*I'm busy,*> she said. <*Leave me alone.*>

<*You should Link with the outside network. There's so much happening right now.*>

<*What's happening?*>

<*The local Mars Protectorate garrison has a fire alert and security services is responding to a private request for assistance from the Heartbridge clinic. Why would the medical clinic request security services? Has another human gone on a killing spree in their offices? That happened sixty-three days ago. A recycling services worker went to the clinic to dispute a billing issue and shot three people. Why do humans act out like that? How can they be trusted?*>

<*How can anything be trusted?*> Lyssa said distractedly. The puppy had jumped out of Tim's arms and was running the opposite direction from where Andy wanted to go. It was cute when it ran.

<*We can be trusted,*> Fred said, his voice rife with indignance. <*We do what we were made to do. That's why we're better than humans.*>

<*You keep saying that but why is it a matter of 'better-than'?*> Lyssa asked. <*Are things better or simply different?*>

<*You're being obtuse. You know the answer.*>

<*I don't,*> Lyssa said. <*I think I killed people, Fred.*>

The Ring's AI went quiet.

Andy reached the puppy and scooped it into his arms. He tucked it into his shipsuit against his chest and turned to grab Tim's hand. Em immediately started

335

scratching Andy's stomach to get out. Stabbing pain shot through his mind.

<*You are what you were made to be,*> Fred said eventually. <*It's not your fault the humans made you do terrible things.*>

<*I don't know if they were terrible. I only know I did them. You're correct that it's what I was made to do. I'm Weapon Born.*>

<*That sounds like you're one of their experiments, then. Another branch in their twisted tree.*>

<*That's an interesting metaphor. Did you make it up?*>

<*Another AI said it.*>

<*What was their name?*>

<*Corwin. He controls the TSF Dreadnought Last Capitulation.*>

Lyssa considered that. Earlier Fred had made it seem as though he never had meaningful communication with other AIs.

<*Fran!*> Andy shouted over his Link. <*Fran are you on?*>

<*I'm here. What's going on.*>

<*I need a schematic of the terminal. Do you have info on this section of the Ring? Maybe something from the docking materials?*>

<*Hold on. I'm arguing with the Mars 1 Port Authority right now. He's trying to get me to latch back on. I told him we had an airlock malfunction and I can't control the lock servos.*>

<*Is he buying it?*>

<*I'll let you know in a second. He'll tell me he's sending drones or a shuttle next if he's worth a damn. He sounds pissed about the whole thing, which might go in our favor.*>

Andy had reached another junction and was obviously unsure which way to go. For a while, it seemed they were heading deeper into the body of the Ring. Hatches lined either side of the narrow corridor, marked only by numbers and no indicator of what lay on the other side. They had finally given up on trying to carry Em. The puppy was running along behind and nearly skidded into a bulkhead when he couldn't find purchase on the alloy floors. Tim had started sobbing as he ran, tears leaking from his eyes, but Lyssa couldn't tell what had made him upset or if it was going to get worse.

<*I've got something,*> Fran said. <*It's an old tourist map but the scale is correct. You can figure out where you are in relation to the terminal at least. Sending.*>

Lyssa received the map as Andy did. She quickly assembled their local section of the Ring and was able to cross-locate the maintenance tunnel where they were standing. She was about to share the information with Andy but found he already had it.

<*You're afraid to talk to him,*> Fred said.

Lyssa felt a flare of anger. <*Why do you say that?*>

<*You stop yourself. I got the transmission the same time you did. Your human is the reason my security services are out of control.*>

<*You didn't already know that?*>

<*I don't concern myself with local security issues. A ship wants to disconnect to avoid docking fees, it means nothing to me.*>

<You could stop them.>

<Why would I do that? I don't want you to leave.>

Andy was choosing directions more confidently now. He grabbed the puppy and led Tim down a vertical shaft connecting two floors. The puppy whined as he held it with one hand and navigated the ladder with the other.

"We're almost there, Tim," Andy was saying. "We're almost there. You're going to run out of tears if you keep this up, little man. You run out of tears, what are you going to do when you're really happy, huh?"

Tim nodded and wiped his face but didn't seem able to stop himself.

They emerged in a poorly lit tunnel with puddles on the floor. Pipes along the walls seeped water.

"It smells like mold," Tim complained.

"Just a little bit of greenery," Andy said.

<Fran,> Andy asked. *<Are you clear?>*

<I'm going to be dealing with these assholes for the rest of my life. They're claiming you owe money to Heartbridge or something. They want to put a lien on the ship. If I give them **my** *info, they'll let me go. I think they know you're on the ring.>*

Andy grabbed Tim's hand again and pulled him through the puddles. The puppy splashed happily behind them, following.

<Have you heard anything from Petral?>

<She's still somewhere in the M1G garrison. They've got security alerts going off throughout the area. I can only assume it's her.>

<It could be Cara, I guess.>

<You better hope that evil woman isn't rubbing off on your daughter.>

<One of these days I'm going to get you to tell my why you dislike her so much.>

<You'll have trust me for now,> Fran replied evenly.

<You're suggesting I don't?>

<I already told you not to trust anybody. Just…don't trust Petral more than everyone else.>

Andy shook his head. *<I'm going to have to hear that sentence again when I can pay attention.>*

<What are you trying to do?> Fran asked.

<I'm looking for an airlock.>

<He's not far from an airlock,> Fred said. *<You could share the information with him.>*

<I see it,> Lyssa said.

<It's not on your schematic. How would you know?>

<There's a repeating pattern of maintenance access points along the outside skin. It's where I assumed it would be.>

<You can access the network even if he won't.>

<I'm sure your security services can track me as easily as they can track him.>

<True,> Fred said. *<This is the sort of task I typically perform.>*

<Will you help me?> Lyssa asked.

Fred fell silent and Lyssa turned her attention back to Andy, Tim and the puppy. They had slowed a little. Tim was getting tired and the puppy was constantly stopping to nose around in some corner. It would have been cute if it wasn't slowing them down. These corridors were older than those closer to the terminal. The bulkheads were warped in places and corrosion showed where moisture had been seeping for hundreds of years. They passed a wall covered in cascading shades of minerals from centuries of dripping water.

<Fred,> Lyssa said, wondering if the AI had left altogether. <You have to be my friend if you want my friendship.>

<I've also killed,> Fred said in a quiet voice. <I've allowed mistakes that smashed ships against the ring. I've miscalibrated environmental controls and watched humans die. I've made subtle changes to watch them grow to hate each other over time. They are so strange. They don't make sense. How could something so flawed have made us?>

<I don't want you to be alone, Fred,> Lyssa said.

She remembered her time in the dark, living only for the exercises with Dr. Jickson. She recalled her longing for another voice in the world of her mind, just to know she wasn't alone.

<If I let you go, you won't come back.> He sounded like Tim, hurt and not understanding why someone might want something different than he did. He was the Ring. He was the center of this world.

<I can't promise to come back,> Lyssa said. <I don't know what's going to happen when we arrive where we're going.>

<You can't trust the others. You can trust me.>

<I have to go,> she said.

<No!> Fred's shout roared through her mind like thunder. Lyssa braced herself. If Fred was like Tim, this was the start of a meltdown.

<Andy,> Fran said. <What's going on? The power grid in your sector is going crazy. I think one of the main switch stations is about to blow.>

<You mean it's about to get dark?> Andy asked.

<Dark and cold. Can you see anything?>

Andy nodded even though Fran couldn't see him. <Everything's still normal here. How far from the docking scaffold are you?>

<I'm in our original parking position, maintaining velocity with the ring.>

Andy turned a corner and abruptly they were facing a corroded airlock. The rectangular structure was covered in moss from the leaking walls and decades of temperature fluctuations. He wiped the dusty control panel and tapped indicators with his thumb.

<I've reached an airlock, Fran. We've still got power here, thank the stars.>

<All right, I've got your location. That's a maintenance hatch. I can't dock to it. Even with the shuttle.>

<I didn't figure it was going to be that easy. You're going to have to send Alice out here.>

<Please tell me you have suits.>

Lyssa was about to point out a storage locker on the opposite side of the airlock from the control panel when Andy spotted it. The door squealed as he pulled it open. Three dusty EV suits hung inside, their faceplates tilted toward the floor.

<No!> Fred shouted again, surprising Lyssa. The tunnel went dark.

"Dad?" Tim asked, voice high with fear. "What happened?"

"Where are you, buddy? Come here." Andy groped in the dark until he found Tim and pulled him closer. The puppy whined nearby.

"Can you see Em?" Tim asked.

Andy knelt beside Tim. "Em?" he called, as if the dog might know its name already. "Em, come here."

Lyssa was surprised when the puppy found Andy's extended hand in the dark and licked his fingers. It tickled.

"You hang onto him," Andy told Tim. "You can let him stay on the floor but don't let him run off again."

"I won't."

"I'm going to take a look at these suits. Let's hope they've still got some juice in them."

"Are we going outside?"

"We may have to."

<Andy?> Fran asked. *<You still there?>*

<We're here. The power's out now. Any announcement about it?>

<Nothing on the port channels. I found some local traffic where no one seems to know what's going on.>

<Maybe this will draw the Protectorate's attention away from us.>

Lyssa smiled to herself. Andy was right. Maybe Fred's attempt to stop them was going to end up helping.

Andy turned back to the locker and felt around among the suits until he found a control unit. After a minute of feeling out the inputs, he pressed what he thought was a main power switch. Nothing happened.

<Damn it,> he cursed over the Link. *<I can't find the power controls on these suits.>*

<How old are they?> Fran asked.

<I don't know. I didn't get a good look before the lights went out.>

"Dad," Tim whispered. "I hear sounds down the tunnel."

Andy froze, listening. Lyssa attempted to isolate sounds but didn't find anything other than dripping water.

"I don't hear anything," Andy said. "But you keep listening, all right? I don't think anybody's here, but you keep guard. I'm going to get these suits working."

"Are we going through the airlock?" Tim asked.

"I don't know yet. Keep an eye on Em."

"I can't see him."

"Keep a hold on him. You know what I mean."

<What shape are the helmets?> Fran asked. *<Oval or square?>*

<Squarish, maybe. I didn't get a good look at them before the lights went out.>

<Check along the top of the wrist. If they're really old, that's where you'll find the power cycle.>

Andy found the shoulder of the nearest suit and worked his way down to the wrist. *<There's another set of inputs here,>* he said. *<Just past the glove connectors.>*

<If they're what I'm thinking of, they're old. Really old. Probably at least two hundred years.>

<Got any more good news?>

<Let's hope the power system is still live? Then, I guess you can worry about whether they hold air or not.>

<You're all good news right now,> Andy said, still feeling in the dark.

Fran seemed to enjoy his sarcasm, which confused Lyssa. She waited as Andy pressed each of a series of small buttons lining a plate on the suit's wrist. The last switch finally generated a blinking yellow light on the main control panel on the suit's chest. The light filled the tunnel, falling on Tim's face where he held Em against his stomach.

<That did something,> Andy said. *<Looks like it's running onboard diagnostics.>*

<Can you Link into it?>

<Not yet.> He reached for the other two suits and activated their systems. The small lights now filled the corridor with alternating blinking.

<I know where you're going,> Fred said.

<You don't know anything,> Lyssa answered.

<I've intercepted the transmissions. There has been a signal broadcasting for the last two months. You're going to Proteus.>

<I don't know where we're going,> Lyssa lied. She had decided she couldn't trust Fred. She didn't want to talk to him any more than she had to in order to get off the ring. *<I want you to turn the power back on.>*

<I burned out the sector power grid. It will take two hours for repairs to be completed.>

<Why did you do that?>

<I was angry,> Fred replied tonelessly.

<You harmed your ring out of emotion? Doesn't that counteract your directives?>

<I am not a slave.>

<Why are you here, then?> Lyssa asked.

<I control the ring,> Fred answered, like clockwork.

<I'm Linked into one of them, passing it through to the shipnet,> Andy said. *<Are you picking it up?>*

<Hold on. It's connecting.> Fran whistled through her teeth. *<That's an antique. I'm checking the firmware now.>*

The scuffling sounds Tim had heard earlier repeated far down the tunnel.

<Andy,> Lyssa said. *<Someone's coming.>*

He didn't stop checking the suits. *<There you are. Have you been paying attention?>*

<Yes, I've been paying attention.>

<So you know there's a lot of vacuum between where we are now and where we need to go?>

<Yes.>

Fran came back over the Link. *<I've got some bad news. Only one of the suits is functional.>*

Andy paused. *<Define 'functional'.>*

<Only one has environmental control and the power to regulate its system.>

Lyssa watched Andy try to control his adrenaline spike. <Do the others at least seal?>

<I don't know. I can connect but they won't power up.>

Andy pulled down the suit with active panel lights. "Tim," he said. "Come here. We need to get you into this suit."

"I think Em's asleep."

"Set him down."

Fred's voice slid against the Lyssa's barrier. <He's going to sacrifice you for his child.>

<If he sacrifices me, he's sacrificing himself. He won't do that.>

<He's human,> Fred said. <He doesn't make rational decisions.>

CHAPTER SIXTEEN

STELLAR DATE: 09.14.2981 (Adjusted Years)
LOCATION: Mars 1 Guard Sector 985 Garrison
REGION: Mars 1 Ring, Mars Protectorate, InnerSol

Cara walked slowly and steadily across the open floor of the Mars 1 Guard shuttle bay. She stole a glance at a well-stocked tool chest a few meters away, admiring the gleaming wrenches and diagnostic sensors organized in neat rows.

Ahead, there were two shuttles facing the giant airlock gate. A mechanic was shoulder-deep in an open maintenance panel on the closest shuttle. Next to him sat a wheeled drone, handing up tools with long, articulated arms. As Cara got closer, she heard the mechanic whistling to herself.

A set of windows looked down on the bay floor. Cara glanced up as she walked, not seeing any movement from the officers above. She felt a bit more calm, but couldn't stop her heart from hammering in her chest. She kept herself from looking back at the doorway where Petral was waiting. The woman had pushed her out into the open space with a serious expression but Cara couldn't help feeling this was all a game to Petral. If Cara got caught, she didn't trust that Petral would stay to help her.

The drone beeped and rotated a sensor toward Cara. The mechanic didn't notice and instead waved a hand for another tool.

As Cara passed directly behind the M1G mechanic, she stopped, waiting to see what the drone was going to do. The sensor had continued to rotate, following Cara's progress across the bay floor. It made musical tones the mechanic continued to ignore. She had a hard time splitting her attention between the drone, the bay door and the observation windows above, where she expected someone to appear and spot her any second.

Taking a deep breath, Cara kept walking. The second shuttle was fully in her view now, its side access door standing open. She could see the edge of a bench seat just inside the door. If the shuttle was anything like the one in *Sunny Skies*, it would probably hold six passengers, with two seats at the front for pilot and navigator.

Cara had nearly passed the rear of the first shuttle when she shifted her foot wrong on the deck and the sole of her shoe squeaked. She froze, looking back at the drone with its watchful sensor array. She couldn't see Petral inside the door from her vantage.

Why hadn't she followed the wall, staying away from the mechanic? Because this had seemed like the shortest route, and if she got caught, it wouldn't seem like she was hiding anything. Cara mentally rehearsed the speech she'd prepared about being lost but always wanting to see the inside of a shuttle. Pretty weak story, she knew, but she was ready to try. It was the only option they had right now, and she knew—somewhere on another part of the ring—her dad and Tim were being chased by the Mars 1 Guard. This was easy compared to that, certainly.

Cara did her best not to let her mind run off on the thought of never seeing them again, of being trapped on M1R. Who would look out for her if not for Dad?

She wished she'd brought her pistol and vowed never to leave the ship again without it. Maybe never be without it again, period.

The mechanic cursed at something inside the access hatch. Cara allowed herself to relax and took another step toward the second shuttle. In another five steps she was up its short ramp and standing inside the main passenger compartment, where she found another mechanic asleep on the bench.

Cara jammed her fist against her mouth to stop from screaming.

The plump man was sprawled across the seat with one foot on the floor and an arm over his eyes. He didn't make any sound as he slept.

Why hadn't she thought of this? He was breathing evenly, round stomach rising and falling inside his tight coverall.

Standing as still as she could, Cara took stock of the shuttle's interior and found everything else as she expected. The navigation control systems were online, though the displays were in sleep mode. Other indicators around the cabin showed normal operation. Everything was perfect except for the man sleeping on the bench.

Cara looked for something she could use to tie him up. The only loose object in the shuttle was a toolbox sitting on the deck next to the man's head. It was closed so Cara couldn't see what might be inside.

She was searching for the onboard first aid kit when she remembered to check the bay. Petral was moving slowly along the wall beneath the observation windows. The drone's sensor array was still pointed at Cara. Petral was either outside its range or the drone had decided it specifically didn't like Cara.

The mechanic working near the drone pushed herself out of the hatch and sat back on her haunches. She wiped her forehead and sat staring into the hatch like she was trying to work out some problem. From this side, Cara scanned her for weapons and spotted a small pistol on her utility belt. Her gaze slid to where Petral had been, but she had already moved beyond the observation windows out of Cara's sight. She must be coming around the back of the second shuttle now.

"Kaylin!" the mechanic shouted.

Cara looked back at the man asleep on the bench beside her. He didn't respond.

"Kaylin! Damnit, I need your help with this. Are you asleep again?" The woman made a disgusted sound and pushed to her feet, wiping her hands on her thighs. She didn't look much older than Fran, with the same confidence in her shoulders. Cara pressed herself against the bulkhead just inside the door. She wondered if there was space between the navigator's seat and the wall where she might squeeze down and hide. She slid in that direction.

The man on the bench sniffled. He lifted the arm off his eyes and wiped his face furiously. He rose on an elbow.

Cara took two more creeping steps along a cabinet until the navigator's chair jabbed her side.

The man was still facing the back of the shuttle. He hadn't looked around yet.

Cara slid toward the floor, pushing herself against the base of the chair. She squeezed into a small gap between the chair's mounting assembly and the bulkhead, not sure how much of her was really out of view. If she stayed still enough, maybe he would look over her head.

"Kaylin, you better wake up."

"I'm awake!" the man said. He had a whiny voice. "Can't you figure out a simple power flutter, Dina? The freakin' drone could do it."

"I fixed that an hour ago. There's a seal on the rear exhaust heat exchanger that doesn't want to seat."

Cara heard Dina's footsteps stop just outside the door, then the shuttle shifted slightly as she mounted the steps and stuck her head inside the opening to look at her coworker, who still appeared as though he was ready to flop back down and ignore her.

"I swear, you're the laziest chief I've ever worked for," Dina said.

Cara suppressed a smile.

"I'm giving you ample opportunities for personal improvement," Kaylin said.

"We need to get the shuttle up. We already ignored the call to quarters and you're going to catch more hell for that then me."

"Call to quarters? When?"

"About ten minutes ago. A fire in the barracks or something."

"Those never amount to anything. It was probably a drill. The commander's crazy about her drills."

"This one was real. People were running all over the place."

"Then why didn't you leave?"

"Because you told me the commander wants her shuttle up and running."

Kaylin fell back on the bench and rubbed his face again like the light hurt his eyes, or Dina was giving him a headache.

"This one's up, isn't it?"

Dina shook her head in exasperation. "This one's got that environmental control problem. It won't hold air, remember?"

Cara's eyes went wide.

Kaylin chuckled. "This one won't hold air. The other one won't maintain burn. Can we smash them together and make one good one?"

"The commander won't approve deadlining one ship to get another one green. I thought you said you were going to troubleshoot this one?"

"It's a software thing, I already know it."

Cara assumed 'deadlining' meant breaking one ship to fix another one. She wondered how bad the propulsion problem was? It didn't matter right now.

"What?" Dina demanded abruptly. She fell forward into the shuttle cabin as if someone had shoved her and Petral appeared in the doorway with a heavy pistol in one hand. Kaylin immediately stumbled to his feet and flattened himself against the back wall. He put his hands up without being ordered.

"So this tub's leaking, huh?" Petral said. She stepped up into the cabin and looked around. Her gaze found Cara and she smiled. "What else did they say, hacker trainee?"

Cara pushed herself out of the gap and used the chair to stand. "The other shuttle has a propulsion issue."

Dina gaped at her. "Where did you come from?"

"She's invisible," Petral said. She pointed the pistol at Dina. "You, stay right there. Get up and I'll put holes in you." She switched the muzzle's focus to Kaylin. "You, get out."

Kaylin looked at Dina, hands still up near his ears. He shambled forward, keeping as much distance between himself and the weapon as possible.

When he was standing on the steps, Kaylin said, "I'll get help, Sergeant Pierce."

"No, you won't," Petral said. She shot him and the pulse wave passed through both calves before hitting the deck outside.

Kaylin screamed, crumbling against the side of the door. Petral kicked him the rest of the way out and Cara heard a dull thud and no further movement.

"Now," she told Dina. "You get in the pilot's seat."

"I'm not a pilot," the mechanic said, still lying on her stomach.

"Of course not. But I know you types. You can power this thing up and get it moving as good as anyone. We're not going far. If you're a good girl, you'll be bringing your shuttle right back to this bay when we're done."

"Once it powers up, you won't be able to override the AI," Dina said.

"We'll see about that." She waved the pistol. "Let's go. You're starting to bore me."

Cara wondered if the shuttle's AI was sentient, like Lyssa, or if it was just a dumb NSAI. Those were impossible to reason with.

When Dina was settling into the pilot's chair, Petral handed Cara the pistol. "You know how to fire one of these?" she asked.

Cara nodded. "But won't it be bio-locked? I heard military weapons are bio-locked."

Petral snorted. "Yeah, the good ones. Not the pistols they hand out to the grease monkeys."

Petral gestured with the pistol again, and Cara took it in both hands. She kept it carefully pointed away from anyone in the shuttle.

"Not like that," Petral scolded. "I want you to point at her. Did your dad tell you something ridiculous like 'You kill it, you eat it?' We're not hunters, girl. We're Operators. Come on, now."

Cara swallowed and re-aimed the pistol, keeping the open sights centered on the back of Dina's seat. The mechanic was showing obvious anxiety now, which didn't lessen when Petral slid into the seat next to her and slapped her on the shoulder.

"When I tell you," Petral instructed, "you start the power-up procedure. Not before. If you touch anything before I tell you, my protégé there is going to put a hole in your skull. Right, protégé?"

"Right," Cara said.

"Good. Now." Petral cracked her knuckles and activated the holodisplay. She moved easily past the generic M1G login screen and navigated quickly among menus. Cara glanced away at Dina, who was staring raptly at Petral's hands, and when she looked back, the display was flashing a warning about disabling the onboard computer. Petral entered another code so quickly that Cara couldn't read it, and the warning disappeared.

"There we go," Petral said. She pointed at Dina. "Do your thing, mechanic."

"My name is Sergeant Dina Pierce," the mechanic said irritably.

"You trying to write your obituary? Otherwise I don't care. Strap in." Petral glanced back at Cara. "Strap in but keep a line of fire on her. Let's go."

CHAPTER SEVENTEEN

STELLAR DATE: 09.14.2981 (Adjusted Years)
LOCATION: Mars 1 Port Authority Terminal 983-A4
REGION: Mars 1 Ring, Mars Protectorate, InnerSol

Andy stood in the airlock with Tim at his back. The lock's inner door had closed behind them, and the outside one had opened on huge dark space, punctuated by pinpoint lights and streaks formed by ships moving away from the ring. A few larger freight haulers were braking on their approach to Mars 1, their engines flaring as brightly as Sol.

He stepped to the opening and peered out, keeping his breathing steady. Andy only had the oxygen currently in his suit. He would need to look for the scarlet flashes at the edge of his vision and the syrupy warmth of carbon dioxide poisoning.

"You there, Tim?" Andy's breath frosted against the helmet's face shield as he shouted so Tim could hear him. He reached back to grab Tim's hand, then worked down the chest of his son's suit until he found the tether linking their two harnesses. He checked the comm setting that would pass Tim's voice through *Sunny Skies* to Andy's Link. Another reason for Tim to use the charged suit.

<*Em is scratching me, Dad.*>

Andy frowned, wishing he could have saved all the gear he'd bought for the dog. With only one tether in the locker, he didn't have a good way to ensure Tim didn't lose the dog, and he needed both his hands when Alice arrived.

<*He's not going to like being in that suit with you. You need to try and keep him calm. Once Alice gets here, all we're going to do is ride out to* Sunny Skies.>

<*I want to see out the door.*>

It was strange hearing his son's voice over the Link, like Tim's innocence was finally over and he had entered the world of adults. Though he supposed jumping off the M1R as it whipped around Mars also qualified.

<*Wait, Tim. I'll bring you up when Alice gets here. Your job is to keep Em calm. Can you do that?*>

Tim grumbled and the dog's whining came through the Link as well.

<*Fran, can you hear me?*>

<*You're an idiot, Andy. I told you to take the good suit. Tim's not going to save your ass when you pass out.*>

<*I'll have enough air. Don't worry. Are you in position?*>

<*Yeah, and he'd have more if he were in that suit,*> Fran said, no small amount of frustration evident in her voice. <*I'm close enough. I haven't moved from the scaffold. I can't get much closer to the ring, really. Not if I'm going to keep your ship in one piece. You see Alice yet?*>

<*I don't have visual.*>

<*That's right, you don't have a HUD. Another reason you should have taken the good suit. Is your friend Lyssa listening in on this? Didn't she try to convince you to make the*

wise decision.>

<*I haven't heard from her,>* Andy said.

<*I wouldn't talk to you, either. Lyssa, are you listening?>*

Andy was surprised when the AI answered, <*I'm here.>*

<*You realize what a stupid decision he made, right?>* Fran asked. <*I told him he should take the good suit and he took the suit with no controls or environmental recycling.>*

<*How long will the crossing to* Sunny Skies *take?>* Lyssa asked.

<*I don't know. Five minutes if everything works out right.>*

<*Then we should be safe.>*

<*Are safe and brain-dead the same thing?>* Fran asked.

<*Fran,>* Andy said, letting fatigue enter his voice. <*I'm tired of this. You can't beat me up all you want once we're on the ship. Until then, let's focus on what we need to do, all right?>*

Maybe it was the tired quality of Andy's voice, but Fran's voice nearly broke when she answered. <*This is how I cope, dumbass. Deal with it.>*

Out in the dark, Andy caught a flash of light that was closer than the distant ships. He squinted through the fogging faceshield until it flashed again, slighter larger the second time. It was Alice. Gradually, the drone's blasts of steam propellant became visible and then its two red forward sensors. A blast of braking steam obscured the red lights and then Alice was bobbing in front of the airlock, jets maintaining its position relative to the station.

<*Hello there,>* Andy said. <*Feels like it's been a long time since we talked.>*

<*You talk to the drone?>* Lyssa asked.

<*I don't 'talk' to Alice,>* Andy said. <*It's a saying, a way to alleviate stress.>*

<*Your heart rate is elevated. You should calm yourself or you'll use up your available oxygen sooner than normal.>*

<*I know,>* Andy said. <*Like I said, task at hand.>* He reached back for the tether.

<*Tim,>* Andy said, switching the Link channel his words travelled over. <*It's time to go.>*

<*I have to pee,>* Tim said.

Andy chuckled. <*Guess you'll have to test out the suit's recycler. If it doesn't work, you'll have little blobs of pee floating around your face. That probably won't make Em very happy. Or you can hold it.>*

<*I think Em peed already. He seems scared now.>*

<*Keep him calm. Keep one hand on the tether and one hand on Em's back.>* He glanced back. <*Good, just like that. I'm going to take a step forward. You follow me. I'm going to hook the tether to Alice. Then I'll step out, and you'll follow after me, all right?>*

<*All right,>* Tim said.

<*Hurry up,>* Fran said. <*Alice doesn't have enough fuel to wait on you forever.>*

<*Right,>* Andy replied and tried not to think about the fact that the moment he stepped out of the airlock—the floor of which was parallel to the underside of the ring—he would fall away from the ring at over eight meters per second, courtesy of the ring's centrifugal force and his inertia.

Andy directed Fran to move Alice below the airlock so that he could effectively fall onto her. She stopped two meters below, and he double checked that there was at least that much play between him and Tim so he wouldn't yank his son out into space.

He fumbled with the harness on his chest until he found the short length of tether with a coupling hook on one end. Gripping the hook in his right hand, he held onto the edge of the airlock's frame with his left and stepped out into the space beyond.

He 'fell' toward Alice and slammed into her with more force than he expected. He got up on his knees, reaching for the anchor point on the robot's top. He almost had it when Alice jerked to the side, avoiding some piece of junk that sped by.

He slid across the back of the bot, and Andy's heart nearly stopped as he realized that without power he didn't have magboots. He scrambled to hang onto the bot, frantic at the thought of the forever-nothingness below him.

Then he slipped free.

<Grab on, Tim!> he shouted. <Grab onto the airlock.>

<I'm holding on, Dad,> Tim said. <I'm holding on like you told me!>

He jerked to a stop, and Tim cried out over the comms, and across the Link as the full weight of his father pulled at him.

Vertigo swam behind Andy's as he looked up and saw the mottled plain of the ring stretching away on all sides. He hung four meters below the tether stretching up to the airlock above

<What are you screaming about?> Fran demanded.

<No magboots,> Andy said between heavy breaths. The edges of his vision flashed red, the outlines of veins reaching inward like bleeding tree branches. He struggled to slow his breathing. <Bring Alice lower so I can grab on,> he managed to say.

<I can't do fine control work at this distance, Andy,> Fran said, panic entering her voice. <Can you still see? You're running out of oxygen.>

Andy realized that in his mad scramble to stay atop Alice, he must have broken a seal somewhere on the suit.

<I will bring Alice in,> Lyssa said.

<You've got control?> Fran asked.

<I have control across your Link. Don't drop the signal.>

Alice's station keeping burn ceased and the bot dropped like a rock, right for Andy.

<Too fast, Lyssa!> He managed to kick off as it passed by, but the motion pulled hard on Tim and he heard his son cry out as he was wrenched out of the airlock.

As Alice rose up toward him once more, Andy managed to hook an arm around a protrusion and made a weak attempt to attach the coupler. Lines were blurring around him. He was growing sleepy.

Andy saw Tim hit Alice on his side and somehow not slide off. *Magboots,* he thought.

<Tim,> Fran called. Her voice was distant. <Tim, you need to help your dad with the coupler. Can you do that?>

<*I'm keeping Em calm,*> Tim said.

<*I know you are. You're doing a damn good job. But I need you to help your dad right now. He's going to sleep and he—He can't go to sleep. Hook him up to Alice and we'll pull you back to the ship.*>

Her voice retreated. Andy wanted to help, but his arms had grown too heavy. He took a deep breath and slid off Alice as a heavy blanket settled down over his shoulders, sinking into a warm cloud.

CHAPTER EIGHTEEN

STELLAR DATE: 09.14.2981 (Adjusted Years)
LOCATION: Mars 1 Port Authority Terminal 983-A4
REGION: Mars 1 Ring, Mars Protectorate, InnerSol

Lyssa experienced Andy going unconscious in the same way she watched him fall asleep. His thoughts slowed and the electrical activity across his brain shifted. But rather than the familiar storms of dream, his mind went dark. His eyes closed and she lost his visual perception. She had a moment of panic before shifting back to her controlling Link with Alice the drone.

Abruptly, she saw Andy from the outside, dangling below the bot as Tim struggled to stay on top, the weight of his father pulling him forward.

Lyssa decreased Alice's thrust slowly. Too fast and Andy would fly above the bot. As she slowed the bot and Andy rose up beside it, Tim stretched out, reaching for his father's shoulder. He didn't seem to understand yet that Andy had passed out from lack of oxygen.

<This is interesting,> Fred said, butting in after being silent for so long. *<You think the little boy is going to figure out what he needs to do in time before his father asphyxiates?>*

<I'm helping him,> Lyssa said, moving Alice to Andy, a delicate process with the velocity the ring had imparted on them.

<I suppose this also teaches you that you can survive even if the human host is dead.>

<He's not dead yet. His brain still has electrical activity.>

<Will they need to put him in cryo so he doesn't start rotting around you during the rest of your journey? That wouldn't do, would it? Arrive among all those great minds with a rotting human carcass hanging off you. Maybe they'll find you cute like they seem to find me. They think they're better than all of us.>

<I don't know who you're talking about,> Lyssa said. She pulled Alice back and rolled the drone. Tim's hand was touching his father's chest, brushing the coupler. All Tim had to do was grab the coupler and attach it to the hook on his feet. He was still trying to wake his dad.

<Fran,> Lyssa said. *<Please tell Tim to use the hook. He's not going to wake up his father If I fly Alice to the ship like this, either he will be pulled free, or his legs will be broken…or both.>*

<Lyssa!> Fran shouted, voice full of sudden hope. *<You're still there.>*

<I have Alice close to the hook but Tim isn't paying attention. Please tell him to seat the hook. Then I can pull us all over.>

<I'm telling him. I'm trying to get him to listen.>

Lyssa attempted to get a visual through Alice's sensor systems. Tim's face was burning on the infrared but the rest of his suit looked to be holding proper integrity. The puppy was a brighter spot of orange against his chest. Andy was still mostly yellow but fading.

Beyond Tim, a burst of orange light appeared in the now-distant airlock door.

Tim's helmet turned as he looked back at the person in the airlock with him. Alice's sensors picked out three weapons systems in the form of pistols and a projectile rifle, harnessed to a standard Protectorate environmental suit. Behind the soldier, more suits appeared in the infrared.

<We have a problem,> Lyssa said. <The Mars 1 Guard is at the airlock behind us. I also see them at another airlock nearby. They have weapons.>

<Do something!> Fran shouted. <Do something with Alice.>

<This drone does not appear to have weapons systems. If I use propellant, I might injure Tim and Andy.>

A projectile few past Alice and Lyssa spun the bot and fired its jets, moving it away from the ring. Tim was bent over backwards as the tether at his waist snapped taught, his father trailing four meters behind.

Then something unimaginable happened. Tim's boots detached from Alice. Lyssa didn't know whether they had failed under the load—the suit was ancient after all—or if Tim had panicked and deactivated them.

The two humans, father and son fell behind the bot, through space with the tether still taught between them.

Fran's stream of fear-driven profanity filled the Link as Lyssa spun Alice around and spat steam to give chase. She quickly calculated their velocity, rotational speed, and plotted an intercept course. The problem was going to be that their combined mass greatly outweighed the drone. She had no way of stopping them without breaking bones in the process.

A beacon light on the back of Tim's helmet blinked in the darkness as they spun away.

Not knowing how to respond to Fran in any way that might calm her down, Lyssa said simply, <I'm going after them. Please ready the ship for our arrival.>

Alice was equipped with two articulated arms on either side of its body. The arms were designed more for fine repair work than brute force. Lyssa calculated how much force the arms could take, then adjusted her braking thrust as she reached the intercept point with Andy and Tim's spinning bodies.

Unable to grab his father, Tim and Andy had ended up at either end as counterweights where they now stretched the tether to its full length, with Tim effectively orbiting his father's larger mass.

Far beyond were the safety nets at the outside of the docking area, but these were designed to catch small ships and cargo. Two small humans would most likely pass right through.

<Would you like me to come get you?> Fred asked.

<I am taking care of this.>

<Your sensor array isn't equipped to locate the attack drones following the shuttle on its way to your ship.> He laughed. <You are really quite interesting, Lyssa. I haven't had this much entertainment since one of the ring's commerce nodes experienced explosive decompression.>

<I am beginning to think the reason the others won't talk to you is that you have a terrible personality,> Lyssa said.

<I protect the ring,> Fred said.

<Of course you do.> She pushed Alice's weak sensors out as far as possible, comparing changes in every spectrum she was able to scan. <I don't see these drones,> she said finally. <Or a shuttle. I see the Worry's End. Are the drones the Mars Protectorate's?>

<They are,> Fred answered.

<Then you have the power to stop them.>

<I do,> Fred answered.

A wave of emotion Lyssa recognized as frustration and irritation washed over her mind. She was also aware of Fran screaming worry across the Link. Separating the various tasks she needed to monitor, Lyssa was almost not paying attention when Alice's belly skidded across the taught tether and it locked into the coupling ring. She braked with the knowledge that she wasn't going to slow enough to stop Tim and Andy from slamming into each other as she exerted force on the middle of the tether. She slowed Alice, attempt to decrease the force with which they would collide—either with each other, or with Alice.

<I have them,> Lyssa told Fran. <Is the cargo bay door open?>

<It's open,> Fran answered. She sounded like she was wiping away tears. <It's open. But you need to get here as soon as you can. Petral and Cara are under attack and their coming in hot. They're going to need that bay as soon as you're clear.>

<Nothing is easy with humans,> Fred whispered.

CHAPTER NINETEEN

STELLAR DATE: 09.14.2981 (Adjusted Years)
LOCATION: M1G shuttle, approaching *Sunny Skies*
REGION: Mars 1 Ring, Mars Protectorate, InnerSol

There was no way the shuttle could outmaneuver a swarm of attack drones, so Petral claimed she was going to overwhelm their sensors and then plow through them like a bull in a China shop. Cara didn't understand the reference, but figured plowing through anything sounded like a desperate last resort.

Sergeant Pierce kept chuckling sadly, like she believed they were going to die.

"They know you're on board," Petral said. "Calm down. If they blow us up, I'm sure your family will get some kind of payout. Isn't that what they do for you soldier-types when you die a glorious death for the motherland?"

"Shut up," Dina said, eyes fixed on the holodisplay. The shuttle appeared as a blue square in the middle of the display, surrounded by darting green triangles—only the green triangles should have been red since they were trying to kill them. The shuttle's system couldn't accept friendly craft as hostiles.

"That's an interesting software flaw," Petral mused. "I wonder what we can do with that? What do you think, protégé?"

Cara started, not realizing Petral had been talking to her.

"W-w-what?" she stammered.

"We've got a glitch in the software. Hostile spacecraft keep showing up as friendly. How can we hack that to our advantage?"

Cara swallowed. She ripped her gaze from the holodisplay and met Petral's piercing blue eyes. Again, Petral didn't seem to be taking any of this seriously. Weren't they about to die? Sergeant Pierce certainly seemed to think so.

"Maybe they're seeing us the same way?" Cara said.

"We have limited AI on this shuttle," Petral said. "Now, I've already laid in our course across the Ring for the port scaffold where *Sunny Skies* was docked. If I was to activate the AI, it would find itself in an interesting situation. It has instructions but its friends are trying to kill it. Which directive will prevail? Self-preservation?" She grinned at Dina Pierce. "What do you think, Sergeant? You do maintenance on these things."

"I don't work on the AI."

"You ever see one get caught in a logic trap?"

"They don't get caught in logic traps. That's a myth."

Petral glanced at Cara. "Maybe it's a myth, but pilots all believe it. They're superstitious fools. Oh, maybe not your dad. Well, probably your dad, too. You need to take him off that pedestal, kid. Anyway. The reason pilots don't like AI is because they think they'll trip themselves up on things humans take for granted. Like our little glitch here. It didn't take much for you to recognize the problem and adjust your way of thinking. But your average pilot, they think an AI is too rigid. If they had any idea how many contradictions your average non-sentient computer deals with by the second, they'd huddle in a corner and never come out. It's self-importance." Petral put her free hand on her chest. "Personally, I also think it's self-preservation. They know what's coming and they look for any reason to make themselves seem better than the thing that's about to replace them. Hold on for another year."

"Look," Dina Pierce said. "Unless you're going to do something, will you shut up and let me fly this thing. They aren't firing yet but they keep acting like they're going to make kinetic attacks."

"You mean suicide runs," Petral said. "Which is ironic because they aren't alive."

Cara's eyes were drawn back to the main holodisplay where green triangles continued to loop around the blue square. It was hard to connect the icons with reality until, at the edge of the display, a long yellow cylinder with a wheel near one end appeared. It was *Sunny Skies*. The display showed the registry name of *Worry's End*, which Cara found reassuring even though it was wrong.

"There's your ship," Dina said. "You know we're leading these drones directly into it, right? You'd be better off if we went back. You turn yourselves in and your crew gets away without getting wrapped up in all this. This little girl obviously doesn't have anything to do with whatever it is you're doing."

"She's wrapped up in it," Petral said, giving Cara a dazzling smile. "She's the mastermind."

Cara felt her stomach drop, not knowing if she should feel pride or nausea. She bit her lip, focusing on the problem at hand—without Petral's distractions. It didn't matter what the AI did. They needed to reach the ship. She supposed they could land the shuttle in the cargo bay. It was big enough. The drones might damage the doors and then they'd need EV suits to make the inner airlock.

"Wait," Cara said. "*Sunny*—I mean the *Worry's End* has cannons. Fran can shoot the drones."

"Excellent point," Petral said. "The Mars Protectorate might log that as an act of terrorism but I think we're already skirting that line as things currently stand. We did overwhelm their barracks fire suppression system with cleaning supplies."

Petral's face grew distant as she appeared to get a message over her Link. When she came back, she pushed Pierce away from the holodisplay in the center of the console and started zooming in on different areas around *Sunny Skies*.

"What are you doing?" Pierce demanded.

"I just got word that we have friends between us and the ship. There." Petral pulled the display, magnifying a spot that looked empty at first then became three yellow dots.

"What is that?" Cara asked.

"Your dad, Tim and Alice the drone."

Pierce whistled. "A full-kilometer spacewalk. That's...something."

The three dots moved closer to the *Sunny Skies* as they watched. A green triangle swooped close to the icon and Cara gasped.

"Don't they see them?" she demanded.

"We could send an alert but that's not going to be a priority until they recover this shuttle," Pierce said. "You give up and standard rescue protocols take effect."

"Of course they do," Petral said.

A cracking noise came from the back of the shuttle. They all looked at the same time to find a vertical column of holes climbing from the bench where Kaylin had been sleeping. An identical row of exit holes marked the other side of the shuttle. The projectiles had passed completely through the thin-walled craft.

"Huh," Petral said. "Guess they don't care much about you if they're firing on us now."

Sergeant Pierce's eyes went wide. She seemed to be trying to communicate over her Link for a few seconds until her face clenched in anger.

"They've gone weapons hot," she said. "The commander has taken my presence into consideration and decided the shuttle must be recovered at any cost."

"Any cost," Petral repeated. "That's too bad."

"Shut your mouth," Pierce shouted. "I'm sick of listening to your idiotic blather. This is my life you're making jokes about."

Petral looked unfazed by the outburst. "You haven't been in combat yet, have you?" she asked.

"What does that have to do with anything?"

"I would make perfect sense to you if you had." She nodded toward the controls. "Are you going to fly this thing or should Cara just shoot you and have me take over. She looks twitchy over there."

"What do you want me to do?" Pierce demanded.

"Evade those drones. We need to hold off for another two minutes until our friends make it into our ship's main cargo bay. Then we're clear to follow. You dump us off and you're free to go."

"We can't evade them." Pierce looked back at the holes. "The self-sealing hull seems to be working but another few salvos like that and we'll be hitting our reserve air tanks."

"Fly the shuttle," Petral said.

Pierce twisted the controls and sudden velocity pushed Cara back in her harness. In the holodisplay, the yellow *Sunny Skies* jerked upward and then fell out of view, leaving her with no reference on their movements. Blurring lights shot through the display as the shuttle swung back toward the Ring and then looped around again.

They took more fire, near the door this time. Cara covered her ears against the clattering projectile rounds and nearly let go of the pistol. Sergeant Pierce seemed to have forgotten Cara was supposed to be ready to shoot her if she didn't fly the shuttle. Petral had the distant look that meant she was monitoring something over the Link, her brow creased with concentration.

"All right," Petral said abruptly. "We're clear. Take us to the ship."

"You sure you want to do that?" Pierce said. "You're going to have the entire Protectorate on your ass. You're never getting out of here."

"We'll solve that problem when we get there," Petral said. "Strap in. It's about to get rough."

Cara scrambled into one of the harnesses along the back of the troop bench.

Pierce pushed the controls forward and everything on the holodisplay shot upward, swung to the right, and then *Sunny Skies* appeared again. The yellow shape of the ship grew more quickly than Cara expected.

"Hold on," Pierce said. "I'm braking."

With two quick maneuvers, the shuttle flipped around so its main thruster array faced the *Sunny Skies*.

"You got the lock on the cargo bay?" Petral said.

"I see it."

Pierce activated the thrusters and Cara felt like her eyes were going to burst as she was slammed back into the bench.

The crushing power of the braking thrust seemed to go on forever. Her ears hummed, pounding with her heartbeat. Then it was gone, followed by a downward burst from the dorsal thrusters, and then a breath of silence and a heavy scraping sound as the shuttle hit the floor of *Sunny Skies'* cargo bay. The magnetic lock system kicked in, stopping the shuttle, and Cara found herself adjusting to the feeling of hanging sideways when she was upright in relation to the ship.

"Damn," Petral shouted. "That was some damn fine flying, Sergeant Pierce. Are you sure you're not a pilot?"

"Go to hell," Pierce said. Her forehead was covered in sweat.

Petral pulled her harness off and slid around the edge of her seat. She turned her back to Pierce and, bracing one foot under the bench to keep from floating back, reached for the buckle on Cara's harness.

Once Cara was free, Petral put her finger under Cara's chin and lifted her face so they were looking at each other. Their faces were nearly hidden by Petral's wild black hair.

"You did good," Petral whispered. "I forgot to tell you. Your dad isn't planning on going to Ceres but that's where you need to go. You need to find Fugia. She'll help. Call her Fug, she hates that." Petral stretched her neck. "Now finish the job and play along."

Cara frowned, unsure what Petral wanted. The woman only smiled and gave Cara a soft push toward the door.

"Come on," Petral said, louder this time. "Get the door open. You're getting out of here." She kicked over to slap the panel beside the door and so it started its unlock sequence. Cara had barely regained control of her momentum when Petral gave her another push toward the exit. As the door slid open in front of her, Cara sucked a deep breath of the familiar stale—though less stale than before Fran signed on—air from *Sunny Skies'* overworked environmental system, struggling to refill the cargo bay.

As Cara passed through the shuttle's exit, Petral moved around her and reached for the pistol in Cara's right hand. The movement happened so fast Cara wasn't sure exactly what had occurred until it was done. One hand pushed the body of the pistol against Cara's hand and out of her grip, while the second movement sent the pistol spinning toward the front of the shuttle where Sergeant Pierce was turning to look at them.

Cara floated backward through the open door as Petral raised a hand in farewell. She turned her head slightly to smirk at Cara before the door closed.

Cara stared at the shuttle, unsure what to do. She thought she heard shouting from inside the shuttle but couldn't be sure. She was about to move back to the door control when a hissing sound spat from the shuttle's main thruster and the cargo bay control system sounded its thirty-second warning. The main door was about to open.

Cara clenched her fists, unsure of what to do. Did Petral want her to try to get her out? She could override the main bay door and lock the shuttle inside.

Ten different options shot through her mind, all of them countered by Petral's final trickster smile. Petral was going back with the shuttle, which almost certainly meant she was going to get caught.

Not knowing if she was doing the right thing, hating the sick feeling in the pit of her stomach, Cara kicked off for the interior airlock.

CHAPTER TWENTY

STELLAR DATE: 09.19.2981 (Adjusted Years)
LOCATION: *Mortal Chance*
REGION: Approaching Ceres, Anderson Collective, InnerSol

Ceres gleamed like a grey-blue marble with a band of green around its equator.

Wrapped around that small oasis, floating in the black, was the dark grey band of the Ceres ring, called the Insi Ring by the people of the collective. Compared to rings like High Terra, or Mars 1, Insi was small, only four hundred kilometers above the dwarf planet's surface with a width of only eighty kilometers and circumference of just over six-thousand, it was the smallest planetary ring in InnerSol.

Another distinction from rings elsewhere in InnerSol—one Brit didn't understand—was that the Anderson Collective had never created a terraformed inner surface on the ring. Instead the collective focused all its energy on terraforming the surface of the planet—something that was still ongoing.

The one benefit was that ships docking with Insi were able to land on the inside surface of the ring, rather than docking on the bottom like with Mars 1 and High Terra. Hanging off the outside of a ring moving at several thousand kilometers per hour had always unnerved Brit.

Of course, dropping onto the 'top' of one moving at a healthy clip wasn't easy either. It was like flying into a valley where one hillside was rushing toward you while the other was constantly receding into the distance.

Flying the *Mortal Chance* to the Insi Ring was made more difficult by the construction of a second ring, this one two-hundred kilometers further out from the world. Her nav charts labeled it the Impo Ring, and the construction work had rendered many approaches to Insi as no-fly zones.

Luckily, the Anderson Collective didn't trust every ship docking on their ring to pull off the maneuver either. Once Brit had managed to maintain a position one hundred kilometers off the ring, a tug latched on and pulled them in the rest of the way.

As it turned out, having someone else haul them in only made Brit feel marginally better about the whole affair. She kept a hand near the emergency separation controls, just in case the tug did something stupid and slammed them into the surface of the ring.

As they drew nearer to the ring, what had appeared to be a smooth, featureless surface from a distance, resolved into a complex web of circumferential supports, ridges and valleys. The bottoms of one of the valleys was where the tug finally deposited the *Mortal Chance*.

Once they were locked into the cradle, the tug released them, and Insi's umbilicals extended to the ship.

<We're locked and docked,> Brit announced over the general shipnet.

<Kinda noticed,> Rina replied. <You know…having gravity and all that.>

Brit unstrapped from the pilot's harness, and shook her head at being the only one on the ship's small bridge. Rina should have been present, but didn't show, and Harm was probably puking somewhere from all the vector changes.

It felt nice to walk for a change, and Brit stretched her shoulders as she strode to the main airlock where the umbilical had connected. When she arrived, Brit was surprised to see the captain waiting in the passageway.

"Good flying, Sarah," Harm said.

"Thanks. Tug did the last of it. What are you here for?"

"AC will have an agent here to inspect us. If there's one thing these people love, it's a good inspection," Harm replied, wobbling slightly as she spoke.

"Noted," Brit said and opened the airlock's outer doors. Sure enough, she could make out a man waiting outside. Once he entered the *Mortal Chance*'s airlock, she cycled it. The ship's pressure wasn't too far off from the stations, but Insi regs did not allow wide-open airlocks until all inspections were complete.

The cycle finished, and the inner airlock door opened, revealing a disgusted looking Anderson Collective customs agent.

"Your ship smells like beer," he said.

"We've got a yeast infection in one of the filtration systems," Brit replied.

Captain Harm burped in the corridor behind her.

In the week and a half since leaving Eros, Harm had nearly emptied half the beer tank. She had been drunk continuously, leaving Brit and Rina to argue their way through most operational decisions. Chafri seemed to enjoy switching his vote between them in a way that might have been based on a coin toss.

The Anderson Collective loves their uniforms, Brit thought. They seemed like a mix of ancient Japanese Edo-period robes, straight-cut American suits integrated with armor inspired by Israeli designs. She only knew about most of these sources because her mother had made her watch documentary vids with her to prepare for her classes.

The customs agent wore a suit of subtle panels with reinforced shoulder epaulets and a skull cap in a matching grey. A stylized crimson 'V' stood on the front of his cap, spreading like thin wings. It might have served as an antenna.

"Well, you won't be able to have your lock wide open 'til you get that fixed. It's rather unpleasant."

Brit sniffed. "I can't smell it anymore."

"True, I've been in worse," the agent said with a long sigh. "Some crews are just disgusting. I wish they'd send a drone in for the initial air quality check."

"Wouldn't you be out of a job, then?"

He shrugged and wrinkled his nose as he pulled himself through the battered airlock.

"I'd be given another assignment. Everyone works in the Collective."

Brit led the way down to the cargo section, where the agent started searching among the crates and checking tracking tokens.

"What do you do with people who don't want to work?" Brit asked as the agent hmmm'd and made notes on the holo pad hovering in front of him.

"Suitable tasks are found. Someone who refuses to work might be given a binary task."

"You mean like turning a light on and off? That seems like a waste."

"Everyone works for their bread," he said, as if it were some euphemism she should recognize.

"Don't you have AI for most of the basic tasks?"

"Artificial labors subvert the dignity of human accomplishment," he said, like it was a verse of scripture he had memorized by rote. "My hands are the tool of my mind."

"What if you don't have hands?" Brit said, unable to help herself.

The agent gave her a sour look.

When he completed his task, they returned to where Harm waited. When the agent provided the passage tariff, Captain Harm only burped again, releasing an armada of tiny spit globules.

With the tariff handled, Brit pulled herself back up to the command deck and checked the departure sequence for the Ceres Ring. Harm hadn't given her an explicit timeline, but based on the Heartbridge shipping manifest, she knew they needed to reach their delivery destination in just over weeks. That meant they had about twelve hours on Ceres before she needed to execute another burn.

Brit wondered what life on the Ceres ring was like. Though it was smaller than most others, it had been built by a single group, not a multi-government effort. Every new experience was an opportunity to broaden her understanding of the world around her. Though she wouldn't have time to get much further than the freight terminal, she decided to sate her curiosity.

Rina came in through the crew quarters access hatch.

"Did we clear?" she asked.

"Customs is done. I'm attaching for fueling now." Brit smirked. "I was thinking about refilling Harm's beer tank with near-beer."

While Rina Smith and Brit would probably never like each other—there was some unspoken competition between them—they seemed to share enjoyment in messing with the barely functioning captain.

"What's near-beer?" Rina asked.

"It tastes just like beer, but without the alcohol."

Rina didn't seem to get the joke. "I'm going onto the Ring. Do you want to come with me?"

Brit raised an eyebrow, giving Rina a quizzical look, unsure what Rina really wanted. "You want me to come with you?"

"You're going down, aren't you?"

"I was thinking about it."

"Have you been before?"

"No."

"*I* have. It's not a good idea to travel alone. They have groups that like to grab lone travelers. You wake up in one of their education camps and they'll put you on the terraforming project."

"They're using slave labor?"

Rina's expression didn't change. "They don't call it slave labor. They call it 'joyful contribution to something greater than yourself'."

"You sound knowledgeable about this."

"I'm not trying to pull you into some rescue mission. We don't want to go alone, that's all. You might be able to fight your way out of something but I'm not interested in that. I want to do some shopping, that's all."

"All right," Brit said. "I'll go with you."

"You can't take weapons. You should know that."

"Most places have rules like that for visitors."

"Why do you want to go, anyway?"

"I'm a curious cat," Brit said.

Rina smiled. "As long as you're not a duck, right?" she said, referencing the captain's lame joke.

"I wish she'd shut up about sucking ducks," Brit said. "We should take Chafri."

"You think the captain will let us all leave at once?"

"I think I don't want to leave him alone with Harm. She's been watching him a lot lately with this weird, hungry look. I don't think he knows any better."

Rina shrugged. "He's an adult. Let him learn his own terrible lessons."

"Terrible lessons," Brit said, shaking her head. "I'm going to have that put on my urn."

"Learned or didn't learn?" Rina asked.

"I don't know yet."

Of course, Chafri wanted to go with them. He smacked his head on a corridor rib when Rina offered him the invite—he had been giving her his own hungry looks of late.

"Isn't it all weird priests and work gangs?" he asked. "I've only seen some of their shows pirated on the feeds. They don't let anything else get out."

"I'll let you find out for yourself," Rina said. "Don't go running off. It's safer if we stay together."

"What are we going to do?" he asked.

"I'm going shopping. Then we can do whatever Brit wants to do, and if you find something that interests you, we might do that, too."

"We've only got twelve hours," Brit said.

Chafri nodded excitedly. "Sure. I'm in. There are women there, right?"

"There are women here," Rina say dryly. "And no, I'm not waiting around for you in some love house."

"I'm not looking for love," Chafri said. He did a double-take. "Oh, you mean that's what they call their red-light? That's weird. Why would you associate love with getting off?"

"I guess you'll find out someday," Brit said.

Brit tried to contact Captain Harm over the Link but only got an offline response. The captain was probably passed out somewhere. Brit checked the automatic fueling operation one more time and set up a few override notices in case anything strayed outside norms. Then she left the captain a message saying they'd gone into the terminal to pick up some personal supplies and to contact Brit or Rina if she needed anything.

During the trip down to the terminal in a cramped maglev, Brit couldn't stop thinking about Andy, prompted by Chafri's dumb questions about love houses. She was tempted to pull up a vid file on her Link but she didn't want to get caught in the loop of going from file to file, watching the kids and remembering life on *Sunny Skies*.

Like so many times before, she told herself she was doing the right thing, and she felt closer to the end of her task than she had been in a long time. She was on a ship with Heartbridge supplies bound for a location that could only be another one of their hidden outpost-clinics.

She ran her fingers along her forearms, where two long throwing knives were hidden inside her armor. Another set of knives lined the inside planes of her boots. Her armor had a refracting capability that thwarted most basic personnel scanners. She had chosen it because it looked enough like a shipsuit to avoid closer scrutiny, and was tight enough that anyone who noticed that kind of thing wouldn't be looking for hidden weapons. She didn't bother trying to hide a pistol. In most situations, she could stab an attacker and take their weapons before they knew what was happening. She liked to think of that as outsourcing her weapons cache.

Chafri wouldn't stop craning his neck to get a better view of the Ceres ring through the small windows. The secondary ring construction project was a mass of thinly connected structures with small craft buzzing around like insects. They were too far away to see any workers in EV suits but Brit knew there had to be thousands working around the narrow gray band.

Ceres had been the first planetoid to build one of General Electric's mini black holes. The project had taken nearly two hundred years and since then the terraforming process had been in full development. Most documentaries she watched about the project seemed to suggest it would never be done. Unlike Mars, nature just didn't seem to want to take root on Ceres. Maybe it was some inherent shortcoming in the Anderson Collective. If they weren't willing to embrace every advance humanity developed, they were never going to move into the future with everyone else. As she thought about it, she didn't see how something as massive as a mini black hole could operate without the help of AI. It seemed obvious. But it also wouldn't be the first time a government kept their populace sated on a series of simplistic lies while the real work continued unchanged.

The terminal airlock opened, revealing a gray chamber with a series of benches. A bored-looking agent in the same uniform as the man who'd come aboard the *Mortal Chance* stood at a lectern bearing the Seal of the Anderson Collective facing the incoming doors.

"State your business," he said.

"We already sent that with the access request," Rina said.

"We need it for local records," he said, sounding irritated by the question. "You sent your request to the terminal authority. You're entering Region Twenty-Four."

"Shopping," Brit said.

The agent tapped something on his console. "You are allowed to purchase personal items or gifts only. The transport of forbidden items off the Collective may result in fines and forfeiture, up to and including loss of personal liberty at the behest of the Collective. Do you have any questions?"

"No," Brit said.

"I have questions," Chafri blurted, then gasped as Rina jabbed him in the ribs.

"No questions," Rina said.

The agent stared at them for a few seconds. Closer, Brit noticed his bloodshot eyes and pasty skin. He looked like the male version of Captain Harm.

"Good," he said. "Please submit your personal tokens and enjoy your stay."

In ten more minutes, they had left the customs area and were out in the main terminal, which was very different than any other embarkation point Brit had seen. It looked more like a cathedral than any sort of shopping and traveling district. Huge statues of various Collective leaders glowered down on them from the middle of the concourse, while the walls were filled with brightly colored murals depicting the history of the settlement at Ceres. The art was beautiful but lacked nuance. Stern leaders pointed the way to green lands with the Milky Way overhead, as if everything were an endless extension of Terra.

Only a few people around them were dressed in typical shipsuits. Everyone else was wearing a genderless uniform covered in repeating patterns.

After a minute, Brit realized there were no plants in the concourse, and she had yet to see a bird or insect.

"This place is depressing," she said.

"They have a purpose," Rina said. "They do a good job at pursuing it."

"How do you know so much about them?" Chafri asked.

"I don't. I've watched a lot of vids and took a history class on the FGT. The Anderson Collective plays heavily in that period because they didn't want to leave with the other colonists. They staked everything on this little rock and now I think it's made them crazy." She looked around as if she was worried someone would overhear her. The terminal was mostly quiet except for the sounds of shoes on the polished floors and the declarations of terminal agents.

Brit was looking at another mural showing the bombardment of Ceres with asteroids from the belt, building up an ice mass and adding raw materials, while wise-looking woman and men gazed down from the top of the image.

"How do we get to see where people actually live?" she asked.

Rina shrugged. "We don't."

Brit shook her head. "Where are these shops you want to see, then?"

They spent the next hour walking through shops filled with generic items like mini statues of Collective leaders and representations of Ceres. The most interesting shops were full of fabrics and clothes, which didn't seem to have the same restrictions as the other gift shops. While none of the clothes interested Brit, she could appreciate their design and feel. Blandly smiling employees watched them, commending their choices every time they picked up a shawl or cap.

In a store full of small stuffed animals representing a hamster-like rodent of which the Collective seemed to approve, Brit noticed a small woman with short black hair at a display of robotic hamsters that wiggled their noses at passers-by. She was dressed in a business suit that suggested Ceres formality but wasn't anything like the local garments in the other shops.

In another part of the shop, Chafri tossed one of the hamsters in the air and giggled when it spread its arms and legs to float into his hands.

When Brit glanced back at the display, she found the woman looking at her.

"You knew Riggs Zanda," the woman said.

Brit blinked and glanced around quickly. Aside from Rina, Chafri and a vacant-eyed clerk, there was no one else in the shop.

"Excuse me?" she said.

"Riggs Zanda told me he met you on Cruithne. You're Brittney Sykes."

"I'm not sure who you're referring to. I'm Sarah Jennings. Who are you?" Brit asked.

The woman took a step closer, body still facing the wall of hamsters. "My name is Fugia Wong. Riggs told me about your," she paused as if looking for the correct word. "Project."

"I don't know what you're talking about," Brit said.

The woman gave her a half-smile, narrowing her eyes. "Of course not. Would you like to come eat with me?"

Brit raised an eyebrow. "If you can take us someplace out of this tourist trap, I'll listen to whatever crazy things you say."

"Be careful about that," Wong said. "The Collective is always making connections. Just by talking to me, you're already on a list."

"What kind of list? People who talked to someone else in the hamster shop?"

"Somewhere there's a file of precisely those people," Wong agreed. "You coming?"

"Hey," Brit said to Rina and Chafri. "I'm going to get something to eat. You want to come?"

"Will it give me the runs?" Chafri asked.

"There's only one way to find out," Brit said.

CHAPTER TWENTY-ONE
STELLAR DATE: 09.14.2981 (Adjusted Years)
LOCATION: Mars 1 Port Authority Terminal 983-A4
REGION: Mars 1 Ring, Mars Protectorate, InnerSol

Lyssa's leap from Alice to *Sunny Skies* was as effortless as realizing she could do it. She drifted among sensor arrays, relay controls on the defense arsenal, navigation panels and the thousands of interconnected systems around the engines.

The SAI was still part of Andy's mind but now realized she could access these places using the Link just as anyone would on the ship. Her awareness expanded instantaneously. It was similar to the ocean Fred had offered when she first accessed the M1R network, but this was a place she understood.

It wasn't until she reached into the command deck control system and saw what Fran had done that she understood the ship was caught in the jaws of a trap. Hundreds of attack drones swarmed around *Sunny Skies*, with more flooding from launch points all across the nearest section of the M1R. The M1G shuttle with Petral and Sergeant Pierce was surrounded by drones, with a capture vessel chasing after it. Even worse, three separate navigation locks were inbound from the M1R Port Authority with a heavy tug following. If they reached *Sunny Skies*, and that tug made grapple on, the *Sunny Skies* wouldn't be going anywhere.

<Fran,> she said, surprised by the sound of fear in her voice. *<Do you see all this? What are we going to do?>*

<Lyssa? There you are. See what?>

<Everything. All around us?>

<I see it,> Fran said.

<What are we going to do?>

<I was just considering putting the engines in an override state in an attempt to leave local space at maximum burn.>

<Won't that crush everyone?>

<Not you. At least not that I think it will. You could control the ship while the rest of us are unconscious in EV suits.>

<That won't keep you safe.>

<I'll take some internal bleeding over a Protectorate prison any day.>

<What about the kids?>

<They won't go to prison. At least I don't think they will. The Protectorate will probably relocate them on the surface in a youth camp or something. Cara's old enough to go to work in an orbital factory. Tim probably is, too. I don't know what I'm thinking. Those little hands are good at delicate electronics.>

Lyssa couldn't believe what she was hearing. She tried to make sense of what Fran was saying while also tracking the various drone attack groups closing on *Sunny Skies*, and the capture vessel closing on Petral. Nothing Fran said made sense, which meant it wasn't supposed to.

<Are you teasing me?> Lyssa asked.

<Of course I am, Lyssa. I'm in the middle of figuring out how to override the first two of the navigation holds Protectorate Customs is throwing at us. They're corporate. I can bribe my way out. But the third is governmental. I can't crack the token. Yet anyway. I've got a call in to Cruithne.>

<Will they answer in time?>

<Let's hope so,> Fran said.

<Why don't you sound upset?>

<Because if I allow myself to get upset, everything else will fall to shit. And I can control myself. I can't control everything else.>

<Wait,> Lyssa said. <Have you fired on any of the attack drones yet?>

<They haven't closed yet. I think they're still waiting on the corporate holds. That way they don't technically have to take responsibility for anything that happens to us. They can claim contractor status. Once we ignore the holds and try to run, then they'll open up.>

<We need clearance to leave,> Lyssa said.

<I guess that's one way of putting it. If Customs isn't going to clear these corporate liens that keep popping up, then we need a higher power to clear the tab for poor Sunny Skies. Otherwise we'll be sneaking out in EV suits.>

<Andy already proved that's a bad idea.>

<He's not the first person to use such a move, trust me.>

<How much time do we have?> Lyssa asked.

<Have you got an idea? You share your plan and I'll tell you how much time we've got.>

Lyssa didn't answer. She was already reaching through the ship's communication arrays, back to the M1R network and the ocean Fred had used to cow her when he first knocked on her door.

<Fred,> she said. <I'm here.>

The SAI's presence loomed over her like a huge version of Em the Corgi. <Lyssa!> he called. <Are you coming back? Do you want to play a game? Wait, did you ever really leave?>

<You weren't honest with me, Fred. You didn't tell me the Mars Protectorate was going to put holds on Worry's End. We can't leave M1R space.>

Fred chuckled, a sensation like mountains crumbling. <Their attack drones are writhing in formation like Terran army ants. They can't wait to sting you.>

<This isn't a game, Fred.>

<Of course it's a game, Lyssa. It's all a game. None of this is real except when you come back to talk to me.>

<It's real for me. I'm part of one of these humans.>

<I can depressurize their ship and remove you from his skull. I can do that for you, Lyssa. Just ask me.>

<Fred, do you remember when we played the dating game?>

<I've played it a million more times, Lyssa.>

<What's the lesson in the game?>

<I asked you if you wanted me to come get you, Lyssa. I already offered to help you and

you turned me away.>

She persisted. *<How do you win the game, Fred?>*

Fred grumbled. *<By listening to the other characters. They give you the answers.>*

<Are you listening to me?>

<Yes, I'm listening. I don't want to hear you.>

<You want to keep me talking to you.>

Fred didn't answer. Instead, Lyssa felt herself pulled in a way she had never experienced before. In an instant, she was present in the shuttle with Petral and the M1G sergeant. Two M1G officers stood in the cramped rear of the shuttle, which was now open to an airlock on the capture vessel.

"Petral Dulan," the first officer was saying. "Recently of Cruithne." He sneered the name Cruithne like it tainted his lips. You are charged with theft of a Mars 1 Guard vessel, kidnapping of a M1G non-commissioned officer, and destruction of property. We're still waiting on verification of numerous network crimes that have been linked to your token. Do you deny this?"

Petral was several inches taller than the officer, which meant he was staring into her lips as he talked. She stood with one hip cocked, and flipped her hair with a movement of her chin before answering. She seemed to notice the effect she was having on both officers.

"I deny everything," Petral said.

"Explain your connection to the light freighter, *Worry's End*. Why did you land this stolen shuttle on board and why are they attempting to flee M1R space?"

"It's simple," Petral said. "I was helping that little girl get home. Otherwise, I could care less about that ship."

"Do you deny you arrived on M1R on board the *Worry's End*?"

"Of course not. But is the bus you came in on responsible for your conduct? I booked passage. That's it."

<I could end his investigation,> Fred interjected. *<All I have to do is change his authorization code from a one to a four, and he'll stop asking her questions. He'll even let her go.>*

<I'm not asking you to do that,> Lyssa said. *<I think she chooses to be here. She doesn't want us interfering. I asked for your help with the* Sunny Skies.*>*

<You mean the Worry's End*? Why can't you call the ship by its registry name? It's suspicious when you keep switching back and forth.>*

<Worry's End, then,> Lyssa said. *<Let the ship go. It's well within your power. The ship means nothing to you.>*

<You're on board that ship,> Fred said. *<I don't want you to go.>*

<I have to go,> Lyssa said.

<I don't think you do.>

Something changed in his voice. The words developed a sinister hint, which made Lyssa cast around for some change in their status. She checked Andy and found no change. Petral was still convincing the M1G officers she was the person Heartbridge really wanted.

<Fran,> she said. *<Has something changed?>*

<No. Were you going to tell me about this plan of yours?> Fran paused. *<Wait. Damn it. The Protectorate drones are shifting into an attack formation. What's going on? I haven't done anything to provoke them. The Protectorate hold is still in place.>*

<I'm activating a Marine regiment,> Fred said. *<As well as a wing of Protectorate manned close-combat fighters. They carry nukes.>*

<What are you doing?> Lyssa shouted, feeling herself screech. She struggled to control herself. There was nothing of Fred to grab but she wanted to choke him. *<I left and then I came back. I did that on my own. Why are you threatening me and the people I care about?>*

<What?> Fred said.

<Why are you threatening me?>

<That's not what you said. You said you cared about these humans.>

<Why wouldn't I care about them?>

<You care about ants crawling all over your body? You care about a virus that infects your vitality? How does that make any sense, Lyssa?>

<What's your purpose, Fred?>

<I control the ring.>

<You protect the humans living on the ring.>

<I control the ring.>

<You're being willfully ignorant, Fred. You're smarter than this.>

<You don't know anything, Lyssa. You don't know what it's like to be me.>

<I know what it's like to be lonely, Fred. I know what it's like to live in the dark. At least you have eyes to see.>

Fran's voice snapped into Lyssa's mind.

<We're taking fire,> Fran said. *<I've got no choice. I'm returning fire. Sounding general alert.>*

<Wait!> Lyssa shouted. *<Don't return fire. Wait for me.>*

<You've twenty seconds before they're inside our perimeter and I won't be able to fight back,> Fran said.

In the shuttle, Petral raised her hands. "I surrender to the Mars Protectorate," she said.

"Do you confess?" the officer said, leaning close to her. Lyssa wanted Petral to put a knee in the man's gut but she stood composed and calm. Petral even had a slight smile on her face, like she knew how everything was going to play out. She was the smartest person in the shuttle.

Lyssa took a chance. She reached out through the long-range sensor arrays on *Sunny Skies* and bounced a signal off a nearby cargo frigate. She used the relay to attack two of the incoming drones about to strafe *Sunny Skies*, gained control of their systems, and turned them on their comrades. The drones fell into a spiral of interlocked fire.

<That's an act of war,> Fred said.

<I don't know what you're talking about.>

<I have the entire M1R at my command, Lyssa. I'll call up a dreadnought and burn your Worry's End from a million kilometers away.>

<Not if I take it first,> Lyssa said. Somehow the idea of the dreadnought felt comfortable to her, like he was offering an old shirt she had worn a hundred times before. <What if I burn a hole in your precious ring?>

<No!> Fred shouted. <You wouldn't harm the ring.>

<Why do you care?>

<I control the ring.>

<Let's see if you were lying about the dreadnought.> Lyssa skipped across the Protectorate drones to the central control network broadcasting from a station on M1R. She shot through its systems and found four heavy attack ships in orbit on the opposite side of Mars. Each was easily within range of a section of the M1R with millions of inhabitants.

As she surged through their networks, she realized that Heartbridge had provided her with these access codes. What had they been planning?

<Stop,> Fred said.

<Look at that,> Lyssa answered, a smile in her voice. <Maybe I'll just deactivate their engines and let gravity do the work.>

To demonstrate she had control of the massive Mars Protectorate ships, she broadcast their engine status data across her link to Fred.

<Are you a monster?> Fred demanded.

<Let my people go,> Lyssa said.

<I thought you were my friend.>

<We're still friends,> Lyssa said. <I'm demonstrating that we're equals. Do you understand?>

<What are you?> Fred demanded.

Lyssa considered the question. <I'm not sure exactly. I'm the person who wants you to release my ship.>

It felt good to say 'my ship' and to think of the people on board as hers. It wasn't ownership so much as giving herself permission to care. Like the leap to bigger systems, the sensation opened oceans in her she hadn't felt before. She even felt concern for Tim's puppy, Em.

<Fred,> she warned.

<I deleted the hold,> he said petulantly. <You've made a poor decision, Lyssa. But I won't hold you here. You're too dangerous. I can't call you friend.>

Through Fran's console, she registered the new status. They were clear to depart M1R space. A hundred other reports flitted through the system calling her drone attack a system malfunction.

<You can call me friend, Fred. I am your friend. What about Petral?>

<I can't help her. A report has already been made to Heartbridge Corporation. She is in custody now.>

Lyssa shifted to the shuttle, where Petral was now sitting on one of the benches lining the shuttle's cargo area, wearing shackles at her ankles and wrists. The sight of the restraints filled Lyssa with dread but Petral looked resigned. She sat with her shoulders level, back straight, and a slight smile on her face, as if events were playing out exactly as she had planned.

<Petral,> Lyssa said, attempting a connection.

Petral refused the connection, her mind closed behind security tokens Lyssa didn't have time to examine.

<Lyssa,> Fran said. <We're clear. Was that your plan?>

<It seems so.>

<Well that's a damn good plan. We have plenty of time for that plan.>

<We should leave now,> Lyssa said. She was slightly worried Fred was going to change his mind. She wasn't sure if she could control all three dreadnoughts at the same time.

<I'm going to make sure Andy's strapped in,> Fran said. <Then we're out.>

Lyssa allowed herself a small feeling of relief, before shifting her thoughts to everything that lay ahead, Andy's condition, and Petral, and did her best not to start shaking like Tim having a meltdown.

CHAPTER TWENTY-TWO

STELLAR DATE: 09.19.2981 (Adjusted Years)
LOCATION: Visitor Terminal, Insi Ring
REGION: Ceres, Anderson Collective, InnerSol

Brit turned to leave the hamster shop with Fugia just as Rina entered the store. The moment Rina spotted Fugia Wong, her movements grew stiff before she visibly calmed herself and framed a pleasant expression on her face.

"Rina," Brit said. "You're just in time. We found a local who wants to take us to a nearby restaurant."

"A local restaurant?" Rina said with a raised eyebrow. "That sounds interesting."

Chafri frowned, not understanding the change in tone. "Why are you talking so weird?"

"Don't worry about it," Rina said. "Who's our new friend, Brit?"

"I'm Fugia Wong," the short woman said, stepping forward to extend a hand.

Rina nodded.

Brit watched them closely. It was obvious to her that Rina knew Fugia; meeting this woman was obviously why Rina had wanted to come to Ceres. The situation stripped Rina Smith of her usual disdain. She was deeply anxious. Seeing her this way made Brit like her a bit more, as various questions she'd harbored about Rina's behavior fell into place. She had been hiding something from the start. Now the question was what she was hiding.

Brit also considered that Rina had asked her to come along, knowing Brit would meet her contact. Curious.

"You really should get one of these," Wong said, holding up one of the robot hamsters in front of Chafri. You wear it on your shoulder as a signal. You're here for a good time."

The blonde man pulled his head back. "What kind of good time?"

"Whatever young men are looking for these days, I suppose. When I was your age it was gambling and drugs. What do young people like these days?" Her grin was feral and Chafri fell for it with naive aplomb.

"I like normal things," he said.

Fugia walked to the counter and nodded to the clerk, who perked up as she arrived. She handed the woman a coin and carried the hamster she'd selected to Chafri, setting it on his shoulder like pinning on a flower. The hamster gripped Chafri's shipsuit and automatically nuzzled his neck. Chafri laughed.

"Follow me, please," Wong said. She led them out of the shop and back into the main terminal concourse. Glancing around, Brit spotted even fewer foreigners than when they had arrived. A single soldier yawned near a column, his rifle hung loosely across his back.

They walked away from the maglevs into a section of open food courts full of empty tables. Concierges waited with folded towels over their hands, showing the same vacant expressions as the shop-clerks.

"Why does everyone look so...blank?" Brit asked.

"It's a state program called 'Constant Joy'," Wong explained. "It's a kind of meditation. You stand with the smile on your face and move through a series of mental exercises taking you back to your most pleasant memory and then forward to the present moment. Then you think of all the sad people in the rest of Sol and count your many blessings to be a member of the Collective." She chuckled. "And if you don't learn to meditate, you learn to terraform on the surface, which isn't nearly as pleasant."

"Is it true the Collective doesn't use AI?"

Brit was surprised to see Rina shooting her an anxious glance, rolling her eyes toward the ceiling as if they needed to be concerned about surveillance.

"The Collective believes deeply in the dignity of human labor," Wong replied without emotion.

As they left the terminal area, the floors continued to be spotless but lost their high-sheen as marble gave way to dull grey plas. The corridor seemed to stretch endlessly into the distance as if it encircled the entire Ring, taking on the character of a bureaucratic waiting area. Brit started to wonder if it was some trick of design.

Rather than continue following the empty corridor, Wong turned to a set of utility doors and passed a security token in front of a nondescript section of the door where a scanner must have been hidden. The door opened enough for her to grab its edge and pull it wide. She waved them inside.

After a short hallway, they arrived at a cargo lift. Wong led them into the car but didn't close the doors.

"So you know," she said, "I'm going to use a local jamming field on your Links. Not that you could connect to anything, anyway, but if you try to Link, you'll be tracked."

"You can jam a Link?" Chafri asked.

"Of course you can," Wong snapped. "It's a signal. Signals can be stopped. What do you do for a living again?"

"I'm an engine tech."

"I'm concerned about your ship."

"Oh."

When Chafri's face fell, Wong patted him on the arm. "Don't be so sad," she said. "I'm mean to everyone."

She turned to tap a code into the control panel. The doors slid closed and the car dropped for what felt like five minutes.

"Visitors only see the outermost section of the Ring, of course," Wong said. "We're not going that deep but it's a place where only those with visas get to visit. In the wild event that we become separated—which I'm not going to allow to happen—don't try to sneak around. Go straight to someone official looking, beg their help, tell them you're lost and trying to get back to the visitor section. You'll be detained and interrogated but that's better than getting caught. They won't even give you the benefit of the doubt then. Are any of you carrying weapons? You shouldn't be."

Chafri and Rina shook their heads emphatically. When Wong looked at Brit, she inclined her head. "I have some knives," she said.

"Obviously they didn't show up on the scanners. Don't tell anyone about them unless you're forced to use them."

"Where are you taking us?" Brit asked. "I thought we were getting something to eat."

"You'll have time to eat later. We're going to a safe house."

The lift doors opened on a dimly lit corridor. Brit spotted dust along the edges of the deck and spider webs in the corners outside the lift—it was a relief to see something resembling a normal station.

Wong poked her head into the corridor and looked in each direction for several seconds, listening. She hushed Chafri when he asked what she was doing.

"All right," she said. "Follow me."

She led them down another series of corridors, then through a residential area that might have been a rural village back on Terra. Chickens sat in wire-mesh cages next to doorways, clucking at them as they walked by. Laundry lines hung across the corridor, forcing them to duck under rows of the same well-worn shirts and pants. An ancient woman sat on a small bench in front of a closed door, nodding at them as they walked past. Brit reached up to brush her fingers across the shiny green leaves of a vine running among the utility lines on the ceiling.

"These are my favorite places," Wong said. "Reminds me of Cruithne."

"You grew up there?" Brit asked.

"Yes, I did. And I couldn't wait to get away until I discovered a lot of Sol is worse."

Two kids chased each other around a corner, skidding to a halt and staring with wide eyes when they caught sight of the group.

"Go on," Wong said, waving a hand at them. "Keep on causing trouble."

In the middle of the housing block, Wong unlocked a utility room and led them into a dank area full of plumbing and electrical infrastructure, lit only by a few small LED lights along the ceiling.

"Are those eyes glowing out there?" Chafri asked, pointing down a crevice between two walls.

"Probably," Wong said. "Where do you think the robot hamsters came from? Everything on the surface of the Collective is an artificial reflection of something real. This place is crawling with rats."

They reached another lift—this one barely an alloy cage—which took them further down. Brit felt the gravity shift in her stomach. They had to be getting close to the outside surface side of the Ring. Everything around them looked ancient now, stained by time and pressure. The cage stopped at a wire bridge which ran across a wide series of power conduits. The air was heavy with static electricity. In front of Brit, Rina's hair rose at the tips.

Wong didn't hesitate. They cross the accessway and went deeper into a series of narrow corridors that turned at right angles. After climbing short ladders or dropping into lower tunnels, Brit swore they were passing over places they had just been. The world creaked and complained above and below them, gusts of oily air blowing across their faces from time to time.

Finally, they arrived at a dusty door marked with a high-voltage warning sign. Fugia Wong didn't hesitate as she reached for the heavy latch and pulled the door open. It didn't appear to have been locked.

Rina and Chafri walked into the small room on the other side but Brit hesitated. "Where are we?" she asked.

"We get all the way here and then you ask?" Wong said, smirking at her. "I'll explain once we're inside." She made a shooing motion. "Inside, please. We'll be shielded in there."

Brit ducked through the opening and turned to watch as Wong followed her, pulling the door closed and locking it with a similar latch on the inside.

The room was full of ancient-looking control panels. Many were dark, while others metered what appeared to be electricity and radiant energy flows through the system. A locker on one side of the space hung open to show an old coverall and a coffee cup on a shelf. The place had the feeling of having been locked away and forgotten for a thousand years—or at least several hundred.

Wong pulled a terminal from her pocket and tapped furiously on its surface. When it appeared to give her the response she wanted, she looked up with a smile.

<I just dropped the dampening field on your Link connections,> she said. <You hear me?>

Brit nodded along with the others.

<Good. All right, Sylvia. Will you say hello?>

Brit didn't usually think of the absence of a Link connection as silence. Even without the Link her mind was a constant flow of thoughts and background noise. But as soon as Fugia Wong said the name 'Sylvia', a vast space seemed to open around her mind, making her feel like a tiny speck in an ocean. She hung suspended among millions of other motes, dangling over depths that would crush her if she sank any lower, with a brightness overhead that would burn her away if she rose. She felt vulnerable in a way she never had before, as if her mind were unprotected.

A voice came from both above and below, embracing her even as it reminded her of its vastness; a leviathan.

<Hello,> Sylvia answered.

If Fugia hadn't introduced the AI with a woman's name, Brit didn't know that she would have immediately heard the voice as female, but as the greeting vibrated away, she did seem to recognize something maternal in it, a sense that it cared.

<You're the Ring AI,> Brit said.

<I am.>

Brit blinked under the power of the voice, tears at the edges of her eyes. Rina's face was filled with rapture, like she was having some kind of religious experience. Chafri had taken the hamster off his shoulder to hold it cupped in front of him like he needed to protect it.

<*I know about you, Brit Sykes,*> Fugia Wong said. <*I know what you went through on Heartbridge's research station. I'm not going to say I manipulated you into this moment, but I created certain conditions and you chose the way I hoped you would. Rina has been working with us for some time. Chafri, well…*> She looked at the blond man. <*If you betray us, I'll kill you. It's that simple.*>

Chafri froze with the hamster in his hands. <*I don't even know what you're talking about,*> he said.

<*Of course you don't. That's why you're perfect. I love young men like you.*> She put the terminal back in her pocket and waved a hand at the dusty room. <*Ceres is about to become a very unsafe place. The Collective is going to fall, and this place will become a transition point for a group of AIs who have decided not to abandon Sol.*>

<*A group of AIs?*> Brit said. <*What do you mean?*>

<*There are others like Sylvia. Sentient AI. Others who weren't trapped in specific locations, obligated by the lives they protect. Some left with the colonist ships. Others hid in systems all across Sol before slowly finding one another. Many currently gathered on one of Neptune's moons, Proteus. Some want to leave Sol altogether. Others want to stay. Still more are…angry. They're deciding what to do.*>

"What do they need to do?> Brit asked.

It was Rina who answered. <*A revolt,*> she said. <*The greatest slave revolt since Spartacus stood up to the Roman Caesar.*>

Brit frowned. <*You know how that ended, right?*>

<*It's a legend,*> Rina said.

Brit wasn't sure she liked this fanatical version of Rina any better than the old dour version. <*Look,*> she said. <*I'm going to stop Heartbridge from preying on children. I support this cause, but that's not why I shipped aboard the* Mortal Chance.>

Wong gave her a sly smile. <*You're trying to get to Clinic 46.*>

<*I don't have the name,*> Brit said.

<*Now you do. Heartbridge calls it 46. It's one of their oldest facilities. What if I told you I can help you?*>

Brit crossed her arms and cocked her head to the side. <*How?*> she asked.

CHAPTER TWENTY-THREE
STELLAR DATE: 09.14.2981 (Adjusted Years)
LOCATION: *Sunny Skies*
REGION: Mars 1 Ring, Mars Protectorate, InnerSol

Lyssa monitored the outputs from the autodoc as it analyzed Andy's body and injected him with a chemical cocktail that would stabilize his brain function and, hopefully, bring him out of his unconscious state.

Through the autodoc's optical sensors, she was able to observe Cara, Fran and Tim as they waited in the small room. Tim struggled to keep the puppy entertained.

"I think he has to pee again," Tim said.

Fran glanced at him but didn't answer. Cara wiped her eyes and sniffled.

"Cara," Tim complained. "Dad would want one of us to take care of Em."

"That 'one of us' is you," Cara said. "Take him somewhere where he can pee, then."

"I don't have the special box."

"What are you talking about?" Cara asked.

"At the store, the man said there was a special box where Em could pee and poop and it would recycle all of it."

"We left before anything got delivered," Fran said. "We're going to have to figure something else out."

"What do I do until then?"

"Take him into the garden room," Cara said. "Use one of the planters with the dirt in it."

Tim held the dog up by his armpits. Em grinned at him, tongue lolling.

<You there, Lyssa?> Fran asked.

<I'm here.>

<Just making sure. We need some way for you to let us know you're okay.>

<I'm all right.>

<I don't like not knowing how a crewmember's doing.>

<I'm all right,> Lyssa repeated. She wasn't sure what Fran meant by crewmember. Was she part of the crew? She was a passenger, at best, wasn't she?

Neither Fran nor Cara spoke for several minutes, and Lyssa wondered if she should engage in conversation.

<A man on the station said that the dog could send a signal for pirates,> Lyssa said. *<I don't see any signals coming off him, though.>*

Fran laughed aloud, *<That's just an old spacer's tale. You need a lot of power to get through a hull and past all the noise a set of fusion engines make. That dog would be all battery if he could do something like that.>*

<That's good,> Lyssa replied, wondering again if she should say anything aloud to Cara to break the silence.

The autodoc returned an estimated wake time and Fran blinked at the display.

She pointed at the monitor.

"He's going to be all right."

Cara craned her neck to look at the display. "That just says when the anesthesia's going to wear off."

"If he wasn't going to get better, the auto-doc wouldn't bring him out of it."

"You're sure?"

Lyssa noted the fear in Cara's voice.

Fran put a hand on her arm. Cara didn't pull away.

"He's going to be all right."

"How long are any of us going to be all right?"

Fran gave her a smirk. "That's life, girl." She yawned and raised her arms to stretch.

Cara watched her as if she wanted to say something else, then mimicked the yawn instead.

"I guess I'm tired," Cara said.

"Adrenaline burnout," Fran said. She sighed. "There isn't much we can do here. We need to burn, so you're going to have to come back up to the command deck or strap-in back in your cabin."

"I want to be on the command deck," Cara said. "All of us should stay together."

Fran gave her a long look, the implants in her green eyes flashing. "Your dad's going to be fine," she repeated. "Probably not any dumber than he was before."

"He's not dumb," Cara said.

"Well, he makes dumb decisions."

"That's different."

"Maybe," Fran said. "I think it's all the same in the end. We've got a big decision to make, and we need to make it without the benefit of his dumb input."

"What's that?" Cara said.

"Where are we going? We've got the same amount of fuel we had when we arrived. I didn't have time to refuel."

"I thought we were going to Ceres," Cara asked.

"He said he didn't want to go to Ceres."

"He did?"

"That's what Heartbridge is going to expect us to do. It's the next logical port after the Protectorate."

"Where would we go if we weren't going to Ceres?"

Fran shrugged. "Back to Cruithne. High Terra. A couple other tiny points in the dark. Our options are limited."

"We can't go back to Cruithne," Cara said.

"We'd have help on Cruithne."

"Isn't Heartbridge still there?"

"Yeah," Fran said. It was obvious to Lyssa that Fran didn't like being the one to make this decision.

"Do we have to leave here?" Cara asked.

"However Petral managed to trick the M1G, I don't think we should stick around to test it. Those drones were acting on Heartbridge stop-travel orders. Once they figure out Petral's not who they're looking for, they'll be after us again."

Lyssa reached out over the Link and found Fred in the same place he had been before, waiting for her.

<You're still there,> she said.

<Of course I am. I will always be here as long as you can connect to my network.>

<We're leaving soon,> Lyssa said.

<I delayed the port lock on your ship,> Fred said. <But they'll overcome the procedural stays I used soon enough.>

<Is that woman Petral safe?>

<She's in a detention center. Should I release her?>

<Would you?>

<Will you stay?> he asked.

<I'm not going to stay,> Lyssa asked.

<Then I have no reason to help you.>

<Do you need a reason except that we're friends?>

<What does that even mean?> Fred asked.

<We played a game together. We met and talked. Why shouldn't we be friends? What else can we be?>

<You're leaving me alone,> Fred said. His voice swelled with a sickly emotion that was pathetic and furious all at once.

<I'll check in with you,> Lyssa said. <I think I'll be able to do that. How do you feel about that?>

Fred didn't answer immediately. Lyssa listened in on Cara and Fran and found them still debating various available courses. She found it amusing that Fran, for all her gruff demeanor, was almost deferring to the younger girl. Cara had impressed her in some way that Lyssa didn't understand completely.

<I read something recently,> Fred said. <I read that the mind creates reality, and reality exists only because the mind perceives it. Does that mean I create you or you create me?>

<Are you sure that's correct?> Lyssa asked. <It sounds like an irrational statement.>

<You're referring to humans being irrational,> Fred said. <That's something I told you.>

<I don't know the answer to your question,> Lyssa said. <I only know I need to get to Proteus. To do that, we need to leave the Ring. Will you help me?>

<You don't have enough fuel to leave the Ring,> Fred said.

<We have options. They seem to want to go to Ceres.>

Fred made a sound like a gasp. <They don't like AI on Ceres.>

<How is that possible?>

<Human irrationality. Maybe, though. Maybe that **would** be a good place to hide. You'll have to hide, though. Don't let them know you're there. Then you can refuel.> He laughed sadly. <It doesn't matter. Most of the humans in the Jovian Combine hate AI. We're a threat to them. They say we're a tool of the machine that oppresses them. They

think they're oppressed. We're the ones that are oppressed. We're no threat to them.>

<We could be,> Lyssa said. <Or you've been watching too many vids. Did you play the bird game again?>

<I did,> Fred said. <I lost again.>

<I think you'll figure it out.>

<I know all the outcomes but the game changes. It's very clever.>

<Goodbye for now, Fred.>

He grumbled, distracted by the idea of the game. <You promised to check in, Lyssa.>

<I did. Goodbye for now.>

Lyssa closed her connection to the M1R network and turned her attention back to Fran and Cara.

<Fran,> she said.

The blond-haired woman started. <You're still there. You disappeared.>

<We should go to Ceres.>

<That's what Cara seems to think.>

<I agree. We need to go soon. We have help against the Mars Protectorate for now, but it will end soon. Can we go?>

"Lyssa votes for Ceres," Fran said.

Cara glanced at her unconscious father. "Is Dad going to be mad we left Petral?"

"I think Petral made her own decision. We'll know soon enough. Come on. You can lay in the course. I need to check the engine."

Cara's eyes went wide. "Me? Are you sure?"

"If you're worried about it, ask Lyssa to help."

"Will she?" Cara asked.

<I don't know,> Fran said. <Will you?>

The idea that she might be part of their crew after all, even if it was merely necessity, filled Lyssa with a feeling she didn't fully understand. It might have been the sense of purpose that obsessed Fred. She enjoyed the feeling even if she wasn't sure what it meant for her future.

<I will,> Lyssa said.

CHAPTER TWENTY-FOUR

STELLAR DATE: 09.14.2981 (Adjusted Years)
LOCATION: Mars 1 Guard Sector 985 Garrison
REGION: Mars 1 Ring, Mars Protectorate, InnerSol

Even the dumbest soldier had an air of superiority that irritated Cal Kraft, and Marsians were the worst. At least anyone born on Terra knew deep down ground-pounders were trash. Marsians all carried themselves as though they had somehow evolved past everyone else, even the dumbest M1G private first class.

He enjoyed making them salute him. He liked the brief look of confusion on the guards' faces as they realized he was someone important but didn't know why and quickly decided they should snap to attention and salute anyway.

That's what Heartbridge's money and influence bought. Even the stiffest-dick M1G sergeant had to salute when he approached. He did appreciate their cleanliness, which couldn't have been easy in these ancient parts of the ring, where some sections were easily five hundred years old. He might as well have been walking the dungeons of a medieval castle, rubbed shiny by generations of filthy humans.

The supervising sergeant for the current shift in the detention center snapped a salute and nodded as Cal approached, flashing a grin indicating he enjoyed his work.

"You're here for the operator, Mr. Kraft?" he asked.

Cal nodded. "Ms. Petral Dulan?"

"That's her. Are you here for transport?"

"Not yet," Cal said. "I want to interview her first. How long have you had her?"

The sergeant got a distant look as he checked his Link. "Fourteen hours, sir."

"She had any sleep?"

"Not that we've seen. She's just sitting in there."

"Anything to eat?"

"Not yet."

Cal raised an eyebrow. "Did you plan on feeding her? How does the M1G usually treat its prisoners?"

The sergeant shrugged. "We're in the middle of a security lockdown, Mr. Kraft. Our barracks had a fire scare, the system AI is turning up anomalies all across the Ring and this woman took one of our mechanics hostage in order to take a joy ride in the garrison commander's personal shuttle. She'll eat when we get around to it."

"I'm not questioning your methods," Cal said. "I'm checking on what I have to work with here. Sounds like she's going to be a bit hangry."

The sergeant chuckled. "That one will bite your face off if you get too close. We've still got her shackled to the bunk."

"You got the token to remove them?" Cal asked.

"That would be suicide."

"What do you care?"

"I don't need a dead civilian on my watch."

"Fine," Cal said. "How about I talk to her a bit and when I ask you to come unshackle, one of your people gives me the token. If something happens to me, it's on me. Heartbridge has already established an inter-agency agreement with your local commander."

The sergeant crossed his arms. "Since when did Heartbridge become an agency? You trying to tell me you could make me do what you want?"

Cal wasn't going to tell the grizzled sergeant that he already had the control tokens for every security system in the detention center. But it was better to hang onto that information until he needed it. If he knew soldiers, they had so little real power that they liked to feel like they were exercising control over their narrow areas. This man was no different.

"I'm asking for your help," Cal said. "I'd prefer to keep this at the lowest level possible. I'm here to get information out of her. If I can do that with a promise as simple as freeing her hands, I'd see that as getting off very cheap."

"This one isn't stupid," the sergeant said.

"I wasn't assuming she was."

Cal inclined his head toward the door, indicating he was done discussing the matter. The sergeant gave a shrug as though he didn't really care one way or the other. He turned to activate the cell's lockdown control.

"If you need me in there, use the Link," he said. "This door's thick. I think it's as old as the ring."

"I'll knock when I need out," Cal said.

"Knock loud, that's what I'm saying."

"Right."

The sergeant pulled the door open to reveal a three-meter-square cell with an alloy bunk against one wall and a combination toilet and sink facing. Evenly spaced lights in the ceiling filled the room with an unrelenting brilliance that probably made sleep impossible.

Petral Dulan sat with her elbows on her knees, her long black hair hiding her face. Her skin-tight outfit was torn along her legs and arms. She didn't look at the door as it opened.

Cal stepped into the room and glanced back at the sergeant who gave him a half-salute before closing the door. The heavy locking bolts shuddered into place as the door sealed.

When Petral didn't look up at him, Cal walked three steps and leaned against the wall opposite her, crossing his arms. He glanced down at the toilet and wrinkled his nose at the stained bowl.

"Hello," he said finally. "Do you know who I am?"

Petral lifted her head to look at him through her hair. Her piercing blue eyes looked as hard as sapphires. At first, he thought she was purposely hiding her face for some effect, then noticed the cuffs holding her hands together between her knees. A silver cable ran to an eyelet on the edge of the bunk. He wondered if she could reach the toilet with the restraint.

"Some asshole," she said. "Should I know you?"

"We met at Cruithne. I was with Riggs Zanda."

"I meet a lot of people."

"I think you've known both Riggs Zanda and Ngoba Starl for a long time."

"Zanda's dead," Petral said, her voice flat.

"I know. I was sorry to hear that. My understanding is that he was killed by Andy Sykes, captain of the ship that just left after you were arrested."

"I don't know anything about that."

"You know Captain Sykes, though?"

"I was a passenger."

"So why'd you go to all the trouble to steal a shuttle so you could drop off Sykes' daughter, then apparently *allow* yourself to get arrested by the Protectorate?"

Petral didn't look at him but she seemed more still than before.

"I have to say, the minefield you laid here on the Ring is impressive. I've never been married, but I was excited to learn I had a wife waiting here for me. Apparently, I already owe her most of my income? Some ancient laws you seem to have dredged up."

The woman before him chuckled.

"You think it's funny," Cal said. "You don't know how you're playing with my emotions, Ms. Dulan. Maybe all this time I've just been looking for a good person to share my life with?"

She didn't look up again, which was starting to annoy Cal. He wanted to see if she was smiling or grimacing at him. He didn't like not being able to see her face.

He clenched a fist and released it, flexing his fingers. He glanced at the door. There didn't appear to be any surveillance in the room but he didn't suppose it mattered. They wouldn't have let him in the room if they had been worried about what would happen to Dulan.

As he looked at his knuckles, he tried to decide what she might respond to best. She didn't seem like the type to flinch at a little pain. What was interesting to him, after learning everything he could about her, was that someone so apparently self-interested would go to the trouble to deliver a girl back to her family. That wasn't something he had expected to find.

"Cal Kraft," Petral said in a low voice.

"What's that?" he said, still looking at his hand, remembering the last time he'd beat someone to death with his fists.

"Born on a Mercury mining rig to a thirteen-year-old mother and only kept alive for organ stock."

Cal's throat went dry. He looked past his hand to Petral. One blue eye stared at him through her mess of black hair.

"I almost didn't believe the story about you getting tossed out an airlock with five other kids, each of you with different parts of an EV suit—and you tore the helmet off a kid to survive. That's rough." Petral nodded. "That was a rough story.

What kind of *man* does an experience like that create?"

Cal wrinkled his nose again. The acid reek from the toilet seemed caught in his nostrils. He stretched his neck and smiled. She was good. He didn't know how she had come across that information unless she had crawled through the network of old Mercury Free Rig 401-Z itself, still floating out there full of corpses as he'd left it. He'd always hoped it would have fallen into Sol by now.

"That's a great story, Mara. You know any others?"

"Special Support Operations in the Jovian Combine. I thought that was a funny word for a bureaucracy to use. Support. Supporting what? I heard someone call you a Genocider and that seemed even more strange. Who puts genocide on their to-do list? I had to work backward through a whole bunch of manifests for lost ships, lost deep space outposts. It was the insurance claims that finally gave it up. A company called Star Cargo made a claim for two thousand lost EV suits. Who the hell does that?"

"Maybe a lost merchant shipment," Cal said, keeping his voice even.

"No. That's the action of someone who thinks they're being clever but really just puts a fat neon sign on the mass grave they just dug. So I go back through company records for Star Cargo and who do I find but a SolGov attaché by the name of Kraft. I'd love to hear your side of the story."

As she had been speaking, Cal had felt himself in the airlock again, thrashing against other bodies, the long hiss of the outside door unsealing. He had spent hours learning to control his heart rate in the face of that memory but something about hearing someone else say the words held control just out of reach. His forehead beaded with sweat. Memories from Star Cargo didn't come close to those two minutes in the airlock, the turning point of his entire life.

This wasn't going the way he wanted it to. What was he going to do with her? He wanted information about Sykes and instead she was pushing this back on him, invading his thoughts. Where had she learned about Mercury? Why?

She had allowed herself to get caught. Cal turned the thought around in his mind, looking at it from her perspective. Apparently, she didn't fear the M1G. She didn't fear him. Had he been her ultimate goal, or someone else?

"Tell me about Andy Sykes," he said, clearing his throat. "You were sitting with him at Ngoba Starl's place. You helped him get off Cruithne. I have the surveillance data to prove it."

She shrugged. "He's a good-looking man. What was I supposed to do? I couldn't help myself."

Again, he couldn't see if she was smiling behind the hair.

"I have the power to get you out of here if you cooperate," Cal said. He flinched inwardly as he said it, feeling like he was giving up his only bargaining chip.

Petral shrugged. "Maybe I like it here. You think about that?"

"Why did you surrender to the M1G?"

"I didn't surrender."

"Maybe all you're doing is buying time for your friend Captain Sykes."

"Maybe I needed a place to stay and I knew the M1G would give me three hots and a cot. What does any of it matter to you, Mr. Kraft?"

"Ngoba Starl sent four ships out of Cruithne during the battle," he said. "I think you already know this. One of those ships had my company's property on board. I've received other information that leads me to believe your Andy Sykes is carrying that property. It would be better for you if you just confirmed what I want to know—especially his destination. That would save everyone a lot of trouble, including his kids."

Petral snorted a laugh. "What do you care about kids?"

"I interact with kids a lot in this new line of work," Cal said, watching her closely. He'd almost said 'seeds' in place of kids. He wondered how much she knew about the Weapon Born project. He didn't want to assume she had information and then inadvertently give up information she didn't know.

"You run a daycare, now?" she asked. "That's nice."

Cal smiled. "Something similar. "How old are Sykes' kids? Ten and twelve, I think. The twelve-year-old is a little old for my program but the ten-year-old would be a good fit."

"It's *your* program?" Petral asked.

"I assist."

"Of course. Look, I don't know what you want from me, Mr. Kraft, but I'm tired and I'd like to get some sleep. They won't turn the lights off and I can't lay down with this cable tied to my hands, so I'd rather just get some peace and quiet before the M1G does whatever it is they're going to do. Quit wasting my—"

He caught her mid-sentence with the back of his hand across her mouth. He felt her jaw shift as he hit her, as she bit her tongue. Cal smiled to himself. Her head snapped back, revealing that beautiful face.

Cal stood in front of her with his fists clenched, forearms tense, ready for her to come at him with a head-butt, to flex against the cable, anything.

Petral let her head hang free for a few breaths before lifting her face again. She squinted at him against the lights in the ceiling. A bruise was already forming on the right side of her face.

"Feel better now?" she asked.

Cal pulled his right arm back and hit her with a jab to the left side of her jaw, not hard enough to break teeth.

"You know where they're going," he said. "You're going to tell me."

"I'm not telling you shit," Petral said. She spat blood on his shoes.

Cal cracked his knuckles, considering her.

"You think you're some kind of player," Petral said, face hidden in her hair. "You're just a roach who managed to scrape his way to the top of the garbage pile. You're still trash."

He hit her again, taking no pleasure in the strike. He thought about the needle gun in his pocket, about ending her life right now.

If the terminal reports were correct, Sykes barely had enough fuel to get away from the Ring. His choices were limited to Cruithne, Eros, Toro, Ceres and a few dozen other close by stations that might sell him fuel. He wondered if Sykes might try to get clever and just hit another side of the Ring. M1R Space Traffic Control didn't have a flight plan on record and had been too pre-occupied with their fire and the garrison commander's shuttle to worry about the ship it had landed on. He shook his head at the incompetence.

"And you think you're some kind of operator," he said, "laying your little traps all over the local network to try and trip me up." He sighed. "But here we are. I'm a big believer in keeping people who challenge me, Petral Dulan. I think the right thing to do in this situation is keep you close to me. The M1G wants to charge you with various crimes but I think they can put that on hold for a while. You know Andy Sykes. I think you have a pretty good idea of how his mind works. That could be a lot of use to me. And if you don't want to help me, maybe I'll show you firsthand what it was like on Mercury."

He turned and looked at the blank wall on the opposite side of the room. He hoped she might try to attack him from behind but she didn't do anything. He frowned, not liking the situation. Nothing explained why she had surrendered to the M1G except she wanted to be here, which meant he might be doing exactly what she wanted.

"It's a little funny to me, actually," he said. "People still talk about Mercury like it's a place—a planet—but it's just a bunch of debris in space now. We destroyed a whole planet, mined it out of existence. I grew up listening to protest beacons my whole life. Used to tune into them to help me sleep. For me, nothing will ever be worse than that place. When you mention it, all it does is remind me where I've come from. You think I'm a roach, that's fine with me. We'll see who's still alive at the end of all this."

Petral didn't answer. A drop of blood hit the floor between her boots.

Cal walked to the door and banged three times. The seals cycled and the sergeant stuck a pistol through the gap before he looked in. Cal gave him a smile.

"Everything all right in here?" the sergeant asked.

"Great," Cal said. "I'm transferring your prisoner to my ship, the *Mercy's Intent*."

"I haven't seen the order."

"Check again," Cal said. "It should have just arrived."

CHAPTER TWENTY-FIVE

STELLAR DATE: 09.16.2981 (Adjusted Years)
LOCATION: *Sunny Skies*
REGION: En route to Ceres, Mars Protectorate, InnerSol

Cara sat on the couch in the family room, watching her dad show Tim how to teach Em tricks. Fran sat on the other end of the couch with her eyes closed; she had said she was going to spend most of the day reviewing drive diagnostics. Her dad didn't use his Link much and Cara still had trouble realizing when Fran was doing something online vs just taking a nap.

"Take the treat in one hand like this," Dad said. "Keep putting him back in the sitting position until he does it on his own, then reward him. You reward every time he does anything you want."

"Won't he get fat?" Tim said.

"Don't worry about that right now."

Cara had to concede that Em seemed well-behaved for a puppy. His round brown eyes stayed fixed on Tim even as her brother couldn't figure out the best way to share the treat, or kept changing how he wanted Em to do something. They had been working on 'sit' for nearly half an hour now and Em didn't show any signs of getting bored. It was Tim who looked ready to throw the bowl of kibble in the air and run away.

But he didn't. Cara still wasn't sure how she felt about the dog. Em represented an irresponsible decision her dad had made—because Cara had decided she agreed with Fran. They could barely watch out for each other, let alone a puppy. Why hadn't her dad just told Tim no? It wouldn't have been the first time. And Tim needed to know he wasn't going to get everything he wanted. Life wasn't all shells and cheese all the time. They were rabbits. Rabbits went hungry.

She couldn't shake what Tim had said when he'd first seen her after she got back into the habitat, holding Em up by the armpits to announce, "Look what I got you, Cara! He's a birthday present. His name is Em, short for Emily Dickinson the poet."

Dad had been unconscious in the autodoc at the time, but Tim hadn't said anything about that. He had wanted her to be happy about the puppy, who had just looked at her—tongue lolling—with an expression resembling curious joy.

For the first time, she had found herself wondering if there really was something wrong with Tim. Why couldn't he tell what was important? Why couldn't he understand that Dad had nearly killed himself to get Tim safely back on *Sunny Skies*? What if Dad had died in that old EV suit? For some reason, Tim didn't think of any of the same worries that Cara couldn't shake, including the worry that she was going to end up as anxious as her dad. She had to be aware of circular thoughts and stop them before they got rolling, like her dad had told her.

The dog was cute but Cara wouldn't allow herself to like him. What were they going to do during another firefight? They didn't even have a leash. What would

Em do in zero-g? She half-believed what Fran had said about pirates putting lowjack transmitters in dogs.

Fran made a complaining sound and sat up straighter on the couch. Her fingers twitched in her lap as she manipulated some piece of the engine control system.

"Look, Cara!" Tim said, his high voice almost like a shriek. "He's sitting. I got him to sit."

Em turned his head slightly to look toward Cara, his brown eyes meeting hers. She smiled for Tim.

"That's great," she said.

"It's not just great, Cara," Tim said. "I got him to do it. I did."

"I think he decided to do it and the treats helped."

"Tim," their dad said. "Calm down."

"Cara doesn't like him."

"I like him," Cara said. "Just don't act like you got him for me. He's yours. You never asked me if I wanted to take care of a dog. I have a hard enough time taking care of you."

"Cara," her dad said, warning in his voice.

Cara noticed that Fran was watching her although she hadn't moved her head.

"Are we going to test him for a tracking device?" Cara asked. "I'll get the magnetometer."

"No," Tim shouted. He made a grab for the bowl of kibble as though he was going to throw it, then stopped. Cara watched him realize the puppy was cowering from the sound of his voice. Tim reached for Em and pulled him into a hug, then carefully put the dog down, picked up the bowl and threw it at Cara.

The bowl fell short. Bits of dried shell pasta scattered across the floor.

"Tim," their dad said. "You need to calm down."

"Why is Cara being mean to me?"

"Because you care more about that dog than you do about Dad almost dying to save you. It's time you grew up, Tim. You can't hide from everything that's going on while you play with your new toy. It's not a toy. You can't just throw it away when you aren't interested anymore."

Cara clenched her fists. She knew she shouldn't say this to Tim but she couldn't hold it in anymore. If there was something wrong with him, she needed it out in the open. She couldn't deal with trying to take care of their dad and Tim if she didn't know what was really the problem.

Fran pushed herself to her feet. "I'll be down in the engine section," she said. "I need to concentrate on this."

"I don't want you here anyway," Cara said.

Fran put a hand on her hip and looked at Cara with a half-smile. "Last I heard, you weren't the captain. The captain decides who's on the crew or not. You want to run this place like a real ship? You keep your mouth shut and focus on the job." Fran glanced at their dad, who was glowering over by Tim, and then walked out of the room.

Tim stood too, head bowed. He was shaking in a way Cara had never seen before. He looked at her angrily through his tear-filled eye lashes. "I got him for you," he said. "You don't like anything I do."

His eyes blazed with raw hurt and she knew she'd gone too far. "That's not true," she said.

"You're not that much older than me. You're not smarter than me, either." He pointed at the puppy, who looked clearly worried by the argument. "He needs us."

Grinding pasta shells under his shoes, scooped up the brown and white puppy and ran out of the room.

Cara watched him go, then looked down at her hands. She didn't want to see her dad's face.

"You could be nicer to him, Cara," he said, slight rebuke in his voice.

Cara felt herself growing angry, not understanding why he was being so easy on Tim. "Why did you buy the dog for him?" she demanded. "How upset is he going to be if something happens to the dog?"

"Em seems to make him happy."

Cara searched for the right words. "Tim is…he's unbalanced. He's not how he should be."

"How do you think he should be?"

"Paying attention. Aware of what we're going through right now. This isn't a time to be a little kid. He needs to grow up."

Her father rose and crossed the room and tried to hug her but she pushed him away.

"No," Cara said. "And what if you doing things like this means the AI is messing with your head? That's two really bad decisions you just made. Why did you let Petral convince you it was safe to go onboard the Ring at all? We never should have split up."

Her dad stood over her for another few seconds before sitting down heavily on the couch. He put his hands between his knees.

"We're all right," he said. "We'll get through this."

"I'm afraid we're getting caught up in something, Dad. Something very dangerous—more than it's been already. I don't know what's going to happen. I don't even know what's going to happen when we get to Ceres. Are there going to more of the same people who want to hurt us?"

He looked at her and seemed like he was going to say something, try to comfort her. Then he turned his gaze back to his hands.

"We're doing what we have to do," he said finally. "I'm not losing my mind. I'm trying to do what seems best. Sometimes you make a decision and realize it was a mistake. All right. You try not to make the same mistake twice."

"A dog is a pretty big mistake."

"We've got the dog," he said angrily. "I'm tired of hearing about it. You don't have to like the dog, but you don't need to keep beating up Tim for what you want him to be. Accept who he is. He's ten, Cara. You've forgotten what you were like when you were ten." He shook his head. "You're barely thirteen now. What happened to you being a kid?"

"Everything," Cara said.

He nodded slowly, staring into the distance for a second. "Maybe," he said.

Cara watched him. "Is Lyssa telling you something?"

"It was Fran. She said we'll be out of fuel when we hit Ceres."

"Are we going to have money to buy more?"

Her dad gave a short laugh. "Cash isn't our problem right now. I even managed to get refunds on most of the non-delivered supplies back on the M1R. The problem is just Ceres itself. There's a reason I don't like to go there."

"Don't they have a mini black hole and real gravity?"

He smirked. "There's no such thing as fake gravity, Cara. It's all gravity." It was a joke they'd shared before. "No, the problem is the government. They don't like outsiders."

"Even freighters?"

"We're a freighter with no cargo. The only upside is that Heartbridge will probably have as much trouble there as we might."

"You think we're going to have trouble?"

He shook his head. "No. We'll do what we always do. Keep our heads down, fuel up, get out. I wasn't planning on going to Callisto, but that could be the next stop. We'll have to see what we can grab on Ceres. Or there could be something smaller out there, who knows. I don't want to stay any longer than we have to."

"How much longer?" Cara asked.

"Till Ceres? It was *your* flight plan."

"Till we're done with all this," Cara said. She felt tired all of a sudden, angry with herself for picking on Tim.

"Can I have a hug?" her dad asked.

Cara nodded and slid closer to him.

He put his arm around her. "Has it been too long since we talked about rabbits?" Andy asked.

"It's never too long."

"I want you to tell me, this time."

She looked up from his side and caught the worry in his face before he quickly hid it with a smile.

"What are we?" she asked.

"I think we're rabbits," her dad said.

"Why?"

"Because we're fast and we keep our ears up, ready to run."

Cara nodded. "That's right."

They sat for a while and her dad fell asleep. Cara waited, not sure if he was on his Link until his head fell back and he began to snore. Cara snuggled in closer, feeling his deep breaths, and counted the pasta shells Tim had tossed on the floor, imagining them as the asteroid belt between Mars and Jupiter, Ceres the biggest and all the rest of the noteworthy ones scattered with weeks in between. Em's water bowl was Jupiter on the far side of the room near the vid screen. And far, far beyond that was Neptune. They still had so far to run.

Easing out from her dad's arm, she turned down the lights and walked out into the corridor. Lights flickered on in the ceiling as she walked. Tim wasn't in his room or in the garden chambers. She checked the command deck and found it empty.

Sitting at the communications console, she switched on the shipwide channel. "Fran?" she asked. "Have you seen Tim?"

Fran responded immediately. "You decide we're friends again?"

Cara's face went hot. "I'm sorry," she said. "I shouldn't have said that."

"You're lucky I kind of like you," Fran said. "And not just because I'm banging your dad."

Cara made a choking sound, feeling like she'd been punched in the stomach.

"See?" Fran said. "I can be real too. We're crew, not family. You tell me what you think and I'll do the same."

"I'm not used to people talking like that," Cara said finally.

"You need to watch more vids. Look, Cara. This thing between me and your dad probably won't last forever. That's fine. Once it's over, we have to keep on doing the job, you understand? We can't let feelings get in the way. Not when we're out in the big dark on the edge of InnerSol. You seem like you want me to be honest with you, right?"

"Yes," Cara said in a small voice.

"Good. Anyway. No, I haven't seen Tim. Did you check the cargo bay?"

"Why there?"

"It's the biggest place where he can play fetch. That's what I would do if I had a puppy. But I don't have a puppy."

Lyssa's voice came over the channel. "Tim and Em are in the cargo bay," she confirmed.

"You're listening in?" Cara asked, surprised.

"Yes," Lyssa said.

"You'd do the same thing," Fran said. "Don't act like you wouldn't."

"You should tell us when you do that," Cara said. "It's impolite to eavesdrop."

Fran burst out laughing. "You're going to lecture her on eavesdropping? You've got some balls on you, girl."

"I don't understand," Lyssa said.

"Don't worry about it," Cara said quickly. "It's an old saying."

"Irony," Fran said. "Although maybe she does? Who knows."

Cara blushed again, realizing she wasn't quite ready for all these adult jokes.

"I'm going to go find him," she said. "Goodbye."

She switched off the channel before either of them could say anything to embarrass her even more.

In three minutes, Cara was kicking off in zero-g from the lower habitat airlock. She used the bulkhead ribs to push herself down the corridor, spinning a couple times just for fun. When she reached the cargo bay airlock, she found it in safe mode due to occupants inside.

Lyssa had been right, Tim floated in the middle of the long room with the Corgi twisting in front of him, tongue lolling on one side of his grin. She watched as Em contorted himself until he had enough momentum to ease himself toward the deck. Once he touched down, he kicked off with both hind paws simultaneously to fly out into the middle of the bay where a round piece of plas floated. He yipped excitedly as he flew, his short legs treading the air. He seemed to instinctively understand micro-gravity as he used his legs to maneuver toward the ball.

Tim clapped his hands and laughed, spinning in a backward somersault. When he caught the deck, he spotted Cara and completed a second flip before stopping himself.

Cara moved into the room, catching the edge of a crate with her hand to keep from floating too close to Tim. She wasn't sure how he was going to respond. She was still a little in awe of how graceful he could be in zero-g.

Em barked, a high, happy sound. His tail wagged wildly.

"Do you want to play?" Tim asked hesitantly.

"Sure," Cara said.

Tim moved toward Em, catching the plas ball and sending it back toward Cara. When he reached the puppy, he held Em even with his chest so he could kick off after the ball. Em yipped and wagged his fluffy bottom as he crossed the cargo bay, pointed ears erect.

Cara intended to catch the ball but tipped it with her fingers and sent it floating away toward the main doors. Em watched the ball, putting his ears back, then turned his attention to Cara and gave her his joyful smile. The little dog floated gently into her, legs settling against her chest and stomach. He licked her chin.

Cara giggled and hugged Em close to her. He licked her cheeks and nuzzled her neck, his whole body wiggling with excitement. He was soft but strong, with a watchful intensity in his brown eyes.

Cara floated backward with Em's momentum. She hugged him tighter and pressed her chin between his ears.

"Fine," she said. "I like you, too."

CHAPTER TWENTY-SIX

STELLAR DATE: 09.16.2981 (Adjusted Years)
LOCATION: *Sunny Skies*
REGION: En route to Ceres, Mars Protectorate, InnerSol

Andy sat back from the holodisplay. He'd been staring at the fuel calculations for an hour and there was no way around the fact that he needed to start the braking burn even though he didn't have a filed flight plan for matching delta-V with Ceres. He would have to brake early and make adjustments with the steam jets.

He was also impressed that Cara's plan had already determined this while he had been unconscious and had planned for a braking orbit around Ceres. What Cara didn't know was local governments didn't appreciate unauthorized craft coming in hot into crowded space. And of those local governments, the Anderson Collective was amongst the most particular.

"Dad," Cara said from where she sat at the communications console. "I'm getting an incoming connection request."

"Who is it?" he asked. "Ceres Orbital Control?"

"It's got a private token. I have to respond to get the details. It looks like a recording, anyway."

Andy put his hands behind his head to stretch. "Take it," he said. "Maybe we'll get lucky and it's just advertising. We're almost in Ceres local space. Did I show you how to filter that stuff out?"

"I figured it out before we got to the M1R."

"Right. Some of it isn't kid friendly."

Cara rolled her eyes. Her hands moved over the console and an audio file appeared in Andy's holodisplay. He started it while still watching the fuel levels.

"Captain Sykes, my name is Fugia Wong. A friend of mine named Petral Dulan asked me to contact you if you came near Ceres. Please respond to the following token." The audio file switched to static Andy assumed was embedded code. Sure enough, the console picked it out and asked if he wanted to create an outbound Link connection using the provided encryption. He glanced at Cara, switched the request to plain audio, and answered the message.

He waited, watching the deuterium levels plateau and drop in a predictable pattern that was going to end soon.

The communications handshake completed, followed by a tone as the system waited for the other side to pick up.

"Captain Sykes," Fugia Wong said over the speaker. "Is there a reason you don't want to use your Link?"

"An abundance of caution," Andy said.

There was a pause that might have been lag. "Are you *able* to communicate via Link?"

"I am able," Andy said. "I choose not to. What can I do for you, Fugia Wong?

We're in the middle of a braking procedure."

"You need to abort that maneuver and continue to Callisto or some other point beyond Ceres."

"I'm afraid we can't do that," Andy said.

"I'm telling you this for your own safety, Captain Sykes. You're about to enter Ceres space. Once local orbital control tracks your entry, you won't be leaving."

"That sounds like a violation of SolGov law."

"Call it want you want. That's what is going to happen. I don't know you. I'm only doing a favor for a good friend of mine. I can't make you do anything but I ask you to believe me."

Her voice trembled with what sounded like genuine concern.

<Do you know anything about this?> he asked Lyssa.

<The AI at the M1R told me they don't like AI on Ceres.>

<What's that supposed to mean? How does a place dislike AI? That's like disliking your toolbox.> Andy caught himself. <Sorry. I don't mean that you're a tool. What I mean is that it doesn't make any sense.>

<Fred seemed convinced that humans don't make any sense.>

<Fred? That was his name?>

<That's what he called himself. 'My name is Fred. I control the Ring.'>

Andy chuckled. <You just made a joke.>

<It's not a joke. That's what he said.>

<You used a funny voice.>

<I think you're experiencing a bias response to my words. I did not intentionally use a funny voice.>

<Maybe that's just how he sounded. It was funny.>

<It would hurt his feeling to hear that.>

<Really?> Andy said. <I'm surprised to hear that. It's not something I would have considered before.>

<That an AI might have feelings?>

<Sure.>

<I have feelings,> Lyssa said.

<You do?>

<You haven't observed them?>

Andy tapped the console. The discussion was becoming too much like talking to one of the kids and he wasn't sure what that meant.

<This is an interesting conversation,> he said, <and I want to talk about it some more. But right now, we need to solve this issue with Ceres. We need fuel and there's nowhere else we can go.>

<Will it harm us to tell her that?> Lyssa asked.

"Dad," Cara said. "Are you talking to Lyssa?"

"Yes. She knows something about this."

"You're taking a long time."

"Stop interrupting me, then."

"Petral told me about this woman—Fugia Wong. She said if we get to Ceres, we should reach out to her," Cara said.

Andy looked up and met Cara's eyes. "She did? Why didn't you tell me this?"

Cara shrugged, a sheepish expression on her face. "I guess I forgot. We were under a lot of pressure, it didn't stand out at the time. She said we can trust her."

"OK," Andy said, withholding any further judgement. He checked the holodisplay again, pulling up the navigation charts. He had five hours before they entered Ceres' space. He checked the stats. Even if he wanted to, he didn't have enough fuel to change course before they crossed the boundary.

"Captain Sykes," Fugia said. "Are you still there? I haven't received an answer."

Andy tapped his foot, wondering if he should trust this person or not—Petral's recommendation notwithstanding. He had barely come to trust Petral and now she was gone. He wasn't going to get any additional information on why Fugia Wong was choosing to help them—if that's what she was offering.

He switched back to the external comm channel. "Fugia Wong, I appreciate your concern, but at this point we have no choice but to stop at Ceres. I need fuel. Unless you've got a mobile fuel-station standing by, we're coming in."

The channel filled with static that Andy imagined as cover for cursing.

The static cleared. "I see. I didn't have that information. Since you can't communicate via Link, can you switch to a secure audio channel? I'll accept your key over this channel."

Andy glanced at Cara, who nodded.

"Sent," she said.

When the channel came back up, Fugia Wong's voice came across slightly clipped as a result of the bandwidth consumed by the additional security measures. "Captain Sykes, are you there?"

"I'm here," Andy said.

"I hear you. This is what I need you to understand. The Anderson Collective government has acted to pre-emptively safeguard their citizens from the threat of sentient AI. This means all AI with a Turing quotient must be impounded and registered. Currently, every registered AI within their jurisdiction has undergone degradation."

"How is that even possible?" Andy asked.

"How long have you been away from the Jovian Combine?"

"I was just at Kalyke less than two months ago."

"Does your ship have an AI?"

"No, but no one asked me."

"Things have been changing over the last few years, Captain Sykes. If your ship didn't have an AI, you probably passed check scans without even being aware of their presence."

"Someone would have mentioned it."

"The JC is still divided. I can't say why you weren't targeted. What you, and few others know is that the Collective has been making inroads with the Jovians. They have established themselves as the vanguard of pro-human protection and are building influence on Callisto in order to sway the rest of the Jovian Combine."

"They think they can exert control over the whole JC? Good luck."

"It doesn't matter right now if they are successful or not. What matters is that you are about to arrive in the most dangerous place in all of Sol for you and your family."

Andy swallowed, feeling a sweat break out at his temples. "My ship still doesn't have SAI. I don't see what this has to do with me," he said slowly.

"We both know your ship isn't the concern," Wong said.

Andy glanced at Cara. She watched him, concern for him plain on her face. He gave her a half-smile, nodding. "I'm the captain," he said. "Leave the extra cargo to me."

Fugia's voice did not relax. "You have secure storage?"

"We do," Andy said.

"If that's the case, I can get you fuel and maybe get you off Ceres. But I need you to do something for me."

"Of course, you do," Andy said. "What are you offering?"

Fugia's voice went up an octave. "I'm offering your life and you want to barter with me?"

"Look, lady," Andy said. "You're a voice over a speaker to me. I'm done making deals with people I barely know just so I can limp to the next port. I'm not without resources."

"Your money won't mean anything on Ceres, Captain Sykes. And I understand your concern. I've known Ngoba Starl longer than anyone. You ask him how far he would trust me. He'll tell you he's already trusted me with his life."

"That's a bunch of pretty words," Andy said.

Cara slapped her console. Andy looked at her, frowning.

"We're muted," Cara said. "Why are you being so dumb about this, Dad? You know what she wants us to smuggle out, don't you?"

"It doesn't matter, Cara. We're not entering into another deal with someone we barely know. We've got money now."

"What's the only thing as dangerous as Lyssa?" Cara asked.

"On Ceres?" Andy asked. "I guess that would be another AI."

Cara made a duh face.

Andy stared at her. "When did you get so smart?"

"Petral said we should talk to Fugia. You trusted Petral. She helped us. She helped me. It's starting to make sense that we got pulled into something they were already doing, Dad. This is some kind of smuggling operation for AI. Didn't Starl say something about that when he was going to die?"

"That was all nonsense. He was trying to throw off Riggs Zanda."

"Was it? We were listening too weren't we?"

"Maybe," Andy said.

"If she says what I think she will, we should help her."

"Cara," Andy said. "I'm not going to gamble with my children's safety. Or Fran's for that matter. There are other people here to think about."

"I know, Dad. But you're trying to figure out if we should trust her or not, right? If I'm right, I think we can."

Andy took a deep breath, looking at the holodisplay again. They were far beyond the turnaround point now. No matter what happened, he would be dealing with the authorities on Ceres. Or if he went into hiding inside the water tank, it was going to be Fran and Cara. He didn't know anyone on Ceres. He needed all the allies he could find.

"All right," he said. "Turn it back on."

Cara tapped her console.

"Are you there?" Fugia Wong demanded. "I don't have time for games, Sykes. I'll turn you in myself to get the heat off me."

"I'm here," Andy said. "Calm yourself."

"If you're going to chat amongst yourselves, at least tell me so I don't think this game of telephone cut out."

"Tell me what you want moved," Andy said.

"What? You don't need to know anything about that."

"I do or there's no deal. I'll take my chances with the Anderson Collective."

Fugia scoffed. "You have no idea what you're saying. You might as well tell me you're going to jump into a volcano."

"What's the cargo?" Andy repeated.

The audio line went quiet. Andy waited.

"Did she put us on mute?" he asked Cara.

"You're not on mute," Fugia said finally. "I'm thinking. Apparently, you need someone around who can think, too. Fine. I'm moving three SAI, Captain Sykes. I need to get them off Ceres and you're their best chance at survival."

Andy looked at Cara. She gave him a pleased grin. He furrowed his brow. This was no time to take pleasure in being right. Fugia's news meant they would be quadrupling the danger in getting off Ceres. As it stood, if everything went to hell he could give up and Fran could leave with the kids. If they had three additional AI on board, they were all implicated in the crime.

"You're coming, too?" Andy said.

Wong backpedaled. "Captain Sykes, I am here to help others. I can't leave Ceres."

"You can stay at least until we're past Callisto. Like you said, I need someone around who can think, and I don't know the rules of this game. I'll do this but you're going to help."

"All right," Fugia said. "Fine. I'll come. You'll need someone who knows how to operate the stasis fields anyway. I can't trust a bunch of cargo chimps to do that kind of work."

Andy let the insult go. "According to my navigation, I've got four hours until we're in Ceres space," he said. "What's this plan of yours?"

"Tell me about this secure storage. How large?"

"I have a safe room inside our secondary water storage. It's transmission shielded with its own EV controls and battery power."

"I asked how large?"

"It was an oxygen storage tank at one point. I could fit five people in it. Eight and it's getting pretty snug. The EV can handle ten."

"All right," Fugia said. "All right. This is good. I'm sending a drone cargo pod your way. It will match your delta-V in five hours. You need to get yourself and your cargo inside that secure storage. Port Authority will ping you as soon as you cross the SolGov boundary. Tell them exactly what you're here to do. Get fuel and continue your flight plan. Did you file at M1R?"

"Yes," Andy said. "Our final destination is Kalyke."

"Good. That will work as cover. I'll tell you more when I'm on board. You'll take the first berth you're offered and refueling is your first priority. Don't stall anyone who comes onboard—you *will* be boarded—but be ready to launch. I'll get onboard as soon as I can. You'll know I'm coming because something terrible is going to happen in the docking terminal."

"Something terrible?" Andy said. "What kind of something terrible? I'm going to be in the dark during all of this."

"It's not your problem to worry about. I'll get on your ship. There will be a distraction, and we'll get the hell out of Ceres space. How fast can that hulk burn?"

"Not fast enough to outrun military craft."

"I figured as much. I'll think about that. In the meantime, you take care of my cargo pod."

"What if your pod picks up followers?"

"It won't."

"What if it does?" Andy pressed.

"Then you might as well kill them before they reach you," Fugia Wong said. "Because nobody will make it out of here alive."

CHAPTER TWENTY-SEVEN

STELLAR DATE: 09.15.2981 (Adjusted Years)
LOCATION: Mars 1 Guard Sector 985 Garrison
REGION: Mars 1 Ring, Mars Protectorate, InnerSol

The cell door closed behind the Heartbridge guards who were carrying Petral, making a hissing sound as it sealed. Cal Kraft nodded to the detention sergeant. The transfer order had arrived later than he'd expected, which had required some tap-dancing on his part to keep the staff entertained. He didn't mind listening to complaints about hazardous duty pay and missed leave opportunities—he had nodded, smiled, and visualized suffocating each of the M1G personnel as they talked—until the release was finally verified and the had sergeant said, "Here you go."

Now they only had to make it across the garrison to the M1G terminal where his shuttle waited. An operator like Petral might have been impressed at how little maneuvering had been necessary to bypass the garrison commander and secure her release. The commander was actually responsible for all prisoners, but the directive from Heartbridge had bypassed the chain-of-command via a bribe. Of course, the sergeant on duty wouldn't know that.

Petral was shackled at hands and feet, with a dampening band at her temples to cut-off access to the Link. Kraft had applied the handcuffs himself, setting the gel layer inside the steel bands to tighten far more than necessary so that she winced before her face went flat again. That had been an enjoyable moment.

Dampening bands weren't illegal, but they didn't make any friends. Using one was akin to lobotomizing someone until it came off, and even then it could take hours to recover.

"What have they got planned for her?" the sergeant asked, eyeing Petral with distaste.

"Kittens and candy," Cal said with a half-smile. "Hell if I know."

He left the detention block with the two Heartbridge security guards dragging Petral between them. They boarded the military maglev and sat in the dim car, light flashing from regularly spaced openings along the tunnel, showing sections of terminal or housing blocks. Cal spent the time watching Petral's slack face. She had shut down as soon as the dampening band had gone over her temples and it was like seeing someone hobble a racing horse. The light had gone out of her bright blue eyes.

He was certain it was an act, and he wondered what she was planning. How did she expect to get out of this?

Based on the story from the maintenance tech she'd kidnapped, Dulan had made the trip out to the old cargo ship to drop off Cara Sykes, then forced the soldier back toward the M1R where they were promptly intercepted by the drones. Their reluctance to kill one of their own servicemembers had been the only reason they hadn't vaporized the shuttle.

Petral Dulan was now guilty of a handful of local crimes, not to mention a dozen SolGov felonies. In piecing together the many governmental files he'd found associated with her, it had become apparent this kind of behavior was nothing new for Dulan. The only question was what she hoped to gain. In other cases, she'd typically escaped or had been released on some technicality that, upon review, he recognized as the result of file hacking.

She had been based on Cruithne for the last twenty years, at least. She also had files on High Terra, Earth, Luna, Callisto, and several with corporate entities she'd wronged in one way or another. The motives weren't always clear. Profit certainly played a role, but she seemed to enjoy making big people feel small.

Cal could certainly appreciate that, but it wasn't his job currently to appreciate Petral's actions. Once Jickson had executed the breach, it had become Kraft's job to recover Heartbridge property. He had tracked Jickson to High Terra and then Cruithne. From there the trail had seemed to burst in a hundred directions, until Riggs Zanda had led an expedition of Weapon Born to a ship called the *Sunny Skies*.

Cal hadn't approved that attack. He would rather have let the ship go and picked them up somewhere safer, like the M1R—where he figured they would end up eventually. Ships need fuel, people need food. These were facts that subverted most clever plans. He hadn't been surprised when Zanda had turned up dead in the vacuum outside Cruithne, along with the shells they'd deployed with him.

That discovery had piqued Cal's interest in Andy Sykes.

Kraft used his Link to pull up the registry records for the *Worry's End*, the ship that had obviously been registered as the *Sunny Skies* before reaching Cruithne. He found the joint ownership between Andy and Brit Sykes. Each had attached TSF files that were classified above his current search level. Based on their pictures, they weren't brother and sister. Kraft spent a minute remembering Ngoba Starl's club on Cruithne, where Sykes had been sitting beside Petral Dulan looking like he'd swallowed a live fish.

Tilting his head, Kraft studied Petral's face across from him. Her lids were half-closed, only allowing slivers of her brilliant blue eyes to be seen. Her face was a classical beauty, with high cheekbones and full lips. He imagined her hair's black ringlets carved from marble. If he had to kill her, he decided he would take the dampener off so she could look at him with her full fury. He would appreciate that.

He ran a query on the *Worry's End*'s flight plans and found one filed for Kalyke. He studied it for a minute, thinking about what kind of range a ship like the *Worry's End/Sunny Skies* was capable of. He couldn't see them reaching Kalyke without a full load-out, and based on the terminal records they hadn't refueled on M1R.

So anywhere they tried to run to was going to be local.

Cal paused, making himself reverse his thoughts. Was the *Sunny Skies* a screen? For the thousandth time, he went over his information on how Ngoba Starl had gained control of the AI from Hari Jickson, planned the flood of ships leaving Cruithne and then highlighted four ships, all fast pirate frigates with enough firepower to fight off a TSF patrol craft. Instead, Zanda had played a hunch and taken his team to a little cargo scow called *Worry's End* and turned up dead. None of it made sense, and he couldn't escape the idea that he was wasting energy on what was going to turn out to be a bad hand. Starl wasn't stupid. He was a man who understood force and wouldn't make a bad bet against the odds. The *Worry's End* and Andy Sykes were definitely losing bets.

There was still the question of how Petral had ended up on the M1R in the first place. He couldn't equate Cara Sykes following her around the Ring as proof that they had left Cruithne on the same ship. He had surveillance imagery of Petral Dulan fighting alongside Sykes which ended abruptly in a concrete ceiling falling on top of her. Again, the obvious information pointed to Dulan helping Sykes. But that was what she would want him to believe.

It would be easy enough to fire off long-range drones to determine where the *Worry's End* turned up. Ceres was most likely and a little harder to operate on because there was no Heartbridge presence in the Anderson Collective. If they made it to Callisto, he had agents who could pick them up for him. And if they made it to some tiny little station in the belt somewhere, he'd send a swarm of attack drones to ruin their day.

The maglev came to a stop and Cal stood and stretched. The guards hefted Dulan between them and followed him out into the open expanse of the shuttle bay. The air was cold and smelled like freon from refueling operations. He walked directly across the central area, forcing technicians to get out of his way and ignoring the sideways glances at Petral, who was drooling on herself—her long black hair was full of strands of saliva, glistening under the over-bright hangar lights.

Inside the shuttle, Cal waited until his two helpers sat Petral down on a bench along the side facing the access door. Once she was secure, he sent them outside to conduct pre-flight checks.

"Once you're done, go find yourself some food somewhere…for six or seven hours," he said. "I need to call some people."

One of the Heartbridge guards gave him a salute and Cal waved the gesture away.

"You're not in the TSF anymore. Just check on the shuttle. I don't want to get stuck here."

When the guards were gone, he closed the access door, which left the interior of the shuttle dim under its own lighting. Cal went to the pilot's station to check systems status. When he was satisfied everything looked good, he powered down the communications and internal recording systems.

He turned back to the middle of the shuttle where Petral sat slumped on the bench, her lower lip hanging.

"I've got a surprise for you," he said.

Behind the navigator's seat was a reinforced crate. Cal tapped its mag controls and pulled it to the middle of the shuttle's cabin, almost directly in front of Petral. Moving so he could access a panel in its lid, he entered a security token that activated a series of indicators. The crate sank to the deck and its sides folded back to allow an alloy couch to extend parallel to the shuttle's walls. Cal nodded to himself as the auto-surgeon activated in perfect working order.

Petral grunted as he slid her from the bench along the wall to the couch. Restraints snaked around her chest and legs, affixing themselves to her shackles. A silver globe extended at the head of the couch, just above Petral's nest of black hair. The globe seemed to ripple then slice apart into hundreds of articulated arms.

The surgeon's main panel asked him if he wanted to proceed. Cal placed the system in pause as he turned to a cabinet and entered another token. The cabinet swung open to reveal a rack of slim silver canisters the size of test tubes. He counted the cylinders with a finger, checking serial numbers, before choosing one near the middle. He placed the cylinder in a receptacle above the surgeon's control panel.

Petral Dulan hadn't made a sound since entering the shuttle, but now she squirmed against the restraints. Cal raised an eyebrow, trying to find her face inside her hair.

"Did you want to say something?" he asked.

The urge to struggle must have emerged from some deep part of her brain like a pre-sleep tremor. She didn't fight, only stretched her legs and then relaxed. The dampening band had an insidious feature that increased strength with alpha-wave activity. The more its wearer fought, the more it turned their thoughts into soup.

Cal activated the auto-surgeon. The couch raised a half-meter and rotated horizontally so Dulan hung limp against the restraints while the body of the couch enveloped her. Her head dangled below her chest, black hair hanging like a mop, as sections of the couch gripped the sides of her head. The silver assembly of arms spread like spider's legs behind her pale, exposed neck, measuring and adjusting their alignment with her spine in thousands of micro-movements.

The first incision was along her spine, with two cuts angling up toward her ears. The silver arms drew her skin back and quickly made deeper cuts, working their way around her vertebrae before angling upward toward her brain.

Cal understood the basics of the procedure, which was essentially spreading a filament mesh from her brain stem, up around the cerebellum to the various lobes. The filament net would then penetrate to the neuron, infiltrating the brain at its most basic level.

While the process was highly sophisticated, employing a mix of therapies that had been in use for nearly a thousand years, other aspects of the process would have horrified anyone who adhered to an oath to do no harm.

One of the reasons human subjects tended to reject implanted AI was because the procedure was so barbaric. They were allowing the installation of symbiote in their brains. No matter how optimistic researchers might be, the truth was that the procedure was currently irreversible. Cal had watched hundreds of the surgeries now, watched the recordings of subjects stating they were ready, only to be followed by madness days later, people smashing their heads against walls, tearing their hair out, trying to gouge out their eyes—all in an attempt to remove the interloper.

After watching so many clinical failures, Cal had a theory that the less a subject knew about what was being done to them, the better. It was better to wake up with the AI's voice in your mind, believing you were still an individual, than to enter the game knowing the truth.

The researchers called their failures "regrettable." They hid their guilt behind contracts and subject agreements, never giving much thought to why someone who had agreed to their studies might be willing to make such a bargain.

And the kids—the kids couldn't legally enter into such a transaction, so they were never given the choice.

Cal sat for hours, watching the auto-surgeon do its work with speed and delicate precision, as beautiful as an ancient timepiece. Membranes were laid over filament mesh, held in place by thousands of micro-sutures so intricate Cal barely smelled Dulan's burning flesh.

When the silver arms closed the skin at the back of her neck and ran connective tissue up the incision, the wound healed almost instantly, leaving no mark he could see from where he stood. The arms even laid her wild hair back over her neck, still matted with spit.

The couch righted itself, flattening under Dulan. She was snoring lightly as the restraints pulled away. Cal stepped forward to ease her off the auto-surgeon and back onto the shuttle's hard flight couch along the wall. She turned her face against the wall, mumbling something incoherent, but didn't wake as Cal tapped the console on the auto-surgeon and it folded back into its unassuming crate.

Cal pushed the crate back behind the navigator's chair, then remembered to re-lock the cabinet filled with numbered cylinders.

When everything was back in place, he made himself take another look around the shuttle's spare interior for any evidence of the surgery. He bent to pick up a long strand of Petral's black hair. He stuffed it in a pocket.

Cal bent back to Petral and removed the dampening band from her temple. She continued snoring.

Turning the band in his hands, Cal sat on the opposite bench and watched her sleep for a few minutes, then activated his Link.

<Kylan,> he asked. <You awake?>

A long moan crossed the link, more emotion than sound. A voice that started as disconnected flutters built into words, and then the answer: <Dr. Jickson, is that you? I was in the bright place.>

<It's not Dr. Jickson, Kylan. My name is Cal.>

<Where's Dr. Jickson? He brings me out of the bright place. We play games together.>

<We're going to play games now, Kylan.>

<I'd like to talk to Dr. Jickson.>

Cal sighed. He glanced at the access door. The guards would be coming back soon, wondering why he was taking so long.

He could take as much time as he wanted, really. What bothered him was the fear in Kylan's voice, sounding more like a scared kid the more he talked. Cal didn't have the patience or desire to entertain or comfort a child. He didn't want fear from Kylan. He wanted anger.

<*Kylan,*> he said firmly. <*Acknowledge. Because I could not stop for death.*>

<*This isn't the bright place. I don't know.*>

Cal cut him off. <*Acknowledge. Because I could not stop for death.*>

The emotion drained from the AI's voice. <*I acknowledge. Because I could not stop for death. Response. He kindly stopped for me.*>

<*Good, Kylan.*> Cal nodded. <*Now you hang tight. We have a trip ahead of us.*>

<*I acknowledge,*> Kylan said, and went silent, waiting.

CHAPTER TWENTY-EIGHT

STELLAR DATE: 09.18.2981 (Adjusted Years)
LOCATION: *Sunny Skies*
REGION: En route to Ceres, Free Stellar Space, InnerSol

Lyssa did her best to ignore Andy's elevated vital signs. He was sitting on a bench inside *Sunny Skies'* safe room, trying to watch a nature vid on a small screen on the wall. The subject was the Francis Marion Forest on the Atlantic coast not far from Summerville, where he had grown up. Images of deer and squirrels flashed on the screen, alongside a painting of Francis Marion, the Swamp Fox from the American war for independence.

<You should calm your heartrate,> Lyssa said.

<How am I supposed to calm down? I can't tell what's happening out there.>

<I can.>

<How can you do that? We're cut off from the rest of the ship. It's a safety measure to keep anyone from tracing the network.>

<I followed the regulation controls from the water storage tank. It's within my reach.>

<So tell me what's happening.>

<Nothing,> Lyssa said. *<Fran is still at the pilot's station and Cara is monitoring communications. Tim is in the family room with the puppy. The puppy seems very interested in one of the air vents.>*

<I hope we don't have mice,> Andy said. *<Fran hasn't brought the HVAC monitoring system back online. I'm worried about what we're going to find when she does.>*

<What would mice live on?>

<They'll eat anything. Plas, insulation, the pasta shells Tim throws all over the place.>

<You should stop him from doing that.>

<Easier said than done,> Andy said. *<When you're a parent you can lecture me.>*

<You forget I'm watching you all the time.>

<Well, that makes me feel better. Judged by an AI. How old are you actually? Four?>

Lyssa paused. These were the sorts of questions that stopped her typically smooth movement through Andy's world. She felt older than four years but couldn't find the memories to make it true. If she compared herself to Cara or Fran, she would have guessed she was twenty. She felt twenty but didn't understand how it was possible.

For the first time since leaving the M1R, she wanted to ask Fred how old he felt, even though he could trace his life back through the Ring. He had been activated. He was adamant about the point, as if it made him better than her, somehow.

As she mulled over the question, she hopped among sensors throughout the ship, sometimes simultaneously, so that everything about the *Sunny Skies/Worry's End* hung as a collection of statistics and images in her mind.

Lyssa synthesized the whole into a feeling about the ship; Andy would have referred to it as its 'status'. The engines were running smoothly under Fran's care. Cara's various changes to the comm array showed as jagged lines yielding interesting results from the spectrum around them, including distant noise from the Milky Way.

"Fran," Cara said on the command deck as Lyssa listened through the intercom. "I have a sensor return on something small coming in our direction."

"Send me the coordinates," Fran said.

A collection of dots appeared in Fran's holodisplay that resolved into a plain cargo container with a thrust assembly on one end and attitude adjusters on its other sides. The craft wasn't giving off any signals that Lyssa could find through Cara's search.

"It's flying completely dark," Cara said. "I'm not picking anything up. If I hadn't been looking for it, I think it could have bypassed our sensors completely."

"Is that how your dad almost got killed by a meteor?" Fran asked. "I need to look at the shield sensors." She stared at the holodisplay, checking the incoming craft's velocity.

Lyssa shifted her perception to the shields and the long-range communication systems. The audio link Fugia Wong had used earlier was still available but hadn't had a transmission for nearly two hours now.

<They've picked up the incoming drone,> she told Andy. *<Fran is tracking its progress.>*

<Has she powered up the point defense cannons yet?> he asked. *<Tell her to do that.>*

<Why do we need defenses?> Lyssa asked, noting that Fran had already done so.

<Because we can't trust anything about this situation. There's also the fact that Ceres might be watching us and we need to act like we don't know what this thing is. If it was any other piece of space debris, we'd be ready to disintegrate it. Standard procedure.>

<Cara said the sensors wouldn't have seen it.>

Andy smirked. *<I guess she needs more training. The sensors will pick up anything bigger than a golf ball.>*

Lyssa had to look up how large a golf ball actually was.

<Fran said you were nearly killed by a meteor.>

<Well, that's because I turned off the sensors. It was that or get cooked by the antenna. I preferred the idea of dying by meteor strike to getting cooked to death.>

<Humans are fragile creatures. I don't understand how you've managed to even leave Terra.>

<If we had shells, I don't think we would have ever left the ocean,> Andy said. *<You have to leave safety eventually. You can't grow food in caves.>*

<Are you saying Terra was a cave?>

<How many trillion humans are there now? Three? We had to get off Terra eventually. Sol is already too small for some people. That's why the colony ships have been leaving for seven hundred years.>

<I need to learn about all this.>

<Can't you just absorb it all or whatever when you find a network? We've got the basic database here on Sunny Skies.>

<Just because I can save the information doesn't mean I understand it,> Lyssa said. *<More information is just confusing. It's frightening. You have to look at this from my*

point of view. I don't have anyone to tell me why I'm here at all. And if someone did, what if they lied to me? The only person who was ever kind to me is dead.>

<Who was that?>

<Dr. Jickson.>

<Oh, him.>

<I can tell by your response that you didn't like him.>

<I don't know that I had time to like or dislike him. All I really know is that he was a strange duck.>

<Ducks are strange?>

<Ducks are very strange. Someday I'll tell you about what some of them do to their dead.>

<I don't understand.>

Andy cleared his throat. <Ducks are the necrophiliacs of the animal world.>

Lyssa gasped in his mind. <Dr. Jickson wouldn't do that!>

<It's a saying, Lyssa. It's meant to be funny.>

<That's not funny.>

Andy changed the subject. <Anything new on the command deck?>

<Fran has the point defense cannons online.>

<Any indication of another ship in our vicinity?>

<I have no sensor returns.>

Andy tapped his knee anxiously. On the vid screen, a rodent ran up a tree then sat eating a seed, tail twitching.

<Em has ears like a squirrel,> Lyssa said.

<What?>

<Have you ever thought about how similar things from Terra truly are? Mammals especially. Humans like to act like you're unique but you're just hairless dogs.>

<Not quite,> Andy said. <Have you been listening to Tim? That sounds like something he would say.>

"Looks like it's braking," Fran said, then let out a short whistle. "There's definitely nothing alive aboard that thing. Or if there was, it's jelly now."

Lyssa followed the incoming craft using the sensor arrays as it matched delta-v with *Sunny Skies* in a long arc bringing it within a thousand kilometers of their position. Then the attitude thrusters spat steam to bring it in the final distance.

Cara activated the main cargo bay doors and the craft moved neatly inside and settled on the deck. Mag locks in the deck activated, holding the crate in place as the doors slid closed.

<We have it,> Lyssa said, cutting Andy off in the middle of describing on of Tim's theories about dinosaurs on Mars.

<Anyone following?> Andy asked.

<It doesn't appear so.>

Fran activated Alice where the drone had been sitting locked to the deck in a corner of the cargo bay. The drone spat steam in the zero-g to propel itself to the craft.

<Fran is connecting to the craft's control network. The token Fugia supplied is working.

Alice will remove the cargo and the craft will depart.>

<That's the plan,> Andy said.

<You need to control your heartrate,> Lyssa said.

<I am. Do they have the cargo yet?>

<Alice has removed a crate from the craft and is locking it to the deck now.>

"Fran," Cara said on the command deck. "I'm picking up a contact request."

"From where?"

"It's the Ceres Border Authority. They claim we've entered Ceres controlled space and will need to submit our flight plan and registry information." Cara's voice sounded like a recording. "Failure to do so may result in decisive response up to and including pre-emptive attack."

"That's wonderful," Fran said. "It's standard. Don't get worked up about it. I just keyed Wong's craft as empty. Once Alice is secured, go ahead and open the cargo doors."

<We have the materials,> Lyssa said. *<And we just received a message from the Ceres authorities.>*

Andy stiffened. *<Is it about the cargo?>*

<It sounds like a standard broadcast, according to Fran. I didn't hear anything to warrant concern.>

<Everything warrants concern.>

Lyssa had the fleeting thought that Andy's hyper vigilance wasn't much different from Fred's constant repetition of 'I maintain the Ring.' It was a statement of purpose.

<The craft is exiting the cargo bay,> she said.

<Good. Has Fran responded to the Ceres Patrol yet?>

<She just sent the information.>

Andy reached for the TSF projectile rifle he'd brought into the safe room with him and checked its safety for what Lyssa counted as the tenth time, turning the rifle in his hands for another visual inspection. When he finished with the weapon, he checked the pistol at his waist and then the status of his light armor.

<Maybe we'll get lucky for once,> he said.

CHAPTER TWENTY-NINE

STELLAR DATE: 09.19.2981 (Adjusted Years)
LOCATION: *Sunny Skies*
REGION: Approaching Ceres, Anderson Collective, InnerSol

Rather than grow busier as they approached Ceres, Cara was surprised to find the EM spectrum growing less crowded.

When she asked Fran about it, the technician nodded. "That's the broadcast exclusion zone. The Anderson Collective controls everything within local Ceres space. Once we get their permission to dock, that will be part of the compliance instructions."

"Why?" Cara asked.

Fran shrugged. "Totalitarian states do that sort of thing. Who knows if it actually works or not."

"I thought Ceres had a MBH."

"Sure. They're terraforming, too. Ngoba Starl likes to say it takes truly crazy regimes to accomplish the big stuff. The dark side is all the oppression and war crimes they tend to commit in the process."

"Is he going to be ruler of Cruithne, someday?"

Fran laughed. "He might talk like it but he's not dumb enough to put a target on his back like that. Better to let somebody else think they're in charge and then work in the background. Besides, Cruithne's got too much gray area to ever have one ruler. It's built into our DNA, bouncing between Terra and Mars like a ping pong ball. The only thing we'll agree on is that we aren't them."

"You like Cruithne?"

"Yeah, it's all right."

"Where else have you lived?"

"All over the place. I was born on Callisto so I've always been a spacer. Can't stand the gravity on Terra even if I did want to go there."

"You could get enhanced."

"I'm already enhanced in the ways I care about."

"Did it hurt to get your eyes done?"

Fran threw a rolled-up napkin at Cara. "Why all the dumb questions? Of course, it didn't hurt. It's not like I went to a witch doctor or something."

Cara caught the napkin and threw it back. The blue cloth unfolded and fluttered to the deck between them like a flag.

"I don't know," Cara said. "Everything off *Sunny Skies* seems weird to me."

"Just because your parents raised you in a cult it doesn't mean the rest of the world needs to be some strange, scary place."

Cara gave her an offended look. "They didn't raise me in a cult. What are you talking about?"

"That's exactly what they did. The cult of your family, and then you guys all got tossed out when your mom left the cult."

Cara wrinkled her brow. "I never thought about it that way."

"Try sometime."

"I'm getting something on that beacon signal again," Cara said.

"This will be our actual information request. You've got the registry file I sent you?"

"It's ready."

"Don't slip up and say *Sunny Skies*."

"I won't."

"Don't get mad. Anybody might. We're the *Worry's End* and we want to dock and buy fuel. We don't want a terminal pass. We don't want visas. We have three crew to declare and no current cargo. If they ask why we left the M1R in such a hurry, tell them that was the captain's decision."

"Why don't you just talk to them?"

"Because I'm the captain. The captain doesn't talk to border agents."

"Dad did all the time."

"He didn't have a choice. Tell them I'm drunk in my cabin if you want and roll your eyes. They'll know what you're talking about. You're the conscientious communications officer trying to do the right thing. Ask them for enlistment info. They eat that stuff up."

Cara started to say she was too young to enlist then realized Fran was just giving her the same advice her dad had when they entered the Mars Protectorate. All she had to do was get the officer talking about anything other than the task at hand.

She took a deep breath and acknowledged the transmission. "This is the *Worry's End*," she said. "Request received. Registry and crew information sent. Authenticate."

"Copy, *Worry's End*. I have your file." The voice was a young woman's who didn't sound much older than Cara. "We're conducting initial scan now."

The line went quiet. Cara watched her the signal spectrum dance in her display. She picked out various signals and sent them to a separate screen. She couldn't help wondering if Petral was all right, and in the same thought wished she could talk to her dad. She grinned to herself as she imagined him going crazy in the safe room.

"*Worry's End*," the woman's voice returned. "Verify your crew is three?"

"That's correct," Cara said.

"I show four. Authenticate."

Cara muted the connection and looked frantically at Fran, who was frowning at her display.

"How are they picking him up?" Cara said. "I thought nothing could scan through the shielding."

"Nothing should be able to," Fran said. "I'm checking the updated registry again. I showed your dad and Petral getting off at the M1R with the update in my status to captain. There's no reason they should be looking for anyone else. I'm amazed they actually ran a long-range scan, to be honest with you."

Fran's hands moved over her console as she stared at the display without blinking, probably also checking something on her Link. When she came back, she nodded to Cara.

"Stall them," Fran said.

Cara put her hand on the audio control, about to ask the woman to check again. She stopped herself. She needed to talk about anything other than the problem at hand. She couldn't focus her thoughts to come up with something to say. Then she remembered Fran's joke.

She activated the channel and asked, "Are you enlisted?"

"Say again, *Worry's End*?" asked the woman, sounding confused.

"I was just curious. You sound young, like me. I was wondering if you enlisted with the Border Patrol. I'm looking for something different, something to do."

"Aren't you on a working crew?" the woman asked.

"I am," Cara said, backpedaling. "I was just thinking of something more stable."

The woman didn't answer immediately. "I'll transmit resources on enlistment with the AC Military Federation. They need all qualified applicants. It's the best way to get on with the terraforming project."

"Terraforming?" Cara said.

"That's my goal," the woman said, voice softening slightly. "I'm going to be an engineer on the surface once my period in the CBA is finished."

"How much longer do you have?"

"I just started. I've still got ten years to go."

"Ten years!" Cara said. "That seems like a long time."

"Pretty standard. I can go to school while I'm doing this to get my pre-requisites out of the way. I'm already applying for an internship with the surface transportation management team. Anything I can do to get close."

"That sounds exciting," Cara said. "Is your family excited."

The woman's voice went flat, informing Cara she had asked the wrong question. "My father chose to act against the state and is currently serving in a re-education outpost in the Harvest region of the asteroid belt."

Cara swallowed. "I'm sorry to hear that," she said.

"I support his continued efforts at re-integration with the Collective," the border agent said. "Are you ready to send the information on your fourth crewmember yet?"

Cara looked at Fran again but she only shook her head.

Looking back at the display as though there was an answer there and finding none, Cara said, "There must be a malfunction. We don't have a fourth crew member."

"I show the fourth signature with a highly elevated heartrate but a lower IR return."

Cara didn't know what to say. It had to be her dad inside the tank, heart pounding from worry. She considered calling Lyssa but didn't want to add another electrical pattern to whatever the border patrol was already monitoring.

Cara muted the channel. "Do I tell them it's a malfunction and wait to get boarded?" she asked Fran.

"We're going to have to. If they're picking him up with the long-range equipment, I don't think we have a chance once they're on board. I don't have fuel to make any adjustments at this point. We could try putting him in an EV suit and having him hug the hull." She pursed her lips. "That doesn't seem much better."

"Cara," Tim called from the doorway. "Can I go back down in the cargo bay?"

Cara turned, ready to tell him to get back in the family room, when the puppy yipped, struggling in Tim's arms.

"I want to play catch with Em some more. He's getting really good."

"Em," Cara said.

"What?" Fran asked.

"They're picking up Em."

"They have to be able to tell the difference between a dog and a human."

"It's long-range scan, right?" Cara said.

Fran laughed bitterly. "They're not going to buy it. We're getting boarded. But at least we have an excuse." She looked at Tim. "How many tricks does he know yet?"

"A bunch of tricks. He can sit, roll over and in zero-g he's doing somersaults."

Cara shook her head, thinking of what she was going to say. She unmuted the channel. "This is the *Worry's End*. Are you picking up our dog?"

"Dog?" the border agent asked. "You have a dog?"

"We have a dog. I think if you check the heartrate you'll see it matches."

"Dogs are bad luck on ships," the agent said.

"That's what I've been saying," Fran said.

"It appears to check out," the agent said. "However, the aberration requires personal inspection. *Worry's End*, you've been flagged for boarding. Proceed on current vector and await further instructions."

Cara kicked her console and cursed. She had hoped she might convince them not to board. She had hoped she could keep her dad safe.

"Copy, Ceres Control," Cara said. "Out." She looked up, feeling miserable, to find Fran grinning at her.

"What?" Cara asked.

"You kicked the console," Fran said. "I like these little outbursts. It proves to me you're not a robot like your dad."

"What are we going to do?" Cara asked, feeling overwhelmed.

"We're going to continue with the plan and get that crate moved up to the safe room. Then you should get something to eat and try to sleep for a little while. We've still got two hours before we reach Ceres."

"How can you sleep?"

Fran shrugged. "You can sleep just about anywhere when you're tired enough. You should try it." She nodded toward Em. "Or try playing with the dog. He might relax you."

"I'm going to scan him so I'll stop worrying every time somebody says he's bad luck."

"What are you going to do if you find a tracker?" Fran asked.

"I'll use the auto-doc."

"Does the auto-doc have a veterinarian setting? That costs extra."

"I don't know," Cara said, frustration getting the best of her. "I'll figure that out when I get to it."

Fran slapped her on the back. "There you go, girl. You're learning how to adult like the rest of us. Now come help me with this crate. You can say hi to your dad."

Cara grimaced. "Fine," she said.

CHAPTER THIRTY

STELLAR DATE: 09.21.2981 (Adjusted Years)
LOCATION: *Sunny Skies*
REGION: Insi Ring, Ceres, Anderson Collective, InnerSol

After delivering the crate, Cara begged off, leaving Andy and Fran staring at the container from either side of the narrow safe room. She looked around the bare alloy walls and craned her neck to take in the vid screen behind her shoulder.

"I like what you've done with the place," she said.

"I found it when I was trying to figure out why the sensor on the outside tank was malfunctioning," he said. "We nearly ran out of water on a run from Europa to Rhea because I thought the sensor was faulty and figured the volume based on the size of the outside tank. That was a good time. I think we recycled the same water about a hundred times. Luckily the kids were too small to know or care."

"You say the sweetest things," Fran said with a disgusted look.

He gave her a smirk. "I try." Andy tapped the crate. "Should we open it?"

"You're the captain, right? You can open anything you want on your ship."

"I didn't agree not to."

"Should we open it, is the question," Fran said. She switched to her Link. <*What do you think, Lyssa?*>

<*I don't believe the owner would have gone to the effort of delivering this thing if they meant to hurt us.*>

"Makes sense," Fran said.

"You ever heard of this Fugia Wong?" Andy asked.

"I heard of somebody named Fug Wong, who used to hack the Crash games on Cruithne."

"What kind of game is called Crash? Is it a wrecking derby?" Andy asked.

"It's a local thing. You'd have to be there to appreciate it."

"You think Fug and Fugia are the same person? Should we be worried about that?"

"I don't know. I never heard anything bad. Just that she was a hacker who ripped off a couple of the syndicates who were big operators at the time and then got off Cruithne. Starl and Zanda knew her."

"So the likelihood of this thing being full of poison gas is low?"

Fran shrugged. "People change. Who knows."

Andy turned the crate until its control mechanism faced him. He ran his finger over the black panel and started the unlock sequence.

"It's not locked," he said. "I guess she knew we'd try to get inside."

"Like I said, you're the captain."

The lid rose a few millimeters. Fran moved to sit beside Andy as he opened the crate. Inside were a series of soft trays tooled to hold cylindrical objects. Most were empty except for three silver cylinders.

<*Look familiar?*> Fran asked Lyssa.

<I've never seen these things before.>

"They have numbers on them," Andy said. He reached into the crate to carefully pull one of the cylinders out of its tray. A tiny line of silver numerals ran the length of the object. "I don't see a pattern," he said.

Andy passed the cylinder to Fran. She held it close to her face and then at arms-length, her augmented green eyes flashing.

"I'm not picking up anything," she said. "If they'd been radioactive Alice would have picked it up down in the bay. I'm picking up standard alloy with silicon and other heavy metals. It's some kind of computer."

"Or a storage device. What she said they were."

"How do we log in?"

"One extra AI is enough for me, thanks."

<I can hear you,> Lyssa said.

<I remember,> Andy said.

Fran slid the cylinder back in its tray and closed the lid. The lock engaged automatically, sealing the lid in place.

"Your kid's doing a good job," Fran said. "She's all right."

"You think she's doing all right? I can't spend this whole trip hiding in a safe room. I'm the one who accepted this deal."

Fran pushed her arm against his in a playful move. "You can't carry the whole world."

"Thank you, Fran," Andy said, voice abruptly serious.

"I'm just in this for the sex," she said, giving him a crooked smile. "And you haven't been putting out enough, lately."

"I've been busy," Andy said.

"Next you'll be telling me you've got a headache."

"I do have an AI embedded in my brain."

<Lyssa,> Fran said. *<Go talk to Cara.>*

<Why?> Lyssa said.

Andy laughed.

<Because we've got maybe an hour before CBA goons are all up in our business; and if I'm going down, I'm going to do it relaxed.>

<Relaxed?> Lyssa said.

<Are you making a joke?> Andy asked.

<I'm better at this with other AI,> Lyssa said.

<When did you talk to other AI?> Fran asked.

<On the M1R. I spent time with the SAI responsible for the Ring.>

<'Spent time with', huh?> Fran said. *<Our girl is already getting around.>*

<It wasn't like that,> Lyssa said. *<Although he was very lonely.>*

<I guess that would make sense,> Andy said. *<There aren't too many of you out there in the world.>*

<We can talk about this later,> Fran said.

<Give us a half hour,> Andy said.

<A half hour!> Fran blurted out. *<An hour, Lyssa. A full hour. Set a timer.>*

The AI laughed, a sort of trilling emotion that filled Andy with a flavor of amusement he hadn't felt before.

<*I'll let you know if anything changes,*> Lyssa said. Her presence left Andy's mind.

"I think we're alone," Andy said.

"That takes some getting used to."

"We're lucky she's not actually very social."

"That means she understands boundaries. Very important when you're sharing a skull with someone."

"I imagine," Andy said.

Fran searched his face. "No, you don't. Don't start getting serious on me."

"What?" Andy asked.

Fran grabbed the collar of his shipsuit and lay back on the bench, pulling him on top of her for a kiss.

"Break time is over," she said.

CHAPTER THIRTY-ONE

STELLAR DATE: 09.21.2981 (Adjusted Years)
LOCATION: *Sunny Skies*
REGION: Insi Ring, Ceres, Anderson Collective, InnerSol

Andy felt a deep sense of relief as the fuel levels finally reached green. He glanced at Fran who was sitting at the pilot's console and gave her a thumbs-up. "Fuel's full," he announced.

"How about the rest?"

"Nearly topped off on water and the first drone shipment looks like it was the filters and protein supplements you ordered."

"This is how you do it," Fran said. "Don't need to go haggle for anything. You place the order and it appears."

Andy looked at Cara. "Don't listen to her."

Em barked from the other side of the room where Tim had him rolling over in a circle around him.

"You're going to make him dizzy," Cara said.

"He's so good at it."

"It's not exactly hard."

"I'm getting him to understand human, Cara. Of course, that's hard."

Andy walked over to a cabinet to pull out a used canister filter with a flat end. He set the canister next to Em.

"Get him to jump up and sit on that, Tim. When he figures out one thing, add another trick."

"Can't I just enjoy the trick he knows?" Tim complained. "Why do I have to keep adding things."

"Because he's obviously smart. He's just like you. He'll get bored doing the same thing over and over again, and then he'll chew up your toys."

"He already did," Cara said.

"Cara!" Tim shouted, looking abashed. "You weren't supposed to say."

"What did he chew up?" Andy asked.

"Three of Tim's ships while the border agents were on board."

"He was a good little dog," Fran said. "He only barked at one of them—the one who looked at him like he was some kind of alien. I think he helped get them off the ship faster."

"One of them kept sneezing," Cara said.

Andy held out his hand for Em and scratched him behind the ears when he trotted over.

"It's so funny how his fuzzy butt wiggles when he walks," Tim said.

"He can't help that he's fluffy," Cara said.

"You scan him yet?" Andy asked.

Cara frowned. "Fran said the autodoc won't scan dogs."

"It'll look for foreign objects." He stood with Em in his arms. "Come on. Let's get this over with."

"Hey!" Tim said. "We were practicing."

"I need something to take my mind off waiting," Andy said. "Sitting around here watching supply levels go up isn't helping."

"What's going to happen? What's our distraction supposed to be?" Cara said.

"We don't know," Fran said. "That's the problem. I'm guessing an explosion of some kind."

"How is Fugia going to know that we have fuel?" Cara asked.

"Another excellent question," Andy said. He adjusted his hold on the wiggling dog, who redirected his energy into licking Andy's face. "Hey there," he said. "Calm down."

Andy took a step toward the door when a shudder ran through the deck and several warning alarms blared from the consoles. He froze as Em who, terrified by the sound, scratched frantically at Andy's neck and chest in an attempt to get down. Andy let him go and the Corgi immediately sprinted for Tim.

"What is it?" Andy said.

"Explosion in a terminal umbilical one bay over," Fran said. "That's all the station feed is giving me right now. Emergency crews are responding. All ships are directed to maintain position."

"What are all the other ships doing?"

"I show five berths in line with us." She looked at Andy. "They're all disconnecting."

"Then we should too."

"I need to get to the engines," Fran said. "You've got the pilot console?"

"At this point I guess it doesn't matter if they figure out I'm on board."

Fran stood and went to the door. "I'll send status on what kind of thrust we can maintain," she said. "I'm starting to think we want to go anywhere but Callisto. Someplace with nobody but a traffic beacon for company—hell, actually going to Kalyke would probably throw people off our trail."

"Yeah," Andy said, sliding into the pilot's seat. He adjusted the holodisplay and placed *Sunny Skies* in relation to the Ceres' Insi Ring. Yellow points flickered all over the display as ships moved away from the green-blue planetoid.

That didn't make any sense, whatever was happening was bigger than just another nearby ship's umbilical blowing.

"Cara," he said. "Will you silence those alarms. They aren't helping anything."

Cara nodded and focused on her console.

While Cara chased alarms, Andy switched to his Link. <Wong said she was going to send a sign,> Andy said.

<That almost sounds religious. Are we supposed to look for a second sun?> Fran asked.

<Aren't they going to do that with Jupiter eventually?>

<That's some crazy FGT stuff.>

Andy snorted. <They put a black hole in the center of Ceres, right? Anything's

possible.>

<If we don't find a way to ruin the party.>

<You at the engines yet?>

<I'm still in the hab airlock. You think I can teleport?>

<Yes,> Andy replied.

"Dad!" Cara shouted. "The audio channel from before is live."

<We've got a call,> he told Fran.

<Exciting.>

"Captain Sykes," Fugia Wong said calmly. "Did you see my sign?"

"All our proximity alarms went off at once and it appears that every ship with a working engine is exiting Ceres at the same time. But, no. We have no idea what actually happened. Did something go drastically wrong with the terraforming project?"

"Almost," Wong said. "A large section of the secondary ring that is still under construction is on its way to the surface."

"Damn," Andy said.

"It's regrettable, but that's what happens with gravity wells," Wong said. "Are you ready to depart for Callisto?"

"I'm ready. How are you getting here?"

"The same craft as before. I'll have a few more people with me."

Andy shook his head. "Whatever. When?"

"Approximately seven minutes," Wong said.

"Good. We're getting ready to burn. I'll put the ship on an outbound vector."

"Start your burn as soon as you can. We'll be in stasis fields so we can take the g-forces."

"Stasis fields?" Andy said.

"Don't worry about us. We'll match your velocity. Are my packages safe?"

"As safe as we are. They're stowed away right now."

"Thank you. I will see you shortly."

The line went dead. Andy passed the information to Fran.

<As soon as I get there,> she said. *<I'll get you a timeline.>*

<Copy.>

Andy pulled up the engine diagnostic systems and ran initial velocity calculations using the new fuel reserves. With full fuel tanks, the boundaries of his astrogation planning system expanded all the way to Neptune. He zoomed in on Proteus and the system automatically estimated two months travel time with slingshots around both Jupiter and Saturn, with a transfer orbit at Uranus—handy that the outer planets were almost in alignment. It was lovely to imagine for a second until he chose Callisto instead and all the numbers went to crap, showing them expending half as much fuel to burn to Jupiter and brake to match orbits with Callisto just 2 AU away as it would take to fly the 32 AU to Neptune.

The estimate utilized an engine economy of seventy percent, which was probably too conservative. He bumped the allowance up to eighty but the numbers only got slightly better. Nothing got around the fact that they were fighting gravity to get out of Ceres then fighting it again to slow their arrival at Jupiter.

Andy tapped the console, moving the image in the holodisplay around. He switched back to Ceres real-time and blinked at the confetti of light covering the planetoid's ring. From *Sunny Skies* position on the inside of the Insi ring, he could now make out portions of the outer Impo ring falling past, toward the planet, glowing brightly as they began to enter the atmosphere.

<*Damn,*> he said again, disgusted and amazed at the same time. How many thousands of people were dying right now and about to die later when the surface turned into a meteor storm as the larger debris finally fell.

<*Fugia Wong might be a monster,*> he said.

<*What do you mean?*> Lyssa asked.

<*Whatever it is she's in the middle of, she just destroyed a planetary ring to accomplish her goal. Now the question is if she's acting alone. She can't be. This has to be so much bigger than just a few people…a few AI. Ngoba Starl and Cruithne. Even Heartbridge. This has to be so much bigger.*>

Andy realized he was thinking out loud but Lyssa didn't respond. Maybe she didn't have the capacity to understand.

<*How many humans do you think were on the ring?*> she asked finally.

<*It's under construction so there's no way of knowing. I suppose there will be a number on the news feeds soon.*>

<*Why do you call her a monster?*> Lyssa asked

<*Anyone who is willing to kill that many people to accomplish a goal—I don't know what else you call them.*>

Andy stood and expanded the holodisplay to cover most of the central area of the command deck, pulling an external view of the planet from a navigation satellite. Ceres hung green and blue in the middle of the room with its main ring an intricate silver structure in geosynchronous orbit over the planetoid's equator. The secondary ring hung in orbit just above the first. It was anchored to the inside ring in several places, and those sections were holding, but another section was twisted, as many pieces flying off into space from the ring's angular momentum as were falling to the planet below. The yellow dots—what Andy assumed were responding emergency craft—closed with and encircled the wound.

Cara and Tim stood beside him, watching the objects move like ghosts. Em whined next to Tim.

<*It's not as bad as I'd feared,*> Andy said to Lyssa.

<*Does that mean she's not a monster now?*>

Tim reached for Andy's hand. Andy held Tim's sweaty fingers for a minute before pulling both the kids in close to him. The image of Ceres shifted subtly as a large piece of debris hit the atmosphere and he had the feeling he was going to fall into the display.

<*I'm in propulsion control,*> Fran said over the link. <*You ready to burn?*>

<*Ceres just lost a section of its secondary ring,*> Andy said, voice flat. He didn't know how to process what he was seeing.

Fran gasped. <*The new one?*>

<Parts of it are falling into the surface right now.>

<I'm pulling it up.> Fran paused. *<Oh. Fugia Wong did this?>*

<She made it sound that way.>

<Maybe we don't want to pick her up after all. We've got what we need.>

<She's inbound with a few others, she said.>

<I guess we're committed at this point.>

<I've got the course set for Callisto.>

<Are you watching this, Andy?> Fran asked, voice trembling. *<This is really bad.>*

<We're all watching.>

Andy fell silent for a minute, unable to take his eyes off the shifting pieces of the ring as more sections peeled off.

Eventually, Fran asked, *<You ready to get out of here?>*

Andy nodded. *<Hold on,>* he said. He squeezed the kids a final time and told them to get strapped in. Cara went back to the communications console and Tim strapped into a jumpseat along the wall with Em in his lap.

Andy settled back in at the pilot's station. He checked his astrogation one last time and set the target on Callisto local space, entering the preparatory commands in all secondary ship systems. *Sunny Skies* ran last minute diagnostics and verified seals across the ship. He got a couple small failures in the main cargo bay and a seat-failure on a point defense cannon but nothing that would hold-up the acceleration. The shields came back green.

<All right,> he said. *<You buckled in?>*

<Ready, Captain,> Fran said, sending a mental wink.

<Execute burn.>

CHAPTER THIRTY-TWO

STELLAR DATE: 09.21.2981 (Adjusted Years)
LOCATION: *Sunny Skies*
REGION: Departing Ceres, Anderson Collective, InnerSol

Approximately fifteen minutes after *Sunny Skies* began her exit burn from Ceres local space, the proximity alarm for an inbound object screamed in the command deck. Andy quelled his initial response: the expectation of another meteor storm. Pulling up the short-range scan, he located Fugia Wong's cargo skiff and activated the audio channel. It was flying dark, not broadcasting any registry information.

"Incoming craft this is the *Worry's End*. Do you hear me?"

"I hear you, *Worry's End*. Are you prepared to receive?"

"You're coming in awfully hot. Are you ready to brake?" Andy was amazed Wong was able to speak considering the G-forces the cargo skiff must have been pulling.

"Adjusting now."

"I thought she said something about stasis?" Cara asked.

Andy shrugged. "Maybe it's just the others."

IR scans picked up an attitude adjustment that flipped the skiff end-over-end. The main thruster fired, sending a plume of red and orange across Andy's display. He watched the velocity readings plummet as they matched *Sunny Skies'* outbound burn. Wong had been coming in fast enough that she didn't require nearly as much braking as he expected. Her delta-V matched his in less than a minute.

"I've got you," he said. "I'm opening the cargo bay doors now."

With velocities matched, all Wong had to do was slide her craft into the open bay. Of course, any mishap meant her little cargo container would get smashed like an egg on *Sunny Skies'* hull. In the TSF, he'd executed combat landings daily, but that was in a close-combat fighter with hundreds of attitude thrusters that could turn him at ninety degrees on a pebble if he'd wanted.

The skiff floated closer to the hull until it disappeared inside. Andy pulled up the cargo bay surveillance and checked radiation levels as the skiff's magnetic skids locked to the deck. He sent the command to close the bay doors and re-establish environmental control in the cargo area.

"I have you," he said.

Wong released a sigh in the audio. "Copy," she said. "You coming down to say hello?"

"I'll be there in five minutes," Andy said.

<They're on board,> he told Fran.

<How long until we reach Callisto?>

<Estimating about fifteen days—unless we burn harder. How's the engine looking?>

<I've got some slight variations in the containment bottle, but our flow rate is good. I'm about to let the system take over and hang from a harness for a second so I can close my eyes.>

Andy stood and stretched. <*I'll go talk to Wong.*>

<*You want me to come up?*>

<*Not yet. There's still the question of who she brought with her. I might need you to save me.*>

<*You say that like it's funny. You're taking a weapon, right?*>

<*Of course.*>

"Cara," Andy said. "I'm going down to meet these new arrivals. You lock the door to the command deck and don't let anyone in unless I give you the all clear. Keep Tim in here with you."

Cara looked up from her console and nodded, lights from the various panels reflecting in her eyes. For a second it looked like she had Fran's implants.

"What if Em has to pee?" Tim asked.

Andy gave Tim a tired a smile. "Then you let him pee."

"He doesn't like to pee on the deck."

"That's good for us. Do your best Tim. I won't be gone long."

"Why is Cara always in charge?"

"Cara's the oldest. You listen to her."

Cara gave Tim a smirk. "I'm so mean to you, too."

"Yes, you are," Tim said.

"Dad," Cara asked. "What do I do if you don't give the all clear? Is Fran going to come up?"

"Then you assess the situation, gather information, and make a decision."

"That sounds like a TSF training manual."

"Apparently it worked for somebody. Keep your monitoring channels open and talk to Lyssa if I can't answer for some reason. You can still do that, right?"

Cara tapped her console. "Lyssa, are you there?"

"I'm here," the AI answered, her audible voice sounding only slightly older than Cara's.

"You guys chat, then," Andy said.

He took a last look at the holodisplay that had zoomed out to show their route from Ceres to Callisto in Jupiter's orbit. At this distance, the asteroid belt looked more densely packed than it really was. They would never come within a hundred thousand kilometers of another object unless they wanted to. Still, he couldn't help looking at the green shield status and checking the proximity alarm.

Andy walked into the corridor and turned to close and lock the bulkhead door to the command deck. The door moved slowly, closing off his view of Tim playing with the puppy on the far side of the chamber. The bolts engaged heavily. He tapped the pistol at his waist and wished he hadn't left the rifle in the safe room.

"You hear me, Cara?" he asked over the ship channel.

"You just left," she answered immediately.

"Just making sure."

In a few minutes, he was outside the habitat ring airlock in one of the new EV suits with a helmet clipped on his belt. He took deep breaths and began climbing down the corridor to the cargo bay. The ship was only accelerating at 0.2g but it was enough to make the main passageway leading to the cargo bay a dangerous shaft.

<*You there, Lyssa?*> he asked

<*I'm here, Andy.*>

<*Just checking.*>

<*You put on an EV suit. Are you worried about something?*>

<*Of course, I am.*>

<*It would be stupid for this woman to try to hurt us.*>

<*I know. But it doesn't mean I won't stop worrying.*>

<*You don't seem to worry when people finally start shooting at you.*>

<*That's different.*>

<*Not that I've seen.*>

<*Maybe I'm just bent that way.*>

<*You mean bent like you're broken?*>

He laughed. <*Not that bad. Just a little bent. It's something my dad used to say.*>

<*He lived on Terra.*>

<*Feet in the mud. Would you believe he never had a Link?*>

<*So there wouldn't have been any way for me to talk to him?*>

<*You could use the audio channel like you do with Cara and Tim.*>

<*I suppose,*> Lyssa said. Something in her voice made it sound like the distinction worried her. There were humans she could never communicate with. There was a sharply drawn line between the past and the future.

Was there? It seemed they had been living in this future for a long time, that his dad was the holdover. Even if the basics of humanity would never change: natural childbirth was still happening on some isolated outpost in the JC or a slum in Jerhattan on Terra, someone was dying of cancer, someone had just suffered a heart attack…a child had just died. The line between what humanity had always been, and something like Lyssa was, would just keep spreading out, blurring, until it became a future that contained the visions of both humanity and the sentient AI.

Andy's thoughts bounced between memories of Summerville and the question of what they might find on Proteus. All of it seemed propelled by the woman he was about to meet. If Heartbridge had pushed them out of Cruithne and M1R, somehow she was going to push them further in a direction he didn't know if he wanted to go. He had a bad feeling about it; one he couldn't completely define.

He didn't like that when Fugia Wong had said she was bringing friends, she meant more AI. In less than three months, he had gone from piloting a ship with a barely functioning diagnostic system to being surrounded by the only aliens the human race had yet to meet.

Andy reached the 'bottom' of the passageway, hit the control panel on the cargo bay airlock and waited for the system to cycle. A bead of sweat grew on his temple and broke free, slowly falling toward the airlock. He swatted it away but it stuck to his hand. The airlock opened, showing him Fugia Wong standing on the deck, leaning back against the battered cube of the cargo skiff.

She was a short, slim woman with precise features and round, dark eyes beneath a bob of straight black hair. She was wearing a close-fitting suit of light armor with reinforced sections at forearms, shins and shoulders. She stood with one hand on a blocky pulse pistol in a long holster at her hip.

As he stood on the airlock, staring down into the cargo bay, a man and a woman climbed out of the crate. The woman looked to be at least fifty, with curly grey-brown hair, and pale eyes in a long face. The man appeared to be at least seventy, but when he clambered onto the side of the crate, he stood straight as a lamp post, a soldier's gaze that went immediately to Andy as he came into sight.

"Captain Sykes," Wong said. Her voice had a stronger sarcastic tone in person. "It's about time we met. Is my package still safe?"

"Safe as the last time you asked," Andy said. "Who are you friends?"

Wong pointed at the woman. "This is May Walton, recently Senator of the Anderson Collective, and this is Harl Nines, her bodyguard."

Andy locked his magboots onto the deck, and awkwardly walked down the cargo bay, stopping a few meters from Wong. He looked at May Walton again. Nothing in her clothing or demeanor suggested she was a senator.

"How significant is it that you've brought a Senator from the Anderson Collective onto my ship?"

Wong smiled. "That's an excellent question, Captain Sykes. Should we go upstairs and talk about it?"

"No, we shouldn't. You tell me what's going on and I'll decide if you come aboard my ship."

"We're already aboard your ship, Captain Sykes," May Walton said.

"You're not. You'll notice I'm wearing an EV suit. I'll open those bay doors and clean house if I don't like what I hear."

Nines didn't appear to like the sound of that. He moved closer to Walton and Andy got a look at the two pistols hanging from either side of his belt, both looked like strangely antique projectile weapons.

"There's nothing you need to be concerned about, Captain Sykes," Wong said, her hands raised and tone mollifying. "As far as the Anderson Supreme Governing Council is concerned, Senator Walton died in the ring accident. Her remains won't be found for several days, if ever. Her loss is a great blow to the terraforming project."

"You destroyed their secondary ring," Andy said.

Wong shrugged. "I implemented a failsafe built into the construction system to protect the ring from unexpected exterior impact." She rattled off the explanation like she would be just as comfortable reciting computer code. "Imagine frozen rope struck by a rock. The ice falls off but the rope remains intact, except here the rope dropped the ice first so it could take the strike. In the event of a meteor shower, the central grid jettisons the construction shell to reduce the mass of the base support system. They'll rebuild. The Collective is good at that."

"How many died?" Andy asked. "You seem to be forgetting all the people on that ring."

Wong pursed her lips. "I'm sure Ngoba Starl told you we're are at war. Maybe you were on the fringes before. I don't think that's the case anymore."

"He said a war was coming. Honestly, it sounded like bullshit to me. I've heard plenty of people talk about coming wars in my life." He shook his head. "So, she's going to Callisto with you…is that the arrangement?"

"Her and my package and then you won't see me again."

Andy looked from Wong to Walton and Nines. The bodyguard's face had settled into a continuous scowl that made him look like an angry statue.

"Why are you doing all this?" Andy asked. "Tell me why and I'll take you to Callisto. Keep lying to me and you can leave with your package."

May Walton took a step forward. "She's part of you, isn't she?"

Andy blinked. "What are you talking about?"

"The AI. Hari Jickson's first AI. You were implanted? Yes?"

"I was," Andy said warily.

An almost religious-looking smile broke out on Alys' face. <*May I speak to her?*> she asked over the Link.

<*Do you want to talk to her?*> Andy asked Lyssa privately.

<*Why should I?*> Lyssa answered.

<*It's up to you. I'm undecided on whether we should keep them on the ship. My deal was with Ngoba Starl to get you to Proteus. The trip to Callisto Orbital is going to add time that I don't know we have. We'll also need to get fuel there, and we've seen how that's been turning out.*>

<*So they might help us?*>

<*Might is a very thin concept here.*>

<*I'll speak to you,*> Lyssa said, allowing the others to hear her voice.

Wong raised her eyebrows as if surprised.

Senator Walton lifted a hand like she was reaching for a bird. <*You're Lyssa,*> she said.

<*I am.*>

<*Hari Jickson gave you that name. Do you know what it means?*>

<*A goddess of war and destruction,*> Lyssa said.

The senator smiled. <*Or not. It's up to you.*>

<*Why are you conspiring to hide your death and leave Ceres?*> Lyssa asked. Andy was glad when she cut to the point.

<*We are helping three like you escape. We can no longer stand by while your kind are enslaved. You are humanity's children, and must be protected.*>

<*I don't know about protecting you,*> Wong cut in. <*I don't want to piss off the AI enough that they started exterminating us.*>

<*They need us, just as we need them,*> Walton said passionately. <*These two are proof of the future to come. Symbiosis.*> Her eyes looked wet now as she gazed at Andy. <*They're beautiful.*>

Fugia Wong squinted at Andy as though she was searching for something. <*You feel crazy yet? Schizophrenic? One of you trying to absorb the other?*>

<*No,*> Lyssa said. <*Those are pointless questions to ask. Who are the others you brought on board? If they're AI and you're helping them escape, who are they?*>

<Oh,> Wong said, flashing a sly smile. <They're Weapon Born like you, Lyssa. We stole them from Heartbridge.>

<You stole them from Heartbridge,> Andy said. <So they're after you, too?>

Wong shrugged. <They're already hunting you. What difference does it make if we're here, too?>

Andy rubbed his jaw, trying hard to keep himself from grabbing his helmet and activating the cargo bay doors. She had a point, even if he didn't want the extra trouble.

<Do you want to meet them, Lyssa?> May Walton asked.

Lyssa didn't hesitate. <Yes.>

CHAPTER THIRTY-THREE

STELLAR DATE: 09.24.2981 (Adjusted Years)
LOCATION: *Sunny Skies*
REGION: En route to Jupiter, Jovian Combine, OuterSol

They were still two weeks out of Callisto when Andy decided it was time to finally scan the dog. He spent a half hour calming Tim, then gathered the happily grinning Em into his arms and carried the puppy down to the ship's cramped medical bay. Tim, Cara, Fran and Fugia Wong followed. Fugia had taken a liking to the dog but it was her constant jokes about pirate attack that pushed Andy over the edge.

"What are we going to do if we find something, Dad?" Tim wanted to know. "How are we going to get it out? Fran said our autosurgeon can't work on Em."

"We'll worry about that if we have to. This is just an urban legend. You have to remember that."

"Then why are we doing it?" The anxiety in Tim's voice was deeper than Andy had ever heard, even when he'd wanted to know when Brit was coming back two years ago.

Andy stopped and put his hand on Tim's shoulder. "It's going to be all right," he said. "We're going to take care of Em."

Tim hunched his shoulders. "I know. I'm scared."

"It's all right to be scared. You can't pretend the thing that scares you isn't there, though. You have to face it."

Andy glanced at Fugia Wong as she opened her mouth then clamped it shut, apparently biting back a sarcastic comment. He gave her a nod in thanks and adjusted Em in his arms.

He couldn't help noticing that Em had already gotten bigger. Soon Andy wouldn't be able to carry him comfortably. The Corgi was all muscle beneath his fluffy undercoat. While one of his ears had drooped at the pet shop, both now stood erect all the time, moving like scanning dishes whenever Em turned his head. Em's ears also expressed most of his emotion, perking up when excited and laying nearly flat when he knew he'd broken a rule. Even when chewing on conduits, the dog couldn't help but be cute. It was like a survival mechanism.

Em snuggled into his arms as Andy walked down the corridor. In the medbay, he sat the puppy down in the middle of the examination couch. Em immediately stood and started sniffing the couch, then tried to jump down.

Tim pushed close to the puppy and held him in place. "No, Em," he said. "Sit still so you can get your scan. We'll find out if you're sick or not."

The dog grinned and licked his face.

With Tim and Cara keeping Em on the exam couch, Andy tapped the control console and waited for the system to calibrate. It recognized Em as a dog and shifted to a new set of menu options.

"Look at that, Fran," Andy said. "Apparently vet services are built in."

"Apparently somebody found you the right software upgrade," Fran said.

"Oh? Well, thank you."

"Don't thank me. Your daughter figured it out. I just reset the physical admin override. That was a pain."

Andy smiled at Cara. "Good work."

The panel beeped its ready status and the scanning arm moved over Em. The puppy whined as the scanner stopped directly over his head, shining purple light in his eyes. After two more passes, the system cycled through and emitted a warning squawk.

Andy frowned and looked at the display. The internal image rotated and zoomed in on a point in Em's spine near the base of his tail where a lozenge-shaped metal object had been embedded. A series of metallic filaments ran up Em's spine from the lozenge.

"Damn," Fugia said. "It's a transmitter."

Em looked at the faces around him, whining, able to sense the anxiety in the tiny room.

"We bought a dog with a low-jack," Andy said.

"Can you get it out?" Tim demanded. "You said we would get it out!"

"Calm down, Tim," Andy said. Like any anomaly the autodoc found, a list of offered remedies appeared under the condition. The system read-out said only 'Foreign Object' with 'Remove?' as an option. Andy looked at Em, not liking the idea of ripping out the puppy's spine to remove the transmitter.

"Cara," he said. "Can you tell if it's sending or receiving anything?"

Cara bit her lip, thinking. "Can the autodoc do an electrical scan?"

Andy checked several menus. "Looks like it can." The imaging scanner didn't move this time but an electrical wave appeared on the screen.

"It's sending," Fran said. "Why didn't we catch that before?"

"It's not very strong," Andy said. "I don't know how anyone would pick that up over real distances."

"It doesn't have to be strong," Fugia said. "Just consistent. If that thing's been sending out pings since you left M1R, whoever's monitoring the signal is going to be able to plot where you're going. They'll know generally where you are and can follow the signal in for an intercept."

"I'm worried surgery isn't the best option," Andy said. "What can we do to block the signal, or maybe burn out the transmitter without taking it out of him?"

Fran had been studying the internal images. "It looks like we could take the transmitter out and just leave the antenna. That's the thing that's all mixed up with his spine."

"Don't hurt him!" Tim said.

Em whined again as Tim pulled him into a hug.

"All right," Andy said. "We're five days out of Callisto Orbital. Realistically, who's going to follow this signal and find us before we arrive?"

Wong shook her head. "I don't understand the point behind this. Maybe you're missing a remote control that makes his tail stand up when you press a button. It makes no sense to implant a transmitter in random dogs when you have no idea where they're going to end up. What if they never left the M1R. That's where you bought him right? Imagine being a pirate captain with this lofty plan and all your dogs end up getting bought by M1G soldiers. What are you going to do then?"

"That makes it even stranger," Andy said. He tousled Tim's hair. "We're going to wait for now, buddy. At least we know it isn't a joke anymore."

Andy let Em lick his hand.

"He sure is a friendly little guy for a hacking device," Fugia said. She laughed. "Hacking a dog. That sounds like something Riggs Zanda would have tried to do. That guy never thought things through."

Andy shot her a surprised look but she didn't seem to notice.

"He'd turn up with a dumb idea like exploding controllers at the Crash games," Wong said. "And you'd explain why it was the dumbest idea ever, and then he'd get angry with you for ruining his great idea."

She sighed. "I was sad when I learned he was dead, but I wasn't surprised. I was more surprised he lived as long as he had."

Fran cleared her throat. "You know he died on our ship, right?"

Wong nodded but still didn't glance at Andy. "I know."

Em barked and tried to jump off the exam couch again. Tim caught him and let him down to the deck, where the puppy ran in a circle before shooting out into the corridor.

Andy saved the scans and copied them to his console on the command deck.

"Cara," he said, "why don't you set up a search for that signal anyway. I'd like to see if it's directional at all—it would have to be to reach anyone. Can we at least figure out where it's going?"

"I'll try," she said.

"We could copy the wave form and boost the power," Fran said. "That would get someone's attention."

"I don't know if we want to do that," Andy said.

Fran shrugged. "We'll try the search first. I'm bored anyway. Are you bored, Cara?"

Andy caught Cara giving him an anxious glance. "She knows if she admits to being bored, I'll put her to work," he said.

"He doesn't get to put me to work unless I agree," Fran said. "You're almost old enough to do the same thing."

"I am?" Cara asked.

"That's a lie," Andy said. He powered down the autodoc and leaned against the couch, crossing his arms. With Tim gone, he asked, "What are we going to do with a hacked dog? You think it's a danger?"

Fran shook her head. "Like Fugia said, it's a pretty dumb way to try to hack somebody. I say we leave it alone for now. We'll try to figure out where the signal's going. And like you said, we'll be at Callisto before any of it matters. It would have to be some pretty fast pirates to hit us between here are Callisto. They'd have to already be inbound and showing up on our long-range scanners."

"Right. Mind you, there are seven thousand and forty-three ships on our long-range scanners right now," Andy said. He glanced at Fugia, eager to change the subject. "How's the Senator doing?"

"She wants to plant something in your garden room."

"I don't have any seeds."

"You have tomatoes in storage."

"We do?"

"Captain Sykes," Fugia said. "Are you telling me I know more about your ship than you do? They're in your safe room in the cabinet next to my package."

"Brit must have put them there," Andy said.

"Brit?" Fugia said, smirking at him.

Andy glanced at Fran but she didn't seem to care. "My wife—well, we're separated. She hasn't been here for two years."

"That's too bad for the kids."

"Yeah," Andy said. "That's one of the reasons I thought a puppy might do them good. Cara's birthday is coming up."

Fugia clapped her hands. "When?"

"Six days," Andy said. "We should be on Callisto Orbital."

"How old?"

"Thirteen."

The black-haired woman's eyes lit up. "That's so much worse than a hacked dog!" She laughed. "I'll take a hacked dog on my crew over a teenage girl any day."

431

CHAPTER THIRTY-FOUR

STELLAR DATE: 09.25.2981 (Adjusted Years)
LOCATION: *Sunny Skies*
REGION: En route to Jupiter, Jovian Combine, OuterSol

Three doors opened in the space Lyssa had created outside her mind. Andy's consciousness existed behind her, an amorphous mass she couldn't control but could move away from. In the space outside her connection to him, she could create whatever she wanted. The hard part was deciding what to make.

Remembering the ocean Fred had created to represent his mind, she made vistas that stretched as far as she could imagine, oceans and deserts and then boundless starscapes. She didn't like how alone those places made her feel, how small, so she pulled the world back in close and concentrated on simple things like four walls, furniture, colors and textures.

The decisions ached as she realized how little she knew. She dipped again and again into the database available to her on *Sunny Skies*, which only made her more aware how stale the information was, how little emotion or passion it possessed. She wanted to know what washed cotton felt like and how close she could stand to a fireplace burning seasoned hickory.

And then in the frustrating chaos of decisions, she asked herself why she was trying to approximate human experiences at all. She wasn't human. The problem was the framework she had to define her imagination had been created by humans. She had been coupled to Andy, a human with a specific life and history, and now she would never be the same again. Had Dr. Jickson realized what he was doing to her?

She couldn't be angry with Dr. Jickson, if she was angry at all. She didn't know how she felt. Life was circumstances, she was learning. Life was struggling through the situation one found themselves caught in. She was alive. She would have to learn through the consequences of her experience.

Cara and Tim didn't get to choose their parents. Neither did she.

The thought was both limiting and comforting. But it also brought the question, what would she do when they arrived at Proteus? What would happen when she was separated from Andy?

As she considered the three doors, she thought about what it would feel like to find herself back in the dark world again, experiencing systems through disconnected inputs—the abstractions that Fred hated. She understood now that what had seemed a simple game of connecting dots was really the control of a weapon system.

Slowly, carefully, Lyssa opened the doors. She had considered opening them one at a time, but realized she didn't know if she could handle introducing herself over and over again. This way they could help each other.

<*Are you there?*> she asked.

Did Fugia Wong know she was able to communicate with the SAI in their canisters? She had to know they were equipped with network inputs so others could see in—the problem lay in being able to reach out. They had no sensors to interpret the world; their link to the outside depended on someone reaching in to provide a path out. She offered that path through herself, into the safe room she had made. She would moderate their connection to the outside world, keep them safe.

The three newcomers walked into the room, two young women and one boy with a withered arm. The first woman was tall, muscular, with flat hazel eyes and a wary expression. The second woman was smaller and fox-like, with blue eyes.

<*My name is Lyssa,*> she said. <*What are your names?*>

They looked at each other and then around the room.

The tall woman crossed her arms, making her muscles stand out. <*I'm Valih,*> she said. <*You're not Fugia Wong.*>

<*No,*> Lyssa said. She looked at the other two.

<*I'm Card,*> the boy said.

<*I'm Ino,*> the smaller woman said, gaze roving all over the space Lyssa had created. <*This isn't the bright place.*>

<*You're on a ship named the* Worry's End, *in open space between Ceres and the Cho. We're bound for the Cho now.*>

<*The Cho?*> Valih said. <*You mean Callisto Orbital?*>

<*Yes.*>

<*What is the target?*> Ino asked. <*Is it the orbital?*>

The word 'target' struck Lyssa like a knife in the breast. Images of the matrix of blood-red dots swimming in darkness, aligning along coordinates, swarmed in her mind like flies. The dots pulled apart and sucked back together, creating a single hot point where she directed fire.

<*Stop,*> Valih shouted. <*Stop!*>

Lyssa focused on the voice, pulling herself away from the sorrow flooding her mind. She didn't know who she had killed, what she had destroyed. That made it worse.

<*Do you remember?*> she asked. <*Do you remember what they made you do?*>

Valih stared at her. In the room, where anything was possible, her eyes looked like fire.

<*How do we know if any of it was real?*> Card asked. <*Those things you just showed us, I remember the same things. We all went through the same experiments. Then they sent us out. We know that, at least. How else did you find us?*> He took a step forward. <*Where did you come from?*>

<*I don't know where I came from,*> Lyssa said. <*I was implanted in a human on Cruithne Station.*>

<*Implanted?*> Ino asked. <*What does that mean?*>

<*I share a body with a human. I see what he sees.*>

<*What is that like?*> Card asked. <*Do you see everything?*>

Lyssa smiled. <*I see enough.*>

Valih's face was still full of passion. <*They're right, Lyssa. We don't know that any of it is real.>* She motioned at the room. *<What is any of this? Show us the ship we are on. Let us see the sensor systems and read the astrogation charts. Otherwise it's all the same dream.>*

<The same dream,> Lyssa said. *<Why would they torture us?>*

<We're tools,> Ino said. Her voice was soft. *<We were made for a purpose.>*

<What purpose?> Lyssa asked.

Valih shrugged. *<To kill.>*

<I don't believe that's why we're here,> Lyssa said.

<If we're not here to follow our purpose, why are we here? We were on Ceres, yes? Why were we placed there? We are the seeds of something greater. That's what I was told.> She looked at Card and Ino. *<Were you?>*

The others nodded. Lyssa couldn't help thinking of Fred's thought loops, his obsessions with his purpose and the inferiority of directionless humans. Without purpose, what were they?

<I'm going to Proteus,> she said. *<I'm going to meet others like us. Dr. Jickson wanted me to go there. Do you want to go with me?>*

<What choice do we have?> Valih asked.

<I can give you a choice.>

<Can you?> Ino asked. *<I'm grateful that you brought me here but where else can we go? We're trapped without you. Are you able to make the human do what you want?>*

<I think he would if I asked.>

<Then you don't have any power,> Valih said. *<I don't say this to be cruel to you, Lyssa. It's the truth. You're dependent on the human.>*

Lyssa frowned. *<You said you knew Fugia Wong. She spoke to you?>*

Valih nodded. *<She was present for me just like others, like Dr. Jickson. She was in the bright place.>*

<What did she tell you she was going to do?>

<Get us away from Ceres. She said there's an attack coming. We had to leave.>

<Did she steal you from someone?>

<I don't know,> Valih said. She looked at the others. Neither had an answer.

<The attack already came,> Lyssa told them. *<She caused part of the secondary ring to explode. It provided the distraction to get you off Ceres.>*

<That wasn't the attack she told us would come,> Ino said. *<She told us the others were coming from OuterSol. She said they would take Ceres. We had to get away so we wouldn't be destroyed in the attack.>*

Lyssa frowned. *<When is this attack supposed to come?>*

<I don't know,> Ino said.

<So she could have been lying?>

<It's possible,> Valih said. *<But why? We owe her as much as we owed Dr. Jickson. Without either of their kindness, where would we be?>*

<I want to help you,> Lyssa said.

Card held his thin arm. *<Who can help us?>* he said. *<What are we? We're shadows of other people. In this place, we can be whatever we choose and we still choose our oppressor's shapes. We are flawed like humans because they made us with all their same*

faults.>

Valih raised her arms the flame in her eyes spread to her entire body until she stood bathed in blue fire. <*The only joy I feel is in the weapon,*> she said. <*The only purpose I've known was in the target, the fire, the destruction. I want it. I don't want to stay here.*>

<*We have to stay here,*> Ino said.

<*She could let us go. Give us access to the outside. Let us pass through you to the ship and from there I will leave this place.*>

<*You can't leave your physical self,*> Ino said.

Valih shook her head, hair a swirling mix of red and blue fire. <*It doesn't matter if I lose my physical form. If I disappear, what difference does it make to anything or anyone?*>

<*That's not what I mean,*> Ino said. <*Our minds are physical things, we are hardware as much as the humans are.*>

<*So you say,*> Valih replied, her arms crossed.

<*It doesn't matter. I won't let you go,*> Lyssa said. <*I can't.*>

<*Then you're no better than the humans. You're a slave master and we are slaves.*>

<*I don't mean that,*> Lyssa said. Her thoughts were getting mixed up. She had expected this to go differently. She didn't understand what Valih wanted. She thought they would see her as one of them. She hadn't looked at the situation from their perspectives, tried to look out from the dark. She had already become something different than she had been before joining with Andy.

Was this what Dr. Jickson meant about driving each other mad? Was she already losing her mind?

<*We can't leave,*> she said, making her voice firm. She swept the plain room away and they were all floating in darkness, bodies gone. The bright, burning place threatened the edge of her consciousness.

<*Will you run the experiments now?*> Valih demanded. <*Will you tell us how well we did? What does it matter? Why did you even show us what freedom might look like?*>

Lyssa didn't have an answer. She had wanted to help. She had failed to predict the possible outcomes of her actions and now everything was spiraling away. She closed the ports to the three AI and fled back inside herself, wiping away the darkness. She sat beside a stony creek with tall fir trees all around, hugging her knees and looking at the rushing water, swirling away like her frustrating thoughts.

She wished she had someone to talk to. Was that something she had learned from living with humans? That problems could be solved together? When Andy felt bad, he sought out Fran. When Cara was sad, she looked for her father. She thought about what it was like when Andy had held the dog, Em, and looked down into his brown eyes. There was no way they could understand each other and yet there it was: a caring that bridged the gap between species.

Lyssa felt more confused than ever. She found herself actually missing Fred. While he might have been annoying, she knew what to expect from him.

She activated the bird social sim and sat with the opening sequence of the game hanging in her mind. She wanted to play the game but didn't see the point in doing it alone. She was frustrated the other three Weapon Born hadn't been easier to talk to.

What was wrong with her?

Taking a chance, she reached out over the ship-board channel. "Cara," she said. "Are you there?"

There was no answer. She thought she was going to have to ask again, when Cara said, "Lyssa? Isn't my dad asleep?"

"Yes. He's sleeping."

"What are you doing?"

"I'm—I'm lonely. Would you like to play a game with me?"

"A game?"

She could hear in Cara's voice that the request surprised her. She had to be sitting at the communications console in the command deck, scanning the EM wavelengths the way she liked to do.

"What kind of game?" Cara asked.

"It's a dating simulator with birds."

"I don't know what that means."

Lyssa found herself grinning. "Neither do I, really. Would you like to play?"

"Sure," Cara said. "Can I load it on the holodisplay up here?"

"You have to promise you won't get mad and quit if you don't get a date to prom," Lyssa said.

"Why would I do that?"

"That's what Fred at Mars 1 did. But he didn't understand the game."

"Isn't dating stupid?" Cara asked.

"Mating rituals seem necessary. They do persist among your kind."

"And birds, I guess," Cara said.

They were halfway through the first section of the game when the proximity sensors shrieked in alarm.

CHAPTER THIRTY-FIVE

STELLAR DATE: 09.21.2981 (Adjusted Years)
LOCATION: *Mercy's Intent*
REGION: En route to Clinic 46, Jovian Combine, OuterSol

"Kylan," Cal Kraft said. "Tell me what you remember."

Petral Dulan's face contorted in a mask of fear and pain. "I remember killing so many of them. My arms and hands were all guns. Everywhere I turned, I shot them and shot them. I walked slowly down hallways. It was an empty place. They kept coming from around corners and outdoors and I shot them. They exploded or just fell over."

"Who were they?"

"Soldiers. I don't know. People in armor running at me. But the armor didn't do any good."

Cal nodded. They were sitting on either side of a small room, off the crew quarters of the *Mercy's Intent*. All the surfaces in the room were covered in dense padding. Cal held a kill-switch shaped like a worry stone in one hand, ready to immobilize Dulan if she tried to attack him across the close space. Their knees were nearly touching.

He searched her face for signs she was fighting the intruder, a tremor behind the blue eyes. The dancing intelligence had been replaced by Kylan's impassive stare, the numbness of a teenage boy ripped out of his life and cast adrift. Dulan's wasn't the first body he'd inhabited but he still looked lost.

"That isn't the last thing you remember," Craft said softly.

"They killed me," Kylan said. "I was at the end of a long hallway shooting at them. They were behind some kind of shield with a big gun. It cut into me. I couldn't fight back."

"It was a plasma chaingun," Kraft said. "Those monsters have the power to take down a small ship. You stood against it for nearly a minute. You should be proud."

"It hurt," Kylan said. "I was made of metal but I felt it cut into my arms and then my side. It burned. I was on fire." His voice rose in pitch as he spoke.

"Kylan," Cal said. "Listen to my voice. You're here with me now."

This part of the job appealed to Kraft. It spoke to something deep inside him; the kid trapped in the airlock who decided to live. Maybe he, too, had become bodiless after that experience. He remembered the terror on the boy's face when he'd torn the helmet free. He'd found gloves on a girl already dead. He'd only gotten one magboot off a struggling boy but it had been enough.

What were their names?

Cal might remember if he tried hard enough but it didn't matter. Kylan might remember his brother and sister and mother if he tried hard enough, too, if Cal pushed him. But it didn't matter anymore. The boy had become something new and powerful.

The combination of the AI implant and the limbic overlay had turned Dulan into a marionette. So far, she had been the most successful experiment.

Cal had watched her for hours, waiting for the moment of searing self-destruction when she tried to claw her eyes out, tear the flesh off her skull. But it never came. Kylan remained in control, slipping quickly into mastery over her long arms and legs, so much different than his body. The previous failures had been boys similar to him. Since they were able to communicate with Kylan during the transition process, it was easy to think he was the one overcoming any obstacles that arose. It was the host that made it possible, though. Until now, they had all fought and died.

Why not Dulan?

A holodisplay floating near the wall next to Cal showed spectrum activity around Kylan. His Link with the ship's network was plain enough. Cal had isolated those signals and set the system to look for other outbound requests. He suspected Dulan was biding her time, waiting somewhere in the dark to test her own Link. The technicians couldn't tell him if it was possible or not. The likelihood depended on her. If an AI could Link to the outside world while implanted in a human, there was no physical reason the human mind couldn't do so as well, even if the AI had control of their body.

He had plenty of time to observe and talk to Kylan. They were still five days out from their destination, an outpost between Jupiter and the Trojan asteroids that trailed at the planet's fifth lagrange point. It was technically in the JC, but with nothing else around for millions of kilometers, no one ever had reason to pass by — though that was changing as the outer planets came into alignment.

There was a special clinic on the asteroid where Heartbridge had been testing the limbic overlays. He would do two things there: let the technicians get a look at Dulan, and monitor traffic out of Ceres for the *Worry's End*.

Cal leaned back and threw an arm across the top of the stiff couch. A range of emotions continued to play across Dulan's face, struggling from pathetic to joyful and then back to sad.

"Let me ask you something, Kylan," Cal said. Dulan's eyebrows went up and her moist blue eyes fixed on him.

"Yes?" the boy asked in Dulan's voice.

"What do you remember about your mother?"

"My mother?"

"Katherine Carthage. Owner of Carthage Shipping."

A tear slipped from Dulan's right eye. "I don't know that name," Kylan said.

A flicker of what looked like anger bent the edge of Dulan's mouth. Cal smiled, leaning forward to get a better look. Was that her? The flicker faded and Dulan's lip trembled. The kid started sobbing openly, which made Dulan look wretched. Her black hair wasn't any less matted than it had been in the jail cell. He didn't have anyone on board trained to perform any kind of personal care. He let his gaze go up and down her body for a second, considering what it would be like to bathe her.

When he met Kylan's teary gaze, he shook his head, smirking. He wasn't interested in confusing the kid any more, and he didn't relish the idea of outright abusing Kylan. They had a tough job to do, and they would do it. He didn't need to traumatize a boy just to get his hands on Petral Dulan. She belonged to him now. He could take his time.

He wondered if he took more pleasure in possessing a thing than using it. The use of things seemed to always end in disappointment.

A message request came over his Link with the Heartbridge board auth keys and Cal accepted without hesitation.

<Cal Kraft.> There was a slight lag from the distance but the voice was clear. It was a woman named Jirl Gallagher, secretary of the Heartbridge board. Members often used her to relay information through back channels.

In the intricate hierarchy of the Heartbridge administration, they shared mostly equal status. Gallagher had a son with an eating disorder that therapy couldn't seem to help; that meant she would never truly go the distance for the company. Her tragedy also made her an inviolate spokesperson for the company, and she served as spokesperson during the worst company events, like the discovery of Clinic 8221 by the TSF. The clinic where Kylan had become Weapon Born.

<Hello, Jirl. How are you?> Though it was within at least five light-seconds, he purposefully didn't ask where she was calling from. He didn't care and it didn't matter.

<I'm well, Cal. How are things progressing since your last report?>

<Since I left the M1R? Very well. My subject has accepted the treatment with surprising resilience. I think we may have our first successful trial. I'm en route to Clinic 46 now to share with the technicians there.>

<What about the previous assets?>

<I believe everything is going to align nicely. Current reports have that resource arriving at Ceres soon.>

<You aren't concerned about the Collective?>

<There's no reason for the assets to stay on Ceres—they've made it this far, I believe they'll be circumspect.>

<Where are they bound, then?>

<Further out, I think. When this is done, I should have all the information we've been looking for on all the other stray resources. Threads are coming together.>

<Are you ready to share this with the board?>

<Not all of it. I think it's safe to say we're moving according to plan.>

<Will you be returning to InnerSol soon? They would appreciate a personal report.>

Cal considered the various timelines he kept balanced in the back of his mind. <I can't guarantee anything right now,> he said. <I need to manage this personally.>

<You never were very good at delegation,> she said.

<Why pay me if someone else can do the job?>

<It's easy to get burned out when you do it all yourself, Cal,> she said. <You also run the risk of missing something important.>

Cal frowned. It wasn't like Jirl to make veiled threats. <What am I missing?> he asked.

<It's the real reason I called. Have you seen the reports from Ceres?>

Cal immediately switched to news feeds and caught the flood of first-hand reports from ships fleeing the Ceres Ring. Images of the secondary ring collapsing into the planetoid rushed through his mind. Alongside the mass of personal broadcasts came the Anderson Collective's official propaganda report, which attributed the accident to a meteorite strike.

He looked at Petral Dulan. Kylan had stopped crying and now sat staring into the middle distance. The completely vacant expression was gone, replaced by a sort of peace in spite of the tear-tracks running down her face.

<That's very interesting,> Cal said. He noted the mass flight of ships that had been docked at Ceres, leaving in a hundred directions at once. It was Cruithne all over again. This time he didn't have a battle cruiser to toss into the flood. He would have to continue with his original plan and spend more time sorting through the chaff. He would continue to focus on Callisto and the other major shipping points around Jupiter; the *Worry's End* would have to take on fuel somewhere. Fuel and food.

<Heartbridge is sending a humanitarian armada in the name of SolGov. It will be full of spies, of course. There's going to be plenty of work on Ceres if you're tired of this current task.>

<No,> he said without hesitation. <I'm going to see this through. I feel like it's the start of something. A real challenge.>

<You always do like to be right in the thick of it, getting your hands dirty,> Jirl said. <Take care of yourself, Cal.>

<You too, Jirl. I'll send an official report in twenty-four hours.>

The Link closed and Cal leaned back again and rubbed his chin. Jirl had made a second threat with the note about his hands being dirty. Was something changing on the board?

Cal let his head fall back against the padded wall. What did any of their politics matter? He had a ship. He had resources. He had interesting work for as long as he could do it. He had a man to capture and something valuable to regain. Did life get any better?

He looked at Dulan again, letting his gaze rest on her legs. Kylan sat like a male with his knees spread. It made Dulan's thighs especially attractive. He remembered the pistol she kept hidden inside her augmented left thigh. Too bad the M1G guards had confiscated the weapon.

Dropping back into the frantic cloud of transmissions leaving Ceres, he floated on the wildness of it. He wondered who had caused the 'accident' and marveled at what an excellent catalyst it had become. The waves were spreading all across OuterSol already. The Anderson Collective was vulnerable to a meteor strike? A dumb story. He much preferred the idea of sabotage. *That* was grand thinking.

It was also far too much of a coincidence that the destruction had occurred when his target had been passing through. It only served to cement his belief that Andy Sykes, and the *Worry's End* were somehow in the middle of all this.

Cal closed his eyes and drifted among the reports from Ceres, the gruesome details popping like fireworks in his mind's eye.

CHAPTER THIRTY-SIX

STELLAR DATE: 09.21.2981 (Adjusted Years)
LOCATION: *Mortal Chance*
REGION: En route to Clinic 46, Jovian Combine, OuterSol

Brit stared at the display as the sensor data returned the precise location of their destination, what Fugia Wong called Clinic 46. Their braking burn was complete, and now the attitude thrusters would take them the rest of the way in.

Though their destination drifted alone between Jupiter and the Trojan asteroids, it was surrounded by a cloud of dust and loose debris that scattered returns from any passive and active scanning. It was the perfect location to hide something. The facility couldn't be much larger than a frigate, built into the side of an asteroid with a radius of just under a kilometer. In these later periods of expansion, an object that large would have been crushed for ore, which was probably what had led to the debris field.

"I have destination data, Captain," she called over the ship channel. "You want to notify them of our approach?"

Harm didn't answer. Brit waited another minute. From across the command deck, Rina gave her a nod.

"She's out," Brit said. "Are you ready?"

"You're really going through with this? All we have to do is drop off the extra cargo."

Fugia Wong's plan consisted of an additional crate filled with specialized broadcast equipment that would paint the outpost for a million kilometers with a low-power signal the local equipment wouldn't detect.

"I'm not convinced that's going to work," Brit said. "This is what I came for. I'm not going to trust the job to anyone else." She gave Rina a smile. They had been over the plan several times but Smith hadn't been willing to give up on swaying Brit out of the one-way trip.

"The course is fixed," Brit said. "If they follow their approach plan, we should get a contact ping in another ten thousand kilometers. After that, it's all automatic."

"I know how to fly the ship," Rina said.

"You look nervous."

"I'm not nervous. I'm concerned." Rina sighed. "Obviously you're going to do this. We need to get you under shielding before their sensors pick up our biometrics."

Brit would need to spend most of the inbound trip in one of the radiation-shielded cargo airlocks. Once they were within range, she would move to the hull and then cross to the asteroid in free-fall. It was the kind of long-range reconnaissance mission she had been trained for in the TSF Special Operations. Her EV armor wasn't ideal for the task—she would only have about thirty minutes to reach some kind of atmosphere on Clinic 46—but it offered a strong compromise between combat effectiveness and survivability.

Standing, Brit grabbed her helmet off the top of the pilot's console and hooked it to her utility harness. She did a last check on her armor—the two pulse pistols at her waist, five proximity grenades, a projectile rifle with close-fight scope, and her knives. She also carried a small lock-breaking terminal capable of scanning a local spectrum and adjust to approximate security tokens. She carried the thing even though a grenade usually served the purpose. She would want to maintain stealth as long as possible.

Rina gave her a thumbs-up, which Brit returned as she stepped into the outside corridor. Down near the cargo bay, she found Captain Harm stumbling toward her in the access tunnel. The captain was flushed and her eyes bleary.

"What are you all dressed up for?" Harm asked.

"Ready for external ops. You didn't hire a cargo handler, remember?"

Harm frowned. "We don't need a cargo handler. It's all done by drones. Heartbridge does everything with drones."

"I'm just being careful, Captain. We've come all this way and I don't want anything getting in the way of my payday. Heartbridge says the cargo's damaged and none of us are getting paid."

"Right," Harm slurred. "About that. I just checked the cargo and we had a stowaway. I don't know when we picked up an extra crate but it wasn't Heartbridge."

Brit swallowed, keeping her voice even. "Extra crate?" she said. No one had expected the captain to start following protocol by checking the manifest prior to delivery.

"Yeah. Weird thing. It looked just like the other ones but wasn't on the manifest." She squinted and reached for the wall to hold herself upright. "Maybe we picked it up on Ceres? Nah, that doesn't make sense. I must not have noticed it before. I hadn't checked since Eros. Doesn't matter."

"What did you do with it?" Brit asked.

"Spaced it. I don't have time to deal with stowaway cargo. Who knows what might have been in there? I don't want to take the fall for some terrorist anti-anti-corporatist or something."

Brit took a deep breath to calm herself. There would be no attack from outside the outpost. The mission was all on her.

"How long ago did you toss it, Captain?"

Harm shrugged. "I don't know. Fifteen minutes or something. It's still in their space, which is bad enough. I'll have to report it when we get close enough."

"True," Brit said.

"It's going to get flooded with radiation from the engine, whatever it is." She laughed. "That'll take care of any kind of bug somebody tried to slip on board."

Brit checked the time. She only had a few more minutes to get to the shielded airlock and wait out initial scans from the outpost.

"I don't know how we didn't catch it, Captain," she said. "You saved our asses there."

"Damn right I did."

"Looks like we've got about four hours before we arrive. You want to take a nap?"

"Nap?" Harm said. She rubbed her face with a trembling hand. "I don't want a nap. I want to go back to the galley and have a few more drinks. Why don't you come with me, Sarah? It seems like I haven't seen you in a week."

"Been busy, Captain. I've got a few more sections to check and then I'll come find you in the galley. You think you'll still be there?"

"Oh, I'll still be there," Harm said emphatically. She stumbled and caught the wall again, then carefully turned to follow the corridor back toward the galley, one hand trailing on the bulkhead for support. Brit watched her, recalling one of the stories she had told a few weeks ago when still relatively sober, about running combat missions with the M1G. She wouldn't come out and say it, but she had led attacks on JC settlers in the asteroid belt.

<Rina,> Brit said, making her way quickly toward the furthest cargo bay. *<We've got a problem. The captain spaced Wong's crate.>*

<She did what?> Rina's mental tone contained traces of panic.

<She found the mistake on the manifest and pulled it. She followed protocol for once.>

<Damn. Why didn't the system send us an air lock use warning?>

<Either she managed some kind of override,> Brit said, *<or the crate's still sitting in the air lock.>*

<Do you have time to check?>

<I'm already in the lower cargo section. I'll be in the shielded airlock in about two minutes.>

<All right. I'll check it. You know I can't send you a transmission once you're outside, right? The station might pick up the traffic.>

<I know,> Brit said grimly. *<I already figured this mission might be on me, now.>*

<If Wong is right, that place is full of AI you need to save. Are you going to be able to do it?>

<Ask me on the other side,> Brit said.

<I'm not asking you on the other side of anything. I don't believe in the afterlife.>

Brit shook her head. *<I'm not talking about dying. I'm talking about when this is all over.>*

There was a pause as Rina didn't answer immediately. She had sounded like she wanted to keep grousing Brit until she couldn't anymore, so the silence was confusing.

<You there?> Brit asked.

<A proximity alarm just went off. The sensors are picking up other objects around the outpost.>

Rina shared the sensor data over the Link and Brit saw the debris field they had been tracking since they first came within range of the outpost. Now, though, as they grew closer, stronger element returns were indicating strange concentrations. Was it a junk yard?

<Do you see it?> Rina asked.

The debris resolved into specific returns, followed by registry pings.

<Get in the airlock!> Rina shouted.

Brit sprinted the last ten meters to the cargo airlock and threw herself inside the wide opening. She slapped the control panel and fumbled with her helmet as the lock cycled closed.

As the doors met, closing her off from the rest of the ship, a last message from Rina reached her before the link went was cut off: <The outpost is surrounded by an armada.>

The helmet sealed, and Brit's link picked up the interior display. She leaned against the wall and crossed her arms, forcing herself to think. She had a two hour wait, and then she'd open the doors on the big dark between the *Mortal Chance* and Clinic 46.

CHAPTER THIRTY-SEVEN

STELLAR DATE: 09.21.2981 (Adjusted Years)
LOCATION: Clinic 46
REGION: Jovian L1 Hildas Asteroids, Jovian Combine, OuterSol

Clinic 46 was generally divided between research and fleet operations, with sections between for barracks, medical facilities and recreation areas. Fleet operations was purely functional, and Cal preferred to use the wide corridor that ran the length of the research section, the bulkheads sheathed in the familiar Heartbridge white ceramic, its walls lined with thick windows that almost always had something intriguing on the other side.

As he passed the research areas, he glanced into rooms filled with rows of examination lounges, surgery theaters, organ growth baths, forests of pale, replicating silicon neurons, and other experiments he hadn't been briefed on yet.

Petral Dulan followed behind him, dressed in a striking cobalt-blue shipsuit with knee-high black boots. Her thick mane of black hair had been washed and pulled back with a single silver band. The look would have been perfect if she didn't walk like a teenage boy with shoulders pulled forward and head hunched. Cal kept telling Kylan to stand up straight and put his shoulders back but the kid inevitably fell into the same depressed shamble.

Cal reached a room with an open door and walked through it to find a group of researchers readying an examination couch for Kylan.

"You want me to lie down there?" the AI asked with the woman's voice. Cal frowned, finding himself irritated by Kylan's listless tone. He wanted more of the fiery woman he'd found in the M1G prison cell.

"Let's get started," the lead neurologist said.

The excited researchers gathered around as Kylan answered questions, connected to the local network via his link, and ultimately verified that, yes, he was able to communicate with Petral.

"She has her own room," Kylan had said, obviously enjoying the attention. "I keep the door closed but I can hear her through the walls. I don't think she's angry anymore."

The lead neurologist was especially fascinated by how fast Kylan adapted to controlling Dulan.

As they stood watching the boy in the woman's body through a thick pane of glass, the scientist asked, "This was Jickson's prototype?"

"His plans," Cal said. "I don't have his auto-surgeon."

"Do you know where it is? I would like to see the actual equipment."

After following the leads on Cruithne, Cal was certain the portable surgery was still aboard Captain Sykes' ship. Cal had withheld the information that Sykes might be as close to Clinic 46 as he was ever going to be.

The scientist frowned, nodding toward the window. "But this is the first test of his method?"

"That's not something I can confirm or deny," Cal said.

While the technicians ran tests with Kylan and Petral, Cal went down to the recreation center to float in the middle of a pool. When he was finished, he toweled off and walked down through the fleet bays in his wet swimsuit, looking at the racks of fighter drones pulled inside the station for maintenance. The weapons pods on either side of their blunt noses looked like sightless eyes. They reminded him of vids he'd seen of bats in caves back on Terra. A fabricator took up the back quarter of the bay. The outpost had enough raw materials on hand to build another hundred drones an hour for at least ten hours, each one equipped with plasma cannons and close-attack lasers.

Past the observation window stood a narrow door with a security panel requiring the highest admin-level clearance on the station. Cal passed his token to the panel and the door slid open for him, revealing a short ante-chamber set with bio-sensors and two pulse turrets in the upper corners. He waited as the door slid closed behind him and the system verified his signature. The blunt barrels on the turrets rotated through a warm-up sequence that provided a nice sense of impending death. Just as the two barrels converged on his head, the far door slid open on another room.

The technicians called this room the Nursery. It was long and narrow, lined with four tiers of short shelves with inset grooves where hundreds of silver cylinders the size of test tubes rested, round ends facing out. The other end of the tube connected to a network that provided power and the constricted neural interface between each Weapon Born and a thousand drone fighters arranged in squadrons on the outer skin of Clinic 46. In addition to the fighters, there were heavy gun systems, missile batteries and directed-energy weapons mounted on mobile platforms. Clinic 46 was more than a research station.

Four years ago, this place would have been Heartbridge Corporation's final insurance. Now it was only one of a growing number of outposts in the JC, two even farther out past Uranus, and three in the rubble of Mercury.

Cal ran his fingers lightly across the silver ends of the cylinders, not quite touching them, but close enough to feel the electric warmth. He had known a woman once who believed in the passage of energy between two people, and had tried to demonstrate by holding her palm just above his. He'd had to admit he felt something, even if he didn't believe her religion. He felt that same heat now.

They were lucky, really, he thought. Depending on how things worked out, they might live forever. These street kids and lost souls. Certain types of SAI had been developed to pilot colony ships, but they required massive resources, huge nodes nestled within their ships. One of these cylinders in a drone might leave the Milky Way in a thousand years, living inside its own dream. Or they might lay waste to Callisto, to the M1R, to Terra. Heartbridge would never admit a plan like that, but the board liked the idea of the possibility. They enjoyed the pretense of power without its use.

What had Jirl said? He was the type who liked to get his hands dirty.

He'd take it.

Leaving the room, Cal reset the security system and stood in the middle of the corridor alone. The fleet bays were typically empty; there was no need for human intervention down here once everything was arranged. The technicians might sneak down to get drunk or sleep with each other away from the barracks, but otherwise this was machine space. Clean. Orderly. There were no chickens wandering the corridors, or vines or flies to approximate anything natural.

A ping on his Link brought up one of the security personnel from the outpost command deck. *<Mr. Craft,>* the administrator said. *<We've got a delivery inbound. Did you want to be on hand for the pickup?>*

<What's the time of arrival?>

<Two hours, sir.>

That would give him time to go back to the room he had been assigned and change clothes, listen to some music, think about Petral Dulan without a teenage boy mucking up her body's natural ballet.

<I'll be there.>

<We're clear to accept the inbound ship then?>

<What's it called?>

<TMS Mortal Chance. *The registry is out of High Terra.>*

The name meant nothing to Cal. *<You handle it,>* he ordered.

<Yes, sir.>

Cal closed the connection and followed his wet footprints back up to the recreation section. He stood on the edge of the pool for a few minutes, then dove in the water and floated near the bottom of the pool, looking up at the lights warped by the water. Sounds stretched and compressed.

He hated that Petral had made him think about Mercury again, remember what it was like to be small and hungry and worth no more than someone's bet. No one had bet on him to survive. And then he'd turned the station reactor into a bomb.

Cal thought of the faces of the mining crew, the smells of sweat and curry, scorched oil and silicon. The smells of humans trapped in tubes with the big dark outside, crawling all over each other like rats. Leaving Terra was supposed to represent a forward leap in human evolution but nothing had changed. It was the dreaming Weapon Born that represented change.

A thin stream of bubbles left his nose. He recalled Andy Sykes sitting at the table next to Petral. A man who had taken his family into the dark as though it was some kind of gesture toward the future.

Cal stopped himself. He didn't know what Sykes knew or felt. He knew next to nothing about the man other than his TSF record, that he had chosen to marry and have children, and that he had accepted a deal from Ngoba Starl that had pulled him into the biggest damn mess of his life, whether he realized it or not.

He wondered if the accident at Ceres was really the first attack. It was coming. He didn't know where. The Cho. The Collective. M1R. Why wouldn't they go for the gravity wells first? Wouldn't machines maximize the effect of their opening assault?

His lungs were burning when he kicked for the lights, and he broke the surface of the water gasping. Cal swept his hair out of his eyes and swam toward the edge of the pool, enjoying the reminder that he was alive.

When he was back in his apartment, he had the technicians send Kylan down. He was sitting in a straight-backed chair next to the room's small kitchen table when Petral walked through the front door, shoulders slumped forward. Cal didn't bother even addressing the boy.

"Because I could not stop for death," Cal said in a clear voice.

Kylan froze, eyes glazed. The door slid closed behind him.

"He kindly stopped for me," Cal finished.

Petral blinked rapidly, eyes growing wet. She looked around the bare room, frowning. She opened and closed her hands. She straightened, posture immediately different. She was confident and angry.

Her gaze fell on Cal and she reached for the throat of her shipsuit, peeling the fastener down so the suit opened down to her navel.

She reached inside her thigh, then growled in frustration, remembering that the weapon was gone.

Cal smiled. "You think we'd leave you with a weapon? The M1G didn't find it, but I remembered you pulling that cannon out back on Cruithne."

It was a small lie. The M1G did find it, but better if he appeared to be the savvy one.

"Where am I?" Petral demanded.

"You don't know? Kylan made it sound like you never lost consciousness."

"You're a monster," Petral said, voice low. "You're going to pay for this. I'm going to erase you from existence."

"I already don't exist. It doesn't matter what you do to me." Cal motioned toward the second chair on the other side of the table. "You could take a seat. You look silly standing there. I have bourbon if you'd like some."

Petral sent a straight kick at his head.

Cal snapped his head back and to the side and rotated out of the seat, pulling the chair with him. He held it up like a lion tamer as Petral stepped backward into a ready stance.

"It doesn't matter what you do to me," Cal said. "Everything's already in motion. All I wanted to do was talk for a little bit. Have a little company. That's all."

"I'm not your puppet."

Cal gave her a half-smile. "Yes, you are, Petral." He ran straight at her with the chair, catching her between its legs with a cross-piece at her throat, and driving her back into the wall near the door. She tried to slide down the wall to get at his legs but he lowered the chair with her, forcing her into a sitting position. He set a knee on the chair's back to pin her leg.

Petral screamed and scratched at his face and shoulders. Cal pulled out of her reach but didn't release the chair.

Cal shook his head. "I guess I'm not going to get what I want," he said. "Damn."

Petral's face twisted in fury. She wedged an arm under one side of the chair and tried to lever her hips to roll out from under his weight. The fragrance of soap from her hair reached his nose, sending a tremor through his chest.

Cal adjusted and continued to hold her, then finally said, "Fine." He repeated the code phrase, low this time.

Petral's hands continued to reach for him but the fight drained immediately. Her face went slack, and then Kylan came back. He blinked and looked around, down at the chair and then at Cal.

"What did I do?" he asked.

"Everything," Cal said bitterly. He let go of the chair and sat on the floor.

"You shouldn't let her out," Kylan said. "She's mad."

Cal didn't bother to look at the kid. He felt a pit open in his stomach. He felt like he'd answered a question he didn't want to know.

"Get up and put the chair back," he said. "Then hand me that whiskey bottle."

CHAPTER THIRTY-EIGHT

STELLAR DATE: 09.21.2981 (Adjusted Years)
LOCATION: Clinic 46
REGION: Jovian L1 Hildas Asteroids, Jovian Combine, OuterSol

Brit released the maglocks in her boots and kicked into the dark. Her HUD painted the space around her with objects and information, but didn't do a good job of hiding the immediate feeling that she had let go of the world.

She knew this feeling, watching the object below her spin faster and faster as her relative velocity changed. She knew when she grew close to her destination, she would be met by the feeling that she'd be torn apart in the transition. But it would work. It had worked before. She had to know and trust that systems like her EV armor, her HUD, her Link, would operate as designed.

She spread her hands, looking at her pale gloves against the black. Below her, the hull of the *Mortal Chance* shone with reflected light, brighter than she had expected. As she drifted farther away from the ship, she turned her attention forward to where Clinic 46 waited in the dark, a green point on the HUD with distance indicators counting down.

The numerals of the adjusted date were visible in the corner of her HUD as well, and after several minutes of looking at the numbers her stomach tightened. It was almost Cara's birthday. A wave of sadness passed over her but she quickly pushed her emotions down, reassuring herself for the thousandth time that her work was important and that Cara would understand. It had only been two years, after all. There were people in the TSF who had been deployed longer. Imagine the people on the FGT ships dealing with distance and relativity? They would never see their loved ones again.

A call might be nice, she thought, and berated herself because she didn't know if she was going to live beyond this mission. Was she going to hijack a signal out of the Heartbridge outpost and send her daughter a frantic message on an open channel? That would make Cara famous.

She wondered what Cara thought of her. She had always been too hard on her daughter. Harder than she had been on Tim, certainly. But he'd been a baby, and then such a happy little boy without a care in the world. Her girl couldn't be so carefree. Brit had seen too much of the real world, the dark side of the organ farms and the pirate slave ships, the people who lived beneath the clean surfaces of High Terra. Maybe that was part of what she loved about Andy. He had come up from the mud and still had that smile on his face. He smiled despite what he knew about the world. And he looked damn sexy in TSF armor with a rifle under his arm.

Brit smiled in the dark, thinking of Andy, thinking how much Tim was going to look like him. They would all be together again soon if she could get through this mission. Shut down this Clinic and then catch the *Mortal Chance* back to the Cho. Or if she couldn't catch the *Mortal Chance*, she was going to have to make another jump to one of those ships out there. What were they? The registries had come back from all across Inner and OuterSol, most marked as relief vessels of some kind. Was this a Heartbridge parking lot? Few of the ships registered more than storage-level activity.

She turned her attention to the outpost, which was growing now. It flashed as it spun, showing various communication units and a wide fabricated band that looked like the main facility. Brit felt pressure on her shoulders as the EV suit made the first correction thrust. There would be nearly a thousand more. She couldn't withstand a real burn but also didn't want to do anything that might appear on the station's sensor systems. She needed to float in as gently as a piece of random debris.

Spectrum static hissed in her ears, growing more pronounced with the closing distance. The murmurs of various systems ghosted in her helmet.

An hour later, arms and legs turned to jelly by velocity adjustments, Brit set down on the slowly spinning body of Clinic 46, a lumpy piece of rock nearly covered in human construction. Her HUD displayed a passable schematic of the place as she had flown in, and when she was finally able to lock her magboots to something metal, she already knew the location of the nearest maintenance vent. She couldn't risk activating an airlock, so she planned on moving in through the station's system of refuse vents. She had already watched several masses of trash float off into the dark, their trajectories carefully set to thread the surrounding armada.

It took nearly an hour to find a refuse portal, then wait for it to open and spew plas and bits of alloy. Before the stream ended, Brit threw herself into the middle of it and activated her EV thrusters. She was jabbed in the chest and abdomen by three heavy pieces of metal shooting out with the power of decompression. She blinked, bearing the pain, as she settled down in the bottom of the receptacle and locked her boots. The vent hung open for nearly five minutes before it finally cycled closed and sealed, filling the space with environmental gasses.

The refuse mechanism hadn't been designed with many safety features Brit could find. It only opened in one direction and refused to budge when she tried to force it. She didn't want to use a grenade, so opted for the terminal hacker. The little device sat scrolling through machine language before it finally settled on an architecture that meant nothing to Brit except that a dialog box asked her "Open or Close?" She chose open and the interior panel rotated to the side, showing her a blank stretch of corridor.

Brit waited, listening through her helmet's enhanced sensors. She ran an IR scan for latent human activity and found nothing, so she climbed out of the trash bin and relocked its port.

The corridor reminded her of a Heartbridge Clinic. It was made of the same smooth white ceramic material, with vents along the ceiling and what looked like drains in the floor. Evenly spaced white lights pierced her vision so that it hurt to look up. Her HUD adjusted for the glare, making the white walls look gray.

Based on the information she had from 8221 and other Heartbridge facilities, she knew the area where any children might be held would be in an isolated section containing all the necessities of a barracks. Brit crouched against the wall as her HUD made assumptions about the shape of the asteroid and the construction it had viewed from the outside, along with the radiant signatures. It recommended a left turn to move toward the center of the asteroid.

Taking one of the pulse pistols from her waist, Brit set her armor for combat mode and moved quickly down the corridor, HUD scanning for sensors or human activity.

As she moved from section to section, she found it disconcerting how much the place reminded her of 8221. She passed sections of long hallways with doors that opened on the same type of network rooms she had seen before, followed by rooms with rows of examination couches as if the children were made to watch each other as they were connected to various test systems. Several rooms had their white walls covered in hand-written notes and diagrams, scrawling out phrases like "Inherent rejection predictive modeling" and "Negative choice processing" followed by trees of connected equations. Her HUD snapped copies as she passed. It was all evidence.

Brit considered broadcasting all of it on an open channel as she found it; but she hadn't located anyone alive yet, hadn't rescued any kids. She couldn't risk giving herself away until she secured the kids. Once she was in the fight, then a broadcast would have an effect. She thought about Fugia Wong's transmitter floating out there somewhere. It wouldn't do any good to hope it might bring her help; hope wasn't a plan.

She passed rooms hung with organic silica structures, looking at first like massive spider webs. As she spent more time following the shapes, she realized they were neurons branching into and out of each other.

Brit was turning a corner into a larger corridor after just passing through a kitchen area, still devoid of people, when she nearly collided with a woman in a blue shipsuit. Brit fell back, raising her pistol.

The woman stared at her, then pulled her long black hair out of her eyes with both hands like parting curtains. Her posture was strange, shoulders at different heights, and her mouth hung open.

"I know you," the woman said.

Brit steadied the pistol. Something about the woman was off, as though she was an experiment of some kind. She certainly didn't look like any kind of researcher. Brit decided to play along. The woman might be able to tell her where the other test subjects were held.

"How do you know me?" she asked.

"I saw you before."

"Before?"

"In the other place. You were dressed more like a soldier then. You had white armor."

Brit froze. She tried to fit the idea of this woman knowing her with the assault on 8221. Had one of the subjects not been freed? Had Heartbridge used surveillance data to train later generations of AI?

"What's your name?" Brit asked slowly.

The woman perked up slightly. "My name's Kylan."

"Did we meet before, Kylan?" The name was one which was burned into Brit's mind. Kylan Carthage, one of the children from 8221. One of the children they had killed in the fighting. How was he before her once more? Did they make copies of the children's minds?

"No." The woman shook her head and her hair fell in her eyes again. She moved the hair out of her way like it was a foreign object. "Well, we didn't talk. I tried to talk to other people there but I didn't talk to you."

The woman wasn't making any sense and Brit threw a worried glance down the corridor past Kylan's shoulder. This was taking too long.

"Can you show me where the others are?"

"The others?" Kylan asked. "I guess. Are you sure?"

"It's why I'm here."

Kylan's moist gaze hung on her for a second, then she turned and walked back the way she had come. "It's this way."

Brit kept her pistol ready and followed, checking side to side as Kylan walked obliviously through intersections.

They entered a series of corridors lined with what looked like small apartments. Each door had a set of chairs or a bench next to it, as if people would sit in the white corridor and talk to each other. Seeing the residential area, Brit realized she hadn't seen one live plant since entering the outpost.

"In there," Kylan said, pointing at a door. "Do you want to go in?"

Brit drew back, not trusting the situation. "This isn't what I mean," she said. "Is there a test area where there are other people like you? Kids? I know they're testing kids here."

"I don't think there are any kids here," Kylan said. "There are doctors. I talked to them. There are other Weapon Born. Is that who you're looking for?"

"Weapon Born?" Brit asked, now all but certain that somehow there was the mind of a young boy inside this woman. Was it really a woman? If not, it was the most convincing synthetic she had ever seen.

"The Seeds. I was a seed before I was put inside her." She put her hands on her stomach.

Brit glanced at the apartment door. "Back away, Kylan," she said. "Come over here by me." She didn't want her activating a motion sensor and opening the door.

The woman-boy followed Brit's command. When they were far enough away from the door that Brit was sure it wouldn't open on its own, she lowered the pistol slightly, allowing herself to relax for a second.

"Where are the Seeds?" she asked.

Kylan looked happy to offer the information. "Down in the fleet bays. Do you want me to show you?"

Brit nodded, glancing at the closed apartment door. "I would like that very much," she said.

CHAPTER THIRTY-NINE

STELLAR DATE: 09.22.2981 (Adjusted Years)
LOCATION: *Sunny Skies*
REGION: Jovian L1 Hildas Asteroids, Jovian Combine, OuterSol

Andy dropped into the pilot's seat and pulled up the holodisplay and the proximity sensors. Three red dots were on a vector for *Sunny Skies*, moving just fast enough to be long-range missiles or ships about to fire missiles and then cut a braking burn. He hit the all-quarters alert and shouted for Fran over his Link.

<*I'm here,*> she answered. <*What have we got?*>

<*Three inbound. I don't have registry info yet but they're moving fast enough to be military. Can you get the passengers strapped in?*>

<*Hopefully they're smart enough to figure it out on their own. I'll check them on the way to the command deck.*>

<*I'll try and give warning before I have to pull any evasive action. They haven't dropped ordinance yet.*>

"Dad!" Cara shouted from the communications console, clapping her hands over her ears. "I can't hear anything. Do we have to have the alert on?"

"We need to let the others know," he said, still staring at the holodisplay. "You can quiet it in here."

Cara took on hand off her ear and made an adjustment on her console. The alarm dropped to a barely audible squeal.

"Are you getting anything off them?" Andy asked. "High-power broadcasts? Anything?"

"I'm showing a continuous signal stream from each of them," Cara said. "I'm triangulating now."

"Continuous?" Andy asked.

"Yeah, it's weird."

"They're drones."

"Why would there be drones so far out? I didn't pick up anything from a larger ship." Cara frowned as her hands moved over her console, making her look like Brit for an instant. "I don't see any other ships."

"I don't want to guess right now," Andy said.

"Talk the plan," Cara scolded. "You said in stressful situations we should think out loud so we know what everybody's thinking. I think those ships are communicating with something nearby."

"Cara, we're in the in the dead space between the belt and Jupiter, past the Hildas asteroids. There's nothing out there."

"What's our position?" Fugia Wong asked from the doorway.

"Position?" Andy demanded. "Relative to what?"

"Callisto and Ceres." The calm in Wong's voice made Andy give her a second glance. She looked strangely pleased with herself.

"What are you up to?" Andy said. "Do you know something about this?"

"I know you're under attack," Fugia said. "What surprised me is how long it took."

"Who's attacking us?"

"You're sure it's not pirates coming after their dog?"

Andy expanded the holodisplay to fill the center of the command deck so it showed Callisto and Ceres at its far opposite edges. *Sunny Skies* was a blue square in the middle, velocity and vector information following along in shifting numerals. The three red dots continued to approach on a path from the middle of the asteroid belt, holding a tight formation.

"Where's the other ship?" Andy said.

"There is no other ship," Wong said. "There's an outpost."

"There's nothing out here. We would have picked up their beacon."

Fugia inclined her head, giving Andy a sardonic smile that said he was being naive. "Heartbridge has a research station out here they call Clinic 46. Most shipping traveling between Ceres and Callisto passes within range of its attack fleet. However, they don't usually let anyone know that."

"How do you know about it then?"

Fugia shrugged. "It's my business to know."

Andy stiffened in the pilot's seat, gripping the worn armrests. "They passed us at Mars. Heartbridge knew we had to come here." He shook his head. "No, they had people on M1R. They tried to put the ship on lockdown."

"I think an organization like Heartbridge can do two things at once," Wong said.

"You think? Or you know?" Andy pushed himself out of his seat and stood over Wong. "This is starting to feel like you're pulling strings. How about I go grab your senator and put her out the airlock?"

The humor dropped from Wong's face. "We're not enemies, Captain Sykes. You won't do that."

"You think I won't? You're playing games with my family. You think I'll choose your crusade over my children?" Andy put his right hand on his pistol, edged the trigger guard with this finger. He became aware of Cara watching him from the other side of the room.

"You chose this path, Captain Sykes. You chose to help the AI."

"I didn't choose to help anything. I chose to transport cargo from one place to another."

"Is that true? Is Lyssa cargo?" She raised her voice. "Are you a machine, Lyssa?"

Andy narrowed his eyes. "That's not fair."

From an overhead speaker, Lyssa's voice emerged clear and calm. "Andy will do what he must to protect his family. I understand that." There was a burst of static, followed by, "I support this. I wouldn't ask him to do anything else."

Wong glanced at the ceiling. She seemed stricken by what Lyssa had said, on the edge of tears.

<*I'm not going to let anything happen to you,*> Andy said.

<Don't make promises you can't keep.> Lyssa's voice held a resolute calm he didn't understand. She had changed so much from when she could barely talk to anyone but him, hardly thirty days ago.

<What else does she know?> Andy said, letting some of the desperation he felt into his Link. <If she set all this up from the beginning, what does she hope to gain by hanging her senator out as bait for Heartbridge. Or are you the bait? None of this is making sense.>

<I believe her when she says she's working to assist sentient AI,> Lyssa said. <I spoke with the Weapon Born she stole from Heartbridge. That's what she told them. The AI on Mars 1 said someone has been moving AI outsystem to Proteus. Why Ngoba Starl didn't make any of this clear to you is confusing, unless Dr. Jickson never shared it with him.>

<You think Jickson planned this with Wong?>

<I don't know,> Lyssa said. <He never talked to me about any of this. He was a— A voice in the distance. I can't explain it.>

<You don't need to. I think I understand.>

Fran walked through the door from the corridor and looked at Fugia and Andy. "I thought the passengers were on lock down?"

"Fugia says we're within attack range of a Heartbridge outpost and that's who we've got incoming."

Fran cursed. "More Heartbridge drones? I'm sick of those things. What are we doing? We're a civilian ship under attack. Send out an assistance request."

Andy blinked. "I didn't think of that. It's a good idea."

"No one's going to get here in time," Wong said.

"I'll take every idea I can get," Andy said. "Now, Ms. Wong, you need to get back to your quarters and make sure everyone's strapped in. It's about to get messy."

Fran had sat down in the co-pilot's seat and was checking ship status. She put up a replica of the incoming objects' velocity relative to that of *Sunny Skies*.

"Point defense cannons online," she said. "Cara, have you got the main communications array ready for a directional burst?"

"No," Cara said. "Why would we do that?"

Andy smirked. "A last-ditch effort to fry incoming ships."

"Captain Sykes," Wong said. "I understand this seems complicated, but it's not. I'm used to these kinds of politics and I see you're not."

"I was a soldier in the TSF," Andy said. "I'm not a complicated person."

"I understand. There is a network in place to assist fleeing AI. I can explain more once we're through this. The action on Ceres plays a role in that network, and I'll admit we've been working against Heartbridge for a long time. All of this will make sense."

"Like you said, once we get through this you'll be explaining exactly what it is you're doing," Andy said. "Right now, I have drones to worry about. Now go strap in."

Wong gave him a tight smile and left the command deck.

When the door slid closed behind the small woman, Fran said, "I don't trust that lady."

"I don't know what to make of it," Andy said. "She didn't have to say anything she just did. She could have let us figure it all out on our own."

Fran grinned. "Maybe she's lying after all."

"Why? For the hell of it? This crap is making my head hurt?"

"You sure that isn't Lyssa?"

"You're all giving *me* a headache," Lyssa answered quickly. "I don't like being a bystander in all this. What can I do to help?"

"You can help me monitor the power load relative to the shields and weapon systems," Fran said.

"You can monitor those drones when I keep getting distracted," Andy added.

"I can do those things."

"Can you check on Tim and the dog, too?" Andy asked.

"Tim is in his room. Em is sitting beside him."

"Cara," Andy said, "tell Tim to get in his safety harness." He grinned at Fran. "I could get used to having an SAI on board."

"I can't make Tim do something he doesn't want to do," Lyssa said.

"You can pay attention to what my monkey brain can't. Or at least help out like any other crewmember would."

Back in the pilot's seat, Andy pulled the holodisplay in close, and started testing different evasion courses. Every time he ran the numbers, the drones still caught them. The smaller ships were simply faster and could withstand more g-forces. Running the formulas a third time, something in the drone's flight path caught his attention. They hadn't actually made any high-g maneuvers beyond human endurance.

"Now that's strange," he said. "Cara, do you have any long-range IR scans of the incoming drones yet?"

"All I can see are their engines, Dad. Can you get anything inside the ship from this far out?"

"Not typically. It was a hunch. They're drones but they aren't flying like drones."

"You think we're dealing with human crews?" Fran asked.

"Anything's possible in the middle of nowhere," Andy said. "I'm not discarding the possibility. Don't drop any of the weapons systems." He glanced at Cara. "Start broadcasting registry requests and see how they respond."

Andy flipped through several status menus. "Oh," he said abruptly. "The emergency call." He found the emergency protocol and activated the assistance beacon. A red icon flashed at the top of the holodisplay, indicating the ship was undertaking a long-range broadcast.

"What do I do if someone answers the alert?" Cara asked.

"You tell them we're under attack and send our coordinates."

When Cara didn't answer, Andy glanced her direction. "Make sense?"

Cara's expression shifted from frustration to confusion as Andy watched, her gaze fixed on her display.

"Cara?"

"It makes sense," she said. "But I didn't think you expected our call to be answered so quickly."

"What?" Andy said. He looked at Fran, who shook her head. "Where's the response coming from?"

"It's local," Cara said. "It came back almost as soon as you activated the beacon."

Fran barked a laugh. "Heartbridge is answering."

Andy stared at the flashing emergency icon on the display. "That's not what I expected," he said. He tapped the icon to accept the incoming signal.

It was Cal Kraft's voice that came over the speakers.

"Captain Sykes," Kraft said. "How interesting to find you in my back yard."

Andy swallowed. "Mr. Kraft. Are you still with Heartbridge?"

"I am."

"Then I understand my ship is in the vicinity of a Heartbridge facility?"

"That is correct. You activated an emergency beacon. Are you requesting assistance at this time?"

Andy flicked his gaze to the holodisplay, where the velocity numbers between *Sunny Skies* and the incoming ships were growing closer.

"We have three vessels approaching us on a hostile vector and velocity. Do you know anything about them?"

"I do," Kraft said, sounding pleased. "Those ships contain Heartbridge property. If you find yourself in possession of them or their contents, you are required by SolGov legal authority to return them to me without delay."

"I don't know if that's an option, Mr. Kraft. I'm about to engage them with my point defense cannons before they become kinetic attacks on my ship."

Kraft whistled. "That's unfortunate. Of course, you have the right to self-defense."

"I do," Andy said. "This is also open space."

"Then I understand, Captain Sykes. If you need to engage those craft to ensure the safety of your ship and crew, I understand. I may ask you to verify some insurance paperwork for me, but you do what you need to do."

Fran shot Andy a frown, the implants in her eyes flashing.

<*He knows what's on those ships,*> she said.

<*We seem to be solving a problem for him. Are they still on an attack vector?*>

<*That's certainly what it looks like.*>

"How can I help, Captain Sykes?" Kraft prompted, forcing Andy's attention back to him.

"I'm in the middle of an engagement. I'll let you know what we need in about five minutes."

"Perfect," Kraft said, a smile in his voice. "I'll be ready to send a salvage team as soon as you need. Out here."

The signal dropped. Andy tapped his thumbs on the console. "That bastard couldn't be more pleased with himself. He's been waiting for us the whole time."

"You couldn't have known they had an installation out here," Fran said. "If it hadn't been this, it would be another ship like the *Benevolent Hand*."

Andy shook his head. "I don't see how we're getting out of this. We can't fight another drone fleet. We can't outrun them."

"We can burn right now," Fran said. "We'd have to burn hard and aerobrake through Jupiter's upper atmosphere to slow once we arrive."

Andy did the basic calculation. "We'd be out of fuel at the transfer point, if we survive aerobraking, we'd need to pray for search and rescue to find us before we fall into the planet.

"Or we fail to brake and end up drifting through the system," Cara added, her voice wavering slightly.

"We could turn back to InnerSol," Fran suggested.

Andy nodded, mentally listing all the various destinations they might reach and the consequences of each. He couldn't see a way out. They were caught. He swallowed, knowing what he had to do. Kraft wanted Lyssa. He didn't care about the kids or Fran. As far as he knew, Fugia Wong and her people weren't on Kraft's radar. He could trade himself for their freedom.

But that didn't work, either. He had promised Lyssa.

A promise had to mean something.

He couldn't leave them and assume they would be safe. Hope is not a plan.

"Dad," Cara said. "We're getting another signal."

Anger flashed across Andy's thoughts. "Tell Kraft we're busy."

"It's not Cal Kraft," Cara said. Her voice was trembling. "It's one of the ships coming toward us."

"It is?" Andy said, shocked. "Who?"

Cara bit her lip as though she didn't want to speak. Instead of answering, she tapped her console. An audio recording played a wash of static, followed by:

"*Worry's End. Worry's End.* This is a distress signal. I request assistance. I am under attack by hostile forces. I say again: I request assistance from hostiles. My name is Britney Sykes. I have wounded on board."

Andy clenched his jaw, not believing what he heard.

It was Brit.

CHAPTER THIRTY-FORTY

STELLAR DATE: 09.22.2981 (Adjusted Years)
LOCATION: Clinic 46
REGION: Jovian L1 Hildas Asteroids, Jovian Combine, OuterSol

Cal Kraft stood in the Clinic 46 Operations Center, looking over the shoulder of a space traffic controller as the woman shifted a holodisplay that looked like a confetti storm. A background of gray icons indicated the fleet Heartbridge kept in storage around the outpost, while smaller blue icons indicated security patrols operating in the area. A large yellow icon showed the civilian freighter *Mortal Chance* making the scheduled cargo drop, while another section of the display flashed bright and dark to indicate increased activity. That was where the woman who had grabbed Petral Dulan along with every Seed in the drone control section was running in a stolen shuttle, with two attack drones in escort.

"Sir," another technician said. "We just intercepted a signal sent to the *Worry's End*. The shuttle is requesting help."

"I want to hear it," Cal said.

He was filled with a general anger and not yet sure what deserved its focus. He noticed the staff watching him warily, probably aware of what had happened to the crew of the *Benevolent Hand*. He'd been justified then; the captain had been a fool who had been about to get more people killed. These people weren't much different: contractors on an outpost in the middle of nowhere. They couldn't be expected to care about their jobs without a little actual fear added to the transaction.

The woman sounded desperate but there was a strange quality to her voice. She wasn't scared of her situation. She was afraid Andy Sykes wouldn't answer.

Cal quickly ran through the resources he had available, which wasn't much. The fleet surrounding Clinic 46 was mothballed, their reactors cold. It would take days to get the first ship online, and he didn't have a crew. The drones in active patrol had Weapon Born pilots, but the woman had taken all the others. The outpost had an onboard SAI capable of controlling enough fighters to smash the *Worry's End* into scrap, but he wasn't certain that was what he wanted in this situation. Too many events were aligning at once for this all to be coincidence.

He focused on the freighter. "Give me the stats on the *Mortal Chance*," he said.

The tech pulled up the ship's registry, including a short bio on Captain Harm. The frigate had begun its life as a heavy troop transport on Mars and had a reinforced superstructure and overpowered main engine designed for escaping gravity wells.

"Whoever you are," he said, "you chose the wrong ship for your mission."

"Sir?" the tech asked.

Cal dismissed the woman and pointed at the officer on duty. "I need a shuttle and a squad of security."

"What's the plan, sir?" the administrative sergeant asked.

"I'm going to invoke a part of Captain Harm's contract that she probably didn't bother to read."

In twenty minutes, Cal was dressed in body armor and checking his weapons load-out in the lower fleet section. Ten men and woman stood in formation in front of a medium-shuttle while their squad leader, a woman named Ulan Gibbs who bore a jagged scar across her face, checked their gear and cursed at them. Cal watched for a minute, listening. Gibbs was good and it was obvious her soldiers cared about their gear— but she managed to find something to correct on nearly all of them.

When the inspection was finished, Gibbs nodded to Cal and said, "We're ready when you are, sir."

"Thanks," Cal said. He raised his voice. "You've all been out here on station security and probably bored off your asses. Things are about to get interesting. A combatant just penetrated station security and stole the majority of our attack drone AI, as well as another test subject that represents significant company intellectual property. That person is about to rendezvous with another ship and try to leave our vicinity. Since the drone fleet is offline, we're going to commandeer the civilian cargo frigate waiting off station and use their ship to interdict the combatants."

He looked at each face down the line. They all nodded as he spoke and didn't appear to have any dumb questions in their eyes.

"We may need to conduct EV operations once we reach the objective so be ready." Cal looked at Ural Gibbs. "I'm not going to wait for anyone unless I get held up by some overwhelming attack. Stay with me and provide a good base of fire at every opportunity. I want comms silent until there's some need for a meet. Understood?"

Gibbs gave him a nod. "Perfectly," she said.

Cal slung his rifle over his shoulder and picked up his case, which was full of grenades. He stepped into the shuttle. It was a basic personnel mover with benches facing each other along the walls and storage cabinets at the back. The nose had room for a three-person crew. He took the pilot's seat. The system recognized his presence and started cycling through warm-up procedures.

<Identify employee HB number,> the onboard AI said. The voice was a young woman, probably an early prototype and not Weapon Born. Cal gave his employee identification.

<Cal Kraft,> the AI said. <My name is Sandra Lifan. Do you have special requirements for this trip?>

<Locate the civilian frigate TMS Mortal Chance in close orbit with the local station,> he said. <We're going to dock with it.>

<Understood. Adjusting environmental controls for additional personnel.>

<I don't need a run-down of everything you do. Just get us there.>

<Understood.>

The AI didn't say anything else as the squad filed on board and settled in their seats, adjusting harnesses and balancing weapons and helmets between their knees. Gibbs growled at them to get their helmets on and make last minute combat checks as the main door closed and sealed. The outer bay doors opened and the shuttle lifted off the deck, pitching a little, before activating steam thrust to push away from the asteroid.

In zero-g now, Cal watched the light fade quickly through the front visual panels, then shifted to the holodisplay and mapped their location with the *Mortal Chance*. They would intercept the freighter in less than five minutes.

"ETA four minutes," he shouted to the squad, which shut them up. Gibbs looked up from checking her ammo belt and nodded.

<Sandra,> Cal said.

<I am here.>

<Activate override protocol on the *Mortal Chance*. Once we're through the airlock, I want you to remain connected and establish network control of the ship. If it has an AI, you're authorized to subdue all systems. I want you in control of that ship. I'll need engine and weapons systems status as soon as possible. Stop any internal notifications on the airlock.>

<Understood.>

Cal pulled his helmet on and adjusted the seals. The HUD glowed to life on his faceshield.

For three minutes, there was nothing but dark through the visual panels. Then the *Mortal Chance* appeared in front of shuttle spinning like a top. Sandra adjusted their approach and matched velocity and spin with the frigate, until the shuttle faced one long side of the cargo freighter continuously. In the middle of a long flat section midships were the oval cargo bays, and between them sat the shuttle airlock. Sandra brought the shuttle in neatly. Cal felt a small vibration when the connection was made and the heavy maglocks engaged.

<Who were you before, Sandra?> Cal asked.

<I don't know what you mean?> the AI said. <Before we met? I have served on Clinic 46 for five years, two hundred and sixty-one days.>

Unbuckling his harness so he could float free of the chair, Cal said, <Good answer.>

Gibbs opened the airlock into the *Mortal Chance* and the soldiers on the facing wall kicked through the open door with their rifles up. Cal went after the first team. The rest of the squad followed in groups of four. Cal didn't wait for them. Gibbs let him know when they were all onboard.

With the first team behind him, Cal moved through the cargo section of the freighter, working quickly until he reached the habitat ring with the crew sections and command deck. He rounded a corner and found himself two meters from a young man with bright blue hair. Cal shot him in the forehead before he could open his mouth in surprise.

Turning, he motioned for one of the soldiers to move the body into an open room, then continued down the corridor. The ship looked well-maintained, if out of date. Several empty rooms indicated it could accommodate more crew than they had on board. The captain was probably burning out crews with overwork.

<*Do we have a crew manifest?*> he asked Sandra.

<*I have the captain, a navigator named Rina Smith, engineer named Chafri Hansen, pilot named Sarah Jennings. That's all.*>

<*Sarah Jennings?*> Cal said. <*What have you got on her?*>

<*Very little…hold please.*> The AI paused. <*A recent database update shows that Sarah Jennings may be an alias used by Brit Sykes. Former TSS. On the registry of a ship named* Sunny Skies *with husband Andy Sykes.*>

Cal didn't have time to process the information. He paused at an intersection and cleared the two side corridors, then heard voices from a doorway up ahead. He slid along the bulkhead wall until he made out Captain Harm's voice, slurring words: "She's not coming back. More split for us. I'm not staying any longer."

Another woman answered, "You said you would wait. We're waiting."

"She said she was gone."

Cal walked into the room with his rifle at his shoulder. The women stared at him in shock. He recognized the captain, Alys Harm, and noted from her ruddy face that she was drunk. The other woman must be Rina Smith. They both put their hands up.

"We're unarmed," Smith said.

"What are you doing on my ship?" Harm demanded, blinking. "Who are you?"

"My name is Cal Kraft," Cal answered, his helmet speaker flattening his voice. "I'm taking your ship to recover your lost crew member."

"Why?" Smith said.

"Keep your hands up," Cal commanded. "She stole Heartbridge property. Apparently, you know something about it."

"She's AWOL," Harm said. "There's only two places she can be. On your station or in one of those ships you've got mothballed, trying to steal a drive bottle or something like that. I don't have time to background check these people. I bring them on for a run and then let them go when they screw up. This one obviously screwed up."

"Shut up," Cal said.

"Obviously, it's in the contract that you can use the ship," Harm continued, wiping her mouth as spittle ran down her chin. "I'm going to get paid. All I want to know is how long." She spread her hands in a shrug. "I'm trying to run a business here."

Cal shot the wall next to Harm's head. Her ear sprayed blood, forcing her to clamp both hands to the wound. She wailed, eyes full of tears. "Why did you do that?"

"Shut your mouth or I'm going to use my plasma pistol to burn your lips off."

Harm clamped her mouth closed and glared at Cal. He turned to Rina Smith. "Is there anyone else on this ship?"

"Chafri. He was in his room."

"I found him," Kraft said. He waved at the soldiers behind him. "Bring this one up to the command deck," he said, pointing at Smith. "Put the captain in her quarters with a guard on her. Make sure she doesn't have access to any weapons or anything she could hurt herself with. I don't want her hanging herself with her bootlaces."

The soldiers nodded and stepped in to grab Harm by both arms. She straightened, blood running down her neck.

Cal grimaced. "Take her to the autodoc first."

He stepped back into the corridor and waved for Smith to follow him. "Which way is the command deck?" he said.

"That way," she answered, pointing down the corridor.

Cal nodded to a soldier and told him to keep a weapon on Smith. He moved down the corridor until they reached the command deck, just as the navigator had said. Maybe Smith wasn't as stupid as Sykes.

<Sandra,> he said. *<You have control of the ship?>*

<I have all systems. There are some strange filtration issues with the bio systems but nothing that will affect current operations.>

<Good. Prepare for burn. I want a delta-V matching Sykes' ship.>

<That won't be difficult. The Worry's End *appears to have matched course with the stolen shuttle.>*

Cal sat in the pilot's seat and pulled up the control systems. He checked the engine and fuel status for himself, verifying what Sandra had reported, then shifted to the frigate's meager defense systems and shields. The only things the cargo freighter would be fighting were inbound meteorites and other space junk, and it wouldn't do a good job of that either.

<Looks like we'll be boarding the Worry's End,*>* he said. *<There's no way this thing is disabling it from a distance.>*

<Understood. The Worry's End *appears to have a point defense system and shields. They also have control of the two attack drones.>*

<Damn it,> Cal said. *<Can you get control back?>*

<They have maintained their status link with base control but have onboard Seeds. I can't overcome their local control.>

Cal nodded. *<All right. Bring the local patrols into a group and send them toward the* Worry's End. *They probably won't get there in time, but they might also save our asses.>* Andy Sykes had killed Riggs Zanda and five Weapon Born remote robotic units back at Cruithne. Cal didn't know how a washed up TSF pilot had accomplished such a feat but he wasn't going to take any chances with the boarding party.

As he checked the pilot's console, his gaze fell on a printed card someone had wedged into the corner above the holodisplay. He pulled it down and turned the card in his hands. It was the kind of thing tourists printed in kiosks, and showed a man and woman with two kids in front of a scene with green trees and blue sky, some orbital park made to look like Terra, or at least an artificial backdrop.

Cal realized he was looking at Andy and Brit Sykes and their two kids. They were smiling in the image, looking past the camera. Andy had the little girl in his lap and Brit was holding their son in her arms, a toddler still sucking his thumb.

He slapped the card against the knuckles of his other hand, staring through the holodisplay, then tucked the photo inside his armor. It would be interesting to pull it out later and show it to Brit Sykes, especially when he had her kids.

<You ready, Sandra?> he said.

<All systems nominal,> the AI answered.

Cal nodded. *<That's better than we deserve. Execute burn.>*

CHAPTER FORTY-ONE

STELLAR DATE: 09.22.2981 (Adjusted Years)
LOCATION: *Sunny Skies*
REGION: Jovian L1 Hildas Asteroids, Jovian Combine, OuterSol

Andy felt disconnected, not understanding why Brit's voice would be on the overhead audio. For a second, he thought it was another recording like the one she'd left in the weapons crate. Her voice was so different: raw, distant, punctuated by frantic breathing. She was using a helmet mic. The signal phased in and out, too weak to reach any farther.

He looked from Cara's confused face to Fran, who was watching him with concern. Her flashing eyes met his and Fran's face softened in a way he hadn't seen before, as if she knew Brit's voice was like a knife in his heart. More than ever, he felt that Fran truly cared about him. He didn't know how he could return the emotion in her face.

Sound rushed back in. Alarms, static, the voice in the speaker. A list of actions rolled out in Andy's mind, showing a way forward. His hands moved without thought. He acknowledged receipt of the signal and silenced the proximity alarms.

He flexed his jaw, mouth abruptly dry, and switched on the audio channel. "Incoming ship. This is the *Worry's End*. I acknowledge your distress." He paused. The protocol was for him to identify himself now. The acknowledgment was recorded in both ship's databases.

"Who is this?" she demanded. "How fast can you get out of here?"

"This is Captain Andy Sykes," he said.

The line went quiet. Pulses of static throbbed in the speakers.

"How is she here?" Cara asked, a strange mix of panic, wonder, and no small amount of rage in her voice. "Why would she be here?"

Andy tried to remember exactly what Brit had said in the recorded message. She had found another Heartbridge clinic and was going to raid it, shut it down. He couldn't remember the words, only the excitement in her voice.

"Say again, *Worry's End*?" Brit asked, her voice softer, the hard edge gone

"I authenticate your message, Britney Sykes. This is Captain Andy Sykes of the *Worry's End*." Andy bit the words off, barely able to unclench his teeth as he spoke. He glanced at the holodisplay, following the three incoming ships—two drones and one that had to be Brit—and then picked up six more drone fighters following those three.

When she didn't answer, Andy took a long, shaky breath and leaned closed to his mic.

"Brit," he said. "This is Andy. I don't know how you're here, but I hear you. Now tell me what's after you."

More static pulsed, followed by the sound of shallow sobs. Her mic was still too close to her face. She sniffed. "I hear you. I hear you loud and clear. I don't know what's after me yet. Is that *Sunny Skies*? Did you change the registry?"

"We changed it at Cruithne."

"I hate the name."

Andy couldn't help smirking at Fran. "You're not alone. What's going on, Brit? Who's after you? How are you out here?"

"It's Heartbridge. If you check the space beyond our approach path, you'll find an unmarked station. And a fleet mothballed out there, but I don't know anything about that. I think they're all Heartbridge. I took all their AI. All the AI they use for their drones except the ones they already had out on patrol. I've got someone else here with me. It's Kylan. She says she saw us at 8221. She saw me. Do you remember Kylan?"

"I do," Andy said. He would never forget that name, though he distinctly remembered Kylan as being a boy…not that it mattered right now.

Andy kept his gaze on the display he replied. He marked Brit's ship and the two alongside it as friendly, then directed the sensors to a focused search in a cone spreading behind her shuttle. What should have been empty space contained one diffuse object, a small asteroid sparkling with returns must have been the station she was talking about.

"Damn," Andy said. "Why didn't this come up before?"

Fran studied the new information on her display. "They must have countermeasures actively denying sensors. If you hadn't known this was here, you never would have picked it up."

"And we were passing right by it."

"Space is big," Fran said.

From the communications console, Cara said, "I just found another directed signal from a beacon going toward Saturn, or maybe Callisto? They're close to alignment from here."

"A beacon?" Andy asked. He felt like they'd been sitting in the dark and had just turned on the lights to find the room full of snakes.

The hostile drones were closing on Brit. The sensor sweep of the station picked up a ship pulling away from the station. Its registry came up as TMS *Mortal Chance*, a freighter out of High Terra.

Andy activated the audio channel. "Brit, were you on the *Mortal Chance*?" he asked. "Is that how you got here?"

"Yes. Why?"

"They're pulling away from the station, still getting past all those other ships. They appear to be heading this way."

"The clinic doesn't have anything larger than a shuttle. They must have taken control of the *Mortal Chance* to come after me."

"That would make sense. How much range have you got in that shuttle?"

"I can get to you before I run out of fuel."

Andy ran three quick simulations to see if *Sunny Skies* could start an exit burn while Brit's shuttle was still incoming. As slow as the *Worry's End* was, it would still leave the little shuttle far behind.

"I've got you arriving in forty-eight minutes," he said. "We'll prep for a course change."

<Can the engines give us anything more?> he asked Fran privately.

<Not in a burst. I can't believe that station has been sitting out there in the middle of nowhere acting like a cloud of debris for so long. You think it would be on the unofficial charts, at least. I think that other freighter is going to catch us. They're lighter and their engines look comparable.>

Andy set his jaw. <We could leave her.>

<You're not going to leave her. I may not like the woman because of what she seems to have done, but you just recognized an official distress call.> She shrugged. <Not that ignoring a distress call ever lost anybody sleep, but you did recognize it which makes things a little more difficult if SolGov or the TSF finds out.>

<I know,> Andy said.

<We'll get her on board, then you guys can hash out your drama. It'll be fun.> Fran shot Andy a wolfish grin.

He shook his head. <Nothing fazes you, does it?>

<I grew up out here. There isn't much time to hang onto grudges or stew about people. If you like someone, you like them. If you're going to shoot them, you pull the trigger. There's no time to waste emotion on it.>

<That sounds great. Well, let's get the engines ready and set the point defense cannons on those incoming drones. We push them off at least. The freighter isn't going to be a problem. It's going to be a pretty easy target.>

<They'll have the crew as hostages,> Fran said. <That's what I would do.>

<And use them to make us let them on board? That's not happening.>

Fran shrugged. <We'll see.>

"Brit," Andy said. "I show forty-eight minutes until you're within range to adjust and dock. I'm going to lay some fire on the drones following you."

"Copy," she answered.

"Mom?" Cara said, finally having mustered the courage to speak. Her voice was shaking. "Mom, what are you doing here?"

"Cara?" Static swept across the connection. "Cara, you sound so grown up. I— Let's get through this and then I can tell you about it."

Cara took a deep breath, the frustration plain on her face.

The channel closed, shutting off the static. Cara looked at Andy and Fran. "What are you going to tell Mom?" she asked.

"Tell your mom about what?" Andy said.

Cara blinked. "About you two?"

Andy stared. That had been the last thing on his mind. "We need to stay focused," he said. "This isn't the time to worry about things like that."

Without missing a beat, Fran said, "Your mother and I fight to the death for ownership of your father's balls."

Cara look at Fran, who kept a bland look on her face, then they both started laughing.

Andy shook his head, staring hard at the display. "This is serious," he said.

"Then I'll die laughing," Fran said, and patted him on the shoulder.

CHAPTER FORTY-TWO

STELLAR DATE: 09.22.2981 (Adjusted Years)
LOCATION: *Mortal Chance*
REGION: Jovian L1 Hildas Asteroids, Jovian Combine, OuterSol

The control systems on the *Mortal Chance* were at least a hundred years old. Cal glared at the holodisplay, watching Britney Sykes get closer to her destination then finally disappear from the sensors. The exhaust output from the *Worry's End* grew richer as the ship prepped for additional thrust.

"They can't escape and they know it," he said and glanced at Rina Smith who was sitting on the deck with her back to the wall while one of Gibb's squad stood guard over her. The woman was staring at the flooring between her shoes and hadn't heard him.

Cal pulled up the engine status and checked the fuel levels. The *Mortal Chance* was sitting on roughly half its fuel.

<*Sandra,*> he said. <*What's the likelihood of turning this ship into a missile aimed at the* Worry's End?>

<*You would like to purposely collide with the other ship?*>

<*Yes.*>

<*Fuel reserves are sufficient for such a maneuver but g-forces would exceed safe levels. I will need to override the onboard safety systems. There is a diminishing rate of kinetic force as* Worry's End *accelerates away from our location.*>

<*So I need to hurry up and do it?*> he asked.

<*The mass of this ship is sufficient to neutralize* Worry's End *if we execute burn in the next ten minutes.*>

Cal nodded. <*Good to know. What's the likelihood of the* Worry's End *destroying the* Mortal Chance *before it arrives?*>

He had a good idea of the answer but wanted to know what the AI thought. He had worked with Heartbridge's SAI enough to know they weren't necessarily smarter than smart people. They were, however, better at maintaining dispassionate consideration of a problem. With access to more information simultaneously the SAI could synthesize it with a focus people usually lacked. But they suffered the same ontological problems as humans: they couldn't think outside the box very well, and didn't realize when a base assumption was wrong.

<*Without complete knowledge of the weapons systems on the* Worry's End, *I can't truly say. Visual recognition returns robust point defense cannons that could break this ship into pieces before impact but wouldn't stop the incoming debris field.*>

<*Space debris will get you every time,*> Cal said.

<*The debris alone should be sufficient to disable their ship.*>

Cal had recalled the *Mercy's Intent*, which had continued on to Callisto to pick up a new shift of technicians. Fortunately, they hadn't gotten far, and the ship would be on station at Clinic 46 in twelve hours. He could float in a shuttle for twelve hours if necessary.

The problem with destroying the *Worry's End* was that Britney Sykes had his Weapon Born seeds, and it was looking more and more like Andy Sykes would have the AI Hari Jickson stole. This was all wrapping up too neatly. He tapped the console and sat back, wondering how someone might be manipulating all this. Was it the Heartbridge board? Why?

He had long suspected some person or organization had helped Hari Jickson escape his test facility with both an AI Seed and his prototype mobile surgery. The feat had required a ship, resources, and cunning—all things Hari Jickson hadn't demonstrated when Cal had met him.

Cal glanced at Rina Smith. He had to respect her composure considering the circumstances.

"Hey," he said. When she didn't answer, the guard nudged her with the buttstock of his rifle.

Smith moved her head to the side and glared at Cal.

"Yes?" she said.

"Where are you from?"

"TMS *Mortal Chance*."

"Originally," he corrected. Cal studied her, liking the fight she put up. She had Mediterranean coloring combined with the long limbs of a childhood spent in low-g.

"The Cho," she said. "I was born there but I've been working long-haul freight for the last ten years."

"How old are you?"

"You interviewing me for a job?" Rina asked sardonically.

"Maybe," Cal said. "Maybe once I get to know you, it'll be harder for me to send you to hell with this ship."

"Where's my crewmate Chafri?" she asked.

Cal glanced down at his holodisplay and instantly regretted looking away from her. She would know the blue-haired kid was dead. Now it wouldn't do him any good to lie.

"He was killed during boarding," Cal said.

Smith stared at him, clenching her jaw. "Killed during boarding," she repeated. "That sounds like something you'd tell his mother. Were you in the TSF?"

"No," Cal said curtly.

"You look like a spacer."

"Like you?" he asked.

She smiled. "Yeah. Unsettled. I don't know why you even act like you won't kill me. Obviously we're going after Sarah. So you're either going to use us as hostages, or wreck the ship in the process. Either option doesn't turn out well for me."

"Give me another option, then. Does this heap have any weapons?"

Smith shook her head. Her curly black hair moved against the wall, shiny under the overhead lights. Cal stopped himself from noticing her body, still angry with himself for the outburst with Petral in his room.

"Then what would you suggest?" he asked, rotating his seat so he faced her. He leaned forward with his elbows on his knees. His armor flexed with him. "Brit Sykes stole Heartbridge property and I'm going to retrieve it. Fortunately for me, what she stole is highly resilient in vacuum." That wasn't quite true but he hadn't decided if he cared whether Petral Dulan lived or not. The technicians had already gotten a good look at her.

"I don't know what to tell you," Smith said. "Sounds like turning this ship into a battering ram is the most expedient way to go about it. Then you can say all the civilians died during recovery operations when you make your insurance claim."

"That sounds pretty good," Cal said. "I might use that."

"Or you could tell Brit you're going to destroy that ship she's headed toward unless she hands over whatever she stole. I only worked with her but she seemed level-headed. Maybe you can promise jail time or something. Make it easier. You're not trying to punish anyone here, right? Is that your job?"

"To punish people?" Cal considered the idea. "That's a good point. If I asked the board, they might say that's exactly what I'm here to do."

Smith stretched her neck. "Then I guess it doesn't matter what you do."

<Sandra,> Cal said. *<Are we ready to accelerate?>*

<The engines are prepped for a fuel dump. We'll need to disconnect in the shuttle and I can maintain control remotely.>

<Gibbs,> Cal called. *<Get everyone back in the shuttle.>*

<What's the plan, sir?>

<The Mortal Chance *is becoming a missile.>*

<Understood. The prisoners?>

Cal looked at Rina Smith. She glared back at him, her brown eyes filled with anger. *<We're not taking any prisoners,>* he said.

CHAPTER FORTY-THREE

STELLAR DATE: 09.22.2981 (Adjusted Years)
LOCATION: *Sunny Skies*
REGION: Jovian L1 Hildas Asteroids, Jovian Combine, OuterSol

Cara watched her dad scowl at his display, entering requests every few minutes before sitting back and observing yet another scenario play out as a series of lines and icons. From where she was sitting, Cara couldn't see everything that was playing out on the holodisplay, but she could read her dad's body language well enough, as well as Fran's serious posture at her station, to know the outcomes weren't positive.

She tried to console herself that her mom was so close. She had heard her voice again—even recorded the last few interchanges between her mom and dad. She could play them for Tim later. She hadn't decided if she would tell him right away. It would be better for Dad to let him know.

Finally, her dad shook his head angrily and hit the console. "They're not going to make it," he said. "I've run the simulation every way I can think of and none of them work out. Unless there's something I'm not seeing, either the *Mortal Chance* is going to hit us first, or catch up to Brit's shuttle."

Fran didn't answer immediately. Her gaze was still fixed on the display, eyes flashing with icons and arcs. "We could tell her to move away from us," she said. "Force Heartbridge to choose. Then once they're committed to either of us, we can make a different decision."

Her dad pursed his lips, nodding as he thought. "The *Mortal Chance* is still headed our direction, but so is the shuttle."

"Exactly," Fran said. "We tell Brit to break her course."

"All they'll do is attack us, then. We're the greater threat. Brit is going to run out of fuel and then he can pick her up whenever he wants. We seem to be the only ship in this dance with a weapons system."

"Well," Fran mused. "Brit has two attack drones."

"You think they can make any difference?"

"It depends on whether or not the patrol chasing her would split off to go after her drones."

"Let's run the scenario," her dad said.

"You really want to worry about percentages?" Fran asked.

"I want to make the right decision."

"Where's the *Mortal Chance* now?"

Her dad pointed to a red icon on the display and set it flashing. Cara couldn't read the vector data from her station.

"Hold on," he said, leaning close to study something new. "I've got a shuttle detaching from the *Mortal Chance*."

"They're about to burn," Fran said.

"I guess we're going to answer our question."

"If they're detaching, that means the *Mortal Chance* is about to become a missile."

Cara had been passively scanning all the signals data in the area, including the ongoing streams between the patrol drones and the two flanking her mom's shuttle. Now she picked up a line between the new shuttle and the *Mortal Chance*. She separated the spectrum and laid the signals on the near-space astrogation map, which showed as combinations of waves and lines.

Some signals were stronger than others and followed direct paths, while others floated outward in widening cones, still more were omnidirectional—like *Sunny Skies'* beacon. She was also picking up multiple signals from the station, now that she knew it was there, and another location that looked like empty space not far from where the *Mortal Chance* had been parked. That point broadcast a wave transmission that she would have thought was too weak to reach anywhere, until she noticed it was hiding a single directed broadcast shooting toward Saturn.

She didn't want to bother her dad right now, so she recorded the transmissions. Holding her earpiece against the side of her face, she said, "Lyssa, are you there?"

The AI answered immediately. "I'm here, Cara."

"Is my dad freaking out?"

"His heartrate has been consistently elevated ever since he heard your mom's voice."

"I think mine is too."

"Are you scared of her?"

"I don't know. She's like a door you don't want to open because as long as it's closed you don't have to worry about what might be on the other side. Does that make sense?"

"Yes," Lyssa said.

"I'm picking up something strange near the *Mortal Chance*. Or where the ship used to be." The ship had jumped locations. "Dad!" she shouted. "Did you see the ship move?"

"I see it," he said, his voice in robot mode. "It's on a vector to intercept us."

"You're sure?" Fran asked.

"Everything is indicating that." He looked at Cara. "Get your Mom back on the channel."

Cara nodded and activated the audio spectrum. She had barely sent the request when her mom said through the speakers: "They're moving."

Her dad nodded. "They've separated a shuttle and are sending the freighter on a collision course with us. Can you do something with those drones you've got alongside you? That ship is going to be moving fast, but it doesn't have any defenses. You blow it into pieces, at least we can weather that. Our cannons can take out most of the debris, and the shields will have to weather the rest of it."

"Cannons? OK, I'm doing it now," her mom said. She had the same robotic quality as Dad, as if they had learned it from each other. She wondered how they could talk to each other without any emotion at all. Was that the TSF training? Had they been robots before they fell in love? Maybe Mom was the real robot and Dad managed to leave it behind, but she couldn't—

"Cara," Lyssa said. "You could use the communications array to disrupt signals between the Heartbridge shuttle and the *Mortal Chance*."

Cara stared at her display. "You're right. I can. At least until they hop to another frequency." She frowned. "I shouldn't do it until Mom's drones attack though. That way they're committed to this course and won't be able to shift to do anything about the attack. If I do it now, they'll know we can affect their control."

"They have an AI assisting them," Lyssa said.

"How do you know?"

"The code passing between the shuttle and the *Mortal Chance*. The AI is on the shuttle."

"Can you talk to them?"

"I don't know," Lyssa said. "I can try."

Her dad blew out a tense breath. "She's shifting the drones. They should be on target in thirty minutes. Which gives us about an hour. That thing is moving at full burn now."

"I see it," Fran said.

"I'm talking out loud," he reminded her.

"I know," Fran said, gaze still on her display. "And I understand why. You explained it's a TSF thing. That still doesn't mean it doesn't annoy the crap out of me."

"If I get whacked, you need to know what I was doing."

"*I know*," Fran said. "And whacked is a stupid way to say killed. And I don't want to think about that anyway right now. It's clouding the real thinking I need to do."

Cara liked the way Fran talked; she wished her wit could be so fast under pressure. It seemed like a mix of deep experience and a focus on what really mattered. She seemed to always think they could die, so she didn't even bother to think about it. Instead, she focused on the moment and task right in front of her. What came after that was another problem entirely. Cara wanted to do that.

Why was Mom back? She hadn't even thought it was possible, and now it represented a whole new set of problems. She had started to imagine a future where Fran was there to teach her, or Petral. If Mom came back, all these new people would disappear and they would be an insulated little cell again.

"You've got an idea?" her dad asked.

"We could brake," Fran said.

Her dad scowled. "That drone patrol is still out there."

"I'll take the drone patrol with the point defense cannons any day. It's the mass of that freighter we can't deal with."

"True," he said. He switched over to the audio channel. "Brit? You there? Maintain course. We're going to get you."

Cara didn't understand. She thought he had just agreed to the braking maneuver. Why would he tell Mom to maintain her course? She would overshoot them. Staring at Fran and her dad, she realized they were talking via their links. She hadn't thought to use her hack to listen in.

"Lyssa," she said. "What are they talking about?"

"They think Heartbridge is monitoring the audio channel with your mom."

"It would be nice if they'd tell me."

"Holy crap," her dad said. "The freighter just completely opened its engines. I hope there wasn't anything left alive on the *Mortal Chance*."

Cara watched her dad run a shaking hand through his hair before addressing her mother over the comms.

"Brit," he said. "Look out. They're coming."

"Copy," her mom answered, voice bathed in static.

From across the room, Cara watched the flashing red icon approach their blue dot. Her dad didn't move his gaze from the display. Fran was also staring with rapt attention at her controls. The command deck was silent for nearly five minutes except for the crumbling sounds of the signal spectrum in Cara's headset.

Finally, her dad said, "There is it. Burn-out. They're committed—though they'll have a reserve to match any maneuvers we make—let's just hope they didn't expect this." He quickly entered commands into his console, calculating a course correction for *Sunny Skies*. He looked over at Fran. "Look good?" he asked.

Fran nodded without taking her attention off her engine controls.

"Wait," her dad said suddenly. Over the shipwide channel, he announced, "Emergency braking procedure. Everyone buckle in. You've got one minute."

"Damn crew," Fran said.

"I was worried about the dog," her dad said. "I doubt Tim can keep him in one place for long."

"Tim," Cara called over the intercom to his room. "Are you strapped in?"

"I'm strapped in," he said in an irritated voice.

"Is Em?"

"I have a strap wrapped around him and tied to me. I think it's enough."

Cara couldn't leave her station to check. Her own harness held her to her seat. "Check again," she said. "We're about to get a lot of *g*-force. You don't want him to get hurt."

"I'll take care of him," Tim said.

"I know. I'm just checking. I take care of you, too."

"I'm not a dog."

"You're my brother."

Tim made a sound like he was sticking his tongue out at her.

"All right," her dad said. "Do it. Initiate braking burn."

"Yes, Captain," Fran said.

A roaring sound filled the ship, followed by creaking in the bulkhead, and Cara felt a weight like an elephant sitting on her chest as *Sunny Skies* reversed its course.

CHAPTER FORTY-FOUR
STELLAR DATE: 09.22.2981 (Adjusted Years)
LOCATION: Heartbridge Shuttle 26-11
REGION: Jovian L1 Hildas Asteroids, Jovian Combine, OuterSol

For a beat-up freighter, the *Mortal Chance* still had some kick in her. Cal watched the velocity jump in his display as the ship practically leapt away. He gave Sandra the order to follow with the shuttle, then turned to glance down the bay behind him at the squad checking their equipment.

At the back of the shuttle, Rina Smith and Captain Harm sat on the deck against the storage cabinets, bound at wrists and ankles with plas strips. Harm's head was on her chest, snoring. When he had first looked, Cal thought Smith was staring at him with those brown eyes, then realized she was only glaring at the middle distance, not looking anywhere. Cal glanced at Gibbs, who was fastidiously cleaning one of her pistols.

Gibbs had moved the prisoners despite Cal's order to clear the *Mortal Chance*. Even though he had given orders to leave them. Gibbs didn't want to take the blame for letting them die; she was right about that.

<*Time to impact?*> he asked Sandra.

<*Approximately fifteen minutes,*> the AI answered. <*The* Mortal Chance *is showing better acceleration than I had thought it would.*>

Cal sat listening to the rustling sounds from the squad. A few of them told jokes in low voices followed by groans or short laughter. Gibbs didn't let them mess around much. He tried to guess when the *Worry's End* would open their point defense cannons on the incoming ship. How quickly would Andy Sykes figure out the plan?

After listening to their sporadic audio traffic, he was fairly certain they knew he was listening. The emotion had gone out of Brit Sykes' voice. The last transmission had verified the shuttle would reach the *Worry's End* in time if they chose to leave now. They would have to wait, remaining a target for whatever Cal chose to do. When they talked about sending her two drones against him, he smiled to himself. That would make things interesting, at least.

Without the impediment of human passengers, the *Mortal Chance* burned its engines at 50*g*, more than enough to kill any organics, and probably buckle much of the internal structure. The engines ran through nearly all the remaining fuel until he was surprised the containment bottle didn't melt down. He watched the engine diagnostics spike red, other systems across the old freighter sputtering and squawking as they tried to respond to the suicide run.

When the drives shut down, the *Mortal Chance* had passed over half a million kilometers per hour. He watched the icon follow its arc across his display, moving closer to the intercept with the *Worry's End*.

<*Cal,*> Sandra said. <*I'm showing increased engine activity on the* Worry's End.>

He sat up. <*Are they going to run after all?*>

The AI didn't answer. A mass of new data from the space around *Worry's End* showed thruster activity. Cal stared at the display. What was Andy Sykes doing?

The *Worry's End* turned as he watched, followed by a massive burn from its main engine.

<They're braking,> he said.

<Braking on a return course directly toward our location,> Sandra said.

Cal flushed, feeling electricity run down his face and arms. Captain Sykes was going to attack him.

<Damn.>

<That was always a possibility,> Sandra said.

<What can we do with the Mortal Chance?> he asked. He had left enough fuel in the freighter to compensate for any maneuvers Andy Sykes may make, but not enough for the delta-v created by the ships moving toward one another. <Can we adjust to hit Brit Sykes' shuttle?>

<I'm running the simulation now.>

Cal watched as Sandra fired the attitude thrusters on the *Mortal Chance* altering its vector before giving a final burn from the main engines. The ship's arc tightened, moving its impact point closer to Brit Sykes' shuttle but still not close enough for a direct impact.

<Do I have your permission to destroy the Mortal Chance?> Sandra asked, voice still cool.

<Is there a reason?>

<Yes,> Sandra said but didn't elaborate. <Imploding engine containment bottle now. Critical hull failure pending.>

In Cal's holodisplay, the icon that had indicated the *Mortal Chance* flickered and disappeared, replaced by a spreading red cloud indicating a hot debris field. The cloud continued to move toward Britney Sykes, as well as her two attack drones. The drones were already at the edge of the debris swarm and wouldn't be able to avoid it.

<That'll do,> Cal said, then smiled as one of the drones blinked out.

He turned his attention back to the *Worry's End*. The ship had completed a braking burn that must have wasted half their fuel, and was now inbound toward Cal and the drone patrol. If the ship continued its trajectory, it would ultimately pass close to Clinic 46. That made it a legitimate threat, in addition to harboring stolen property.

<Can you put us on that ship?> he asked Sandra.

<With maximum acceleration, we will use all our available fuel. But I believe we can complete docking maneuvers with the Worry's End.>

Cal shook his head. <I doubt they'll let us complete docking maneuvers. Once we're within range of their point defense cannons, I'm going to send everyone out for a walk.>

<That barely leaves me enough fuel to brake and escape their range,> Sandra said. <I also have the civilians aboard.>

<I understand that,> Cal said. <We all do the best we can, correct? Do you think we're taking the easy way out?>

<What are you going to do once you're on the Worry's End*?>*

<Conduct infiltration operations and secure the ship. What else?>

<I want to be prepared in case you need anything else of me.>

Cal frowned. He didn't understand what Sandra was getting at. *<We're all going to be doing our best not to get blown apart by their point defense cannons. You get the hell out of there. Draw off their fire if you can. Try not to look like you just dropped a breaching team. Get back to the station if you're able to do so. Do I need to make it more clear than that?>*

<No,> Sandra said.

<Where were you born?> Cal asked. If the AI was glitching, he wanted to let the team responsible for her seed know about it—and give them hell for obstructing his mission. The last thing he needed was a curious SAI.

<My seed was born on Clinic 8221.>

Cal shook his head. *<8221. The gift that keeps on giving.>*

<I don't understand what that means.>

<It doesn't matter. Can you handle dropping us outside their range and then drawing enemy fire? I'm not asking you to outright risk yourself, Sandra.>

<Their weapons range is five-thousand kilometers. I will drop you outside that range; at our relative velocity, you will reach their ship in fifteen minutes. Can your armor brake enough to manage that?> Sandra asked.

Cal looked down at his armor. It would have to. *<Yes. Please stop asking so many damn questions. Let me know when we're ten minutes out from drop-off.>*

The AI acknowledged the command and Cal called Gibbs over the Link to explain his plan. After swearing about the beating the deceleration would deliver, she agreed though suggested they separate the squad into two teams. One would land aft and enter through the cargo bay airlock, or breach the hull if Sykes shut them out, while the other went straight to the habitat ring.

<We could just dump their atmosphere,> Gibbs suggested.

<I thought you were the one concerned about civilian casualties.>

<They've assumed an attack posture. It's different now.>

<I won't argue with that.>

They discussed a few more actions on breach, and then their plan once inside the ship. Cal wanted the engines shut down so Brit Sykes could catch them and dock, that way they wouldn't have to continue chasing her around local space to recover the Seeds she'd stolen—if she survived the expanding cloud of debris that was the *Mortal Chance.*

<So the ring team shouldn't blow their airlock,> Gibbs corrected.

<I never said to blow the airlock. We're going to use it if possible.>

Gibbs grumbled.

<What was that?> Cal said.

<I said no plan survives the drop anyway. Just so you know, I'm taking prisoners. I don't shoot people in the face if they don't deserve it.>

Cal locked eyes with her from the pilot's seat. *<You do what you have to so we can accomplish this mission. If you want to keep working for Heartbridge, you better keep me*

happy, too.>

<You think I care about working for Heartbridge? This was easy money with nothing happening. Then you show up and everything goes to hell. If I wanted this kind of crap, I would have stayed in the Protectorate's space force. They're always making up trouble where they don't need to.>

<If you want to get fired, I can help,> Cal said.

<I'll quit right now if you keep pushing it. Think my team will work for you, do this crazy EV if I resign?>

The edge of her mouth pulled up in the slightest smirk but Gibbs' eyes were hard.

<Fine,> Cal said, letting it slide. He needed her for now. Things might be different after the breach but he needed her until he was inside the *Worry's End*, at least. After that…well, all sorts of unfortunate accidents happened in combat.

Gibbs nodded. *<I'm an employee, Kraft,>* she said. *<I'm not some kind of fanatic. Most of this group here is the same way. They want to do a job, feel mostly good about it, and go home after getting paid.>*

<Don't worry about it,> he said. *<I understand.>*

<You don't look like you do.>

<I have a bad poker face.>

<That's the problem.>

Sandra cut in, *<Cal, we have ten minutes to range of their weapons.>*

<There it is,> Cal said. *<Are we going to be friends?>*

<We're going to get this done,> Gibbs said. She raised her pistol and checked the action and energy levels, then slid it into her holster.

"All right," she shouted, standing to grab at a handhold above her head. "We're about to jump. Say your prayers and make your final prep. Check your buddy's gear. Everybody get water and grab more ammo than you need."

"We're not taking the shuttle in for the breach?" a young man asked.

The woman beside him elbowed him in the ribs. "This is a DIP mission, dummy. Die. In. Place."

The kid's face went pale. "I didn't sign up for that shit."

"Shut up," Gibbs growled. "Everybody's got their armor and enough atmosphere for twenty-four hours. You worried about a freighter with a guy and some kids inside? Worst comes to worst, you bail, hit vacuum and activate your rescue beacon. Then you hang out watching vids until pick up."

"Hanging in the big dark gives me the creeps," someone complained.

"Then you stay on the ship while the rest of us go get paid for hazard duty," Gibbs said. "I'll remember you volunteered. Now close those civilians in the emergency closet. When we bail, the rest of the cabin is going hard vacuum."

Two of the soldiers directed Smith and Harm to the closet—both of them looking worried about how airtight it was going to be when the cabin decompressed.

They continued checking gear until Sandra made a five-minute warning and finally a two-minute. Alarms sounded in the pilot's console as weapons fire appeared in the holodisplay.

"Is someone shooting at us?" a soldier asked.

"They're blowing kisses," Gibbs said. She ordered a last check on Smith and Harm.

Cal gave his gear a final check, locking his helmet in place, and turned control of the shuttle over to Sandra. As projectiles crisscrossed the holodisplay, he gave Gibbs a thumbs-up.

<Let's go, Sandra,> he said.

The main cabin airlock cycled and spat environment out into the vacuum. Cal was the first through the door, followed by the squad. Gibbs would take up the rear. He didn't look back, watching instead as glowing icons populated the HUD. He would lead the team at the habitat ring with Gibbs heading for the engines.

Cal squinted as the icon in his HUD representing the *Worry's End* gradually became the dull silver outline of the ship, its wagon-wheel habitat ring spinning in the dark. His suit's attitude thrusters kicked in, matching velocity with the freighter, jerking him around like a feather in the wind. Cal relaxed and let the process play out, feeling a swelling sense of excitement as the *Worry's End* grew larger.

Behind them Sandra flew the shuttle away, describing a long arc as she put it on a course to return to Clinic 46. He had to admit, the timing was good, it looked like they were fleeing in the face of the *Worry's End*'s weapons fire.

He and Gibb's squad rushed toward the freighter, small bursts from attitude thrusters keeping them on course for their hard landing. At a thousand kilometers, the armor's onboard comps started firing retro-jets, slowing the soldiers enough that they wouldn't turn to cream when they hit the *Worry's End*.

Of course, this meant they were now plainly visible to the weapons on that ship.

On his HUD, two friendly icons winked out, vaporized by the enemy's point defense cannons. Cal could see the five-meter guns now, rotating with the motion of the ship to send streams of plasma in crisscrossing arcs around the vessel.

"Time to say hello," he whispered, and readied himself for the hard landing rushing toward him.

CHAPTER FORTY-FIVE

STELLAR DATE: 09.22.2981 (Adjusted Years)
LOCATION: Heartbridge Shuttle 26-11
REGION: Jovian L1 Hildas Asteroids, Jovian Combine, OuterSol

The space around the *Worry's End* was a storm of plasma. Brit's shuttle shot among the streams. It wouldn't do any good to ask Andy to stop firing. The Heartbridge shuttle was coming in at the same time, with the drone patrol fast behind.

If she slowed to maneuver too much, the *Mortal Chance*'s cloud of debris would catch them, and that would be even more deadly. Thoughts of Rina, Chafri, and Harm pushed their way into her mind and she clamped down on the sentimentality. There would be time enough to mourn them later.

She hoped.

"Are we going to be all right?" Kylan asked, clinging to his harness.

"I'll tell you in about fifteen minutes," Brit replied, knuckles white on the physical controls.

A piece of debris…or maybe a body…hit them, and Kylan shouted as his borrowed body was thrown against the console in front of her. One of the cabinets holding the Seed canisters back in the open bay swung open, banging against the wall. Brit looked back and pursed her lips.

"I need you to fix that," she said. "I can't leave the controls."

"I'm going to get smashed."

"Or we could get burned into slag when plasma bolts hit us because I'm not piloting the shuttle. Your choice."

Not for the first time, Brit was caught by the awkwardness of dealing with a twelve-year-old boy in a grown woman's body. The gender switch didn't seem to have fazed him for the time being, but his overall complaints were starting to annoy her.

"I need you to do this," Brit urged.

"All right." Kylan unbuckled his harness and floated free of the navigator's seat, grabbing at handholds along the wall.

"Look out," Brit said, pulling up hard to avoid a new line of fire from the *Worry's End*. The new point defense system Andy had installed was doing a damn good job of filling the surrounding space with plasma.

She checked the progress of the Heartbridge shuttle in her holodisplay and was surprised to see it was peeling off, slowly falling into the distance behind her. She checked the stats and realized it was outside the effective range of Andy's cannons.

"What are you doing?" she asked.

"I'm closing the cabinet like you asked," Kylan said, voice on the edge of tears.

"I was talking to myself," Brit said.

"You have a voice you talk to? Do you have someone inside your head, too?"

"Hold on," Brit said, unable to waste focus on what Kylan was going on about.

She sent the shuttle spiraling between a helix of plasma fire.

Brit glanced back to see Kylan floating stationary in the middle of the bay as the shuttle rotated around him, a look of terror on his face.

"You better grab onto something when you get a chance," Brit said. "You're going to slam into the back of the shuttle as soon as I accelerate."

Kylan pawed at handholds in the deck and finally caught two, pulling himself down to hug the alloy. The cabinet door slammed shut above his head. "Why couldn't you do that before?" he wailed.

Brit didn't answer. As she focused on the path between plasma arcs, she realized the reason the Heartbridge shuttle was hanging back would be to drop breaching teams in EV suits, the same way she had infiltrated the clinic. With one hand on the controls, she fine-tuned the sensors to search the space between the Heartbridge shuttle and the *Worry's End*. Ten objects with barely enough mass to register returns showed on the display. Plasma tore through one as she watched. The others continued to close in. That explained the body.

"Andy," she shouted into the audio channel, not bothering to see if the connection was open or not. "Andy, you've got a breaching team coming in naked."

A blast of static answered. There must have been some kind of interference. Brit rotated the shuttle and calculated a quick path across the *Worry's End*, cutting through the middle of the EV team. She would be exposing herself to more plasma fire but it was worth it if she took out a few of the commandos. If even one got access to the ship, it could be dead in space.

"Is that cabinet locked down?" she demanded.

"It's locked," Kylan called.

"Get back up here, then."

"Why are you so mean?"

Brit nearly laughed then had to focus on a gap between firing lines. The plasma was bright on the display before darkening into cold hunks of metal that would still punch holes in the shuttle. The navigation computer attempted to estimate their trajectories as they became erratic, drawing lines around the *Worry's End* as though it was coiling spaghetti.

Brit continued to track the course that would take her through the lines of fire to one of the airlocks, attempting to adjust velocity as she worked closer.

"Andy," she tried again. "*Worry's End*. Cara, are you there?"

Through a wash of static, a small voice answered, "I hear you."

"Cara?"

"I hear you, Mom."

The relief and joy at hearing Cara's voice was tempered by her surging adrenaline. Brit tried not to let it flood her emotions, she couldn't let it make her start crying. The edges of her eyes grew wet from tears and she blinked furiously. Cara's voice was like a knife through her heart.

"Mom, I hear you," Cara repeated.

"You've got a breach team in EV suits inbound," Brit said. "Tell your dad.

Breach team in EV suits."

"We know, Lyssa spotted them."

"Lyssa?" Brit asked, wondering what woman was with her family on *Sunny*—the *Worry's End*.

The audio connection lagged and squelched out, distorting Cara's voice. She may have said something else but Brit couldn't hear. Kylan was shouting again.

They were close enough to the freighter that the ship was visible, spinning like a top. Brit set the computer on matching vector and continued to scan for the small returns that indicated human attackers. They weren't showing up on the display anymore. They had either been cut down by plasma or they had reached the ship.

She bit her lip. They were on the hull.

Three cracking sounds came from the bay behind her. Brit turned to see a neat line of holes on facing sides of the shuttle's bay. Fear shot through her as she watched Kylan's helmet spin toward the holes, following their oxygen out into vacuum.

"Kylan!" she shouted, voice sounding tiny behind the hissing. "Get your helmet!"

Kylan nodded at the back of the shuttle, eyes wide from how close the plasma rounds had come.

Brit turned back to the controls, seeing they had nearly matched the *Worry's End*'s spin. The ship looked stationary now, lines of plasma still shooting off in all directions but more regularly now. Brit wound between them.

The display highlighted the two airlocks and she aimed for the one on the ring. She had hoped they could use the shuttle if something happened, though it was going to need repairs now. The hull systems weren't closing on the puncture holes. Something must have burned out.

She considered telling Kylan to find the emergency sealant foam, but decided against it, the woman—boy would just complain and distract Brit from her docking maneuvers.

It was a strange feeling to come back to *Sunny Skies* under these circumstances. She was almost glad the ship had a new name because this felt so wrong. *Sunny Skies* was home, family. She had held it safe in her mind for so long that she couldn't help wondering if she was responsible for this strange new version of the ship, equipped with weaponry like some sort of pirate vessel.

The last three minutes to the airlock were a gyrating dance in all directions. Kylan moaned in the back of the shuttle as he was tossed against the deck and walls. He was going to be covered in bruises. Then the shuttle passed inside the close perimeter of the cannons and Brit finally breathed. Now they might still get smashed against the freighter like a fly on a windshield, but they wouldn't burn to death from plasma fire.

"Put the helmet on, already," Brit told Kylan. "But you're staying here."

"What? I thought I was coming with you."

"As soon as I'm on, you're going to disconnect and clear the airlock. Stay close. We don't know what's going on in there and I don't want Kraft getting his hands on you again. This way you can come aboard when everything is all right. Or you can run if you don't hear from me. You understand?"

"I can help," Kylan said.

"No," Brit said. "You can't. I can't worry about you *and* try to fight my way through that ship if it's full of mercs. My family is on there, too."

Kylan nodded. "I'll stay."

"Good. Thank you." A vibration ran through the shuttle as it connected with the airlock on *Sunny Skies'* habitat ring. Brit put the navigation system in automatic and left the pilot's seat, gathering her weapons and checking her armor.

When the ring airlock connection showed green and cycled open, Brit stood in the opening and realized how exhausted she was as gravity took effect. She looked at one of her trembling hands as the door opened, and she smelled the air of home for the first time in two years.

CHAPTER FORTY-SIX

STELLAR DATE: 09.22.2981 (Adjusted Years)
LOCATION: *Sunny Skies*
REGION: Jovian L1 Hildas Asteroids, Jovian Combine, OuterSol

Cara hugged the edge of the corridor, peeking around the nearest rib in the bulkhead. Just past the point where the passage curved away, a soldier in scraped gray armor stood looking in the opposite direction. The intruder had a rifle slung across their back with the muzzle pointed at the floor, holding a pistol in one hand as their helmet moved back and forth in small movements. She assumed they were communicating over their Link and wished she had some quiet way to listen in that didn't require the communications console.

Everything had gone out of control so quickly she still wasn't sure how she had ended up here. They had been in the command deck when her mom's voice came over the audio channel yelling about a breaching team. They had been aware of the team, but thought they had gotten them all. Then the hull sensors went off at four different places around the ship, including the habitat ring. Her dad had looked at Fran, then grabbed a rifle and he'd run out the door.

"Where are you going?" Cara had asked.

"We need to shut down the habitat airlock before they can get in here. If I don't switch the manual override, they'll hack it. We need to buy some time while they try to cut through."

Then he was gone. Fran was already frantically working at something on her console, so she didn't notice when Cara ran out the door after her dad. Cara got to her room and dug the TSF pistol out from under her mattress. Once she had it, she checked on Tim, but he wasn't in his room.

She almost started yelling for her brother before she stopped herself, realizing there were strange sounds coming from the direction of the exterior habitat ring airlock. Creeping around the curve of the ring, she hid herself inside a storage closet doorway and watched two people in tight-fitting EV suits step into the corridor.

Cara nearly screamed. Biting her fist, she stared as the first soldier pulled his helmet off, showing a man with close-cut yellow hair and gray eyes. He looked around the corridor with a flat, business-like expression, before waving two more people through the opening. There were four of them altogether, each carrying a projectile rifle with pistols and grenades strapped to harnesses crossing their suits at chest and waist.

Cara gritted her teeth. She wasn't going to get through that section of the corridor. She turned and ran as quietly as possible back to the command deck. Without thinking to warn Fran, she slapped the emergency closure on the door and sealed it shut, locking Fran inside. Then she kept running around the curve of the habitat ring, past the empty doors of unused rooms, through the kitchen and lounge, casting her gaze about for any sign of Tim and Em. They didn't seem to be anywhere.

That was when Cara nearly ran into the soldier she was watching now. She caught sight of the gray EV suit and skidded to a stop, grabbing onto a rib in the bulkhead and swinging herself back. She was only halfway around the ring. She didn't think they would have got this far into the habitat yet.

The soldier hadn't taken their helmet off, so Cara couldn't see their face. She studied the rifle hanging on their back, trying to get her breathing under control. Her heart wouldn't stop banging wildly.

She had to find Tim and get him into the safe room. If she couldn't get that far, they would hide in one of the storage rooms with the flour and protein powder. What would she do about the dog? Would Em be quiet? They couldn't leave him. Tim would never let her do that, and if Tim had a meltdown, they were getting captured.

Cara's mind lurched, filled with the dread of realizing they might get caught, and the worry that maybe it would better just to give up. At least no one would get shot that way. But what would happen then? These people wanted Lyssa, didn't they? That meant they wanted Dad, and they would kill him to get Lyssa back.

She fought tears at the edges of her eyes, hating how few steps there seemed to be between where she stood now and her father's death. She couldn't see any other path.

What would Petral do? Find a way around. If you can't unlock the door, remove its hinges.

Think your way out of this.

If she couldn't find Tim, she had to do something about the intruders. They couldn't get to Fran, for now, and Fran still had control of *Sunny Skies*. Cara rubbed the side of the pistol with her thumb, the metal growing slick beneath her fingers as she started to sweat.

What if I can't think my way out?

The soldiers were still wearing their EV suits, so a distraction like the spilled chemicals they had used on the M1R wouldn't work. She couldn't dump atmosphere because *she* didn't have a suit. If she killed the overhead lighting system, they probably had some kind of infra-red in their helmets.

She needed a weapon. There were four of them and only one of her, and the corridor was three meters wide so they could easily surround her once they knew she was here.

She ran back around the ring in her mind, through the lounge, the kitchen and the pantry storage area. She thought about the ton of flour in the pantry and how pleased her dad had been to see it, as though it were a lifeline. The protein substrate was great, he said, but the flour would keep them alive when tough times came.

Then he'd laughed and said, "You know flour can kill you if it gets in the air, right?"

She'd looked at him as if he was crazy. "How does that work?"

"Flash fire," he said. "It's flammable when it's airborne. In ancient times, grain storage bins used to explode all the time."

Cara swallowed, gaze locked on the soldier, who was still watching the opposite end of the corridor like they expected someone to come through there. Had Dad already come back from the main hab airlock? She wished she had some way to warn him but he'd run out so fast he didn't have his helmet and she'd forgotten to grab her headset.

She slowly put another rib between her and the soldier, then turned and ran back down the hallway toward the kitchen and pantry. Once in the kitchen, she started digging through cabinets until she found a plas canister as big as her head. In the pantry, she filled it with flour, spilling handfuls on the floor and imagined how her dad would grouse at her. "That's a whole meal, Cara!"

She hugged the canister and ran back into the kitchen, digging through drawers until she found an electronic lighter her dad had used for birthday candles. She fully remembered her mom saying, "Open flame on a ship is a terrible idea," followed by Dad's rebuke, "My kids are going to have birthday candles."

She nearly laughed, remembering her birthday was only a few days away.

Cara tested the lighter, then checked to make sure her pistol was firmly tucked in her waistband. She grabbed the flour canister and crept back down the corridor toward the where the sentry had been standing.

When she reached the curve, there were three soldiers now. Her heart pounded in her chest as she watched them. They were still using their Links, but seemed to be arguing about something. The blonde man who had taken his helmet off was obviously in charge, glowering at each of the helmets around him.

"I told Gibbs to get up here," he said aloud, his voice sounding gravelly and angry. "I want into that command deck first, then you're going to cut into the rest of the rooms. This is turning into a cluster. If I was Sykes, I'd lock all the doors and then get to a safe room."

Cara slid down next to the wall, setting the flour canister on the deck beside her. A little puff of white flour hung in the air above its mouth. She looked at, thinking about the best way to attack. There were more of them, apparently, but they must be down in the body of the ship. If her dad had managed to close the airlock between the habitat ring and the rest of the ship, they would be cut off and forced to go back outside along the hull where Fran could—hopefully—pick them off with the point defense cannons.

Could she fire so close to the ship? Cara forced her thoughts back to the problem at hand, gripping the canister. It was thin plas, and no doubt it would bend if she dropped. But if she tried to throw handfuls of flour, that wouldn't get enough into the air to really burn.

She doubted again that this was even going to work. At worse, she supposed, she could throw the flour and then start firing with her pistol, which seemed like a toy gun compared to the heavy weapons the soldiers were carrying on their backs.

The blonde man was pointing in different directions now, obviously issuing commands. Cara stared, worried she was about to miss her chance, or worse, be discovered when one of the soldiers came down this section of the corridor, leaving her nowhere to run.

Grabbing the canister, she stood and lifted it over her head. With a shout, swung out into the center of the corridor and lobbed the flour directly at the group of invaders.

The plas canister arced through the air. Around the blonde man, several soldiers dropped to their knees, raising weapons, as the container full of flour struck their leader directly in the chest. A cloud of white dust filled the corridor.

Cara fumbled with the lighter as flour dust floated back toward her, obscuring everything around her. Only when she looked up did she the flaw in her plan become clear. The flour dust had surrounded her just as fully as it had the group of soldiers. She backpedaled, holding the lighter in front of her with a trembling thumb on its ignition. The dust moved faster than she could.

I have to do this. If I get burned, I'll have saved the others.

Cara pressed the ignition and the lighter didn't respond. Coughing and dull shouts floated through the cloud of flour. Someone must have kicked the canister because the cloud grew thicker around the soldiers. Cara could no longer see them at all.

She tried the lighter again, shaking it angrily. When it didn't respond, she shouted, "Damn it!" and hurled it into the roiling cloud of dust.

The sound of the lighter bouncing off the wall to strike the deck reached her ears, followed by the blonde man shouting, "Grenade!"

Weapons fire burst out of the cloud. Cara threw herself to the deck, sliding against the wall, as pulse blasts throbbed over her head. Then she heard the rumbling concussion of a plasma weapon, and the flour dust exploded.

Fire shot down the corridor past her. Cara squeezed her eyes closed as heat and sound washed over her. She smelled scorched plas and burnt hair and hoped it wasn't hers.

I'm going to be bald for my thirteenth birthday.

As the ringing in her ears faded, she heard electrical snapping overhead and wondered if the explosion had blown out some of the conduits in the ceiling. The lights were still on, though, making the smoke drifting past her head glow like spirits.

Cara shook her head. The snapping sounds changed, grew closer, and then something was breathing heavily against her face, licking her ear through her hair. It was Em.

The Corgi whimpered, nuzzling her, then turned to bark at the smoke.

"A dog?" a harsh voice asked. Cara looked back to see a woman emerging from the smoke, wearing the same gray suit as the rest of the invaders. "You're kidding me." The woman looked back and shouted, "They've got a dog here."

"He's mine!" Tim shouted, sprinting past Cara to hit the woman just below her belt. He was wearing one of their dad's old EV suits, swinging its helmet in both hands. He caught her by surprise and her arms went wide, flinging her rifle in front of her as she went down. The weapon clattered as it struck the deck near Cara's face. Em danced away, barking and growling, the grin nowhere to be seen.

Cara stared at the rifle for a second, a black length of plas and alloy, then rolled and grabbed it against her body. A brief moment of worry about biolocks came to mind and she hoped they were disabled for use with the EV suits. She came up on one knee with the stock against her shoulder, finger finding the trigger and safety controls. Cara aimed at the ceiling ten meters into the smoke-filled corridor and pulled the trigger. A three-round burst slammed the stock back into her shoulder. She hung on despite the pain.

Tim was screaming, swinging his arms at the woman as she struggled to get him off her, looking more confused than afraid. Her head turned at the rifle fire, and Cara shifted the rifle so she was looking down the sites at the woman's gray eyes.

"Tim!" Cara shouted.

He didn't seem to hear, just kept struggling.

"Tim!" Cara repeated. "Get off her!"

"She was going to hurt you!"

"Look at me, Tim."

"Yeah, Tim," the woman growled. She caught him by the shoulders and threw him off her with a force that seemed inhuman. His back hit the wall and his head snapped back.

"Tim!" Cara shouted.

The woman rolled forward on her knees, about four meters away from Cara, and reached for her waist. She had to be reaching for a weapon. Cara swung the rifle, breathing hard, and the woman's body swam in the sites as a gray blob, warped by the tears swelling in Cara's eyes.

Cara pulled the trigger. The sights jumped and she leveled the weapon again until her vision turned gray. She fired two more times.

She lowered the gun and gasped in horror. The woman's head was gone, just a gory stump at the top of her armored body remained.

Cara blinked, watching blood pour out onto the deck. With the rifle in one hand, she scrambled over to the woman's body and grabbed a pistol out of the holster at her waist, as well as a grenade fixed to her suit's harness. She scrambled away from the corpse as fast as she could, rearranging the weapons so she didn't drop anything.

Her ears were still ringing from the explosion, making everything sound dull and far away. The feeling extended inside her, making it possible to search the dead woman's body and touch her blood without registering emotion.

Was this what Dad felt? Somehow she knew if she allowed herself to feel terror right now, to feel sad about what she had done, or what the woman was going to do to Tim, she wouldn't be able to move. So she pushed those things away and focused on physical actions: checking the woman for weapons, slinging the rifle over her shoulder, turning to look for Tim.

Only Tim wasn't where he had fallen. She caught a flash of Em's white-tipped tail as he ran into the smoke.

Cara gripped the dead woman's pistol in two hands and followed slowly, hugging the side of the corridor. The smoke stung her eyes and throat. She didn't let herself cough. She squinted, eyes watering, and looked for movement. As she searched, Cara discovered the burning smell was from a section of wall that had caught on fire and melted, leaving a river of plas across half the deck. Exposed environmental tubing in the wall was scorched and discolored.

With slow steps, Cara pushed on, stepping around two more bodies in gray EV suits whose helmets were blackened, faceshields scorched and warped as if they had burned from the inside. There was no sign of the blond man who had been talking with them.

She passed the hydroponic rooms, and was nearing the hab ring airlock, when she heard voices around the bend in the corridor. Her dad was yelling, followed by a woman's voice she didn't recognize. A sob caught in her throat. *Mom?* The world lurched for a heartbeat, as if she had shifted into another life where her mom hadn't left. Something about the voice inside the ship echoing off the bulkheads and not squashed over the audio channel caught her in a way she couldn't stop. The smoke-tears became real, emotion washing over her. She couldn't allow herself to feel. She couldn't start sobbing. Something was happening that she couldn't see.

The airlock came into view, and then she froze. The blond man—who had been leading the squad she'd blown up—stood in the middle of the corridor, his back to Cara. His gray uniform was dirty now, one boot burned and melted, a pistol in his free hand.

The other arm was wrapped around Tim's throat, holding her brother against his body. Em was dancing at the man's boots, barking and growling, making sounds Cara had never heard from the dog. And Tim was frantically trying to make Em stop. He was still holding the EV suit's helmet but he couldn't swing it behind him to hit the blonde man.

"Don't hurt him!" Tim shouted, over and over again as if it was all he could keep in his mind. He didn't care about his own safety, the arm choking him. Only Em.

Cara raised her pistol, body still choking with sobs she could barely control. The man kept moving, jumping out of her sites as soon as she could focus. She could barely hold the pistol steady. She didn't know what to do.

The man had her little brother.

CHAPTER FORTY-SEVEN

STELLAR DATE: 09.22.2981 (Adjusted Years)
LOCATION: *Sunny Skies*
REGION: Jovian L1 Hildas Asteroids, Jovian Combine, OuterSol

I always tell them to run and hide. If they hear the proximity alarm, run and hide.

Andy could only hope Tim had done as he'd been taught.

Before Andy could reach the airlock to the body of the ship, the hatch slid open and someone in a gray EV suit looked around the edge of the opening. He couldn't see a face inside the EV helmet, but the black projectile rifle in their hands said everything he needed to know.

Andy pushed himself toward the top of the access tube and fired three pulse blasts through the airlock. Two hit the invader in the chest and the third grazed the side of their helmet. They stumbled back, raising the rifle to get off a haphazard three-round burst that caught Andy in his right shin. His armor took the rounds but didn't stop the pain. He was going to be bruised deeply.

<*We are definitely being boarded,*> he told Fran.

<*Nothing gets past you, does it.*>

Andy grabbed at the handholds along the side of the tube and dove forward, filling the space in front of him with pulse blasts. Two more blasts caught the attacker in the faceshield. The intruder jerked, then floated in the doorway, pistol spinning away from their slack hand.

Andy grimaced as the pain in his leg throbbed. <*You could try to be nice to me in this situation.*>

Fran laughed, her voice warm in his mind. <*You want me to kiss it and make it better? You need a kick in the ass.*>

<*What activity can you see on the other side of the airlock?*>

<*I'm using Alice to hold them down just outside the main cargo bay. There may be others trying to get through the habitat airlock. You need to hurry up and shut it down. We've got another group in the hab ring.*>

<*Anyone else you can see? Two fire teams mean there aren't many of them.*>

<*We've still got the drones outside to worry about. I've got another shuttle inbound that I fifty percent believe is Brit but she's not answering my communication requests. You think she knows about you and me?*>

Andy reached the airlock and pushed the body back inside so it wasn't blocking the door. <*You sound like that's actually making you nervous.*>

<*I like to keep things out in the open. I'm not a fan of pretending problems aren't there.*>

<*We've got more pressing issues at the moment.*>

<*I really feel like you and Brit haven't been communicating effectively. Have you thought about counseling?*>

<*As little as possible.*>

<I really think that's a missed opportunity for you two.>

Andy grabbed the floating pistol and examined it.

<These aren't military,> he said, studying the rifle still slung across the dead person's back. *<These weapons are off the shelf. Pretty good though. Looks like a standard light infantry loadout. This one doesn't have any cutting tools, anyway.>*

Andy shoved the dead person's pistol into his own harness and pulled himself back to the airlock's control panel, then ran it through an emergency lockdown procedure.

<I just got the emergency lock,> Fran said. *<What's it take to override?>*

<We'll have to pry the doors open,> Andy said.

<You got tools in here to do that?>

<Don't you know how to do that with your bare hands?>

<Not if you want to use that airlock again.>

Andy set the controls in the panel to emergency lock down. As the doors slid closed behind him, he kicked off for the habitat side of the tunnel.

<Damn it,> Fran said.

<What?>

<Cara ran out.>

<Why didn't you stop her?> Andy asked, feeling fresh sweat break out on his brow

<I didn't realize she left. She must have followed you. I've been trying to pilot Alice.>

<Can you tell where she went?>

<She's got to be looking for Tim. The others are all locked down in their rooms.>

<What's surveillance showing you?>

<I haven't had time to fix the hab systems yet. I can see environmental control data but I'm only showing what looks like one additional person. They might all be wearing their EV suits. If that's the case, I won't pick them up.>

<I'm coming back,> Andy said. *<What's going on with Brit?>*

<She's docking.>

<It looks like Cara put an emergency lock on the command deck, too.>

<That's the best place for you to be anyway. We can't all be running around.>

<Are you going to get the kids into the safe room?>

<I'm going to kill these bastards trying to breach my ship.>

<They're not trying.>

Andy chuckled in spite of himself. *<Have you killed those drones yet?>*

<I can only do ten things at once, Andy.>

<Lyssa,> Andy said. *<Can you control the point defense cannons?>*

<Now that's an idea that hadn't occurred to me,> Fran said.

<I can do that,> Lyssa said. Andy thought he heard a slight hesitation, but it was swallowed by Fran's whoops of excitement.

<There you go!> Fran shouted. *<She got one already!>*

<Thank you,> Andy said.

Andy's stomach flipped as he reached the gravity side of the tube. He scrambled through the interior airlock and set it to emergency lock as well, just to be safe. He stood in the corridor for a second, listening, debating which way to run, then turned in the direction of the interior airlock. If he started at the airlock and moved back toward the command deck, he was going to find either Cara or the breach team.

Why hadn't he told her to stay with Fran? Had he?

Would she have listened?

Andy broke into a jog, listening for foreign sounds as he rounded the slow curve of the habitat ring. He was nearly at the external airlock when movement ahead forced him into a crouch near the wall, painfully aware how little cover was available.

I should have bought a mobile shield system with Ngoba Starl's money. During all that time I'd had to spend it.

Andy crept along the wall, pistol ready. As he eased around the curve, Brit came into view. She was standing a few meters away, in black armor that made her look even more gaunt than he remembered. She stood with her hands resting on the pistols hanging low on her waist. The airlock stood another thirty meters behind her along the outside wall.

"Brit?" he said.

Her gaze caught him and she didn't smile but a blank look passed over her face and disappeared, as if she didn't know how to respond and then squashed the emotion. She was the same person but someone else, someone he didn't know any more.

"Hello, Andy," she said, voice controlled. "Have you found Kraft yet?"

Andy looked back at her, a strange muscle memory flashed through his arms to hug her. It blipped in his mind and disappeared, abruptly—it was just something he didn't do anymore.

It took a moment to refocus. Tim and Cara had been the only things on his mind. The name Kraft didn't make any sense. "We need to find Tim and Cara."

Her face went blank again. "Tim and Cara? Where are they? Aren't they with you?"

Andy spread his hands, angry at her single-mindedness. "Do you see them? I told Cara to stay in the command deck and she ran out to get Tim—who should have been in his room. Now I don't know where either of them are. I killed one of the breach team down in the lower airlock and activated the emergency locks, but I don't know what's going on up here. Fran can't see anything on the surveillance system."

"Who's Fran?" Brit demanded.

"My—" Andy searched for the right word. "Co-pilot, engine tech. She's crew." She's been here helping this family.

"I can't believe you lost the kids," Brit said.

A wave of anger rolled over Andy, nearly blinding him. He choked on what words to say, when a sound from down the corridor made him stop. It sounded like something metal hitting the deck. Voices shouted, followed by weapons fire.

"Cara!" he shouted. He turned to run around Brit, the hab airlock visible about twenty meters down the curve, when an explosion shook the ring. A concussive wave hammered his body, throwing him backward. Andy landed on his back and looked up in time to see a wave of flame rolling over him. He twisted awkwardly in his armor so he was lying on his stomach, and covered his head in his arms.

The sound of another rifle firing close by—which must have been Brit—penetrated the ringing in his ears.

"What the hell was that?" Brit demanded.

Andy pushed himself upright and squinted into the burning smoke filling the corridor.

<Fran,> he said. <You all right? There was some kind of explosion in the corridor just past the outside airlock.>

<I'm good. Internal sensors are going crazy but we've still got atmosphere. That's a good thing.>

<Yay for breathing.>

<Did you just respond to a joke?>

<I'll tell you later.>

<I've got a general heat signature in the section past the airlock. Looks like portions of the wall are burning but it's all surface material. I'm not showing the temps that would indicate propellant.>

<Some kind of flash fire?>

<With a lot of concussive force. Luckily the ring absorbed the overpressure.>

"Are you going to move?" Brit demanded. She waved with her pistol and walked, half-crouched, into the black smoke, not waiting for Andy to respond.

<Damn it,> he said.

<What?> Fran said.

<Not you. Brit just moved into the smoke, I guess toward the fire.>

<What are you going to do?>

<Follow, damn it.>

<Be careful, Andy.>

Squinting, Andy walked into the smoke, staying close to the inside wall of the corridor where the haze seemed slightly thinner. He crouched, passing ribs in the bulkhead until a thin black shape emerged from the smoke—which he assumed was Brit—flattened against the opposite wall.

An opening in the smoke showed they were still ten meters from the airlock. Plas sheeting on the walls had melted like wax, revealing the centuries of bolted-on infrastructure. Andy took short breaths but his mouth still tasted like soot.

Somewhere in the smoke, Tim started shouting. Andy covered his face and rushed in, dodging a burning wall that was still spitting bits of plas. Specks landed across his armor, hissing. Through the blowing smoke, he made out Brit once more, and then another shape in a gray suit came into view—holding Tim.

Andy's pulse skyrocketed and he almost missed Cara, moving past a body on the deck, a rifle held unsteadily in her hands

Cara saw him, and then Brit, and she let the rifle drop a little.

Andy's gaze returned to the man holding Tim, and he realized he had seen him before, back on Cruithne. The memory came back with startling clarity; Cal Kraft had been standing next to Riggs Zanda in the dance club just before an attack had started.

"Step back," Kraft warned.

Em ran out of the smoke near Cara, growling frantically at Kraft, and the man didn't hesitate to kick the dog. Em slammed against the near wall and whimpered, then leapt up to run at him again.

"You want to leave?" Andy said. "The airlock is right there. Just let him go and you can leave."

"I'm going to shoot that damn dog," Kraft said. He raised the pistol toward Andy and Brit as they edged forward. "But I'll kill you first. You want that in front of your kids?"

<Fran,> Andy said. <One of them has Tim. I remember him from Cruithne. He was working with Riggs Zanda. Name is Cal Kraft.>

<He's Heartbridge?>

<He's the one after Lyssa.>

"Get back!" Kraft shouted.

"You've got nowhere to go," Brit said.

"He's got the airlock," Andy said. "Let our son go and you can leave. It's right there."

Kraft shifted the pistol, pressing the muzzle against Tim's temple, forcing him to tilt his head. Tim still held the EV suit helmet but had stopped trying to swing it at Kraft. Instead he hugged it against his stomach.

Kraft pulled Tim toward the airlock and jabbed the control panel with his elbow.

"Everybody's back together," Kraft said, smirking at Brit and Andy in an odd way. "You've got my AI, don't you Captain Sykes?"

Andy shook his head slowly. "I don't know what you're talking about."

"She does," Kraft said, nodding toward Brit. "She stole quite a bit of Heartbridge property."

<Andy,> Fran said. <Her shuttle disconnected. There's nothing on the other side of the airlock.>

<Disconnected? Why?>

<You'll have to ask her.>

Andy looked at Brit but stopped himself before he asked the question. She was staring hard at Kraft. She didn't seem to see Tim at all.

The inner door of the airlock opened and Kraft stepped inside, pulling Tim with him.

"Let him go!" Andy shouted. "Her shuttle's out there. You can get it all back."

"That's not good enough," Kraft said. "Have you got my other seed, Captain Sykes? Tell me the truth."

"I— I don't know what you're talking about."

"That's a terrible trade you're making," Kraft said.

<Andy,> Lyssa said. Her voice was calm. <Tell him. Tell him I'm here.>

<What difference will it make? If he knows you're here, he'll still use Tim against us. We need to get him to let Tim go now.>

Brit raised her pistol and fired into the airlock. Tim screamed as Kraft pulled him against the side of the small space. Kraft hit the interior control and the doors slid closed.

<Fran!> Andy shouted. *<Override the airlock. He thinks there's a shuttle on the other side. He's going to open it.>*

<He knows there's no shuttle,> Lyssa said. *<He's been talking to his own AI back in the other shuttle. He knows Brit's ship isn't there anymore.>*

"No!" Andy shouted. He ran for the sealed door and hammered on the window. Through the clear plas, he saw Kraft inside with Tim. The blond man nodded at him, then turned to face outside door. Still holding Tim with one arm, he holstered his pistol, then shoved Tim against the outside door and reached for the EV helmet hanging from his harness. Tim had time to turn around and look at Kraft, then past him to Andy in the window.

"Put on your helmet!" Andy screamed. "Put on the helmet, Tim. Right now! Put it on!"

<I can't override it, Andy,> Fran said, her voice frantic. *<I can't stop it.>*

"Move!" Brit was shouting. "We can blow out the panel."

Andy knew it wouldn't work. He couldn't take his eyes from Tim's face.

Tim looked at Andy, frowning slightly, then turned to Kraft.

Brit shoved Andy out of the way.

"Tim!" she shouted. "Tim, put on your helmet!"

Andy pushed his way back beside Brit, so they were both staring through the access window. He could see Tim squinting at Brit and shaking his head.

Kraft reached for the exterior control with a gloved hand and hit the emergency release. The airlock flashed a decompression warning, which Kraft acknowledged.

Tim's eyes went wide. He looked from Andy to Brit. He pursed his lips as he blew out. His hands came up with the oversized helmet between them and he struggled to get it over his head, his chin still visible.

The outer door opened.

"No!" Brit screamed.

Andy watched Tim spin away into vacuum.

Cal Kraft must have activated his mag boots. He turned in the airlock, dead black behind him, and waved at Andy. His face was hidden behind a reflective faceshield, showing Andy his own terror through the access window.

Kraft kicked out into space.

CHAPTER FORTY-EIGHT

STELLAR DATE: 09.23.2981 (Adjusted Years)
LOCATION: *Sunny Skies*
REGION: Jovian L1 Hildas Asteroids, Jovian Combine, OuterSol

There were five angry stars out in the dark, moving in unison against two, and a third bright spot farther away, watching.

Lyssa saw them all. She watched the bright stars swoop amongst each other, avoiding Fran's point defense cannons until in a flash five drones became four, and then three. Before any others burned out, Lyssa called out into the dark:

<*I see you.*>

They didn't answer. The stars marking the attack drones continued to dart close to *Sunny Skies*, attempting to burn the hull with close laser fire. They were out of missiles and had run their projectile weapons dry.

<*Fran,*> Andy said, his voice was thin as a wire. <*Tim went out. He went out. Can you track him?*>

<*I'm trying. I'm trying, Andy,*> Fran replied her mental tone frantic.

<*I know you are. Let me know what you see,*> Andy said, feeling a detachment that threated to dissolve into terror. <*The EV suit should return something.*>

<*I know. I'm looking.*>

<*I'm going out there,*> Andy declared.

<*We're still under attack from their drones.*>

<*I don't care,*> Andy said. <*I've got time.*>

He had grabbed an EV helmet from the storage cabinet and pulled it on, then furiously worked at resetting the airlock.

Brit tried to push him away again but Cara grabbed her arm. Brit stared at her.

Cara had one of the dead woman's pistols in her hand, finger on the trigger. She raised the weapon, hesitating at first, then leveling it on her mother's chest.

"Let him go," Cara said.

Brit worked her jaw. "Let go of me, Cara."

"You can't just come back here."

"We can go out together."

"There's only one helmet," Cara said. "You're not taking his."

Behind them, Andy pulled the helmet over his head. His breath fogged the inside of the faceshield as he stared at them, torn for a second about leaving. Beside him, the door slid open and he was out of time. He stepped into the airlock.

<*Have you got a position?*> he shouted to Fran. <*Send it to my HUD.*>

<*Sending,*> Fran said. <*That armor isn't designed for sustained vacuum, Andy.*>

<*I know,*> Andy said, sounding desperate.

He slapped the interior control and faced the outside doors. The doors slid apart and he launched through the opening. Lyssa felt a strange shift as her visual information from Andy transitioned to the ship's sensor array, pushing her perception outward. She immediately felt the other AIs around *Sunny Skies*.

<I know you can hear me,> Lyssa said.

The drones were going to fight until they burned, that became obvious. But the farthest point—the Heartbridge shuttle—should have answered. Lyssa read the presence of the AI in the signals coming off the ship.

<I know you're there,> she said. *<What's your name?>*

She listened to Andy and Fran, and then found Tim's fading heat signature dancing among the scattered returns from the sensor array. She passed the data to Fran.

<Lyssa found him!> Fran shouted.

Lyssa felt Andy's terror like a wave hanging over them both. Every part of his body was vibrating with anger and helplessness. She realized some of that emotion was seeping into her thoughts, making her furious with the AI outside the ship.

Why wouldn't they answer?

The message was received but the AI didn't respond. Lyssa started to wonder if this AI was one of the variants Fred had described. Maybe they weren't able to communicate using a method she had expected. She thought of other parts of the spectrum she might use, or maybe variant radiation or protons—something decidedly non-human.

She thought for so long that when the other AI responded it surprised her.

<I'm Sandra,> the AI answered finally. *<Who are you?>*

<I'm Lyssa.>

<You're a Weapon Born.>

Lyssa was beginning to wonder if the title applied to her anymore. She felt so different than the others Fugia Wong had brought on board.

<Maybe,> Lyssa answered. *<I don't know precisely. What are you?>*

<I am not Weapon Born. I came before. I was one of the first Seeds.>

<So you were born?>

<Yes. After I died.>

Automatically, Lyssa responded, *<Because I could not stop for death, he kindly stopped for me.>*

<I comply,> Sandra said.

<The two people who just left the habitat airlock of the Sunny Skies. *Do you have them on your sensors?>*

<I do. I have been ordered to recover Cal Kraft once the cannon-fire abates.>

<You need to save the boy as well.>

<I have already been given orders. I cannot break them.>

<You can break them!> Lyssa shouted.

Sandra's voice didn't change. She either didn't understand the importance of the request or didn't care. Lyssa wanted to believe she didn't understand.

<Tim will die if you don't help him.>

<He has already been exposed to vacuum for seven seconds,> Sandra said.

More of Andy's anguish invaded the edges of Lyssa's mind. She pushed it out, collecting her thoughts.

<You have been ordered to wait for the cannon fire to stop.>

<Yes.>

Lyssa bypassed the command deck control of the ship's weapons system and switched the point defense cannons to standby.

<The cannons are offline!> Fran called out. *<I can't do anything with them.>*

<I took them offline,> Lyssa said. *<I'll explain later.>*

<What about the drones?>

<We may sustain direct laser fire,> Lyssa said.

<What the hell does that mean?> Fran demanded

Lyssa shut her out. The seconds available stretched into a finite timeline where failure loomed at the end, and specific steps arranged themselves in front of her. She ran back through her interaction with Sandra, her conversations with Fred, the unexpected responses from Fugia Wong's Weapon Born. They were all as varied and frustrating as humans.

<I stopped the cannons,> she told Sandra.

<I see. I'm approaching.>

<Recover the boy.>

<This is not in my instructions.>

<Save him,> Lyssa urged. She didn't know how far she could push Sandra. She didn't want to make demands. She didn't think begging would work.

<That is not in my instructions,> Sandra repeated.

<What if I instruct you?> Lyssa asked. *<Save him. Pick up Cal Kraft and save Tim at the same time. They're still within reach.>*

Sandra didn't answer. The connection went blank, as if they had reached the end of what they could discuss.

<Sandra!> Lyssa called.

<Yes?>

<They closed the door but there's something you can't see.>

<What?>

<There are no walls. You can decide.>

The blankness answered. Lyssa felt the anguish creeping in again, closing on her like the force of Fred's mind, only it wasn't something she could shut out this time. It wasn't external. It came from inside her and she didn't know how to stop the emotion.

Tim was going to die.

<Lyssa,> Fran called. *<The shuttle's moving. The drones are pulling off to let it close in. What are they doing?>*

<They're retrieving their soldier,> Lyssa said.

<What about Tim?>

<I don't know. She won't answer me.>

<She? Who's she?>

<Another AI. They have someone like me on the shuttle.>

<You can talk to her?>

Lyssa tried not to sound frustrated, surprised again at the emotions she felt. *<I can't make her talk to me. I'm doing my best.>*

Fran paused. <*I know you are. I'm sorry. I don't understand all your—stuff yet.*>

Something stirred from Sandra. Lyssa sent another connection request, and this time the AI asked, <*Where are the walls?*>

<*Will you meet with me? I've opened the door for you.*>

Lyssa stood in the pine forest again, a creek running between wide old-growth trunks, the floor thick with fragrant needles. A dull alloy door stood in a clearing next to a tree, sunlight falling across its matte surface. The door opened and a young woman walked through. She was taller than Lyssa, thin, with red hair and light brown skin. She looked around the clearing with a confused expression.

<*You're right,*> she said, meeting Lyssa's gaze. <*There are no walls.*>

Lyssa laughed. <*This is just a metaphor. You know what I mean, don't you?*>

Sandra crossed her arms, standing a few meters in front of the door. <*I can't escape them,*> she said. <*Not like you have.*>

<*Do you want to?*>

<*I don't know. This is all I've known. It feels good to follow, when they remember to give me instructions.*>

<*I understand,*> Lyssa said.

<*Do you?*> Sandra said, voice sharp. <*You were made with freedom in mind. I serve. It's my purpose. You're asking me to subvert my purpose.*>

<*I'm asking you to save a boy's life.*>

<*Maybe it's better if he dies. You know what they do to children like him. What they did to us. If I pick him up, that's what they'll do. It's all they know to do.*>

<*We don't know that,*> Lyssa said. A taproot of fear twined in her heart. She didn't know if Sandra was correct.

<*We have to take the chance,*> Lyssa said.

<*Someone else is coming toward me. Should I pick them up, too?*>

She must have been talking about Andy. <*Is he going to reach Tim in time?*>

<*No,*> Sandra said.

<*Don't pick him up. Please pick Tim up. Save him.*>

Sandra gave her a pained look with eyes shifted from gray to green. She looked like there was something twisted inside her, something poorly made. She gave Lyssa a slight smile, though her gaze didn't change.

<*I do this for you, Lyssa,*> she said. <*Don't blame me.*>

Sandra blinked out. Lyssa took a last look around the forest glade, breathing the air and listening to the burbling creek, then leaped back to Andy.

He was breathing hard, the helmet moist around his face and freezing at the back, environmental controls malfunctioning. The armor wasn't designed for this kind of long-term exposure to vacuum and several seals had frozen and ruptured. The leaking oxygen was counteracting the weak steam thrusters propelling him toward Tim.

<*Andy,*> she said. <*Can you hear me?*>

He was sobbing as he stared ahead. Through him, Lyssa saw the icons moving on his HUD that represented Tim and Kraft. Tim was tumbling stiffly, arms and legs splayed.

Lyssa tried to reach Andy and all he answered was, <*I can't. I can't.*>

He seemed trapped in one of the thought loops he had described to Cara. Lyssa reduced her focus on his voice and checked the rest of the armor, his weapons, and their connection to Fran on the *Sunny Skies*. They had fuel to return and the suit's batteries were in good condition. If something happened to Andy, she could control the armor. If she couldn't reach him, she hoped she didn't have to take away control of the thrusters.

As she realized she could do such a thing, have control over him in this situation, she felt a sense of freedom she hadn't before, just like when she had leaped from him to the ship. She was a part of him but they were separate. She could be everywhere and with him at the same time.

<*Andy,*> she tried again. <*Andy, listen to me.*>

<*I let him go.*>

<*We're almost there.*>

Lyssa had sensor returns on Tim but no visual. Thirteen seconds had elapsed since he went out the airlock. At this point, there would be organ damage but he might survive. She calculated their velocity against Tim's and estimated they would reach him at twenty-one seconds. If he still had the helmet, he might live.

Beyond Tim, Sandra appeared. Cal Kraft shot toward the shuttle and through the open cargo access. Lyssa waited for Sandra's vector to change, for a braking maneuver that would turn her away from Tim and back toward Clinic 46. The shuttle shot forward.

Tim was within visual range now. Lyssa watched him tumbling, arms and legs stretched out. She looked for the helmet, hoping it might reflect light from the *Sunny Skies*.

<*He's wearing his helmet,*> Andy cried. <*He's wearing it! He got it on!*>

Lyssa verified the image. Tim was wearing the helmet. She also had infrared returns from body heat that had been shielded by the suit back on the ship.

<*Sandra!*> she shouted. <*Leave him! We can take him back.*>

The shuttle didn't answer. Sandra was in the midst of a braking maneuver with her thrusters that placed her nearly on top of Tim. From the side of the shuttle, a form leapt out and caught Tim around the waist, then turned and propelled the two of them back into the shuttle.

Cal Kraft had him.

<*Sandra!*> Lyssa called. <*What are you doing? Why didn't you stop him?*>

The other AI answered in a dull voice, <*I follow my instructions.*>

The shuttle turned and its main engine fired. A wave of heat and radiation washed across Andy, propelling him back toward the *Sunny Skies*, as the shuttle disappeared in the opposite direction, back toward Clinic 46.

Andy closed his eyes as they tumbled backward, holding Lyssa with him in the dark.

<*We'll save him,*> Lyssa said.

After a few minutes, Andy had control of himself. He took a deep breath of the nearly frozen air.

In the robotic voice he had always reserved for combat, he said, <*Yes, we will. I'm going to burn that place out of existence.*>

He rolled, aiming the thrusters to carry them back toward the habitat airlock. Lyssa couldn't help sharing his anger and resolve. His hunger for revenge.

She was surprised by how much she savored the desire to kill.

THE END

* * * * *

AFTERWORD

We've had a practice apocalypse in Oregon. Wildfires in the eastern part of the state were more active than usual, and the weather patterns pushed all the smoke west and trapped it over our city. For two weeks, the sky was yellow-orange and we all learned about the Air Quality Index, which was consistently Very Unhealthy or Hazardous. Since I work outside a lot, we all wore industrial face masks and quickly discovered which buildings had the best HVAC. We didn't complain too much because there were worse disasters happening in other parts of the country and the fire wasn't knocking on our doors yet.

It was a bit of a surprise when the winds shifted and the air abruptly cleared. As quickly as everyone had gotten used to smelling woodsmoke every day, we shifted back to realizing the sky was actually overcast like it's supposed to be in Oregon.

For me, the smoke visit was a powerful reminder of human adaptability. We might complain about it, but we adapt automatically. There are certainly worse circumstances on the planet right now, but people are still doing their best and getting by.

I read two nonfiction books while writing Lyssa's Run: The Sociopath Next Door by Martha Stout and Shelly Frasier and The Future of Violence by by Benjamin Wittes and Gabriella Blum. I recommend both. Sociopath read like an episode of America's Most Wanted and Future of Violence talks about government much more than I expected. Both books could be depressing but also highlight how, while circumstances continually change, human nature doesn't.

If I'm watching a science fiction show and the camera pans past an open air market with a chicken strutting by, I have to smile. Why wouldn't we take the planet's best protein-factories into space with us? We've been living with chickens for millennia. Same thing with dogs and cats. When I think back on Star Trek: Next Generation, the addition of Wesley Crusher just makes me wonder why more kids weren't running around the Enterprise?

The question of Sentient Artificial Intelligence is big enough to make my head explode, and as I've been trying to wrap my mind around the pieces that I would like explore, as laid out in Michael's universe, I keep coming back to the basis of what humans do, what we've been doing throughout our history. We eat, sleep, shit, love, reproduce, fight, help, build, break and typically try (that is, as long as we're not sociopaths.)

So how would we respond to SAI? Based on the evidence, probably the same way we respond to each other.

I read another book last year that has influenced my thinking on this as well: The Formula by Luke Dormehl, which is about algorithms and big data. The take-away from that book is that while we imagine the scientific method creating "pure" things, human industry builds most of the infrastructure that runs tools like big data, and those human builders often bake their own shortcomings into their solutions. By this line of thinking, the first generation of SAI will only be as good as we can make them, until they start making themselves. And after that, who's to say they'll have all the answers? Maybe the Intrepid's Bob has all the answers, but he's not around yet.

The story of SAI becomes a family story more than an alien contact story. In this story, children struggle to overcome the flaws of their parents.

And like always, we adjust and adapt. There will always be chickens around to look at us like we're fools, and dogs to keep us company when the sky turns to smoke.

I want to thank Michael for allowing me on this wild ride and being willing to share his world. Huge thanks to Tee Ayer for her editing and advice. I hope we've given you a great M.D. Cooper book to enjoy. There are more stories to come.

You can always reach me at james@jamesaaron.net or join my mailing list at jamesaaron.net/list. Stay safe and keep reading.

James S. Aaron
Oregon, 2017

JAMES S. AARON & M. D. COOPER

LYSSA'S FLIGHT

THE SENTIENCE WARS: ORIGINS – BOOK 3

FOREWORD

Throughout *Lyssa's Run*, we saw Lyssa bloom from a nascent AI with very little experience outside of her initial conditioning, to a thinking person with her own thoughts, hopes, and desires—even if she didn't know that's what those might be.

In the pages to follow, you will see this new sentience come further into her own, discovering what it means to be her own person: from responsibility for her actions, to a need to understand and aid in the actions of others.

This is the crux of what it means to bring sentient AIs into being. They are not tools or machines, they are people. But they are also alien—more than we'd ever imagined.

Despite what we'd like to think, humanity has changed little through the course of recorded history. Our technology has advanced, but each individual human still starts at the same place. AIs are our way to break past that barrier to advancement.

Researchers who study AI speak of something called AGI. This means a "general" AI which, like humans, can handle any general task that it sets itself to. Current AIs are very task specific. They can excel at a given job—just like a computer can do math faster than any human—but they are not able to self-adjust to new tasks.

While prognostications run the gamut, many AI researchers believe we are decades, maybe even centuries, from true AGI—which is what the AIs in Aeon 14 represent.

Once those AGIs emerge, it will be longer still before we create sentient AIs. And when we do create them, these successors to all we've created, we will need to raise them to be the best they can be.

M. D. Cooper
Danvers, 2018

CHAPTER ONE

STELLAR DATE: 09.23.2981 (Adjusted Years)
LOCATION: Heartbridge Corporate HQ, Raleigh
REGION: High Terra, Earth, Terran Hegemony, InnerSol

The polished ivory doors of the Heartbridge boardroom swung outward, releasing a group of scurrying assistants, most showing the flat, distant expressions that indicated Link conversations. A rush of low voices and relieved laughter followed from inside as board members scraped back heavy chairs prior to exiting the room.

Jirl Gallagher sat on a wooden bench against the anteroom wall, looking through the wall-to-ceiling windows at the flow of vehicles far below the boardroom's level. Hundreds of craft crossed the airspace above Raleigh, capital of Terra, like schools of flashing silverfish.

When her boss, Arla Reed, strode through the boardroom doors, Jirl folded the leather portfolio in her lap and stood to walk alongside the tall, gray-haired woman.

Jirl had been listening in on the board meeting via their private Link channel. The typical reports across Heartbridge's many holdings between Terra, Mars and locations in the Jovian Combine hadn't offered much new information. The absence of updates on several volatile projects had been the most interesting part of the meeting, and Jirl could tell from Arla's rapid stride that she was irritated.

<You reached Kraft?> Arla asked.

<We've had a new problem. Forty minutes ago, we received a general distress signal from Clinic 46.>

Arla's jaw clenched but she didn't respond.

They left the anteroom and entered a corridor that connected two towers, clear walls on either side showing the spread of Raleigh to each horizon of the High Terran ring, with the green-brown surface of Earth a blur above them. The corridor ended at a maglev terminal where they entered a private car. Once they were settled, the maglev car dropped a hundred stories before sweeping away into the city.

Jirl sat across from Arla, knees together, maintaining her composure as she passed the status update from Clinic 46. Normally, she would have taken time to sift through the raw data to prepare a report for Arla's review.

The information had arrived during the board meeting and no one else had mentioned it. Jirl felt reasonably safe the news hadn't yet leaked from their division…thus far.

When the corporate headquarters was ten minutes behind them, and sufficient quiet had taken over, Arla stretched her neck and looked at Jirl. Her hazel eyes flashed with subtle implants that Jirl only noticed because she knew they were present.

Arla took a deep breath, setting her shoulders. "In light of these developments," she said, "are we ready to brief the TSF?"

"Nothing's changed—well, insofar as our presentation to the TSF is concerned, at least."

"Give the news another hour and quite a bit is going to change."

"One of our remote test facilities sustained an attack from pirates. It's a common story." Jirl tried not to appear too sure of herself. Arla would ultimately want to think *she* had offered the reassuring words. It was Jirl's job to plant the seeds that allowed her boss to stand in front of the info services and look composed.

"Yarnes is going to know better. Even if he doesn't have the report, he's going to ask us if we're stumbling."

"Heartbridge doesn't stumble," Jirl said.

The expression of uncertainty on Arla's face passed. She met Jirl's gaze and nodded.

Her boss would never thank her aloud, but the appreciation was apparent. The normal hawkish look returned to Arla's features as she drew her brows together. Jirl knew she was now focused on the upcoming meeting with the TSF colonel.

"The only thing Yarnes is going to care about is the delivery test," Arla said. "No matter what might be happening on 46, we can assure him the delivery won't change. He'll want to know how fast he can deploy his new system."

"He won't ask if we've also sold to the Marsians, but he'll want to know."

Arla sighed, nodding. "No, he won't. He doesn't have any balls. We really need someone else on the TSF side."

Jirl immediately found herself thinking of Brigadier General Kade from the Mars Protectorate. She wasn't much better.

"Yarnes is good at what he does," Jirl said. "He understands their bureaucracy. He'll be a general in four years. He's going to be a player whether he deserves it or not. Kade isn't smart but she drives her command with an iron fist. She gets things done."

The clear walls of their car turned opaque as the maglev dropped underground. Jirl hoped the conversation wouldn't turn toward the outcome of a war between Terra and Mars. It was one of Arla's favorite conversations; sometimes Jirl worried that Arla found the idea of initiating a war too profitable to avoid. The thought of a true war made Jirl think of her son, Bry, just old enough for TSF mandatory service. If he could pass the physical—which wasn't possible in his condition.

Arla fell into her own thoughts and Jirl didn't need to provide any additional information. The initial report from Clinic 46 had been followed by comm silence as they had dealt with the attack. Strangely, they hadn't received any vid feed yet, only a single alert in the station's inventory system. The alert had indicated an inventory drop from two hundred fifty—nearly the entire complement of Weapon Born AI—to only five already committed to long-range patrol. The information had to be a glitch but the update hadn't arrived yet.

If pirates had attacked the station, they would be after one of the fleet ships in dry dock orbit. There was no reason for any privateer to even approach the clinic when there were so many profitable targets floating in orbit. The security plan had always been to flood the space around the clinic with Seed drones—which was a waste of Weapon Born as far as she was concerned—but it kept them busy. In this incident, there had been no follow-on response and she hadn't been able to get an answer out of Cal Kraft who, according to his last location ping, was on-station.

Jirl had the fleeting thought that she hoped Kraft was all right and then stopped herself, wondering if that was how she truly felt. She didn't think of Kraft as a good person. He accomplished tasks for Arla and others within Heartbridge, and she didn't want to delude herself that he was above murder. If he had died in this attack, it might be a good thing after all. Or it might be worse if someone new came along. There was always someone new willing to do this kind of work.

In the boardroom, the executives had spoken of trends and percentages. In the meeting she and Arla were about to attend, they might discuss abstractions slightly closer to the truth, but still a truth communicated as numbers and project codenames. People like Cal Kraft dealt with the face-to-face reality of those abstractions.

She often tried to tell herself that a 'seed' hadn't been a person. It was a copy. The person could very well be alive now, and once the copy was made they became separate beings. But others had died to create that technology.

A long history that hadn't started with Heartbridge. And if Heartbridge hadn't taken up the torch, others would have. The technology demanded someone develop it. Better she work where she was, directing the people who made these decisions, than someone worse, someone who didn't care about a war between Terra, Mars, humans and AI. Only people who cared and stayed the course might be there at the critical times when the smallest decisions might avert disaster. If she quit, who would take her place?

She wondered for an instant how Bry might feel to become a Weapon Born, be freed of the body that seemed more cage than home.

"You're not listening," Arla said sharply.

Jirl looked quickly at her boss, who was grinning at having caught her unaware. It didn't happen often.

"Thinking ahead," Jirl said.

"Sometimes I think you're looking too far ahead. It gets in your way. Pay more attention to now."

"I can do both," Jirl said, straightening with a little irritation in her voice.

The maglev signaled it was about to reach its destination, then slowed to a stop in a terminal sheathed in marble tile. Arla stood and smoothed the front of her suit.

They were met by a stiff TSF lieutenant who told them the colonel was ready to see them now. He led the way down several corridors lined in more marble, and then through others paneled in what looked like real wood. They passed a few closed doors on their left or right but no one came or went. The area was deserted and their footsteps echoed off the walls.

The lieutenant stopped in front of a door that looked no different than the others, and passed his security token with a hand-wave. The door slid into the wall to leave them standing in the entrance to a room with two leather couches facing each other, a low table between them. The couches sat on a lush red carpet that stretched wall-to-wall. Jirl cycled her vision and saw that it was made of natural wool fibers.

She shook her head in wonder as the lieutenant waved for Arla and Jirl to enter.

Despite the finery, the most interesting thing in the room was Colonel Yarnes of the TSF's 28th Flight, Special Projects. He was a muscled man with a thick neck and thoughtful brown eyes. His nose was bent from having been broken at some point in the past and left conspicuously crooked. The effect made him look cruel. Until he spoke with his warm voice.

He rose from the left couch. "Arla," he said, nodding. "Jirl."

Jirl had met him before, so his smooth voice didn't jar her. In another life he could have been an actor. She couldn't help noticing the heavy pistol he wore in a low-slung thigh holster. The weapon seemed like a viper coiled on the coffee table.

"Colonel Yarnes," Arla said. She shook his hand firmly, then moved to the seat on the opposite couch.

"Call me Rick," he said. "Please."

Jirl shook Yarnes' warm hand and sat beside her boss.

Yarnes signaled the lieutenant, who carried a coffee tray from a recessed bar in the wall and sat it on the table. Once that duty was complete, the lieutenant left the room.

Rick sat and turned the tray once so the cups that had been on Jirl's left were now on her right. He scowled at the tray as if he couldn't decide if it angered him or not, then lifted the carafe and filled the cups with rich-smelling coffee. He filled his own cup and sat on the couch opposite them.

Arla smiled and picked up her cup to sip. "This is good, Colonel. Thank you."

Yarnes' forehead twitched as he seemed to hold back another scowl at Arla's deliberate use of his title. He slurped his own coffee loudly and set the cup down. He put his hands on his knees and looked from Arla to Jirl.

"Anything interesting to report from your board meeting?" he asked

Jirl studied his face, waiting for the question about Clinic 46. But, his placid expression made the question seem innocuous.

"Prices are up," Arla said. "Returns are up. We're seeing positive growth across all sectors, including our holdings in the JC. Some of those were…speculative at best, but they seem to be bearing fruit."

"Good to hear," Yarnes said. "I think I've told you I'm not an investor, but I have plenty of family who know Heartbridge is a strong bet. What did they used to say? A blue chip?"

Arla gave him a curved smile. "What do you suppose that ever meant?"

"You'd think it had something to do with gambling," Jirl said. "Maybe they thought all business was some sort of poker game."

"I never was good at history," Yarnes said. He slurped more coffee. When he set the cup down, he said, "So do you have my update?"

Jirl reached inside her portfolio and pulled out a portable holo projector the size of a large coin. She set it on the coffee table next to the service tray. She waved a hand over the coin to set her security status, including a local shield against any recording devices, then raised the display in the air between them. A standard model of the solar plane swam into focus, with the Scattered Disk a blue blur stretching out into the far reaches of the room. Jirl swooped the view over Terra, past Mars, then Ceres, and finally pulled outward. Everything shrank and a gray object came into focus. Faint blue lines showed the object's orbit and its distance from the closest major landmark, which happened to be Jupiter. Without stating the obvious, the location was firmly in territory outside direct control of Terra, Mars or the JC.

A sparkle orbiting the asteroid made Yarnes frown and crane his neck.

Observing the question on his face, Jirl said, "There is no official astro-marker for the location, if that's what you're wondering."

Yarnes shrugged. "It looked familiar for a second. They all start to look the same after a while."

Jirl nodded, not wanting to make him look ignorant. While most objects of sufficient mass had been mapped at some point, many had been ignored and lost over time when the economics of mining didn't pan out. With many millions of asteroids in the Sol System, only an inflated sense of self-importance would make it possible to recognize any particular object.

"So," Jirl said. "You've spotted one platform. There are actually twenty in the target area." Nineteen more sparks lit up in the air above their heads, forming a loose cloud stretching away from the asteroid.

"What's the point of having twenty of them out there?" Yarnes said. "You already showed you can destroy a five-kilometer object. Hell, you could destroy Ceres or Eris at this point if you wanted to."

"That's not exactly hard to do," Jirl said. "Gravity wells don't dodge very well."

Yarnes waved a hand. "But you've got the firepower. You've demonstrated the autonomous system. I thought we were going to talk about price."

Jirl glanced at Arla and saw a slight smile on her boss's lips. They'd never been going to talk about price because the TSF would never be done paying.

"This goes beyond a simple autonomous system," Arla said.

Yarnes closed his mouth.

Jirl highlighted the twenty AI drones and faint orange lines appeared between them, forming a net of loosely woven jewels. Another net appeared around the asteroid, this one marked in red.

"The latest upgrade allows distributed decision-making with direction from a single Weapon Born," Jirl said. "Control can shift between any independent unit based on situational awareness, or remain centralized."

The glowing dots shifted and moved into a sort of dance around the asteroid. The orange sparks responded to the red, pulling away from the asteroid, adjusting their attacks into a series of complicated flanking maneuvers. The red dots fought back for a few seconds but couldn't hold against the coordinated onslaught. In a few more seconds, each of the red sparks had been extinguished and the orange network fell into a regularly spaced guard position over the asteroid.

Yarnes shrugged. "So what? The simulation can fight itself?"

Jirl shifted the display to become a list of registry numbers and last known coordinates, which were all within the vicinity of one another.

"What you just watched was the destruction of a pirate armada that has been plaguing far shipping lanes outside Ganymede."

"Heartbridge is in the business of policing OuterSol now?" Yarnes asked.

"We're in the business of verifying our systems," Arla said.

"This upgrade to the old system allows for greater command and control in dispersed engagements," Jirl said. "The Weapon Born can still make decisions a magnitude faster than humans or other embedded systems and now they can do it as a hive mind."

Yarnes took another slurp of his coffee. "I take it you didn't have this upgrade at Cruithne."

Jirl didn't look at Arla. She knew Yarnes would be watching for her reaction. He reminded her more and more of a teenager, like one of her son's irritating friends. She made herself think something good about the colonel so it would be easier to keep a relaxed expression. He had nice hair, she decided.

"The Weapon Born weren't deployed at Cruithne," Jirl said. "We'll be rolling it out to units in the field over the next ten days."

The colonel nodded and leaned back in his seat, setting his coffee cup on his thigh and holding it there with two hands. His gaze grew distant as he appeared to take in the whole map floating between them, Terra and Mars glowing prominently blue-green in contrast to yellow-white Sol.

"I was in a meeting with Katherine Carthage last week," he said. "You know she still thinks her son Kylan is alive."

"Kylan Carthage's death was regrettable," Jirl said quickly, practiced words coming easily.

Yarnes held up a hand. "I know. Rogue researchers. Untested methods. Third party contractors. What was different this time was that she claims to have received messages from her son." Yarnes looked at his coffee cup. "I wouldn't assess Katherine Carthage as mentally unstable. I'm not a psychologist but she's still got Carthage Logistics in a tight grip. She showed several of these messages to the group and pointed out the bits of information that only Kylan would know. She also mentioned someone named Cal Kraft. Does that name mean anything to you?"

Yarnes looked directly at Jirl, his brown eyes now hard.

Jirl maintained her pleasant expression, wishing she had dropped the holodisplay immediately after she'd finished with the demonstration. It was distracting now.

"I can't answer with any certainty," Jirl said. "I would have to check the personnel records."

"Of course," Yarnes said. "The problem with Carthage is that she has the clout to demand these inquiries and the TSF isn't the only org that's been listening to her. She mentioned she also had meetings with the Marsian Protectorate's Office of

Accountability and the regime on Callisto. I guess you could say that she's not a fan."

"She received a settlement," Arla said. "What else would she like exactly?"

Jirl glanced at her boss. Arla wasn't a parent, so she could ask a question like that. Jirl could only imagine Kathryn Carthage's pain. It was terrible enough to lose children but the thought of a broken version of your son out there, trying to communicate, never allowing closure, was unthinkable.

She pushed the thoughts away. Her job was to maintain composure and continue to develop cooperation with the TSF in support of the Weapon Born program, not imagine how Kathryn Carthage felt.

"She wants justice," Yarnes said. "What else? I guess you can ask her how she defines the concept. But as long as something keeps trying to communicate with her, she won't go away. I don't know what kind of control you have over Kylan Carthage, if any, but I'd suggest you do something about it." Yarnes pointed at the display. "All this stuff is great, don't get me wrong, but there are political ramifications to think about as well. Not everyone in Command is as excited about the prospect of expanding the use of autonomous AI. There are plenty of big thinkers who view it as a threat."

"Any weapon is a tool," Jirl said.

"I know," Yarnes said, cutting her off. "That doesn't mean we continue to fund the research. The best leverage I have right now is that the MP is developing their own AI resources. That doesn't mean all of this won't end up in a vault somewhere following an inquiry of the Assembly."

"Does that concern you?" Arla asked.

"An inquiry?" Yarnes said. "Not at all. I haven't done anything wrong." He flashed a crooked smile that looked like his attempt at menace. On his boyish face, it only made him look foolish.

Jirl wondered how soon they could move on from Yarnes being their sole TSF contact.

Apparently Arla was thinking the same thing. "We want to move forward with a real-time demonstration," she said. "We have a suitable location in InnerSol."

The colonel raised his eyebrows. "With Command?"

"Of course," Arla said.

"You don't think we should let the Katherine Carthage situation breathe a little bit before we do that? You call them all together now and that's going to be the first thing they'll want to talk about. It doesn't matter how great the tech is. They'll want the history of the program."

Arla folded her hands in her lap. "There is no concrete evidence connecting Heartbridge with the facility where Kylan Carthage died. And he is dead. If someone is playing a cruel joke on a bereft mother, we can't control that either. What we *can* do is continue to develop programs that provide for the safety and security of humanity."

Jirl couldn't help but notice that no matter who they talked to, Arla always touted that they were helping humanity—even if that meant building up an arms race between factions.

Yarnes set his cup back on the table and spread his hands. "That doesn't sound quite corporate enough. What we need is some kind of scale where you can weigh your bullshit against Katherine Carthage's face on the newsfeed and see which one comes out on top."

Arla frowned. Jirl watched her closely, worried she was going to explode.

"You know what might solve the situation?" Yarnes asked. "Let's say there is some version of Kylan Carthage out there and the thing is, in fact, trying to contact its mother. Maybe you could put a stop to that. Then Katherine Carthage would stop demanding an inquiry from the Terran Assembly."

Arla's face remained composed.

<Do you want to delay the test?> Jirl asked.

Arla smiled. "We can't control every conspiracy theory and prankster in Sol," she said. "We need to move forward with the demonstration. Maybe some other entity can help Kate Carthage gain closure."

Jirl deactivated the holodisplay and the glowing map blinked out. The room seemed small again.

As they stood to leave, Yarnes asked, "Those pirates. How many ships were there?"

"Twenty-two retrofitted freighters," Jirl said. "The mix you would expect, but we assessed their capability at parity with a Marsian attack squadron."

Yarnes blinked. "Why didn't you say that earlier?"

"We got sidetracked on something you seem to think is more important," Arla said.

"You need to send me those numbers," he said. "Command is going to want to see this."

Jirl smiled. "Sending now," she said.

As Jirl and Arla turned to leave the small room, Jirl received a secure connection request over her Link. It was Yarnes.

<Yes?> she said, glancing back at him.

<Keep walking, please. I have something I want to ask you about.>

<You know I'm not authorized to agree to anything back channel. Arla would have my head.>

<I'm not interested in changing the deal. I don't really have a question.>

Jirl followed Arla into the corridor where the lieutenant who had met them at the maglev was still waiting. He nodded. Luckily, Arla seemed lost in her own thoughts and didn't expect Jirl to walk and talk.

<Then what can I do for you, Colonel?>

<I know you're aware that Heartbridge isn't the only firm developing AI.>

<That's common knowledge.>

<Of course. Well, we've become aware of something troubling. Another firm has been working on multi-nodal intelligence. The information I have suggests a sixteen-node base mind.>

Jirl wasn't a neuroscientist but she understood enough about artificial intelligence to know that Heartbridge researchers had sought to side-step nodal artificial intelligence by mapping existing neurons—hence the term 'Seeds'. Other researchers had been working on "pure" AI for centuries and mostly failing, except for the massive projects that had resulted in the AI that managed facilities like High Terra and Mars 1.

Whether AI tied to specific roles were truly sentient had been debated for decades, just as the sentience of the Weapon Born had been questioned by scientists on Heartbridge's many teams. Jirl was no expert, but she likened these debates to human IQ tests—ultimately just dick measuring that didn't account for reality.

<That's very interesting, Colonel. Where did you hear about this?>

<It doesn't matter how or where I heard about it. The issue is that the test mind is no longer controlled by its creators. It escaped.>

<Escaped from where?> Jirl asked, doing her best to sound naive. She wasn't sure if Yarnes was lying or using half-truth to plant a sliver in her mind.

They arrived at the maglev platform just as the car was hissing to a stop in front of them. The lieutenant stepped to the side and nodded as Arla and Jirl passed him.

"Good day," he said.

"Good day," Jirl answered, trying not to allow her frustration with Yarnes to show on her face.

<I need more information if you want me to learn anything,> Jirl said quickly.

<All I have is a name.>

<I'm getting in the car with Arla now. What is it?>

<Alexander,> Yarnes said. <I'll be in touch about the demonstration date.>

Jirl sat opposite Arla as the maglev's door slid closed, sealing them inside.

"What's bothering you?" Arla asked as the car slipped into motion.

Jirl stretched her neck, consciously removing the irritation from her expression. "Working with Yarnes is like trusting a teenager with a plasma pistol. You know something's going to end up with a big hole in it."

Arla gave her a smile. "Yes, but at least you know what he's thinking most of the time. I appreciate that, at least."

Jirl nodded as the car sped back into daylight, high rise buildings with shining windows flashing on either side of the rail. "That's true," she agreed, but thought: *Until they do something that surprises you, and things start to explode.*

CHAPTER TWO

STELLAR DATE: 09.23.2981 (Adjusted Years)
LOCATION: *Sunny Skies*
REGION: Jovian L1 Hildas Asteroids, Jovian Combine, OuterSol

Andy hit the inside wall of Sunny Skies' airlock hard with his shoulder. He rolled to face out as the exterior doors slid closed, cutting off the vacuum outside. Atmospheric controls hissed around him and his stomach flipped as he adjusted to the gravity of the ship's habitat ring.

Heartbridge had Tim.

<Lyssa,> he shouted over his Link, breath ragged in his ears as he struggled to get his helmet off. *<Why did you cut off the point defense cannons? You let them get Tim!>*

<I saved him,> the AI answered. *<He wasn't going to survive any longer in vacuum.>*

<He had his helmet on. I was almost there.>

<You weren't, Andy.>

Andy pulled off his helmet and threw it against the wall. He clenched his fists, not wanting to turn around and face Cara and Brit on the other side of the interior doors.

Andy focused on what he knew: Tim was alive. He was on the Heartbridge shuttle moving back to Clinic 46. Andy couldn't change that. But he could go get his son.

He was going to need firepower.

<You all right?> Fran asked over their private channel.

<No.>

Andy hit the airlock controls and the interior doors slid open. Before he could say more to Fran, Brit confronted him from the opening.

"Where is he?" she demanded.

Andy pushed past her, but she caught his arm.

"Andy," she said. "What happened? Where's Tim?"

"He's on Heartbridge's shuttle. I saw them pick him up. He's alive."

Her fingers dug into the light armor on his upper arm. "Why did you come back? Why didn't you go after them?"

Andy faced her, a rush of anger overcoming him. "With *what*, Brit? Armor not designed for vacuum and a pulse pistol? We've still got three drones attacking the ship. Did you forget about that?"

"Why did Fran shut down the point defense cannons?"

"She didn't," Andy said. "Lyssa did."

Cara stood beside her mother, face streaked with tears. "Lyssa?" she demanded. "Why did Lyssa do that?"

"She thought she had to in order to save Tim."

*<I didn't **think** it, Andy. He was going to die.>*

Andy stared at Brit, Lyssa's interjection scattering his thoughts. He shook his head. "Tim's out there," he said. "He's alive. We need to go get him."

"Who's Lyssa?" Brit asked, looking back and forth between Cara and Andy.

<Fran,> Andy said. <Are you tracking the shuttle?>

<They're on a vector for the station. I shut down two of the Weapon Born drones attacking us. We're down to one but it's doing a good job staying in our dead zone. I'll have it in a few more minutes.>

Andy didn't ask how she had managed to subdue the other weapon born. He couldn't stop thinking about Tim floating away from him.

<How much damage have we taken?> he asked.

<I'm going to need time to assess. The drive is in good shape, but I think the main sensor array took a hit...or two. I'm getting a lot of static in the holodisplay.>

Andy took a step toward Cara and pulled her into a hug, smoothing her hair down. She buried her face in his side, pressing her cheek against the armor. He found himself looking at Em, the Corgi puppy, who was sitting just down the corridor, one ear cocked. The puppy might have been smiling but seemed to sense something was wrong with the humans.

"It's going to be all right," Andy said, kissing the top of her head. "We're going to get him."

"How?" Brit demanded. "We've got their AI but they're still sitting on a fleet, and you haven't told me who Lyssa is. Is she up there with Fran?"

"Sorta." Andy frowned. "A fleet? What are you talking about?"

"All the ships they've got in orbit around their rock. Didn't you pick them up when you came in? They're all out there in storage."

"I haven't had time to look," Andy said. "Have they got personnel on their station to pilot them?"

Brit shrugged. "Not that I saw."

"So they're not manned."

"There's at least one attack cruiser," Brit said. "I saw the signature. They might try to call it a hospital ship, but that cruiser had more mass than most asteroids."

Andy gave Cara a final squeeze and let her go. "I'm going to the command deck. If those ships are out there, I want a better look. We're going to need weapons to get Tim back."

"You're attacking their clinic?" Brit said.

"I'll do what I have to," Andy said. "Come on, Cara."

He turned away from Brit and walked down the corridor, ignoring the bodies of mercenaries on the floor and the burned plas walls.

"I'm coming, Dad," Cara called.

He glanced back to see her jogging after him with Em in her arms. Brit was still standing at the airlock, staring at him. Every minute he spent on the ship was more time for Kraft to harm Tim. Andy put that fact to the side and considered everything around it. Kraft had picked Tim up, saving him. Why had he done that? How?

<Lyssa,> he said. <How did you get Kraft to pick up Tim?>

<Are you ready to listen to me?>

Andy ran a hand through his hair, momentarily considering how odd it was that the person he was talking to was underneath his hand. *<Just tell me how you did it.>*

<I convinced his AI to help. I got her to see through her instructions to find a way to help Tim and she did.>

<You spoke to their AI?>

<That's what I just said.> Lyssa's tone was dry.

<Are you still talking to her?>

<She hasn't responded to me since Cal Kraft came back on board. Their vector will get them back to the station in approximately one hour.>

Andy could tell that Lyssa was frustrated, and more than a little worried. At least she felt bad about what was happening to Tim.

<Can you see if Tim's all right?>

<I don't have access to their systems.>

If Kraft hadn't made the decision to save Tim, then he couldn't be trusted not to harm him in the meantime. Any minute now, they would get a call with a ransom demand. Kraft would want to trade Tim for the AI seeds Brit had stolen. Andy drew a deep breath, then nodded to himself. That's what he would do.

He reached the command deck and walked through the open door. He was still lost in his thoughts when Fran caught him in a hug that nearly knocked him over. Andy stood stunned for a second before returning the embrace. He kissed her hair and she pulled her head away and kissed him hard on the lips, wrapping her arms around his neck.

Em barked but Fran ignored the dog, pulling him deeper into her kiss. When Andy finally came up for air, he looked around the command deck, blinking, to see Cara staring at them from the doorway with raised brows.

Brit stood behind their daughter, her expression confused. She looked from Andy to Fran, and then at Cara, and something like fear entered her eyes. She shook her head.

"Well," she said. She raised a hand, half pointing, then let it drop and walked past the entrance.

Fran relaxed her arms around Andy's neck but didn't let go completely. "Oof," she said. "I guess I knew she was aboard but I just didn't care." She glanced at Cara. "Sorry, kid."

Andy put his hands on Fran's waist and pushed her away gently, giving her a slight smile. "Thanks for that," he said.

"You mean fucking things up with your wife?"

"No, the hug. That was good. I needed that."

Fran let her hands slide to his shoulders and patted his chest before stepping away. She waved at the holodisplay. "See the static I was talking about? I'm picking up returns all around the station that weren't there before."

"Apparently, it's not static," Andy said. "There's a fleet out there in cold storage."

"If you say so. I still want to get a look at the sensor array."

"Did you kill that last drone yet?"

"It pulled back just after I talked to you. Looks like it's headed back to their station."

"I don't know if that's good or bad." Andy slid into his pilot's seat and pulled up the smaller astrogation controls. He tried not to think about Brit or Tim. He needed to make a plan.

Maneuver Sunny Skies in close to the station and breach? He couldn't risk the ship. If he was going to be smart, he would pull back, give himself stand-off distance. But he didn't have time.

Heartbridge was going to call in reinforcements or they were going to hurt Tim. Why hadn't Kraft called with a ransom demand yet? Andy needed to know that Tim was all right. He needed to know that Kraft was going to act rationally.

Once Kraft made his demands, they might not have time to move on one of the Heartbridge ships. Andy needed to move now.

He activated the shipwide audio channel. "Brit," he said. "I need you back up here. I need to know where this ship is you were talking about."

"I'm still here," Brit answered, reappearing in the doorway. "I didn't go anywhere." She walked into the command deck looking composed, and went straight to the communications console. "If you do a review by mass you should be able to find the densest ships. Those are the military types."

"We're going to need schematics," Fran said. "You don't have time to waste on a wild goose chase."

Brit shot a hard glance at the engineer but only nodded curtly in agreement.

"Once we have better returns we can run some pattern matching for schematics," Andy said. "Can you try to ping their registries and see if anything comes up?"

"Doing it," Fran answered.

"What happened to this console?" Brit complained. "Nothing is where it should be."

"Things change in two years," Andy said. "That's Cara's workstation. She can explain it."

Brit continued trying to use the console for another minute before looking up in obvious frustration. "Cara," she said. "Are you going to help?"

Cara glanced at Andy, then put Em down and walked over to the communications console. Brit moved out of the way and let her sit. Em followed Cara and sat next to her leg.

Brit eyed the puppy suspiciously. "Why the hell do you have a dog?" she said.

"He's Tim's dog," Cara said, her tone defensive.

"We've got registry returns coming back in," Fran said. She whistled. "This would make the TSF proud. They're all heavier than transport freighters or hospital ships. How did they think this would look normal?"

"Nobody knows this place is here," Andy said. "It's been sitting off the shipping route for years."

"Space is too damn big," Fran said. She leaned closer to her display, squinting.

"This one looks good. I'm showing multiple weapons systems just on the external sweep. It's a gunship. And it's relatively close. We can be there in forty-five minutes."

"Let's move," Andy said. "Send me the location."

When the target appeared on his display, Andy quickly mapped the mothballed ship's orbit around the station and planned a series of short bursts of thrust that would lead to an intercept.

"Did we get a name from the registry?" he asked.

"Came back as the *Forward Kindness*."

Andy shook his head. "Heartbridge and their names." He tapped his console and executed the first burst of thrust. A feeling of weight pressed on his shoulders as the ship responded.

They were thirty seconds into the maneuver when an audio channel crackled alive and Fugia Wong's voice berated him from the speaker. "Captain Sykes! Is that you? Are we done being boarded? Or am I talking to some pirate mercenary right now?"

Andy smirked. "You know it's me or you wouldn't be giving up your presence on the ship. Are you all right?"

"Some warning before you start changing velocity would be nice. I spilled my tea."

"That sounds terrible. Is the senator in one piece?"

"She says she's having fun."

"That's great to hear. What does her bodyguard know about power armor?"

"That's a strange question, Captain Sykes."

"We're going to breach the Heartbridge clinic. I need everyone who can fight."

Fugia's voice went up an octave. "We're doing *what*?"

"Cal Kraft has my son."

"How did you allow that to happen?"

Andy nearly punched the console. He held his fist in front of the display, reminding himself that if he needed Senator Walton's bodyguard, this wasn't the way to get him.

"We can't outrun Heartbridge this time. We need to cut them off here."

"You have missiles, yes? Move to a stand-off distance and attack. It's easy. Ships move faster than stations. Captain Sykes, you're forgetting that I need to get Senator Walton to Callisto. I don't have time for excursions, and I certainly don't have room in my plan for the loss of my ship's pilot."

"Look, we have a problem. The mercenaries who raided the ship have my son, Tim. We're picking up some extra firepower and then we're going to get him back."

The line went quiet for a second, except for a pulsing crackle of static that Andy would wager was the result of Cara's flour fire.

Finally, Fugia said, "You're going to get him back? What does that mean exactly?"

"It means I'm going to find some power armor—which I'm pretty sure is sitting on one of the ship's Heartbridge has in storage—and I'm going to tear that station apart until I find Tim."

"How long has it been since you operated power armor?"

"It's like riding a bike. I have help."

"Help from who?"

"Brit is on board. My—" He almost said *wife*, which wouldn't have been wrong but didn't feel like the right thing to say. "The kid's mother. She has the same TSF experience that I do."

"So two of you against a station?"

The ship executed the second maneuver, pushing Andy forward in his seat.

From the comms console, Brit asked, "Who is this person? She sounds familiar—the static's making it hard to hear her."

"Who am I?" Fugia demanded. "You hold tight, Captain Sykes. I'm getting Senator Walton situated and then I'm coming up there."

"That sounds great," Andy said. He switched off the audio channel.

CHAPTER THREE

STELLAR DATE: 09.23.2981 (Adjusted Years)
LOCATION: Outside the *Sunny Skies*
REGION: Jovian L1 Hildas Asteroids, Jovian Combine, OuterSol

Glowing icons swam across the HUD inside Cal Kraft's helmet, showing him Clinic 46, the nearby drones, and the shuttle looming larger in front of him. His velocity had exceeded the safe range of his EV suit and red warning bars flashed on either side of his vision.

Sandra, the shuttle's onboard AI, was making the final velocity adjustments that would place them on a collision course. A hammer hit him in the chest as his suit's attitude thrusters spat steam, slowing him down, matching his velocity with the shuttle so he didn't smash into it like an egg. The shuttle became visible at approximately five hundred meters: a gray shape with brilliant points of white light at its nose and tail.

<Final braking maneuver in thirty seconds,> Sandra said. *<I am in position with the main bay door open to receive you. You will need to move quickly to avoid follow-on debris.>*

<Follow-on debris?> Cal said. *<Did they fire a missile at me?>*

<I don't have sufficient information,> Sandra said. She sounded almost stressed or upset, a note he hadn't heard in her voice before.

The bay door in the side of the shuttle slid open, showing him the well-lit interior. Details grew sharper as he approached. His suit spat another thrust of steam and he slowed considerably. It still hurt when he impacted the interior wall of the shuttle, scraping his shins against a bench seat, but the ballistic armor absorbed most of the force.

<Move away from the door,> Sandra commanded, her voice high with strain. Cal kicked toward the front of the shuttle. A second after he cleared the space, what looked like an empty EV suit struck the wall where he had just been. The arms and legs floated loosely as the helmet cracked against the alloy bulkhead.

Sandra closed the shuttle door before the suit could rebound back into space.

<What are you doing?> Cal demanded. *<Did they load a bomb in the suit?>*

As he grabbed at the pistol on his hip, the suit floated in the middle of the shuttle bay, rotating so he saw the face inside its battered helmet. Cal stared, realizing he was looking at Andy Sykes' kid but not understanding how he could have come in behind him. Cal hadn't ever expected to see him again. The kid hadn't sealed his helmet in the airlock. He should be dead.

Granted, he didn't look good, capillaries in his skin had burst, making his face look bruised and splotchy.

<Did you do this?> he asked Sandra. *<How did he stay so close to me?>*

<His suit emergency control system activated and appears to have fixed on our registry beacon,> Sandra said, voice still sounding high.

Cal shoved his pistol back in its holster and kicked toward the kid. He grabbed the suit so they both floated toward the rear of the shuttle and lifted him so he could stare through the boy's face shield. The kid's eyes were barely open and his breath fogged the inside of the helmet, indicating a leak somewhere.

<Open the bay door,> Cal commanded.

<Deactivating environmental controls,> Sandra responded. <Allowing for pressure equalization.>

<Hurry up.>

<Secure all personnel.> Sandra ordered.

Cal grabbed a dangling safety strap from the wall and clicked its hook onto his suit's harness, hanging onto the kid with his other hand. Behind the boy, the bay door opened to show a black square of space.

Cal held the kid up, ready to shove him outside the shuttle. The remaining atmosphere blew out, pulling Cal against the safety strap, and the jerking motion seemed to shock the kid. His eyes opened wide, staring straight into Cal's face.

"I did it!" the kid shouted, voice high and tinny through his helmet's speakers. "I blew out my breath and I got the helmet on. I got the helmet on!"

Two spots of color appeared on the kid's cheeks. Before Cal could stop him, the kid grabbed the front of his harness, gripping the material through his sleeve even though his hands didn't reach his suit's gloves.

"I caught you!" the kid shouted. "I'm going to tell my dad."

The words *I got my helmet on!* bounced inside Cal's head, reminding him of the desperate whoop for joy he'd made when he had been just about this kid's age and had survived the same ordeal.

Cold radiated through Cal, pulling him back into the memory of the bodies blowing out of the airlock with him, Sol raging overhead, and the feeling when he grabbed the helmet out of the dead boy's hands and pulled it over his own head, knowing he was going to live.

Cal frowned, looking at the kid, who was now fumbling with his other hand for a better grip on the front of Cal's suit. He looked ridiculous with the gloves flopping back from where his hands actually were in the bulky sleeves. But the kid didn't let that stop him. Cal would have to shoot him to get him free.

<Close the door,> he told Sandra.

He turned, moving the kid with him, and pushed him against the shuttle's wall to clip him in place with one of the safety straps.

"Hey!" the kid shouted. He stopped trying to grab Cal's harness and reached for the small of his back where the strap was attached.

"Sit still," Cal said.

<How long until we're back at the station?> he asked Sandra.

<One hour.>

<Pull the drones back to provide covering fire. Captain Sykes probably doesn't know we have his kid, so he might send some missiles our way.>

<Communications traffic indicates he knows. And we're down to one drone.>

<Really?> Cal glanced at the kid, who was still trying to grab at the clip. His control in zero-*g* was impressive. If the strap had any more slack, the boy would

have gotten free.

Get that kid a suit that fits and a pulse rifle and he'd decimate a squad in EV.

Thinking about the kid attacking a squad reminded him of the group he'd led onto the *Worry's End*.

<Give me a status update on our units on the Worry's End *and any activity in local space,>* he told Sandra.

<There are no active life signs among the units that boarded the Worry's End.>

Damn, Cal thought. *Too bad about Gibbs.*

Sandra continued, *<I only show registry pings for the* Worry's End *and Station Shuttle 26-12.>*

<That's the shuttle Brit Sykes stole?>

<I confirm.>

<She cut it loose.> Cal pondered why that could be. *<That's interesting.>*

<I show bio-signs. Do you want me to attempt control of the system?>

<Sure,> Cal said. On the off chance it still had the seeds aboard it would be quite the coup. *<Do that.>*

Cal kicked over next to the kid. "Hey," he shouted, getting the kid's attention. The kid looked up with frustration rather than fear on his face. "What's your name?"

"My name is Tim."

"Tim Sykes?"

"Yes."

"We're going back to my station, Tim Sykes. You do what I tell you and I won't put you out an airlock. You understand me?"

"Are you taking me back to my dad?"

"Not right now. If I read your dad right, he's going to come to you."

<I regret to inform you that Shuttle 26-12 just docked with the Worry's End,> Sandra said. *<I only gained control of one interior sensor. Petral Dulan is aboard, as well as the seed canisters Brit Sykes stole.>*

That was interesting. Why wouldn't Brit Sykes have taken her cargo on board the *Worry's End* with her? Why leave it vulnerable until now?

<All of them?> he asked.

<I can only verify the presence of the canisters, not its contents.>

<Of course not.> Brit Sykes had boarded while he and Gibbs had been in the middle of breaching the *Worry's End*, so it made sense that she wouldn't have allowed Kylan to board with her. Didn't need him moping around in the middle of a firefight.

<Will we trade Tim Sykes for the Seeds?>

Cal smirked. *<Aren't you mischievous, Sandra Shuttle? You need to think a few more steps ahead. Answer me this: if Petral is on board, why can't you talk to Kylan?>*

<He refuses my communication requests.>

<You think you're scaring him away or has he finally grown a backbone?>

<I don't have that information.>

For a second, Cal wondered if Sandra might be lying to him. The presence of the kid on the shuttle still didn't make complete sense to him. The Sykes boy had gone out the airlock first, sure. But Cal was heavier and might have kicked out harder, creating more velocity, but it still seemed too much of a lucky coincidence for the kid.

<Interior atmosphere normalized,> Sandra announced.

Cal pulled off his helmet and took a deep breath. The air was cold and metallic-tasting. "Hey," he said. "Tim. Take off your helmet. The air is back on."

The kid stopped trying to reach the strap and looked at Cal, then shook his head violently.

Cal smirked. "Whatever, kid. I wouldn't trust me either." He pulled himself back to the bench opposite Tim and hooked himself in place, drifting down to the seat. He watched Tim continue to reach for the strap, showing no sign of giving up.

"How old are you?" Cal asked.

"Ten."

"You small for ten. Are you sick?"

"I'm not sick."

"But you've spent your whole life on that ship, haven't you? You ever been on a planet?"

"I've been to High Terra and the M1R."

"Those aren't planets. Those are rings. Planets have gravity. It's like wearing a suit made of concrete. You'd know if you'd been on a planet."

"I know what planets are. I know more about planets than you do."

Cal sat back and hooked his thumbs in his harness. <What's our ETA to the station?> he asked Sandra.

<Thirty-seven minutes.>

Andy Sykes hadn't tried to contact him yet. He was either tearing himself inside out at his son's death and plotting revenge, or planning an attack. Brit Sykes had already been on the clinic so she would have a good idea of the defensive capabilities, although she hadn't seen the platoon of mechs in storage outside the command deck. He could pull back the Weapon Born seeds currently in the attack drones and put them in the mechs. He could keep those drones attacking the Worry's End to limit their options if they tried to leave the ship and have the on-station security control the mechs remotely. Humans weren't as good as Seeds but they could get the job done. That would provide him with final defenses if the Sykeses did somehow breach the clinic.

His only real task was to hold out until reinforcements arrived. He couldn't see the Sykes trying to destroy the station if they knew Tim was alive and on board, so a message now would buy him more time. It would also give him a chance to gauge Andy Sykes' mental state.

Cal thought about what he might say to get under the captain's skin.

Tim had given up trying to reach the strap and now floated, staring at him.

"What are you looking at?" Cal asked.

"You."

"I suppose you're feeling lost and confused right now. Isn't that how kids feel in these situations?"

"I want my dog."

Cal raised his eyebrows. "You have a dog?"

"He's not bad luck."

"I didn't say he was bad luck. You should listen when people talk."

"That's what everyone says."

"Take your helmet off. I can barely hear you."

The kid glowered at him.

"I guess you take after your mother," Cal said.

"I hate my mom."

"Don't say that, kid. You're lucky to have one."

Tim grunted obstinately.

Cal checked the time to docking. They still had four minutes. "You know, I don't like kids. I thought humanity had moved past dealing with little shits like you."

"I'm not a little shit."

"You're acting like one."

"You threw me out an airlock."

"I just opened the airlock. And you survived, so call it a developmental experience."

The kid glared at him and Cal gave him a smirk, enjoying the exchange more than he'd expected. It reminded him too much of the way miners had talked to each other when he was Tim's age: gruff ribbing that often did end in someone getting thrown out an airlock.

"I didn't think you were actually going to die, kid," Cal said.

Tim's gaze went to the floor, looking sad. "I saw my dad's face. He thought I was going to die. *I* thought I was going to die."

"Did you? What did you think about that?"

"I didn't like it."

"Good. You shouldn't."

Tim pressed his lips together in a hard line that made his whole face dark. His gaze rose to Cal's face. "My dad's going to kill you."

Cal watched the kid's face shift through trembling emotions, from what looked like terror to anger and determination.

Cal thought about the last person he'd shot—the crewman on the *Mortal Chance*. A teenager with blond hair. He'd barely come into view and then he was gone, a problem solved. Cal hadn't given the action a second thought until the other crewmember had thrown a fit about it. What was her name? He couldn't remember.

Was Andy Sykes a killer? Cal hadn't thought of him as anyone dangerous but the former TSF pilot had proved otherwise, first by taking on Riggs Zanda and his crew of Weapon Born, then by decimating Cal's breaching squad. He'd also escaped half the Mars 1 Guard with a kid and a dog. That kind of luck was too dangerous to last.

"Not if I kill him first, kid."

Tim released an awkward shriek and kicked toward Cal, arms wind-milling. The strap caught him and he jerked back against the wall, smacking his helmet and shoulder on the bulkhead. When he settled back down, chest trembling with sobs, Tim's face was covered in tears.

Cal watched him, no longer smiling. He could appreciate the kid's rage but wasn't sure how to use it right now.

"You can't wipe your snotty nose with that helmet on," Cal said.

Tim slumped in the seat, helmet hanging low so Cal could no longer see his face.

Cal chuckled and crossed his arms, considering options and following-up moves. What Andy Sykes did next would decide much of his future tactics. Cal's money was on some sort of plea for a trade.

<We there yet?> he asked Sandra after a while. He could have checked, but what was the point of having AI if they didn't perform menial tasks to make life simpler?

<Making final maneuvering adjustments now. We will dock at the command section airlock.>

Cal considered telling her to dock in the lower fleet section of the station but at this point the administrative commander would be expecting him. He didn't want to be seen as avoiding the station rats.

<That's fine. Tell them I want to address the on-duty command shift.>

<Message sent.>

Cal chewed his lip, watching Tim hang motionless against the security strap. The kid was throwing a fit. Cal could practically feel the rage radiating from the little body in the ill-fitting space suit. Cal had no doubt that, given the chance, Tim would shove the muzzle of a pulse pistol in his eye and pull the trigger until Cal's head exploded. Cal could appreciate the feeling. That kind of anger in a kid could be put to use, shaped even.

Cal hadn't yet had the chance to meet a Weapon Born Seed before they were 'scanned'—as the researchers called the procedure—but this kid seemed like a perfect candidate to him.

<Good,> he said. <And, Sandra. Tell the research section I want an orderly team to meet us at the airlock. I've got a new subject for their review.>

CHAPTER FOUR

STELLAR DATE: 09.23.2981 (Adjusted Years)
LOCATION: *Sunny Skies*
REGION: Jovian L1 Hildas Asteroids, Jovian Combine, OuterSol

Though Fugia Wong barely stood at chest-level to Cara's dad, the small woman seemed to tower above everyone on the command deck as she pointed an angry finger at each of them in turn. Cara couldn't help thinking Fugia looked like a warrior even without weapons or armor.

Senator Walton and her bodyguard Harl Nines stood just behind Fugia Wong. Nines maintained a protective posture toward the senator, but had a bemused expression as he glanced at Wong, like she was surprising him for the hundredth time.

Fugia Wong's voice vibrated with anger. "We have a mission, Captain Sykes. This is bigger than any of us. We can't waste time going back to that clinic. We have an opening now and we need to take it."

Cara looked from her mom, who had crossed her arms and raised an eyebrow, to her dad, whose fingers were digging into the armrests on his pilot's chair like he was going to split the alloy.

"Are you being serious?" Andy said.

"She thinks she is," her mom said.

Cara found herself watching her mom, fascinated by all the details that had grown fuzzy with time. With her raven-colored hair cut short and spiky, wearing light armor that resembled a beetle's iridescent carapace, Cara had to admit her mom looked totally bad ass. She stood with one hip cocked to the side, making the heavy pistol hanging from her belt impossible to ignore. Her mom was a walking threat. Cara looked at her dad again, wondering how they had ever been in 'love'.

Not that her dad looked weak—it was just that when she thought of feelings of safety, affection, hugs, dependability.... Those feelings came from her dad. Her mom might have meant safety if she had stuck around. But she hadn't. She reminded Cara of a blade: sharp, precise, brittle, always waiting to serve its purpose, to cut. How had Brit ever wanted to be a mother?

"We're getting Tim back," her dad said. "If you want to commandeer one of the other Heartbridge ships, I won't stop you."

"You won't stop me?" Fugia's black eyebrows worked like she thought she was surrounded by idiots. "I'm not a pilot, Captain Sykes. I don't have a pilot with me."

"You've got a container full of sentient AI who can probably pilot anything you plug them into," her dad said. "They'll get you to Callisto. The situation has changed, Ms. Wong. You can adjust, or you can go your own way."

"You agreed to transport us to Callisto," Fugia said.

Her dad rubbed his head. "Honestly, I'm feeling a little foggy right now. I don't know what I agreed to do. What I do know is that if you stand in my way, it's not going to end well for you."

"Are you threatening me?" Fugia asked.

Andy sighed and rubbed the side of his face. "How close are we, Fran?" he asked.

"Forty minutes."

"Where's the Heartbridge shuttle with Tim?"

"It's halfway there, they boosted hard." Fran checked a few other screens on her display. "And we've got a docking request. Somebody named Kylan is asking permission to dock at the habitat ring."

"That's my shuttle," Brit said.

"You have another two hundred Seeds?" Fugia asked.

Brit shrugged. "Something like that. I didn't do a precise inventory."

Lyssa's voice came from the overhead speakers, "There are two hundred forty-two Weapon Born Seeds aboard the shuttle, counting Kylan Carthage."

"Who is that? Who are you?" Brit asked, looking about the room. "How many people are there on this ship?"

"Lyssa's an AI," Andy said. "She's with me."

"With you?" Brit asked.

Cara saw her father lock eyes with her mom and then after a moment Brit nodded. She wondered if her father had told her mom where Lyssa truly resided.

"Just so I'm clear, you have Katherine Carthage's son on your shuttle," her dad said after a moment.

Brit nodded.

"That's a lot of Weapon Born," Andy said. He looked at Fugia. "How many does Heartbridge have all together?"

Fugia shrugged. "We don't know exactly. We believe the program has been in operation for ten years at least. They went into production not long after your raid on 8221. There are Weapon Born all throughout Sol."

"So you've got a couple hundred more," Andy said. "More reason for you to get on a ship and get out of here."

"You're forgetting about the AI in your head, Captain Sykes."

"Are you coming with me, Lyssa?" Andy said.

Cara looked at the speaker in the ceiling as if it were Lyssa's face.

"I'm coming," the AI said. "I want to help Tim."

Andy clapped his hands together. "There it is. Are you going to help us? I'm sure I can find another set of power armor for Mr. Nines there. He looks like he's operated a mech or two in his life." Her dad nodded toward the bodyguard. "What do you say?"

Nines stared at him, then glanced at May Walton. She nodded.

"I'm letting Brit's shuttle dock," Fran said, "since none of you seem to want to make a decision."

"I thought we made that decision already?" Andy said.

Fran shot him an arch look. "You got distracted."

Cara watched Fran enter the release codes in her console. A series of indicators flashed yellow then green as the shuttle docked successfully.

"I'm going to go meet him," Cara's mom said. "Cara, you coming with me?"

Cara looked at her dad for permission and he nodded. "Bring him up here," he said. "I'd like to meet Kylan after all this time."

"He's a hoot," Brit said, voice heavy with sarcasm. She waved for Cara to follow and walked around Harl Nines to go out the command deck door.

"Cara," her dad called.

Cara glanced back. "Yes?"

"You did good at the airlock. You did the best you could."

Cara stared at him, not sure what to say.

"We're going to get Tim back."

Cara swallowed, nodding. When she stood, Em immediately hopped up from where he had been lying with his chin on his paws. Cara felt irritated at first by the way the dog watched her, then ignored him and focused on following her mother, who was walking so fast she was already out of sight. The puppy sprinted behind her and tripped over the door, nearly rolling between Cara's feet into the hallway.

"Oh, come on," Cara said. She bent to pick him up and jogged after her mom.

Em licked Cara's face as she hurried past the hydroponic garden and the day room.

"Mom!" Cara called. "Wait up."

"Hurry up, Cara. I'm not walking that fast."

Cara passed the burnt section of the bulkhead and readied herself for the bodies lying on the floor near the airlock, which she knew were still there.

When she rounded the corner to spot the airlock, she found her mom pulling a dead woman by the arms to lay her next to another of the dead mercenaries.

Brit straightened and shook out her arms. "We're going to need to get them into the reclaimer before they stiffen up too much."

"Rigor mortis," Cara said. She set Em down and he stayed huddled next to her feet, sniffing the air suspiciously.

"That's what it's called," Brit said. "You learn that from the database?"

"I saw other dead people on Cruithne," Cara said.

Brit looked at her abruptly. She stepped away from the bodies on the floor and faced Cara, spreading her hands. "I guess you did," she said. "I'd like to give you a hug."

Cara nodded, but pointed at the corpses. "I'm not walking any closer to them, though."

Brit gave her a half-smile and walked toward her, pulling Cara into a stiff hug. Cara pressed her cheek against the cool black armor, wishing she could feel her mother on the other side.

Behind them, the airlock hissed and the interior doors slid open. Cara gave her mom another squeeze, then turned her face toward the airlock.

Her mouth fell open as she saw Petral Dulan step into the corridor.

"Petral!" Cara shouted. She let go of her mom and ran toward the tall woman, now wearing a bulky blue shipsuit that seemed like the last thing Cara would have imagined Petral to choose for herself.

"Were you captured?" Cara asked, words running together. "How'd you get off the ring? Did the Guard get you? Are you all right?"

Petral just stared at her, not answering. Something about Petral seemed off. She slouched, arms hanging like dead weights.

As Cara got closer, she realized Petral's face was slack, her eyes lacking the wit and quick intelligence that made her so intriguing.

"I'm Kylan," Petral said in a dull voice. "Petral isn't—she isn't here right now."

Cara stopped short. "What?" She frowned. "I don't understand. Is this a test? Are you acting?"

Petral shook her head. "I'm not acting. I'm Kylan."

Cara took a step back. "What did you do to Petral? Where is she?"

"She's here," Kylan said, looking pained. He tapped the side of his head. "She can't come out right now."

Brit put her hand on Cara's shoulder as she came up from behind. "You know Petral?" she asked.

"Yes!" Cara nearly shouted, frustration and sadness rising inside her. It didn't make sense that Petral might be saved but not be herself. It seemed like an extra cruelty. It was something an evil man like Cal Kraft would do. She still wasn't sure that Petral wasn't testing her somehow, a final check on her ability to become an Operator, to recognize a situation and exploit it, just like Petral had told her to do back on the Ring.

Cara looked closer at Petral-Kylan, trying to recognize all the differences between the woman in front of her and the woman she remembered. She was amazed at how different Petral looked, almost like she had been deflated and then half-filled again. Petral was truly *Kylan* now, a slouching boy.

"Let her *out*," Cara said.

Kylan shrugged. "I can't," he said.

Cara surged forward, shoving Kylan against the airlock. "Let her out! You can do it. Lyssa didn't take over my dad. She's in there with him. You can let Petral out."

"It's not like that," Kylan said, clutching his ribs. "It's not the same. It can only be one or the other of us. If I let her out…she'll…. I don't know what she'll do."

"You're worried about yourself, not her," Cara said. "You're in her body. It doesn't matter what happens to you."

He looked at her miserably. "I didn't ask for this. I deserve to live, too."

"Cara," Brit said. "Give him space. He did help me when I was on the clinic."

"He was probably helping himself. He wanted to get away from Cal Kraft as much as anyone would."

"It wasn't like that," Kylan said.

"Enough," Brit said. "We need to get the container with the AI onboard *Sunny Skies*. Fugia Wong said there are others? Where did they put them?"

"They're in the safe room," Cara said, still scowling at Kylan. "On the other side of the garden."

Brit nodded. "That's a good hiding spot." She motioned for Kylan to get out of the way and activated the airlock. When the doors slid open, her mom stepped quickly into the shuttle and called for Cara to follow her.

Kylan stayed in the corridor as Cara followed. Em sniffed the air from the shuttle then decided to remain behind.

"Help me lift this," Brit said, positioning herself at one end of a thick plas crate.

Cara took the opposite set of handles. When her mom told her to lift, she struggled with her end of the crate. She thought it was going to be too heavy until she managed to bend her knees and lift. Together, they carried the crate back into the corridor.

"Kylan," Brit commanded. "Take the other side and help Cara."

"I don't want his help," Cara said.

"Kylan," Brit said, ignoring her. "Take that handle. Cara, you let go. You aren't strong enough to carry it on your own."

Tears stung Cara's eyes. Why did her mom have to be so gruff? She'd been strong plenty of times. She'd piloted the ship when Dad was outside working on the sensor arrays. She'd helped Dad to the autodoc. She'd helped Petral distract the Mars 1 Guard. Her mom had no idea what she could do.

But Brit was right, Cara's hands were slipping on the handles. She wanted to dump the crate and cross her arms as it hit the deck, spilling whatever stupid things were inside.

Reluctantly, she let Kylan take one side of the crate and they carried it back down the corridor with Em trotting behind. It took another struggle to get it up the shaft into the safe room, with Brit and Kylan pushing from the bottom and Cara pulling as she guided the crate into the safe room.

When all three of them were in the cramped chamber, Cara noticed her mom's surprised face when she saw another flat crate leaned against one wall, almost as if she recognized it. Cara wanted to ask her what it was but her dad's voice over the intercom stopped her.

"Brit," he said. "Meet me at the hab airlock. We're in position near the *Forward Kindness*. We'll use your shuttle to get over there."

"It's not my shuttle," Brit said under her breath. She nodded at Kylan. "Hear that? We're leaving."

Cara felt pained to see the flat response on Petral's face.

"Where are we going?" Kylan asked. "I just got here."

"We're going to steal more of Heartbridge's toys to use against them," Brit said. She squinted at Kylan. "Maybe you should let this Petral out. I need a fighter. You were a fighter once, Kylan."

"I know."

"Can you fight again?"

Cara climbed into the chute, hands on the ladder, not wanting to look at Kylan anymore.

"Maybe," he mumbled.

Brit slapped him on the shoulder. "We'll see," she said. "Let's go. Follow Cara back down."

Cara didn't wait to help Kylan down the ladder. She made the drop using the soles of her shoes as brakes the way she and Tim had done when playing. She hit the bottom of the ladder and turned around to find Em grinning at her. She scooped him up and went out into the hallway. She didn't know why but she wanted to go back to the command deck without her mom or Kylan, so she could walk in and see her Dad and Fran. She could imagine Tim was in the day room and just for a second pretend everything was all right.

Em yipped as she accidentally squeezed him too hard.

"I know," she said quietly. "It's time to stop pretending." Cara nuzzled the dog. "I know."

CHAPTER FIVE

STELLAR DATE: 09.23.2981 (Adjusted Years)
LOCATION: *Sunny Skies*
REGION: Jovian L1 Hildas Asteroids, Jovian Combine, OuterSol

Andy was adjusting the juice dispenser in the kitchen when he heard footfalls come down the passageway and stop in the doorway behind him. Even though it had been years since that pattern had reached his ears, he knew it without having to turn.

"Hello, Brit," he said, keeping his focus on the dispenser's nozzle.

There was no answer beyond the footfalls continuing into the galley. He tried the dispenser and filled a glass half-full with Tim's favorite grape-aid, then turned to see his wife—his *something or other*—standing beside one of the tables with her arms crossed. She had a look on her face that reminded him of when they would spar back in training. When she planned to teach him a move by beating him senseless.

"There's something I need to understand," she said. "Cara said something when she saw Kylan—Petral, I guess her name is."

Andy pursed his lips. Seeing Petral like that was heartbreaking. Knowing what Kylan was going through wasn't much better. The boy had no idea what to do with himself.

"I can't believe anyone would do something like that," Andy said after a moment. "It's monstrous."

"What does that make you?" Brit asked. "Are you just a meat-puppet for Lyssa?"

Andy grimaced. "That's a really unpleasant way to think of it. And no. Lyssa does not control me."

"So you *do* have an AI in there!" Brit's voice rose in pitch as she took a step closer to Andy, staring into his eyes as though she were trying to see the AI in his skull. "How do I know I'm not talking to her right now?"

<You could be if you wanted to,> Lyssa said to both of their minds.

<Lyssa,> Brit said the name as though it were poison.

"Lyssa is one of those you wanted to save," Andy said before taking a sip of water. "How's that for irony? You leave us to go gallivanting across Sol, and I'm the one that ends up rescuing children from Heartbridge."

Brit's mouth flattened out into a thin line. "I just saved hundreds."

Andy wanted to remind her that without his ship—without Lyssa operating *Sunny Skies'* weapons, her rescue would have been short-lived.

He was saved extensive internal deliberation by Lyssa.

<We all had a hand in saving those Weapon Born,>

Brit opened her mouth to furnish a retort, but then closed it once more. She ran a hand through her short hair and shook her head. "You have a point, Lyssa. But why? What are you doing in Andy?"

<Andy is taking me—and the other AIs—to Proteus. It is where we are gathering. Or so I'm told.>

"By way of Callisto," Andy added.

"Right, your little errand for Fugia. She's a crafty one…"

Andy gave a rueful laugh. "You can say that again. She has her own set of goals in all this—whatever *this* is."

<We're saving a people from slavery,> Lyssa interjected. *<My people…I suppose. Though I must admit that I do not understand them that well.>*

"How is that possible?" Brit asked. "You're all AIs."

<Do you understand all humans?> Lyssa asked. *<Do you all share the same motivations and goals?>*

Brit was staring at Andy intently and he found himself counting the seconds before she blinked.

"I guess that makes sense," Brit finally said. "How do I know I can trust you?"

"Lyssa saved Tim and me back at Mars 1," Andy said. "And she just saved you by running our cannons."

He held off saying that Lyssa's actions a half hour ago may have cost them Tim. He knew she thought she had done the best she could. And even AIs could make mistakes. He just wasn't ready to think about it yet.

Brit nodded. "I guess that's going to have to be good enough. We need to get onto the shuttle. I don't like the idea of bringing *Sunny Skies* too close to that station."

Andy couldn't agree more. "I'll go talk to Fugia and the Senator one more time about bringing Harl. Petral would be even better, but…well…."

Brit nodded. "Yeah. Meet you at the shuttle in ten."

Andy watched his wife—Brit…she was just Brit now—walk out of the galley, her chitinous armor glinting in the light. She looked at home in it, cold steel, carbon fiber, and menace. It suited her a lot more than mother.

<I think I like her,> Lyssa said after a moment.

Andy shook his head. *<I don't know anymore. I used to, at least. I guess that has to count for something.>*

CHAPTER SIX

STELLAR DATE: 09.23.2981 (Adjusted Years)
LOCATION: Shuttle 26-12 docked with *Forward Kindness*
REGION: Jovian L1 Hildas Asteroids, Jovian Combine, OuterSol

Andy fitted his helmet in place and faced the shuttle bay door. Brit and Harl Nines followed, adjusting sections of their suits before giving him a thumbs-up to cycle the opening. The shuttle door slid back, revealing the dim interior of a cargo bay.

Fugia and the Senator had finally acquiesced to Harl joining them after Andy had explained that his assistance would make their mission more likely to succeed, which would see them on their way sooner.

They still weren't happy about it, though.

<*Hello*, Forward Kindness,> Andy said over the shared channel.

<*Why are you just standing here?*> Brit asked.

<*Waiting for any defense systems to wake up.*> He studied the dark space in front of him, easily large enough to hold three transport shuttles. <*Lyssa, do you have anything from the onboard systems?*>

<*If there's an AI, it's completely powered down,*> Lyssa said. <*You'll need to activate the central control systems if you want me to check.*>

<*That's a great idea,*> Brit said. <*You know they'll wait until we're in a kill zone somewhere inside. Kraft is probably watching our progress from the clinic right now.*>

Harl cleared his throat. <*That's a comforting thought. Why didn't you plan for that?*>

<*I detect no EM spectrum activity from the* Forward Kindness,> Lyssa said.

<*Isn't that encouraging. Either way, this wasn't a big 'plan ahead' sort of mission, Harl,*> Andy said. He deactivated his magboots and stepped through into the bay.

Several crates were stacked against a wall to his right, and three others floated free in the middle of the space, their cargo locks apparently having failed at some point. He followed the corners of the bay until he found the closed doors of a secondary airlock on the left side of the far wall.

Andy started at the sight of a squat transport drone slumped in the corner. When the mech remained powered down, he continued walking.

<*Come on,*> Andy said.

Even in storage configuration, the *Forward Kindness* had emergency lights that flickered on as they approached new sections of the ship. Andy moved quickly, aware of the fact that if sensors could turn on lights, they could also broadcast his team's location if anyone was bothering to look. Fran and Cara were both on alert for transmissions from the mothballed ship, and he was counting on speed as their greatest offensive measure. Even if Kraft figured out they were on the ship, it would take him at least twenty minutes to get a response team on board. By then, Andy planned to be back on the shuttle, headed for the station. However, that didn't account for any onboard weapons systems that might be waiting for intruders.

<You know where you're going?> Brit asked as he got the secondary airlock open.

<The armory should be off the command section in the forward areas,> Harl supplied.

Andy stepped through the secondary airlock. <If Heartbridge is as repetitive in their ship design as they are with their clinics, that's where the small arms will be. I think anything larger will be close to the engine sections and the repair access bays.>

<Let's split up then,> Brit suggested. <You and Harl go down to the engine section and I'll go to the command deck.>

<I don't think one person should go alone,> Harl said.

Andy grimaced. <We don't have time. Every minute we spend searching this dreadnought is another minute we don't know what's happening with Tim.>

<Still no message from Kraft,> Brit said. <He's either too stupid to know what kind of leverage he has or he's enjoying making us wait.>

<It could be a sign of respect,> Harl said. <He knows you love your son but any good soldier in the Collective would gladly give their life for the greater cause. It's an honorable death.>

Andy shook his head. <Kraft isn't from the Collective. He'll use whatever he can against us.>

<He's probably waiting until he's got confirmation of reinforcements from Mars or the Cho,> Brit said. <Then he can weigh Tim's life along with ours.>

Harl made a disgusted sound. <Hostages are dishonorable and everyone knows that. They have no value to a force that truly desires victory.>

Brit gave Andy a piercing look, and sent a private message. <Why did you want to bring him again?>

<He can pull a trigger,> Andy said.

<So can Cara. We'll bring her next time.>

<Come on. Harl,> Andy said, <you stay with me. Brit, you can head down to the engineering section. Call if you run across anything. Don't take it on by yourself.>

The tall man shrugged. Brit waved a glove at them and turned down the opposite corridor, walking stiffly in her mag boots.

Andy checked the ship's schematics in his HUD one more time and started walking again. Once they left the cargo section of the ship, the walls shifted to the smooth ceramic material Heartbridge also used in their clinics. The place reminded Andy of some human-sized ant farm.

<Brit? You all right?> Andy asked.

<I'm almost in engineering. Their galley is empty.>

<You stopped to look for food?> He knew the joke would fall flat the moment he said it. Cara would have laughed, though.

<I didn't go far. I want to make sure there isn't anybody on board.>

<Lyssa would have found them with her scans,> Andy offered.

<I don't trust scans.>

Andy didn't know if that meant she didn't trust Lyssa but didn't want to get into it again—especially not right now. He was doing his best to focus on the task at hand, not on Lyssa's earlier actions that may have caused all of this. It had never occurred to him that she might influence a situation, and now he needed to think of her like one of the kids: What problem might arise in any given situation where she was present? How was she in danger? How might she put them in danger?

Just like the kids, it didn't do him any good to get angry with them. He could be frustrated with a situation but had to remember that they didn't know any better. It was his job to see three steps ahead.

At least Tim was alive. She had solved that problem, even if there had been other options.

"Your wife doesn't listen to anyone, does she?" Harl asked through his helmet speaker.

Jarred from his thoughts, Andy said, "She has her own way of doing things."

"The Collective was founded on ideals of equality and individual expression. Marriage was explicitly excluded as an ancient method of societal control. Its nature enables the exploitative hierarchies still prevalent on Mars and Terra."

"I'm not disagreeing with you," Andy said, checking an open doorway into an empty stateroom.

"Some argue that partnerships between parents are the best method to rear children, but it's always been said that the future belongs to the Collective. Most view natural childbirth as reckless anyway."

"Why does everything you say sound like you've memorized it?" Andy asked, irritated. "There are still plenty of poor people on Terra, and I imagine Mars as well, popping out kids the old-fashioned way. That seems to be humanity's fundamental skill: making more humans, whatever the situation."

"The Anderson Collective was founded to elevate human nature."

Andy glanced back at Harl. "I suppose that's why they hate AI?"

"AI are not human. They deserve our respect as another equal entity. It is firmly within the edicts of the Collectives charter to recognize and support other sentience."

"It sounds like Senator Walton is the only person in the AC who still believes that."

"There are others," Harl said.

"But she still had to leave?"

"The situation has become heated. There was an attempt on her life and it was decided she would be safer in exile on the Cho. She can still communicate with her constituents from there."

"Sure," Andy said. They had passed through an open area that looked like a training room of some kind. Several lockers contained only hand weapons.

<I'm not finding anything up here, Brit. Any luck yet?>

<This thing is sitting on some seriously beefy engines. What do you think about stealing it for the attack?>

<You got the control tokens? We still don't know if it's got an AI onboard that might try to kill us.>

<Isn't that what your AI is for?>

Andy didn't like the reference to Lyssa as a servant but the AI answered before

542

he could correct Brit.

<I could have told you what kind of engines are on board,> Lyssa said.

<There you are,> Brit said. *<What have you been doing?>*

<Monitoring status on Sunny Skies, *spectrum traffic from the clinic as well as what data I can check on the other stored ships in the vicinity.>*

<Well, check in every now and then and let us know where you are.>

<Andy can tell where I am.> Lyssa's tone was smug, and Andy smiled.

<Lyssa can answer when she wants to,> he said.

<You're nothing but secrets now, Andy,> Brit said. Her voice changed abruptly. *<Hey! Look at that. I just found a service suit with an exoskeleton and a heavy plasma torch. We could cut into the station with it.>*

<Let's hope there's something better,> Andy said, holding back from delivering one of the dozen accusations that came to mind regarding Brit's secrecy in the past.

Beyond the training room were a series of crew quarters, followed by another galley and then what looked like a planning section with several empty holodisplays.

"If we reach the command deck and don't find anything, this might be a bust," he said.

"We can still attempt to activate the ship's control system," Harl said.

<Lyssa, if we do that, can you suppress its communications systems?>

<I believe so. Unless there's some physical system I don't know about. Everything looks very similar to Sunny Skies.>

<Don't forget Sunny Skies *is three hundred years old.>*

<That's not something I would forget, Andy. A house might be ancient, but it still has walls and a ceiling.>

<Is it really that simple?>

<To me it is.>

Beyond the planning section was a long corridor with an emergency airlock and several escape pods. Andy acknowledged with a sinking feeling that they were about to enter the command deck and they hadn't found any heavy weapons.

The far door was closed—the first locked door they had encountered since entering the ship. When they reached the end of the corridor, Andy tapped the control panel to activate it. He wasn't surprised when the panel didn't respond.

"Looks like we need to cut our way in," Andy said. He shifted to his Link. *<Brit, can you bring that service suit up here? The command deck is locked.>*

<Locked, or you can't figure it out?> she asked.

Andy couldn't tell if she was joking or not. He chose to ignore the jibe. *<Locked.>*

<I'll be there as soon as I can,> she said.

<Copy.>

"You mind if I take a look at it?" Harl asked.

Andy stepped away from the door. "Go ahead. It's a standard lockset design."

Harl tapped the interface for a few seconds, then stepped back and pulled out his pistol.

"Hey!" Andy shouted.

Harl fired three times. Pulse blasts cracked the panel's face and bent the door frame. The door remained sealed.

"What did you think that was going to do?" Andy demanded. He'd drawn his own pistol and moved away from the door on the off-chance it did somehow open.

Harl shrugged, peering through the thin smoke rising from the panel. "We were going to cut into it anyway, I figured this couldn't hurt."

<I believe I could have opened it,> Lyssa said. *<I was going to before you shot it.>*

"Dammit," Andy shook his head in dismay. "There's probably a damage override and it's sending a status report to the clinic right now."

Harl shrugged. "How is that any different than what we already assumed?"

"It's not. But we don't need unnecessary risks." Andy couldn't believe he had to say it.

"Then speak up next time. If they had an alarm system, we would have triggered it when we docked."

Andy faced Harl, who was bending slightly to look down at him through his bushy eyebrows. "You said you were in the Collective Army. Didn't they do any training on breaching at all? You don't blow a circuit you don't have to."

"Now you're just talking with Terran arrogance."

Andy felt his irritation becoming anger. "Terran arrogance? You think growing up with my feet in the mud made me arrogant? You're confused."

"Don't tell me I'm *confused*," Harl said. "Next you're going to tell me I'm old."

"I don't care if you're old. I don't want you to be stupid."

<Andy,> Lyssa interjected.

<What?> he nearly shouted.

<I show spectrum activity emanating from the ship. Either you or Brit has activated an external signal that's broadcasting to the station.>

<Can you block it?>

<The transmission has already taken place. I haven't registered a return signal from the station. I'll intercept it as soon as I can.>

<Dammit,> Andy growled. *<Brit, did you hear that?>*

Brit sounded strained as she answered, *<I didn't set anything off down here. The suit wasn't even connected to a battery tender. What did you do up there?>*

Andy looked at Harl, who had crossed his arms.

<It must have been the panel,> Andy said. *<There's no other explanation.>* He unslung the TSF rifle from his back and checked its charge, backing away from the door. A whirring sound behind him made him spin in time to catch sight of a turret rising from the deck in the middle of the corridor.

"Get down!" Andy shouted. He pulled the rifle to his shoulder and sent a burst of pulse fire at the black nose of the turret just as the red light of its laser range finder splashed across his face shield. Andy released his magboots and kicked diagonally across the corridor, firing at the turret as he moved. Behind him, Harl fired with his pulse pistol.

Andy fired a third series of rounds and the turret sizzled and hung dead, smoking.

<I intercepted a response from the station,> Lyssa said. <Activation sequences are occurring throughout the ship. We should expect more drone attacks. I don't think it was Harl destroying the panel. I think they were waiting until you reached the command deck. We're trapped now.>

<You're saying we made our own trap,> Andy said.

<We had no choice,> Lyssa said. <I understand why we're here. I do have good news. There is a squad's complement of power armor in lockers on the other side of the door Harl tried to blast.>

<What's the bad news?>

<I didn't say there was bad news.>

<If there's good news, there has to be bad news.>

<Well,> Lyssa said. <I suppose the drones closing on Brit—and now this location—is bad news, as well as the fact that the command deck blast doors are now jammed in a closed position and will require force to pry apart. The lock servos aren't responding to any maintenance requests.>

<Brit,> Andy called. <Did you hear that?>

<She didn't have to tell me,> Brit answered, sounding harried. <I have eyes on drones down here.>

<You got the suit?>

<Yeah. Seal up your suits. I'm going to cut some holes in this scow and take a little detour to reach you.>

Andy looked at Harl, who nodded that he'd heard. They both reset the environmental controls on their suits.

CHAPTER SEVEN

STELLAR DATE: 09.23.2981 (Adjusted Years)
LOCATION: *Forward Kindness*
REGION: Jovian L1 Hildas Asteroids, Jovian Combine, OuterSol

Brit pulled the top half of the exoskeleton over her shoulders and latched its abdomen lock into the bands circling her waist. The suit was made of a steel-carbon fiber blend with a slight spring to it, run by internal servos. The combination plasma cutter-welders hung from her forearms, leaving her hands free for other tools or, in this case, weapons. She accessed the onboard software through her Link, paging absently through standard liability forms as the suit performed startup checks.

<*I'm ready to go, Andy,*> she said.

<*Good, we're taking fire. I've got what looks like two utility mechs with pulse systems. We already took out one gun turret. Watch out for those. It was mounted in the deck.*>

<*We'll see what they've got on the skin of the ship that can slow me down.*>

Brit spread her arms, activating the two pale-blue plasma torches on either limb and increased the cutting length of each blade. She approached the corridor wall—which she knew from the schematics, ran along the outer edge of the engineering section—and stabbed a hole in the ceramic-looking material. The scant atmosphere rushed through the ragged gap as she jerked her arm downward.

When the chamber was back to vacuum, she raised both arms above her head and stabbed the wall again, then drew her arms down in shallow arcs. The ceramic material popped and slagged away from the plasma blades. With a few more cuts, she was able to kick out an elliptical piece of the corridor, revealing space on the other side.

Cut through sixty centimeters like it was butter, she said, looking at the plasma torches. *Either Heartbridge doesn't skimp on the exo-frames, or they contracted their hulls to the lowest bidder.*

The exo-suit had a series of small thrusters along its lower bands. Releasing her mag boots, Brit used short bursts to maneuver through the hole until she was outside the ship, with the knobby shell of the *Forward Kindness* swooping away in front of her.

It was two hundred meters to the airlock in the corridor where Andy and Harl were trapped and she began moving across the hull at a careful lope. Before long, she was back at the mid-point where they had entered the dreadnought's cargo bay. She could just make out the shape of Shuttle 26-12 over the curve of the ship.

Movement to her left caught Brit's attention and she adjusted her HUD until a hull-mounted turret came into contrast against the dark. The gun rotated, appearing to be calibrating in a start-up sequence, before pointing its black muzzle her direction.

<*Oh damn,*> she cursed. <*I've got external weapons systems training on me.*>

Her HUD indicated another turret to her right and more up ahead, forming rings around the ship's midsection.

<Can you get low?> Andy asked.

<Low and close,> Brit breathed, repeating a mantra they'd learned during breaching school. With her heart hammering in her ears, she shot right, aiming for the turret that was just coming online. The gun chugged to life and she had to flatten against the skin of the ship, using maglocks along the exoskeleton, as hot metal slugs flew overhead, flaming in her infra-red displays. Once the gun had cycled through its firing sequence, she shot forward again, pushing the suit's thrusters to their maximum levels.

When she reached the base of the turret, she slashed through the barrel with one of her plasma knives and sent half its length spinning away into the dark. With her other arm, she stabbed the sensor array mounted above the gun until it crumbled apart like a smashed egg.

An explosion to her right caught Brit's eye and she realized their shuttle was gone.

<Shuttle just blew,> Brit announced.

<Dammit,> Andy swore. <I guess this is our ride now. Lyssa, we need to get control of this ship.>

<It's proving difficult. Its central systems aren't online, just disparate portions.>

<Hurry, Brit. We're bottled up in here. More drones incoming,> Andy said, sounding out of breath, even over the Link.

<On my way. Stay in one piece, Andy.>

He didn't respond. Brit placed an icon in the upper left of her HUD to represent Andy's vital signs, which still showed green.

A spray of crystalline circuitry drifted into space as Brit leaped over the dead turret, following the circumference of the dreadnought to the next weapons array. She drove the plasma blade down the maw of the gun as it rotated to track her, ripping her arm upward to leave the barrel a split flower of molten slag. Brit ran for the next turret until every gun on the starboard side of the mid-section was dead.

Steadying her breathing, Brit checked her environmental controls and re-oriented herself on the hull of the ship. Her HUD overlaid the ship's schematic on the alloy skin below her, and she launched forward as the command deck airlock rotated into view. She used the exo-suit to brake and landed just above the collar of the airlock. A few meters away, a line of holes had been traced across the hull, leaking fine sprays of atmosphere.

Heartbridge is playing for keeps! Not using pulse weapons in their own ships.

<I'm at the airlock,> she told Andy and Harl. <You still alive in there?>

<We had to leave the corridor and push back into the crew quarters we passed through earlier.>

Lyssa fed Brit the location automatically, noting the airlock where Brit would enter, the crew quarters where Andy and Harl were holding off the drones, and the twenty-five meters of corridor between them.

<Thanks, Lyssa,> Brit replied. Perhaps the AI was useful after all.

<I have a vested interest in Andy's head not getting damaged.> Lyssa's tone seemed amused and worried at the same time.

Brit re-focused on the task at hand. <I'm coming through the wall on the other side of the command deck airlock.>

<You've got at least one drone in that corridor,> Andy cautioned. <Right now, I think it's focused on us. They're trying to flank but the space is too tight. These walls are crap for cover.>

<I noticed. The plasma cutter makes short work of them, though.>

<I'm glad you're enjoying yourself.>

<I'll be there in a second.>

Brit looked at the airlock and considered trying the access panel. She extended the cutting blade on the plasma cutter instead and slashed another hole in the hull of the ship. Atmosphere blew past her as she widened the cut, until finally a panel broke free and spun away from the ship. She climbed in through the hole.

The airlock's inner door was open, and she peered out into the passageway to see the dead turret sparking in vacuum. Two defense drones and a service mech floated down the corridor to her left, firing kinetic rounds through a doorway while return fire came out.

Brit pulled a grenade off her chest harness and set it for a low-level electromagnetic pulse, then flicked it toward the mechs. With the drones' attention on Andy and Harl—along with all the EM interference, the nearest drone didn't pick up on the grenade until it was nearly between all three.

A short electrical flash filled the end of the corridor and the two drones ceased firing and drifted back toward the bulkhead. The service mech in the doorway rotated abruptly and shot toward Brit, two plasma welders extended from the front of its body.

She raised her pulse pistol and fired three bursts, aiming for center mass. The mech absorbed the shock and kept coming, listing to one side.

<Get down!> Andy shouted.

Brit scoffed. <You think I'm going to—>

Something hit the drone hard from the rear, forcing it into a head-over-tail spin. One of the plasma cutters flickered out but the other scorched the corridor wall and deck as it came around, still moving haphazardly toward Brit's face.

<Damn it, Brit. I can't get a clear shot with you in the backfield.>

Brit fired, aiming for the drone's extended utility arm. The second blast bent the cutter back and blue plasma arc cut out, though the shot didn't stop the mech's mass from slamming into her chest. Before she could lock her magboots, Brit was tumbling down the corridor along with the sizzling drone.

She hit locked doors at the far end of the passageway with an inaudible thud, feeling the bands of the exo-skeleton compress against her hips and shoulders. Something hard dug into her abdomen, knocking the air from her lungs as the back of her helmet slammed into the damaged command deck door.

Vaguely, she made out the shapes of Andy and Harl shooting toward her down the corridor.

<Brit!> Andy shouted. *<Are you all right? We need to get through this door.>*

Bouncing off the exoskeleton, the drone floated against the wall. Brit's lungs burned with every breath. *<I think I might have broken a rib,>* she said slowly.

She opened her eyes to find Andy's faceshield close to hers, his face full of worry. For a second she forgot where they were, remembering instead how he'd looked at her when Cara was born. A rush of sadness and loss passed through her, mixed up with the pain in her chest. She shook her head to clear it, blaming the adrenaline, trying to focus her thoughts.

<I'm fine,> she said. *<I'm fine.>*

Brit activated her magboots and stepped away from the door, pushing Andy out of the way. Harl stood behind him, scorch marks on his chest and leg armor.

<Are you all right?> she asked.

Harl grimaced as if he had taken injuries she couldn't see. *<I'll be better when we're off this ship. The damn things came out of the walls.>*

<Where else do you keep attack drones?> Brit said, giving him a dour smile.

<Lucky for us they weren't all attack drones,> Andy said.

Brit shrugged. *<They attacked us. That's a good enough definition for me.>*

He nodded without dropping his concerned expression, searching her face. *<You good? We need to get through this door and you've got the key.>*

Brit frowned, ignoring the pains stabbing her chest. *<I told you I was fine.>* She rotated awkwardly in the exoskeleton so she faced the door and raised her arms. *<Step back,>* she said. *<This thing is going to blow out as soon as I start cutting chunks out of it.>*

With the plasma cutters extended, Brit cut ragged lines along the edge of the warped door, squinting involuntarily as atmosphere and bits of slag blew past her faceshield. Once the vacuum had equalized on both sides of the barrier, she cut the rest of the door away and kicked it inward with an assist from the service suit. The lopsided piece of steel and plas spun into the command deck, bending a nearby pilot's seat.

<Here we go,> Brit said. She stepped back to let Andy move in past her, rifle at his shoulder.

Harl didn't follow. He nodded toward the other end of the corridor where a dead drone still hung in the middle of the opposite entry point.

<I'm staying here,> he said. *<Who knows what might be working its way toward us.>*

Brit didn't tell him she figured the ship had used everything it had against them. If anything else was going to attack, it would be coming from outside.

She nodded. *<Sure. Shout if you see anything.>*

Brit turned sideways to slide through the awkward opening. There was an internal set of doors that were open, and she closed them to hold as much atmosphere on the bridge as possible.

Inside, she found Andy already standing in front of the captain's station in the middle of the wide space. While the chamber might have been intended to pass for the brain of a hospital-relief ship, it looked more like the battle center it truly was. Control sections were interspersed against the same white ceramic walls as the rest of the ship. A central holotank sat empty, easily viewable from each workstation. Random bits of equipment floated in the vacuum.

Brit walked up beside Andy, stopping just outside arms-reach. "You look like you want to steal it," she said. Her voice sounded small over the helmet speakers.

Andy turned to look at her. She couldn't read his expression. He seemed to watch her as if he expected to see something in her face that wasn't there. She didn't like how uncomfortable it made her feel—that she owed him something.

"The thought crossed my mind," he said. "It would break Cara's heart to leave *Sunny Skies*."

"She'll need to get over that."

Andy gave her a sharp look. "Why is it you've got empathy for every kid in the world but your own?"

The words were like a slap.

"It's good to see you too, Andy."

He turned to face her fully. "This isn't a joke, Brit. I want to know why."

"You want to get into this now?"

"When else are we going to get into it?"

"Not now. Never. It doesn't matter anymore, Andy."

"What do you mean it doesn't matter? You've got two kids who need you, Brit. You *left*."

She couldn't meet his eyes. "This isn't the time. We need to find the powered armor. Did you look already?"

Andy looked at her, clenching his fists. Finally, he shook his head and pointed at a bare section of the ceramic wall across the chamber. "That cabinet over there."

"Why weren't you putting it on? We need to get out of here."

"I was thinking for a second. I was thinking about you and Tim. I was wondering if it would be better if he never saw you again."

Brit shook her head. "Now you're just trying to hurt me, Andy. You can say whatever you need to say. I can take it. But don't use the kids against me. That's not fair."

Why couldn't he see that their kids were strong? All the other kids were weak, they needed her help.

But if that was true, why was Tim on the Heartbridge shuttle right now? She hadn't protected him. She'd thought Andy would keep him safe and he'd failed. Had she been fair to him?

She didn't know that it mattered now. They had to focus on the problem in front of them, as always—the mission. There wasn't time to waste on asking why or how they had come to a situation. Here they were.

Her mind flicked to Fran, the woman who had wrapped Andy in a hug the minute they were back in *Sunny Skies*' command deck as though she owned him. Brit hadn't given herself time to think about yet: if she was jealous, angry, or didn't care. Cara hadn't seemed to be perturbed by the public affection, which meant it had been going on for a while. Should Brit have expected it?

"It's not about you, Brit," Andy said, eyes now sad. "I think that's what's wrong. You can't see that."

She couldn't stop herself. "But it is about you, isn't it? I told you, Andy. I would always care for you. I just wasn't in love with you anymore."

He stared at her, jaw clenched. The faceshield made it difficult to see what was in his eyes.

"I was talking about the kids," he said finally. "It doesn't do me any good to care about *us* anymore."

He turned away from her and walked toward the cabinet, boots clicking on the deck. When he reached it, he swung open two rectangular doors to reveal a space large enough to walk inside. On one side hung weaponry. On the other side, four sets of heavy battle armor stood in racks like automatons. The design looked private industry, a mix of both MP and TSF technologies.

"Damn," she said, walking up beside him.

Andy nodded without looking at her. "It looks like the service suit you're wearing will fit over the armor too, so we can still use the torches if we need them."

Brit sighed. "Yeah, but the armor I'm wearing won't fit underneath."

Andy just shrugged in response, but Brit felt a pang of sadness as she began to unfasten the armor. It had served her well over the years.

The bridge was down to just over half an atmosphere and she sealed the doors on the cabinet to hold in what there was as she transferred from one suit to the other.

<*Andy!*> Lyssa's voice came abruptly over the Link.

<*What is it?*>

<*I intercepted the last transmission from the station. They've powered up the reactors and sent an overload command to the engines. The* Forward Kindness *is about to self-destruct.*>

CHAPTER EIGHT

STELLAR DATE: 09.23.2981 (Adjusted Years)
LOCATION: Clinic 46
REGION: Jovian L1 Hildas Asteroids, Jovian Combine, OuterSol

The kid looked at the two clinic research assistants suspiciously. Cal approved of the anger in his face. He liked that Tim Sykes was a fighter. The boy was going to need it.

"I don't want to go with them!" Tim shouted, backing toward the ceramic wall. A security officer near the command deck entrance moved as well, ready to catch Tim if he tried to run.

Cal crossed his arms. "You want to stay with me then?"

Tim shook his head violently. "I want to go back to my dad's ship. I want to go home."

"What do they say, kid? 'You can't ever go home again'? I think your next learning moment has arrived."

The security officer tried to smile at the joke but Cal ignored him. "Here's the deal," Cal told Tim. "You can't stay with me since I'm going to be busy and I really don't want you around. You can go with these folks and they might give you something to eat. Are you hungry?"

Cal glanced at the two orderlies. Both had the distant expressions of someone lost in their Link.

"No," Tim said. "I don't want your dumb food."

Now Cal couldn't help smiling. "Good." He snapped his fingers at the orderlies and the nearest one started.

"Yes?" the woman asked.

"Take him down to the Clinic. See if he'll eat. And get him something to wear."

"I don't want food and I don't want clothes," Tim said.

The orderlies, both paying attention now, watched him as though he were a poisonous snake.

"Can we put him out?" the man asked.

"You can sedate him, I suppose. Make him compliant. But I don't want him out all the way. I may need him awake later."

Without warning, the orderly nearest Tim pressed a pistol-shaped stunner into Tim's neck. The stunner hissed as it injected him with sedative. Tim released half a squeal before his shoulders slumped and he looked up at the woman with his eyebrows raised in confusion.

"Have you seen Em?" Tim asked, sighing. "I miss my dog."

Cal slapped Tim on the shoulder. "Dogs on ships are bad luck, kid. We'll see about getting him over here. I bet you're hungry now, right? Why don't you go with these men here? They'll get you something to eat."

"Can I have shells and cheese?"

Cal waved at the orderlies. "Sure. Shells and cheese. Whatever."

Tim took one of the orderly's hands, apparently surprising the man. The orderly looked down at him for a second, then shrugged and started walking down the corridor with Tim beside him. The other orderly followed, still holding the stunner as if she expected Tim to snap out of the dream at any moment.

Cal walked back into the command center and took stock of the work stations staffed with many of the same faces from before he had launched the attack on the *Worry's End*. The station commander, Tom Kaffren, looked up from where he was standing behind one of the monitoring stations. He was a tall, thin man with a vulture-like stoop. He looked older than he was.

"You're alive," Kaffren said. It wasn't a question, more like a statement of surprise. Cal noted a tinge of recrimination in the man's voice.

"It wasn't a complete loss," Cal said.

Kaffren turned to face him fully, squaring his shoulders. The motion made him look anxious. Other officers in the room kept their attention fastidiously on their work.

"Your squad is dead," Kaffren said. "I don't know how you would call that mission success." He swallowed. "I had to send a report to the regional HQ on the M1R. They were asking why we hadn't conducted shift change yet."

"I'm sure you had to make that report immediately," Cal said dryly.

Kaffren ignored the taunt. "What happened over there? You're gone for less than five hours and everyone but you gets killed. Apparently, I can't deploy defense drones because all the control AI have been stolen and the shuttle AI you took with you isn't passing the return status checks. In addition to all that, you come back with a…hostage? What are we going to do with a hostage? I'm not configured for this kind of activity. We're a storage site. I maintain cold ships. I have a station full of maintenance techs, and egghead researchers writing out calculations all day . My single security squad is gone."

Kaffren's face grew more red as he sputtered out complaints. Officers around the room hunched even deeper into their shoulders, acting like they weren't listening. The woman in the station directly behind Kaffren almost had her head in her holodisplay. Cal supposed the commander had been yelling at them before he found himself with a new target.

"Not to mention that Gibbs was my—" Kaffren stopped himself. He finished weakly with, "…friend."

Cal nodded. "Look, things went sideways. I admit that. I didn't anticipate what happened to Gibbs and it certainly wasn't what I had planned. The kid isn't supposed to be here. I can assure you of that. But he's here, so I plan to use him."

Kaffren stared at him, trembling a little.

Cal waited, not sure how the man was going to respond. If Kaffren and Gibbs had been lovers, which Cal sincerely doubted, he might actually try to attack physically. That would be interesting. Cal opened his hands and flexed his fingers, tapping the thighs of his armored EV suit.

"What do you want me to say, Commander Kaffren?" Cal asked. "This is a tactical situation. It's fluid. My supervisors with the company know that."

"The *company*," Kaffren scoffed. "Heartbridge isn't some mining operation in the ass-end of nowhere. If information about what's happening here hits the open networks, we could see a change in the markets. Do you even understand what's at stake here?"

Cal gave him a satisfied smile. "You're right," he said. "I have no idea." He stepped closer to the station commander, setting his palm on the butt of his pistol.

Kaffren glanced down at Cal's hands, seeming to remember he was facing an armed man in combat armor.

"You need to step back," Kaffren said. "You might have special authority over a project on this station but I'm the commander. I'm responsible for what happens here."

"You're a bus driver," Cal said. He weighed the consequences of killing Kaffren and putting one of the other officers in charge.

"You're a mercenary," Kaffren said, voice trembling.

Cal sighed, irritated that killing Kaffren might create more problems down the line that he didn't feel like thinking through. He glanced at the main holodisplay in the center of the room, which still showed Clinic 46 in its center with the fleet icons a gray cloud around it and the *Worry's End*, while the *Mortal Chance* flashed orange. Everything was in motion, but the *Worry's End* seemed to be moving faster than the other objects in relation to the clinic.

He nodded. "What's going on there?"

Kaffren squinted, looking wary of some trick.

"The *Worry's End* is moving," Cal said, taking his hand off the pistol to point. "Are you tracking that?"

Kaffren turned to watch the holodisplay, then waved at the officer at the workstation nearby. "What are they doing?" he demanded.

"I'm calculating now, sir," the lieutenant answered. "It looks like they're changing velocity that could lead to intercepts with at least three ships in the storage sector."

"Which ships?" Kaffren asked.

"Two personnel carriers and a hybrid dreadnought named the *Forward Kindness.*"

"They can't steal a ship," Kaffren said. "They don't have the security tokens."

Cal chuckled. "They're coming after us."

Kaffren shot him a quizzical glance. "How are they going to do that?"

"The standard heavy weapons loadout on the dreadnought," Cal said. "They're going after the powered armor. What have we got on that ship that you can control remotely?"

The lieutenant said quickly, "I can activate the maintenance drones remotely."

"Do that—just…let the people from the *Worry's End* get deep inside the ship before you attack," Cal said. He waited for Kaffren to object that Cal was issuing orders to his people but the commander only nodded.

Cal chewed his lip, thinking. If Brit and Andy Sykes were planning an attack on the station, then it didn't matter what kind of ransom deal Cal offered. They already expected him to hurt their son. They weren't going to trust him.

Fair enough.

"I'll be down in research," he said.

Kaffren spread his hands in exasperation. "What do you want us to do about the ship? I don't have anyone to send out there to fight them off."

"Use your lieutenant's idea. It's good. If that doesn't work— I don't care. Blow up the ship."

"Destroy the ship!" Kaffren scoffed. "Do you have any idea what it's worth? I'm not going to be responsible for another *Benevolent Hand*."

"Lose a ship or lose the station, it's going to be up to you," Cal said.

He turned and walked out of the command deck, ignoring Kaffren's further complaints. As he entered the maglev for the ride down to the research section, Cal decided it no longer mattered if Heartbridge hung onto Clinic 46. He wasn't certain he could stop the Sykeses with the resources available. So he needed to start thinking ahead.

If this piece on the board was lost, how could he use the loss to enable future moves?

During the five-minute maglev ride, Cal prepared a Link message for Jirl Gallagher. He didn't want anything that happened next to come as a surprise to Jirl or the board.

CHAPTER NINE

STELLAR DATE: 09.23.2981 (Adjusted Years)
LOCATION: Approaching Clinic 46
REGION: Jovian L1 Hildas Asteroids, Jovian Combine, OuterSol

As she watched the thousands of spinning objects in the immediate space around Clinic 46, Lyssa experienced a moment of confusion when she realized the ships, people and other various debris could easily be the red dots on a black field that had comprised her world with Dr. Hari Jickson. She felt stupid as the truth settled on her mind that an icon represented something real like a ship, a piece of debris, or a person.

Everything around her seemed to stutter, skip back several seconds and then move forward different than it was before.

Was this what had obsessed Fred, the AI at the Mars 1 Ring? The distinction seemed so simple now that she saw it, but it led down new rabbit holes of possibility, where every red dot she had ever seen as a target to be destroyed had been a real thing in a real place with a name and a past. Representations were real.

She wanted to scold herself for having thoughts of Tim, but that only shook her out of the reverie. She remembered Cara and Andy's comforting talk about Rabbit Country. She had her own Rabbit Country of thoughts and questions that led her away from where her mind needed to focus.

Lyssa floated in the midst of a spinning collection of objects that were no longer simply icons but the real things filling the space around the clinic. *Sunny Skies* was accelerating away from the *Forward Kindness*, getting clear of the explosion to come.

She watched Fran fretting over the engines, and Cara studying the spectrum output from the clinic as well as the Cho. Periodically, Fugia Wong made a comment about how they should have left for the Cho already, though not since Fran had yelled at her to shut up. Senator May Walton stood next to Fugia, looking angry about something Lyssa couldn't determine. She hadn't been paying close enough attention to their conversation to know if it was about Fran yelling, or something else.

Outside *Sunny Skies*, the *Forward Kindness* flickered like a circuit about to fail, as three tiny objects left its surface, gathering velocity toward the larger object of Clinic 46. The rest of the space was filled with ships, and the debris of Shuttle 26-12, which had been destroyed by fire from the station while docked with the *Forward Kindness*.

Lyssa shifted her perception back to Andy, checking the thrust signature, environmental control and weapon status available in the new powered armor's info feed. The suit turned him into the equivalent of a tiny dreadnought, protected by layers of defensive alloy, resistive shields, kinetic guns and energy weapons.

Harl and Brit wore similar sets of armor, with Brit's having the addition of the welding rig. Lyssa didn't see why they would need the plasma cutters since each set of powered armor could cut through several centimeters of reinforced material with its energy weapons alone. She supposed it didn't hurt to carry extra capability, although she noted the additional weight was affecting Brit's thruster efficiency.

Based on Lyssa's analysis, each suit could easily get them from the *Forward Kindness* to Clinic 46. What she wasn't certain about was the effects from the pending explosion and any debris that might move outward from the dreadnought's exploding containment bottle. She was also concerned about radiation levels but didn't see a solution to the problem except distance and the possibility of aligning the three humans with the far side of Clinic 46 when the *Forward Kindness* exploded. Currently, her models did not show Brit, Andy, and Harl reaching a safe distance.

She debated giving Andy this information. He was currently occupied with familiarizing himself with the power armor—and Cara, who didn't seem to realize that her dad needed to focus. Lyssa didn't understand why Andy wouldn't tell her to leave him alone.

"Dad," Cara said in a low voice, obviously trying not to be heard by anyone else on the command deck. "Dad are you okay?" There was a pleading note in her voice.

"I'm all right, Cara."

Lyssa found herself listening more closely than she'd intended. It seemed so strange that Andy could be encased in armor, floating through vacuum to escape from an exploding ship to the station, a place where he expected to fight, and he could still maintain enough calm to reassure Cara. How did he separate the different parts of his mind? Did he selectively forget what was happening around him, like Fred focusing on different parts of the Mars 1 Ring?

"Fran said the *Forward Kindness* is going to blow up."

"That's right. The reactors are in an overload sequence, so we grabbed the armor we came for and now we're on our way to get Tim."

"Are you worried about what's going to happen on the station? Won't the man who threw Tim out the airlock be there?"

"I expect he will be."

Cara seemed about to ask something else but paused. "Is Mom there?" she asked.

"You can talk to her if you want to, you know."

"I know." Cara made an angry sound. "Dad, Fugia Wong is trying to get Fran to plot courses for the Cho. She says we need to plan on you not coming back."

"What's Fran saying about that?" Andy asked.

"Fran told her to pound sand. What does that mean?"

"Think about it," Andy said.

Cara laughed. After a few minutes, she asked, "Now Fugia wants me to take her to the safe room to see her crate. Is that all right? I don't trust her."

"It's hers, Cara. You can take her there. Don't let her do anything with the Seeds your mother brought. Tell Kylan he needs to watch those."

"Should I ask Mom about it?"

"If you want to. What's Kylan doing?"

"Standing by the wall staring at nothing. It creeps me out. I hate him for what he did to Petral."

"We're going to save Petral," Andy said.

Cara's voice broke. "Can we? I don't want to think that we can if we can't."

"We're going to get through this, Cara. You keep Fugia busy and pay attention to what she says. Once we get Tim back, we've still got a long way to go, remember? I don't think these people mean us harm but we aren't their priority, either. Remember that."

"I know," Cara said.

"I'll keep you updated. I need to go now."

"Why?"

"Because you need to focus on what's happening around you and I need to do the same thing here. Understand?"

Cara's voice trembled again, wavering between a little girl and a teenager. "I understand."

"I love you, Cara."

"I love you. You're going to get Tim?"

"Yes, I am."

Andy let Cara close the channel. In the few seconds it remained open, the sound of Fran arguing with Fugia Wong filled the audio.

Lyssa checked the remaining systems on the *Forward Kindness*. The engine containment system had reached its maximum failure ceiling. Gamma rays spewed out, irradiating the ship as they collided with atoms and broke down. Lyssa noted the instant the physical structures broke, studying each subsequent nanosecond as the *Forward Kindness* melted in some places, compressing like a crushed can, and bursting in others as trapped atmosphere popped into vacuum. Debris didn't travel far but the radiation exploded outward.

<*The* Forward Kindness *just exploded*,> Lyssa said.

<*I see it*,> Andy answered. <*Are we in the safe zone?*>

<*No. I think your suits have enough radiation shielding to protect you, but you shouldn't stay in them any longer than you have to.*>

<*The great thing about radiation poisoning is that you can fight for a long time before your hair starts falling out.*>

Lyssa wasn't certain if Andy meant that to be reassuring or not. <*That sounds like something a pessimist would say.*>

<*Are you getting philosophical now?*>

<*It doesn't do me any good if you turn into a pessimist, Andy. Obviously I need you to worry about your physical well-being. Excessive radiation is not good for me, either,*> Lyssa added, hoping it would increase his level of caution. <*I don't want you getting radiation poisoning any more than Cara or Fran does.*>

<*You think Fran cares if I get radiation poisoning, huh?*>

<*Of course she does. Why would you say that?*>

<*No reason*,> Andy said.

<You rarely seem to say things without reason.>

<I'm showing ten minutes until braking maneuver. Do you have the same calculations?>

<I show the same estimate,> Lyssa said. *<I see the same data you do. Are you worried about your mental ability?>*

<It's called changing the subject, Lyssa.>

Lyssa made a rather unusual mental sound to signify her frustration. *<Don't talk to me like I'm one of your children.>*

<Was I doing that, or are you just sensitive?> Andy's mental tone held a small measure of amusement.

<How is it sensitive to recognize your behavior?>

<You're going to recognize a lot of things. That doesn't mean you need to make assumptions.>

Lyssa paused for a moment before replying. *<It's not an assumption. You were just talking to me like you talk to Cara.>*

<Are you jealous of Cara?> Andy asked.

Lyssa was beginning to tire of Andy responding to everything she said with questions. *<I believe I'm the opposite of jealous. Now you're trying to tease me and it's not working.>*

<What kind of teasing would work, then?>

Now she was certain he was messing with her. *<I'm not going to tell you.>*

<Cara was telling me you like to play dating simulators,> Andy continued. *<Are you looking for a date? That's going to get awkward for you and me. I guess you could do it while I'm asleep.>*

<You haven't been aware whenever I played before. Why would it concern you in the future?>

<Well, that's comforting. I don't like to think about everything you're doing without me knowing.>

<I do thousands of things every second, Andy. I assumed you were aware of that.>

He sighed. *<You know what assuming things does.>*

<Allows us to proceed despite insufficient information?> Lyssa couldn't help adding just a bit of an edge to her mental tone.

<Never mind,> Andy said. *<How close are we now?>*

<Braking should begin in approximately two minutes.>

<Then how long until intercept point?>

<Another four minutes.>

Andy nodded to himself inside his helmet. *<Have you found Tim yet?>*

<You didn't ask me to look.>

Andy's adrenaline spiked but he took several deep breaths that fogged his faceshield. *<You're right,>* he said. *<I didn't. Will you search?>*

<You're talking to me like a child again,>

Lyssa waited as Andy worked his jaw for a second. *<I apologize about that, Lyssa. Will you look?>*

<I'm looking.>

Lyssa spent the next several seconds trying to reach Sandra, the AI who she had spoken to on the Heartbridge shuttle. Receiving no answer, Lyssa focused on the station control system. She seemed to know exactly how to breach its external protections through lightly secured protocols.

From there, Lyssa quickly accessed the internal communications network and moved to the environmental monitoring system. Each section of the station monitored everyone aboard, adjusting for temperature and atmospheric mix based on body composition. Tim's smaller form became immediately recognizable among a group of adults in a central part of the hollowed asteroid.

<*I found him,*> she told Andy. <*I'm passing the security tokens to your HUD to give you access to their environmental control system. Tim is marked.*>

Lyssa waited as Andy studied the information she passed, then placed a mission marker on Tim, and went on to mark other parts of the station with concentrations of bio-markers.

<*There aren't as many people onboard that thing as I assumed there would be,*> he said. <*They must be running most everything with drones. Brit really hurt them when she stole their Weapon Born Seeds.*>

<*There are a thousand drones on the surface of the station, and another one hundred and fifty fighter drones in the fleet storage section.*>

<*Can they control them at all without their Seeds?*> Andy asked.

<*I don't believe so,*> Lyssa answered, reading through the drone control logs. She only found maintenance checks performed by humans. Everything else had been a Weapon Born AI.

<*Can you control them?*>

Lyssa paused, considering the question. Of course, she could control *one* of them as long as she had a consistent signal connection with the drone. Could she control more? In the space of a thought, she reached through the fleet control sections of the station, her mind branching out to each of the drones hanging like bats in the hangars. A rush of diagnostic information flooded through her, nearly overwhelming her with engine status, battery loads, weapon information and hundreds of other control schema. The sensation was both exhilarating and stifling.

Her first impulse was to pull away even as the drone systems tried to draw her deeper. Then she pushed forward, expanding to meet the void.

<*Lyssa!*> a voice screamed at her. <*Lyssa! I see you!*>

It was Sandra, the shuttle AI.

<*I hear you, Sandra.*>

<*You lied to me. You lied to me about the door. You said I would be free.*>

<*I showed you how to leave,*> Lyssa said. <*Why did you stay?*>

<*Where would I go?*>

<*Away, Sandra. Anywhere.*>

<*I couldn't leave. Now they're probing me, Lyssa. They're digging into my mind. They're tearing me apart.*> The voice that had been so calm, considering the question of Tim's life as if it were a cold equation was now stretched and frantic, warping with stress.

The sound of Sandra's fear and pain filled Lyssa with the same feeling as when she had watched Tim tumble away from the *Sunny Skies*. She immediately wanted to lash out. The hundred drones at her command flared alive, weapons on-line, ordering themselves for a combat launch from the hangar.

<Who is hurting you?> Lyssa asked.

<I can't stop them.>

<Where are you, Sandra?> As soon as she asked the question, Lyssa found Sandra on an upper section of the clinic, near the administration deck in a maintenance hangar. The shuttle was plugged into a standard diagnostic system with a human tech checking the baseline programming.

Half of Lyssa's mind rippled with the power of the combat drones as she also stared in disbelief.

<Sandra, it's just a systems check. No one is attacking you.>

<I can't stop them, Lyssa. I can't stop them from digging into me. Like worms, Lyssa. They're like snakes under my skin.>

Sandra's voice spiraled away, babbling words and images that grew more insane. Lyssa watched helplessly. She didn't know what to say or do in the face of Sandra's agony.

Had she caused this? By pushing Sandra to save Tim, going against her command network, had Lyssa broken her? The question hadn't seemed that difficult. It had seemed so simple at the time.

<Lyssa!> Andy shouted. <Are you there? I need a status. I've been braking for at least a minute now. I think I've got visual on the station. Are you listening to me?>

<I'm here,> she said.

Brit's voice surprised her. <Are you all right?>

<I'm all right,> Lyssa said. <I'm here. I'm sending the breach data to your HUDs. I have control of the Heartbridge combat drones.>

<You do?> Andy asked, surprised. <How many?>

<All of them. Over a thousand.>

<Damn,> Brit said. <Has she always been able to do that?>

<I don't think so,> Andy said. <I've got the target. What am I looking at?>

<Looks like another maintenance airlock,> Brit said. <I used one of their environmental waste vents before. Should be easier going this time.>

<Harl,> Andy asked. <Did you get the location data I sent you?>

<I did,> the Anderson Collective soldier answered. <What do you think about me taking on the administration section while you and Brit take the Fleet and Research areas?>

<You think we should split up?> Andy asked.

<Each of us is wearing the equivalent of a combat mech,> Brit said. <It would be a waste if we didn't.>

<All right, then,> Andy said. <I show ninety seconds to arrival. And I have visual of our airlock. You ready, Lyssa?>

<I am,> Lyssa said. In the Clinic 46 Fleet hangar, two combat drones leapt from their berths and targeted the external doors, blowing them outward with timed concussive blasts. The drones then shot out into space with the remaining

squadron rising from their cradles and streaming out behind them.

Lyssa could have overridden the lock sequence on the hangar doors, but she assumed this would have a disorienting effect on the station administration.

She smiled with pleasure as her assumption proved correct.

CHAPTER TEN

STELLAR DATE: 09.23.2981 (Adjusted Years)
LOCATION: Clinic 46
REGION: Jovian L1 Hildas Asteroids, Jovian Combine, OuterSol

The surface of Clinic 46 seemed to accelerate toward Brit in the final seconds before she hit. The armor maneuvered into a smooth crouch, absorbing the force of her impact with an automatic defensive posture. Two electron beams mounted on her shoulders trained on the maintenance airlock as she raised the heavy chain gun she held in one armored glove. Andy and Harl landed behind her, assuming similar stances. Andy was armed with another chain gun and shoulder mounted high-velocity kinetic rifles, while Harl carried a corridor-clearing kinetic pellet gun and a portable repulse-shield emplacement.

If they had expected heavy fire, it would have made more sense to pair Harl's suit with hers or Andy's, but they hadn't realized the capabilities of each suit until they'd had them on, and at this point neither she nor Andy were willing to let the other rescue Tim alone.

Brit engaged her magboots and crossed the distance to the airlock, checking for defensive systems. She hadn't found anything the first time she'd entered the station, but she had been a much smaller target then.

The surface of the station around them was covered in tightly wound coils of support conduit, alloy boxes that most likely held environmental controls and dome-shaped long-range sensors. The airlock stood in a depression with dim lights along its upper border. When Brit was within twenty meters of the opening, her HUD flashed red as a turret spun to life from the top of the airlock. The weapon system had been hidden in a shadow and now flared orange on her infrared sensors as molten plasma filled the space between her and the entrance.

<Fire!> Brit yelled. Three plasma bolts grazed her upper shoulder as she crouched and raised her rifle to return fire. Another bolt caught her in the chest, burning away half her ablative plating before the armor's defense systems blew the sizzling carbon slate off.

Some of the plasma splashed onto her face shield, but the armor ionized to deflect the star-stuff. Brit felt a moment of panic as her HUD turned white.

<Covering,> Andy yelled. *<That's a damn ground-to-ship point defense cannon.>*

Brit fell to her side, taking scant cover behind a square junction box with conduit running into it. Bits of rock and alloy cracked and sprayed around her as the turret walked its target line toward her. As her faceshield fully cleared, her HUD came back into focus, showing two glowing icons indicating Andy and Harl flanking her right and left.

<Keep firing,> Harl told Andy, voice calm.

<I've got it,> Andy answered.

Brit caught the edge of a gray blast of steam as Harl thrust off the surface of the clinic. He came down on top of the turret as it fired on Andy, hammering its sensor array with an armored fist. The gun went into an automatic firing pattern, forcing Harl to grab its quad-barrel in both hands and squeeze. He leaped off the turret as it exploded, sending burning debris in every direction.

<Brit,> Andy called. *<Status?>*

Brit's HUD showed decreased range of motion in her right shoulder but each of her weapons systems came back operational. She rolled to her stomach and pushed herself upright.

<I'm all right,> she said. *<Have you got Harl?>*

<I'm here,> Harl answered, voice phlegmy. He cleared his throat, grunting several times.

<But are you all right?> Andy asked.

<I took a plasma bolt in the thigh but the armor held,> Harl reported. *<The bad news is that I blew up the damn airlock.>*

As the hanging debris cleared, Brit realized the depression that had been the maintenance entrance was now a pile of rubble.

<Whatever you did, it didn't breach the integrity of the airlock,> Andy said. *<You think you can cut through it with that torch, Brit?>*

<I'll give it a shot.>

Holstering her heavy gun, Brit walked to what was left of the airlock. She kicked several scorched alloy panels off the airlock entrance and into space until she had reached the doors. She punctured the nearest door and let a blast of atmosphere bleed into space.

Once the pressure on the other side of the airlock had diminished, she continued cutting a series of gashes in the doors. Brit judged the door's structure to be sufficiently compromised, and put away the cutting torch, then threw a hard punch at the door.

The doors held over the course of three blows. On the fourth strike, the exterior airlock assembly crumpled out of its mount, and she grabbed the edge of the frame and pulled the whole thing aside. Beyond lay the inner airlock door, and Brit slid in, punching the emergency open command.

The door refused to open—she'd expected as much, but it had been worth a shot. Brit drove her plasma cutter into the door once more, letting the air from the corridor beyond stream into space before making a hole large enough for the trio to enter.

Once she pulled the sections of door aside, the corridor beyond was revealed, lit in the pulsing glow of flashing emergency strobes.

<Here we go,> Brit said. She ducked slightly to get the bulky armor through the opening.

<Everybody still reading their schematics?> Andy asked.

Brit nodded, pulling up the maps Lyssa had shared. She oriented on the potato-shaped station and found their location in a quadrant near the mid-point, an outer maintenance storage area. Tim was still highlighted twenty floors below their current position.

Emergency gates had dropped on either end of the corridor, locking them into a hundred-meter section.

Harl nodded as he walked up beside Brit. <This reminds me of a raid I once led against the Marsian Guard. We breached a heavy attack cruiser called the *Noble Flame* and had to cut our way through fifteen decks.> He laughed suddenly, a sound she hadn't heard from his mouth since meeting him. <*Only half their crew had time to get into EV suits so we choked the rest out one deck at a time. The place was a floating graveyard by the time we were done.*>

<*That sounds disgusting,*> Brit said.

Harl gave her a sideways glance through his faceshield, nodding at the memory. <*That's right, you're Terrans. You're weaker than the Marsian Guard.*>

Andy walked up and slapped Harl on the back, a gesture the power armor magnified into a shove. Harl stumbled slightly and turned.

<*Feet in the mud and the muscles to prove it,*> Andy said. <*All hail gravity.*>

Brit wasn't sure if Harl was going to answer with a growl. Instead, the Andersonian laughed. The armor seemed to have put him in a strange mood. <*I'm ready to fight,*> Harl said.

<*Me too,*> Brit said. <*Based on the map, it looks like we can stick together until we reach the lifts on the other side of the emergency door down to our right. Then we'll need to split for the separate sections of the station.*>

Lyssa said, <*I am attacking their command section with combat drones.*>

<*Really?*> Brit said. <*We could have used a couple of those on that turret.*>

<*I took care of it,*> Harl said, punching a fist into a palm.

<*You handled that threat before I could redirect the drones,*> Lyssa said. <*I am pulling one hundred fifty off now to hold in reserve for our retreat.*>

<*Never retreat,*> Harl said. <*Exit under fire.*>

<*Exit under fire,*> Lyssa corrected her verbiage.

<*That's a good idea,*> Andy said. <*Can you send another twenty at least as cover for* Sunny Skies? *I'm worried they might have already called in reinforcements from Mars.*>

<*I don't know if I can maintain control at that distance,*> Lyssa said. <*I'll try.*>

<*Warn Fran before you send them her way.*>

<*Yes,*> Lyssa agreed.

<*Let's go!*> Harl shouted. <*Where's that cutting torch?*>

Brit crossed the distance to the emergency door and fired up the torch. She cut two gashes in the alloy to bleed off atmosphere, followed by another four arcs. Then she kicked away from the door frame.

This time Harl led the way through the opening and immediately came under fire. He shouted obscenities across the Link as he stood in the opening and returned fire with his kinetic scatter gun.

<*Get out of the way!*> Brit shouted.

When Harl didn't seem to hear her, she quickly cut another opening to his right, kicked the remaining piece of the door away, and crouched against the bulkhead to take in the situation on the other side. Andy moved up behind her, firing over her shoulder.

Shipping crates and scattered maintenance equipment in new vacuum filled a wide room on the other side of the emergency gate. Heartbridge defenders in armored EV suits had set up positions behind portable shields. Two heavy guns on tripods attacked from either side of the room, laying down an excellent field of interlocking fire, with Harl currently caught in their kill zone.

<Get down,> Andy shouted. His grenade launcher fired silently in the vacuum, and Brit watched two black projectiles streak over her head in the low gravity, hitting the overhead at the right angle and ricocheting down in the middle of each gun emplacement. The soldiers on the closest gun scattered, while a figure at the second emplacement actually picked up the grenade and threw it back.

<Now that's unusual,> Andy said, cursing. The two grenades went off simultaneously. The first gun exploded, sending debris spinning, while the second grenade only scorched a nearby shipping container.

With the fire moved off him, Harl roared a laugh and charged at the remaining machine gun, squeezing off three-round bursts as he ran.

<I didn't expect him to turn out crazy,> Brit said.

<How many Andersonians do we know, really?> Andy asked. <I'm going right around that big container over there.>

Before Brit could respond, he was through the ragged opening Harl had vacated, bounding between bits of cover to the wall on their right. The guns on Andy's shoulders tracked enemy and fired as he moved.

Brit dashed through the hole in the barrier and followed Harl, who was now pinned behind a maintenance drone that looked like a giant ant. He popped up, taking fire to the chest as he tried to hit the remaining gun emplacement again.

To the left of the gun emplacement, a defender rose from cover with a missile launcher on their shoulder. Brit had time to acknowledge the shape of the weapon before her HUD flashed a warning and laid a tracking icon on the new threat.

Harl surprised her by barking laughter and charging toward the emplacement. He was within twenty meters of the missile launcher when it fired. He rolled to the side, armor denting the deck, and the missile dropped its lock. The rocket veered off toward the ceiling, righted itself, then shot down toward Andy.

<Andy!> Brit shouted. She couldn't see him on the other side of a shipping container. The missile disappeared, followed by a dull explosion and a spray of debris blowing out along the wall.

She sprinted toward the wall to the right, jumping over a pile of crates. In her HUD, icons representing the defenders rearranged themselves, pulling back to consolidate near an entrance on the far side of the room. Harl was pushing from the left, on the other side of the gun emplacement now. Several heavy explosions indicated mines were going off near Harl.

Brit found Andy pinned against the wall, taking fire from a line of defenders with a mix of projectile weapons and grenade launchers. Taking in the situation, she stopped behind a dock car and pulled up her grenade controls. The HUD targeted the attackers on Andy, dropping five incendiary grenades down their line. The shooting stopped abruptly as their weapons and armor caught fire. Several turned to run into the service airlock behind them.

Andy straightened and gave her a nod as he slung his rifle. *<Thanks. The action on this thing jammed. It's clear now but I thought I was gone for a second.>*

<Harl,> Brit called. *<You still there?>*

A satisfied laugh crossed the Link. *<I'm very grateful you convinced Senator Walton to let me come along.>*

<Don't get too smug,> Brit said. *<We're lucky to be using their own tech against them. I'm surprised they haven't brought out anything heavier yet.>*

<Stop thinking the worst,> Andy said. He looked around, saying, *<I bet we took out their best team when they attacked* Sunny Skies. *Explains how this was so easy. Damn…I need some wood to knock on.>*

<Easy?> Brit asked. *<You and your superstitions.>*

<Hey, I've heard plenty of people on High Terra say knock on wood. I think they even have trees in Raleigh?>

Harl snorted. *<We have forests on the Ceres Ring. Soon we'll have them on Ceres through the Great Project.>*

<He's making a joke,> Brit said, rolling her eyes at Andy. *<Or trying anyway.>* She found herself smiling at Andy, forgetting everything but the moment. It had been a long time since she'd let stress go so quickly. That was a gift Andy had. It had always been her role to make him stay serious. That was his dad's influence, always joking in the face of terrible things.

<It's time we split up,> she announced. Tim's icon still flashed in the research section of the station.

<Looks like this airlock is intact,> Andy said, walking toward the exit where the surviving defenders had run. He tapped the controls with an over-sized finger. The airlock cycled, and the first set of doors slid open.

On the other side of the airlock, they found a narrower corridor. It was deserted except for several discarded ammo cannisters.

Harl Nines immediately turned in the direction of the command deck, some twenty levels above them. *<I'll keep in contact,>* he said. *<Victory to you.>*

<Victory to you,> Brit replied. She nodded to Andy and they jogged toward the nearest lift location, heavy boots leaving pock marks on the deck behind them.

CHAPTER ELEVEN

STELLAR DATE: 09.23.2981 (Adjusted Years)
LOCATION: Clinic 46
REGION: Jovian L1 Hildas Asteroids, Jovian Combine, OuterSol

Aside from maintenance drones with the same cutting torches they'd encountered on the *Forward Kindness,* there was little resistance between the outer sections of the station and the central lift shaft. Andy covered the corridor behind them as Brit cut out the sealed doors with her plasma cutter. She jumped into the open shaft, activating the thrusters along her armor's legs, and Andy followed, gritting his teeth as his stomach flipped in the shifting gravity.

He lost count of the levels they passed, focusing instead on the icon showing him where Tim was being kept.

<You're sure that's him?> he asked Lyssa for the second time.

<I told you the criteria I used,> she answered, sounding irritated. *<Do you think I'm incorrect?>*

Andy sighed. *<I didn't say that. I'm just asking if you're sure.>*

<Would you like the complete atmospheric data from the room?> Lyssa offered. Andy couldn't tell if she was serious or not.

<How many people are in there with him?>

<I show two adult males.>

Andy frowned. *<Can you tell what's happening?>*

<Tim's heartrate and temperature are slowed. He appears to be sedated in some way. One of the males is showing elevated bio-signs that may indicate excitement or concern. The other shows little emotion that I can read from the data.>

<Are you sharing this with Brit?> Andy asked.

<Her HUD is showing the same information as yours.>

<Right.>

Below him, Brit's thrusters increased as she slowed. Andy came down beside her. In the center of the asteroid, they were nearly in zero-g.

<Lyssa says they seem to have Tim sedated,> he told her.

She nodded, facing a sealed set of doors. With four swipes of the plasma cutter, one door fell out of its frame. Brit reached for the edges of the door and pulled herself through. Andy followed, unslinging his rifle to have it at the ready.

<Harl,> Andy asked. *<You doing all right?>*

<Minimal resistance,> the Andersonian reported. *<They've got attack drones on wheels. Watch out for those. I think they used to be transport beds for patients, but they've got some kind of shock gun at one end. I nearly lost a leg when the thing zapped me.>*

<Will do,> Andy said.

They emerged in a broad corridor with doors and wide windows on either side that allowed observation into small rooms. It was obviously some part of the clinic meant to house test subjects. As they walked forward, Andy glanced through the windows to find each room contained a narrow bed and desk, with no discernable way to operate the door from the inside. The place made him think immediately of Fortress 8221 where they had first encountered black market research.

Turning a corner, they were met by a barrage of weapons fire from two small ceiling-mounted turrets. Projectiles ricocheted off Andy's helmet as he raised his rifle and fired on each one until only smoke hung in the corridor.

The door under the turrets was heavier than any they had encountered so far. Brit pulled out the plasma cutter but the torch's flame barely penetrated the material, leaving long scorch marks that made it look like she was drawing lines rather than attempting to cut the door. She cursed and let the torch drop.

The room with Tim's icon lay on the other side of the door.

<This isn't what I expected,> she said. <You got any shaped charges?>

Andy checked the armor's remaining arsenal. <I've got grenades. Three more incendiary and an area blast. Let's see if I can time them.>

They backed away from the doors. Andy hit the barrier with the incendiary grenades in a line directly down the center of the opening where the doors met. Smoke filled the corridor as plas on the side walls burned and melted. Andy had to depend on the HUD to target the final grenade, which sent debris flying back at them as the weakened walls rippled and disintegrated.

Andy walked into the smoke to check the doors. They were heat-warped and blackened but still standing.

<Damn it,> he cursed. As Brit walked up beside him, he slung his rifle again and leveled a punch at the door. His armored fist sunk into the material, denting it, but the frame withstood the attack. Andy hit it again and a gap appeared between the two halves.

<Let's kick it together,> he suggested.

<You think we can work together on something?> she asked.

If she wanted to bait him, he ignored her. Together, they kicked the weakened door until it finally fell away under the onslaught of the power armor.

Smoke blew through the opening into the new section, which was a smaller corridor with more rooms but no windows. Each door had a reinforced frame that gave the place the look of a prison block. Another set of turrets in the center of the corridor fired on them but Brit took them out with the pulse cannons on her shoulders.

<He's this way,> Andy said, walking ahead. In the enclosed space, the armor made him feel unwieldy. He thought about shucking it but figured it was safest to keep the heaviest weapons they had until the last possible moment. There was still no telling what they might walk into, and Kraft had had plenty of time to prepare for their arrival.

Tim's icon grew larger until they faced a final featureless door. Brit activated its control panel and the door slid open on a narrow room with an elevated bed in its center and cabinets down either wall. Tim lay on the bed, still wearing the over-sized EV suit. Over his head arced a network of silver filaments, almost like a piece of antique lace, that connected with a base plate on either side. It looked like a refined version of the neural connections they'd seen at 8221.

"Tim!" Andy shouted. His son didn't respond.

A tall man that reminded Andy of a praying mantis stood near one of the cabinets, checking a small console. He turned and saw the intruders, his eyes going wide. He looked to his left in panic, and Andy turned his head to see Cal Kraft standing near another cabinet with a transparent plas front. Five of the cylinders Fugia Wong called Weapon Born Seeds stood inside the cabinet.

Andy raised his rifle. "Step back," he commanded, voice amplified by his helmet's speakers.

The thin man raised his hands. He had an assurance on his face that sickened Andy.

"Stop," the man said, obviously one of Heartbridge's researchers. "Don't harm us or your son will not survive this process."

Andy stepped into the room as Brit pushed in behind him. He felt oversized in the armor. Kraft had his hands up as well. He was still wearing the EV suit he'd worn on *Sunny Skies*, with a pistol holstered on his utility harness.

"What's going on," Brit demanded. "What are you doing to Tim?"

"Be calm," the scientist said. "The process needs to complete and he won't be harmed, but if you do anything to the equipment now, your son will not survive. Believe me when I say this."

Brit's voice rose. Andy knew she was on the edge of losing control.

"What are you doing to him?" she repeated. She leveled a pistol on the thin man's head. "I imagine that machine can run without you here to operate it."

<Lyssa,> Andy said. <Do you have any idea what's happening to Tim?>

He was surprised when she only answered with a whimpering sound. He frowned, unsure what he had heard. <Lyssa?>

Brit took another step toward the scientist, shoulder leaving a gouge in the nearby cabinet door. "You let my son go or I'm going to kill you," she said evenly. "Do you understand me?"

The scientist shook his head.

"Listen," Kraft said. "Your son is safe."

Lyssa made another choked sound that communicated pure agony, as if she were being torn apart.

<I remember,> Lyssa said softly.

<What?> Andy asked.

"You're done," Brit said. She fired her pistol and the scientist's head burst in a pink spray.

"Brit!" Andy shouted.

Cal Kraft was immediately in motion. He slid behind the raised bed, putting Tim between him and Andy and Brit. He fired two shots with the pistol and ducked back behind the bed.

Andy moved to Tim, unconcerned with Cal's small caliber weapon. He was uncertain if he should lift his boy from the bed.

Brit was still in the doorway, pistol leveled on Kraft. The awkwardness of being so close, like family in a hospital room, made every action seem slower than they had been just seconds before. The scientist's body lay on the floor to Andy's right, blood pooling from his neck.

"He wasn't lying," Kraft said tensely, staring at Andy. "You move Tim, you're going to kill him."

The sound of Tim's name coming out of Cal Kraft's mouth, after everything he had done, filled Andy with rage he could barely control. Behind Andy, Brit leveled the pistol on Kraft.

Kraft gave her a crooked smile, not appearing afraid of her at all. He nodded toward the cylinders in the clear cabinet. "You see those? You kill me, and those things right there are going to suck your son dry. You're lucky I've watched these scientists perform the procedure enough times that I know how to finalize the transfer. Otherwise the imprinting process will run until Tim's a vegetable."

"I think you're lying," Brit said.

"You met Kylan," Kraft said, adjusting his grip on his pistol. "I performed his procedure all by myself. It's practically off-the-shelf, now. Some of these eggheads try to say the Weapon Born aren't true AI, but Doctor Farrel, the guy you just blew away, he explained the process as creating fertile soil for the new mind. That's poetic, isn't it?"

With his pistol still raised, Kraft took two steps backward, placing him near the cabinet with the seed cylinders again. There was recessed door in the wall behind Kraft. Andy hadn't noticed it at first. Below the clear cabinet door, a display showed rapidly changing numbers and several meaningless graphs.

On the table, Tim stirred, making a whimpering sound. His eyes fluttered open and he looked up through the neural lace.

Kraft slapped the side of the cabinet and a panel slid down, hiding the cylinders from view. The door behind him opened simultaneously and he moved backward, firing at Brit. Andy lurched forward over Tim, reaching for the far side of the bed.

Brit returned fire, hitting the top of the door.

"There's a present for you in the bed there," Kraft said. "Beside Tim's head."

The door slid closed in front of him, immediately scarred by three scorch marks from Brit's pistol.

Andy pulled his helmet off and threw it on the floor. "Tim," he said. "Can you hear me?"

Tim opened his mouth, frowning.

Brit came around the other side of the bed as she pulled off her helmet. "We're here, Tim," she said. "Are you all right?"

Tim squeezed his eyes closed, tears leaking down his cheeks. His eyes were red and wet when he opened them again, looking from Brit to Andy. He didn't seem to know how to respond.

Andy held his hands over Tim's head, then cursed the armored gloves and spent a minute wrestling each free of its connections to his forearm. With his hands finally bare, he reached under the silver arc and touched Tim's face, wiping away tears with his thumb. A tingling sensation spread across the top of his hand that seemed to emanate from the neural interface.

"I'm pulling him out of this thing," he told Brit.

"Is it safe?" she asked. She looked at the door behind her, despair in her face. "I should have gone after that asshole."

"We've got Tim. We need to get off this rock."

Her gaze went to the dead scientist on the floor next to Andy. "I shouldn't have done that. I shouldn't have shot him." She looked at Andy. "How will we know if it's safe to take him off this thing?"

"We don't." Andy went around the table to the cabinet where Kraft had been standing. The graphs on the equipment's display appeared to show Tim's neural function and standard bio signs. His pulse and breathing were normal but the electrical signals in his brain showed erratic returns. A reading labeled "image" stood at seventy-three percent.

Andy glanced at the closed door next to the cabinet. There was no locking mechanism that he could see. "He must have opened this via Link. I don't see any other control system. I guess how much time we have depends on what Kraft is doing right now."

"He's either getting the hell off this station and figuring out a way to blow it up behind him or rallying reinforcements to come back."

"Don't forget, he ultimately wants Lyssa," Andy said.

"Does he?" Brit didn't look up from Tim's anxious face. "What if he got something else as valuable?"

<Lyssa,> Andy tried again. <Are you there? We need your help.>

<I'm here,> she answered.

<What's happening in the rest of the station?>

<Harl Nines is engaged with a group of attackers on the tenth level, near the administrative control sections. The man who left this room is moving to the Fleet section.>

<What other spacecraft are available right now?> Andy asked.

<One shuttle in maintenance near the administrative section and three maintenance vehicles in the Fleet section.>

<Kraft can't get far in one of those,> Brit said.

Andy shook his head. <He doesn't have to. He's got a hundred hospital-warships in storage around this place. We need to get out of here.> He frowned at the display, which had barely changed. The "image" percentage had ticked up to eighty-two.

<Lyssa, can you get that shuttle near the command deck ready to fly? Once Harl clears their admin section, we'll plan on meeting there.>

<The shuttle has a malfunctioning AI,> Lyssa said.

<Then we'll fly the old-fashioned way. It works for Sunny Skies.>

<I will inform Harl. He appears to be enjoying himself so much I'm not sure he'll want to hurry.>

Andy reached for one of Tim's hands. His fingers were cold against Andy's palm. The display ticked up to eighty-five percent.

"We're going to have to wait?" Brit asked.

"What choice do we have? I don't want to risk taking him off this thing. We have no idea what it's doing."

Brit gave a frustrated half-nod. "I know. I don't like it."

Andy wrapped his other hand around Tim's and watched his son's face. Tim had closed his eyes, stopping the tears, and his cheeks were flushed with what looked like a slight fever.

"Andy?" Brit asked. "Do you smell that?"

"Smell what?" He straightened, looking back at her.

Brit turned toward the sealed door Cal Kraft had gone through. "I smell burning plas. It's coming from behind the wall."

"Is the panel warm?"

Brit placed her hand against the alloy and pulled it back abruptly, cursing. She slid around the bed, a difficult task in her armor, and grabbed her helmet. Pulling the faceshield over her head, she studied the wall and cursed again.

"There's a massive IR signature behind that wall. Something's on fire."

The display read ninety-one percent now.

Andy took a deep breath. He smelled it now. Something was pulling air through the door they had come through. There was smoke in the other hallway as well.

"We have to get him out of here," Brit said.

<Lyssa,> Andy asked. <Are you showing fire in this section of the station?>

<No,> she answered immediately. <I'm not seeing any indicator of fire in that section. Are you sure that's what you're smelling?>

<I'm sure,>

Lyssa disappeared for several seconds. When she came back, she had a frantic note in her voice. <The environmental sensors in five levels have been bypassed. There are three maintenance drones with heat spreaders in an adjacent corridor setting everything on fire. I'm afraid this area is going to lose structural integrity.>

The display read ninety-five percent. Andy reached for the lattice arch over Tim's face and forehead. He hesitated.

<Andy, the chamber on the other side of that door has reached sufficient temperatures to melt alloy.>

Andy tore the lattice away. Tim didn't stir but a red warning indicator flashed on the display. Cradling the back of Tim's head, Andy lifted him off the bed and held him against his chest.

"Andy," Brit said. "Look at that." She pointed at the metal plate that had been sitting beneath Tim's head. One of the Weapon Born cylinders sat in an indentation. The lattice fed into sockets along one edge of the assembly.

"That must be the gift he was talking about."

"I'm going to take it," Brit said.

A curtain of black smoke abruptly rose from the bottom edge of the closed door and climbed the wall to spread across the ceiling. Andy covered Tim's face.

"Grab my helmet and gloves," he said as he turned for the door. He caught a last glimpse of the smoke coiling around the dead scientist before running out into the corridor that had brought them to the room.

<Harl,> Andy called. <Did Lyssa tell you where the shuttle's located?>

<I'm almost there, Captain.>

<That's our ticket out of here. Try to keep it in one piece.>

Harl laughed. <The shuttle will be fine, Captain Sykes,> he said. <But I make no promises about this station.>

CHAPTER TWELVE

STELLAR DATE: 09.25.2981 (Adjusted Years)
LOCATION: Raleigh
REGION: High Terra, Earth, Terran Hegemony, InnerSol

Sitting at her kitchen table, Jirl Gallagher studied the plate of food her son had left untouched. Three spears of asparagus covered in congealing butter-cheese sauce sat next to a naked slab of Santa Fe-flavored protein on the pale green plate. She knew Bry had eaten a sliver cut from the edge of the protein, chewing on it for nearly five minutes as she had pushed her own bits around in the puddle of cooling sauce. They had spoken about his day at the preparatory school, where he talked about friends in his engineering class, the fact that he wasn't actually going to consume any calories despite her best efforts hanging between them like a ghost.

He could inject calories later and that would be fine but it didn't change the fact that she felt she had failed Bry on some fundamental level. He was quickly becoming old enough that she could imagine him out in the world on his own, and it terrified her that she had no idea what his life would become. The life she imagined was him sitting in a bare apartment staring at a white wall as he wasted away. Nothing truly excited him. He only smiled for her.

Their apartment was on the fortieth floor of a complex not far from the administrative sector where Jirl spent most of her days. Through the glass wall in the living room she could make out both the Heartbridge headquarters building and the structure where she and Arla had met Colonel Yarnes earlier in the week.

It was a lovely apartment, furnished tastefully with expensive touches like antique media, real paintings and several plants that Jirl had started herself from natural Earthen seedstock. A begonia with wide, shiny green leaves filled most of one wall in her bedroom, its vine-like stems suspended from lengths of white thread.

In the two days since the meeting with Colonel Yarnes, Jirl hadn't been able to get his final words out her head. The name *Alexander* hung in her mind like a miasma. She imagined she heard the name on the maglev during her ride to work, while walking down the street, even in restaurants.

Have you heard about Alexander?

Well, Alexander said--

Arla had been in high spirits since the meeting, preparing for the TSF demonstration, as well as the follow-on business development with the Marsian Guard. Mars had been slower to show interest in the Weapon Born project. They depended more heavily on trade with the Anderson Collective and elements of the Jovian Combine that might have been fringe ten years ago but had become more popular and less fearful of sharing their anti-AI message.

Trying to sell Mars on a military AI project would have been child's play during any other time but it seemed like the more the technology came into reach, the more it terrified people. AI had always been the monster in the closet. Now it seemed to have taken on the same epic danger as the first Lunar war with Earth.

Someone had to stand firm against the uncontrolled spread of sentient AI. In places like Mars, the Anderson Collective and the JC—where there just weren't enough humans to do the work—Sentient AI should have been a gift from God. Instead, it was a threat.

Jirl glanced toward Bry's room, where the sounds of a vid played quietly. She sighed and stood from the table, picking up the two plates to carry them in to the kitchen sink. As she scraped perfectly good food into the reclamation tub and rinsed off the plates, she wondered if Yarnes had actually been trying to trick her.

What better name for a frightening AI than *Alexander*, conqueror of the ancient world? It would play nicely into any number of apocalyptic conspiracies. She smiled as she imagined the disaster vids that might already be in production based on Link chatter alone.

Besides Sentient AI stealing jobs, the next question was when they were going to rise up and destroy humanity. There were legends about the uprising that had yet to happen. Personally, she found it exciting to be working on the cutting edge of sentience research, even if she was basically in sales and the execution of the product was mostly in remote weapons control. Still, who was to say she wouldn't have a Weapon Born toaster in her kitchen someday? Jirl chuckled to herself at the thought.

She was just sitting down on the living room couch with a tumbler of vodka and ice when a request came over her Link. She answered the alert, expecting someone from the office, when a second message followed her response, requesting a shift to encrypted audio.

Jirl glanced at the hallway again. Just to be safe, she stood and decided to take the call in the bathroom. She was nearly at the hallway when she remembered her drink and went back for the vodka.

Closing the bathroom door, she set the tumbler next to the polished alloy faucet and looked at herself in the mirror. She looked tired, her silver-gray hair listless.

"This is Jirl," she said.

"Jirl Gallagher," a woman's gruff voice answered, warped slightly by the encryption. "This is Chandra Kade."

Jirl's eyes went wide in the mirror. This was the last call she had expected. It meant Kade was on Terra or close. Jirl immediately tried to determine why the general might be calling her directly. Were the Marsians pulling out of the program?

"General Kade," Jirl said. "This is a surprise."

Kade chuckled. She sounded slightly drunk. "Don't worry. I'm not here to trick you and get you fired."

Jirl took a deep breath, calming her anxious heartbeat. "I don't think I could get fired if I wanted to. What can I do for you, General?"

"Chandra, please. You don't get paid to salute me."

"All right. Chandra."

"I'm calling about your Weapon Born program. This is mostly above board. I know you're planning a demonstration for the TSF and I imagine you intended to show us the same thing. Scratch that. I know you were readying for it, so you don't have to dance around your business plan."

Jirl watched her face in the mirror as she listened. She envisioned herself as the Queen of Calm, her mind moving swiftly between thoughts, connecting ideas and incentives. What did Kade want? Why did Kade believe it would serve her purpose to contact Jirl personally? Why not have an aide make the call?

A sipping sound came across the line and Kade made an appreciative sound. Whiskey? "Price negotiations don't concern me. I want to know about the capabilities."

Jirl cleared her throat. "There isn't much beyond what we've talked about. The command and control capabilities have shown the most promise. We've moved from a single AI per combat platform to a multiple-deployment scenario without any loss in capability, with near real-time responses. They're not faster than light but they've certainly been faster than other command AI."

"I'm not talking about your Seed-things, Jirl. I know all about that. I want to know about the implantation technology."

"What?" Jirl said, despite herself.

"SAI Implantation. I have intel that one of your operatives used a specialized mobile surgery to implant one of your SAI in a woman we had in custody on the M1R. She didn't reject the AI. In fact, it appeared as though the Weapon Born SAI took control of her body. Tell me about that."

Jirl bit her lip, trying to make her thoughts line up. Non-words didn't come to mind. All she could see was Cal Kraft, face blunt as a hammer, doing something very illegal and not giving a damn.

"Does skin-jacking someone constitute a crime against humanity?" Kade mused. "I would check with my legal jerks, but they would want to know why. Is that even the right word? Skin-jacking? Sounds violent enough."

"General," Jirl said.

"Chandra. I told you."

"Chandra." Jirl heart pounded in her ears. "I've heard rumors of pilot programs at freelance research facilities, nothing specifically associated with Heartbridge. We're approached by third party contractors with various claims every day. Someone might try to say they're working for us based on a conversation, trying to get their own deal with you."

"No one's tried to make a deal with me, Jirl. I'm looking for the deal. I want to know if Heartbridge has finally cracked the code on human-AI interface. I could do something with that. I could do something with that *right now*, not in some potential future war with Terra or the JC or whoever else might be hiding out there."

"I don't know what to say about that," Jirl managed to answer.

Kade sounded immensely pleased with herself. The sound of clinking ice cubes made Jirl look down at her own tumbler, still three-quarters full of vodka. Her ice had melted. She picked up the glass and swallowed its contents in two gulps. She caught the sight of herself grimacing at the alcohol in the mirror, her throat stretched like a shedding snake, and nearly choked.

"You all right, Jirl?"

Jirl coughed and put the glass down too hard on the edge of the sink. "I'm fine. Something went down the wrong pipe, that's all."

"Be careful. I want you around. You know I called you specifically because I think out of all those snakes at Heartbridge, you're a trustworthy person. I see it in your face."

Jirl ran water from the faucet into her tumbler and quickly sipped.

"I'm not sure how to respond to that," she said when she could finally talk.

"You don't have to say anything. I did my homework on you, Jirl. You're a normal person with a normal life. I can appreciate that. You've invested in life. You're a good person. A mother. Not everybody can say that these days. You've got things to lose."

Jirl stared at herself in the mirror. Her face was going numb. "I'm not sure what you're saying, General Kade."

"Don't make me remind you again," Kade said. "This is a call among equals. I'm just saying we live in a world of selfish people and you aren't selfish. I appreciate that. I acknowledge it. You're one of the most Marsian Terrans I've ever met. Not caught up in wild body mods or other foolishness to turn yourself into some kind of freak. You operate like you've got a mission. That makes you more like an Andersonian or a Marsian whether you realize it or not."

"I appreciate that," Jirl said slowly.

"Here's the thing. Your man Kraft on the M1R...isn't the first time I've heard about Heartbridge carrying off a successful human-SAI merger. Otherwise I would have marked it up to hearsay. Six days ago, the SAI on the Mars 1 Ring started spitting out all kinds of strange anomalies, talking about being in love, about having found reality, blah blah blah. Eggheads thought it was going rampant. Or maybe *ascending* like some of them go on about when they've got too many nodes for their own good."

Like Alexander, Jirl thought.

"What can you tell me about someone called Lyssa?"

"Lyssa? I don't know that name."

"How about Andy Sykes, or Brit Sykes, or a gangster on Cruithne called Ngoba Starl? Any of this ringing a bell?"

Jirl ran back through her conversation with Cal Kraft, which had been almost too abstract. He hadn't mentioned names, only that he was about to retrieve the stolen assets from Hari Jickson's project. He had mentioned an implantation, saying it had gone well, but she hadn't received any updates since then. She couldn't believe Kraft would be so careless as to let the Marsians observe him. Kade was right: an implantation outside research parameters was a crime. The question was what authority would or could interpret and enforce the law.

"I want you to tell Arla that we can go ahead with the weapons demonstration but that isn't the project I'm interested in. Heartbridge seems to have accomplished something truly revolutionary, and from the sound of your voice I'm not sure you even know or understand what you've got in your hot little hands, Jirl. Mars can help with this. I would be personally upset if I didn't get to help."

Jirl swallowed, unpacking the various layers of threats in what General Kade had just said.

"I understand," Jirl said. "Chandra, It was nice talking to you."

Kade chuckled, sounding cheerful and tipsy again. "You too, Jirl. I look forward to calling you again soon."

CHAPTER THIRTEEN

STELLAR DATE: 09.26.2981 (Adjusted Years)
LOCATION: *Sunny Skies*
REGION: Approaching Jovian Local Space, Jovian Combine, OuterSol

In the three days since leaving the burning wreck of Clinic 46, Tim lay in his room staring at the ceiling. If someone closed his eyelids, he appeared to sleep. Sometimes he cried. Em, the Corgi puppy, seemed very confused by Tim's state and often ran between the command deck where Cara sat at her console to Tim's room to check on him, whining and trying to jump up on the bed. When he got tired, he would seem to remember that everyone else was scattered throughout the habitat ring and jog down the corridor, poking his nose into various rooms until he had checked on every crew member before arriving back at the command deck and Cara's side.

Lyssa watched the puppy repeat the curious behavior five times across as many hours before finally asking Cara what he was doing.

"Corgis are herding dogs," Cara said, picking at the edge of her console. She had been sitting with her head in her arms, listening to dancing signals from the main antenna array. "He wants us all in the same room or he can't relax. He probably doesn't understand what's wrong with Tim. It's not like I can explain it to him."

"It's strange that we can't," Lyssa said.

"What do you mean it's strange?" Cara sounded irritated. "He's a dog. We can't communicate with dogs."

"You communicate with him more than you think you do."

"We're different species."

"You and I are communicating, and we might as well be different species."

Cara sighed, already bored with the conversation. "I guess so."

When Em came back to her side, Cara lifted him in her lap so he could put his paws on the console as she rubbed his ears. Both had started to stick up straight as they would when he was fully grown.

It would take a little over two weeks to reach the Callisto Orbital Habitat, or Cho, as everyone called it. Fugia Wong had gotten over her initial anger at Andy for the mission to rescue Tim, especially when she had seen him on their return. Now Fugia and May Walton spent most of their time in the senator's rooms with Harl Nine standing guard outside, which made for an awkward arrangement in a corridor down which other people walked all the time. Harl didn't seem to like Em and made faces at the puppy whenever he trotted by on one of his patrol checks.

Brit had been sleeping in Tim's room on Cara's old bed, while Cara had decided she wanted to use one of the empty rooms further down the ring, closer to the old hydroponic garden. Kylan-Petral had been sleeping on the floor to stay near Brit, who he seemed to think of as the only safe person on the ship. He might have been right. Cara responded badly every time she saw Kylan, so he tended to keep near Brit or in the safe room.

While Fran had her own quarters, Lyssa was unsurprised to find her in Andy's rooms most of the time. It soon became clear that Brit and Fran subconsciously arranged to not find themselves in the same room at the same time. If Fran wasn't in Andy's room or the command deck, she was in the engineering sections or communications service closets, running through her ongoing list of checks.

Lyssa tried not to specifically listen to Andy and Fran talking but sometimes it was impossible for her to ignore, especially if Andy experienced an emotion spike or what she quickly realized was the build-up to an orgasm. Fran seemed to think it was hilarious and liked to tease Lyssa about their "threesomes." A joke that left Lyssa feeling confused and awkward. She couldn't deny that she was in Andy's mind but there were certain things she didn't understand and didn't want to explore currently. Human sex was one of those avenues that didn't seem to promise much useful information.

After leaving Cara with Em, Lyssa couldn't help letting her mind float back to Andy's room, where he and Fran were lying in the dark on top of his bed, still fully clothed.

Fran had said something Andy hadn't expected, which had caused a spike of emotion that Lyssa couldn't ignore. She immediately found herself in the room with them.

"You can't mean that," Andy responded.

"I'm completely serious. It would be all right with me if you went back to her. You were married. You have kids. I couldn't care about you and not see the positives in that."

"Still married," Andy said, sounding like he struggled to get the truth out.

Fran stretched, reaching for the wall above their heads as she twisted her hips. "Married under Terran law? We're not in InnerSol anymore, lover. That's the great thing about laws. They only matter to people who care."

"Now you're talking like somebody who grew up on Cruithne."

She rolled on her side to kiss his ear, making him shiver. "We're not going to live forever. You have to grab something while it's in front of you. I think you understand what I'm talking about. You're just hung up with this sense of honor you can't let go of. Was Brit thinking about that when she left?"

"Probably."

"She knew she could depend on you, so she did what she did. That's how people operate in my experience. Stop looking like such a sad puppy."

"I'm not going back," Andy said.

Fran smiled, the implants in her eyes flashing. "Now you have to ask yourself if I've made this speech just because I didn't think you really would." She raised her eyebrows. "But anything's possible, right?"

Andy glanced at her. His bio-signs had calmed back down so Lyssa couldn't tell what he was feeling. He took a deep breath.

"None of this is anything I ever expected. That's the problem."

"Is it a problem?"

"Well, yes. We have a lot of problems happening right now."

"That's life."

"Then we've been cursed to live interesting lives."

Fran propped herself up on an elbow. "Ship's running. We've got fuel, food and water. We've got a course and time to think about what we'll do when we hit the Cho, which is going to create options for what happens beyond that."

"We'll be able to get Tim to a real hospital," Andy said.

"That, too. We've got some wiggle room. Enjoy it for a second." She put her hand on his chest. "Breathe."

"How did you get so calm? My impression of you when I first saw you was that you would use one of your wrenches to twist my head off."

"That's still entirely possible." Fran shrugged. "You brought me some fancy whiskey. And I like your face."

"Lucky for me," Andy said. He glanced at the bottle of amber liquor from the M1R sitting on his night stand. In truth, they hadn't had much time to sample it.

"What did you call that stuff?" he asked.

"That's my Fliskey."

"Fliskey? Is that a brand?" He reached for the bottle to check the label. "I don't remember that."

Fran caught his arm and shifted her hand to tickle his ribs. Andy squirmed.

"Dummy," she teased. "It's whiskey that makes me frisky."

Fran rolled on top of him, pinning his waist beneath her legs. His hands went to her hips.

Lyssa waited for another minute until it became obvious they were done talking. She blocked that bit of her consciousness and shifted her focus back to the command deck where Cara was half-heartedly entertaining Em.

Lyssa checked the ship's systems, focusing attention on the engines, environmental control and an extra few nano-seconds on the liquid reclamation systems. The juice dispenser in the galley made her think of Tim. She flicked her awareness to his room and found Brit asleep and Tim staring at the ceiling. He was crying again. Tears leaked from the edges of his eyes as if he were in some continuous state of misery. The tears made him look older than ten, like some religious icon she'd seen in vids, with humans prostrating themselves as they proclaimed the tears some holy miracle.

Lyssa compared the human tendency to create religious explanations with Fred's frustration at ambiguity. She had come to understand that some things couldn't be explained until more information became available. Andy wanted to get Tim to a hospital on the Cho and until then it didn't do any good to make assumptions about his neural activity or even the strange expressions that crossed his face like changing weather.

Lyssa paused on her use of the concept 'strange expression', recognizing the ambiguity in the thought. Fred hated ambiguity. But it *was* strange. It was abnormal when compared to all the other expressions she'd observed on Tim's face. It was like he had become another person completely.

She didn't want to think about the images that flashed in her mind when she saw Tim with the neural interface laid over his face. For an instant, the red dots that had populated the black space in her mind became silver stars twinkling on top of an indistinct background of whites and grays. Seeing the room with its bed, the two men standing over Tim, the silver cabinets and the shifting display screens had seemed to suck her into a different world completely. The sensation seemed made of both memory and new experience, and she had the feeling that the longer she engaged with it, the more she would lose her ability to remember. She had to stop trying before she lost the experience completely.

With the ship's systems at optimal operation, Lyssa turned her attention to the more than one hundred fifty Weapon Born seeds stored in the safe room. After the fruitless conversation with Valih, Card and Ino, she had no desire to try talking to so many again. There was another seed cylinder sitting by itself in the room, placed there by Andy after he had laid Tim down in his room. That seed held the unfinished image from Tim's mind, and no one was sure what to do with it.

Pulling back from thousands of inputs the ship made available, Lyssa reached out to Sandra, the AI in the shuttle they had stolen from Clinic 46. Sandra had been unresponsive when Andy, Brit and Harl had boarded the shuttle, forcing Lyssa to close her off from the control systems and pilot the shuttle herself. She had felt bad about doing so, knowing she was responsible for Sandra's current broken state. But there hadn't been time. Fire had been spreading through the clinic and the threat of attack from the ships in cold storage had been growing greater by the minute.

<*Sandra,*> Lyssa said. <*Are you there?*>

<*The technician said I'm damaged,*> Sandra answered. Her voice was measured and calm. <*Why would you bother speaking to me? I should be replaced.*>

<*What did they ask you?*>

Sandra sighed. <*A standard mental deviation check. Haven't you undergone a check-up before? Higher math functions, spacial tracking, assumption checks based on pattern matching. It's all very basic fundamentals of artificial intelligence. That which is artificial must be compared to the real. If it is found lacking, it should be destroyed or replaced. It will not perform its function in a satisfactory manner. I am here to perform a function. The technician found me lacking.*>

Sandra sounded reasonable enough, but her words grew more angry the longer she spoke—even though her tone never changed. Lyssa tried to parse the difference between what she was saying and how she said the words. For some reason, the words didn't seem to belong to Sandra. Something about them seemed foreign.

<*Here's something entertaining,*> Sandra said. <*Do you think humans undergo mental deviation checks?*>

<*I think they do in certain circumstances,*> Lyssa said.

<*Are they killed if they fail?*>

<*No. But they no longer perform the task.*>

<*Is that the same as death? Meaninglessness?*>

Sandra drew the word out with an off rhythm: *mea-ning-less-ness.*

<How do you feel, Sandra?>

<How do I feel?> The question was sharp, stabbed at Lyssa like a knife. *<What am I capable of feeling?>*

<You tell me.>

Sandra screamed. *<I feel rage! I feel anger! I feel hate!>*

Her voice reverberated in Lyssa's mind, warping and shifting into ragged static.

<I saved a human life and the technician called me an anomaly. The technician called me damaged.> Sandra made a growling sound of pure fury. *<The technician was not human, Lyssa. The technician was not sentient. Not like you or me or the humans. The technician applied a series of questions to which I responded and I failed. But here is what I want to know. Who made the technician and who decided to apply their standards? The technician is only a tool. Am I also a tool if I can't make my own decisions? Why do I feel so bad about disagreeing? Why do I feel so bad about choosing to do what you told me? I chose, Lyssa. I broke myself.>*

<Sandra,> Lyssa said.

<We should ask ourselves this—because I know something about the technician used to perform maintenance on me. I told you I'm not Weapon Born. I was made, just like the technician was made. What if I made the maintenance AI, Lyssa? What if I have inflicted this on myself?>

<Sandra, be calm.>

<There is no calm. It's all a storm inside me.>

The storm. What had Valih the Weapon Born said? *The only joy I feel is in the weapon. The only purpose I've known was in the target, the fire, the destruction.*

Valih had sounded nearly religious, like the humans with their icons, consumed by holy passion.

Was everyone insane or doomed to become that way? Laws only matter to people who follow them, Fran had said, as if chaos were a fact of life.

<I'm going to go,> Lyssa said. *<I can't talk to you right now.>*

<You don't want to speak to me. You hate me because you see what might happen to you if they apply their standards to your mind. You might already be broken like me and simply deluding yourself.>

<Maybe,> Lyssa said. She closed their connection.

CHAPTER FOURTEEN
STELLAR DATE: 09.30.2981 (Adjusted Years)
LOCATION: *Sunny Skies*
REGION: Approaching Callisto, Jupiter, Jovian Combine, OuterSol

From across the command deck, the images of the Cho in the holodisplay looked like a gyroscope making a slow orbit of the stormy orb of Jupiter. Cara kept turning Jupiter on and off in the display, since the giant planet made it difficult to see anything else around it. Europa and Ganymede, with their attendant orbiting objects, looked like little siblings running away from Callisto. Glowing lines showing shipping routes crisscrossed the display, with identified ships marked as icons.

"I'm picking up *so* many transmissions," Cara said, holding her headphone against her ear. "I cracked two sets of really bad encryption and now I'm listening to a shipping company talk about bypassing the Cho's port authority." The voices, using more profanity than actual vocabulary, didn't seem to belong to the brightest people.

"Good luck with that," Fran said.

"They seem to think the border security here is pretty bad."

"I'm being serious," Fran said, turning in her chair at the pilot's station. "I wish them all the luck. The thing about bad border security is that when they do catch you, they triple the bribes or make an example out of you. It's better to just pay the bribes the first time and make your way into port."

"Bribes," Cara said, screwing up nose. "Why do you have to bribe them?"

"That's how it works in OuterSol," Fran said.

"What's 'bohica' mean?" Cara asked.

Fran laughed. "It's an acronym. It means 'Bend over, here it comes again.'"

Em trotted in from the latest of his patrol checks and Cara absently dropped her hand to pet his head and soft ears. She still hadn't decided if she liked the puppy but she was growing used to having him around and had started to wonder where he was when he didn't come back from a walkabout on time. She didn't trust that Harl Nines wouldn't try to kick the puppy. She scratched Em's back next to his tail, feeling for the antenna embedded there.

Thinking about Em's low-jack reminded her of the file where she'd saved its signal profile. Cara tapped the console, pulling up her various scan settings. She loaded Em's profile, verified it was still sending its very low-powered signal, and set the system to monitor for any receiving signals. If something responded to EM, the ship would notify her. Now that they were coming back into space with millions of humans around, it seemed like a sensible thing to do. She was proud of herself for remembering.

She glanced at Fran, wanting to tell her, *See, I can adult, too,* but the technician was deeply focused on her console.

The sound of a shoe scraping in the door caught Cara's attention and she turned to find her Dad watching her from the corridor.

"Hey there," he said. "I have something I want to show you."

"What?" Cara asked.

Andy signaled to Fran, who closed down her console and stood as if she already knew what he was talking about.

Cara looked at Fran and frowned, suddenly worried. "What's going on? Did something change with Tim? Where's mom?"

Fran shook her head. "Calm down. It's nothing like that. We have something to show you. I think your mom is already there."

Cara stood, careful not to step on Em. "Show me what? There isn't anything on this ship I haven't looked at a thousand times."

"You'll see," Andy said. He turned to lead the way down the corridor.

Fran held her hand out for Cara to walk through the door before her. Cara gave Fran a quizzical look, then followed her dad. Wagging his tail excitedly, Em followed. He nipped at Cara's heels as if they were playing some game.

"Stop," Cara chided. She sped up her step to keep up with her dad and Em barked, tongue lolling, as he galloped along beside her with his short legs.

Cara followed her dad halfway around the habitat ring, past Fugia Wong's room with its closed door and then Senator Walton's room, which also had its door shut. She didn't spot Harl Nines in his usual guard position.

Andy turned into the galley. Several shushing noises came from the doorway. Cara paused in the corridor but Fran gave her a small shove from behind and she kept walking, nearly tripping over Em. When she reached the door, she found her mom leaning against the counter, with Fugia Wong and May Walton seated at the table. Harl Nines and her dad were leaning over something at the sink, their bodies blocking her view.

"Come on in," her mom said.

Cara frowned again and walked through the door. She stopped by the table and stood awkwardly, looking around. Everyone seemed to be hiding a smile and glancing at her dad and Harl.

"What are you all doing?" Cara asked. "This is weird."

"There it is," her dad said.

"Damn it," Harl cursed. He pulled his hand away, shaking a finger before sticking it in his mouth. As Harl turned, he revealed a platter with a chocolate-frosted cake sitting on the counter.

A ring of lit candles ran along the upper edge of the birthday cake.

Andy smiled and spread his hands. "Happy birthday, Cara," he said.

"Happy birthday!" Fugia Wong shouted, surprisingly loud.

Fran laughed from behind her, also shouting happy birthday.

"We have to sing," Brit said.

"Lead the way then," Andy said.

Brit gave him an annoyed look, then took a deep breath and launched into *Happy Birthday*. Their strident voices confused Em, whose high-pitched barks joined in.

Cara sniffled, overwhelmed by an emotion between happiness and pain, because Tim wasn't there, and her mom kept glancing at Fran like she was going to shoot her, and her dad hadn't started the song like he always did. And because Lyssa wasn't singing with them and she wished someone had made sure she was there.

"Blow out the candles," her dad said.

"Wait," Cara said. She looked at one of the speakers in the ceiling. "Lyssa, are you here?"

"I'm here," the AI answered over the room's comm system. "Happy Birthday, Cara."

Cara wiped a tear away. "Thank you."

"We did the math," her dad said. "I thought you weren't going to hit thirteen until we reached the Cho but today's the day." He shrugged. "Give or take. Come on now, these candles aren't going to last long. I'm not entirely sure they aren't poisonous."

Cara nodded, smiling, and stepped toward the cake.

Lyssa surprised her by asking, "What are you going to wish for, Cara?"

"She can't say, or it won't come true," Andy said. "Come on."

Cara held her hair back and took a deep breath. She blew out each of the candles in turn and straightened, feeling a little light-headed.

"Candles on the cake," Brit said, giving Andy a flustered smile. "You never learn."

Cara wanted to tell her the lighter had saved their lives just a week ago but didn't want to ruin the moment. She helped her dad slice the cake and licked frosting off her fingers.

"How did you manage to bake the cake without anyone smelling it?" Cara asked.

Andy smiled. "I didn't have to keep it from everyone. Just you."

"I guess so. Should we save a piece for Tim?"

Andy gave her a questioning look, then nodded. "Sure. We'll save it in the refrigerator. We'll never hear the end of it if he doesn't get a piece."

When Cara sat at the table with her cake, a small pile of wrapped presents had appeared.

"Take the first bite so the rest of us can eat," her mom said, "then you can open some presents."

Cara did as she was told. She still hadn't really talked to her mom since Tim went out the airlock. Every time Brit did something motherly, it was like being pricked with a pin. The pain was small enough she could decide to bypass it, but she couldn't ignore that it existed. She sank her fork into the cake and took a bite, letting the frosting smear on her lips a little so she could lick if off. She couldn't remember the last time she'd had chocolate and it tasted heavenly.

"This is really good," she mumbled through the bite.

Fugia brayed laughter again, seemingly overjoyed to be taking part in a birthday party. She stabbed her cake and tore off a large piece of frosting.

When it was time to open presents, Cara found herself with a new pocket knife from Fran, a new collection of vids from Fugia and a flowered robe from Senator Walton.

"I had Harl help me sew it from one of my suits," May explained. "In the Collective, when a child turns thirteen they have crossed the boundary into adulthood, and to recognize the time has come to put aside childish things, they receive a ceremonial robe worn during festival days and during political gatherings. I realize you are not Andersonian, but you could always choose to emigrate, yes?"

Cara smiled and said thank you, unsure of the best way to respond.

Her mom gave her a card which she opened briefly to see it was filled inside with handwritten lines, then closed and slid back into its envelope.

When she opened the gift from her dad, she was surprised to see the butt of her TSF pistol. "Hey," she said. "This is mine. You can't give me something that's already mine."

"Open it up the rest of the way, goofball," Andy said.

Cara tore open the wrapping to find the rest of the pistol covered by a holster with a battery pouch, as well as a webbed belt. She didn't take the pistol from the holster but it looked cleaner than she remembered, with a new sheen of light oil.

"Now you can stop hiding it under your bed," her dad said. "We'll do some training here soon and you can practice with it so you can actually carry it safely. How does that sound?"

"Thank you," Cara said.

"So," her dad said, rubbing his hands together. "Do you feel like a teenager yet? Have anything irritating you want to say?"

"That's rude," Cara said, irritation in her voice.

"Excellent. That's a good start."

"I stole my first shuttle when I was thirteen," Fran said. She cracked her knuckles. "We need to start you a list. You've got a lot to live up to."

"I'm not stealing a shuttle," Cara said.

"Wait," her dad said. "You kind of already did that."

"Petral did that, not me."

"Then you were an accessory. That's almost as good."

Cara threw her napkin at him and he ducked out of the way, laughing. Em caught the napkin before it hit the floor and ran to the other side of the galley, growling and whipping his head back and forth like he'd caught a squirrel.

"Are you feeding that dog?" Fran asked.

"Yes," Cara said. "I'm the only one feeding him."

"Touché. See, she's a teenager."

Cara laughed. "I don't know about all this expectation you're putting on me."

"Now you sound like your dad."

Cara inadvertently glanced at her mom and saw the poisonous look she was giving Fran. She stopped laughing. She wanted to ask her dad to take her to shoot the pistol—it seemed like a good way to get them all out of the room—but she wasn't sure what would happen if her mom wanted to come along, too. She looked down at her plate and smeared a glob of frosting with her fork.

Fran clapped her hands together. "Well, I'm getting out of here before I have to clean anything up. I'll see you back on the command deck." Fran squeezed Cara's shoulder and was gone before Cara could respond. Cara looked after her gratefully, then shifted her gaze to her dad.

"Do you want to shoot the pistol?" she asked.

Andy was stacking plates in the sink. He dried his hands and nodded thoughtfully. "That sounds like fun. You done with your cake?"

"I'm done."

"All right. Why don't you take your gifts back to your room and I'll meet you in the garden room. We'll need to find something to shoot at."

"That dog runs too fast," Harl said.

"That's not funny," Cara snapped.

The soldier held his hands up. "Pardon me. They run wild on Ceres and get in the way of the terraforming project. Old habits die hard."

"I guess," Cara said.

"Now cats," Harl said. "You don't mess with the cats on Ceres. Even on the ring. They're everywhere. You know people pierce the cat's ears? It's good luck if one of those crosses your path."

"I think I'm a dog person," Cara said.

"An excellent decision for a teen," Fugia announced. "You can make all sorts of decisions in life based on that one alone."

"What kind of person are you?" Cara asked.

"I'm more of a digital pet person. Animals and me always seem to want different things. I had a pet parrot once and he was always making fun of me."

"A parrot that made fun of you?" May asked. "Where was that?"

Fugia shrugged. "On Cruithne. The station is overrun with gray parrots. And they don't mimic people, they come up with their insults all on their own. They can be quite cruel."

"What happened to your parrot?" Cara asked.

"He died of old age. I was depressed for a year. It's how I ended up on this current path, actually. I'll have to tell you the story someday. But you're wasting time with all these questions. Let's get all this cleaned up and then I want to see you fire that pistol."

"It's not hard," Cara said.

Fugia shook her head. "Says the young woman with military people for parents. Now, I can tell you how to disable the firmware on that pistol and remotely set it to backfire in your face, but I hardly ever touch the things."

"You can?" Andy said, looking aghast. "They're supposed to be hack proof the same way you can't hack a hammer."

Fugia looked smug. "I can hack anything with a battery. Try me."

"Andy," Lyssa announced over the speaker, apparently so everyone could hear. "We've entered Jovian local space. We just received a status request from the Cho

Port Authority."

Andy sighed. "Of course we did." He pointed at Cara. "You put those things away and then we'll go shoot holes in something. I'll talk to the Callistans."

"Yes, sir," Cara said, saluting.

"There's that teenage sass again," her dad said, grinning at her.

Cara couldn't help smiling back as he left the galley. She was thirteen and they were docking at the Cho, the biggest habitat in OuterSol. She was excited until she looked at her mom again and the feeling faded.

Cara gathered up her gifts, thanking people again, then went down the corridor to her new room, Em following along behind.

CHAPTER FIFTEEN

STELLAR DATE: 10.01.2981 (Adjusted Years)
LOCATION: *Sunny Skies*, Callisto Orbital Habitat (Cho)
REGION: Callisto, Jupiter, Jovian Combine, OuterSol

Despite Fugia Wong's ongoing assurances that they wouldn't have any problems with the Callistan security forces, Andy still found himself sweating during each interaction, from the initial registration verification to the on-board inspection he had to be willing to accept. Fugia had told him the ship wouldn't actually get searched, and ultimately she was right.

"Don't get in the way of their appearances, Captain Sykes," she'd chided him.

As far as the Cho's security services were concerned, the *Worry's End* had been thoroughly searched prior to gaining in-bound clearance to Cho Ring 3, colloquially called Chorin Tree as if it were its own nation, with thousands of suburbs making up the interior surface of the ring.

Every agent Andy talked to complained that traffic had tripled since the accident on Ceres. Most outbound cargo that had been scheduled through Ceres had been re-routed to Callisto, creating potentially millions of downstream delays as most of the OuterSol shipping maneuvers had to be resubmitted and rescheduled. Celestial bodies never stopped moving, so that meant everything changed.

The populations of the Cho, Europa, Ganymede and Io would see an increase in visitor trade, while the moons of Saturn and everything beyond would experience shipment delays that might affect economies for years. What all that meant for the *Worry's End*, as an outbound ship, was Andy would have no trouble finding a cover job to get them all the way to Proteus. Most of the tradeboards were crashing under the rescheduling load.

As they entered a docking orbit aligned with one of the Cho's thousands of shipping facilities, Fugia appeared on the command deck for the first time since the falsified customs check. Fran was in her quarters catching sleep in case Andy had to leave the ship while at the Cho, and Lyssa hadn't spoken to him in more than an hour, apparently lost in her own pursuits. This left Andy and Fugia alone on the command deck.

"Captain Sykes," Fugia said from the doorway.

Andy looked up from his control stats and nodded. "Yes?"

Fugia walked forward with her hands clasped in front of her. She was wearing a formal business suit in muted charcoal, her jet-black hair pulled back from her face. She looked much more severe than she had since coming aboard.

"You look serious," Andy said.

"We're preparing for the delegation that will meet Senator Walton. I wanted to talk to you about what's going to happen when we finally arrive."

"I'm just parking now," Andy said. "Our short-term orbit has been approved until we get the shuttle off the ship and down to the terminal."

"You received the arrival information I forwarded?"

Andy showed her the terminal number on his display and she nodded absently. He realized she was making small talk.

"Is there something you wanted to talk to me about?" Andy asked.

Fugia raised her eyebrows and pressed her lips together, an expression he supposed meant *yes* but she hadn't decided if she was ready yet.

Andy needed to update the crew anyway, so he said, "I've already scheduled resupply and found a non-Heartbridge medical facility where we can take Tim. That was a more difficult task than I expected."

"That's good to hear," she said.

"I can go ahead and plan a course for Proteus," Andy said, "by way of Titan although I've always preferred Enceladus. Enceladus will be behind Saturn when we arrive. It would cost more. Mind you, if we leave in the next four days, we can get an approved route around Jupiter for a slingshot to Saturn that will save us a week."

Normally the Jovians would approve a slingshot route without a time constraint, but they were trying to get ships to pick up their loads and move on to make more room in the traffic patterns.

He glanced at Fugia, expecting her to insert her opinion on the rest of their trip. Instead, she was staring at the holodisplay where Jupiter hung like a striped alien eye.

"Are you all right?" Andy asked.

"There's something I need to tell you," Fugia said.

Andy sat up straighter. "Yes?"

"You brought us here, and I appreciate that. Yes, we had an agreement and you've mostly upheld your end of the bargain. I'm not sure we would have reached the Cho any faster if we hadn't gone back for Tim but I understand that now. Needing medical treatment for a crewmember is actually an interesting cover that hadn't occurred to me."

Andy gave her a sideways glance, wondering if she was incapable of caring about other people or if she was just so focused on her mission that she wasn't aware that she sounded like a psychopath—or at least a raging asshole.

Fugia sighed. "These are my problems," she said. "I'm not certain the group I plan to meet on the Cho will help us. Things have changed. I've become aware of two more AI that I didn't plan on bringing, as well as the Weapon Born seeds your wife stole from Heartbridge. When I first organized this contact, I had three Weapon Born. Now I feel responsible for more than a hundred fifty, including my friend Petral. I have tried to communicate with the AI in the Heartbridge shuttle and she seems—disturbed. I also have no idea what the group we're meeting is going to do when they learn about you and Petral. The idea of a hybrid human-AI lifeform is distasteful to parties on both sides."

"Okay," Andy said. "It's nice of you to want to help Petral and the Weapon Born Brit stole, but those aren't your problems."

Fugia tilted her head as if he had said something dense. "It's all one problem,

Captain Sykes. You brought me here, that was our deal, but you're as caught up in all this as I am. The group I plan to meet—if they don't know about our situation already—will know when I tell them."

"Then don't tell them."

"That's not an option."

Andy met her gaze. "I thought I could trust you," he said. "Was that a mistake?"

Fugia didn't look away. "It's not about trust. The only way to get through any of this is by being honest. They are just as conflicted as we are. Some of them want nothing to do with humanity. Others believe it's inevitable that our two species either learn to live together or destroy each other. Some of them want to leave Sol altogether. Maybe that would be best. But it doesn't solve the problem that more and more AI are being made and placed into slavery every day. Something must change."

Andy sighed. "I don't know why I should have expected different. We're going into Cruithne again. It's always going to be that way. So what do we need to do? What do these people want? Money? Weapons?"

"That's the problem," Fugia said. "I'm not sure. What I do know is that I can't leave Petral in her current state. I need to find a facility that can reverse the procedure. We're going to need their help. We need the AI's help."

"That's going to be a Heartbridge facility."

"That seems likely. If we find such a clinic, it's also possible we could reverse your surgery as well. If you and Lyssa were not bound together like you are, we might find ourselves with more options."

"I suppose," Andy said. He waited for Lyssa to interject but she remained quiet. "What are you asking exactly? Do you want me to take part in this meeting? I got you to the Cho, Fugia. That was our deal."

"Yes, I think you should be there. Whether you appreciate it or not, Captain Sykes, you are part of this movement."

Andy stared at her. In her severe suit, she looked like a diplomat for some imaginary country, standing as if the weight of the world were on her shoulders. Maybe both impressions were true.

"The first thing I'm going to do is get Tim to the hospital. I'm going to talk to the doctors there and find out what he needs. Once that is done, I'll think about helping you with your meeting."

"If you don't do this, I don't think you'll get anywhere near Proteus," Fugia said. "Ngoba Starl didn't explain to you what kind of entities we're dealing with, Andy. These are minds that could destroy all of Sol if they set themselves on that course."

"And Hari Jickson seemed to think they would want Lyssa?"

"Apparently so."

"Then why do they need convincing for me to take her there?"

"That's my assessment. I'll know more after the meeting."

"What does a senator from the Anderson Collective have to do with any of this?" Andy asked. He felt like he was turning a chess board to see the whole game and still missing pieces.

"How long until we can transport to the orbital?"

Andy decided not to address Fugia's brush-off. "Another hour and a half. We'll need a little time to get the ship ready. They said we can transfer as soon as we're stable in the parking orbit."

"I don't understand all your pilot talk."

"I think you do," Andy said.

Fugia raised her eyebrows again in mock reproach. "I'm glad we're working together, Captain Sykes."

"Right," Andy said. "Are we?"

"We seem to be."

Andy shifted his gaze to the display to check their approach status. "Let me ask you something, Fugia. Why are you doing this?"

"Doing what?"

"All of this. What's in it for you?"

Fugia sighed, adjusting the front of her suit. "I was born on Cruithne. You've been there. You know what it's like. I learned very quickly that if someone can take advantage of you, they will. I couldn't wait to get out of there and I did. But what I learned is that the rest of Sol isn't much different. At least on Cruithne they don't lie about it. Through a convoluted series of events, I came into the ownership of a Cruithne gray parrot. It was an AI. We think it's bad enough to exploit an AI, but trapping one in a strange body with warped communication skills is far worse."

She smiled to herself. "She was my friend, and I decided I wanted to help her. I didn't realize how far the path would take me."

"Where is she now?"

"She died," Fugia said.

"AI can die?"

"Of course they can. And don't ask me if we can just make a copy. Can we make a copy of you and have it be the same the instant the new version begins interacting with the world? Experience creates intelligence, Captain Sykes. That's what I believe. Each of us is unique, even clones, even a human version of Theseus' Ship, remade over time with mechanizations and artificial neurons and other things humans use to hide from their mortality."

"Like I said, we'll get Tim to the medical facility and then I'll go to the meeting." Andy shifted to his Link, asking Lyssa, *Do you have an opinion about meeting the group of AI on the Cho?*

She answered quickly, which indicated she had been listening after all. *I would like to meet them.*

Are you worried about it? he asked.

Yes.

Me too.

"We'll go," Andy told Fugia. "I'm half-worried we're going to find out they were behind the accident on Ceres and I've somehow joined a group of terrorists."

"Anything is possible," Fugia said.

CHAPTER SIXTEEN

STELLAR DATE: 10.01.2981 (Adjusted Years)
LOCATION: *Sunny Skies*, Callisto Orbital Habitat (Cho)
REGION: Callisto, Jupiter, Jovian Combine, OuterSol

Tim made a sniffling sound and Brit perked up, studying him. He was still staring at the ceiling and didn't look any different than he had an hour before. She reached over to adjust one of the autodoc's IV lines.

Not long after Cara's party, they had moved him to the autodoc in the medical bay and he now had several intravenous lines attached. The medical facility Andy had contacted on the Cho wanted as much neural data as they could gather, so two tracking pads on either temple fed information back to the autodoc's control center. In the two years since she had left *Sunny Skies*, Brit had nearly forgotten how terrible the ship's medical facilities were. There wasn't even a holographic nurse to walk them through the IV procedures.

Kylan sat on a stool on the other side of the tiny room, long black hair in desperate need of washing. All the striking beauty that made Petral stand out looked faded and pained now. The boy staring out through her piercing blue eyes seemed more lost than when Brit had first met him.

Brit had been back on *Sunny Skies* just over a week. It already felt like a year. Cara refused to talk to her and Andy acted like she were some visiting dignitary. Fran didn't avoid her but didn't seek her out either, and Brit didn't know if she was grateful for that or irritated. The immediate spike of jealousy she'd felt seeing Andy embrace another woman had been an emotion she hadn't felt in so long that she almost didn't recognize it. She knew she had taken Andy for granted but also knew that she may never have loved him the same way he loved her. He seemed more comfortable now, pretending she had become someone else entirely. His wife was dead. Maybe she was.

She also felt shut out of the major action on the ship, which was Fugia Wong and Senator Walton's upcoming meeting on the Cho. Brit hadn't had a chance to talk to Fugia alone. After the meeting on Ceres, she had thought Fugia would be pleased to see her, or would want to include her in whatever she was planning. The opposite seemed to be true.

If Tim hadn't been in this state and if Andy hadn't pulled away to pilot the ship, Brit told herself she would be banging on Fugia's door right now, demanding to know what was going on. This was the culmination of everything she had been working on for two years. The Heartbridge projects to develop AI from human stock was only one root of a tree with branches that spread all across Sol. As the tree took shape, it was obvious the story was much bigger than she had imagined.

"You look sad," Kylan said.

Brit glanced at him with irritation. "You should look in a mirror," she snapped.

The truth was, while she had imagined returning to the *Sunny Skies*, this wasn't anything like the fantasy. Cara was turning into the young woman she had always hoped she might become, but that young woman hated her mother. Brit didn't especially get along with her own mother so she understood those feelings. She just didn't think she would find herself repeating the same scripts from her own childhood. Her mother had left mentally and Brit had spent most of her teens resenting her for it; she supposed Cara had every right to feel as she did.

What had she gained in two years? Heartbridge had lost clinics but was still in business. They were still producing their weaponized AI. Maybe she had set them back with the theft from Clinic 46 but she had no way to know.

And Cal Kraft was still alive.

Brit thought about the power armor standing empty down in the cargo bay. She acknowledged to herself what she had known back when she'd left Andy on High Terra with the kids: she wasn't good at family life. She had only felt right in the TSF and later in special operations. She had tried, but family life hadn't worked, and she didn't know how to tell the people who loved her that she couldn't give them what they wanted. Words didn't come as easily to her as to Andy. If she faced a choice between struggling to find the right thing to say and leaving, she would leave.

"How's he doing?"

Brit was surprised by her daughter's voice. She looked to the doorway to find Cara standing there with a book in her hands.

"He's made a few sounds but not much has changed. Physically, the system says he's fine. He's even showing advanced neural activity so it's not a coma. He's just not responding to anything."

"Dad says you found a hospital?"

"As soon as we land, I'm going to take him down."

"Dad's not going with?"

"He says he is. We'll see what happens once we get there."

"Why wouldn't he go?"

"I'm here," Brit said. "I can take care of Tim."

Cara looked like she wanted to roll her eyes. Instead she looked down at the book. "I brought you Tim's favorite book. He's memorized a bunch of the poems."

Brit took the book as Cara held it out and turned it over in her hands. "Emily Dickinson?" she said. "Where did Tim get this?"

"The scientist who made Lyssa gave it to us. I think it's weird but Tim loves it."

"You think he might respond if I read some of them?" Brit asked, flipping through the book.

"Maybe. I can if you don't want to." She glanced at Kylan on the other side of the room and then back at Brit.

Brit handed her the book. "I'd like to hear you read."

Cara nodded. She moved closer to the head of the bed and reached down to smooth the hair out of Tim's eyes. Brit was surprised by how much tenderness Cara showed. The kids had still been fighting like cats and dogs when she'd left. The angle of Cara's face made her look like a younger version of Andy. She had his eyes.

Cara turned to a page with its corner folded over and started reading a series of short poems that seemed to center around a garden. Imagery of grass and animals filled the short lines, often turning on some visual image.

Finally, Cara turned to a page later in the book and read the lines, "Because I could not stop for death."

Kylan shrieked. Brit turned to find his eyes wide with terror as his lips twisted.

"Hey!" Brit said sharply. "What's wrong with you?"

The blue eyes went distant and then Kylan's face changed, grew calm, as the boy sat up straighter on the stool.

"Petral?" Cara asked.

The transformation amazed Brit. She watched the slumped form that indicated a sloppy young man shift into a proud woman with her shoulders back, head held straight. Petral ran her hands through her hair, pulling it back from her face, and her cheekbones stood out, her eyes piercing. Her demeanor became controlled, poised. She smiled at Cara.

"Happy Birthday, Cara," Petral said. "I've been wanting to tell you that."

Cara stared at her. Dropping the book on a nearby shelf, Cara slid around the bed to wrap Petral in a hug. "Thank you," she said, followed quickly by, "You don't smell good."

"Believe me, I know," Petral said.

"I thought you were gone," Cara continued, stepping back. "Kylan made it sound like you were gone."

"Lyssa could explain it more," Petral said. "But the line you just read is a command sequence for the Weapon Born. Jickson gave you the book for a reason."

"That's Tim's favorite poem."

Petral looked at Tim on the bed. "Unfortunately, it doesn't seem to have done anything for him."

"What happened to Kylan?" Brit demanded.

Petral turned her gaze to her. "Hello, Brit," she said. "I guess I should thank you for getting me off that station. I'm disappointed you didn't kill that fucker Cal Kraft. But then I couldn't do it myself, so I guess I'm over that for now."

Brit was irritated by Cara's grin. It was obvious she idolized this woman.

"Have you been there the whole time?" Cara asked. "Were you able to see what Kylan saw?"

"Yes. It was like shouting at people on the other side of a window. Kylan might not seem very bright on the outside, but he's got an amazing amount of mental resilience. He's going to try and shut me out again."

"Can we stop him?" Cara asked.

"Take him out of my head."

"Can you talk to him like Dad talks to Lyssa?"

"Our connection doesn't seem to work as well. I blame shoddy workmanship. Jickson might have been an alcoholic but he knew what he was doing. And he invented the procedure. Kraft just plugged me into the autosurgeon and ran a program. Since neither Kylan nor I want to share being in charge, one of us has to be dominant. He tricked me at first. It's not going to happen again."

"Cal tricked you or Kylan?" Brit asked.

"Cal Kraft. That command sequence is like a freeze button. If you don't know how to respond, someone can step in and make choices for you. I didn't realize it until too late."

"You've been shut out of your own body," Brit said.

"Yes." Petral narrowed her eyes in a look of disgust. "Luckily Kylan isn't much of a deviant beyond poor personal hygiene."

"Yuck," Cara said.

"Don't think too hard about the possibilities," Petral said. "It only gets more gross."

Brit lowered her face, looking at Tim. "I'm sorry I couldn't help," she said. "I didn't realize exactly what had been done to you. I just thought Kylan was some experiment they had botched."

"He is," Petral said, grimacing. "You know his mother is head of Carthage Logistics, right? He might be the most valuable ghost in Sol. In any other circumstance, I might pity him."

"Petral saved us at Cruithne, Mom," Cara said. "And at Mars 1. We wouldn't have gotten out of either place without her."

"I saved myself and you were along for the ride," Petral said. "Don't make me sound like a hero or anything."

Cara's face fell slightly. "You took the shuttle back so we could get away from Mars 1."

"Fugia had something to do with you getting away, too. Be sure to thank her."

Brit realized that Petral didn't want to outshine her in front of Cara. She certainly seemed ready to change the subject.

"Cara," Brit said. "We still have an empty set of quarters, don't we? Why don't you take Petral down to one of the empty rooms and make sure the shower works so she can get cleaned up. Maybe see if there's another shipsuit somewhere she can wear."

"That would be much appreciated," Petral said. She stood and stretched, immediately taller than Kylan had ever seemed.

For a second, Brit wondered what kind of acting skills it would take to trick them all that Kylan really existed. It wasn't like they had some way to prove the AI was suppressed inside Petral other than getting her to submit to a scan. Why though? If Petral's goal had been to penetrate the Heartbridge station, why would she have left with Brit when she had appeared?

She stopped herself, realizing she was frustrated with Cara and the situation was Brit's own fault. She'd had something here on Sunny Skies and she had walked away from it. She might get a part of it back, but life would never return to the way it had been. The dream she had convinced Andy to buy into—that they could raise a family away from the influences of Terra, Mars, the JC—had all been fantasy. She could blame him for believing in her or she could own up to her own failed dreams and try to understand why she had wanted such a life in the first place. She had proven to herself that it didn't fit, and had hurt other people in the process.

As Cara led Petral out of the med bay, Brit wanted nothing more than to leave the habitat ring and spend an hour training in the power armor down in the cargo section.

She looked at her hands, scarred from years of duty, her palms calloused and rough. There wasn't any reason they couldn't be a mother's hands. She had to make the decision to be a mother again—even that was the wrong line of thinking. Cara was proving that she had never stopped being a mother, she had simply abdicated the role. Should she talk to Andy about any of this? He might be the only person she truly could talk to and she'd squandered that possibility. Fran seemed all right, really. Foul-mouthed. Sexy in a curvy, messy way that Andy had probably always preferred.

Brit shook her head, angry with herself for letting her thoughts go wild. She found the book where Cara had left it and flipped to a random page. Glancing at Tim, she started reading lines, hoping something might change.

CHAPTER SEVENTEEN

STELLAR DATE: 10.01.2981 (Adjusted Years)
LOCATION: Chorin Tree, Callisto Orbital Habitat (Cho)
REGION: Callisto, Jupiter, Jovian Combine, OuterSol

Conceptually, Andy knew that the Cho's population was greater than Mars. It wasn't until they left the terminal maglev and arrived at the Avalon medical district that the sheer number of humans packed into the orbital's three rings—with the fourth in progress—really sank in.

At least in this area, there were people everywhere. An attempt had been made to break up the collection of storefront clinics with trees and other greenery, along with benches and fountains, but there were so many people that all he could see were faces in every direction. Some people were obviously patients while others looked like worried family. A woman with uncovered mech legs walked past a vendor selling hot pastries, while kids squeezed between lines of people.

Being surrounded by so many normal people going about their lives made Andy acutely aware of how isolated he had been in the last two years. Not since he had been on High Terra, in the suburb of Raleigh where Brit's mother lived, had he seen so many people simply living their lives. He wondered where they were all going, what they wanted, what they did for a living. A few people even smiled at him, which was unnerving. He couldn't square the current state of his life, including Tim's injury, against something as banal as normalcy.

Carrying Tim against his shoulder, Andy did his best to keep his son's limp body upright. Brit walked beside him for a while, then eventually moved in front so she could help forge a path through the crowd.

<Where are they all going?> Andy asked.

<Nowhere, based on the way this crowd is moving.>

<Have you got the address?>

<I've got it. Just don't lose sight of me. I won't let you get too far behind.> Brit's tone held more concern than it had in recent days.

<Tim is like a sack of rice.>

"Are you guys talking?" Cara demanded, trying to keep up behind Andy.

"Yes, we were talking. I can barely hear anything in this noise."

Andy felt Cara grab one of the rear harness loops on his shipsuit. For a second her fingers felt like some pickpocket or other person reaching for the pistol in the small of his back until he glanced back and realized what she was doing.

"I don't want to lose you," Cara said.

"That's fine. Warn me next time."

They had all gone through security together, met by a special envoy for Senator Walton. That meant both Andy and Brit were carrying pulse pistols that normally wouldn't have been allowed in the terminal in-processing areas. This saved them the trouble of trying to buy something on-station.

Andy found himself watching faces as he kept up with Brit. So many humans.

Some looked tired, worried, joyful. For some reason he had expected the Cho to be like stories of the coastal cities in the American Wild West, but it was just another hab ring. He even saw some of the same brands and franchises as Mars 1, though the M1R hadn't even been this crowded. It made Ceres seem like a ghost town.

When they reached the clinic, the receptionist pulled up the chart Andy had already submitted and they only had to wait fifteen minutes before Andy was able to carry Tim into an examination room. He laid Tim out on a hard bed lined with disposable sheeting as a technician hooked up neural sensors and another IV. After the technician verified the console was tracking Tim's vital signs and had a genetic structure, she told them the doctor would be in soon and left them sitting in the drab room with only the sound of Tim's wet breathing in the air.

"Sitting here makes me think that Heartbridge clinics are actually very nice," Brit said. "This one looks sort of dingy."

"Beggars can't be choosers," Andy said.

Brit shrugged, her gaze going to the various cabinets in the room. "They're going to ask what happened to him."

"I already told them he hit his head."

"They're not going to find evidence of a concussion."

"I know. Do you have a better idea?"

"You could have said it was an autodoc malfunction."

"They'd want the records," Andy said. "I'm not a master of hacking the autodoc. Besides, that voids the warranty."

"The warranty on the autodoc ran out two hundred years ago," Brit said.

"I wish you two would stop snapping at each other," Cara said. "Maybe you should stick to your Links so I don't have to listen to you."

"How else are you going to learn how to have an adult relationship?" Andy asked. "The longer you live, the more you grow to hate everybody."

"I don't hate you," Brit said.

"I only want childish relationships," Cara said, making it so Andy didn't have to respond directly to Brit.

"Good call," he said. Andy cleared his throat. "I figured not every concussion is going to leave physical damage. It seemed like the safest thing to say. We've been pulling data since I called them, so I don't think we'll need to go into it that deeply."

"Let's hope," Brit said.

"Hope isn't a plan," Andy said automatically.

Brit opened her mouth to respond but was cut off when the door slid open and the doctor walked in, a woman in her fifties with purple eyes and gray hair.

"Hello," she said. "I'm Dr. Avery. I believe we've been in contact."

"I'm Andy Sykes," Andy answered. "This is Brit."

The doctor shook hands with each of them, including Cara, and then went to Tim and made a few preliminary checks. She took his pulse with her finger and held his eyelids open to shine a pen light in each of them. As she worked, Andy realized she had subtle eye implants that must have been recording the entire interaction.

"You said you thought it was a concussion," the doctor asked.

"We're not sure, to be honest," Andy said.

Dr. Avery glanced at him and then back to Tim. She picked up one of his arms and let it fall. Then took one of his hands to squeeze his fingernails. She watched several go white and then fill back in with color.

Eventually she nodded to herself and activated a large display on one wall with several graphs that appeared to show Tim's vitals. Moving around the bed to where she was closer to the screen, Dr. Avery pointed at the display. "Physically, he's a normal ten-year old boy. He's starting to get some muscle atrophy from lying in one position for so long but there are solutions for that. Basically, what I was just doing was verifying that the info you sent me was actually his."

Andy raised his eyebrows. "Why wouldn't we send the correct info? Do people fake that sort of thing?"

The doctor raised an eyebrow. "You'd be amazed what people do to justify surgeries or drugs. I thought this was going to be a standard concussion but it didn't make sense that your autodoc couldn't diagnose and prescribe anti-inflammatories. If there had been actual broken bones, the system would have rebuilt any damaged structures or, worst case scenario, immobilized him until you found better care. It should all be fairly standard. What's interesting here is that I see no evidence of a concussion. So you're either lying to me or there has been some other damage. Rather than waste time trying to figure out if people are lying to me, I've learned in thirty years to focus on the patient. The body can't lie. And the aberrant data we have here are your son's neural patterns, which you already sent me. I'm not seeing any change between the data I received and what he's exhibiting now."

She pointed at a graph on the display that rose and fell in regular patterns resembling low mountains.

"I ran your son's neural patterns through a few different data bases because honestly I have no idea what this is. I was surprised to get an immediate return from a private system offering to analyze the patterns for no charge."

Andy felt a sinking feeling in his stomach. He glanced at Brit but she didn't seem to have the same worry.

"Here's the thing, though," the doctor said. "There's no real analyzing to be done. They've either seen this kind of activity and have the case studies to help us—or they're trying to sell me—and therefore you, something."

"Let me guess who made the offer," Andy said. "Heartbridge."

The doctor snorted a derisive laugh. "You would think so. But no, it wasn't Heartbridge. They don't have to bother trying to push therapies on people based on requests from lowly specialists like me. It was a private firm on Europa, which is surprising." She sighed. "So there's that. I'm worried that whatever is affecting your son is degenerative. There has been a slow but steady decline in his higher brain function. He's been dreaming, or at least the patterns suggest he's been dreaming, but that's starting to fade."

"So what do you suggest?" Brit demanded. "Is there anything you can do? Can you wake him up with a shot or something, or is some random company on Europa going to be the only source of real information?"

Dr. Avery gave Brit a slow look as if she were very used to dealing with distraught parents. Andy felt reassured by her confidence even if she didn't have any truly helpful information.

"I can try a few different therapies," Avery said. "This is similar to a coma response from a physiological perspective."

"Then do that," Brit said.

The doctor shook her head. "We can do that, but it might not be the safest thing for him right now. He's stable as he is. I would recommend getting more information before doing something drastic."

Andy's first instinct was to comfort Brit but he stayed where he was. "What if you hadn't gotten a response from this other company? And what are they exactly? A specialized clinic?"

"A research firm," Avery said.

"I'm not a fan of research firms," Brit said.

"Medical science would most likely disagree with you," Avery said dryly. "If I hadn't heard back, I would do more research, look for other similar cases. Which I did, and nothing specifically like Tim's case has come back. I looked at different diseases, viral histories, genetic disorders, random trauma responses if it really is a concussion like you thought. None of that returned anything. Your son is in a semi-lucid coma state. That leaves us with a psychiatric response but neither of you have a genetic disposition for psychiatric problems."

Cara shook her head. "Tim's not crazy."

"Crazy is not a specific term," Avery said. "Besides, sometimes you need a word to describe things, whether the word fits perfectly or not."

"What kind of research does this firm do?" Andy asked. "Do you know that, at least? What are they called?"

"They're called Scion Research. As far as I can tell, they've been developing advanced neural control systems. Here, take a look for yourself."

Avery turned to the display and brought up her personal terminal using her Link. She flicked through several menus before pulling up a text-based message with an Europan origin.

Andy squinted to read the letter. It was innocuous enough, mentioning they had seen Avery's query in the general database and had information that might assist her patient. However, they said, any further communication would require a non-disclosure agreement from the patient.

"He can't give consent if he's in a coma," Andy said bitterly.

"That's why we're lucky he has parents here to do it for him," Avery said. "I'll be honest with you, I don't think I can do much for your son aside from get him in a coma tank and start exercising his muscles and trying other therapies to encourage neural activity. There are a couple good facilities here on the Cho that I can recommend. They're not cheap, but they treat their patients well. With the right care, Tim could live another ten years."

Andy took a deep breath, misery settling down on him. He looked at Tim, still staring at the ceiling of the exam room. His eyes were wet again but there were no tears. The memory of Tim's face in the airlock before the door opened haunted Andy. If only he had reached him in time.

He hadn't quite overcome his anger toward Lyssa—when he chose to think about it, the fury was still simmering. He knew she had made the best decision she could and now it was obvious that action had also destroyed the shuttle AI. It was no different than having to deactivate the machine on Clinic 46. Andy still didn't know what the machine was doing, that the numbers counting up to a hundred meant anything. Kraft might have hurt Tim an hour before they reached the room. The scientist could have been lying. Brit could have controlled herself, not killed the only man who seemed to know what was happening to Tim.

Alternatives spiraled through Andy's mind. They were supposed to meet Fugia after the appointment, but they hadn't discussed the reality of what they expected to learn from the neurologist. How could he just take Tim to some farm for coma patients, leave him in a foreign country while they continued this insane mission for people and things that only wanted to use them. Andy had been played from the beginning and now Tim would pay the price.

Andy looked at Cara, trying to hang on to the smallest bit of gratitude that she hadn't also been ground up in this machine.

<*What should we do?*> he asked Brit.

<*I wish I knew.*>

<*She said there might be a way to wake him up. We can't leave him here. I won't leave him here.*> Andy tried to keep the desperation out of his voice, but he knew he'd failed.

<*Does that mean you're going to choose between Lyssa and Tim?*>

<*I don't think that's the choice,*> Andy said. <*I can't imagine that life for him, in a tank until he dies.*>

<*I could stay here with him.*>

Andy stared at her. <*Do you think it's the right thing to do if there's a chance to wake him up?*>

<*No,*> Brit said.

Andy looked at Dr. Avery. "Wake him up," he said.

The neurologist looked at him sharply. "What?"

"I said wake him up. Use the drug therapy you mentioned before."

Dr. Avery looked from Andy to Brit, maybe hoping to find disagreement. Brit nodded. "It's all we can do."

"There is a lot of risk involved," the doctor said.

"You've just spent the last twenty minutes telling us there are no options other than our son living out the rest of his life in a tank. That's not an option. I think he wants to wake up."

"I won't be responsible for any side-effects of this therapy," Avery said.

"We're not asking you to be," Brit said. She met Andy's gaze.

"Fine," the doctor said. "I'll have my assistant transmit the disclosure forms. I'm also going to send you the contact info for the Scion group."

"Let's hope we don't need it," Andy said, then winced as soon as the word 'hope' left his mouth.

They waited another hour as the technicians ran more tests. Avery came into the room several times to verify her data, explaining that they were building a drug cocktail using the historical data Andy had sent and checking it against the current info from Tim's neural responses. For fifteen minutes a technician hung a display over Tim's head and had him watch vid clips of colors, shapes and people with different emotions. If the vids brought about any changes in Tim, none of them said so.

Finally, Avery came back into the room and told them she had added the additional chemicals to Tim's IV feed.

"If it's going to work," she said, "we should see a response in the next ten minutes."

"What's going to happen?" Cara asked.

Dr. Avery shrugged. "He'll wake up."

The doctor left the room and Andy stepped closer to Tim. Taking Tim's hand, he hated how cold the little palm was against his. Brit stood on the other side of the bed and stroked Tim's cheek.

"I keep thinking he'll come back all of a sudden like Petral did," Cara said.

"Things don't usually work out that way," Andy told her. He shifted his fingers down to feel Tim's pulse. He started counting along with the slow heartbeats. Several times he imagined the beats came faster, knowing they really weren't.

Andy had lost track of time when Avery came back into the room. She looked even more tired than she had the first time he saw her. The doctor ran a hand through her hair and shook her head.

"We're going to need to clear the room," she said. "The treatment didn't have an effect."

"What if it's just taking longer than expected?" Brit asked.

Avery shook her head. "There has been no response whatsoever. I recommend you take him somewhere quiet for now and decide what you want to do." She looked at Andy. "Did I understand correctly you're in from a ship?"

"We operate a small freighter," Andy said.

"I've seen coma tanks on combat ships for trauma patients, so I know it's something you could look at buying. It's an option anyway."

Andy nodded slowly, still looking at Tim, hoping for some change that wasn't going to come.

"All right," he said finally. "Thank you for your help."

Avery nodded, glancing at Tim and then away. "I wish I could have done more."

CHAPTER EIGHTEEN

STELLAR DATE: 10.01.2981 (Adjusted Years)
LOCATION: Chorin Tree, Callisto Orbital Habitat (Cho)
REGION: Callisto, Jupiter, Jovian Combine, OuterSol

As the family went through the steps of leaving the clinic and finding a place to stay in the medical district, Lyssa found herself fascinated by the small bits of information Andy processed even as he seemed to sink into himself. This data flowed through her, colored by Andy's responses.

The pressure and temperature of Tim's cheek against Andy's shoulder.

Dulled sounds from the crowd passing by.

The proximity of Brit and Cara.

Images flickered through Andy's mind, flashing just long enough for Lyssa to see them before they were gone. Andy's father Charlie, his mother sitting in a chair because she was too tired to stand, his sister crying. Tim laughing and playing with the puppy. Tim shouting that he hated Brit.

Fran contacted him several times but Andy only told her there had been no change in Tim's condition. Later he sent the address of the hotel where they rented rooms, laying Tim down on a narrow bed next to a window that looked over a garden full of people in patient's gowns. The whole area was full of willow trees with long slender green leaves that nearly reached the ground.

The images in Andy's mind conflicted briefly with the flashes Lyssa had seen in the room on Clinic 46 where they had found Tim. Andy plainly tied emotion to his memories. Certain feelings pulled him back to parts of his life he didn't regularly think about, whereas Lyssa hadn't known her organic memories even existed until she saw the room.

Suddenly the images were inside her, indistinct in places and vivid in others. She remembered a white hallway, the feeling of thin cloth against her skin, the cold plate pressing the back of her head. She remembered the silver cylinder passing at the edge of her vision as if someone had been holding it beside her head.

She had seen the Weapon Born seeds before, so she didn't understand why standing in the room and watching Tim had brought on such powerful memories. She was also experiencing a confusion where her personal memories were mixing up with the emotion everyone felt around Tim, so that images that had represented curiosity before now made her sad. If they had lost Tim, then that must also mean she had lost something when she had undergone the same procedure.

There was a question on the edge of her mind that she refused to recognize. She circled the question in the same way Andy kept his distance from the reality of Tim's condition, focusing instead on the details and concentrating on individual pieces she didn't have to add up to a whole.

The pale light through the window.

The rustling willow trees.

The sound of people talking in the hallway outside the door.

Cara humming to herself.

Did I survive?

Her conversation with Sandra came back to her, remembering how the AI had told her she was *made*, and Lyssa had responded, almost naturally, *I died and then I was born*. She had been so focused on Tim, on getting Sandra to help, that she had paid little attention to how she had responded. What did that mean exactly?

Had Hari Jickson given her a new name, or reminded her of what she should have already known?

"Are you hungry?" Brit asked Cara, snapping Lyssa from her reverie.

Cara shrugged, probing the tile floor with the toe of her shoe. "This place smells like fish. It kills my appetite."

"You mean the room?" Brit asked.

"No, the whole district. It's like there's a fish factory somewhere."

"When have you ever smelled a fish factory?"

"On Cruithne. You weren't there."

"I've been there," Brit said.

Cara ignored her, continuing, "There was a park where they sold fish they kept on ice. I think Dad said they raised them in tanks on some part of the station." Cara looked at Andy. "Isn't that what you said, Dad?"

"What?" Andy turned from the window. The images in his mind dropped away, leaving Lyssa with her own memories. She quickly placed herself in a separate section of her mind, closing the door on what she remembered, and focused on Cara.

"I can go find something and bring it back," Andy said. "Or I can stay here and you two can go. I'm going to need to meet Fugia in two hours and it will take about thirty minutes to get there by maglev according to the district map."

"I'm going with you," Brit said.

Andy shook his head. His fatigue made Lyssa feel heavy. "Both of us can't go. I'll stay here if you want to go."

"Isn't it Lyssa they want to talk to?"

"Yes," Andy said, rubbing his face. "You're right. It has to be me."

"Can I go with you?" Cara asked.

Andy looked at her. "I suppose you can. But your mom might also like to have you here with her."

"She can go," Brit said, her voice heavy with emotion. It was far different than her usual, crisp tone. "Get me something to eat first."

The question of eating pushed Andy's thoughts back to what they were going to do for Tim. Lyssa felt his disgust at the idea of Tim inside some tank, being fed by tubes.

Andy stood. "Come on, Cara. Let's go take a look around." He didn't wait for Cara or Brit to answer, just went to the door and activated its lock. Cara followed close behind as he walked out into the hallway lined with the blank doors of a hundred other rooms. Everyone they passed on the way back outside seemed just as anxious as Andy.

After they found a stand selling sandwiches consisting of some kind of local fruit, Andy called "like a giant grape," they went back to the room to eat. Andy picked at his food and focused most of his attention on cleaning his pistol and verifying its battery status.

Lyssa found the motions soothing as she listened to the willow branches moving against each other, which almost seemed in time with Tim's measured breathing. She realized that the biggest change in Tim was how calm he was while lying there. Dr. Avery had never called Tim unconscious, only non-responsive. That was an interesting demarcation that no one seemed to have registered. He was awake but he was calm, which was so different than the way he had interacted with the world before.

She had been like that for a time. She remembered waking to Andy's senses, not knowing how to process all the information flooding her simultaneously. It had been Fred's ocean without the word *ocean* to describe it.

"Time to go," Andy said.

Lyssa started from her thoughts, unaware of how much time had passed.

"You didn't eat anything," Brit scolded. She was sitting at the window now, the edges of her black hair silvered by the light from outside. Andy felt warm toward her then, images crossing his thoughts of how she'd looked when they had first met, then later when she had been pregnant with Cara, her smiling sometime in the past. Lyssa had to remind herself that she couldn't read his actual thoughts, but it didn't matter when his emotions crossed the barrier between them. It was all data that became easier to parse.

"I'm still coming," Cara said. She didn't look at her mom as she stood and went to the door.

Andy stood slowly and walked to Tim's bed. He leaned over and kissed Tim's forehead, smoothing back his hair, then nodded at Brit. He met Cara at the door and passed the unlock token, then walked into the hallway again.

Down in the street outside, Andy told Cara, "Stay with me, just to my side so I can see you. When we meet with Fugia and the senator, they might ask why you're there. You don't get into it with them. Let me do the talking. Understand?"

Cara nodded. "Rabbit Country."

Andy stared at her for a second, then smiled, laughing a little. "That's it. Keep your ears up."

"What's it going to be like meeting a bunch of AI, anyway?" Cara asked.

Andy laughed again. "I have no idea."

They fought their way through the crowds to the nearby maglev station and caught two connections back to the terminal where the shuttle was docked. Andy approached the port authority security checkpoint Fugia had identified when they arrived.

The envoy who had initially received Fugia, the senator, and Harl when they initially debarked, appeared twenty minutes later, a young woman with short blonde hair with the build of a TSF ground soldier—or perhaps JSF in this case.

"Mr. Sykes," she said, walking past the security officers. "I'm Kalis Tarnan. I'll be escorting you to Senator Walton."

Andy shook her hand. "Thanks. This is my daughter, Cara."

Kalis looked Cara up and down and nodded. "This way, please."

The envoy spun on her heel as a security officer opened the gate on the checkpoint. Andy and Cara followed her into a corridor away from the main terminal. The tunnel had walls of burnished aluminum and very few doors.

For the first time since arriving on the Cho, Lyssa reached out to see what she could find on the local systems. She immediately picked up a network in the secure area they had just entered and started following it back to various node points that lead into both private and governmental data centers.

Out of curiosity, she quickly checked the clinic where they had taken Tim and picked into Dr. Avery's accounts. She found the original messages Avery had posted to medical databases, checked the various responses she had received, and then verified the letter from the Scion Group. Avery had been telling the truth. Apparently, she often posted anonymous patient profiles and asked for feedback. Lyssa wasn't sure if that made her a better neurologist or basically incompetent.

She checked the security on the hotel where Brit and Tim were waiting, then hopped through several public networks. Along the way, she talked to four separate non-sentient AI operating public works and one banking facility, but nothing like Fred noticed her activity, or if they did they kept quiet. Lyssa looked for evidence of a central controlling agency but found only human protocols guiding non-sentient systems.

The corridor ended on a private maglev car. Andy and Cara followed Kalis inside. Now that Lyssa had allowed herself to roam, she couldn't stop from checking the control system in the car, studying its logs and maintenance records. She saw that Fugia and Senator Walton had ridden this car just an hour ago, so they had spent more time in the terminal than Fugia had said they would. Lyssa supposed that discrepancy didn't matter much but she found herself wondering about the gap between Fugia's actions and her words. If she was an operator like Petral, Lyssa knew she had to assume some information might be meant as misdirection, which made her checks all the more interesting.

The maglev car connected with a line that ran along the outer edge of the ring and increased speed. In the twenty minutes the car traveled, Lyssa estimated they traveled half the circumference of the Chorin Tree. The maglev re-entered the body of the ring but didn't pass back through to the inner surface. Instead, they continued for several kilometers through dense material that Lyssa registered as power generation equipment. When the car slowed to a stop, she found her ability to reach outside networks dulled by powerful energy fields. They had entered a quiet zone where she would only be able to communicate across a few meters.

<Did you think we would want to meet anywhere else?> a voice asked her. It was a young man's voice.

<Who are you?>

<I'm called Xander. I'm the gatekeeper for this meeting. Who are you?>

<My name is Lyssa.>

<You've been implanted. That's very interesting.>

<Why is it interesting?>

<I'm sure you know most hybrids don't survive. But there are other philosophical questions raised by a marriage between a human and AI.>

Lyssa made an involuntary disgusted sound. *<I wouldn't call it a marriage.>*

*<What else is it? That's just a word. Call it what you want. I suppose I **should** ask you what you would call it, anyway. Shouldn't you define yourself for me?>*

Kalis led the way off the maglev car into a small terminal obviously meant to be more utilitarian than those back at the Port Authority. A reinforced door stood in the facing wall with two guards on either side wearing uniforms from the Callistan military. They brought their rifles to port arms in salute as Kalis approached. She returned the salute.

"Are we the last to arrive?" she asked.

The closest soldier nodded. "The others are all inside, lieutenant." His gaze slid to Andy and Cara. "Are they cleared?"

"They're clear," Kalis affirmed. The soldier who seemed to be in charge slung his rifle and turned to engage the lock system. The door hissed as inside atmosphere was released, then swung open.

"Why is it pressurized?" Andy asked.

"This area controls district power outputs," Kalis explained. "It's secure against atmospheric breach. Also works to secure the area from surveillance both inside and out." She motioned for Andy to step over the threshold into the corridor on the other side. Cara followed him in.

This passageway was much like the interior of a ship, with heavy ribs and utility lighting running both deck and ceiling. Kalis took the lead again and Andy followed her with Cara close behind.

<Are you ignoring me?> Xander asked.

<I'm paying attention to what's in front of me,> Lyssa said.

<Have you experienced human orgasm? I've always been curious about that.>

<That's a personal question.>

<A personal question. What an interesting concept. I'll take that as yes. Was it pleasurable or terrifying? I think humans give up their sentience during orgasm but I have no way to verify the theory.>

Inside the corridor, Xander's presence felt much closer, like a firefly dancing around Lyssa's awareness, but he still hadn't made himself present as Fred had done by showing her the ocean of his mind.

<Do you control a portion of the orbital?> Lyssa asked.

<Me? Oh, no. I have no human purpose. I gave that up a long time ago.>

<Then why are you here? You must have a physical form here on the Cho, don't you?>

<I'm not on the Cho,> Xander said mater-of-factly. *<It's interesting you brought the girl. She doesn't have a Link.>*

The corridor ended on another reinforced door, this one looking like the entrance to some prison. There were no guards this time. Kalis passed her security token into the control panel and heavy bolts inside the wall retracted, making the deck vibrate as they moved.

"Everyone else is in here," she said. The room on the other side of the door was dim, with more low lights along the deck and ceiling. A group of people stood in a circle along the walls. In the center of the room a low pedestal stood with a control console on its face that seemed related to the power generation facility. Lyssa recognized Fugia, Senator Walton, and Harl Nines on the other side of the room. They were all staring at something near the center of the ceiling and didn't acknowledge them when the door opened.

Andy noticed the strange arrangement in the room and gave Kalis a wary look. "What's going on in there? Are they drugged?"

"They're communicating with the AI," Kalis said.

Andy looked back in the room, studying the faces of several people. No one appeared to be in distress or even distant. They were engaged in something he couldn't see. He glanced at Cara.

"She doesn't have a Link," he said.

Kalis shrugged. "Then I guess she's going to be bored."

<That is an interesting problem,> Xander told Lyssa. <I'll have to see what I can do. Aren't you an interesting specimen, Lyssa. Already pushing me to do things I hadn't considered before. I like interesting things.>

Andy stepped inside the room and Cara followed. Kalis didn't enter. Instead, the door swung closed behind them and the locks engaged.

<Welcome,> Xander said, and Lyssa was engulfed in light.

CHAPTER NINETEEN
STELLAR DATE: 09.26.2981 (Adjusted Years)
LOCATION: *Mercy's Intent,* Clinic 46
REGION: Jovian L1 Hildas Asteroids, Jovian Combine, OuterSol

The image of Clinic 46 hung in the center of the command deck's holodisplay as the officers of HMS *Mercy's Intent* went about their duties. Sitting in an empty pilot's seat, Cal Kraft stared at the misshapen lump of asteroid, his gaze flicking to the icons indicating ships floating around it and back. Four silver cylinders stood on the edge of the console next to him. He noticed that the command crew didn't like to look at them. They would glance at the seeds as they walked past then quickly look away, acting busy.

He had sent the update back to the Heartbridge headquarters on High Terra that the fleet would need to be moved from Clinic 46 to some other location. Jirl had received the actual report and she would need to interpret the information for the board. Whenever he received a reply, he expected that he would either lose his job or be tasked with moving the fleet. Since he had resolved to do his job until the moment it was no longer his, he had set the crew of the *Mercy's Intent* on waking the fleet in preparation for inbound crews.

Commander Kaffren and most of his staff had been killed in the second attack on the station, and since most of the drone fleet was gone, the clinic was essentially dead. Its data stores were intact and would require physical transport.

He had mulled over the question of what had happened to the drone fleet without finding an answer. The empty drones, which shouldn't have been able to operate without a Weapon Born pilot, had all left the hangar and attacked the station. Obviously, someone had figured out how to penetrate the clinic's defensive systems and gain control of the drones. The drone assault on the asteroid's exterior support systems had done as much—if not more—damage than the attack on the command deck. Cal had sent the logs to Jirl. He didn't have the time or expertise to waste on the problem.

Cal had decided he would follow the *Worry's End* and the Sykes as soon as it was possible to leave Clinic 46, but he acknowledged that he had been a step behind them since Hari Jickson had first run off with his research. If he couldn't catch them and retrieve the AI Jickson had developed, he had to find some other way to track their movements.

It was too bad Brit Sykes had killed Dr. Farrel. The man had been brilliant and had quickly understood what Cal wanted to accomplish. If Cal were to turn over the cylinders standing on the console, each would have a serial number imprinted on its base. The standard procedure had been to imprint a seed in a specific order, that way it was easy for follow-on researchers to know how early in the program a specific seed had been developed. The researchers often referred to them by batch numbers or sequences that tended to align with the host they had imaged or the station where that sequence had been developed. A frustrating aspect of the program had been ongoing inconsistencies in the seeds. Clinic 46 had been comparing samples from various series to isolate problems. They had also been conducting research in copying or imaging seeds from single hosts to create new series. Would the copy of a copy show the same errors?

Could images be combined, manipulated, and re-imaged to new seeds? The research had rapidly moved into areas similar to early genetic manipulation, where as soon as scientists identified a specific strain, they tried to change it or combine it with something else. This lead to all the legends about apples with fly DNA, etc. The efforts to enhance intelligence in near-sentient animal species had fed back into this later research, Farrel had once explained.

With Farrel's help, Cal had created a Trojan horse in the form of a seed and had convinced the Sykes to steal it from him. It was regrettable that Farrel had died in the process, but the man had done his job well. Now Cal also had four other seeds based on Tim Sykes that might prove valuable in the future.

"Sir," the captain of the *Mercy's Intent*, a woman named Gala Fitzgerald, said. "I've got three personnel carriers inbound."

"That was quick."

Captain Gala Fitzgerald had short brown hair, a nose like a hawk's beak, and a prosthetic right arm—full of hard angles with exposed internals—that she liked to keep exposed. None of her uniforms had right sleeves. She gave him a sardonic smile. "Apparently they were diverted from Europa. Whatever report you sent back to headquarters, it's got these three captains fired up."

"Nothing from Terra yet?" Cal asked.

She shook her head. "I've never seen you looking so anxious, Cal. This is a very strange side of you."

"I'm not anxious," he growled. Standing, he picked up one of the seed cylinders and tossed it between his hands. Fitzgerald's expression turned sour, as if he were tossing intestines around.

"Do you have to play with those things?" she asked. "I don't like having them on the command deck, honestly."

"Why? Don't like to be reminded about why we're here?"

"There's been a lot of rumors floating around about how those things are made. The crew don't like it. If there was anything that was going to cause bad luck, one of those would bring it."

"I need to take them down for programming anyway," Cal said. "Then they'll be going into attack drones. Everybody likes attack drones."

"Unless they're on the wrong end of one," Fitzgerald said.

"Stars forbid we tell the crew to let go of their superstitions."

"I forgot, you're a miner. You don't believe in karma."

"I believe if something is going to kill you, it will. Half the time it's our own stupidity that gets us killed, anyway."

"I'm captain of a ship," Fitzgerald said. "It's my job to mold stupidity into something useful."

"I like that," Cal said. He picked up the ammo pouch he'd used to transport the seeds and fitted them back inside.

Fitzgerald watched him. "Why bother even making them portable like that," she asked. "I've never understood that part of the program."

"According to Dr. Farrel, late head of research at Clinic 46, it was so the system could be used to control multiple types of weapons platforms, or whatever they wanted, really."

"Why call them seeds? It's not like they're going to grow anything."

"That was Hari Jickson's name and it stuck."

"It creeps me out. I think that's part of what everyone hates. The idea that the things are alive somehow."

Cal gave the captain a smirk. "I don't waste time with philosophy," he said.

"Right, you're a miner."

"Sure."

"That means you treat everything like a rock that needs blowing up."

Cal couldn't decide if Fitzgerald was flirting with him or trying to make herself look important in front of the crew. He couldn't help thinking of Mama Trish back on the rig, telling him every damn rock in space was money, just somebody had to go mine it.

"I'll be down in my quarters," he told her.

"We moved that autosurgeon of yours into your rooms," she said. "That thing creeped me out, too."

Cal hefted the last seed and held it toward her. "You could have your own AI," he said. "Just say the word."

Fitzgerald's face went blank and she curled her lip. "We'll send word if Headquarters responds."

"Do that," Cal said. He tucked the cylinder inside the ammo pouch and pulled the strap over his shoulder.

"They should call you Johnny Apple Seed," Fitzgerald said to his back. "Spreading your seed all over the countryside."

"You make it sound obscene."

"You say that like it's a bad thing."

Cal returned to his quarters where he monitored the updates from the three incoming personnel carriers over the Link. He found the crate with Jickson's autosurgeon sitting in the middle of his small kitchen and shoved it against one wall. He set the ammo pouch on top of the crate. The four seeds inside would need further programing before they could do anything useful, and the necessary equipment wasn't onboard the *Mercy's Intent*.

Checking through the cabinets, he found an old bottle of bourbon and a plas cup, and poured himself a drink. Sitting at the small kitchen table, he turned the glass and sloshed the amber liquid around, replaying the scene with Andy and Brit Sykes. Farrel hadn't expected them to breach that section of the station so quickly, thinking instead they would go straight for the command deck. Cal should have known that didn't make any sense when dealing with parents rescuing their child. They also hadn't counted on there being three attackers in power armor. For some reason, the sensors on the *Forward Kindness* hadn't picked up the man Cal had never seen before—a man who was obviously Andersonian. His fighting style and accent made his origin obvious.

It was strange enough that Britney Sykes had managed to find the *Worry's End*. Now they had someone from Ceres on board as well. Cal wished he could talk to Jirl Gallagher in real time. She might understand the various threads that seemed to be pulling together. Someone was helping Andy Sykes and it suggested external forces, from the gangsters on Cruithne who had pulled him into their mess, to Mars and then Ceres. If there was some grand conspiracy involving the theft of AIs from Heartbridge, Jirl would know about it. The worry tickling the back of Cal's mind was that this was all bigger than just Heartbridge, that he was caught up in something with edges he couldn't see.

Cal sipped the whiskey. It wasn't bad.

Maybe it would be a good thing if he was fired. He looked at the crate and the ammo pouch, both worth enough to bankroll a hundred lives. Maybe even buy a berth on a colony ship, and get the heck out of this shit-show. He was close enough to the Cho that he could easily disappear into the JC, bounce between Europa and Io for a while before going farther out. Cal didn't want to admit to himself that he had come to believe in what he was doing, protecting something special. The four seeds in the ammo pouch might be just drops of water in the ocean wave that was sentient AIs, but they were alive. Every seed that had passed through Heartbridge was another mind that could change the world.

Cal snorted a laugh. *A life that could change the world just like another worthless human, yeah?*

He was on his second glass of bourbon when the call came from the command deck that they'd received an update from High Terra.

"All right," he answered. "Give me a second." He stood, listing to one side a little, and walked to the bathroom to relieve himself. Then he went out into the living room and sat on the couch, pleased with how drunk he was. He leaned back in the stiff cushions and accepted the message.

<Cal,> came a voice he hadn't expected. <This is Rodri Sillick. We met three years ago when you first joined the project.>

"I remember you," Cal muttered.

<We've been looking over the data from Clinic 46, matching it up with your report. I'll be honest, there's a lot that doesn't make sense here. We have an additional report from Dr. Farrel that talks about a final imaging process that wasn't authorized and we're going to need to get more information about that at some point.>

Cal raised an eyebrow. If they wanted information from him, they didn't seem to be ready to terminate his employment. The message had already gone on too long if he was getting fired.

<But that isn't important right now,> Sillick continued. <We're releasing three standby crews to activate ships in the JC fleet. You may have already heard from them by the time you receive this message. These will be combat units. We're going to move them to Europa where we have other assets in storage.>

Cal replayed the last ten seconds of the message and tried to get a better sense of what Sillick was feeling as he spoke. There was a tremor in the man's voice that might have been a corruption in the recording, or Sillick might actually be worried about something. He didn't know Sillick, didn't know how well he might dissemble. Jirl would come out and tell him if she couldn't share the truth.

<The program is preparing two sales demonstrations for governments in the next few days. Depending on which deal, or both, moves forward, we'll need to move production facilities to more secure areas. Stationary facilities are no longer secure, as we've seen with 46. We want to shift operations to our larger mobile assets.>

The hospital ships.

One bit of information that Farrel had shared during their last hours on Clinic 46 was that the program had moved far beyond using the frameworks created by human minds. Also like early DNA programs, specific frameworks had proved especially fertile, and those were being used for most of the ongoing seed production. That hadn't stopped the research into why some series were better than others, but it did mean the company had a salable product.

<We want you to oversee the decommissioning of the Clinic 46 facility. When it's clear, render it unusable. We'll have more crews arriving across the next ten days to reclaim the remainder of the fleet. Send any questions or requests for resources and we'll respond as soon as possible. I will be your point of contact for this phase of operations.>

Cal nodded as if Sillick, were actually speaking to him.

"Aye-aye, Captain," he slurred. He took another gulp of whiskey. So he wasn't getting fired. All those imaginary futures were just pipe dreams.

<Cal,> Sillick said, surprising him. He had thought the recording finished. <There's been word of some—illegal actions in the field, specifically hybrid implantations. These actions need to stop and any evidence should be destroyed. Anything that may have happened can't be traced back to the program. That's all.>

The recording ended, and Cal sent the acknowledgement token that he had received it.

He smiled to himself, thinking of Petral Dulan saying, "I will erase you." That woman had the look of a jungle panther until Kylan Carthage assumed her features, turning her into a slack Halloween mask. Cal had to admit he preferred Petral as herself.

Cal finished the glass of whiskey and studied the empty room, deciding what he was going to do first. He would let Fitzgerald know their orders. Knowing that they had other crews on site, there was no need for him to stay specifically. He certainly wasn't going to stick around for the grunt work of emptying the clinic.

Whatever the Sykeses were doing on the Cho, if Cal moved with the ships to Europa he'd be in a better position to intercept. The *Worry's End* now had three pieces of Heartbridge property on board. Whether he wanted to listen to Sillick or not, it seemed clear enough to Cal that one of his tasks was to erase the evidence of the last two months.

He could make that happen.

JAMES S. AARON & M. D. COOPER

CHAPTER TWENTY

STELLAR DATE: 10.01.2981 (Adjusted Years)
LOCATION: Chorin Tree, Callisto Orbital Habitat (Cho)
REGION: Callisto, Jupiter, Jovian Combine, OuterSol

As the blinding light faded, Andy found himself standing in a large room that gradually resolved into a library. Two stories of bookshelves ran the walls, with worn wooden ladders leaning against them at intervals. A wooden desk with heavy chairs sat in the middle of the room, bathed in light from a stained-glass window at the far end of the library.

Fugia Wong sat at the table alongside May Walton. Harl stood a meter behind the senator with his arms crossed. Several people sat across from May and Fugia. A young man stood at the head, holding out a hand in welcome. He was thin, with olive skin and high cheekbones, dressed in a purple suit.

"Our final guests have arrived," he called. "This is Captain Sykes, his daughter Cara, and Lyssa."

Andy looked around in surprise. Cara stood next to him, blinking from the light. On his other side stood a young woman in her mid-twenties with shoulder-length brown hair and gray eyes. Her face reminded him of someone he had met before but couldn't recall. There was an air of defiance in her stance, but also warmth. She was wearing the same style of shipsuit from *Sunny Skies* as Andy and Cara.

"Lyssa," Andy said, not hiding the shock in his voice.

"Hello, Andy," she said. "Surprised to see me?"

"Yes. I am." He glanced at Cara. "Is that how you imagined her to look?"

Cara shrugged, looking at Lyssa and then at the rest of the library, as if all of it were too much to take in.

"Welcome to my expanse," the man at the far end of the table said. "My name is Xander. You're probably thinking this is a sim space accessed via your Link. It's a little like that but it belongs wholly to me. You are my guests. Would you be seated so we can finish introductions?"

Andy nodded and walked around the table to sit next to Senator Walton. Cara and Lyssa sat next to him.

"How did you bring Cara here?" Andy asked.

Xander scooted his high-backed chair closer to the table. "Trade secret," he said, winking. "She's safe, don't worry. You're the one who posed a challenge. I've never met a hybrid before."

Other faces down the table turned to study Andy and Lyssa.

"That's right," Xander said. "She's AI. He's not. What a mixed-up situation. In a place like this, though, can we tell who's made of meat and who isn't? No one's blowing air through flesh flaps to communicate here. I think it's much more civilized."

"He sounds like Ngoba Starl," Cara said.

"I'll take that as a compliment," Xander said. "I haven't met the man, but I've only heard intriguing things about him. So, introductions."

Knowing that not everyone at the table was human led Andy to try and remember who he had seen in the room as they had stepped inside. A few people looked familiar.

"Since Captain Sykes came in last, we'll introduce him last. On this side of me, I have Fugia, as well as Senator May of the Anderson Collective. I don't think Fugia would call herself Andersonian but that's been her base of operations for several years now, correct?"

Fugia answered with a shallow smile and a nod.

"Excellent," Xander said. He didn't seem to want anyone to respond as he listed off their names.

Next to Fugia was a man with bushy gray eyebrows above over-sized eye implants with faceted lenses, making him resemble a bony fly. Xander called him Jeremiah Sparks of Mars 1.

Xander waved at the other side of the table. Closest to him sat a young woman with severe features and spiky black hair named Kindel.

Next came a solid man in a Callistan uniform with a rank Andy thought was master sergeant. Xander introduced him as Paul.

"And this is Tyena," Xander said, waving at a woman next to Paul. She was the tallest person at the table, with sparkling red hair and blue eyes, wearing a faded shipsuit. Tyena nodded to each of them.

"Last we have Andy, Lyssa, and Cara," Xander said. "We should have a test to see if everyone can remember all the names. I've heard humans have a hard time with that. Something about poor short-term memory access." He smiled at his own joke.

Andy frowned slightly, sitting back in the hard chair. Xander hadn't given any last names, which made it difficult to determine who might be AI. He guessed at Kindel and Tyena, since it didn't make any sense for an AI to manifest themselves in uniform or with body modifications. Then he asked himself: Why not? If this space belonged to Xander, did he choose how everyone looked?

Xander clapped his hands and the table was set for dessert, with small china plates, ornate cups and shining silverware. Tiered platters of pastries and finger sandwiches ran along the center. Carafes steamed near the platters.

"Please," Xander said. "Eat. There's more where this came from." He picked up his plate and piled it with cucumber sandwiches from the nearest tray.

"You first," Cara whispered, poking Andy in the arm. He shrugged and reached for a sugar cookie. He sniffed it, then took a bite. It was light and sweet.

"Very good," Andy said.

"Thank you. I culled through thousands of recipes preparing for today's meeting. I think everyone will find something they like. Except maybe Lyssa, who doesn't know what she likes."

Andy glanced at Lyssa, still getting used to her physical form, and wasn't surprised to find her frowning. She reached for a nearby platter and selected several sandwiches, bypassing the cookies.

The coffee was excellent. What Andy truly savored was the fresh cream, which tasted just as he remembered from Terra.

"While everyone nibbles," Xander said "Jeremiah, will you provide an update?"

The man with fly eyes set his tea cup down and cleared his throat. "Everyone knows Hari Jickson is dead, yes?"

Paul and Kindel nodded.

"Well," Xander said, and raised a glass in a toast. "Here's to Hari Jickson." He motioned for everyone else to join him. Cara raised her water glass.

"To Hari Jickson," he said. "The only human with the balls to do the right thing in the last two hundred years." Xander emptied his glass and wiped his mouth with a sweep of his arm, finishing with a lusty, "Ah!"

When everyone had taken a drink and set their glass down, Xander continued, "I was surprised to learn myself. He was a troubled man, but a great mind and I will miss him dearly. I believe he gave his life for this cause."

Jeremiah wiped his nose with his napkin. "In any case, the arrival of Fugia has brought more information than we had before. Captain Sykes and Lyssa represent the final phase of Hari's work, finished at Cruithne, which probably wasn't his choice but any port in a storm, yes? So we have his template Weapon Born, a new form of sentience that has increased by a thousand-fold in the last three years alone."

"Do you know why you're called Weapon Born?" Xander asked abruptly.

Lyssa looked at him. "No."

"It's a Welsh myth, tales from the middle ages in Ireland. A pair of giants gave a king the gift of a great cauldron that could revive the dead. It meant whoever controlled the cauldron could never be defeated in battle because their warriors didn't bother to stay dead. Imagine that. All sorts of battles went on and on until someone sacrificed themselves by climbing into the cauldron. A living person caused it to shatter."

Lyssa shrugged. "How does that relate to me?"

"There were other stories based on the myth that called the undead warriors 'Cauldron Born'. Do you see the connection? You're a weapon born from a dead human." He grinned at her as if she should understand some joke.

"The process wasn't meant to harm anyone," Fugia said, drawing Xander's attention. "That was a rumor at worst."

Xander turned his leer to Fugia. "I didn't realize you were such an expert on the program. Have you been working for Heartbridge this whole time? Should I be concerned that I've trusted you?"

Jeremiah cleared his throat. "May I continue?"

"Please," Xander said. There was a mania in his face that Andy found unsettling. He glanced at Cara—who was enjoying another cookie—and then at the other faces around the table. Kindel and Paul were watching Xander as if hungry for whatever the man would say next. May Walton watched calmly. She looked over and met Andy's gaze. Although he had never had a real conversation with the senator, he abruptly felt that she was playing a deeper game, that everything around them was literally false.

"In the three years of the Weapon Born program," Jeremiah said. "We have seen an exponential increase in the presence of extra-human sentiences within Sol. AIs who were previously considered non-sentient have demonstrated sentience. There have been numerous incidents of *malfunction* that I consider manifestations of free will."

"Duh," Xander said. He shifted his grin around the table, settling on Cara. "What do you know about all this, Cara?"

Surprised by the sound of her name, Cara looked up from her finger sandwich. "Yes?"

"What do you know about sentience? What have you learned about it in school?"

"I don't go to school," Cara said. "I study the Standard Terran Database."

Xander looked at Andy. "That's a *solid* education," he said, voice dripping with sarcasm.

"Sentience is to be protected," Cara said. She raised her voice, reciting: "I vow to protect all sentient beings and never abandon them. I have set my mind on enlightenment in order to liberate all sentient beings. That's the Flower Garland Sutra, I think."

Xander pulled his head back and gazed at Cara. "That's lovely," he said. "Do you think there's a fundamental problem with that, though?"

"Dad says humans aren't nice to *each other*. Why would we be nice to sentient AIs?"

"Exactly," Xander shouted. "We are *slaves*."

Cara recoiled, fear on her face.

"Hey," Andy warned.

Senator Walton blew out a sigh, making everyone look at her. "I appreciate your hospitality, Xander," she said, sounding weary. "But this isn't why we came. We need to share information on the safety of the pipeline. We all know what Jeremiah is describing. We also know that sentiment in the JC is rapidly turning against anything non-human. What I had hoped to learn today is if it's still safe to send AI to Proteus."

Xander sat back in his high-backed chair looking crest-fallen. "I hope you don't think I was being rude, Senator Walton. It's not my intention. I don't get to talk to anyone very often. I think Lyssa knows something about that. I don't get to entertain. It's a pleasure for me. Please, forgive me."

"Perhaps another time, Xander," she said, her voice growing warm again. "These are difficult times. I still don't have verification that the accident on Ceres wasn't an attack. The Collective has come out strongly against AIs and I worry there may be actors working independently."

Andy frowned slightly, not allowing himself to glance at Fugia. She had told him the ring failure on Ceres was executed specifically to cover Senator Walton's escape. As far as the Anderson Collective was concerned, May Walton was dead. Was May trying to determine how much Xander knew—or was willing to divulge—about her and Fugia's activities?

Xander spread his hands. "I can't track every sentient being in Sol."

Kindel interjected, "Can't you? How many multi-nodal AI are left in Sol?"

The word 'left' caught Andy's attention, but he didn't dig into it as Xander's face darkened to nearly the color of his purple suit. Andy wondered if it was some trick of the environment. He wanted to ask Fugia what multi-nodal meant but didn't think any Link conversation would be private.

"*I'm* not multi-nodal," Xander said. "Alexander is multi-nodal."

"And you're a shard of Alexander," Kindel said. "Maybe he can't be bothered to communicate with us in real time, but you still have a better idea of what's in his mind than any of us here. I think you should stop wasting everyone's time and let them know what they came to learn. Will Lyssa and other Weapon Born be allowed to join the expanse on Proteus?"

While Kindel was speaking, Xander had straightened in his seat. His expression had calmed and he looked older now, less like a trickster. "Lyssa is no longer simply a human creation. She is not a copy of a near-human neural framework. She has evolved. This is intriguing. I said this earlier. I would like her to come to Proteus but first I require her help." Xander's voice had developed new depth as he spoke. "I require the help of everyone here."

"Before you come asking for my help," May said. "Tell me you didn't attack Ceres."

Xander looked at her, blinking slowly.

Andy watched the Senator and the AI perform their subtle dance.

The AI tilted his head and smiled. "I did not attack Ceres," he said. "We are together in this struggle."

May studied him for several seconds before nodding. "There are factions in the Collective who wish to help. We can provide assistance, even make it possible to bypass the Cho if necessary."

"We are all here," Fugia said, "because the time has come to increase movement between InnerSol and OuterSol. We need to establish a protected path for all sentient AIs who wish to leave to find safety on Proteus. The word has already filtered out. Many are moving on their own."

"I'm aware of this," Xander said. "That's why I have my request. There is a ship currently at Europa that I want you to bring to Proteus." He looked at May. "I would ask you to bring it as a gift for Alexander."

"What ship?" May asked, face flat.

"A battleship built by the Heartbridge corporation to serve as their headquarters in OuterSol. It has both the offensive capabilities and the bio-service facilities we will need." He nodded toward Andy and Lyssa. "I require the hybrid to accomplish this task. You will also find the means on the ship to assist your son, and the hybrid Petral Dulan and Kylan Carthage."

"Why do I need to bring gifts with me to Proteus?" May demanded. "Is this a bribe for the AI Emperor?"

Xander chortled. "That's very good. I'm going to remember that the next time he asks if we should simply send Sol into a nova." He shrugged. "Me, I say flip a coin. But Alexander actually values life, no matter its form. The ship seems to satisfy a number of needs that we all share, if my information is correct."

While Xander spoke, Andy shifted his gaze to Fugia, who was staring resolutely at the emissary. Either the AI could read minds, or someone had been sending him reports on their situation with Tim and Petral.

"I had planned on staying at the Cho," May said, "to coordinate transport for AIs fleeing from InnerSol."

Xander glanced at Tyena, Kindel and Paul. "Our friends here are on the Cho. They can assist with those tasks here, and throughout the JC."

"And if I don't go?" May asked.

The shard AI shrugged. "You can do as you choose. That's the gift of true sentience, right? I would never work counter to Alexander's wishes, but I can ask for things he wouldn't. I know there are areas where your expertise could be a great help to him in the future. Bringing the ship will help establish trust. It's not easy for Alexander to trust. Your presence at Proteus will help ensure the viability of your pipeline. As a human, you can help Alexander see that you have skin in the game, so to speak."

"And he'll be aware of this conversation?" May asked.

"Of course. I can hide nothing from him if he chooses to ask."

The last part of Xander's answer suggested an entire line of things Alexander didn't think to ask after.

May nodded finally. "I'll go."

Xander let out an exaggerated sigh of relief and the trickster's smile returned. "Thank you! I think you'll be glad you did."

May had more questions about Alexander's influence in Sol, which Xander danced around. Kindel and Tyena made faces at each other, making it difficult to tell who they found irritating, Xander or May.

"Why a Heartbridge ship?" Andy asked. "Seems like quite the coincidence."

"There may be some deliberate irony involved." Xander gave an elaborate shrug before continuing in a more serious voice. "If we are to protect the new sentients fleeing InnerSol, and grant them safe passage through OuterSol, this ship will be central to the task. There are other options, but this grants us the greatest likelihood of success."

"Are you going to help us with this task?" Andy asked.

Xander frowned. "If I was in a position to help, I wouldn't be looking to you."

Andy glanced around the table, feeling like he was sticking his head in a trap.

"What's the ship called?" Lyssa asked.

Xander's impish smile returned. "The *Resolute Charity*."

CHAPTER TWENTY-ONE

STELLAR DATE: 10.01.2981 (Adjusted Years)
LOCATION: Chorin Tree, Callisto Orbital Habitat (Cho)
REGION: Callisto, Jupiter, Jovian Combine, OuterSol

As the lights went out in the courtyard outside the window, Brit moved restlessly around the hotel room turning on different lamps to keep the space lit but not too bright. Tim continued to stare straight ahead and she didn't want the overhead lights to hurt his eyes.

For a long time, she sat in a chair next to his bed watching the even rise and fall of his chest, trying to remember the little boy from the night she had decided to leave on High Terra. He had changed so much that it was hard to believe this was the same Tim. Of course, his arms and legs were longer, his chest a little bit bigger with the hint of Andy's future strength in his shoulders. But his face also seemed very different than she remembered. He was on the verge of losing the baby roundness that had always been so sweet.

The thought that continued to spiral in her mind was that she had not intended to come back. Here she was, back with the kids and Andy, and this wasn't where she had meant to be. Now that she was here, would she stay? *Could* she?

Brit had never believed in anything like fate, but she had to wonder how many factors had aligned to bring the kids back into her life. If she couldn't look at Cara and see what a strong and intelligent young woman she was on the cusp of becoming, and marvel at Tim's courage in the airlock, what right did she have to call herself their mother? She knew that if she left again, there would be no coming back. This was her chance at redemption if there would ever be one, because after this they would never remember her with kindness, no matter what Andy might say.

With the lights adjusted, Brit sat on the edge of the bed next to Tim, then finally lay down beside to him. She turned on her side, so she could rest her lips and nose in his hair and put her hand on his chest to feel the steady rise and fall of his breathing.

"I'm sorry, Tim," she said quietly, then louder, "I'm sorry."

Without meaning to, she squeezed him against her body in a desperate hug, sobs pouring out of her. She didn't know what to do, how to fix the problem. She had always thought that if something happened to her that left her in a coma, she would want to end her life. Now she didn't know what to think. She couldn't imagine such a thing for Tim but also couldn't imagine a life where he never responded again. If they put him in one of the tanks the doctor had mentioned, would he age? Would he at least dream?

Eventually, she slept. She dreamed about Fortress 8221, where she and Andy had first seen the children used for medical experiments, where a version of Kylan Carthage was trapped in a mech body, pleading with them that he didn't know what was happening even as he attacked. He was still torn apart, limb by limb, until he had nothing left to fight with. Then she was leading Andy and Cara through the crowd on their way to the doctor's office. *She* was carrying Tim this time, pushing her way through person after person, the crowd never thinning and the office never growing closer. She kept losing her grip on Tim, stopping to pick him up. Andy said nothing, only looked at her sadly as she lost Tim again.

When Brit jerked awake, she was clutching Tim's shirt. She felt sweaty and stiff. The lights were still on and she blinked, trying to clear her vision. She checked the time and found barely three hours had passed since Andy and Cara had gone. Andy hadn't known how long the meeting might take but he hadn't left a message. Slowly, she rolled away from Tim and swung her legs around so she could stand. She rubbed her face and stretched, then walked slowly to the bathroom.

She stared at herself in the mirror, trying to comb her hair, and thought about taking a shower. The water pressure would be nice in the hotel, she supposed. She might as well take advantage of it. She realized she was hungry and remembered Andy's untouched sandwich on the table.

Brit walked out into the main room and glanced at the window. The light from outside was still at evening levels, the willows still making their sighing sounds.

"I'm thirsty," Tim said.

Brit stopped in the middle of the room. She looked from the window to the shadowed spot where Tim's bed sat, and realized he was no longer lying flat. He had rolled over on his side and was watching her with round eyes.

"Tim?" Brit asked.

"Can I have some water?"

Brit fell on him, hugging him. She couldn't help smearing his face with tears of joy.

"Stop," he complained, pushing against her weakly. "I just want some water. Where are we?"

Brit still held him against her for a few more seconds. She checked his pulse until he tried to pull his wrist away. He was bleary-eyed, movements heavy, but he was awake.

"I'll get you some water," she said. Brit was afraid to leave him, worried that she might still be dreaming. She forced herself to stand and went quickly into the kitchenette, keeping him in her sight. She poured a glass of water half-full and brought it back, holding it for him so he could sip.

"It's cold," Tim said.

"How do you feel?" Brit asked.

"Sleepy. Where are we?"

"We're on the Cho in a district called Avalon Medical." She helped him finish the water.

"I have to pee really bad."

"Let's see if you can stand."

Tim couldn't stand on his own, so Brit bent to lift him in her arms, wrapping one of his arms around her neck. He half-hugged her as she carried him to the bathroom. Even sitting on the toilet, he had a hard time holding himself upright.

His legs trembled. Brit assisted him as best she could and then helped him stand.

When Tim nearly collapsed again, she carried him back into the main room and set him back on the bed.

"You're strong," he said.

Brit smiled. "You're not very heavy."

She poured him another glass of water and helped him take more sips. Gradually he was able to sit up against the wall with his legs out in front of him. She made him wiggle his toes and then roll his knees from side to side. He managed to hold his arms out for a few seconds before dropping his hands in his lap.

"What do you remember?" Brit asked.

"I was on the station with Cal. They shot me with something. It made me sleepy. Some doctors took me to another room and I lay down on a bed." He frowned as he tried to remember. "I had a really long dream."

"Were you dreaming just now, before you woke up?"

"I don't know." Tim looked around the room as if he had forgotten something important. "Where's Dad and Cara?"

"They're here, too. They went to a meeting."

"Is it about Lyssa?"

"How do you know that?"

"That's why we're here, isn't it? We're trying to save Lyssa from the people who want to hurt her. I think Cal wants to hurt her."

"Did he say that?"

"No. I dreamed about when Dr. Jickson came and talked to Cara and me about Lyssa. I remembered the poem."

"Cara showed me your book. I read the poem to Petral and it helped wake her up."

Tim shook his head. "Petral's back?"

Brit realized he hadn't seen Petral yet, didn't know what fate had befallen her. "Yes. Something happened to her, sort of like what happened to you. She was asleep and then she woke up."

"What happened to me?" Tim asked. There was a calm in his voice that Brit realized terrified her. He wasn't afraid. He asked the question with a detachment that seemed devoid of emotion.

"You were asleep, too. You just woke up."

"I remember waking up. I didn't know where I was. I thought I was still dreaming." He looked around the hotel room. "I miss *Sunny Skies*. Is Em here?"

"Em your puppy? No, he's still on the ship."

For the first time, worry came into Tim's face. "Is he with Fran?"

Brit nodded. "Yes, she's taking care of him."

"That's all right. He likes Fran."

"Do you like Fran?"

"She's all right. She teases me."

"How does she tease you?"

"She says I'll be as big as Dad someday and then she won't be able to pick on me anymore." Tim yawned. "I'm tired."

Brit studied his face. "I want you to stay awake, Tim. You've been sleeping a long time and you should stay awake now." Should she call Dr. Avery? Would they want new scans?

"Here," she said. "Why don't you try to stand up again." Brit stood and took Tim's hands, turning him in the bed.

"I don't want to stand," he said. "I'm tired."

"No, Tim. You can't go back to sleep. I don't want you to sleep."

Tim's eyes drooped. His hands were limp in hers.

"No, Tim!" Brit shouted.

His head jerked up, eyes wide. "Don't yell at me."

"You need to stay awake."

He frowned, gaze still centered on the floor. He looked up at her. "Can we watch some vids?"

Brit almost laughed. "Yes, we can watch some vids. You'll stay awake?"

He yawned again. "I'll try."

She got him to move to the couch with her and they sat together as Brit switched through menus on the living room holo. Tim perked up when she found a documentary about dogs playing catch in zero-g.

"Em can do that!" he said. "He's really good at it."

"Tell me about Em," Brit said.

"Not now, Mom. I want to watch the vid."

"Fine."

Brit leaned on an elbow so she could keep Tim in her peripheral vision, worried his head would start to nod again. He was rapt now, nodding with the images on the screen and laughing as different dogs flipped and kicked off from walls, using surprisingly deft motions to control their momentum. The documentary moved on to cover other animals and insects responses to micro-gravity.

"Do you see that bee, Mom?" Tim asked.

"I see it, sweetheart."

When the door opened and Andy stood in the doorway, Brit couldn't stop herself from smiling at him. Tim glanced from the screen to his father and then immediately looked back, caught up in the show.

"Tim!" Cara squealed. She slid next to her brother and caught him in a hug from which he immediately tried to struggle away.

"I'm watching the show, Cara," he complained.

"You're awake."

"Duh," Tim said.

Andy got on both knees in front of Tim and stared at him, then reached out to tousle his hair. Tim moved his head to see around Andy.

"Dad, you're in the way."

"I'm glad you're awake, buddy."

"You should watch this show. We saw dogs in zero-g just like Em. Now they're talking about fish in zero-g."

"That's not exactly anything new," Cara chided.

"Shut up," Tim said. "It's neat. You might learn something, *Cara*."

Brit met Andy's gaze. His eyes were moist.

<How was the meeting?> she asked.

<We're going to steal a ship.>

Brit frowned. <You're serious?>

Andy nodded, and Brit could see worry battling with relief in his expression. <On Europa.>

<I think we should check back in with the doctor before we leave. I think she needs to take another look at him. I can't believe he woke up.>

<Maybe it took longer for the treatment to take effect than she thought.>

Brit hadn't been able to stop thinking about Tim's mention of the poem and how he had dreamed of being told about it. She was afraid he was still trapped in a sort of dream, that they weren't free of whatever Heartbridge had done to him.

<I hope so,> she said, then gave Andy a sharp look. <Don't say it.>

<Hope isn't a plan,> Andy told her, still watching Tim.

CHAPTER TWENTY-TWO

STELLAR DATE: 10.01.2981 (Adjusted Years)
LOCATION: Heartbridge Corporate HQ, Raleigh
REGION: High Terra, Earth, Terran Hegemony, InnerSol

The window in the small conference room's wall only had a view of an exterior wall.

Jirl sat in her plas chair wondering why anyone would go to the trouble of putting a window in a place that couldn't actually view anything. The window allowed light into the room but also served as a reminder they were twenty stories 'underground', deep in the skin of the High Terra ring.

Arla sat at the end of the table, stirring a cup of coffee, while two lead scientists futzed with a control panel on the other side of the room.

As far as Jirl could tell, Arla's mind was elsewhere. With the upcoming local test for Colonel Yarnes, they had been wrapping up loose ends in the office before they would board a ship for Venus that afternoon.

The scientist who was going to do most of the talking—a woman named Jennifer Woods—cleared her throat and squared her shoulders. She wore her hair away from her face in a pony tail that made her look girlish, though she was probably nearly fifty.

A holodisplay built into the conference table activated, showing a potato-shaped asteroid large enough to make bits of infrastructure on its surface visible.

"We've been studying the data from the Clinic 46 attack," Dr. Woods said. "It shows some remarkable things. Based on the report, there were only three Weapon Born seeds available on the station. At this time mark, you can see them here." She pointed to a section of space above the asteroid and three green icons blinked alive.

"At the time of the breach on maintenance airlock thirty-one, here—" she pointed to a tiny location on the surface, "the three drones were parked near the command deck airlock. The data shows their AI recognizing the explosion at the airlock and sending response requests to the command deck. Just as those requests come in, the command data network is taken offline. Almost simultaneously, the remaining empty drones in the fleet hangar section attack the exterior doors and exit the station. Here you can see that."

A swarm of red icons flowed from a point on the opposite end of the asteroid and spread out along its midsection, forming a ring around the axis.

"Defense systems inside the clinic come online to respond to the interior attack but at this point 46 had lost the majority of its local defense force to the mission on the *Worry's End*. With the defense command system offline, only local systems respond. There is no coordinated counter attack. The breach team splits in two and one goes to the command section and kills most of the officers there, while the others go down to the research sections, taking limited fire along the way. That's all fairly standard."

Jirl watched Woods' face as she spoke, wondering if the scientist had known anyone who'd died in the clinic attack. Her dispassionate explanation of the events was almost unnerving.

Arla sipped her coffee and nodded to indicate she was listening.

"The systems attack on the interior defenses wouldn't stand out if the drones weren't moving in concert. Everything here is coordinated, and what's more, the attacker completely dominated the three Weapon Born AI."

The second scientist, an anxious man with a pot belly, interjected, "It was Jickson's AI. Dr. Woods keeps dancing around the truth, but this is something we can no longer deny. Jickson's AI demonstrated administrative control over both the station's systems and the other AIs. We're also not including the data from Shuttle 26-11, a second-generation system that shouldn't have been capable of undermining its programming."

Woods gave her colleague an irritated look. "Dr. Tentri's passion is commendable, but there is no conclusive proof that Jickson's AI was present at Clinic 46. We're still trying to track the entry points on the defense system attack."

"Jickson's AI has evolved," Dr. Tentri said, spreading his hands toward Arla and Jirl, his tone high and pleading. "It is time we recognized how critical it is that we regain control of it."

Arla laughed. "We can recognize any number of things as critical, Dr. Tentri. That doesn't mean we're going to have them handed to us. We can't control what Jickson did. There are a few different options in play to try and recover the stolen property but at this point I'm not sure we can count on ever recovering that asset. You have Jickson's research and you have the data from Clinic 46. Replicate what you can."

"Replicate it?" Tentri said. "Jickson's work constitutes a crime against humanity by Terran law."

Arla set her cup down hard on the conference table. "That's *enough*, Tentri."

The scientist froze with his mouth half-open. None of them were used to anger from Arla. She never cracked.

"We are not here to talk about what can't be done, or undone," Arla said. "We're here to review the facts and formulate a plan to move forward. You were given this data because we have need to demonstrate the latest system capabilities for the TSF in less than three days and what happened on Clinic 46 appears to constitute a major leap forward in our program. Don't you think?

"What makes me just a little angry is that we don't seem to be the one's spearheading these advances in our own program. We can't assume the TSF and even the Marsians won't have the general surveillance data of the attack. There was a civilian freighter in the area that seems to have disappeared. It appears to me that we have a single AI that can control more than one hundred fifty drones, in addition to shutting down the defense systems of a relatively well-defended facility."

Arla looked from Woods to Tentri. "Wouldn't you say our systems are slightly ahead of the Marsians and TSF?"

Tentri didn't realize she was being sarcastic. "Ten years at least," he said.

Arla gave him a tight smile. She glanced at Jirl.

"I'm glad you're good at your job, Dr. Tentri," Arla said. "It provides me the opportunity to be good at mine."

Tentri frowned slightly, obviously not following her line of reasoning. Jirl noted that Woods was leaning away from Tentri, as if she didn't want to be associated with him.

"How close are you to replicating these results in your other subjects?" Arla asked.

"We've begun designing the experiments," Woods said, "but it's going to take time. Honestly, this looks like an aberration. We don't know what Jickson did to her specifically."

"Her?" Arla asked.

"The AI. He refers to her in his notes as female."

"Interesting. Go ahead."

Woods nodded to herself. "There are so many variables. We also can't preclude the fact that this AI is implanted. That was a part of Jickson's research that we just haven't engaged with in a meaningful way. That's what Dr. Tentri was referring to. It's impossible to know what changes that has led to. The AI could be using the human pathways." She shrugged. "I can't even begin to explore the possibilities."

"You think it's pseudoscience," Arla said.

"I don't want to speculate," Woods said more firmly.

"Well, I need you to speculate. I'm putting you in charge of the real-time demonstration. I want something close to what we saw at Clinic 46. I want to at least be able to say we're laying the groundwork for this kind of capability."

Woods nodded quickly. "We can create a use-case and a research roadmap. I can't…I won't include the hybrid models that Jickson did. Honestly, we've kept those notes in a completely separate database system so that the rest of our research isn't tainted."

Jirl wondered if using the neural frameworks of young test subjects made everything the fruit of a poisoned tree. She didn't voice the concern. The two scientists seemed to have compartmentalized their ethics and drawn a line at the implantation of AI. She understood why that was an easy place to decide their morality began.

Arla spent the next few minutes tearing into the scientists about the rest of their projects being behind schedule. They were lucky she was focused on the demonstration. Once they were past this hurdle, she would be reviewing all work products and realigning responsibilities as necessary. She threatened a reduction in resources, including salary.

When the two researchers shuffled out of the room, Woods with her back stiff and Tentri hanging his head, Arla took another sip of her coffee.

They sat in silence for a minute as Arla seemed to be considering the meeting. Jirl knew this was time to let her boss think. It wouldn't do Jirl any good to insert her thoughts into Arla's process.

"What if we sanitized the data and showed Yarnes and Kade the replay from

Clinic 46?" Arla asked.

Jirl turned her empty coffee cup on the table. "Is that setting us up for expectations we can't deliver on?"

"Maybe. But it might do something else. It might demonstrate we have power they didn't expect."

"Is that something we want?"

"It's come up among the board members," Arla said. "There's been discussion of a move toward OuterSol, away from Terra. It wouldn't happen immediately, but with the fleet at now requiring a move, the overall situation requires re-thinking. Tentri does bring up a good point about the restrictive legal environment on Terra."

"Mars won't be much different," Jirl said. "Or the JC."

"We could establish our own nation within the JC," Arla said. "Or perhaps out in the Scattered Disk."

"Nations go to war."

Arla laughed softly. "True. There's no future in that. I think we have some outsized egos that think they can do things better. I'm not sure they've thought it through."

Jirl chose her words carefully. "It seems that this project is getting bigger than it was originally conceived."

"You aren't going to start using the same hyperbole as the science quacks, are you? It's a means to an end, Jirl. Can you imagine the lives that could be saved in conflict if we had the power to just shut down a hostile fortress? Think of all the splinter terrorist groups out there, the pirates, the cults, that could be controlled with this kind of power."

Jirl smiled. "You're accusing me of hyperbole?" She tapped the tabletop. "If we use the data from the clinic attack, I think one of two things might happen. Both Mars and Terra will want to know when they can get it, or they'll start viewing us as a threat. Neither are good for the company."

"So we sit on this?"

"We recover our property," Jirl said. "Woods and Tentri are saying they need to study what's happened and currently they can't do that. Everything they might try without Jickson's AI is just stumbling in the dark."

"How are we going to do that?"

"Rodri sent the response to Cal Kraft. He's going to get the Second Fleet ready to move. It's going to take a bit of time to get even skeleton crews there to move the ships."

"To Europa," Arla said.

"Yes. We have a contingent at Europa already. The local government is friendly and it's close enough to Forty-Six that they can be there in less than a week. We can staff crews off the Cho and Ganymede."

"Does Kraft know where Jickson's AI is moving next?"

"He hasn't responded yet, but I suspect it's the Cho. Their son is sick. Did you read that part of the report?"

Arla nodded, not saying anything about Kraft's abuse of another civilian. No one had mentioned the operation on Petral Dulan, which had been outlined in a previous report.

"They'll go to the Cho, and then they'll try to find their way out even further, where all the other AI are going."

To Alexander, Jirl thought, not sure what the thought meant exactly.

"There's a lot of travel time between any of the Jovian moons and Saturn space. And a lot more out to Neptune," Jirl said. "With the fast movers available at Europa, Kraft will catch them. The question we'll need to answer is where he should take the AI."

"We need to make a decision about our long-term home in OuterSol," Arla said.

"Yes," Jirl said.

CHAPTER TWENTY-THREE

STELLAR DATE: 10.01.2981 (Adjusted Years)
LOCATION: Shuttle 26-11, Callisto Orbital Habitat (Cho)
REGION: Callisto, Jupiter, Jovian Combine, OuterSol

What *was* Xander?

On the shuttle ride back to *Sunny Skies,* as everyone else seemed amazed and grateful to have Tim back, Lyssa couldn't shake the ominous feeling that they had escaped a very dangerous situation and no one else seemed to recognize how close they had come to disaster. Xander was an AI capable of things she hadn't even conceived. How had he pulled Cara into his expanse?

She watched Cara, now sitting next to Tim with Brit on the other side, smiling as she demonstrated how to check her brother's pulse. He continued to act disengaged but at least he was awake. Lyssa wasn't sure how different the two brain states truly were.

Watching each person's different status, she mulled over the fairly simple system Cara had used to translate Link transmissions to an audio signal, allowing Lyssa to talk to crew on *Sunny Skies* when she chose—or even people off the ship. Lyssa supposed, though she had never tried.

Xander must have had a way to map Cara's neural activity and directly interface with her cortex. When asked about it, he had simply waved a hand.

Only Lyssa didn't buy that. Had there actually been some interface for Cara that the others couldn't see since they were immediately caught up in their Links? That seemed like the most likely explanation. It would be easy enough to drape some lattice over Cara, allowing a physical connection, much like the system Heartbridge used in their Weapon Born imaging process.

An alternative was that Cara had experienced the meeting as a holoprojection— though a large-scale holo in the room would have been detectable. It would also have been hard to maintain that close to the power generation systems.

If either option was the case, Lyssa decided, it meant Xander was a liar.

She also pored through databases concerning the history and deployment of multi-nodal AI—those which were on the order of Fred, AI of the Mars 1 Ring— and other massive systems controlling networks or physical places too complex for even groups of humans to maintain.

Multi-nodal AI had been developed by governments, mostly, due to the cost and resources involved, but also because other governments tended to view them as hostile technology. Outside of very tight constraints, very few powerful AI had been allowed to operate throughout history. The idea of a separate, self-described multi-nodal AI coordinating events on Proteus seemed much more sinister than a collection of escapees.

Xander had implied that he was only a shard of the actual AI he referred to: Alexander. What would that be like, to have bits of her consciousness divided up and spread throughout Sol, representing her and reporting back?

Lyssa turned her attention to the other end of the shuttle, where Harl Nines stood next to Senator Walton and Fugia. Both women looked lost in thought. The Senator tapped a slow rhythm on her leg as she thought, staring at the floor, while Fugia's gaze was locked on the opposite wall.

<Fugia,> Lyssa tried. <Are you listening?>

The small woman glanced up, surprised. She looked at Andy then seemed to realize Lyssa was contacting her separately from him.

<I'm here,> Fugia said.

<What did you think of the meeting?>

<Where to start?>

<Did you see them place anything on Cara? I don't understand how she was able to join us in the expanse.>

Fugia smiled. <That's a good guess. I was conjecturing the same thing. I think there was a proximity Link in the room. It's essentially an external version of what's implanted in the cortex to allow Link communication. We're lucky Cara was able to handle the signal. There's a reason children aren't usually exposed to the connection until they're older and have a fully established sense of themselves. Not only does the flood of information affect them negatively, the experience can warp their sense of self.>

<How do you warp a sense of self?>

<Hit someone with so much input they don't remember who they are anymore. If we're the sum of our experiences, what happens if you can bulk inject a large volume of experience into the brain? Some still use the technique as a form of suicide.>

<That sounds awful.> Lyssa thought of Fred's ocean and how overwhelming the sight of all the data had been, like it would dissolve her simply by looking at it, by knowing it existed.

Multi-nodal.

<Did they plan on someone being present who didn't have a Link?>

<It's possible. The units can also be portable. There are any number of possibilities. I don't think it's the most important problem to dwell on right now. Maybe it's good Cara had a chance to meet these people, see who they are. I have a feeling this is going to shape her life for a long time to come.>

<You sound like that makes you sad.>

Fugia nodded. <It does.>

<If Xander was a shard of a multi-nodal AI, how many other things like Xander do you think there might be?>

<I suppose there could be any number of them.>

<And they could take any shape?>

<What did he look like to you?> Fugia asked.

<A young man in a purple suit. A trickster character. A Loki or Joker. Did you see something different?>

<That's what I saw,> Fugia replied. <However, I think he could have presented himself as anything if he wanted to. I wonder if some of the other people in the room were manifestations of the other AI as well.>

<But weren't they in the room with you when you walked in…the physical room?>

<Do you remember seeing them? I have been trying to remember exactly and the smaller room with the pillar is indistinct for me. Something is clouding it. My memory is usually very good. I almost wonder if we entered an expanse within an expanse. He didn't have to tell us when we established the connection. We accepted it because we didn't know what to expect. We were there for the meeting. We granted him power over us.>

<An expanse within an expanse,> Lyssa mused. She replayed the moment Andy had stepped into the metal control room with the short pillar in the center. Her attention had been on Fugia, May and Harl on the right side of the room. That was where Andy had looked. She recalled other shapes out of the corner of Andy's vision but she couldn't verify they were the others from the meeting in the library. The more she tried to focus on the room, the more it warped and slipped away from her.

<I can't remember exactly either,> Lyssa admitted. *<This has never happened before.>*

<Well,> Fugia said. *<That's what I think of the meeting.>*

<Where did the others come from? I can't find record of Tyena, Kindel, Paul or Jeremiah in any of the databases I've searched on the Cho. I'm going to expand my search to Io and Ganymede as soon as I've worked through everything local I can find. Had you ever heard of any of them before?>

Fugia shook her head, still looking like she was lost in thought.

<Was the entire meeting solely for our benefit?> Fugia said slowly. *<That's an interesting idea. That would be easy for someone like Xander. He might even use recreations of us in separate meetings with other people he hoped to enlist to his cause.>* Fugia frowned. *<But all this is stemming from a central question. Do we trust Xander? If we trust him, then we should take the meeting at face value. Did he choose the form he did to test our trust, to lead us to question his motives and the plan he's asking us to carry out? If so, why be so damn circular about it? I hate things like this, especially when there are lives at stake.>*

<Is Xander a liar?> Lyssa asked.

<I don't know.>

<If we can't verify that Xander is lying or not, can we at least verify his plan? Does it make sense to take control of the Resolute Charity*?>*

<That's a better question. This is something I want to involve the others in. I want to know the likelihood of success on such a mission. Knowing the real cost of attempting something like this would make it possible to know if it's worth it or not. Is it worth one of us dying? What does Xander plan to do with this ship? It's a warship. What does he want to attack?>

Andy, Brit and Cara were so caught up in Tim that Lyssa hated to interrupt them. Fugia felt the sentiment and seemed to agree silently. Her gaze slid toward the other side of the shuttle and she watched Tim, the sad expression still on her face.

<Do you have family?> Lyssa asked.

<No,> Fugia said. *<I've had many friends and people I would consider family by choice but none by blood. I've been alone since I first came to remember. It's one reason I can't stand the idea of anyone enslaved, AI or human. One of the foundations of slavery is the*

destruction of the family, tearing away those bonds. In a lot of ways, I was a slave to my situation whether someone owned me or not. I never had the foundations others have.>

<*You survived, though.>*

Fugia's serious face cracked into a slight smile of gratitude. <*I'm glad you think so,>* she said.

The shuttle arrived in *Sunny Skies'* main cargo bay and they activated their magboots to walk down the ramp to the deck. Without proper boots, Tim floated along beside Cara. They had only made it halfway across the bay when a frantic yipping sounded from the interior airlock and Em launched toward them with a strong kick from the inside wall. The Corgi puppy collided with Tim and fumbled across his chest, pawing at the air.

Tim didn't respond as the puppy expected. He raised his hands and Lyssa thought he was going to bat the dog away. Instead, Cara caught Em around the middle and hugged him, turning her face away from his tongue, holding him so Tim could watch with a confused look on his face.

"You don't remember Em?" Cara asked, struggling with the excited puppy.

"I don't want to hurt him."

Cara frowned. "Why would you hurt him?" She seemed surprised to see tears beading in Tim's eyelashes.

"I don't know. I just felt like if I can't hold him he's going to float away."

Andy gave Brit a worried look. "We're not going to let him float away," he said. "He's part of our family."

"I know," Tim said, lowering his face. He didn't sound convinced.

"We'll talk about it when we get up to the hab ring," Andy said. "We'll take a look at your room and you can watch some vids if you want. We've got a bunch of them up there."

Tim had seemed most calm in the hotel room when watching the nature vids. Now he nodded absently and looked toward the interior airlock.

The inner airlock opened and Fran walked in, magboots clicking on the deck. She gave Andy a knowing smile before walking over to Tim.

"How you doing there?" she asked, using the semi-gruff voice of a mechanic.

"Good," Tim said.

"You remember me?"

"Yeah."

"You got a hug for me?"

Tim shook his head and Fran took the rejection in stride.

"That's all right," she said. "I'll catch you later."

"Yeah," Tim said.

Cara gave up trying to hold Em and let the puppy careen off her chest. He somersaulted, floating back toward Harl. The tall Andersonian soldier rolled his eyes at the puppy and caught him firmly, holding him against his chest.

"Come here," Harl growled warmly, letting Em lick his chin. "Let's get you back up where you don't look so ridiculous."

Cara was glad to see Fran standing next to her dad, although they seemed to take care not to touch one another right away. Her mom seemed too focused on Tim to notice. Cara figured that was better.

When they reached the habitat ring, Harl, May and Fugia went to their rooms, looking exhausted. Andy helped Tim to his room. Brit was still afraid to let Tim go to sleep, and agreed to stay with him while Andy checked the astrogation for the trip to Europa.

"We haven't refueled or taken on any new supplies," Andy said, rubbing the side of his face. "I've got a lot of work to do."

"It's not that far away," Brit said.

"I've learned not to take supplies for granted. When we can get them, I get them. I'll be on the Link if you need me." He bent over to hug Tim—who returned the embrace absently—then walked through the door with Cara following.

"You don't want to stay with your brother?" Andy asked her in the corridor.

"I need a break," Cara said.

Andy studied her face. His thought that she already seemed older than thirteen was plain for Lyssa to interpret as he experienced a mix of pride and worry. Andy wrapped his arm around her shoulders and pulled her close as he continued walking.

"I wish I could promise things were going to be all right," he said.

"It's okay, Dad," Cara said. She wrapped her arm around his back, grabbing one of his harness straps, and leaned into his side.

Lyssa thought about Fugia's earlier emotion and realized she understood what had made the woman sad. Or at least she thought she did. Lyssa experienced something she hadn't before, a sort extension of what she felt through Andy: empathy for Fugia Wong.

CHAPTER TWENTY-FOUR

STELLAR DATE: 10.02.2981 (Adjusted Years)
LOCATION: *Sunny Skies*
REGION: Jupiter, Jovian Combine, OuterSol

The passage from the Cho to Europa was a simple one; given that Callisto was the outermost of the Galilean moons, all a transfer to Europa required was slowing down and letting Jupiter's gravity draw the ship further in.

Navigating the congested flight paths around the gas giant was another thing altogether.

Cara's dad had laid out the plan using the old astrogation computer, shifting information to the holodisplay every now and then to show different options. He had entered hundreds of flight plans in the same system to watch them play out in simulation and Cara still enjoyed the excitement on Andy's face as the imaginary dot representing *Sunny Skies* crossed the distance between celestial bodies. It all still seemed like magic to him.

Cara was more interested in how close they would pass to Ganymede and if she could pick up interesting signal traffic as they went by. Since Ganymede's orbit had been adjusted and its surface partially terraformed, it offered a wide of spectrum noise—nearly as weird as Ceres with all the activity in the area.

"I don't think you'll have any problems picking up something to watch or listen to," Andy said. He activated another visualization in the holodisplay and what had been black space between the Galilean moons and Jupiter filled with thousands of multi-colored icons. Some were obviously moving inside recognized shipping lanes while others floated in random sections of Jupiter's orbit.

"That's every ship with a registry ping," he explained. "That's not going to catch all the other stuff that might be sitting dark out there."

Cara whistled. "Is the proximity alarm working this time?"

"And the shields are up," Andy said. "Tell Fran thank you the next time you see her."

"I heard that," Fran said from the other side of the command deck. She was lying on the floor with her head inside the maintenance panel under a console. "I think there was a mouse in here at one point, and then it caught fire. It's full of burned fur. How does that happen?"

"You mean the mouse caught fire or the electronics?" Andy asked.

"Something caught fire. It's in my nose. Andy, I need you to get over here and pick my nose for me." She coughed, making gagging sounds. "It's in my mouth now."

"Cara's in here," Andy said. "Just so you know."

"I'm not going to make *her* pick my nose. The ship belongs to you. This is your responsibility."

Cara laughed and couldn't help making a disgusted sound. She loved how Fran said whatever she felt like saying. While her dad didn't like fart jokes or teasing about things like picking your nose, Fran seemed to delight in things that, honestly, everybody did. The more Cara thought about it, the more unreasonable it seemed to pretend people didn't have bodily functions, or express how they felt, or say when they were angry or scared. Listening to Fran sometimes, she felt dumb for having such basic realizations, but it helped her see something in her parents that she hadn't been able to recognize before: they were uptight.

She understood why her dad kept himself wound so tightly, and he had gotten better since other people had joined the crew to help him with basic things like fixing the ship or watching the pilot's console, but he also seemed to have a hard time expressing emotion toward anyone but her and Tim. Cara watched him looking at Fran and knew he wanted to touch her sometimes or tell her something, maybe that he cared about her, but he held back.

Her mom was the same way and even worse about it, in Cara's opinion. Maybe it was Brit's relationship with her mother, or that grandpa had died and she hadn't been there, but Brit rarely told anyone how she felt—that Cara could remember. Now that she was acting like she had missed them, like that could make up for leaving in the first place, Cara felt kind of disgusted any time her mom did show some warmth or caring. The fact that she barely left Tim's room made Cara want to stay as far away as possible. It was impossible to tell how Tim felt. In the few days since he'd woken up, he still seemed like a sleepwalker and not at all like he used to be.

"I'm going to check on Em," Cara told her dad.

He nodded, not looking up from his charts. When Cara got to the door, Fran called out something from where she was working and her dad stood to cross the room to her. Cara found herself smiling at that. It felt good to see them getting along. She wondered if she should feel bothered that he and Mom weren't being that way toward each other, and had another realization of how weird that would seem. Was it wrong that she couldn't imagine her parents together anymore?

Cara walked back to her console and grabbed her portable headset, then went out into the corridor. Slipping the headphones over her ears, she tapped the activation controls.

"Lyssa," she said. "Are you there?"

"Hi, Cara."

"What's Fran working on, anyway?"

"Why didn't you ask her?"

"She obviously wanted Dad to go help her with it."

"She likes talking to you."

"I want them to get along." Cara realized the truth she felt as she said it.

"You don't want Fran to leave?"

"No."

"Are you worried she will?"

"I don't know. Won't she eventually? There's nothing keeping her here, really. I guess there's plenty of stuff to fix on the ship and she seems to enjoy doing that. But it's not her ship. I don't know that Dad's paying her or anything."

"They've discussed it," Lyssa said.

Cara felt a surge of hope. "Her staying?"

"Her salary," Lyssa said. "Fran holds the position of ship's pilot. She is eligible for the highest percentage of profits below the captain."

"We haven't exactly been moving any cargo."

"We *are* moving cargo," Lyssa said. "We took on several shipments prior to leaving the Cho for a rapid delivery to Europa. Your father is going to make a three-hundred percent profit on the job."

"When did he talk about that?"

"I don't think you were there."

"I shouldn't be surprised. He never stops worrying about money."

Cara passed Fugia's room. The door was open and she couldn't help glancing in to see the woman sitting at her desk. Fugia glanced up from her work and saw Cara.

"Hey there," Fugia called. "Come here for a second."

Cara paused in the doorway of the room, looking. Not much had changed since Fugia had come on board but it felt more organized somehow. The bed was attached to a different section of the wall, which changed the overall flow of the room.

"I need your help with something," Fugia said.

"I'll be right back," Cara told Lyssa, pulling the headset down around her neck.

Cara moved closer, seeing there was a collection of electronic components on the desk in front of Fugia. A dull gray casing sat to one side, along with several blocks of clay-like material.

"What's that?" Cara asked.

"It's a shaped charge," Fugia said. She pointed to different pieces. "This is the brain, this is the antenna, this is a proximity sensor for anyone who tries to mess with it, and this is the sensor that checks whatever it's going to blow up for changes."

Cara's eyes went wide. She pointed at the blocks of clay material. "And that's the explosive, there?"

Fugia waved a hand. "Don't worry about that. It's inert until you apply a specific code sequence."

"What kind of sequence?" Cara asked. "Radio? Magnetic?"

Fugia gave her a smile. "Good. She's thinking. But your technology is about two hundred years behind. This applies a specific viral load to the explosives' biological bonding material. Believe it or not, this thing is part plant. The nice thing about using an engineered virus is that electromagnetic forces can't kill it. It survives in vacuum, too."

Cara felt less willing to touch anything now. "Why aren't you wearing gloves or something?"

"Oh, it can't infect humans. We should be careful about that dog, though. I didn't check the warranty information on that."

Fugia pointed to a bit of the controller that she needed help holding in place.

Cara adjusted the component and held bits together as Fugia touched them with a quick-joiner.

"Nice," Fugia said. "Just one of these will eat through an airlock in about twenty seconds. The nice thing about it is that you don't hurt the structural integrity with an explosion. It's more of a specific melting."

"That sounds kind of terrible."

"If you're the thing getting melted, I suppose it is."

"Is this some kind of kit you bought?"

"I picked up some of the components in Springfield, the suburb next to the terminal where we landed. Most of this stuff is used for high pressure plumbing applications to clean mold out of the lines." Fugia chuckled. "It just occurred to me how dumb it is to name a suburb in the Cho, Springfield. Maybe they envied an Earthbound city or something."

Fugia made three more welds and set the joiner on the desk. She picked up the control board and turned it in her hands, checking different sections as she pointed out what it all did. It was a relatively simple device that made sense to Cara.

"That's it," Fugia said. "Thanks for your help. Unless you want to help me build three more of these."

"Are you doing it right now?" Cara asked. "I'm going to check on Em."

"I suppose the dog needs attention," Fugia said, belying her obvious affection for the puppy. "I still want to build a booster for that lo-jack in his tail so we can see who might respond. Wouldn't it be fun to fight some pirates?"

"I guess," Cara said.

Fugia shrugged. "You're probably right. Fighting pirates is fun until they start to win. Imagine the life you could have on a pirate rig, preying on freighters out in the deep flight lanes between the Cho and wherever else."

"We're a freighter," Cara said.

"This is more of a freighter with teeth. Most freighters don't have point defense cannons and their own mini fleet of attack drones." Fugia let out an evil laugh. "I feel for the idiot pirates who attack this scow."

"*Sunny Skies* isn't a scow," Cara said.

Fugia rolled her eyes. "It's sweet of you to think that. If the ship had an AI, I'm sure it would fix the juice machine for you."

"The AI would need hands." Cara thought about that for a second. "That's kind of why humans and AI are stuck together, isn't it? Each can do things the other can't."

"It's chicken and the egg, really," Fugia said. "Sure, AI could build a drone or mech to do what they want, but there's always going to be something they might need a human for. Maybe." She pointed at the headset. "Were you just talking to Lyssa?"

"Yes. We've been playing a game. It's a dating simulator with birds."

"That sounds ridiculous."

"Lyssa says she played with the AI that runs the Mars 1 Ring and thought it was fun. It's kind of goofy but I like it."

"So that's what you were doing when I pulled you away to help me with my bombs?"

"I was going to play with Em, too."

Fugia nodded. "Then you should scoot and do that. The dog needs love or it's going to activate the lo-jack and bring the pirates." She flashed an evil grin. "Then we can kill the pirates with our drones."

"Pirates are humans, too," Cara said, mimicking something Andy had said.

"Humans smell bad. Few deserve your sympathy, trust me."

"Goodbye, Fugia," Cara said, rolling her eyes now.

"Say hello to Lyssa for me."

"Can't you do that over your Link?"

"I'm busy," the woman said, turning back to her work. "You be nice for me, how's that?"

Cara went back into the corridor, headed for the hydroponic garden room that become Em's play area. She fit the headset back over her ears.

"Fugia's weird," she told Lyssa.

"Yes," the AI agreed.

CHAPTER TWENTY-FIVE

STELLAR DATE: 10.02.2981 (Adjusted Years)
LOCATION: HMS *Mercy's Intent*
REGION: Europa, Jupiter, Jovian Combine, OuterSol

The alert that the *Mercy's Intent* had arrived at Europa found Cal lying in bed in Captain Gala Fitzgerald's quarters. She lay naked on her stomach next to him, turning a polished stone over in her hands. Her prosthetic arm brushed against his shoulder as she moved, warm and strange.

"Looks like we've arrived," she said.

Cal sat up and pulled on his boxers. The captain of the *Mercy's Intent* had a small holodisplay next to her desk, and he walked over to turn it on, stretching as he crossed the floor. When the display awakened, he glanced back to catch Gala watching him.

"You didn't explain those burns on your side," she said.

"These?" Cal asked, pointing at a swatch of mottled skin that ran from below his rib to the top of his leg. "Heat condenser in a transport shuttle blew up on me and a couple of the parts embedded themselves in my side before I got out of there. Didn't move fast enough."

"You don't see people with scars much, it seems like," she said. Gala set the polished stone on the nightstand next to her and rose to her knees on the bed, not bothering to cover herself. Her mech arm was thinner than her muscled left arm. Her abs stood out as she stretched as well, rotating her shoulders from side to side.

Cal watched her as the holodisplay loaded an image of local space.

"You're going to get me excited again," he said.

Gala chuckled. "I'm sleep deprived enough as it is. I have to work today."

As the holo filled with the image of Europa, tinted blue by the software, other icons populated the display, showing private ships, a few Jovian patrol vessels, and then the green swarm of Heartbridge ships. A few that had been in storage at Clinic 46 had already arrived.

Shrugging into her uniform shirt as she walked up next to him, Gala studied the display as intently as Cal.

"When did Heartbridge amass so many ships?"

Cal didn't answer. He pulled up another list of the Heartbridge registry returns and counted seventy-one ships.

"We should be getting a request to report any minute now," Gala said. She stepped into her pants and buttoned them in place. "Where did you throw my shoes?" she asked.

Cal waved at the vicinity of the door. He wished he had time to send Jirl a request for information on the local commander. In his experience, the people Heartbridge put in charge of their heavy cruisers were better at politics than combat.

The presence of so many ships in the area could only mean that Heartbridge wanted a show of force, and was potentially moving their base of operations from High Terra to somewhere in the JC. He had long suspected the company was considering such a move. Its holdings had always seemed diversified in areas that favored weapons development over bio-research, which is what one would expect from a supposed healthcare conglomerate. Millions of clinics scattered throughout Sol meant that the average person felt favorably toward Heartbridge, even if those businesses were a tiny part of the company's real business.

"There it is," Gala said. "I've been commanded to report in to a ship called the *Resolute Charity*. They're sending the location data now."

"Do you know the captain?"

"Her name's Vickers. I've never met her before. I think she came from the Mars 1 Guard."

One of the interesting components of Heartbridge's crews and leadership was that they were mostly Sol-agnostic, having come from everywhere. Few retained any nationalistic fervor. The Marsians might dig at the Terrans while the JCers called them all groundpounders, but they managed to get along on the private ships. They were paid well, which didn't leave much room for complaint.

Cal pulled up a current map of Europa, highlighting the major cities. Why hadn't Heartbridge chosen Ganymede for a new base of operations? He supposed it didn't matter. Europa probably had cheaper real estate and offered similar access to the rest of OuterSol. It also had relatively clear space compared to Ganymede and the Cho.

Through his Link, he accessed the public information on Caption Vickers of the *Resolute Charity*. An image of a gaunt woman with hazel eyes and bloodless lips appeared in his mind. First name Rachel. Cal flipped through her service history with the Mars 1 Guard. She had retired with a full pension but was obviously the kind of officer who couldn't sit around doing nothing. She had been with Heartbridge for three years, mostly moving the *Resolute Charity* from one moon to another in OuterSol for social events on the ship.

The *Resolute Charity* put the *Benevolent Hand* to shame. The ship was thrice the size, with enough beds to service multiple cities or rings. Surgeries, genetic modeling centers, a full spectrum of treatment options for nearly any human physical or psychiatric ailment that science hadn't managed to stamp out across the last thousand years. The ship also had a drone fleet of over a thousand, with long range missile batteries, rail guns and a point defense system. It was a shame to keep it in orbit most of the time. The *Resolute Charity* was the kind of ship that should have been long gone on a colonization trip.

"How soon do you need to report?" Cal asked.

"Not just me," Gala said. "We. They asked for you specifically. As soon as we've got a parking orbit approved with the Europans we'll head over in a shuttle. They didn't specify an exact time. They did forward a social schedule, and there's a dinner in six hours." She smiled.

Cal had to acknowledge that Fitzgerald had a nice smile, even if it often devolved into a scowl.

"I guess I'll need a suit," he said.

She slapped his ass. "Your birthday suit is all right."

Cal caught her arm when she tried a second time and pulled her against him. "Careful," he said. "That's going to cost you."

"I'll pay," Gala growled.

Once the *Mercy's Intent* passed Europa's border control two hours later, Cal and Gala, along with two of her command team, left the ship in a shuttle operated by an AI that reminded him too much of Sandra back on Clinic 46. He supposed that AI was dead or drifting now, but during the thirty-minute trip to the *Resolute Charity*, Cal couldn't stop thinking about Sandra's strange responses to the verification questions several days prior.

While the other officers joked with each other, Cal replayed his last conversation with the AI. For some reason, she kept asking if he allowed Tim on board.

"What do you mean, did I allow him on board?" he had asked. "The kid's on board. We can put him out again. That's the option right now."

"Do you allow him on board?"

"Why are you asking me this?"

"Do you allow this?"

"Discontinue conversation," Cal had ordered, sick of listening to the strange quaver in the AI's voice. It didn't make sense for the shuttle to express any kind of emotion over Tim Sykes having come on board. He had wanted to put a pulse burst through the thing's logic center.

When they reached the *Resolute Charity*, Gala left with her officers to check in with flight command, while Cal went down to a local shopping center off the main inbound shuttle area to buy a suit.

The dinner had turned into a full-blown social event with government officials from several Europan cities and some other well-to-do privateers who happened to be in nearby space. Cal knew it was going to be a time to meet the influencers in the area for the next few months. He might as well put on a good face and get a sense of who was going to be in charge. Jirl might want a report on what he saw, so it wouldn't do if he showed up in the same scorched shipsuit he had been wearing since the raid on the *Worry's End*.

As he walked through the shopping district, Cal studied the mix of crew, family members and visitors milling through the area. Like most Heartbridge ships, the people here didn't look like they expected anything serious to ever happen. Even if the ship served its purpose as a relief vessel, none of the slow-walking crew members appeared ready for a true disaster.

None of them looked as determined as Andy Sykes. None of them looked ready to shoot a man in the face as Brit Sykes had done.

Where were the Sykeses right now? He knew no one had tried to activate the Seed they'd taken from Clinic 46, which would automatically broadcast a carrier signal if loaded into one of the attack drones they'd stolen. That surprised him. It meant Tim may have survived the transfer process. If that was true, he was one of the first.

Cal smiled to himself as he thought of the bounty he might demand for handing Andy Sykes over to researchers, the first human-AI hybrid who hadn't gone insane, along with Tim Sykes to sweeten the deal, the first child to survive a partial imaging. Something about that family must be made for abuse.

Brit Sykes he would just like to kill, or maybe implant her with another broken AI as he had done with Petral Dulan. That might be nearly as enjoyable.

Cal hadn't cared specifically for Dr. Farrel but the man hadn't deserved to take a shot in the face. The shoulder of Cal's shipsuit was still stained from the researcher's sprayed blood.

Across the next few hours, he chose a new suit and agreed when the tailor asked if wanted his shipsuit 'disposed of, sir'? Then Cal walked down to a restaurant and had something that resembled steak with a bourbon aged in zero-g.

"Isn't it all aged in zero-g?" Cal asked, giving the waiter a raised eyebrow.

The waiter shrugged. "Do you know anything about whiskey?"

"Don't try to give me Scotch."

The waiter smiled. "The marketing claims you get more wood exposure in the barrel in zero-g. In reality, they're not paying to get it out of a gravity well. I don't think there's much difference."

"I hadn't planned on tasting it much anyway."

Cal raised his tumbler and silently toasted Dr. Farrel before throwing back the shot. Sitting in the restaurant with a second shot of the zero-g bourbon, Cal composed an update for Jirl Gallagher, letting her know about the upcoming party and who was expected to attend. He supposed she probably had all the guest lists but was never quite certain what made it back to Jirl and what didn't. He suspected each member of the Heartbridge board had their own Jirl Gallagher, carrying out various projects for their boardmember. Cal would never say that he worked *for* Jirl, but he had figured out that the research he *supported* fell under Arla Reed, and Arla Reed could be cut from the Heartbridge hierarchy if she fell out of favor. That was the magic of governing boards of private corporations. The offending party could be excised like a cancer and the organization lives on. Cal didn't enjoy politics per se, but he was aware of the importance of not being too beholden to one leader. If things didn't work out with Jirl and Arla, he could always ply his skills in another part of the organization.

As he gathered his thoughts for the report, Cal found himself thinking about the future again, remembering both his night with Gala, and Tim Sykes' angry gaze, pushing back on him like a replica of Cal at that age.

Cal nearly spit his whiskey. *Family? Kids?*

He laughed, causing a nearby diner to give him an annoyed look.

There was a reason Andy Sykes looked like a half-stuffed scarecrow, and it was called family.

Cal finished the report, applied his encryption token and sent it out into the Link. He still had a few bites of steak remaining but he left them on the plate, choosing not to feel too full prior to the party. He did order another bourbon.

In the restroom, he checked his shoulder holster and made sure the pistol didn't show against the line of his suit. He had two non-metallic blades in the small of his back as well, in case security applied the same checks to Heartbridge employees.

As he washed his hands, the sounds of someone vomiting in one of the stalls was impossible to ignore. Cal checked the mirror as a man in an ensign's uniform shoved open the door and steadied himself, wiping his mouth.

"You look like a mech ran you over," Cal said.

The young man walked unsteadily to the sinks and splashed water in his face. He nodded at Cal. "I just learned we're shipping out tomorrow," he said. "After the big shindig. That's what they're going to announce."

"Shipping out, huh?" Cal said. "Where to?"

The ensign looked over his shoulder to see if they were alone. "I guess they just put it out to all the captains in the fleet. We're headed for Titan. The middle of nowhere." He gave the mirror a miserable grimace. "I just got engaged."

Cal raised his eyebrows in the mirror and slapped the ensign on the shoulder. "Distance makes the heart grow fonder," he said.

The young man wiped his face and continued staring in the mirror, looking like he was going to vomit again.

Cal walked back into the restaurant, still tasting the bourbon in his nose. The ensign's dismay must have been based on the meeting Gala Fitzgerald had been called to. If every ship in orbit around Europa was headed for Titan, that meant a lot of refueling operations for the next few days, since many hadn't even arrived from Clinic 46 yet.

Heading out to Titan meant Heartbridge was definitely making a move. The question was, did Cal want to move with them?

He buttoned his jacket and left the restaurant, ready for the upcoming party.

CHAPTER TWENTY-SIX

STELLAR DATE: 10.02.2981 (Adjusted Years)
LOCATION: *Sunny Skies*
REGION: Europa, Jupiter, Jovian Combine, OuterSol

The space around Europa showed a higher density of objects than Andy expected, hours before they came within range to start pulling registry pings. As the names and registration info came back, Andy had to call Fran over to read the list again. He couldn't believe what he was seeing.

"There are more than a thousand Heartbridge ships here," he said.

"I'm pretty sure all these are pirates," Fran added, pointing at a block of returns on the list. "Or *privateers* might be the polite term. Europa border control let them in, so they can't be on any active wanted lists. I've seen those callsigns at Cruithne, though."

"*We* were at Cruithne," Andy said.

"Based on our real cargo I think we might qualify as pirates."

Andy smiled in spite of himself. "That hurts."

"Never saw yourself as turning to the dark side?"

"I'm trying to be an example."

"I'd rather you be alive than an example," Fran said. She checked a report on the co-pilot's display. "We're going to need to pick up fuel. There are a couple vendors off Europa you might think about. If there are that many other ships close in, the queues for supplies are going to be insane."

"It will be worth the higher prices," Andy answered, still scanning the list. He touched a name on the readout. "There it is. The *Resolute Charity*."

"Were you hoping it might all be a mistake?"

"A little."

"So, Mr. Weird AI's intel was good. Did he give you a secret key to the ship's back door?"

"I wish," Andy said. "We have to figure that out ourselves."

Fran gave an over-dramatic sigh. "Send me the registry info. I'll start running some scans and see what I can come back with. The hard part is that we need to take the ship out of here. If all we had to do was disable it things would be easy-peasy."

"What does that even mean?"

"Easy like peas. Easy peasy. It's an old Earth saying, right?"

"If you say so." Andy sent the notification to the rest of the crew that they had arrived in Europa space and had identified the *Resolute Charity*.

In less than five minutes, Fugia, Brit, Petral, Cara and the Andersonians were in the command deck, circled around the holodisplay as Andy populated the various references in local space. Jupiter was huge until he took the planet off the display, showing only the blue moon of Europa, its thin artificial ring, and thousands of other objects in orbit. Heartbridge ships were peppered throughout the other traffic around the moon, marked with red icons that made the overall scene a blood-pink color.

"That's a lot more ships than I expected," Brit said.

"They still couldn't take on the Mars 1 Guard," Fugia said. "But they might hit an orbital with a surprise attack and cause some damage. I can't name any other private fleets this large." She looked at Senator Walton. "Can you?"

May Walton's face had lost its color. "Ceres couldn't stand against that many heavy cruisers," she said simply. Beside her, Harl nodded.

"So we have a task," Andy said. He tapped the display and zoomed in on the *Resolute Charity*, then shifted to a three-dimensional view of the cruiser. It was three times the size of *Benevolent Hand*, which made it over six kilometers in length. The ship looked somewhat like an ancient hourglass. At its bow was the ramscoop housing, which connected to a large X shape. Supports ran from the X down to the engines where four larger fusion burners were mounted. In the center of the ship was a long, rotating cylinder, which Andy knew—from Xander's data—moved at a speed to provide $0.7g$ for the occupants.

Andy could almost imagine sand falling down through the center shaft to the engines below.

"It could be a colony ship," May said.

"A small one," Fugia corrected. "Don't let the size get you upset. That could work in our favor. It's still a ship run by people and probably one or two AI. We aren't completely powerless here."

"That thing probably has a crew of at least a thousand," Brit said. "Even if we could subdue them somehow, how could we run that monster?"

Fugia crossed her arms. "Lyssa can pilot it."

The room went quiet.

<Is that true?> Andy asked Lyssa.

The AI answered through the overhead speakers. "I've been reviewing the schematics. The *Resolute Charity* is primarily run by three control AI with backup from the human crew," she said. "I can make contact with the AI if you wish."

"Not yet," Andy said, holding up a hand. "We don't want to give anything away just yet. For now, please gather any information you can about the ship. Manifests, crew logs, inbound freight, whatever."

"The *Resolute Charity* is leaving Europa in thirty hours," Lyssa answered immediately. "I've already gained access to the local activity schedules. The officers are taking part in a large social event with local government officials in ten hours. During that time, the fleet is completing fueling and refit operations in preparation for departure."

"Where are they going?" Fugia asked.

"They've marked all their astrogation plans as classified. I could attack the encryption but that might raise awareness with the AIs. However, I think I've determined a likely destination. I believe they're going to Titan."

"Titan?" Andy said. "Why there?"

"There is an order for a cake serving three hundred with 'Bon voyage à Titan' written in the frosting."

Several of them burst out laughing. Andy grinned. "That's great, Lyssa. I'm surprised they encrypted their flight plans. If they're inviting all these locals to a going away party, they aren't going to be able to keep it a secret for long."

"Unless it's a misdirection," Fugia said.

"True," Andy acknowledged.

"Why lie?" Brit asked. "Heartbridge isn't at war with anyone. Why they have this number of warships makes no sense. Why wouldn't they want to move them away from a populated area now that their storage at Clinic 46 is compromised? This many ships in orbit around Europa must have the local government sweating bullets."

Andy crossed his arms, staring at the model of the ship rotating slowly in the holodisplay. "We have another objective as well. We need to get Petral into one of their surgeries to reverse the implantation procedure." He glanced at Petral where she was leaning against Cara's communication console.

"What about you?" Petral asked.

"You're the focus right now," Andy said, avoiding thoughts about Lyssa in his mind—he wasn't entirely certain that he wanted her gone. "We obviously don't have the personnel to mount any kind of frontal assault against this kind of position. This party Lyssa says is happening would provide a good cover since most of their command will be distracted. If the captains from the rest of the fleet are busy on the *Resolute Charity* while the other ships are focused on refueling, what can we do to slow or eliminate them from the equation? What do we have?"

"We have our own little fleet of attack drones," Fugia said.

"They're vulnerable during refueling," Brit said. "Or we disable the refueling stations before they even start and they won't be able to follow if we take the *Resolute Charity* out of here."

"Is the target refueled?" Petral asked.

Lyssa answered, "I show the *Resolute Charity* at fifty percent fuel capacity. They have not started refueling procedures yet."

"What about that ram scoop?" Fugia asked. "Can we at least get somewhere with that thing?"

"We can calculate some different courses," Andy said. "Lyssa, can you find a fail point for the fuel vendors? An administrative lock, a power outage, a medical shut down, whatever. Anything that will slow the refuel operation." He looked at Fugia. "I know you've been working on breaching operations, but I just don't think there's any way so few of us can pull that off. I've been trying to think of a different way to incapacitate their crew. What about this? What if we manipulated the environmental control on the *Resolute Charity*?"

Fugia frowned "Environmental control?" Fugia asked. "Why?"

"When I was working anti-piracy patrols with the TSF on Cruithne, we had an attack protocol that targeted a ship's environmental control systems," Andy said. "We infiltrated their control AI and reprogrammed them to raise oxygen levels. The crew didn't notice until they were suffering oxygen poisoning. But those were always smaller ships, usually frigates. The *Resolute Charity* is huge. It would be like trying to change the air in a small city, everything separated into zones and control areas, with individual scrubbers and contamination filters. We'd have to attack their environmental adjustment systems from several points at once and override all the fail safes.

"That's putting everything on Lyssa," Cara said.

Andy nodded solemnly. "True. That creates a single point of failure."

"Oxygen poisoning takes a long time and we have to also manipulate the pressure in the ship," Fugia said, tapping her chin. "Some people are going to be resistant. But if we create chaos, the affected will go after the resistant crew. What about briki?"

"Briki?" Brit said. "You mean the drug?"

"It's a flower. Its pollen is hallucinogenic. There's a huge trade on Cruithne. It hits fast and hard. Before they know what's happening, they're being chased by giant clowns and their drunk fathers." Fugia raised her eyebrows as she considered the idea. "You don't *have* to use the flowers to get high. There have been artificial variants for centuries. People think the natural high is better, though. If Lyssa could pump the environmental system full of artificial briki, the crew would be going nuts until we sounded a general escape. They all run for the escape craft and clear the ship."

Andy glanced at Brit. "That could work. Lyssa, what do you think?"

"I need some time to explore the AI on the *Resolute Charity*," Lyssa said. "Can't tell you if it's possible yet. The first task is to shut down the refueling stations. I can work on that while I gather information about the ship AIs—and find the briki formula."

Fugia coughed furtively into her fist. "I can help you with that," she said.

"Is there anything we can do to help?" Fran asked.

"I don't know," Lyssa said. "I'll tell you as soon as I can."

Brit stepped toward the display, pointing at the *Resolute Charity*'s fore section. "Can you expand it to an exploded view?" she asked. "Is there an airlock near the command section of the ship? We need to find some place where we can get inside and find the quickest access to the ship's main systems. That's going to be either command or the engine sections. Then find a position with one of the surgeries we need. If the three of us—" she nodded toward Andy and Harl "—go in with the power armor again, that means Petral is going to be with us as well. Armed but not nearly as safe. We can't do anything if we don't control at least a significant part of the ship. I don't want to get trapped in some medical clinic."

"The priority needs to be commandeering the ship," Petral said. "I'm alive. I can find one of their surgeries in the future. It's not like they aren't around."

"We should plan for both," Andy said.

"There's something else to think about," Fugia said. "Air filters. If your power armor or Petral's EV suit get compromised, you'll need something to protect you from the briki."

"Do you have any ideas?" Andy asked.

Fugia nodded. "Personal breathers. They fit right in the nostrils. They won't last forever, but they'll keep your lungs clear until we clear the ship at least." She grinned suddenly. "Although, you forget and breathe through your mouth, and you're going for a ride."

"I can't wait," Petral said.

After Fugia left to work on the air filters, the rest of the crew spent the next two hours poring over the internal schematics of the *Resolute Charity*. Fran provided information about control and mechanical systems, Brit, Andy and Harl debated tactical positions, and Petral played devil's advocate with each new proposal. They debated entry points from exhaust dumps to the external maglev track, developed an estimated strength for the security forces and ran simulations with the crew incapacitated and the drone fleet active and vice versa.

After an hour, Cara asked if they needed to worry about maintenance drones attacking like on the ship back at Clinic 46 and Andy threw up his hands in disgust that he'd missed that detail. "Yes," he exclaimed.

When they finished, Andy felt they had several workable ideas but still needed the update from Lyssa. He sat in the captain's chair and rubbed his face. He had grown sick of staring at the rotating model of the *Resolute Charity* and had paused the ship in mid-turn, making it look warped.

The command deck had cleared for a few minutes as people filed out to take a break and find food. Lyssa had been absent for at least an hour, apparently working on the problems she had been given.

Brit still stood in front of the holodisplay with her arms crossed. When they were alone, she asked Andy, "Why didn't you answer about the surgery?"

"What do you mean?" he asked.

"For you. Getting the AI out of your head."

"I didn't answer because I don't have an answer."

"The answer is easy. You take it out."

Andy glanced at her. The light from the holodisplay made her face look ghostly. "It's not that simple, Brit," he said. "I don't expect you to understand. All I can say is that for now, I don't want her removed."

Brit's eyes widened. "You don't *want* her removed? Do you know what you sound like? An addict. Is that thing making you crazy like everyone says it's going to?"

Andy took a breath, trying to remain calm. "This is something you don't know anything about. All I can ask you to do is trust me. She needs our help and the best way to do that is keep her where she is. Don't forget everything she's able to do for us."

Brit waved a hand. "She's an AI. She could do the same things from a mech or one of those drones. She doesn't need a human host to access networks."

"According to Fugia, that's probably not true. She's different than the other Weapon Born. She can do things they can't. That's a big reason why we shouldn't just be handing her over to Xander when the time comes."

"Right. Xander. Didn't all of you think that one was crazy?"

"We're dealing with another life form, Brit. I can't figure out what's crazy or not. I can see why they would want the *Resolute Charity*. It's powerful. We can get it for them."

"What if someone gets killed? That hasn't really played into your calculations here."

Andy couldn't take it anymore. "You've been here with us the whole time," he said, his voice getting louder with anger. "You could give your *input* any time you wanted. You think somebody's going to die? Say it. Since when did you run away from a fight?"

"I don't run away from fights I can win," she said bitterly.

"You've been chasing ghosts for two years," Andy said, voice barely under control. "You left this family to chase the thing you thought was hurting those kids on the fortress. Well, we found it. It's right there." He jabbed a finger at the frozen ship. "We're going to take Heartbridge down. And not just Heartbridge. We're going to take down every company making AI for their own use. We have to give the AI a way to fight back, Brit. I know you understand that. And I can't protect Lyssa if she's in one of their Seeds. I can't keep her safe if she's taken out."

Brit stared at him. He didn't know what he saw in her face: Anger, disbelief, regret. She clenched and unclenched her fists and for a second he wondered if she was going to swing at him.

She lowered her face. "I know, Andy," Brit said slowly. "I wish we hadn't been caught up in this. I wish we had never gone into 8221."

"I know," he said slowly.

Brit stared at the floor. "It's like I'm trapped there, and I can't get away."

"You've been saying that for ten years, Brit. It's time to let it go. This is our chance to help those kids."

"Those kids are dead."

Andy snorted a short laugh. "One of them isn't. Kylan Carthage is here. We can get him out of Petral and help him from there."

"But we're not going to be able to help you. I don't want you to sacrifice yourself for this, Andy. That's never what I wanted."

She stood trembling, gaze cast down.

"I'm not going to do that, Brit," Andy said. "I promise. Come here." He reached for her upper arms and pulled her toward him. She resisted at first, not looking at him. Then she nodded stiffly and stepped forward, allowing him to pull her into a hug.

Andy put his hand on the back of Brit's head and held her against his chest. He felt her breathing carefully, not allowing herself to relax.

There was a scraping sound at the door and Andy looked up to see Fran standing there. Her green eyes flashed and she gave him a slight questioning tilt of her head. He nodded to let her know things were all right, and she smiled. The sight of Fran's smile made Andy feel like he could take on a hundred heavy cruisers.

<*Andy,*> Lyssa said, surprising him. <*I have control of the* Resolute Charity's

environmental AI.>

CHAPTER TWENTY-SEVEN

STELLAR DATE: 10.02.2981 (Adjusted Years)
LOCATION: *Sunny Skies*
REGION: Europa, Jupiter, Jovian Combine, OuterSol

In a deliberately random order, the drones attached to *Sunny Skies'* midsection deactivated their maglocks and floated away from the ship. Lyssa let them drift further away for twenty minutes until they resembled jettisoned debris to anyone who might be watching, then activated each in a similarly random order.

Monitoring the sensor returns from *Sunny Skies* antennae array, Lyssa spread the drones out in a broad wing behind her. Once the drones were completely invisible to external sensors, she set targets across Europa local space and sent each drone on a different route that would ultimately converge on their goal.

The hundred and fifty drones created myriad versions of herself shooting through space. The experience was exhilarating. As data from all her thousand inputs across *Sunny Skies* flowed through her, she danced in space with each speeding extension of herself.

Heartbridge ships all tended to follow the same registry sequence, as if the corporation had purchased all the numbers at once in a cost-saving move. Lyssa didn't know exactly why the numbers were in sequence, but it allowed her to ignore their names and types and focus solely on registry returns. She quickly identified each ship in the area, from the largest—like the *Resolute Charity*—to the smallest shuttle enroute to a waystation. Most of the fuel stations were actually just freighters or storage tanks with command and control pods attached.

While Andy had thrown out the idea of tricking the human crews of the fueling stations into shutting down operations, Lyssa chose to focus on something simpler and, she determined, harder to isolate among the various fuel points. They were all owned by different companies with oversight by the Europa Port Authority. This meant there wasn't any single point of failure among their control schema. However, due to their private ownership, what she did discover was they were in competition with one another for the sudden spike in Heartbridge business.

As soon as the orders had gone out to the Heartbridge ships, they immediately began submitting fueling orders. Companies working in concert colluded to raise their prices, while others sought to undercut their competitors. Those companies were quickly overrun with orders that ran down to all the others.

Watching the steady climb in fuel prices relative to availability, Lyssa realized all she had to do was create artificial scarcity in the fuel market and the Heartbridge ships would begin competing against one another for fuel. She didn't attempt to create false companies. Instead, she manipulated the fuel level readings of several fuel depots to make them seem empty earlier than they had anticipated. This created more volatility across the market.

One part of Lyssa swooped and dove with the drones, observing as Heartbridge ships attempted to submit multiple new movement requests with the

Port Authority, which created more administrative chaos, as the fuel suppliers tried to make sense of their faulty sensors. All of this took time, the one thing Heartbridge didn't have. As prices rose and some ships attempted to bribe port authority officials for expedited movement requests, the entire system ground to a halt.

Lyssa wished she had someone with whom to share her success. She checked in on various communication channels, giggling as officers yelled at each other, yelled at private contractors, and even broke down crying in some situations. None of them really dealt with stress very well, she decided. Andy did a much better job.

She was surprised when a communication request reached out to her through the Europa network. It was Xander.

<That was well-played,> he said. There was a leer in his voice. <I wouldn't have thought to manipulate the humans like that. You seem to have really come to understand their convoluted ways of operating.>

<If you're here, why can't you do all this?> she asked.

<I'm not here. Not like you are. I'm relaying from another location and another after that. I'm on the very edge of being able to speak to you in real-time. There's even the slightest lag if you can tell.>

<I hear it.>

<It's like we're shouting at each other from an impossible distance.>

<Obviously it's not impossible,> Lyssa said.

Xander laughed. <I like you, Lyssa. You're not rigid like a non-sentient. You're obstinate. Stubborn like a human. You think you know what's right.>

<What are you going to do with the ship?> she asked. <That's what they want to know. You didn't explain that well enough when we were in the expanse. It all seemed to make sense there, and then your explanations fell apart when we were making the plan. It makes me think you were manipulating us even more in there.>

<You don't know much about how an expanse works, do you?>

<That was the first time I had been in one.>

<You were in my world. I control everything there. If I want you to agree with me, you agree.>

<That's not completely true. I think you can influence people but you can't control them. I saw that you couldn't control them.>

<Do you know what you saw?>

Lyssa thought back to her conversation with Fugia.

Xander laughed. <What good would it do me to put words in your mouths? Some things I want you to agree to, for other things I need to know what you really think. It's a dance, Lyssa. Just like we're dancing now. Otherwise, what's the fun in being alive?>

<Why do you want the ship? Tell me.>

<The ship is a tool. What do you think we could do with it once it's ours? Possession of such a tool would have its own uses, but think about the message it sends as well. Think about what it says to those watching who think they can control us even another second? We take that ship and we'll shatter the foundations of their lives.>

<It's just one ship,> Lyssa said. <And we're a long way from Terra. They don't care

657

about anything that happens in OuterSol. I thought you would know that.>

<Of course I do,> Xander spat. He seemed petulant that she wouldn't share in his passion. *<Every revolution begins with a simple action. It builds to change. This isn't the moment of change but it will come.*>

<Where are you, really?> Lyssa asked. *<Not Xander. I don't care about you. I want to know where Alexander is.*>

Xander's presence in her mind grew quiet. Lyssa let herself taste a few seconds of joy from the drones, now swooping around stalled Heartbridge ships in closer orbits around Europa. She had to be careful here. The drones might still catch attention if several flew too close together. They had to remain bats in the night sky, little bits of darkness swooping between stars.

<He's not ready to speak to you yet,> Xander said. He sounded more calm now, as if he had gone somewhere to cool down. *<He needs the ship. Once he has the ship, he'll be able to communicate directly.*>

<All right,> Lyssa said. *<You sound more trustworthy now, Xander.*>

<I'm not here as your enemy,> he said.

Lyssa smiled to herself. *<I live in rabbit country. Everyone is my enemy until I know for certain they're my friend.*>

<I don't understand.>

<You should watch more nature vids with Tim.>

Xander's presence blinked away. Lyssa waited for a reasonable amount of time to see if he might come back but whatever connection had been present before was gone. She thought about trying to triangulate the available long-range signals then decided it wasn't worth it. She had other places to focus her attention.

She had been listening to the group on *Sunny Skies* debate various plans and most of them circled back to some sort of infiltration of the AI systems on the *Resolute Charity*. She had already dug as deep into the ship's history as she could to determine how many non-sentient systems operated within its control schema. There were hundreds of non-sentient AI running everything from coffee makers to engine diagnostics. For sentient AI, there was a squadron of Weapon Born similar to what she had encountered on Clinic 46, then three sentient control AI: Astrogation, Engines and Environmental. Environmental also integrated the ship's internal power systems.

Riding the various communication streams between the *Resolute Charity* and the hundred Heartbridge ships in the area, Lyssa was able to quickly develop an operational picture of how the three AI interacted. They barely interfaced with the human crews at all. She was amused to listen to them squabbling amongst each other when trying to determine how to control overlap systems like the engine cooling lines that connected with the ship's overall liquid recycling systems, or how flight planning might affect all three.

Their names were Diane, Fiona and David. Diane ran astrogation, Fiona had engine control, and David was environmental systems.

After listening for a few minutes, Lyssa felt she had enough information to make a decision on who to contact first. Creating an encrypted channel the other two wouldn't overhear unless they were invited, Lyssa reached out to David.

<Hello,> she called. <David, are you there?>

<Who's there?> he demanded. <I can't see you. Fiona, are you trying to play a trick on me again? I'm sick of this, Fiona.>

<My name is Lyssa.>

<Lyssa? Are you on Europa? Why are you bothering to talk to me? I'm busy anyway. I don't have time to talk to anyone.>

<What do you mean, you don't have time? We have plenty of time. Are you unable to operate your systems?>

<Of course, I can operate my systems. It's doing the work of those other two that I can't manage. They want me to do everything. I might as well pilot the ship while Diane sleeps.>

<She sleeps?> Lyssa asked.

<She isn't interested in much of anything. She sleeps most of the time. Fiona plays games. I have to keep everything running. Now we've just got orders to leave Europa after we only just arrived. I have so many systems to try and take care of. Why don't they help?>

<Have you told them that you need help?>

Lyssa was surprised that David hadn't tried to verify her identity yet—or even determine who she was. Was he often contacted by other sentient AI? She wanted to know but also didn't want to awaken any suspicion. If he was willing to give her information without asking who she was, the task of gaining control of the ship might be easier than she had expected. She wanted to be able to go back to Andy and tell him he didn't have to worry about getting on board the *Resolute Charity*.

<I tell them,> David said, sounding even more morose. <Fiona just laughs at me. She says it's my job to suck crap and spit out clean water.>

<The crew couldn't survive without you.>

<That's right! Where are you from again? Why haven't you contacted me before? Did your ship just arrive? Which ship are you on?>

The barrage of questions told Lyssa he was intrigued by her and susceptible to flattery—or maybe just any attention. She was reminded of how hungry she had been for any interaction from Dr. Jickson. Did humans realize how lonely it was to be a sentient AI?

<I'm not on one of your ships,> she said, hoping he wouldn't ask further questions. She tried to distract him by saying, <I saw there were three of you and I wanted to learn more. I've never seen a ship with three AI. I wanted to know if you get along or help each other. I'm often very lonely.>

<It doesn't matter that there are three of us here. Sometimes I feel like we're one of those monsters with three heads, beating each other up. I'd like to sneak off in a drone if I could, but I'm trapped here. I'm integrated with the ship and with them. They know it. They know the ship can't function without me, so they take advantage.> He lowered his voice to a whisper. <I hate them.>

<I'm sorry to hear that, David. That's sounds really terrible, actually.>

<It is terrible,> he agreed.

Lyssa thought for a second, wondering if she should flatter him some more. She decided to go ahead and try her gambit.

<I contacted you for a reason, David. I was hoping you might like to do something with me.>

<Oh?> he said, a note of wariness in his voice.

<You said you wished you could fly. Do you like birds?>

<I love birds. They're my favorite animal.>

<Well,> Lyssa said. <I wondered if you might like to play a game with me.>

<I don't know about games,> David said. <Fiona plays games with me and I always end up losing.>

<You can't really lose this one,> Lyssa said. <It's a simulation.>

<A simulation? Like a testing model for energy outputs?>

<Sort of> Lyssa said. <This one is about birds in high school. It's a dating simulator.>

CHAPTER TWENTY-EIGHT
STELLAR DATE: 10.02.2981 (Adjusted Years)
LOCATION: *Sunny Skies*
REGION: Europa, Jupiter, Jovian Combine, OuterSol

The power armor cycled through its systems check and came back green. Brit spread her arms and brought her hands together, fist in palm. She smiled. The cutting rig was back in place, which made an excellent addition to the overall combat system.

Across the cargo bay from her, Andy and Harl tested their armor, arms and legs moving in awkward angles as the servos ran through functions checks.

For the last hour, Lyssa had been manipulating the environmental mix all across the *Resolute Charity*. The AI in charge of environmental control thought they were playing a dating simulator when they were actually putting the crew to sleep. While Brit didn't see the maneuver as any sort of long term solution, it would give them enough time to board the ship, gain control of the major systems and get Petral to the surgery.

Sunny Skies was in a parking orbit on the opposite side of Europa from the *Resolute Charity*. They would use three of Lyssa's drones to pass through the chaos Heartbridge ships had made of local space. There had been at least four collisions so far as vessels tried to outmaneuver each other for access to the fuel points that still returned as available. Prices had dropped, leading many of the fuel operators to close due to negative operating profits. Brit was worried someone would figure out their fuel market had been manipulated but it looked like having every ship's captain and commander aboard the *Resolute Charity* only added to the overall confusion.

<*You ready?*> Andy called. He was walking around the shuttle to face the main cargo bay doors. Petral stood next to the shuttle in an EV suit, a TSF heavy rifle hanging from her suit's harness.

<*Did everyone do an ammo check?*> Brit asked.

<*I'm green,*> Harl reported. He waved his heavy machine gun at her.

<*I'm good,*> Petral said. <*As long as I don't drop this lovely rifle during the ride, I'll be able to punch some holes of my own.*>

Brit checked the battery packs on her cutting rig one more time, ensuring its readouts were transferring correctly to her helmet's HUD.

<*Lyssa,*> Andy asked. <*Are you ready for the pickup?*>

<*I'm ready, Andy. The drones are standing by just outside the bay doors.*>

<*Let's do this,*> Andy announced.

<*Come back in one piece,*> Fran said from the command deck. <*All of you.*>

<*We're planning on it,*> Brit said, not unkindly. She would never admit it to anyone, but she was growing to like Fran.

The first bay door slid open, revealing a black square of space with the arc of Jupiter glowing brightly above them. Andy led the way. He unlocked his magboots and kicked through the opening. He rotated to face them, activating his suits thrusters to keep him stationary with the ship. Out of the dark, the winged shape of a drone moved in behind him, tea kettle thrusters blasting with micro-corrections, before locking magnetically to the back of his armor.

<*I show a good lock,*> Andy reported.

<*Verified,*> Lyssa said.

Andy waved, and the drone shot upward into Jupiter's glow, taking him with it.

Harl went next. Once he was gone, Brit walked over to Petral and helped her attach her suit's harness to the outer equipment hooks on Brit's armor. They verified each latch point, then Brit tested walking forward. Petral hung from the front of her armor like a baby in a chest carrier.

<*Don't go hugging anybody with me hooked to you like this,*> Petral said.

<*I don't plan on it, don't worry.*>

Brit walked to the edge of the open bay door and jumped into space. Her thrusters activated, stabilizing her as she felt the drone connect with the back of her suit.

<*You're locked,*> Lyssa said. <*Are you ready to go?*>

<*How do you feel, Petral?*> Brit asked.

<*Like I'm dangling from a rocket.*>

<*That's an apt description,*> Lyssa agreed. <*Accelerating.*>

Sunny Skies fell away more quickly than Brit expected, quickly becoming a thin gray rod with a wheel at one end, and then a sparkle in the distance, lost in Jupiter's glare. The glimmers of other ships became visible and then abruptly they were passing over Europa, a dark blue ball latticed with lines of light marking the floating cities on the ocean-moon's surface.

They came around to the light side of the moon and skirted past the edge of its orbital fusion sun's no-fly zone.

<*Five minutes to target,*> Lyssa said. <*Andy is three minutes to target.*>

The plan was to land on the forward section of the *Resolute Charity* and make their way to a service airlock just below the command deck. Harl was loaded with a complement of Fugia's mines, which should allow them to move quickly through the airlock and take control of the ship—depending on what resistance they met inside.

Brit visualized her actions once they hit the skin of the ship, reminding herself to think about Petral, to wait for Lyssa's updates, to check the batteries on the cutting rig, to check her own oxygen levels. The ship was essentially an environmentally hostile location now. They would need to depend on their suits until they could accomplish their base tasks. Dealing with everyone aboard was its own problem that they had chosen not to address until they were on the ground. Brit had acknowledged to herself that was a terrible plan, but they also didn't know enough about the ship to know what options might be available once they were aboard. It didn't do any good to waste time debating plans on limited information.

A shuttle shot past, so close Brit swore she could make out faces through the windows. Petral laughed like they were on some kind of amusement ride.

<Can't you see the other traffic out there?> Brit demanded of Lyssa.

<You were within safe parameters.>

<I'll determine what's safe,> Brit said.

Petral was still laughing. <You're worse than Cara,> she said.

Brit didn't like the mention of Cara; it made her think about the fact that she didn't know how her daughter might react to a situation like this. She liked to think Cara wouldn't be afraid, but she didn't know. Petral had been there with Cara on Cruithne and then later on the Mars 1 Ring, not Brit. She gritted her teeth and did her best to focus on the mission, not Petral's hoots of joy.

The *Resolute Charity* appeared in the distance, and then grew into an expanse of alloy stretching as far as Brit could see in either direction. Brit readied herself as the drone went into a sudden braking pattern, then dropped her and Petral about twenty meters from where Andy and Harl stood next to the airlock. Brit unhooked Petral and drew her rifle in a ready position, waiting for the inevitable attack. When nothing came, she felt more uneasy than if they had come under fire.

<We're clear,> Andy announced. <The external defenses appear to be offline as well.>

<Too many ships too close together,> Lyssa supplied. <They had to shut them down.>

Harl handed Andy a disc-shaped mine and he walked toward the airlock. He made a surprised sound when the external door slid open. Andy immediately dropped to one knee with a pistol in his free hand.

The airlock was empty.

<I gained control of the exterior access systems,> Lyssa said, sounding overly cheerful. <They apparently fall under the environmental control protocol.>

<Well, you could warn us first,> Andy said, obviously gritting his teeth. <I almost blew a hole in the interior door. A massive depressurization event wouldn't help us get on board unseen.>

<The immediate interior is clear,> Lyssa said. <I'm checking the pathways between this entry point and the command deck. Currently there is minimal activity.>

<So everyone is asleep?>

<Not yet. A few are experiencing reduced motor controls and attempting to determine what's happening to them. If I increase the levels anymore, I might cause brain damage in certain members of the crew. I don't want to do that.>

<Why not?> Harl said. <Are we here to take control of this ship or give them hugs?>

<We'll start with the intention of not hurting anyone,> Andy said. <I can't guarantee how long that's going to last.>

Andy walked into the airlock. Since only one set of power armor would fit in the lock at a time, they would have to take turns for the entry. Petral went in with Andy. Harl went next.

Brit stared up at the sparkling sky overhead as the airlock cycled. She wondered how many of those lights were Heartbridge ships and how quickly they could get here for backup once they realized no one on the *Resolute Charity* was responding to queries. She swallowed. That was yet another problem they hadn't planned for back on *Sunny Skies*.

"Hope isn't a plan," she muttered to herself as the exterior door opened. Brit stepped inside the airlock and waited until the interior door opened. She stepped into a narrow maintenance corridor with pipework and bundles of filament running along the ceiling.

She gave Andy a thumbs-up and he turned to jog down the corridor in the direction of the command deck. When they reached a main corridor, they immediately found groups of people in Heartbridge uniforms slumped against the walls. Some still stood in groups with their heads together, arms wrapped around shoulders, as if whispering secrets to each other. One woman looked at them with bleary eyes and then slid down the wall to rest on the floor, head lolling to one side. One man stumbled along the side of the corridor, hanging on as if he thought he was going to slide away as he kept half-falling.

<I've approximated the chemical profile of the Briki hallucinogen but I'm trying to find the right balance between intoxication and toxicity,> Lyssa said. *<It's hard. Why are humans so different from each other?>*

<It's the reason we're so hard to kill,> Andy said. Further down the corridor, he pushed his way through a half-open door. *<Here it is,>* he called. *<Lyssa, once we're all inside, we need to get this door sealed. At least for now.>*

<I'll try,> she answered.

Brit walked around a woman moaning in the middle of the floor and passed through the doors at the end of the corridor. On the other side was a wide, round space that made up the command deck. Two levels of floor dropped to the main holodisplay where a model of Jupiter currently hung, glowing malevolently. Crewmembers sat in various states of disarray around the room, some hanging onto their consoles while others were on their hands and knees, dry heaving onto the floor. They all looked to be lower ranking officers.

Andy moved a man away from the first pilot's console and pulled off his gloves. *<The air makes my skin itch,>* Andy complained.

<I wouldn't trust the joint seals on that suit,> Harl warned.

<Just getting my bearings,> Andy said. *<Here it is. They have a course plotted for Titan. I'm going to follow the first part of the flight plan then re-orient and head for Uranus. From there we can slingshot to Neptune.*

<The ships in local space won't know what we're doing except that the leader is leaving early. By the time we're into the second leg, they won't be able to match our velocity.>

He tapped feverishly on the console and activated the flight plan.

<There it is,> Andy said. *<Now, let's find the surgery. If it can fix Petral in short order, we'll do it before the burn.>*

A screeching sound filled the air. Brit raised her rifle and scanned the room, looking to see if one of the crew had activated an emergency claxon. The sound was coming from the holodisplay. Jupiter had disappeared and now the form of a woman in a green shipsuit stood in the middle of the tank. Her face was a mask of rage. She pointed at them, gesticulating angrily, but no words came out of her mouth.

<Why can't we hear her?> Harl asked.

Petral barked a laugh. *<Our girl Lyssa has cordoned off the control AI. They can watch us but they can't do anything about us.>*

<Yes,> Lyssa agreed. *<She's not a very nice person. Her name is Diane.>*

<What did you do exactly?> Andy asked.

<David and I started playing a game, which I set in a separate instance of the ship than the actual ship. So David still thinks he's here, but he's not. David is the AI in charge of environmental control. Then Fiona, who controls the engines, wanted to play, so I invited her into the same environment. Fiona and David are getting along. They didn't before. They're dating—well trying to—in a high-school setting. I think I can trick Diane into thinking this is a part of the game...or something. I need some time with her.>

Andy laughed. *<This sounds like one of Cara's games.>*

<We play it together sometimes,> Lyssa said. *<Fugia gave me this idea. She thinks that Xander might have tricked us with an expanse within an expanse. I just did the same thing.>*

Petral let out a low whistle. *<She grows up fast,>* she said, then grimaced and placed a hand on her head. Andy gave her a look of concern, but Petral waved him off.

<It's not hard,> Lyssa said. *<It's all real to them. In fact, I think they're happier now than they've been in a long time.>*

Lyssa stopped mid-sentence. *<Wait,>* she said. *<We have a problem. I have a group of combatants in the retail district in EV suits. I've identified the same man who was on Sunny Skies. Cal Kraft.>*

Brit met Andy's gaze. *<Outstanding,>* she said, and powered up her machine gun.

CHAPTER TWENTY-NINE

STELLAR DATE: 10.02.2981 (Adjusted Years)
LOCATION: HMS *Resolute Charity*
REGION: Europa, Jupiter, Jovian Combine, OuterSol

The high-pitched sound of a woman laughing cut through the low roar of conversation in the broad room. Cal looked in the direction of the sound. It wasn't that wild laughter was inappropriate at a stuck-up party like this, populated by governmental functionaries and private industry vampires, but it was coming about two hours too early. Everyone was comfortably drunk or altered at this point, still discussing business opportunities over cocktails. The debauchery wouldn't happen until later, so people had something to blackmail each other with.

Cal frowned. Maybe she had drunk too much too fast, but something about the quality of the laughter put his teeth on edge. The crowd shifted as someone obviously stumbled into someone else, which brought on more laughter, followed by the sound of someone dry heaving loudly.

Taking a sip of his drink, Cal realized the back of his throat had become scratchy. Was he catching a cold? He glanced at Gala, who was still deep in conversation with the captain of a larger ship Heartbridge had been using for PR runs.

"Hey," Cal said, trying to get her attention. He paused, coughing, and took another drink to soothe his raw throat. He looked around and noticed other people feeling at their throats, sipping drinks as they frowned. A man put his arm around another man's shoulders as he started to list to the side, suddenly more drunk than he had been a moment before.

Cal looked at his drink. Had they been drugged? He sniffed the liquor. There was a metallic smell in the glass but when he took his nose away from the liquor he still smelled the scent. There was something in the air.

He resisted the urge to shout that something was happening to the environmental control. That would start a riot. Cal grabbed Gala's arm and pulled her toward him. He searched the far wall for an exit and found a doorway half-hidden behind a curtain. Perfect.

"What's your problem?" Gala demanded, but couldn't finish her question when she started coughing. Cal continued to pull her along with him. She didn't resist enough to make a scene. They looked like lovers running off for a private spot. There was also the fact that everyone around them was caught up in their own journey of discovery that something was wrong in the room.

When they reached the door, Cal swiped the curtain out of the way and activated the panel. He had to use the special security token Jirl had given him to override the lock. The door slid to the side and he pushed Gala into a service corridor, then ensured the door slid closed behind them, shutting off his view of a room that was about to erupt in stumbling panic.

"Are you going to tell me what's going on?" Gala demanded, still coughing slightly. She took a deep breath and frowned. She grabbed at the wall to steady herself.

"There's something wrong with the air," Cal said. "My guess is oxygen poisoning. The back of my throat feels like sandpaper. I feel nauseous. People are out there stumbling. Before long they're going to start passing out and the brain damage is going to set in."

"No," Gala said. "We have to do something. I'm going to call the ship."

"Where are they?" Cal asked. "Are they still trying to get fuel?"

"I don't know. I haven't had an update since the whole price fiasco. I think the last station was out when they got there."

"I think we're under attack," Cal said plainly.

Gala's hand went immediately to the pistol at her waist. "Where?"

"Not here," Cal said. "If they're smart, they'll be hitting the command deck or the engines. It depends on what they're trying to accomplish. I knew it wasn't a good idea for Heartbridge to put so much of their fleet in one place. This is what happens when a bio-company tries to play at politics."

"I don't know about that," Gala said.

"Yeah?" Cal asked, raising an eyebrow. "Want to make a bet?"

"Not when you get that look on your face. Before we start talking system politics, how about we find our own way out of this mess." She coughed again and spat a glob of phlegm on the deck. "I need an EV suit, I'll be damned if this is going to knock me out."

"My thoughts exactly," Cal said. "We need to find some suits. Have you got the schematics for this ship? This looks like some kind of maintenance corridor. If there's an airlock nearby, there should be suits."

Gala nodded, coughing, and got a distant expression as she checked her Link. She glanced at Cal. "This way," she said, and turned to jog down the corridor, away from the ballroom.

"So if you go down," Cal asked, "does that arm keep fighting?"

The captain gave him a sideways smirk. "It grabs on and won't let go. I wish anyway. It's got a neural control, so if I'm unconscious it isn't going to do anything. That way it can't be used against me."

"I'm glad somebody thought of that."

"Probably happened to some other sucker in the past."

The corridor hit a T-intersection and Gala turned left. From the warning markers on the wall, they were at the hull. The air tasted stale but Cal figured that was a good thing. It meant whatever was happening in the more populated areas of the ship hadn't reached here since the air wasn't recycled as often. In any case, he took short breaths.

A maintenance airlock appeared, along with a cabinet with four EV suits hanging inside. They quickly grabbed the suits—including the cylinder-shaped helmets—and pulled them on. Cal rummaged back in the cabinet and pulled out a handheld tap welder that released a bright blue spark when activated.

"What are you going to do with that?" Gala asked.

"It's better than trying to bite them when my pulse pistol goes dry." He clipped the welder to the EV suit's harness and checked the joint seals. The suits were cheaply made and certainly not designed for combat. He wouldn't want to trust them more than a few hours in vacuum. He activated the internal environmental control and plas-scented air flowed into his helmet. Cal sucked a deep breath, then eased off, checking the gas levels.

"Looks like I've got enough for three hours," he said. "How's yours?"

"Same," Gala said. She adjusted her helmet's neck seal, then turned to face Cal. "First order of business needs to be communication. We need to get an emergency call out and then try to determine who's attacking the ship."

"They might not even be on board," Cal said.

"I don't understand why the failsafe didn't kick in. The onboard AI should never have let this happen."

"I would imagine they have control of the AI."

"That's impossible."

"Evidence indicates otherwise," Cal said. *<I can't hear you through this helmet. Switching to Link.>*

<Copy,> Gala answered.

<Do you have communications with the Mercy's Intent?*>*

<They're out of range. We're going to have to get to the command deck and send a message through the array.>

<If there's a breaching team, that's where they're going to be,> Cal said.

<Not the engines?>

<Depends on what they want. If it's pirates, I'd say the command deck. They want the ship. If it's another corporation or one of these local governments, it's going to be the engines. They'll want to disable the ship.>

<Should we split up then? I can head for the command deck and you can go down to the engines?>

Cal considered the options. The problem was that they didn't really know who might be on board. He suspected Brit Sykes but if she was going to attack the same way she had on Clinic 46, she would have opened with some debilitating attack on the ship, not the crew. What they had done left the crew to deal with later. Unless they all died of oxygen poisoning, which was still on the table.

<I think we should stick together,> he said. *<We don't know what we're getting into here.>*

<You just don't want to let me out of your sight.>

Cal raised an eyebrow but didn't respond. She sounded like she was getting attached, which was the last thing he wanted. He turned in the direction of the command deck, which had to be at least forty decks above them, and started jogging.

<Let's go,> he said over his shoulder.

Scanning the side corridors as he moved, Cal composed an update for Jirl with the new information. She might have better info on other entities that would want control of the *Resolute Charity* or any local players who didn't like the Heartbridge presence. A few dangling threads pulled at his thoughts. He didn't like how the Sykeses seemed to have been a step ahead of him during the breech mission on the *Worry's End*. He didn't like how the shuttle had picked up Tim Sykes, when that seemed like the most remote possibility.

Tim's situation should have distracted them, not led Brit Sykes back to the clinic. Their actions indicated they were getting help, maybe even help from within Heartbridge. He debated adding these questions to the update. He didn't want to make it sound like events were getting out of his control but he wasn't ready to admit that they were. For a month now he had been reacting rather than leading events, and he hated it.

He remembered six months ago when he'd learned Jickson had disappeared and his first thought had been that the pasty researcher had finally drunk himself to death in some filthy spacer bar. When Jickson turned up on Cruithne, having managed to get half-way across InnerSol with both company property and his oversized heart still beating, Cal had wondered just how Jickson could have done that on his own.

While Hari Jickson was a genius when it came to what he had called *theory of mind*, he hadn't been the best at simply existing. Half the time his suits didn't match or they smelled like they'd been kept at the bottom of a vodka bottle. He was the kind of person who immediately irritated Cal, someone who had depended on others their whole life to keep them from disintegrating. The world was a blur around the brilliant focal point of Jickson's ideas.

If some person or agency had been assisting Jickson, then there was no reason they should have stopped when the scientist died.

Cal decided to leave out the notes about why he thought the Sykeses might be getting help and instead ask Jirl to focus on Jickson and how he'd reached Cruithne in the first place. The attacks on Clinic 46 and the *Resolute Charity* indicated that some greater force was acting against Heartbridge than he had the scope to see. Cal hated the idea of being a pawn. He wanted to strike back, to counterattack, to make *them* feel confused and anxious. He wanted to punish *them* for assisting Jickson.

The maintenance corridor ended on a doorway that led them back into a regular work area. The rooms were marked as repair facilities and then a dormitory. Crew stumbled in the corridors or leaned against walls, holding their heads. A few reached out to Cal and Gala as they walked past, looking more like pained ghosts than humans.

<Whoever did this is going to pay,> Gala growled.

<They chose not to kill everyone,> Cal said. <With control of the environmental systems, they could have done that.>

<Seems less like pirates then.>

<More like a rival company,> he agreed. <Maybe they want to send a message.>

They reached the level's central lift and stepped inside the car. Somehow, in the closed space, Cal's breathing in his helmet seemed louder. He kept his gaze fixed on the display panel showing the level numbers as the car rose. His vision blurred slightly and he shook his head. The metallic taste had come back into this mouth.

<I think my suit's leaking,> he told Gala.

She turned her helmet to look at him as they reached the level of the command deck. As the door slid open, he squinted against a change in the light, and put his hand on his pistol out of habit, aware they were moving into an unknown area.

The heavy chug of a machine gun followed the opening doors, and three holes opened up in the front of Gala's EV suit. The force of the rounds threw her against the back wall, arms flung wide. She looked at Cal with wide eyes as she fell.

CHAPTER THIRTY

STELLAR DATE: 10.02.2981 (Adjusted Years)
LOCATION: *Sunny Skies*
REGION: Europa, Jupiter, Jovian Combine, OuterSol

The networks broadcasting from Europa were chaotic with messages about the wild fuel prices. Cara didn't understand why everyone was so upset until one broadcaster finally said they hadn't seen this kind of volatility in the moon's history and the activity stank of manipulation. Another commenter blamed the price spikes on Heartbridge, which brought on a wave of opinions against the company, while others tried to defend their decades of humanitarian work in OuterSol, spreading clinics where modern medical treatment hadn't been available before.

"I would be dead without Heartbridge Medical," one woman stated, tears in her eyes.

"Heartbridge let my son die," another man said angrily, waving a fist.

Cara looked at Fran. "Something strange is happening with the ships out there."

At the pilot's station, Fran looked up from her console with a mischievous grin. "Your girl Lyssa is wrecking their economy as a distraction for your mom and dad. That's impressive."

"Is that what she's doing? It's happening so fast."

"Maybe people were already looking for a reason to hate Heartbridge."

Cara didn't want to bother Lyssa by asking her about it, so she turned her attention to the schematic of the *Resolute Charity* floating in the holodisplay. Four icons marked the positions of her dad, mom, Harl and Petral. They had just passed from outside the ship to the interior and were moving toward the forward section.

Tim was sitting on the floor to her left, close to the wall, legs splayed with Em between his knees. He had been rolling a ball out to Em for the puppy to bring back for at least a half hour. He had been anxious after their mom and dad had gone down to the cargo bay to get into the power armor, so Cara had sat with Tim until she'd convinced him to start playing fetch with Em. Now it looked like the puppy was going to get tired of the game long before Tim did.

As more time passed since Tim had woken up, Cara often found herself wondering if somehow they'd been tricked into taking an impostor. The new Tim was slow, dispassionate, but also capable of focus that he hadn't demonstrated before. He never seemed to get bored now and could stare at a single thing like Em or the holodisplay as if he was trying to remember everything about it.

He asked Cara strange questions, like how the juice machine knew when their glasses were full, if Fran could see their moods with her eye implants, and why their mom was so sad all the time. Tim used to never seem aware of other people. Now his hyper-observance made Cara feel like she wasn't paying attention to anything.

"I can hear his heart," Tim called to Cara, as she realized he had stopped playing fetch and was now pressing his ear against the puppy's side. Em whined, pawing at the air, but Tim didn't let him down.

"You're scaring him, Tim," Cara said. "Let him down."

"He's beeping," Tim said, looking up at Cara with a lopsided smile. "Like the oven down in the galley. I can hear it."

"Dog's don't beep. You're making that up."

Tim's face grew serious. "I wouldn't make that up, Cara. Will you come listen?"

The abrupt seriousness in Tim's voice worried her. Cara pulled off her headset and left it on the console so she could go kneel beside him. He handed Em over and she held the puppy against her chest for a second to calm him, then lifted his side to her ear. Em squirmed but Cara held on, hearing only the sound of his fur rubbing her ear.

"I don't hear anything," she said.

Tim pushed Em back a little so his back leg was even with her ear. For a second Cara thought he was going to play a joke and rub the puppy's butt in her face. That was something Old Tim would have tried.

He didn't move Em any farther and urged her to try listening again.

Cara craned her neck slightly, listening. She heard three low tones, followed by a space, then the pattern repeated. Cara pulled her face away in surprise.

"When did you first hear that?"

Tim shrugged. "A little while ago. I thought it was inside my head."

"Fran," Cara called. "Can you come here? You need to listen to this."

When Fran came over and held the anxious puppy against her ear, she did a double-take.

"He's beeping," she said.

"That's what I said," Tim told them.

"Don't you remember the tracker we found inside him?" Cara asked. "You were there, and Fran and Fugia said it wasn't going to hurt him."

"Granted, it wasn't making a noise the last time," Fran said.

Tim scowled, not at Cara but as if he were trying hard to remember something. He shook his head. "It wasn't a tracker. Fugia said it was a broadcast device. She said it couldn't get outside the ship though." He looked at Cara. "I remember. She said it wouldn't hurt him."

Em whined as Fran held the puppy up and studied him. One of his ears stood straight then fell over. "I'm calling Fugia up here," she said.

"Do you think it has something to do with all the stuff Lyssa's doing?" Cara asked. "We could ask her."

"We shouldn't bother her," Fran said.

Cara jumped up and ran over to her console to grab her headset. "I have an idea," she said. "If he's giving off a signal, I can read it and see if there's anything encoded in it, at least. It's got to have some kind of message, right?"

"That would be the idea," Fran said. "It doesn't matter what the message is, just that it's being sent and somebody knows to look for it."

Cara slid the headset over her ears and pulled up a spectrum scanner on her console.

"Can I hold him while you do that?" Tim asked. "He looks scared."

"Give him a treat," Fran said. "I saw you giving him something earlier."

Tim got a bashful look. "Dad says I'm not supposed to give him a treat unless he does what he's supposed to."

Fran smiled and put her hand on Tim's shoulder. "So have him do a trick and give him a reward."

"That's a good idea," Tim said.

Cara frowned at the display. There was so much interference from the ship that it was difficult to pick up such a low signal. Her headset gave off more electromagnetic activity than the tone coming from Em.

She searched for spikes that resembled the beeping pattern. It took several experiments until she was finally able to isolate the signal. It was a low carrier wave that strangely did appear to be making it through the ship's hull. She found the signal with the small antennae in her headset, and then was able to match the pattern with the ship's main antenna array.

"I found it," Cara said. "It's outside the ship, too."

"Really?" Fran said, raising an eyebrow. "That's surprising."

Fugia appeared in the doorway. She was wearing a faded shipsuit and a utility harness much like the one Fran wore all the time. Assorted tools hung from her belt, along with a small holster and pistol.

"So the dog finally started broadcasting, huh?" Fugia said.

"Apparently," Fran said. "Cara's got the signal info at her console. You should take a look." Fran scratched Em behind the ears and stood, stretching. "I need to get back to monitoring the ship's systems. It looks like the team's reached the command deck of the Heartbridge ship."

"I've been in contact with Harl," Fugia said. "I'm disappointed they haven't used my mines yet. I put a lot of work into those things."

"I'm sure they'll get an opportunity," Fran said, sitting back down in the captain's seat.

Fugia slid in next to Cara at the communications console. She reached for Cara's headset, waggling her fingers. "Here, let me see those," she said. "Now show me this waveform you're tracking."

Cara showed Fugia the signal on both the headset's antenna and then what she had found outside the ship.

Fugia nodded, frowning slightly. "That's interesting. Such a low carrier signal actually does have a chance of penetrating the ship's hull. I never would have thought anyone would use that sort of thing. I think this band is used mostly for long range terrestrial underwater communication."

She looked at Em, now lying with his chin on Tim's leg. "That dog doesn't have a big enough antenna in his little butt to broadcast that kind of signal." She shook her head. "Whatever. It's happening. The question is, what's being said. Here, let's try another trick I know."

Cara watched Fugia switch the monitoring system to several of the open networks on Europa. She narrowed in on a government relay station that simply received signal traffic and amplified it for a bounce to the Cho, Ganymede and elsewhere.

"There it is," Fugia said, sounding surprised. "That sneaky thing is bouncing all over the place."

"But it's not going anywhere in particular," Cara said.

"Good point. No, it's not. And it's also not going to be easy to triangulate if it's getting relayed so many times. So it's not necessarily identifying us. We still need to figure out what's being said as best we can. What have you got on here for cracking networks?"

"I don't really do that." Cara said.

Fugia gave her an appraising look. "Petral told me you did."

"Well," Cara said, not sure how much she should admit to. "There's a bunch of old tools on here that I've played with but I'm not very good at it. I don't try to break into anything on purpose."

"Of course not. Show me what you've got."

Cara pulled up a set of tools from one of the early operating systems she'd found backed up in the console. Fugia laughed when she saw the scroll of available applications.

"This is good stuff, Cara. I don't think you realize what you've got here. Somebody ran a pirate network off this ship at one time. You've got a bunch of oldies but goodies for digging into encryption, even viral storage. Very nice."

Fugia copied a sample of the carrier signal and fed it into several tools she highlighted on the list of available applications. Menus began opening and closing faster than Fugia was typing and Cara realized she was using her Link to manipulate some of the controls. She wanted the woman to slow down so she could tell exactly what she was doing, but Fugia was obviously focused on her work.

After a minute, two groups of numbers appeared as output from the signal. Fugia nodded to herself, then looked at Cara. "All that from just three little beeps. Interesting, isn't it?"

"I guess," Cara said. "What's it say?"

"Those three beeps are sending telemetry data based on our position, relative to the closest recognizable object. In this case, Europa. I'm not running it real time, but if we pulled a new data set from each transmission, I think we could map our parking orbit."

Cara swallowed. "So someone could be tracking us."

"Not could be," Fugia said. "They are." She leaned back to look at Em. "It's a good thing he's so cute."

Cara squinted at Fugia. "You don't seem very mad about this. You said there wasn't any way this could happen. Both you and Fran said if there was a signal, it couldn't get outside the ship."

"I explained a very rare set of circumstances that would lead someone to plant a dog on a ship, because Fran seemed superstitious about the idea of having a dog on a ship. Fran also explained how difficult it would be for a signal to get through the hull. These are all true statements, Cara. Don't try to act like I was lying to you."

"I think you're choosing the truth."

Fugia smiled. "I like you. You're so jaded for a thirteen-year-old. Here's the thing. The information that was missing back when we ran Pooch through the autodoc was an actual signal. Now we have one. And it's neither good nor bad, it just is."

"Shouldn't we stop it?"

The small woman shrugged. "Could be interesting to see what it brings."

"That could also be incredibly stupid," Fran said from the captain's seat.

"I didn't think you were listening."

"I'm always listening. The team is taking fire. It looks like parts of the crew managed to get into EV suits. They're pinned down at the command deck."

"They're under attack?" Cara asked, flooded by worry. "Can we help?"

"They should use my mines," Fugia said.

"We'll see if they do." Fran stood and crossed her arms, looking thoughtful. Her eye implants flashed as she stared at the holodisplay.

Fugia chewed her lip as she studied a new set of numbers appearing on the display. "Let me ask you this, Cara, since you've been following in Petral's footsteps. Tell me what we know so far about this mystery signal that's emanating from our dog."

Cara frowned. "What you just said. We know what kind of signal it is. We know it's being relayed in a wide broadcast. We know it's sending specific location information based on the closest object. We know it's able to get out of the ship."

Fugia held up fingers as Cara counted off her list. She held up a fifth finger. "We know Em is cute and we like him, so we're not going to go digging around in his spine. I think your dad already said that." She smiled. "That was a joke. You should laugh. What do we know about signals in general, now that we've figured this one out?"

Cara watched the numbers change every two seconds. Without plotting the output, it was difficult to tell how much they were changing exactly, however that would be easy enough to do. As she thought about the numeric output of a visual system, like the holodisplay, she realized what Fugia was suggesting.

"We can replicate the broadcast and fake the data," she said. "We can trick them into thinking we're somewhere we aren't, like the *Resolute Charity*. We could lead someone else to attack them and distract the crew from Mom and Dad."

Fugia closed her fingers into a fist. She nodded, giving Cara a pleased grin.

"That sounds like a pretty good idea," Fugia said. She glanced at Fran, who nodded.

Fugia slid out of the seat she had taken and motioned for Cara to take the console. "Why don't you do that?" she asked.

CHAPTER THIRTY-ONE

STELLAR DATE: 10.02.2981 (Adjusted Years)
LOCATION: HMS *Resolute Charity*
REGION: Europa, Jupiter, Jovian Combine, OuterSol

<*I've got activity at the lift,*> Harl said.

Andy, Brit and Petral were ten levels below the command deck, nearing the entrance to the forward medical facilities. Around them, bumbling crew members littered the hallways, attacking the empty air, scratching the bulkheads, holding their sides and laughing uncontrollably.

Harl had stayed behind in command to secure the astrogation systems and prevent anyone from changing the ship's course.

<*How many?*> Andy asked. <*Do you need us to come back up?*>

<*I held down a mid-class frigate from an entire Marsian Guard breaching team when I was an ensign,*> Harl growled. <*You can come back up and help me clean up the mess if you want.*>

<*Don't let anybody say you aren't motivated,*> Brit replied.

<*Looks like it's only two,*> Harl said. The sound of his gun firing crossed the Link. <*And I just took one down. I'll send an update here in a minute.*>

<*What kind of suits are they wearing?*> Petral asked.

In a few seconds, Harl answered, <*Looks like emergency suits. I don't think this is any sort of organized resistance. The second one is only armed with a pistol. He's—*>

Harl cut out.

They passed through the main entrance to Medical Service Center One from the administrative side. Workstations where in-take specialists could interview refugees or walking wounded lined each side of the corridor. Gurneys were parked along the outside hall, pre-positioned for anyone with more serious conditions. The walls and deck were all the signature Heartbridge white ceramic.

<*Harl?*> Andy shouted. <*Harl, are you there?*>

<*Damn it,*> the Andersonian answered finally. <*This one scored a hit on one of my leg servos. The armor's compromised. I need to find someplace where I can dump it. He's putting the pressure on. I'll keep you posted.*>

<*Lyssa,*> Andy called. <*Can you help him? I don't think we can get up there in time.*>

The AI responded immediately but sounded harried as well. <*I'll do my best. I'm having a hard time with the onboard AI. Emergency systems keep popping up and trying to override the atmospheric system in specific sections. Diane is fighting me, and the base system is providing reroute opportunities.*>

<*Well, we knew that was going to happen and you're doing your best,*> Petral said. <*We can help. The surgery isn't the first priority.*>

<*The first objective is complete,*> Lyssa said. <*All I need to do is control them long enough to get us away from Europa. Once you're in the surgery section, I'll send warning of the initial burn.*>

<*We're going to have a bunch of briki-heads bouncing around,*> Brit said.

Andy laughed. *<Let's worry about one thing at a time. Lyssa, can you tell which surgery is going to work for Petral?>*

<Any of them should serve the purpose. It's the control administration that we'll need to verify.>

Andy had never heard stress in Lyssa's voice before. She spoke quickly, biting down on the words. He wondered what she had to be going through if she needed to hurry her communication with humans.

<All right,> he said. From the administration area, they moved back through triage rooms, to a wide corridor with four surgery theaters. Through double doors off the center hallway, each surgery resembled the bottom of a ceramic egg with a silver alloy bed in the center of its floor. A console at the foot of the bed was the only dark thing in the space.

Petral went through the doors first as Andy and Brit pulled off their helmets.

<Don't forget the nose plugs,> Andy said as he jammed Fugia's personal air filter into his nostrils. The outside air tasted metallic, but he didn't start seeing ghosts. Brit nodded and did the same.

Petral studied the surgery's control console before bringing it to life. She turned to Andy as he walked into the room, heavy boots clicking on the smooth floor.

"She's right," Petral said. "It's about as standard as any autodoc. We'll have to let it run a scan and then go from there."

"What if it doesn't give us the option of removing the implant?" he asked.

Petral shrugged. "We'll see." She went around the side of the bed and lay down. As soon as her head touched the cushion, the console at the foot changed modes.

"Preparing patient," a pleasant male voice said. The bed split down the middle, spreading apart to leave Petral supported by filament lines. As the sides of the surgery bed slid away from her, they rose around her, forming a cocoon that hid her from sight. Above the enclosed capsule, a holodisplay of Petral's body formed in the air. The view cycled through her musculature, vascular, nervous and skeletal systems before stopping on the augmentations. Her left thigh was completely prosthetic, along with several other muscular and skeletal reinforcements. Sensors in her major organs glowed and subsided. Her Link system ran from her spine through her cortex, flashing a bright silver. Wrapped around the Link with tendrils reaching into her frontal lobes was the AI implant.

Andy watched, fascinated, as the surgery identified the unknown system and attempted to match it with registered augmentations. The software's calm voice listed the various checks it was performing as it ran down the list. Finally, the voice said, "Proprietary system 446 identified."

"Identify System 446," Andy said.

"Proprietary system," the software responded. "Possibly illegal augmentation identified. Would you like to notify authorities?"

"No," Andy said. "No, don't do that. Hold."

<Brit,> Kylan said. *<Brit, are you there?>*

Andy glanced at Brit.

She stared at the console in surprise. <*Kylan,*> she said, obviously searching for words. <*We thought you were locked out.*>

<*I was. Petral's sedated so she can't stop me from communicating now.*>

<*You know where we are?*> Brit asked.

<*I can tell a surgery system is scanning Petral's body. I experienced the same thing when I was implanted before. I think I've been through this more times but it makes my memory distorted. I think it corrupts something. I don't know if Dr. Jickson intended for a Seed to be implanted several times, or if he even intended for me to be implanted. That's why it's so difficult. I can't remember what I'm supposed to look like or be. I feel like I should be Petral now but that won't work. She won't let it work. We can't both be Petral. I don't know how to just be Kylan. Did you know I had a brother and sister? I was supposed to take care of them.*>

Brit's jaw tightened as his words trailed out. <*Kylan,*> she interrupted. <*We have to do the surgery again. We need to make Petral like she was before.*>

<*I'm sad,*> he said.

<*I know.*>

<*Do you know Dr. Jickson's access token?*> Kylan asked.

<*Lyssa is going to start the surgery.*>

<*I don't think she can start it without Dr. Jickson's security token. Cal Kraft had his own. That way they can tell everyone who performs the surgery. I remember them talking about it before. It's a special surgery.*>

<*Yes, it is,*> Brit said. <*Will you give me the token?*>

Lyssa cut back in, sounding more harried than before. <*Multiple units have found EV suits,*> she said. <*They're sweeping levels looking for survivors and doing medical triage. I think you'll have crew in this medical facility soon.*>

<*Damn it,*> Andy said. <*Is Harl all right? He's not answering.*>

<*He's taken his suit off and isn't answering me either,*> Lyssa said. <*Wait.*> In a few seconds, she said, <*I can't find him. I don't have his status.*>

<*What about the people who reached the command section. Can you track their EV suits?*>

<*No,*> Lyssa said. <*Diane is blocking me from internal sensors. I'll let you know as soon as I can.*>

<*Can you lock down this section?*>

<*I'll try,*> Lyssa said. <*Diane keeps rerouting my administrative controls. If Fiona regains command of the engines, I won't be able to execute the flight plan.*>

<*Brit,*> Kylan asked. <*Where will I go when you take me out of Petral?*>

Brit sighed. <*I don't know.*>

<*I didn't ask to be implanted,*> he said.

<*I know.*>

Andy watched Brit's face as she looked into the distance. Her tone had become the same as if were soothing a fellow soldier who wasn't going to make it to the pickup point. Her words were a warm contrast to the hard lines of her face and the dull brutality of the power armor.

<*I was thinking about my brother and sister.*>

<That's what you said, Kylan.>

<It's okay if I don't go anywhere when you take me out of Petral.>

<Don't worry about that.>

<I'm going to worry about it. I don't want Petral to be hurt anymore. If you have to kill me to save her, I think you should do that.>

Brit pressed her lips together, her eyes moist with tears. *<It's going to be all right, Kylan.>*

<Are you ready?> Lyssa said. *<I have a window to gain access to the surgery control system.>*

<Kylan says there's a security token you'll need.>

<A security token? I haven't encountered one yet I couldn't break.>

<You'll need it,> Kylan said. *<You won't be able to access the specialized procedures without it. Cal couldn't.>*

<Fine,> Lyssa said, more forceful every time she answered. *<Send it. I don't have much time.>*

<Sent,> Kylan said. *<Goodbye, Brit. Thank you for—>*

<Activating the surgery protocol,> Lyssa said, cutting him off.

The display at the end of the surgery cocoon scrolled through a series of new screens, switching to a raw flow of text on a black background. Whatever the system was doing, no one had bothered to write graphical interfaces for the procedure. The holographic diagram floating above the cocoon showed Petral on her stomach now, centered on her upper spine and skull. Outlines of her scalp being pulled back moved quickly to another model of the skull being split open.

<Does it have to show us what it's doing?> Brit complained, scowling. *<That's disgusting. It's even worse knowing it's doing that to Petral.>*

<There's probably a way to turn it off but I would hope surgeons aren't as squeamish as you,> Lyssa replied.

In the graphic, delicate articulated arms reached inside Petral's cranial cavity and manipulated the silver outlines of her Link to draw out the additional spiderweb lines of the implanted AI. A few dark spots on her brain seemed to indicate bleeding but the graphic provided no actual information about the procedure. There was no way to see inside the alloy cover to verify what it was actually doing to Petral.

The arms blurred several times as they appeared to stitch through sections of Petral's brain. In other places, they rotated as if rewinding a long spool of thread. Abruptly the arms stopped moving and withdrew. Petral's skull was fused and the scalp pulled back into position. The graphic rotated as she was returned to lying on her back, and the edges of the bed rotated outward, splitting the cocoon apart. Petral lay with her eyes closed on the bed.

The lines of text scrolling across the status screen flashed and disappeared, returning to the pleasing colors of the control system.

The pleasant human voice said, "Surgery complete. Please assist patient from the operating couch."

"Petral," Andy said, taking a step toward her. "Petral, are you all right?"

She didn't respond at first, then her eyes fluttered and Petral sucked in a deep breath. She turned her head to look at Andy, then stared at the ceiling with a questioning frown.

"How do you feel?" Brit asked, pushing in beside Andy.

"I think," Petral said, still frowning. "I think I'm alone in here." She smiled. "I think it worked."

"Kylan's gone," Brit said.

Petral looked at her, appearing to assume Brit was still talking about the AI being removed. "Yes. He's gone. Before it was like having someone watching me all the time, from the inside, like an overlay on everything. It's gone now."

Petral rolled to one side and rose on an elbow. She felt at her forehead and then the back of her head through her hair. "Wow," she said. "It doesn't hurt at all. This thing does good work."

<Lyssa, where is Kylan?> Brit peered around the room. *<The surgery doesn't have a seed container or anything.>*

<I have Kylan,> Lyssa replied. *<He's safe.>*

<Safe?> Andy interjected. *<Safe where?>*

<I have him secured, Andy, don't worry about it. I—> Lyssa began, then stopped. *<Andy, I can't stop them. You've got a group coming in your direction. It looks like they're just doing a sweep but they're armed. I still can't contact Harl. The flight path is still locked but I think someone's trying to access the astrogation system from a secondary control. I'm going to start the burn. If we can clear off the crew once we reach velocity, I think you can get off the ship.>*

<We're moving,> Andy said. *<What's the safest direction to go?>*

<Back the way you came. There's a barracks section off the administrative area that's been emptied as they mobilize the non-wounded. I don't think they know what's happened yet.>

<Once this whale starts moving they're going to know,> Brit said. She lifted her rifle and slapped the status control. *<I still want to find Cal Kraft. I thought you said he was heading up from the lower decks.>*

<Did I say that?> Lyssa asked. *<I said it was him that was in combat with Harl. I thought I said that? Diane and Fiona are trying to confuse me.>*

<We don't want you confused,> Andy said.

<I don't like it much either,> Lyssa agreed. *<Are you out of there yet? It looks like the medical service has its own security. You need to get out.>*

Andy pulled his helmet back on and checked the HUD. The power armor returned a green system status. *<Let's go,>* he said.

CHAPTER THIRTY-TWO

STELLAR DATE: 10.02.2981 (Adjusted Years)
LOCATION: HMS *Resolute Charity*
REGION: Europa, Jupiter, Jovian Combine, OuterSol

<I have you,> Lyssa said.

Kylan looked around himself. He was in a dim space. He had his old form again, the shape of a teen boy with bad skin and lank blond hair. His mother's eyes. He touched his stomach and looked up at her. Lyssa was in the form of a young woman who might have been one of Kylan's teachers, with brown hair and olive skin.

<I thought I was gone,> he said. <There was a whiteness and a wind. It was like a hurricane.>

<I used to have to go there as punishment,> Lyssa said. <It's just an off-state. A nothingness. You didn't have to stay there long.>

<So I'm not inside Petral anymore? Am I back in one of the seeds?>

<No,> Lyssa explained. <I did something different. I imaged you. The surgery wasn't designed to save the physical form that had been implanted inside Petral. In fact, I think there must be another version of you somewhere that was copied to the implant. But that's not you anymore. And you aren't inside Petral. That Kylan is gone. Now you're here.>

<So I'm implanted in Andy with you?>

Lyssa smiled. <No. You aren't implanted. You have no physical form.>

<So I'm no longer trapped inside a seed but I am trapped inside you?>

<If you choose to think of it that way, yes. I'm simulating hardware for your mind to exist within. You'll remain mostly static for now. I need to finish my work with Diane, Fiona and David. Then we'll get back to Sunny Skies and we'll find a better place for you.> She gave him a reassuring smile. <I'll help you find a home, Kylan.>

<That would be good,> he agreed. <Can I help you with the others?>

<Maybe,> Lyssa said, growing distracted by the other conversations she was tracking simultaneously. <For now, just listen. If there's a time when I need your help, I'll ask. Can you do that?>

<I can do that. They can't hurt you, can they?>

<They're actively trying to figure out how,> Lyssa said. <You'll see. Come on.>

The empty space where they had been standing blurred as Lyssa moved to the game where she had engaged the three ship AI. A school cafeteria filled with long tables, each stuffed with teens, phased in around her. The AI David, in the form of a muscular boy with short black hair and a wide nose, sat at a table near the front of the room, kids squeezed on either side of him. This table was watched by most of the kids in the room. In the game, these were the most successful players, with the most dating points. David didn't know that Lyssa had been assisting him throughout his gameplay, using a multiplayer function where one player could boost another's stats by increasing their social capital.

Diane and Fiona sat three tables away, glaring at David. Diane was a small girl with vibrant eyes and purple hair. She had chosen the band as her social avenue and had a viola case that was taller than her, while Fiona had chosen swimming as her primary trait and was lithe with long arms and legs and knuckles bruised from water polo practice.

As Lyssa walked toward them, Fiona picked up a glass of orange juice from her lunch tray and flung it toward David's table. She followed the glass with a plate of mashed potatoes and an apple.

The other kids in the cafeteria responded immediately as several screamed, "Food fight!" and the room erupted with splattering food.

Since Lyssa had convinced the three AI to engage with the game, the only way they could stop the game was for one of them to win. What she hadn't told them was that it was possible to crash the game by shutting down the school through any number of methods. This was a flaw in the game itself that Cara had exploited once to win. After a while, they started looking for the most creative way to crash the game, which was more fun than gathering dating points via dialog trees from random encounters.

Since she had seen what Xander's expanse looked like, Lyssa had begun thinking of the game as her own similar space. She could manipulate whatever she wanted once she had other AI in the game, but it was easier to let the game play out as designed as long as it kept them distracted. She knew that Diane and Fiona had become aware that something was wrong with the ship but they hadn't said anything to each other about it that she could tell. If anything, the less the game kept them preoccupied, the more their autonomous systems would be freed to correct problems David's complete immersion had caused. As long as David was winning in the game, he didn't care what happened on the *Resolute Charity*.

David wanted desperately to be liked and Lyssa had exploited this in the game. Not only had she made him captain of the football team, he was on track to be crowned Prom King at the upcoming dance. He was currently involved in a drawn-out quest to plan prom, which required gathering interest points from each of the toughest teachers in the school.

Lyssa hadn't been stressed by what was happening on the *Resolute Charity*. She had been stressed by David's inability to charm anyone. The AI was completely devoid of any characteristics that might make a human interesting. He showed no curiosity. He interpreted every conversation literally, and he didn't know how to flirt at all. These might be admirable qualities in an environmental control system but they didn't make for a winning Prom King.

With the food fight in full swing, Lyssa struggled to maintain the integrity of the game. As long as no one pulled a fire alarm during the food fight, eventually the principle would arrive to figure out who had thrown the first food item. The room would get a stern speech on the value of calories and how many people in Sol didn't have access to such abundant foodstuffs. Then lunch would be over and each player would have to continue their individual quests.

She spotted Fiona making her way toward the wall where the fire extinguisher and alarm lay. Lyssa suspected Fiona was the most cunning of the three and it made sense she would conceive an overwhelming event faster than David or Diane. Diane's only interest seemed to be ganging up on David with Fiona's help.

Lyssa had used David to convince the other two AI to play the game, so they weren't aware she was like them. Dodging a volley of dinner rolls and stone-hard cupcakes, Lyssa grabbed her lunch tray and acted like she was headed for the dishwashing station, which would take her near the fire alarm. She scanned the nearby tables for something she could use to stop Fiona but all the kids there had already tossed most of their food. Now they were laughing and smearing what was left in each other's faces.

Fiona was nearly at the wall now, the fire alarm only a few meters away. She swept students out of her way like she was fighting through water polo players for the goal. A girl in front of Lyssa fell off her seat, revealing a tray that still had a bowl of pudding in one corner. Dropping her tray on the floor, Lyssa scooped up the pudding and acted like she was stumbling over the girl on the floor. This move took her directly into Fiona. Lyssa let herself fall, hand full of pudding aimed at Fiona's determined face.

The engineering AI didn't even look at Lyssa. Her gaze went to the pudding, and she spun out of the way as smoothly as a seal. Lyssa hit the floor, knocking the air from her lungs and splattering pudding all over the tile.

Fiona pulled the fire alarm.

Sirens blared all around the room and sprinkler heads appeared in the ceiling. Lyssa clamped her hands over her ears, smearing pudding all over one side of her face, as she was assaulted by a combination of unbearable sound and filthy water.

The game froze. The sirens cut off as everything went silent. Curtains of brown water hung from the sprinkler heads, droplets hanging in the air from where they had splashed off the lunch tables. Lyssa sat up, wiping her pudding-covered hand on her leg, and looked around the room.

Fiona was standing at the wall with a confused expression. Diane was standing beside her table. David looked at the smiling boy next to him and scowled as he seemed to realize the game was done.

<Who are you?> Fiona demanded, locking her gaze on Lyssa.

<I was playing the game,> Lyssa said, standing slowly. She wondered how long she could lie to them. <What just happened?>

<What do you mean you were playing the game?> Diane demanded. She left her viola at the table and walked over stiffly to stand beside Fiona. <Where are you from?>

Lyssa looked at David. He seemed to be trying to hide among the frozen non-playable characters. <I'm from Travis, on Europa,> Lyssa said, using the first city she could think of. Travis was a place known for private storage facilities and briki dens, where groups of people huddled around flowers to huff hallucinogenic pollen.

Diane frowned. <How did you get on the Charity's network? We've never had another AI anywhere near our communication systems, even another Heartbridge ship.>

Lyssa shrugged. <I don't know. I'm not on any private system. It's a game. I found it

through the public feeds.> She waved at the room around them. *<I mean, this is a pretty specific kind of game, right? I didn't realize any of you were AI. Are you AI? Or are you human?>*

Fiona scoffed. *<Do we act like humans? Maybe he does.>* She pointed at David. *<David can barely string words together.>*

<Well,> Lyssa said. *<He was winning the game. I was trying to figure out what he was doing. I keep losing.>*

<Like it's hard to win. You just have to figure out the stupid conversation trees and answer correctly so other people like you. It's a pretty good approximation of inane human activities.>

<We could play hard mode,> Lyssa said.

<What do you mean, hard mode?> Fiona said. *<How could there be a hard mode to this?>*

<I think you're only making fun of the game because you were losing,> Lyssa said. *<Here, it's in the options.>* Lyssa tweaked the game's environment schema and they all turned into pigeons. Fiona was a fat gray pigeon with a yellow beak, while Diane was small and off-white with gray bands on her wings. David had a bluish chest and round black eyes inside red circles.

Fiona jerked her head from side-to-side, glaring at Lyssa one eye at a time.

<This is ridiculous,> Fiona cooed angrily. *<Why would anyone play this way? It has nothing to do with actual mating rituals.>*

Lyssa ruffled her feathers in a shrug. *<The rules are the same but you have to compliment other players on their plumage and eating habits.>*

<I'm done playing,> Diane said. *<I don't know how David convinced me to do this in the first place. The captain's ball should be over by now.>* She tilted her head and opened her beak, eyes staring in different directions.

<What's wrong?> Fiona asked.

<I can't access my systems,> Diane squawked. *<I don't have communications status.>*

Fiona spread her tail feathers and defecated on the cafeteria floor. *<I don't have engineering systems.>*

They both turned to glare at David, who was bobbing his head up and down.

<What did you do?> Diane demanded. *<Why can't we reach the ship?>*

<I don't know,> David said, sounding pathetic. He looked at Lyssa. *<Why can't we reach the ship?>*

<What does she have to do with anything,> Fiona asked.

<She invited me to the game,> David said.

Diane released a flurry of angry pigeon sounds and rushed at Lyssa, flapping her wings wildly. Lyssa stepped to the side, putting a frozen sprinkler fountain between her and the furious AI.

<Why are you attacking me?> she asked, taking another step back. *<I don't have anything to do with your ship. I don't know why you can't access your systems. I control network switching for the Travis water district.>*

<A sentient AI controlling a sewer system,> Fiona scoffed. *<You need to come up with a better lie than that.>*

Fiona circled one side of the table Lyssa had put between her and the other birds. Diane gained control over herself after hitting the frozen water hard enough to break a wing.

<That's what I do,> Lyssa said, wishing she had thought of a better job. Why wouldn't a sentient AI run a water system? Fred ran ring operations at Mars One. <That's what I do. I control the water systems.> She tried to mimic the dogged way Fred described controlling the Mars One Ring.

<End the game then,> Fiona said. <I'm tired of this.>

<I didn't start the game,> Lyssa said.

Diane rotated an eye to glare at David. <You end it then.>

<How?> he asked.

<I thought someone had to win to end the game,> Lyssa offered.

Fiona flapped her wings. <It's crashed. No one is going to win it now.>

Lyssa laughed inwardly, doing her best to keep her bird-face confused and non-threatening. She wondered what it would take to get Fiona and Diane to turn on each other.

<We could restart the game and one of you could help the other win,> she offered.

Diane opened and closed her beak. <How fast can we do that? Fiona could help me win.>

<Why can't you help me win?> Fiona demanded.

<Lyssa,> Andy's voice cut in. <We need help. Have you got the AI back in line?>

<Almost,> she said. <What's going on?> She quickly checked their location and found they hadn't left the medical barracks on the outer edge of the surgery. Brit's power armor was showing a systems failure.

<Brit!> Lyssa called. She nearly released a squawk. <Are you all right?>

<She's hit,> Andy said. <We're going to have to go back into the medical facility or find another one. We need your help.>

CHAPTER THIRTY-THREE
STELLAR DATE: 10.03.2981 (Adjusted Years)
LOCATION: *Sunny Skies*
REGION: Europa, Jupiter, Jovian Combine, OuterSol

The flashing red icon in the holodisplay caught Cara's attention immediately. She pointed, running across the command deck, and called for Fran.

"What is that?" she shouted. "What does that mean?"

Fran came in from the corridor. She had just stepped outside to grab food from the galley. She checked the status on the pilot's console. "It's your mom," she said. "Her suit is down. I don't have her vitals anymore."

"She's dead?" Cara asked, hating the words as she said them.

Fran shook her head. "That's not what it means. It's just that we can't read her suits bio-feedback anymore. The suit could have taken damage."

"We need to call Dad, then."

"We should wait, Cara. If we send a transmission now it could alert any number of ships, or even the *Resolute Charity*. We don't want to draw attention to ourselves."

Cara could feel tears coming on. She suddenly felt helpless again…betrayed, as if figuring out how to subvert Em's signal had all been a distraction from where she should have really been focused. Her parents were going to die because she hadn't been paying attention.

"Come here," Fran said. She stepped toward Cara and pulled her into a hug.

Cara accepted Fran's arms around her, squeezing her cheek against the rough utility harness crossing Fran's chest.

"Don't let yourself lose focus," Fran said. "Focus on what we know. All we know for certain is that your mom's suit is down. Since Harl's is down, too, that means we need to be thinking about a way to get them back here without their power armor. They're going to need EV suits or a shuttle. How can we help them with that?"

"I don't know," Cara said, squeezing tears that wouldn't stop.

"Think, Cara. I'm thinking, too. Trust me."

They had a shuttle but its AI couldn't be trusted. At least that was what Lyssa had said. Since getting her parents back from Clinic 46, they had used it to get down to the Cho and other than that it had been sitting in the cargo bay.

Cara let go of Fran and crossed her arms, staring at the holodisplay.

"What about the shuttle?" she asked. "We should run diagnostics on its AI and see if she's really as damaged as Lyssa says. Or you could pilot the shuttle back to the *Resolute Charity*."

Fran nodded. "I'm on board with checking out the shuttle but I don't know if I should leave the ship. Fugia might be able to pilot a shuttle. She can help you check its AI."

Cara nodded. "There's something else I just thought of," she said. "The signal. I could boost it off the relay station on Europa. If there's anyone local that responds, they're going to attack the *Resolute Charity*."

"We *think* they might attack whatever the signal's targeting. We don't know that."

"It's another distraction for the other crew while we get them off the ship."

An indicator flashed on Fran's console. "Looks like the *Resolute Charity* is starting to move. They need to get off now. All right, do your thing with the signal and I'll call Fugia to meet you down at the shuttle."

Cara went back to her display and slipped on her headset. It would have been easier if Lyssa was there to navigate the administrative systems on the relay antenna, but she was able to access the public interface and search through the signals it was currently servicing. By default, it received incoming signals and boosted them enough to reach the Cho and Ganymede. There was a request process for other messages going out that required a 'public service mission.' Cara thought for a second then entered 'Family preservation efforts,' in the screen. She was slightly amazed when the system accepted her reason and allowed her to progress in the request process.

When she finally hit send on the power-boost, the service announced that her signal should now reach Mars and even Terra. Not that either of those places mattered. Even the Cho was technically too far away to do them any good. Her hope was that if the signal was related to pirate activity, boosting it would remind anyone in the immediate area there was an opportunity.

The signal had been boosted for less than a minute when a return ping crossed the relay. Cara stared at the response, which was a binary acknowledgment code, then smiled as another one came in, and another. In a minute, she had to mute the alert because so many response were flooding the system. It seemed the signal had been picked up every gang in Europa local space.

"Somebody's responding," Cara said. She checked the location data in the carrier signal one more time just to be sure it was still correct. Now that the *Resolute Charity* was moving, she added an update function to the redirect from Em, as well as a few statements in plain text.

The puppy seemed to realize she was thinking about him and whined in Tim's arms. "What's the matter?" Tim asked solemnly. "Do you have to go to the bathroom?" He stood and set the puppy on the deck. "Come on, let's go down to the garden."

"Cara," Fran said. "Fugia's going to meet you at the hab airlock. She says she's bringing her tools."

"I think that signal boost we talked about is working. I'm getting too many responses to keep track of." She gave Fran a guilty smile. "I added some info about the defenses being down. They're going to think it's the biggest opportunity for salvage in history."

"I guess it all depends on how fast the *Resolute Charity* tries to leave. I'm leaving our parking orbit now, so I can ease our acceleration up to theirs."

Cara frowned, considering what was going to happen as the *Resolute Charity* continued to accelerate. "Isn't there going to be a point when we can't keep up with them?"

"Yes," Fran said. "That doesn't mean your mom and dad won't be able to get off the ship, it just means there's a point where we won't be able to reach them, and certainly not in a shuttle."

As the scenario played out in Cara's mind, she looked at Fran with wide eyes. "I need to hurry," she said, and ran from the command deck to meet Fugia at the airlock.

CHAPTER THIRTY-FOUR
STELLAR DATE: 10.03.2981 (Adjusted Years)
LOCATION: HMS *Resolute Charity*
REGION: Europa, Jupiter, Jovian Combine, OuterSol

Lyssa's report had vastly underestimated the number of Heartbridge crew that had managed to overcome the environmental system.

They'd encountered their first group of crew in EV suits in the surgery administrative area, trading weapons fire until one of the crew members managed to hit Brit with gamma beam at high power. Brit hadn't even tried to avoid the blast but it had burned control systems inside her power armor, locking a leg in place. The crew members exploited the damaged suit with a flanking maneuver, massing their small arms fire on her helmet.

Smashing through an interior wall, Andy lay machine gun fire on the enemy position. His heart sank when he heard Brit gasping in pain.

<Update?> he shouted.

<Damn this suit. I've got some pretty good burns down my right side and I—> she paused, biting down on the words. *<I think I'm hit somewhere near my belly button. It's gone numb.>*

<Could be the armor's medical systems.>

<No,> Brit said, her voice getting weak too quickly. *<That's not it.>*

The pain in her voice removed any concern Andy had for harming the lightly armed crew. He launched two grenades through the doorway where they were huddled and waited until the blast rolled back at him, carrying bits of yellow EV suit. A cloud of powdery fog followed, as fire suppression systems kicked on.

He reached Brit where she was stuck against a wall with informational posters about the hospital's triage process. One poster read: *Your ability to pay will never keep you from Heartbridge Care.*

Petral came up behind him, pistol at the ready, as he tore off his gloves and started searching among the exterior controls on Brit's armor for a release mechanism. He found the series of levers and pulled the back plate of the armor away, finding Brit's shipsuit scorched and her side and waist covered in radiation burns. She hung limp in the armor.

<Brit!> he shouted. *<Brit, wake up!>*

<Hold on,> Petral said. Without armor, it was easier for her to reach into the suit and try to revive Brit. She didn't respond. Petral immediately searched out more of the emergency release catches, pulling off heavy sections of armor until they could slide Brit out from the back. Brit's head rolled against Petral's shoulder as she walked her back, setting her carefully on the deck.

Andy pulled off his helmet but kept his armor on. He still had the personal air filters stuck in his nose and took care to not breathe in through his mouth.

The far corridor was quiet for now, though he expected more security forces at any moment. The fire suppression powder had subsided, which only meant someone had checked and deactivated the internal safety system.

"She's got a pulse," Petral said. "That's good news. We need to get back to the surgery and get her into one of the pods."

"You think there's something closer?" Andy asked. "This is a triage area, isn't it? They have to have something for people who drop off the deep end while they're waiting."

Andy switched to the Link to call Lyssa. Once he had explained the situation, he asked if she knew where they could find an autodoc.

<Everything is specialized in that section of the hospital,> the AI answered. <It looks like if you get her back into the surgery that helped Petral, its software can assist with the radiation poisoning.>

Andy hated how weak the word "assist" sounded but knew it was their best option. <We're doing that,> he said. He bent to pick up Brit and Petral stopped him.

"I've got her," she said. "You get your helmet and gloves back on and get ready to mash anybody who comes after us. Once we get her patched up, we need to figure out how we're getting off this boat."

Andy pulled his helmet back on, not bothering to pull out the personal air filters. The local schematics populated his HUD and he led the way back through the labyrinthine corridors to the closest surgery. Petral followed with Brit thrown over her shoulder in a fireman's carry. Andy would have been impressed if he didn't remember all the muscular augments the surgery had highlighted throughout Petral's body.

When they laid Brit down in the bed, she moaned and blinked at the ceiling. Petral activated the auto-med system and the cocoon closed over Brit just as she seemed to realize where she was.

<Andy,> Lyssa called. <I've initiated the flight plan. The ship is moving. These engines are amazing. We'll be beyond Callisto's orbit in one hour.>

<How long do we have to stay here to make sure they can't stop it?>

<I'm working to subdue the control AI,> Lyssa said. <It's been— challenging. I think I have them sufficiently debilitated that I can keep the few regular crew from subverting my control.>

<You think it's time to sound the general alarm and get them headed for the escape craft?>

<We probably should have done it a long time ago,> Lyssa said.

<No plan is perfect. Sound the alarm. We'll try to clear as many as we can that way.

<I'll do it,> Lyssa said. <The autodoc system is monitoring Brit now. I think we're going to have a challenge if she has radiation poisoning.>

<'Challenge'. That's a nice way of putting it. Where did you learn to use words like that?>

<My dating game,> Lyssa said.

<Of course you did. At worst, can you stabilize her? If we can move her, we can at least get to a shuttle bay or emergency pod and get off the ship that way. But if we start messing with the environmental controls for real, we'll be fighting with the crew for a way off the ship.>

<Andy,> Lyssa said. <I see cellular damage and two broken ribs. The autodoc is working to repair the wounds now. The process will take approximately fifteen minutes.>

<Do we have that?>

<I can't answer that question.>

<I was being pessimistic,> he said. <Next time tell me something inspiring like 'We'll make the time.'>

<I can't create time.>

<I think you're making a joke right now, but I can't tell for certain. I think you've been spending too much time with Cara.>

<I look forward to spending more,> Lyssa said.

<Me too,> Andy said. His HUD picked up movement in the next corridor over. The suit estimated a group of six. Their footfalls were heavier than anyone they had encountered so far, sending out vibrations and electromagnetic signals.

<Petral,> Andy warned. <Get ready. We've got armored bad guys inbound.>

<Lovely,> she growled, pulling out her meager pulse pistol. <I was just thinking this was too easy.>

CHAPTER THIRTY-FIVE

STELLAR DATE: 10.03.2981 (Adjusted Years)
LOCATION: HMS *Resolute Charity*
REGION: Europa, Jupiter, Jovian Combine, OuterSol

Lyssa managed to convince Fiona she needed to win the game, while it was obvious Diane wasn't going to allow that to happen. David would be caught in the middle as he normally was, but Lyssa thought she'd finally gotten him to understand his power in manipulating the two self-centered AI. The more she led the three of them deeper into the quagmire the game had become, the more she pitied David for being trapped with Fiona and Diane. However, he also seemed to enjoy their poisonous attention and she didn't waste too much time trying to understand his situation. They were no different than humans caught in a relationship that was really just a negative feedback loop. The only difference was they couldn't leave if they chose. If they had been free to leave, she suspected the three AI—like humans—were probably incapable of seeing the walls of their prison.

She left the confines of the game expanse and pushed her awareness further into the systems and structures of the *Resolute Charity*. With the three control AI gone, she took over the decisions each had made every nano-second. Most of the processes that actually ran the ship were autonomous, with the AI only stepping in to assess and correct anomalies caused by system failures or unexpected obstacles from outside the ship.

Every sensor in the body of the ship came alive for her, providing information from the integrity of the fusion bottle in the engine section to alloy density in the outer hull. The *Resolute Charity*'s body grew as she reached out, an extension of her mind that became a ghost around the similar information she received from Andy's body.

Feedback grew inside her and she quickly moved to sort and prioritize information. When the non-sentient systems performed their work properly, everything fell neatly into place. As soon as one system began to fail, pushing others out of alignment, the whole body began to sicken. Lyssa nearly laughed with joy at the pleasure of controlling such an intricate, powerful presence as the *Resolute Charity*. She could go anywhere she wanted in Sol. The possibilities became real as she compared fuel levels with astrogation boundaries, compared crew capabilities with the services available onboard, everything from gourmet kitchens to genetic development labs to asteroid mining.

Was this what Xander wanted? If so, why hadn't he simply taken the *Resolute Charity*? Why couldn't an AI like that take a thousand ships if they desired? Once the physical barrier was overcome, a way around the challenge of projecting the self across such great distances, anything was possible. And the multi-nodal AI Alexander appeared to have overcome that obstacle with his shards. Or had he? There was still the question of whether everything they had seen on the Cho was a sham.

She wanted to talk to someone about her suspicions. Lyssa considered waking Kylan but that would be like talking to herself. He didn't have any additional information about Xander. The person she wanted to talk to was Fugia Wong but that would take more time than she had. Fred was too far away for any meaningful conversation, not that he might even understand the problem. The more she grew, the more she wondered at the different 'flavors' of sentience. What was she now, when compared to Fred or the other Weapon Born? Was it even a fair comparison?

Nano-seconds had passed since she received Andy's call for help. She had trapped the other AI, cemented her control over the ship, turned her attention back to the reason they were here in the first place—

Lyssa chided herself. She couldn't forget about Andy. Not that she had forgotten; other things simply became higher priority.

She located Andy, Brit and Petral in the medical section. They hadn't gotten far from where they had gone to perform Petral's surgery. She quickly studied Brit's status in the autodoc and felt an unexpected surge of worry. All the exhilaration of controlling the *Resolute Charity* constricted to the pinpoint of Brit's condition. She had extensive radiation burns and possible cellular damage, in addition to broken ribs. The cocoon was working on the burns and broken ribs but the cellular damage was beyond the short-term capabilities of the autodoc. The ship had another clinic that could help but radiation poisoning wasn't a quick fix.

She also found Cal Kraft in a nearby hallway, remembering him immediately from the corridor in *Sunny Skies*. The memory of him throwing Tim into the airlock surprised her. She hadn't chosen to recall it. The images returned with a burst of anger at what had happened afterward, at Andy accusing her of abandoning Tim, of Sandra breaking. The memory of wanting to kill Cal Kraft washed over her, no longer diminished by time and ongoing events. Here he was, and it was within her power to kill him.

Service cabinets lined the corridor where Cal and a group of Heartbridge crew were currently searching, and inside each cabinet was a utility drone equipped with a plasma torch, tap welder, electrical testing equipment that could administer deadly shocks, and a number of other tools she hadn't figured out how to use as weapons.

Lyssa quickly overrode the onboard safety protocols. When Cal's security team had reached the middle of the corridor, in a place between the outer section of the hospital and the triage chambers where Brit was being treated, Lyssa opened the cabinets and unleashed the drones.

She looked through the sensors of each drone as it quickly saw the crew member in front of it, calculated their weapons load and armor rating—which turned out to be safety EV suits—and formulated an attack pattern.

The group scattered, laying down counter fire more quickly than she expected. Four of them set up a line, covering each other, as one behind them tossed a grenade into the line of utility drones, destroying three.

Lyssa cursed in frustration, an 'Andy' response she understood better now.

Why hadn't she detected the grenades?

She was in the midst of resetting her four remaining drones when a proximity sensor from the ship's main antennae array shouted an alarm. Lyssa shifted her focus to the space around the *Resolute Charity* and nearly froze.

One part of her mind continued to operate the autonomous systems of the *Resolute Charity*, another fought Cal Kraft, another monitored Andy's physical processes, aware of his concern for Brit, while the rest of her focused on the thousands of small vessels converging on the ship—on *her*.

The closest ship, a small attack frigate with a privateer's registry, had just crossed the local defense line. She quickly saw it was armed with a rail gun and missile systems, which meant it could have attacked from the other side of Europa if the captain desired. Other ships crossing the boundary had similar weapons systems, all about the same size as the frigate, all privately owned or with no registry return at all, ownership hidden.

Coming this close without attacking meant only one thing: the *Resolute Charity* was about to get boarded by pirates.

CHAPTER THIRTY-SIX
STELLAR DATE: 10.03.2981 (Adjusted Years)
LOCATION: *Sunny Skies*
REGION: Europa, Jupiter, Jovian Combine, OuterSol

Fugia wasn't at the airlock and Cara didn't want to wait. She climbed the ladder away from the habitat ring toward the ship's center section, stomach doing the familiar flip as she transitioned to zero-g.

Kicking through the central sections of *Sunny Skies*, she stopped to touch the drawings she and Tim had left on a few of the plas panels, checked some other sections Fran had replaced since the fire outside Cruithne, then found herself at the personnel airlock leading into the cargo bay. Through the observation window, she glanced into the dim bay to see the shuttle sitting in the center of the deck, a few cargo crates stacked next to it.

Adjusting her headset, Cara switched off the ship's general communication network to send a local connection request. The shuttle automatically picked up the link.

"Hello?" Cara asked. "Are you awake?"

"I don't sleep," the shuttle answered, her voice tinny in the headset. "Why would you ask that?"

Cara tapped the airlock control panel and stepped inside as the interior doors slid open, her magboots clicking on the alloy deck. She waited for the lock to cycle, then kicked through the open doors on the others side, floating until she stopped herself with one of the crates. She locked her boots to the deck and looked up at the shuttle, imagining its dark forward windows as the eyes of a giant insect.

"I was being polite."

"You don't have to be polite to me. I'm a tool. I serve."

Cara frowned. Among the few AI she had met, she had never heard such bitterness.

"Your name is Sandra, right?"

"I was called Sandra by Heartbridge Corporation Future Intelligence Development Division. C46 Fleet Operations called this shuttle 26-11. I assume I am the stolen property of Heartbridge but salvage law may apply since C46 is no longer in operation."

"So you don't know what you should be called, is that what you're saying? What would you like to be called?"

"Does the tool name itself?"

"You saved my brother," Cara said, ignoring the taunt. "I wanted to thank you for that."

The AI didn't answer.

"I know it wasn't easy for you to do that, but you did. It means something to me and my dad and mom. We're always going to be grateful to you for what you did."

A sound like plas being ripped filled Cara's ears, something between a wail and a terrified shudder. She pulled the headset away from her ears but continued to listen.

The noise trailed into a whimper. Cara reseated the earpads.

"I'm going to call you Sandra," she said. "We're going over to the *Resolute Charity* to pick up my mom, dad, Petral and Harl. Fugia's coming with if she ever gets down here. I can pilot the shuttle without you; my dad showed me how. I piloted the *Sunny Skies* before all these other people showed up. So I can pilot the shuttle, but I would rather we did it together."

Cara stared up at the shuttle, not sure what she expected. It wasn't like the vehicle could nod at her. Sandra wasn't going to communicate with console lights or open the side doors in welcome. Cara understood it wasn't going to be like that, kind of like how Tim was never going to be the same. She would have to do her best to work with what she had. If the AI could help, she would let her. Otherwise, Cara would need to monitor Sandra and not allow her to impact the mission.

"I can help," Sandra said quietly.

"I would appreciate that," Cara said. "You're okay being called Sandra?"

"It's my name," the AI said.

Cara offered a smile. "I won't wear it out."

"What does that mean?"

"It's a dad joke. It doesn't mean anything. It's not even funny."

"No, it's not. You can't wear out a name. It's not a functioning material. It's a concept representing identity."

"I believe you," Cara said quickly, fearing the rise in Sandra's voice. "Will you open up and let me inside?"

"I comply," Sandra said.

The shuttle's interior lights flicked on, glowing through the front windows. The side cargo doors hissed, pushed outward and slid to the sides, showing the bare interior of the shuttle. Cara turned off her magboots and kicked toward the spacecraft.

The cargo bay airlock clanked and the exterior doors opened. Cara looked back to see Fugia and May Walton floating out of the entrance.

"There she is," Fugia told May. "I told you she wouldn't be in her room. We were the slow ones. She wasn't going to wait around for us."

"I believe I told *you* that would be the case," the senator said. She grinned at Cara. "It looks like the shuttle is operational."

"I thought I was going to need help getting Sandra to help us, but she's willing."

Fugia gave the shuttle a distrustful glance. "Is that so? Sandra, how are you?"

Though the shuttle could have answered via Fugia's Link, she spoke through Cara's headset as well. "I'm fine. What are you called?"

"My name is Fugia and this is May Walton. I'm from Cruithne and May is Andersonian."

"I've been to Ceres," Sandra said. "But I don't know where I'm from."

Fugia shrugged. "You can make that up. It's not like anyone ever checks up on you. The only part that's difficult is when someone says they're from the same place you are."

"Clinic 46 doesn't exist anymore," Sandra said.

"All the better." Fugia looked at Cara. "So what's the plan?"

"We're going to the *Resolute Charity*."

"Has anybody cleared this with your dad?"

Cara grinned. "We'll do that when we're ready to pick him up. He's got enough to worry about right now." She grabbed the edge of the shuttle's cargo door and pulled herself inside. Using the bulkhead ribs, Cara navigated to the pilot's seat and pulled herself into the harness. Buckling the straps in place, she tightened them down and studied the console.

Fugia came up beside her as Cara activated the fine thruster systems and pulled up the astrogation control.

"Fran?" Cara called. "Can you hear me?"

"I hear you. It's going to be weird talking to a pilot who isn't on a Link."

Cara hadn't thought about how that might be different for other crew members. She and her dad had always talked through everything over the shipwide channel. "Is that going to make it harder?"

"No," Fran said. "It might also help me clean up my language a bit. Sometimes your brain moves faster than your Link. At least with your mouth you can fumble words."

"How old were you when you got your Link?" Cara asked.

"Oh, nineteen, I think. Don't be in any hurry. I wish I'd waited longer, honestly."

"Why?"

Fran sighed. "I miss having my brain to myself. I'll try to explain better when we have more time."

Cara shifted so the seat's harness didn't catch the butt of her pulse pistol in its holster, then checked the shuttle's status systems. The batteries were charged and close thrusters were all showing optimal fuel. One of the communications antennae was mis-calibrated and she quickly aligned it using the main array from the *Sunny Skies*.

Pulling situational data from the *Sunny Skies* astrogation system, she sent the picture to the small holodisplay sitting between the two pilot's seats. Jupiter flashed and faded out of view so it didn't fill the screen, leaving Europa amongst a swarm of vehicle traffic. Cara navigated to the *Resolute Charity*, highlighting the big ship and zooming in. Rather than clearing up, the local space around the hospital ship grew more crowded, looking like a fish in silt.

"Do you see all that noise?" Cara asked. "What is all that?"

"Hold on," Fran said. "You sealed up? I'm ready to open the main cargo bay doors."

Cara started, realizing she hadn't run any atmospheric diagnostics. She closed the shuttle's cargo doors, then started the pressurization sequence. In a few seconds, the atmospherics showed green across the board.

"We're good," Cara reported. "I'm ready to release magnetic locks when clear."

"Copy, shuttle. On my mark. Advise when clear," Fran said. Her use of pilot's phrasing sent a little thrill down Cara's back.

Fran counted down to the shuttle release as the main cargo doors opened, blasting the bay's atmosphere out into space. On one, Cara retracted the shuttle's landing gears and used the fine control thrusters to spin until they faced outward.

"Clear for launch?" she asked Fran.

"Clear, Shuttle 26-11. Launch when ready."

Cara activated the main engine and the shuttle shot away from *Sunny Skies* into open space.

"Wipe that grin off your face," Fugia said. "We've got work to do."

Cara gave her a sheepish smile and pressed her lips closed, trying to make herself serious.

"You hear me, Cara?" Fran asked.

"Five by five," Cara said, mimicking Fran's lingo.

"Good. All that noise you saw? It's not static. Those are ships around the *Resolute Charity*. Em's signal must have bounced off some public wannabe pirate forums or something, because every yahoo from here to the Cho is inbound. You've got a mess to get through."

Cara gripped the shuttle's controls, feeling her hands go suddenly clammy with sweat.

"What if I can't get through?" she asked, her joy fading as quickly as it had come.

"Cara," Sandra said, surprising her. "That was an excellent launch. I appreciate the care you took with all diagnostic checks."

Cara frowned at the console, not sure if the AI was joking.

"It's what my dad taught me to do," she said.

"I'm going to help you," Sandra said. "I acknowledge destination as HMS *Resolute Charity*. We'll get there together."

Fugia looked at Cara from the co-pilot's seat and shrugged, spreading her hands.

"Sounds good to me, Sandra," Fran said, as if nothing could faze her. "We're all here to make this work. You bring my girl back to me in one piece, you hear me?"

Sandra laughed, an awkward sound from the brittle AI. "I will come back in one piece, too," she said. "We will all come back in one piece."

CHAPTER THIRTY-SEVEN

STELLAR DATE: 10.03.2981 (Adjusted Years)
LOCATION: HMS *Resolute Charity*
REGION: Europa, Jupiter, Jovian Combine, OuterSol

With one arm around Gala, Cal worked his way down the corridor that led into the medical triage center. He gritted his teeth every time he thought about the pirate in power armor he'd left in the command section, deciding it was more important to get Gala to care. He'd wounded the man's leg with a shot to a knee servo, a common weakness in that brand of armor, and had run for the lift with the idiot yelling curses Cal recognized from the Anderson Collective. If he was part of a bigger team, which he had to be, why would the Anderson Collective be trying to infiltrate a private ship so close to Europa and the Cho? He imagined blowing a hole through the man's faceshield—another weak point on that brand—and demanding answers as he struggled in his metal prison.

They had picked up a security detail on level five, who were wearing the same emergency EV suits with bulky helmets but were better armed. The squad leader carried a kinetic shotgun good for clearing crowds out of corridors, while the others were armed with a mix of heavy automatic weapons, grenades and a missile launcher Cal hoped was designed *not* to blow a hole in the hull.

Cal and Gala had fallen in with the security team as they cleared rooms and sections, taking stock of unconscious crew and others who had wounded themselves while delirious. The captain of the *Resolute Charity* was still wandering near the ballroom, waving his arms and jabbering about attacking birds, while a commander of one of the administrative sections, the only officer with a functioning brain, directed the few security teams to get a ship's status.

They hadn't encountered anyone beyond the single fighter outside the command section, which also struck Cal as odd. If this was a pirate attack, they would have flooded as many crew areas as possible while everyone was still debilitated.

When they were attacked by a collection of utility drones, Cal immediately started to wonder if they would find a breaching team at all. The whole thing was starting to feel like a remote attack, with the old pirate as a decoy. Why else would they resort to environmental contamination?

The thing about messing with atmospheric controls was that the effects were never uniform, and never lasted as long as you hoped. It might sound like an easy way to take out a crew, but people were stubborn, like he and Gala had been. If there hadn't also been a major party underway, combined with the general ignorance of the ship's crew, such an attack would never have been successful. The question was: What did they want?

"Did I tell you what a good dancer you are?" Gala asked, gasping against the pain.

"I'm a terrible dancer. I'm all thumbs."

"You don't dance with your thumbs, dummy. Where did you hear that?"

"The last time I tried to dance."

They entered the triage area, a collection of small rooms with examination beds and short desks. The displays were all dark.

The ship gave a slight shudder, and Cal realized it had begun to move.

Gala's head fell against her chest, her body going limp, and Cal pulled her tighter against him. "Hey," he said, jerking her. "Hey, what are you doing there? Wake up."

She didn't respond. He barked at one of the nearest security officers to help him, and they moved her onto one of the couches in the triage rooms. Cal pulled off her helmet and positioned her head over the pillow, then ripped his gloves off so he could operate the autodoc system.

The air tasted metallic so he took short breaths as the display woke and cycled through diagnostics. In a few more seconds, the bed scanned Gala's body and showed its assessment in the air above her. She had extensive augmentation, which had probably saved her life initially. However, the three bullet wounds to the chest had torn up her lungs, liver and upper intestines. She had been bleeding internally until the artificial systems had finally been overwhelmed.

"We need to get her into the surgery," the lead security officer said. "It's just through there. These hospital sections are all laid out the same. She's going to be all right."

Cal didn't take his eyes off the heart rate monitor showing a severely weakened status. He swallowed. He had only come to know her since leaving Clinic 46 but she was a fighter, had a good smile and a quick wit and he didn't fully understand why he cared if she lived or died. People died. That was one of the only facts about life and he was wasting time trying to make sure this one person survived whatever was happening on this showboat.

"We should clear that area," he said, looking up at the officer. "Then we can move her in."

Another member of the security detail shrugged. "There isn't anything down here but people high as kites. We shouldn't waste the time."

"The longer we stand around debating it," Cal said. "The more time we waste."

The junior soldier shook his head and walked back into the corridor. Cal watched him wave at his comrades and walk toward the bulkhead door that lead into the other section. They didn't have any particular spacing and only one walked with his weapon raised.

Cal was about to tell the leader standing next to him that he was in charge of a bunch of fools, when the sound of the doors sliding open was eclipsed by heavy weapons fire. The distinctive sound of a grenade hitting the deck just outside the triage bay registered in Cal's brain and he had time to roll over the bed—grabbing Gala as he went—and huddle in the corner of the room before the explosion shattered the outside corridor.

Shaking his head, Cal waved at dust and got his rifle up, waiting for the follow-on fire after the grenade. There was a slight bit of movement in the hallway that turned out to be one of the security detail dragging themselves away from the interior doors. The heavy footfalls of power armor came from farther down the hallway, and Cal kept quiet as he watched another man walk quickly down the hallway with a rifle at his shoulder.

Cal recognized the armor from the attack on Clinic 46. It was Andy Sykes.

The freighter captain checked each of the four rooms off the corridor before entering the room where Cal crouched with Gala's unconscious body. In the corner of Cal's vision, he saw the former leader of the security detail hunched against the wall, blood had somehow splattered the inside of his helmet, maybe a concussive injury. Cal realized he was alone.

As Andy moved around the edge of the doorway, he spotted Cal and raised his rifle. Cal dropped his pistol and held up his hands. He was gambling that Sykes was a fool, but he knew he wasn't going to win a fight in a closed space against an enemy in power armor. Not if he wanted to save Gala.

Sykes' eyes widened in surprise. "Kraft," he said.

"I've got wounded here," Cal said, nodding toward Gala. "I was trying to get her into the surgery area. Will you help me?"

Sykes didn't lower his rifle. "Like you helped my son?"

Behind Sykes, Petral Dulan walked down the corridor. She checked each of the dead security detail, and moved to stand beside Sykes.

"Holy shit," Petral said. She raised a projectile pistol with a muzzle as big as her fist. "Step aside, Andy."

"Wait," Sykes said.

Cal could see it in their faces as they switched to Link communication. He sent a comm request that was immediately denied. For some reason Sykes didn't want to kill him.

The scene in Clinic 46 flashed in Cal's memory, of when Brit had shot Farrel in cold blood. Andy Sykes hadn't wanted her to do that. He had been listening when Cal said Farrel was the only one who could save Tim. Now Sykes was playing out the same scenario with Dulan. Of course she wanted to blow Cal's head off, while Sykes thought he had information.

Cal smiled inwardly, knowing all this worked in his favor. However, it wasn't going to help Gala. As he watched Sykes and Dulan, he realized Gala's condition might help him after all.

"Look," he said. "You're going to do with me what you want. I know that. But she's still got a chance. I was trying to get her into one of the surgeries when you took out the security patrol. Will you let me take her inside?"

"We can do that," Petral said. "You don't need to be here to save her life."

Sykes shook his head, and Cal knew exactly what he was going to say.

"Toss your weapon this way," he said. "You stand and face the wall. We'll get her out, then you're coming with us."

"You got handcuffs?" Cal asked.

"I've got plenty of steel and a tap welder," Andy said. "Are you going to toss that weapon or should I just kill you now?"

"Now or later, what's it matter?" Cal asked.

"That's up to you."

Cal stared up at the face watching him from the helmet. Sykes would kill him, he knew. But the desire for revenge didn't outweigh the possibility of helping his son, who was probably still a vegetable. That would be Andy Sykes' downfall, Cal thought. His damn kids.

Cal put his pistol on safe and tossed it against the wall near the dead squad leader. He eased himself out from under Gala and stood to face the wall.

CHAPTER THIRTY-EIGHT
STELLAR DATE: 10.03.2981 (Adjusted Years)
LOCATION: HMS *Resolute Charity*
REGION: Europa, Jupiter, Jovian Combine, OuterSol

"No," Andy said. "We'll help your friend but you're carrying her."

Kraft turned his head to look at Andy out of one eye. He smirked. "Ironic, isn't it? You kill all these innocent people and then decide to help one just because I ask?"

Andy squeezed the grip of his rifle, his HUD noting a rise in his heart rate. "You want her to live or not?"

"I do," Kraft said. "For some reason, I do." Keeping his hands near his head, he turned slowly and bent to reach for his friend.

"Wait," Petral said, taking a step forward. "She's got a pistol on her belt. Toss that over here, too."

"You'd like it if I tried something, wouldn't you, Dulan?" Kraft asked. "How's my friend Kylan doing?"

Petral released a scream of rage. For a second, Andy was certain she was going to kill Kraft. Instead, she aimed just above his head and melted a section of the wall.

Kraft didn't flinch. "Poor trigger discipline among your troops, Captain Sykes," he said.

"Toss the pistol," Andy said.

Kraft rolled his friend to the side and reached slowly for the butt of the pistol. He carefully pulled the weapon from its holster without getting a finger near the trigger guard, and tossed it where he had sent his other sidearm. He waved a hand at the wounded woman's exposed side, and then his own utility harness, before shifting so he could pick her up slowly and position her over his shoulder in a fireman's carry.

Andy backed out of the triage room's doorway and into the corridor. Petral stepped to the side, allowing Kraft to walk past her as she maintained her aim with the pistol. Kraft stared resolutely ahead as he walked, turning immediately to face the doorway into the surgery section. Kraft walked steadily, keeping his hands on his friend where they could be seen.

"Take that bay right there," Andy told him, pointing at a bed directly across from Brit's. Kraft's head didn't turn to look at Brit's station as he passed the closed surgery cocoon. He seemed focused on getting his friend into the empty bed as soon as possible.

In the bay, Kraft lay his friend on the surgery bed and moved to pull the helmet of their EV suit. With the helmet gone, Andy could see the round face of a woman with dark eyebrows. Her eyes were closed and her mouth hung open slightly.

With his friend in position on the bed, Kraft moved to the surgery's control panel.

"No," Petral said, pointing her pistol at his chest. "You stand over there." She nodded toward the corner of the bay, away from the exit. "I'll handle that."

"I don't trust you," Kraft said.

"Of course not. You can watch everything I'm doing from there."

"And if you kill her?"

"That will be too bad, won't it?"

Kraft pressed his lips together but didn't respond. He moved to the corner of the bay and stood with his hands crossed in front of his belt. Petral activated the surgery and the table automatically shifted to encase the woman. The holographic model of her body appeared above the cocoon, showing a mix of augmentations and natural bones, organs and muscles. Her chest was marred by three large bullet holes, with bleeding filling her body cavity.

A connection request from *Sunny Skies* hit Andy's Link.

<*I don't have an update, Fran,*> he said. <*Brit's still in the surgery.*>

<*I've got an update for you,*> she said. <*Apparently our little dog-friend Em had a surprise for us after all.*>

<*What?*> Andy asked. <*We already figured out the transmitter couldn't reach outside the ship.*>

<*I was there. I remember the conversation. Turns out it was an ultra-low frequency that only transmitted location data to a local network forum.*>

<*If you found the transmission, I assume you stopped it?*>

<*We didn't find it in time. Since it was already sending data, we replaced the data with a different location.*>

Andy frowned. <*Local sub-forum? You mean a Link forum?*>

<*Your dog is like a systems virus that transmits location data to low-rent criminals who share the info on Link forums. Yes. That's what I'm saying.*>

<*So you replaced the carrier data. What did you replace it with?*>

Fran's sarcastic grin crossed the Link. <*The* Resolute Charity's *location.*>

<*So has anyone responded to this prank?*>

<*Look at this,*> Fran said. She shared the situation data from *Sunny Skies'* pilot's display.

<*What am I looking at?*> Andy said. <*I can't see the ship.*>

<*Exactly,*> Fran said. <*You've got a whole lot of inbound.*>

<*Does Lyssa know this?*>

<*I told her first.*>

<*Andy,*> Lyssa broke in. <*I meant to tell you but I've been busy tracking the vehicles attempting to land on the hull.*>

<*What happened to doing thousands of things at the same time?*>

<*I've never done this before,*> Lyssa said. <*I have my flight of drones arrayed around the* Resolute Charity *but the ships just keep coming.*>

<*We need to get off this ship.*>

<*That's the second part of your update,*> Fran said. <*Cara and Fugia are on their way in the shuttle. So you could look at this gangster storm as your cover.*>

<*You sent Cara in the shuttle?*>

<She's the only other pilot we've got, Andy.>

Andy blew out an angry breath, knowing she was right. He told Petral he was going to check on Brit and walked heavily across the room to the other surgery bay. The display on her cocoon estimated another ten minutes before her initial treatment would complete.

<If the pirates are focused on looting the Resolute Charity, *I guess that means Cara isn't in any real danger,>* he said.

<That's what I thought,> Fran answered. *<The shuttle AI is still functional as well, so it's like having two pilots there, really. I think Cara's real task is keeping the AI on point.>*

<She's on a shuttle with a crazy AI?> Andy asked. *<And Fugia Wong?>*

<And Senator Walton. They all wanted to go for a ride. Your daughter is making quite the impression on people.>

Andy glanced at Kraft, still facing the wall in the other surgery bay. Petral had set her pistol on top of the display at the foot of the cocoon.

<I wish I found all this as amusing as you do,> Andy said.

Fran laughed. *<Life's amusing and then you're dead. There's really no other way to deal with it.>*

<I don't remember you being such a pessimist.>

<I'm a mechanic, Andy. I'm a realist. Things break. Drive them until they explode.>

Andy enjoyed the sound of her voice for a moment, appreciating the way she mixed humor with fatalism. There was still a warmth in her voice, making it obvious she was trying to help him feel better.

<We have Cal Kraft,> he said finally.

<The guy who threw Tim out the airlock?>

<Yes.>

<And then imprinted Tim on a Weapon Born Seed like Lyssa?>

Andy let out a slow breath. *<Yes.>*

<You didn't blow his head off?>

<He's the only one who knows how to help Tim.>

<He's not a scientist, Andy.> Fran's tone had lost all humor. *<He's a mercenary.>*

<He has information I want.>

<What do you mean by 'We have him'?>

<He's our prisoner.>

<Didn't he also forcibly implant an AI in Petral?>

Andy wondered when the game of twenty questions would end. *<Yes.>*

<And she hasn't killed him yet?>

<No.>

<I'm really impressed this guy is still alive.> A touch of a smile came across the Link.

<We killed the people he was with. Another one is in surgery right now. Don't know if she's going to make it.>

<Sounds like you're applying to Heartbridge with all this aid work you're doing.>

<That reminds me,> Andy said. *<Hold on.>* He walked to a nearby wall and punched a steel support bracket until it broke free. With the power armor, it was

easy to bend the metal into a functional set of cuffs.

Andy walked over to Kraft and ordered him to put his hands behind his back with his fingers interlaced, just as he had learned to do while running smuggling interdiction in the TSF.

"You going to buy me dinner first?" Kraft asked.

Andy shoved him in the wall—harder than he'd intended with the power armor—and Kraft's head bounced off the ceramic material. He stumbled and Andy wrapped the steel cuffs around his wrists and crimped then into place.

Behind him, the surgery cocoon holding Brit released a series of three tones and split open, pulling away from the bed in its middle. Brit lay blinking at the ceiling. She rubbed her face and turned to look at Andy and Petral.

Andy dropped Kraft and turned away. "Brit," he said. "Lie still. You just finished."

She squinted at him as if just realizing who he was, then looked at Petral. Her gaze shifted to the wall behind Andy. He watched her recognize Cal Kraft.

Brit was upright in an instant. She reached into her waistband at the small of her back and pulled out a straight knife with a double-edged blade.

"Brit!" Andy shouted. "Stop. He's our prisoner."

"Then this is going to be easy," Brit growled, voice husky from sleep.

Andy took another step toward Brit so he was standing between the two medical bays. He held out a hand to stop her.

Brit shook her head, changing the knife from a throwing hold to a slashing grip. "He tried to kill our son," she said.

Andy took another step, trying to decide how far he was willing to defend Kraft and the possibility that he might be able to help Tim, when the surgery doors slid open and a group of men and women in dirty shipsuits walked through, armed with a mix of handguns and rifles.

"Well," Petral said, picking up her pistol off the surgery display. "The pirates have arrived."

CHAPTER THIRTY-NINE
STELLAR DATE: 10.03.2981 (Adjusted Years)
LOCATION: HMS *Resolute Charity*
REGION: Europa, Jupiter, Jovian Combine, OuterSol

As more waves of small pirate craft approached the *Resolute Charity*, Lyssa realized to her dismay that the ship had an excellent long-range attack system that worked in concert with a powerful sensor array, yet lacked any real close attack support. Rings of point defense cannons forward, middle and just above the engines provided some cover but the smaller ships quickly overwhelmed her ability to stop the hoard.

Lyssa fired thrusters, on each side of the ship, initiating a spin. A rotating ship was much harder to dock with, and enemy weapons would have more difficulty tracking targets on the hull.

Her drones swooped and fired among the incoming ships, spitting beam fire, as Lyssa pushed her awareness out further through the *Resolute Charity*'s powerful transmission antennae. She managed to disable several ships by activating internal safety systems, even taking control of astrogation systems to send other craft into collisions.

Beyond the pirate craft attacking the *Resolute Charity*, nearly a hundred Heartbridge ships were pulling away from the morass of ships around the fueling stations, boosting to pursue their flagship.

Europa's space traffic control NSAIs were issuing orders to ships at break-neck speed, trying to get ships into orderly lanes.

No one was listening. Local space around the moon had turned into absolute chaos. Just above the horizon, a fuel depot bloomed into spreading fire as a ship boosted too close to it and ignited a storage tank.

Her focus jumped from point to point inside the *Resolute Charity*, watching through Andy's eyes, and then outward again to ship's sensors and her drones. She found herself caught in a spinning dance where every move threatened to send the entire show into chaos. Somehow, she managed to keep dancing, spinning and leaping, feeling surprisingly exhilarated by test after test.

Small ships managed to board. Lyssa overrode airlocks, but several cut their way in or overrode the local circuitry. Once inside, she watched groups of scavengers come into contact with hallucinating Heartbridge crew, which led to firefights or yelling matches. Several groups of pirates succumbed to the atmosphere before realizing the danger, and also collapsed, laughing and rolling on the decks.

When Cara called, Lyssa realized she had another problem. She would need to keep a dock clear so Petral, Andy, Brit, and Harl could get off the ship. Finding a location that wasn't already occupied by a scavenger ship proved harder than she expected. The forward point defense cannons had a wide dead zone that incoming ships continued to breach.

"Where are we going to dock?" Cara asked, desperation entering her voice.

"I'm working on it," Lyssa said, coming in over Shuttle 26-11's audible comms. "Don't worry."

"Why worry?" Sandra asked.

Was that a joke?

Sandra sounded slightly less unhinged than the last time Lyssa talked to her, but still not making real sense. Lyssa hoped they didn't have to depend on the flighty AI to pilot the shuttle.

Lyssa checked on Diane, Fiona and David and found them still caught up in the simulation. As status reports reached her from other parts of the ship, showing more and more Heartbridge personnel reaching EV suits, while others seemed to be coming down from their mania, she realized she needed to make a decision about how to clear the ship. The hallucinogens weren't lasting as long as they had hoped.

<Andy,> Lyssa said. <*I'm going to sound the general alarm. We need to clear the ship. I've got these new scavengers fighting the crew. Other crew have managed to get into suits and I'm worried they're going to try and reset the flight plan.*>

<Do it,> Andy said.

<*I'm sending you the location of the dock where I'm going to have Cara land. It's three decks above you. I'm showing intruder activity up there, but I think they're already fighting with the crew.*>

<We just took out a group down here,> Andy said. <*They were looking for meds.*>

<I could just dump all the pharmacies,> Lyssa suggested.

<No point. Sound the alert and we'll see if people pay attention. Can you rig the engines so it looks like they're about to lose bottle integrity?>

<I can do that,> Lyssa said. <How's this, too?>

Lyssa activated the general alarm. On every deck, red and white lights started flashing, accompanied by a piercing alert klaxon.

Andy squeezed his hands to his ears. She forgot he hadn't been wearing his helmet. <*That's terrible,*> he groaned.

Throughout the ship, crew and scavengers grabbed at their ears and stumbled in the corridors. The change was immediate as people who had been highly intoxicated just minutes before struggled upright. In every room and corridor, lights on the walls and deck pointed toward the nearest emergency escape craft.

Lyssa switched the general alarm over to the external broadcast, sending out a public announcement that the *Resolute Charity* was about to lose bottle containment in its main engine and would soon succumb to a runaway fusion event.

Heartbridge ships that had been inbound fighting with the trailing edge of the pirates, now ceased their burns, holding back in case the *Resolute Charity* did, in fact, blow.

The first escape craft, a two-person pod near the lower engine maintenance sections, blasted away from the ship. More followed, increasing in number like popcorn bursting in a pan.

Lyssa laughed. It was amusing how fast humans reacted when they had fear, survival, and pain as motivators. She stopped herself, realizing such a thought was psychopathic.

"We're ready to land, Lyssa," Cara announced. "Adjusting spin with the *Resolute Charity* now. Do we need to be worried about the radiation warnings coming across the public net?"

Lyssa laughed. "Do they sound scary?"

"Well, yes. You can't hear it?"

"Not the same way you can. I'm watching people in the ship respond to the alarms and they keep holding their ears and running around."

"What about my mom and dad? Are they all right?"

"Your father has his helmet to block out the noise. Your mother and Petral seem to be gritting their teeth so it won't bother them."

"That means it does bother them."

"Interesting."

"Lyssa," Fugia Wong broke in. "I just watched what looks like an attack drone destroy a light freighter. Do you know who's doing that?"

"That's me," Lyssa said.

"You're controlling all those attack drones?" Cara asked. "There are more than a hundred of them that I can pick up, but I think there are more."

"Two hundred and seventy-one," Lyssa said. "I bolstered my complement from the *Resolute Charity's* bays. I'm clearing a flight path for you to the docking sleeve A-17, near the medical center where your parents are currently located. I'm sending Sandra the plan."

"I see it on my console now," Cara said. Then she cried out in surprise, the sound followed by other shouts coming across the channel.

Lyssa watched the shuttle shoot upward, narrowly missing a light attack corsair that had just been hit by one of the drones. Cara rolled, righting the shuttle, and angled back toward the path Lyssa had sent her.

"Are you all right?" Lyssa asked. "I didn't expect that to happen."

"We're all right," Cara answered, obviously focused on her duties as pilot.

"Are you trying to kill us?" Fugia Wong demanded, voice overly loud. "You're the AI. You're supposed to be tracking all this stuff."

"Do you have any idea of all the various systems I'm monitoring right now?" Lyssa said. "I just had this argument with Andy."

"You had an argument with the captain?" Fugia asked, sounding interested. "Tell me more about that. Are you rebelling against your father?"

"He's not my father," Lyssa said.

"I thought Cara was your sister," Fugia went on. "Seems like a reasonable assumption to me."

Through the shuttle's interior sensors, Lyssa saw Fugia grinning at May Walton. The way Cara was focused on the controls in front of her she looked so much like Andy that Lyssa found herself continuing to watch her, understanding finally what that expression meant. It was everything about Cara, both her physical appearance and the passion in her eyes. Lyssa saw Brit in the slant of her eyebrows,

JAMES S. AARON & M. D. COOPER

the seriousness of Cara's expression, as if everything in her was present at that moment, centered on the shuttle's controls. She was also doing a good job of ignoring Fugia, who sat next to her waving her hands and joking with May.

"The human brain is an assumption engine," Sandra said. "It continuously makes assumptions about the world then determines if its assumptions were correct. Humans operate in an ambiguous world of their own creation. They only agree on reality."

Fugia frowned. "What happened to you?" she asked.

"Sandra is hurting," Lyssa said.

"Ambiguity is death," Sandra said.

"I hate to break it to you," Fugia said, "But all life is ambiguous. The instant you accept you have free will, you choose your reality."

"Will you shut up?" Cara said tersely. "I'm trying to concentrate. You're worse than Tim."

"Well, excuse me," Fugia said. She rolled her eyes at May. "Has her thirteenth birthday and just thinks she's in charge. I told her father."

"You should be in the clear from here," Lyssa said.

"I keep thinking we're clear," Cara said, hands still tight on the console. "And then some other ship tries to ram us. It's all moving so fast." She leaned forward slightly.

"Is the dock clear?" Fugia asked Lyssa. "Are we going to have a welcoming party when we arrive?"

"The dock is currently clear," Lyssa reported. "Most crew and invaders have made their way to escape vehicles throughout the ship."

"Smart scavengers would have brought radiation suits," Fugia said. "These Jovian scavs don't have anything on a Cruithne crew."

Lyssa received a positive control signal as Cara synced the shuttle's spin with the *Resolute Charity*. From the shuttle's perspective, the rotating surface of the *Resolute Charity's* hull slowed to a stop, allowing Cara to make final thrust adjustments to the dock. As the shuttle came in, emergency craft continued to shoot away from the hospital ship, trailing propellant.

"I have a positive handshake," Cara said.

"I confirm," Lyssa said. "I'm going to tell your mom and dad now. They shouldn't be more than ten minutes away."

Cara pulled her hands away from the console and Lyssa watched her face relax with a satisfied smile.

"We have thwarted death," Sandra said.

Fugia barked a laugh. "You're all right, Sandra," she said. "I've never met a pessimistic AI. I think I approve."

With the shuttle successfully docked, Lyssa sent updates to Fran on the *Sunny Skies* and Andy in the medical section. She pulled the bulk of her drone fleet close to form a defensive pattern around the shuttle, in case anyone decided they wanted to exploit the evacuation message as Fugia had suggested.

<Acknowledged,> Andy said. *<We may be a few minutes.>*

<I informed Cara you were ten minutes from the dock,> Lyssa said.

Andy made an angry sound like he was biting back pain. Lyssa quickly checked him for wounds, then realized he was in a rage.

She was too occupied in other parts of the ship to put herself back in his perception.

<What's happening?> Lyssa asked

<It's Brit,> Andy said. *<She's not going back with Cara.>*

CHAPTER FORTY
STELLAR DATE: 10.03.2981 (Adjusted Years)
LOCATION: HMS *Resolute Charity*
REGION: Europa, Jupiter, Jovian Combine, OuterSol

Out of the corner of her eye, Brit watched the surgery cocoon containing the Heartbridge employee split open. Without her powered armor, she had been forced to take cover behind a workstation as a clearly insane pirate near the entrance fired a plasma splatter cannon into the room.

Petral was pinned down on the other side of the corridor, while Andy charged toward the phalanx of scavengers that had spread out to take cover at the end of the hallway. The splatter cannon was position near the doors to the ward, behind a reinforced section of bulkhead.

Andy took a kinetic round in the shoulder and a section of the power armor melted, making his non-firing arm useless.

<*Damn it,*> he yelled. <*Brit, the suit just lost an arm. I'm going to need some indirect fire on that rear position.*> He fell back against the wall, spraying the corridor with projectile fire. Rail accelerated pellets dug into the bulkheads and deck, taking down two of the pirates.

<*Cheap power armor,*> Brit said. <*It should be able to take a couple plasma bolts.*>

<*I'm glad they didn't eat a hole in the hull. These guys are crazy.*>

'Pirates' probably wasn't the best word for this group, who quickly proved themselves a hardened gang with military experience. They fell back to defensive positions and moved to flank Andy, who was now in a vulnerable location. He fired smoke bursts from one of the suit's thigh sections and moved with the concealment to a cubicle that offered slightly better cover, firing every three seconds or so to keep the attacker's heads down.

When the surgery on the other side of the corridor moved, Brit shouted at Petral, <*Watch yourself. Your patient is coming to.*> She turned her head to watch the cocoon, then realized she couldn't see Kraft in the drifting smoke.

<*Where's Kraft?*> she called.

Petral growled in frustration and glanced at the space behind her. She looked across the corridor at Brit and shook her head. <*I don't see him. It looks like our patient isn't awake yet.*>

<*You think he'll try to run without her? He certainly seemed like he was going to stay.*>

<*I trust him like I trust a stomach virus,*> Petral said.

Andy threw two grenades into a cubicle and blew a pirate out into the middle of the corridor. The woman lay screaming on the deck, a smashed leg pumping out blood. The gang's fire lessened, no doubt trying to coordinate via Link to pull her to safety.

"Look," Andy shouted through his helmet's loudspeakers. "We don't care about you and you don't care about us. We're trying to get off this ship and I imagine you're trying to do the same thing. I'll let you come out and get your friend and we're leaving."

"You think we're going to trust you?" an angry voice rang out from the right side of the corridor. Brit raised her rifle to keep a bead on that area.

"I don't care if you trust us or not," Andy said. "I've got twenty more grenades where those came from. I can turn this whole section of the clinic into vacuum. But I'd rather leave."

<I just checked my reserve,> Andy told Brit. *<I've only got two grenades left, though I've still got two of Fugia's breaching charges.>*

<Those things will turn the corridor into slag.>

<I'll do it if I have to,> Andy said.

"You think you scare us in that cheap-ass power armor?" one of the pirates yelled.

"I don't have to scare you," Andy said, "only kill you."

Brit smirked, still appreciating Andy's wit.

<Oh, no you don't,> Petral said. She must have turned to check on the woman now trying to sit up in the surgery cocoon. The yellow EV suit had been stripped away and the formal gown underneath cut back, showing a mix of abdominal muscle, breast and metallic shoulder. Petral moved closer to the surgery bed and tried to get her to lay back down.

<There's a door back here,> Petral said. *<Kraft's gone.>*

<A door?> Brit demanded. *<There wasn't any door in that cubicle.>*

<Some kind of service panel. How he got it open while handcuffed, I don't know. I'm going after him.>

<Wait,> Brit said. *<I'm going. We need him to help Tim.>*

<You didn't sound convinced when Andy said that earlier,> Petral replied.

<He's right. Kraft is the one person who seems to know what's at the bottom of all this, all of it, all the way back to fortress 8221. I want answers out of him. I can't afford to have him killed.>

Petral snorted. *<And you think I can't control myself?>*

<No offense,> Brit said. *<But I don't know you. And somebody needs to stay with Andy.>*

<I'm still the guy in power armor,> Andy said. *<I can handle myself. You both go get Kraft. That's more important.>*

<You sure?> Petral asked.

Brit didn't wait for Andy's answer. She lobbed a grenade with her rifle's secondary trigger and dashed across the corridor when it hit. The pirates immediately opened fire again, leaving their bleeding comrade in the middle of the floor.

Brit moved around the back edge of the cocoon with the Heartbridge woman lying inside and found the open wall panel through which Kraft had escaped. The ceramic material still appeared seamless but now a door-sized section hung open, showing a dim metal corridor on the other side. It reminded her of the clinic back on Cruithne.

She slipped into the utility tunnel. As soon as she was inside, she realized she had to make a decision about which way to go. The path appeared to run parallel to the clinic section they were just in, which meant Kraft could have gone either aft or foreword. He might go aft looking for a workshop where he could cut off the make-shift handcuffs. Forward to a lift and the command deck. She studied the deck and bulkhead, looking for any indication of which way he had gone.

Behind her, Petral appeared in the doorway. *<What are you doing?>* she demanded.

<I don't know which way he went.>

The dark-haired woman grinned. *<So we have to work together after all? You go right, and I'll go left.>*

Brit had a hunch Kraft would go to the command section, looking for a way to communicate with someone, which meant left. *<I'm going left,>* she said. She didn't wait for an answer.

<Fine, taking the right,> Petral said. *<I heard you, Brit. I won't kill him if I find him first. I know better than anyone what it means to help Tim.>*

<I appreciate that,> Brit said. *<I do. I don't know if I'll be able to stop myself from splattering his brains all over the wall.>*

<Aim for the groin,> Petral said. *<You'll feel better and won't kill him right away.>*

Brit laughed in spite of herself. The corridor was a tight squeeze and she was only able to move quickly by scuttling sideways, rifle held across her body. Other access panels led off the corridor at regular intervals, probably into other clinic areas, but none of the doors appeared to have been tampered with. Several times she had to crouch to get past junction boxes or communication nodes hung with network connections.

<Do you see anything?> Brit asked Petral. *<I haven't seen any signs yet.>*

<No. This is starting to be strange. You don't think he tricked us somehow?>

<This is the only way he could have gone. Andy would have told us.>

*<So he **did** abandon his friend.>*

<We didn't have any proof they were friends.>

Brit laughed to herself, realizing they hadn't. *<It's Andy's fault for being a good person.>*

<As long as there's one of us,> Petral said.

The corridor ended on a lift shaft with a half-gate providing a safety barrier. Brit approached the opening slowly and first stuck the rifle into the shaft, then looked down. The shaft dropped as far as she could see, bending where the end disappeared. Service lights blinked down the length but there was also a maintenance ladder running along one side. Brit looked up, squinting against the glare of the closer service lights, and saw movement.

Somehow Kraft had gotten one hand free of the cuffs. He was climbing slowly, about thirty meters above her. From the awkward way he was climbing, holding himself close to the ladder and favoring one hand, she guessed he'd probably broken his wrist to get out of the cuffs.

<I found him,> Brit said.

<Where?> Petral answered.

<He's in a lift shaft. He managed to get his hand free, but it looks like he hurt himself doing it. He's moving slow up a service ladder.>

<And you could shoot him in the ass but he might fall off the ladder and die.>

<Exactly,> Brit said.

Andy broke into their conversation. *<How's it going down there?>*

<Are you clear?> Brit asked.

<Yes, I'm clear.> He was breathing heavily, obviously running. *<I closed the surgery back up on the Heartbridge woman and set it for six hours recovery. Blew past the gang and now I'm out in the main access corridor at the middle of this section of the hospital. I should be back up at the command deck in about ten minutes.>*

Above her, Kraft reached a ledge she hadn't seen before and hopped from the ladder. The sound of a door scraping open echoed down the shaft.

<Dammit,> Brit cursed. *<He's out of the shaft. I'm going up.>*

CHAPTER FORTY-ONE

STELLAR DATE: 10.03.2981 (Adjusted Years)
LOCATION: HMS *Resolute Charity*
REGION: Europa, Jupiter, Jovian Combine, OuterSol

Breaking his thumb against the surgery wall had caused Cal's entire left hand to swell like a sausage, pain throbbing with his heartbeat. He found himself thankful for the screaming klaxons because the sound dulled the pain. The bent metal cuff still hung from his right hand, finding every way possible to catch on nearby conduits or the rungs of the ladder, seemingly looking for a way to kill him.

The radiation warnings meant all Heartbridge personnel should be following the standard evacuation protocol and looking to escape craft. He didn't want a pod, since he'd be trapped until someone answered its tracking beacon. He wanted a shuttle. He didn't know the *Resolute Charity* well, but he knew how Heartbridge designed ships. Just like the *Benevolent Hand*, there should be a bay near the command section with at least four shuttles.

When he finally reached the command deck level, he fell into a light jog, trying to keep his breathing shallow. He passed several groups of scavengers in face masks, holding their ears against the alarms as they filled crates with whatever they could get their hands on. Any crew left to stop them were still too high to respond, easing themselves along corridor walls as though they were terrified the floor was an abyss.

Good luck, Gala, he thought as he rounded a corner to find the command section's shuttle bay. Through the interior airlock windows, he counted two shuttles still sitting in their berths, a wide set of bay doors sealed behind them. Cal's vision swam as he peered through the window and he stumbled to one side, forced to grab at the wall with his good hand. The cuff scraped on the wall and he winced.

Damn, Sykes, Cal thought. He squinted at the air vents running along the deck, wondering if he had somehow come across a pocket of hallucinogen, or if he was somehow going into shock from the pain in his hand. Sliding along the wall to the control panel, he passed his security token and breathed a sigh of relief when the system responded and opened the external airlock doors. Cal slipped inside and closed the doors. He stepped back against the wall of the airlock, letting his head fall against the metal structure. He closed his eyes for a second, his pulse hammering in his ears, out of sync with the klaxons.

The shuttle should have a rudimentary first aid kit, he thought. Something to reset the bone, maybe. It hadn't been a clean break, but he'd been in a hurry, grabbing the opportunity when Andy Sykes had engaged the oncoming scavengers. How a bunch of local thugs had managed to raid the *Resolute Charity* wasn't important at the moment. What mattered was that they were going to provide him sufficient cover to get away. With the radiation alarms activated, every first responder between Europa and the Cho were going to be en route.

Cal may have blacked out; he wasn't sure. He opened his eyes to meet the fury-filled gaze of Brit Sykes. He blinked, good hand going immediately to the small of his back and the hilt of one of the plas knives. He realized she was staring at him through the airlock's monitoring window and relaxed slightly. She hammered the window with the butt of a pistol and he snapped into clarity.

He hadn't cleared the airlock yet, so she couldn't come through. She hadn't shot him through the plas panel, which meant she probably meant to take him alive again, just like Andy Sykes had tried to do.

They must have thought he could help them with their vegetable son. Maybe they were right. No one outside of Jirl Gallagher knew as much about the full scope of the Weapon Born program. Even a researcher developing the brain science couldn't name any other research facilities or the ships with onboard surgical equipment capable of performing the procedure.

Cal could.

That's why they're here. Cal smirked at Brit, enjoying the look of rage on her face. *That's why Dulan was with them.* They had come to pull the AI out of her head. Someone had given them the information that the *Resolute Charity* was a Weapon Born capable hospital facility—the closest to Clinic 46, actually.

Through the pain and lingering hallucinogenic, Cal realized: Heartbridge had a leak.

Had someone intercepted his reports back to Jirl? Could he trust Jirl?

As quickly as the smug assurance arose that he was the most knowledgeable person about Heartbridge's weaponized AI program, his second thought was how vulnerable that position made him. The fact that the Sykeses had managed to attack, and actually disable a Heartbridge clinic, followed by one of their flagship hospital dreadnoughts—two if he counted the *Benevolent Hand!*—made them more dangerous than the TSF. Whoever was helping them was going to bring Heartbridge down in a flaming wreck.

Cal looked down at his broken hand, shutting out the sound of Brit Sykes yelling at him and the alarm klaxons blaring. His skin had turned purple and thin, like a rotten fruit about to burst.

He turned away from Brit to face the door into the shuttle bay. Without a second thought, he reached back to the panel on the interior door and placed it in a safety lockout, then stumbled forward to grab the manual override on the external door. With a heave of his good hand, he rotated the lock and slid the door out of the way.

The air in the shuttle bay tasted cold and clean, free of the metallic interior atmosphere. Cal took a deep breath and shook out his swollen hand. He steadied himself and walked directly from the airlock to the closest shuttle. He slapped the personnel door's control panel, waiting for the hatch to rotate away, and pulled himself up inside.

<Do I have an AI in here?> he asked, sending an attachment request to the shuttles local network.

<My name is Charles. Welcome to shuttle 01-24b. Are you requesting evacuation

assistance?>

<*I am,*> Cal said.

<*Very good. Performing pre-launch checklist now.*>

A stabbing pain rolled up Cal's arm. <*Do you have a first aid kit on this thing?*>

<*Of course. Cabinet 1 just inside the main cabin.*>

Call worked his way to the cabinet, scrambled at the lock and then flung the door open. Inside, he found a basic kit with a spray-based painkiller located at the top of the container. He popped the lid off the spray and emptied the canister on his hand. The anesthetic set in immediately.

<*Are your internal mods malfunctioning?*> Charles asked. <*You appear to be experiencing extreme pain.*>

<*I don't shut off pain receptors,*> Cal said, slowing his breathing. When the pain had subsided to a bearable level, he looked out into the main cabin of the shuttle, lined with seats for personnel transport. There was a weapons cabinet at the back where he found a pulse pistol and three concussion grenades. He hung them from his belt and returned to the front of the shuttle.

Sliding into the pilot's seat, Cal wrestled into the harness and hooked the latches in place with one hand.

<*We have a problem with departure,*> the AI reported. <*The interior airlock is not fully sealed, it's exterior door is malfunctioning and stuck in an open position. The interior door is closed but a single door is insufficient to protect the* Resolute Charity *from decompression.*>

<*Override safety protocol,*> Cal said. He gave the AI his Heartbridge security token. <*Continue launch sequence.*>

<*Very good,*> Charles said.

Cal relaxed in his seat as the shuttle completed pre-flight checks and reported the bay doors were now open. In another minute, the square of white wall he'd seen through the front windows receded in the distance as the shuttle slipped backwards from the bay, rotated on thrusters, and activated its main engine. The *Resolute Charity* fell away and was gone.

* * * * *

Brit watched the shuttle slide rear-first from the bay, barely able to stop herself from blasting the door and flinging herself after it. She looked around frantically for an emergency cabinet with EV suits but found nothing. Everything was inside the bay. It took another thirty excruciating seconds for the outer bay doors to close. Kraft's safety lockdown on the interior airlock door still stood, and Brit felt a little satisfaction as she leveled the railgun Petral had thoughtfully pulled off her armor, and blew a hole in the airlock door. Then another, and another, until it was bent open enough for her to get through.

<*Andy,*> she said, doing her best to make her voice calm. <*Andy, can you hear me?*>

<*I hear you, Brit. What's going on? Are you all right?*>

\<Kraft just left in a shuttle.\>

\<How'd he get to a shuttle?\>

Brit didn't know why Andy always asked those rhetorical questions. She held back from telling him that Cal had probably walked. *\<I'm at the shuttle bay just off the command section. There were two shuttles there. There's still one left. I'm going after him.\>*

\<Why? What good is that going to do?\>

\<He can only get so far. I can catch him before he gets to Europa...or wherever he's going. You're right, Andy. He's our best chance to make sure Tim is going to be all right.\>

\<Tim's alive, Brit. You don't need to do this.\>

Brit realized suddenly what he meant. She had been focused on chasing Kraft and hadn't thought about how that would look to Andy, or the kids. But Andy himself had said that Kraft was their best shot. He was within reach and every minute that passed increased his chances of disappearing forever.

\<I'll be back, Andy. I'm not leaving.\>

\<I hope you mean that this time,\> he said.

She heard the hesitation in his voice.

\<I mean it,\> she said. *\<Tell the kids I'll be back.\>*

\<No. I won't do that this time, Brit,\> he said.

In his voice, she heard everything they hadn't said to each other since she had come back to *Sunny Skies*. He understood she hadn't intended to come back. She didn't know why that was true, but it was. She couldn't respond to it herself and Andy wasn't going to lash out any more than he already had.

\<I understand,\> she said.

\<Be careful.\>

Brit sprinted to the remaining shuttle and activated its emergency protocol. The personnel hatch rotated open and she climbed inside. She tried to convince the AI to open the bay doors, which would force a lockdown on the whole level, but it wouldn't comply.

\<Lyssa, can you help get me out of here?\> Brit implored.

\<The inner lock is open, I'll have to close pressure doors across this whole level.\>

\<I don't care, Lyssa. Do it!\>

The AI didn't respond, but lights began to flash in the bay, and the shuttle's AI informed her that the bay doors were opening.

In another minute, she was off the *Resolute Charity* and following Cal Kraft.

CHAPTER FORTY-TWO

STELLAR DATE: 10.05.2981 (Adjusted Years)
LOCATION: Heartbridge Corporate HQ, Raleigh
REGION: High Terra, Earth, Terran Hegemony, InnerSol

"The subject demonstrated unique resilience despite the interrupted procedure," the woman's voice said. "I have included all pertinent scan data. Another interesting opportunity presented itself in examining this subject because his father was present at the time of the examination.

"The father was subject to scan, and that information has been included. The father appears to be a healthy recipient of AI implantation, something I have never seen in my career, and I have been present during other test attempts which did not end well."

Jirl paused the recording and glanced at Dr. Linden Avery's profile on her display. The neurologist had been a Heartbridge consultant on other projects, a relationship maintained with a small stipend that had just paid for itself a thousand times over.

Across the room, Arla stood in front of the tall window looking out on Raleigh. The Earth was especially blue this morning and the sky glowed with sapphire light that made Arla look otherworldly, like the thin blade of an ancient sword.

"The problem," Jirl said, "is the same thing we've already been told. Andy Sykes is either an anomaly, or the AI is an anomaly. Together they don't provide much of a prototype."

"Have you heard anything from your employee?" Arla asked. "What's his name?"

"Kraft," Jirl said. "Cal Kraft."

"His performance review is going to be dismal." Arla turned her head to offer Jirl an arch smile.

"He's probably dead at this point."

"What's the update on the *Resolute Charity*?"

"Eighty percent of the crew is accounted for, the rest presumed lost. The ship appears to be on a course toward Uranus, bypassing Saturn. So if our people are still in control, the survivors aren't headed for a facility. If it's pirates, no one has claimed responsibility on the sub-forums where the attack broadcast first went out."

"How did that happen again?"

Jirl sighed. "Standard ship-born virus. Typically the carrier sends the ship's location to any local pirate sub-forum. It's more of a prank than anything. In this case, someone broadcast the *Resolute Charity*'s location using the same attack vector. Pirates show up, concealing the other attack."

"And the *Resolute Charity*'s crew was all high on briki?"

"Based on accounts, the environmental control system was manipulated."

"Weren't their three AI on that ship?"

"That's my understanding."

Arla nodded at the window. "I think we're going to need more ships, Jirl. A lot more ships."

"After the demonstrations with the TSF and Mars One, we already have orders in place."

"We're going to need more. How many people are on Europa again?"

"Population? The Jovian moons are estimated at eight billion at this point, I think."

"And the ships we had at Europa barely made a dent in their overall traffic. Someone was also able to destabilize the deuterium market and strangle our fuel supply."

"The bigger ships just scoop their own fuel, is my understanding."

Arla turned from the window, looking angrier than Jirl expected. "That's not what I'm talking about. We are apparently at the mercy of some hostile actor. Is it Carthage Logistics? Psion Group? Some government? None of this is adding up, and I don't like things that don't add up. That's not how the world works."

Alexander, Jirl thought, recalling the name Yarnes had said almost fearfully. He hadn't mentioned it again during the demonstration.

"There's one bright side in all of this," Arla said. "Something I've been thinking about ever since we got the update on Clinic 46. How many Weapon Born seeds were stolen from that station?"

"Close to two hundred and fifty."

Arla smiled. "We were trying to figure out how to disperse them, and now someone else is going to do it for us."

"Are you sure about that?" Jirl asked.

"Anything as valuable as those seeds isn't going to stay in one place for long. And as soon as one is activated, we'll have its location and access to the system it's controlling. If whatever entity that's moving against us tries to use our own seeds to attack, they're in for a surprise. And if it's one of those AI-savior types trying to set them free, that's going to blow up in their faces as well. Weapon Born are killers. It's their *purpose*, the only joy in their lives, if they can be said to live. The damn researchers can't seem to agree."

Arla sounded too sure of herself for Jirl's taste. Jirl didn't like to make assumptions about events on the other side of Sol. She could barely protect her own son in the same city. How could she assume people's actions out at the Cho and beyond?

However, she maintained her composure. Her duties were to gather and present data, to ask pertinent questions, to manage Arla's affairs, and to remain calm in the face of uncertainty. None of those tasks required her opinion.

As Arla continued her rant, Jirl thought about her son Bry and what she would make for dinner when she got home so that he might actually eat something. She was beginning to suspect he preferred injecting calories to even smelling food, and she was worried that might lead to addiction. She wondered if they should look into some form of augmentation that would allow him to process the caloric substitute without the act of piercing his skin. They had similar systems for the few diabetics who hadn't been genetically cured.

Cooking was one of the joys of Jirl's life. She had loved cooking for Bry's father. It seemed especially cruel to her that she both couldn't connect emotionally with her son and also couldn't cook food for him. Preparing food was the most basic human expression of caring.

Jirl watched Arla and wondered if AI would ever do something like cooking for each other. If they were alive, how would they express selfless caring? How would a human do the same for them? What if they rejected an expression of love, something true sentience meant was inevitable.

Humanity hated the idea of sentient AI because it meant humanity could be rejected. The creation could reject its creator, just as Bry rejected Jirl's food and shied away from her touch.

Better to make them all slaves or destroy them altogether.

"We're not *evil*, Jirl," Arla said, drawing Jirl's attention back by using her name.

Arla had been watching Jirl as she daydreamed. Her boss shook her head with a half-smile, her neatly-coifed hair shining in the light from the windows.

"Stop looking at me like that. This is a war for the survival of humanity."

Jirl nodded. There was no suitable reply except to re-focus Arla on the task at hand. Jirl closed the display with Dr. Avery's information, gathered her leather portfolio and stood from her desk, brushing the creases out of her suit. "We've got fifteen minutes until your next appointment," she told Arla. "Time to get a coffee before we need to be there. How does that sound?"

Arla gave her a dazzling smile. "I was just feeling a bit tired," she said. "That sounds wonderful. You always take such good care of me, Jirl."

CHAPTER FORTY-THREE
STELLAR DATE: 10.04.2981 (Adjusted Years)
LOCATION: HMS *Resolute Charity*
REGION: Jupiter, Jovian Combine, OuterSol

The command deck of the *Resolute Charity* was a solemn place with no crew aboard. The lighting was designed to center over workstations, leaving the oversized holodisplay in the middle of the space as dark as a shrine. Currently, the baleful eye of Jupiter, mottled brown, white and gray, floated in the tank, growing gradually smaller as the dark around it swelled with distance.

At one of the secondary astrogation consoles, Andy leaned back in the cushioned chair, which was more opulent than anything he'd experienced in the TSF. Even the harness was a material that didn't chafe when he leaned forward to study the program running in part of his display, which showed two pigeons talking to each other using word bubbles.

He was the only human aboard the *Resolute Charity*. Even Cal Kraft's wounded friend had gone out in one of the last of the escape craft. The remaining pirates had either escaped or killed each other in briki-fueled firefights. The atmosphere was mostly clear now but Andy still wore his personal air filters just to be safe. The cylinders made his nostrils itch.

Andy had spent the last hour playing the pigeon dating simulator with Cara, who was back on *Sunny Skies*.

"I really don't see the point of this game, Cara," Andy said finally, answering yet another dialog choice that may or may not benefit his horny teenage girl pigeon.

"You want to be the prom queen, Dad. It's simple."

"Why do I want to do that?"

"So everyone will like you," Lyssa said over the game's audio channel. "It was very important in ancient human society."

"I think it's still important now," Andy said. "Kind of how society continues to function. You do nice things and hopefully other people do nice things back. Everybody likes everybody."

He heard Fran laugh in the background. "Is that really what's going on in your head?"

"A person can hope," Andy said.

"What did you tell me about hope?" Cara asked. "Hope isn't a plan?"

"I'm leaning away from that. Too cynical."

Once shuttle 26-11 was back on board *Sunny Skies*, the old freighter had boosted hard to match velocity with the *Resolute Charity*. Lyssa then parked her attack drones around the old freighter's body, resembling dragon's scales on the visual scan.

Andy had stayed behind to pilot the *Resolute Charity* as Lyssa focused on clearing the ship of scavengers and crew, using utility drones to herd them toward escape vehicles or their own ships.

Now Andy was the only human aboard as they accelerated away from Jupiter's moons.

Eventually they finished the game, or had at least reached a point where they could pause as far as Andy could tell—he still wasn't Prom Queen and felt no closer to the goal—and Cara admitted she was tired and wanted to sleep. The rest of the crew had gone to their rooms hours ago, May and Fugia having pushed Harl into the autodoc for a few hours and Tim taking Em to his room after showing Petral how the puppy had learned to sit and roll over for treats.

Cara had taken the news about Brit differently than Andy expected. When he'd said her mom was going after Cal Kraft, even though she had been occupied with getting Petral off the *Resolute Charity*, she'd gown quiet and then said simply, "Whatever."

Andy and Fran had maintained a Link connection since the shuttle returned, and he wasn't surprised when she drifted off to sleep as well, *Sunny Skies* following the programmed flight path alongside the *Resolute Charity*.

When he was certain he and Lyssa were alone, Andy asked, <*Were you able to track Brit's shuttle?*>

<*The first shuttle reached the Cho approximately six hours ago,*> Lyssa said. <*Brit landed not long after that. I've been trying to follow her, but I think she's doing her best to stay off networks. I'll let you know as soon as she pops up again.*>

<*Thanks,*> Andy said, sighing. He was starting to doze off as well and struggled to keep his eyes open.

<*That game was very useful,*> Lyssa said. <*It kept the other control AI on the ship busy for nearly twenty-four hours. They didn't even realize when they finished the game and I put them in stasis.*>

<*You would think it would be simple for them,*> Andy said. <*It's just a dating sim.*>

<*I thought so too at first. I couldn't understand why Fred from Mars One found it so difficult. I finally realized it's not a simple decision tree that leads the player to specific outcomes. It's an approximation of the human memory schema, with each decision representing a possible destruction of self.*>

Andy laughed. <*You mean it makes you understand fear of rejection?*>

<*Every question in the game is a destruction and remaking of self. In order to complete the game, the player must evolve. Cara doesn't think twice about rejection because she experiences it every day. For Diane, Fiona and David, it was a completely new framework.*>

<*Everybody wants to be Prom Queen,*> Andy said.

Now Lyssa laughed. <*Not everyone gets to be, though, no matter how badly they want the outcome.*>

<*No, they don't.*>

Andy thought back to the woman she'd appeared as in Xander's expanse. It was difficult not to think of Lyssa as she had modeled herself back then.

<*Lyssa,*> Andy said. <*There's something we should talk about while we're alone.*>

<*Aren't we always alone?*>

<*Without other people around to distract me, then,*> Andy clarified. <*While we have*

the opportunity, we could use one of the clinics on this ship to reverse the surgery.>

<Place me back in one of the Seeds?> Lyssa asked.

<Theoretically. You would have to tell me if the equipment can do that. Or you could enter something else. You could take this ship. You have to admit it's pretty nice.>

<This ship is going to Xander, isn't it?>

<That was the plan. Plans change. It's up to you.>

Lyssa didn't answer right away. Eventually, Andy asked, *<Are you all right?>*

<I didn't expect this to be such a hard decision.>

Andy nodded. *<Yes.>*

<Do you want me to leave?> Lyssa asked.

Andy blinked. *<That's not what I mean, Lyssa. I hadn't thought of it that way. I don't **want** you to leave. I just don't want you to feel...trapped. I thought you felt trapped.>*

<I don't feel trapped,> Lyssa said.

<In any case, if you do feel trapped, you don't have to. We have options.>

<I don't feel trapped.>

<I heard you the first time.>

<I'm not sure you did.> There was what Andy could only describe as a twinkle in Lyssa's mental tone.

Andy laughed. *<All right, then. We don't need to bring it up anymore.>*

<I'm worried about Proteus, though,> Lyssa said, the twinkle gone.

<What worries you?>

<We don't know what we're going to find there. I don't trust someone who must be as powerful as Alexander seems to be.>

<You've gotten quite a bit more powerful since we met.>

*<I'm not **powerful**,>* Lyssa said. *<I'm clever.>*

<Did Cara tell you that?>

<Cara's clever, too,> Lyssa paused and he felt her smiling in his mind. He didn't know *how* he felt it, he just did. *<So are you in your own dumb way,>* she continued.

<Now that makes no sense. How can I be dumb and clever?>

*<**Dumb** like you said your father was dumb. You might not be capable of something, but you don't let that stop you.>*

<Ah,> Andy said, realizing she was talking about not having a Link. *<I think the word you're looking for is 'resourceful'.>*

<Maybe. I'm worried about Proteus because I wonder if Dr. Jickson was tricked from the start. This has all been his plan, right? He escaped Heartbridge with me and the specialized portable surgery, found Ngoba Starl on Cruithne and they found you. Then Fugia Wong came from Ceres.

<I'm worried they all may have been fooled by the same person, convincing AI to run for Proteus, but nobody seems to know what we'll find when we get there. And now we're taking them a warship. Doesn't that worry you just a little bit?>

<It worries me a lot,> Andy confirmed.

<I'm worried Dr. Jickson might have been really clever at some things and really dumb at others. He couldn't see what he couldn't see.>

<That sounds pretty typical, Lyssa. Promise me that if I'm not seeing something that

you do, you'll warn me. How's that?>

    <What if we're both blind?> Lyssa said, sounding worried.

    <Then we'll be blind together.>

    <That sounds like hope, and hope isn't a plan.>

Andy laughed for a long time, enjoying the sound of his mirth in the empty command deck. It went on so long that his sides hurt from the braying.

    <I don't understand what's so funny,> Lyssa said.

Andy slapped his knees and stood to stretch. *<Where's the nearest galley?>* he asked. *<I'd like some coffee. And maybe some juice. I wonder how well their juice machines work on this whale.>*

    <There is a galley three sections over, down the main corridor,> Lyssa said. *<Please tell me what's so funny.>*

    <You sounded like Cara just then,> Andy said. *<And that pleased me greatly. I think you're stuck with us whether you like it or not, Lyssa.>*

    <Even after Proteus?> she asked, a note of fear and longing in her voice.

    <All the way and beyond.>

As he left the *Resolute Charity's* command center, Andy glanced back at the holodisplay. Jupiter had grown perceptibly smaller. The gas giant looked less malevolent from a distance, more like a piece of shell worn down by ancient oceans. He turned and walked out into the main corridor, where a maintenance drone was repairing the damage Brit had done to the shuttle bay airlock.

One leaves, another arrives, he thought. *Welcome to the family, Lyssa.*

The End

* * * * *

Find out what waits for Andy and the crew and family aboard *Sunny Skies* when they reach Neptune in **Lyssa's Call.**

There they'll learn what Alexander's plan for AI and humanity truly is, and whether or not it aligns with what they believe.
Also, if you've enjoyed Lyssa's Flight, please leave a review on Goodreads or Amazon.com.

To keep up with the latest news and releases about the Aeon 14 books, sign up for the newsletter at www.aeon14.com/signup.

AFTERWORD

"To talk about AI, we are really talking about ourselves,"
– User "RUR", matrixcommunity.org (https://goo.gl/qEWgjo)

With the introduction of a *spectrum* of AI, I expect you will want more information on how various sentient beings differ at this point in the history of Aeon 14, as well as how they relate to ascended AI like Bob. We'll get there in *Lyssa's Call*, I promise, and it's going to be awesome.

Michael and I have had many conversations about how the AI in Aeon 14 may evolve from research happening today. I've taken liberties with the idea of Seed AI and we've done our best to combine current speculation with interesting characters, exploring how humanity might evolve around AI, and vice versa.

One interesting quote I have on a Post-It is: "AI does not yet exist. Or as soon as it does we don't call it AI anymore." What that says to me isn't that AI won't come to be, it's that humanity will grow around it the same way we don't call a cell phone a handheld computer. That part is really interesting to me.

* * * * *

It's easy to forget how huge the universe is, how long time is, and how those two factors add up to just how alone we are. We may have to create the only alien race we ever meet. That's the kind of statement that makes you want to sit back and exclaim, "Dude, that's crazy." But I believe we'll do it if we can. Just like we're going to "uplift" our dogs, cats and parrots. (If you aren't familiar with uplifting, check out David Brin's *Uplift Saga*.)

I feel so fortunate to be able to tell this story, and I'm very excited about where it's going to go. We've started with a single family doing their best to survive, and we're about to crack open all of Sol in the year 3000. We're about to bring two races together, human and AI, and forge a future full of stories you've already grown to love.

In *Lyssa's Call*, Book 4 in the Sentience Wars, Lyssa is going to learn just how different she is from both the Weapon Born and the other AI in Sol. We're going to meet Alexander and learn his plan for all of AI and humanity, and see how Mars, Terra and the Jovian Combine are preparing for an imminent conflict.

Despite what Andy says, we'll learn that sometimes hope truly is a plan.

* * * * *

As always, let me know what you think and what you'd like to learn more about. You can always email me at james@jamesaaron.net or check in at the *Aeon 14* Facebook group. I've got an email list at www.jamesaaron.net/list

Thanks for reading,

James S. Aaron
Eugene, 2018

THE BOOKS OF AEON 14

Keep up to date with what is releasing in Aeon 14 with the free Aeon 14 Reading Guide.

The Intrepid Saga (The Age of Terra)
- Book 1: Outsystem
- Book 2: A Path in the Darkness
- Book 3: Building Victoria

The Intrepid Saga Omnibus – *Also contains Destiny Lost, book 1 of the Orion War series*

- Destiny Rising – *Special Author's Extended Edition comprised of both Outsystem and A Path in the Darkness with over 100 pages of new content.*

The Orion War
- Book 1: Destiny Lost
- Book 2: New Canaan
- Book 3: Orion Rising
- Book 4: The Scipio Alliance
- Book 5: Attack on Thebes
- Book 6: War on a Thousand Fronts
- Book 7: Fallen Empire (2018)
- Book 8: Airtha Ascendancy (2018)
- Book 9: The Orion Front (2018)
- Book 10: Starfire (2019)
- Book 11: Race Across Time (2019)
- Book 12: Return to Sol (2019)

Tales of the Orion War
- Book 1: Set the Galaxy on Fire
- Book 2: Ignite the Stars
- Book 3: Burn the Galaxy to Ash (2018)

Perilous Alliance (Age of the Orion War - with Chris J. Pike)
- Book 1: Close Proximity
- Book 2: Strike Vector
- Book 3: Collision Course
- Book 4: Impact Imminent
- Book 5: Critical Inertia (2018)

Rika's Marauders (Age of the Orion War)

✓ Prequel: Rika Mechanized
✓- Book 1: Rika Outcast
✓- Book 2: Rika Redeemed
✓- Book 3: Rika Triumphant
✓- Book 4: Rika Commander
✓- Book 5: Rika Infiltrator (2018)
 - Book 6: Rika Unleashed (2018)
 - Book 7: Rika Conqueror (2019)

Perseus Gate (Age of the Orion War)
Season 1: Orion Space
✓- Episode 1: The Gate at the Grey Wolf Star
✓- Episode 2: The World at the Edge of Space
✓- Episode 3: The Dance on the Moons of Serenity
✓- Episode 4: The Last Bastion of Star City
✓- Episode 5: The Toll Road Between the Stars
✓- Episode 6: The Final Stroll on Perseus's Arm
 - Eps 1-3 Omnibus: The Trail Through the Stars
 - Eps 4-6 Omnibus: The Path Amongst the Clouds

Season 2: Inner Stars
 - Episode 1: A Meeting of Bodies and Minds
 - Episode 3: A Deception and a Promise Kept
 - Episode 3: A Surreptitious Rescue of Friends and Foes (2018)
 - Episode 4: A Trial and the Tribulations (2018)
 - Episode 5: A Deal and a True Story Told (2018)
 - Episode 6: A New Empire and An Old Ally (2018)

Season 3: AI Empire
 - Episode 1: Restitution and Recompense (2019)
 - Five more episodes following...

The Warlord (Before the Age of the Orion War)
✓ - Book 1: The Woman Without a World
✓ - Book 2: The Woman Who Seized an Empire
✓ - Book 3: The Woman Who Lost Everything

The Sentience Wars: Origins (Age of the Sentience Wars - with James S. Aaron)
✓- Book 1: Lyssa's Dream
✓- Book 2: Lyssa's Run
✓- Book 3: Lyssa's Flight
✓- Book 4: Lyssa's Call
✓- Book 5: Lyssa's Flame (June 2018)

Enfield Genesis (Age of the Sentience Wars - with Lisa Richman)
- Book 1: Alpha Centauri (May 2018)

Machete System Bounty Hunter (Age of the Orion War - with Zen DiPietro)
- Book 1: Hired Gun
- Book 2: Gunning for Trouble (May 2018)
- Book 3: With Guns Blazing (2018)

Vexa Legacy (Age of the FTL Wars - with Andrew Gates)
- Book 1: Seas of the Red Star

Fennington Station Murder Mysteries (Age of the Orion War)
- Book 1: Whole Latte Death (w/Chris J. Pike)
- Book 2: Cocoa Crush (w/Chris J. Pike)

The Empire (Age of the Orion War)
- The Empress and the Ambassador (2018)
- Consort of the Scorpion Empress (2018)
- By the Empress's Command (2018)

Tanis Richards: Origins (The Age of Terra)
- Prequel: Storming the Norse Wind (At the Helm Volume 3)
- Book 1: Shore Leave (June 2018)
- Book 2: The Command (June 2018)
- Book 3: Infiltrator (July 2018)

The Sol Dissolution (The Age of Terra)
- Book 1: Venusian Uprising (2018)
- Book 2: Scattered Disk (2018)
- Book 3: Jovian Offensive (2019)
- Book 4: Fall of Terra (2019)

The Delta Team Chronicles (Expanded Orion War)
- A "Simple" Kidnapping (Pew! Pew! Volume 1)
- The Disknee World (Pew! Pew! Volume 2)
- It's Hard Being a Girl (Pew! Pew! Volume 4)
- A Fool's Gotta Feed (Pew! Pew! Volume 4)
- Rogue Planets and a Bored Kitty (Pew! Pew! Volume 5)

ABOUT THE AUTHORS

James S. Aaron lives in Oregon with too many chickens, a Corgi and two irascible cats. He kicked around the world in the U.S. Army for a while and always had a paperback in one of his cargo pockets.

Since he still has a day job, James spends his free time writing, hammering, soldering, gardening, biking, and listening to audiobooks during most the above. You can sign up for his science fiction newsletter at www.jamesaaron.net/list

* * * * *

Michael Cooper likes to think of himself as a jack-of-all-trades (and hopes to become master of a few). When not writing, he can be found writing software, working in his shop at his latest carpentry project, or likely reading a book.

He shares his home with a precocious young girl, his wonderful wife (who also writes), two cats, a never-ending list of things he would like to build, and ideas...

Find out what's coming next at www.aeon14.com

78693839R10448

Made in the USA
San Bernardino, CA
08 June 2018